Volume 2

James Clavell's

WHIRLWIND

Volume 2

WILLIAM MORROW AND COMPANY, INC.
New York

BOOK THREE

BOOK THREE

THURSDAY
February 22

NORTHWEST OF TABRIZ: 11:20 A.M.   From where he sat on the cabin steps of his parked 212 high up on the mountainside, Erikki could see deep into Soviet Russia. Far below the river Aras flowed eastward toward the Caspian, twisting through gorges and marking much of the Iran–USSR border. To his left he could see into Turkey, to soaring Mount Ararat, 15,500 feet, and the 212 was parked not far from the cave mouth where the secret American listening post was.

Was, he thought with grim amusement. When he had landed here yesterday afternoon—the altimeter reading 8,562 feet—the motley bunch of leftist fedayeen fighters he had brought with him stormed the cave, but the cave was empty of Americans and when Cimtarga inspected it he found all the important equipment destroyed and no cipher books. Much evidence of a hasty departure, but nothing of real value to be scavenged. "We'll clean it out anyway," Cimtarga had said to his men, "clean it out like the others."

To Erikki he had added, "Can you land there?" He pointed far above where the complex of radar masts stood. "I want to dismantle them."

"I don't know," Erikki had said. The grenade Ross had given him was still taped in his left armpit—Cimtarga and his captors had not searched him—and his pukoh knife was still in its back scabbard. "I'll go and look."

"*We'll* look, Captain. We'll look together," Cimtarga had said with a laugh. "Then you won't be tempted to leave us."

He had flown him up there. The masts were secured to deep beds of concrete on the northern face of the mountain, a small flat area in front of them. "If the weather's like today it'd be okay, but not if the wind picks up. I could hover and winch you down." He had smiled wolfishly.

Cimtarga had laughed. "Thanks, but no. I don't want an early death."

"For a Soviet, particularly a KGB Soviet, you're not a bad man."

"Neither are you—for a Finn."

Since Sunday, when Erikki had begun flying for Cimtarga, he had come to like him—not that you can really like or trust any KGB, he thought. But the man had been polite and fair, had given him a correct share of all food. Last night he had split a bottle of vodka with him and had given him the best place to sleep. They had slept in a village twenty kilometers south on carpets on a dirt floor. Cimtarga had said that though this was all mostly Kurdish territory the village was secretly fedayeen and safe. "Then why keep the guard on me?"

"It's safe for us, Captain—not safe for you."

The night before last at the Khan's palace when Cimtarga and guards had come for him just after Ross had left, he had been driven to the air base and, in darkness and against IATC regulations, had flown to the village in the mountains north of Khoi. There, in the dawn, they had collected a full load of armed men and had flown to the first of the two American radar posts. It was destroyed and empty of personnel like this one. "Someone must have tipped them we would be coming," Cimtarga said disgustedly. "*Matyeryebyets* spies!"

Later Cimtarga told him locals whispered that the Americans had evacuated the night before last, whisked away by helicopters, unmarked and very big. "It would have been good to catch them spying. Very good. Rumor says the bastards can see a thousand miles into us."

"You're lucky they weren't here, you might have had a battle and that would have created an international incident."

Cimtarga had laughed. "Nothing to do with us—nothing. It was the Kurds again, more of their rotten work—bunch of thugs, eh? They'd've been blamed. Rotten *yezdvas*, eh? Eventually the bodies would have been found—on Kurdish land. That'd be proof enough for Carter and his CIA."

Erikki shifted on the plane's steps, his seat chilled by the metal, depressed and weary. Last night he had slept badly again—nightmares about Azadeh. He hadn't slept well since Ross had appeared.

You're a fool, he thought for the thousandth time. I know, but that doesn't help. Nothing seems to help. Maybe the flying's getting to you. You've been putting in too many hours in bad conditions, too much night flying. Then there's Nogger to worry about—and Rakoczy to brood about and the killings. And Ross. And most of all Azadeh. Is she safe?

He had tried to make his peace with her about her Johnny Brighteyes the next morning. "I admit I was jealous. Stupid to be jealous. I swore by the ancient gods of my forefathers that I could live with your memory of him— I can and I will," he had said, but saying the words had not cleansed him. "I just didn't think he'd be so . . . so much a man and so . . . so dangerous. That kookri would be a match for my knife."

"Never, my darling. Never. I'm so glad you're you and I'm me and we're together. How can we get out of here?"

"Not all of us, not together at the same time," he told her honestly. "The soldiers'd be better to get out while they can. With Nogger, and them, and while you're here—I don't know, Azadeh. I don't know how we can escape yet. We'll have to wait. Maybe we could get into Turkey. . . ."

He looked eastward into Turkey now, so close and so far with Azadeh still in Tabriz—thirty minutes by air to her. But when? If we got into Turkey and if my chopper wasn't impounded, and if I could refuel we could fly to Al Shargaz, skirting the border. If if if! Gods of my ancestors, help me!

Over vodka last night Cimtarga had been as taciturn as ever, but he had drunk well and they had shared the bottle glass to glass to the last drop. "I've another for tomorrow night, Captain."

"Good. When will you be through with me?"

"It'll take two to three days to finish here, then back to Tabriz."

"Then?"

"Then I'll know better."

But for the vodka Erikki would have cursed him. He got up and watched the Iranians piling the equipment for loading. Most of it seemed to be very ordinary. As he strolled over the broken terrain, his boots crunching the snow, his guard went with him. Never a chance to escape. In all five days he had never had a single chance. "We enjoy your company," Cimtarga had said once, reading his mind, his Oriental eyes crinkling.

Above, he could see some men working on the radar masts, dismantling them. Waste of time, he thought. Even I know there's nothing special about them. "That's unimportant, Captain," Cimtarga had said. "My Master enjoys bulk. He said get everything. More is better than less. Why should you worry—you're paid by the hour." Again the laugh, not taunting.

Feeling his neck muscles taut, Erikki stretched and touched his toes and, in that position, let his arms and head hang freely, then waggled his head in as big a semicircle as he could, letting the weight of his head stretch the tendons and ligaments and muscles and smooth out the kinks, forcing nothing, just using the weight. "What're you doing?" Cimtarga asked, coming up to him.

"It's great for neck ache." He put his dark glasses back on—without them the reflected light from the snow was uncomfortable. "If you do it twice a day you'll never get neck ache."

"Ah, you get neck aches too? Me, I'm always getting them—have to go to a chiropractor at least three times a year. That helps?"

"Guaranteed. A waitress told me about it—carrying trays all day gives them plenty of neck and backache, like pilots; it's a way of life. Try it and you'll see." Cimtarga bent over as Erikki had done and moved his head. "No, you're doing it wrong. Let your head and arms and shoulders hang freely, you're too stiff."

Cimtarga did as he was told and felt his neck crack and the joints ease and when he raised himself again, he said, "That's wonderful, Captain. I owe you a favor."

"It's a return for the vodka."

"It's worth more than a bottle of vod—"

Erikki stared at him blankly as blood spurted out of Cimtarga's chest in the wake of the bullet that pierced him from behind, then came a thraaakkk followed by others as tribesmen poured out of ambush from the rocks and trees, shrieking battle cries and "Allah-u Akbarrr," firing as they came. The attack was brief and violent and Erikki saw Cimtarga's men going down all over the plateau, quickly overwhelmed. His own guard, one of the few who was carrying a weapon, had opened up at the first bullet but was hit at once, and now a bearded tribesman stood over him and gleefully finished him with the rifle butt. Others charged into the cave. More firing, then silence again.

Two men rushed him and he put his hands up, feeling naked and foolish, his heart thundering. One of these turned Cimtarga over and shot him again. The other bypassed Erikki and went to the cabin of the 212 to make sure no one was hiding there. Now the man who had shot Cimtarga stood in front of Erikki, breathing hard. He was small and olive-skinned and bearded, dark eyes and hair, and wore rough garments and stank.

"Put down your hands down," he said in heavily accented English. "I am Sheik Bayazid, chief here. We need you and helicopter."

"What do you want with me?"

Around them the tribesmen were finishing off the wounded and stripping the dead of anything of value. "CASEVAC." Bayazid smiled thinly at the look on Erikki's face. "Many of us work the oil and rigs. Who is this dog?" He motioned at Cimtarga with his foot.

"He called himself Cimtarga. He was a Soviet. I think also KGB."

"Of course Soviet," the man said roughly. "Of course KGB—all Soviets in Iran KGB. Papers, please." Erikki gave him his ID. The tribesman read it and nodded half to himself. And, to Erikki's further surprise, handed it back. "Why you flying Soviet dog?" He listened silently, his face darkening as Erikki told him how Abdollah Khan had entrapped him. "Abdollah Khan no man to offend. The reach of Abdollah the Cruel very wide, even in the lands of the Kurds."

"You're Kurds?"

"Kurds," Bayazid said, the lie convenient. He knelt and searched Cimtarga. No papers, a little money that he pocketed, nothing else. Except the holstered automatic and ammunition which he also took. "Have you full fuel?"

"Three quarter full."

"I want go twenty miles south. I direct you. Then pick up CASEVAC, then go Rezaiyeh, to hospital there."

"Why not Tabriz—it's much closer."

"Rezaiyeh in Kurdistan. Kurds are safe there, sometimes. Tabriz belong to our enemies: Iranians, Shah, or Khomeini no difference. Go Rezaiyeh."

"All right. The Overseas Hospital would be best. I've been there before and they've a helipad. They're used to CASEVACs. We can refuel there— they've chopper fuel, at least they had in . . . in the old days."

Bayazid hesitated. "Good. Yes. We go at once."

"And after Rezaiyeh—what then?"

"And then, if serve us safely, perhaps you released to take your wife from the Gorgon Khan." Sheik Bayazid turned away and shouted for his men to hurry up and board the airplane. "Start up, please."

"What about him?" Erikki pointed at Cimtarga. "And the others?"

"The beasts and birds soon make here clean."

It took them little time to board and leave, Erikki filled with hope now. No problem to find the site of the small village. The CASEVAC was an old woman. "She is our chieftain," Bayazid said.

"I didn't know women could be chieftains."

"Why not, if wise enough, strong enough, clever enough, and from correct family? We Sunni Muslims—not leftists or heretic Shi'a cattle who put mullahs between man and God. God is God. We leave at once."

"Does she speak English?"

"No."

"She looks very ill. She may not last the journey."

"As God wants."

But she did last the hour's journey and Erikki landed on the helipad. The Overseas Hospital had been built, staffed, and sponsored by foreign oil companies. He had flown low all the way, avoiding Tabriz and military airfields. Bayazid had sat up front with him, six armed guards in the back with their high chieftain. She lay on the stretcher, awake but motionless. In great pain but without complaining.

A doctor and orderlies were at the helipad seconds after touchdown. The doctor wore a white coat with a large red cross on the sleeve over heavy sweaters, and he was in his thirties, American, dark rings around bloodshot eyes. He knelt beside the stretcher as the others waited in silence. She groaned a little when he touched her abdomen even though his hands were healing hands. In a moment he spoke to her gently in halting Turkish. A small smile went over her and she nodded and thanked him. He motioned to the orderlies and they lifted the stretcher out of the cabin and carried her away. At Bayazid's order, two of his men went with her.

The doctor said to Bayazid in halting dialect, "Excellency, I need name and age and . . ." He searched for the word. "History, medical history."

"Speak English."

"Good, thank you, Agha. I'm Doctor Newbegg. I'm afraid she's near the end, Agha, her pulse is almost zero. She's old and I'd say she was hemorrhaging—bleeding—internally. Did she have a fall recently?"

"Speak slower, please. Fall? Yes, yes, two days ago." Bayazid stopped at the sound of gunfire not far away, then went on: "Yes, two days ago. She slip in snows and fell against a rock, on her side against a rock."

"I think she's bleeding inside. I'll do what we can but . . . sorry, I can't promise good news."

"Insha'Allah."

"You're Kurds?"

"Kurds." More firing, closer now. They all looked off to where the sound came from. "Who?"

"I don't know, just more of the same, I'm afraid," the doctor said uneasily. "Green Bands against leftists, leftists against Green Bands, against Kurds—many factions—and all're armed." He rubbed his eyes. "I'll do what I can for the old lady—perhaps you'd better come with me, Agha, you can give me the details as we go." He hurried off.

"Doc, do you still have fuel here?" Erikki called after him.

The doctor stopped and looked at him blankly. "Fuel? Oh, chopper fuel?

I don't know. Gas tank's in back." He went up the stairs to the main entrance, his white coattail flapping.

"Captain," Bayazid said, "you will wait till I return. Here."

"But the fuel? I ca—"

"Wait here. Here." Bayazid rushed after the doctor. Two of his men went with him. Two stayed with Erikki.

While Erikki waited, he checked everything. Tanks almost empty. From time to time cars and trucks arrived with wounded to be met by doctors and medics. Many eyed the chopper curiously but none approached. The guards made sure of that.

During the flight here Bayazid had said: "For centuries we Kurds try for independent. We a separate people, separate language, separate customs. Now perhaps six million Kurds in Azerbaijan, Kurdistan, over Soviet border, this side of Iraq, and Turkey." He had almost spat the word. "For centuries we fight them all, together or singly. We hold the mountains. We are good fighters. Salah-al-din—he was Kurd. You know of him?" Salah-al-din—Saladin—was the chivalrous Muslim opponent of Richard the Lion-Hearted during the Crusades of the twelfth century, who made himself Sultan of Egypt and Syria and captured the Kingdom of Jerusalem in A.D. 1187 after smashing the allied might of the Crusaders.

"Yes, I know of him."

"Today other Salah-al-dins among us. One day we recapture again all the holy places—after Khomeini, betrayer of Islam, is stamped into joub."

Erikki had asked, "You ambushed Cimtarga and the others and wiped them out just for the CASEVAC?"

"Of course. They enemy. Yours and ours." Bayazid had smiled his twisted smile. "Nothing happens in our mountains without us knowing. Our chieftain sick—you nearby. We see the Americans leave, see scavengers arrive, and you were recognized."

"Oh? How?"

"Redhead of the Knife? The Infidel who kills assassins like lice, then given a Gorgon whelp as reward! CASEVAC pilot?" The dark, almost sloe eyes were amused. "Oh, yes, Captain, know you well. Many of us work timber as well as oil—a man must work. Even so, it's good you not Soviet or Iranian."

"After the CASEVAC will you and your men help me against Gorgon Khan?"

Bayazid had laughed. "Your blood feud is your blood feud, not ours. Abdollah Khan is for us, at moment. We not go against him. What you do is up to God."

It was cold in the hospital forecourt, a slight wind increasing the chill factor. Erikki was walking up and down to keep his circulation going. I've got to get back to Tabriz. I've got to get back and then somehow I'll take Azadeh and we'll leave forever.

Firing nearby startled him and the guards. Outside the hospital gates, the traffic slowed, horns sounding irritably, then quickly snarled. People began running past. More firing and those trapped in their vehicles got out and took cover or fled. Inside the gates the expanse was wide, the 212 parked on the helipad to one side. Wild firing now, much closer. Some glass windows on the top floor of the hospital blew out. The two guards were hugging the snow behind the plane's undercarriage, Erikki fuming that his airplane was so exposed and not knowing where to run or what to do, no time to take off, and not enough fuel to go anywhere. A few ricochets, and he ducked down as the small battle built outside the walls. Then it died as quickly as it had begun. People picked themselves up out of cover, horns began sounding, and soon the traffic was as normal and as spiteful as ever.

"Insha'Allah," one of the tribesmen said, then cocked his rifle and came on guard. A small gasoline truck was approaching from behind the hospital, driven by a young Iranian with a broad smile. Erikki went to meet it.

"Hi, Cap," the driver said happily, his accent heavily New York. "I'm to gas you up. Your fearless leader, Sheik Bayazid, fixed it." He greeted the tribesmen in Turkish dialect. At once they relaxed and greeted him back. "Cap, we'll fill her brimming. You got any temp tanks, or special tanks?"

"No. Just the regular. I'm Erikki Yokkonen."

"Sure. Red the Knife." The youth grinned. "You're kinda a legend in these parts. I gassed you once, maybe a year ago." He stuck out his hand. "I'm 'Gasoline' Ali—Ali Reza that is."

They shook hands and, while they talked, the youth began the refuel. "You went to American school?" Erikki asked.

"Hell, no. I was sort of adopted by the hospital, years ago, long before this one was built, when I was a kid. In the old days the hospital worked out of one of the Golden Ghettos on the east side of town—you know, Cap, U.S. Personnel Only, an ExTex depot." The youth smiled, screwed the tank cap back carefully, and started to fill the next. "The first doc who took me in was Abe Weiss. Great guy, just great. He put me on the payroll, taught me about soap and socks and spoons and toilets—hell, all sorts of gizmos un-Iranian for street rats like me, with no folks, no home, no name, and no nothing. He used to call me his hobby. He even gave me my name. Then, one day, he left."

Erikki saw the pain in the youth's eyes, quickly hidden. "He passed me on to Doc Templeton, and he did the same. At times it's kinda hard to figure where I'm at. Kurd but not, Yank but not—Iranian but not, Jew but not, Muslim but not Muslim." He shrugged. "Kinda mixed up, Cap. The world, everything. Huh?"

"Yes." Erikki glanced toward the hospital. Bayazid was coming down the steps with his two fighters beside orderlies carrying a stretcher. The old woman was covered now, head to foot.

"We leave soon as fuel," Bayazid said shortly.

"Sorry," Erikki said.

"Insha'Allah." They watched the orderlies put the stretcher into the cabin. Bayazid thanked them and they left. Soon the refuel was complete.

"Thanks, Mr. Reza." Erikki stuck out his hand. "Thanks."

The youth stared at him. "No one's ever called me mister before, Cap, never." He pummeled Erikki's hand. "Thanks—any time you want gas, you got it."

Bayazid climbed in beside Erikki, fastened his belt, and put on the headset, the engines building. "Now we go to village from whence we came."

"What then?" Erikki asked.

"I consult new chieftain," Bayazid said, but he was thinking, this man and the helicopter will bring a big ransom, perhaps from the Khan, perhaps from the Soviets, or even from his own people. My people need every rial we can get.

NEAR TABRIZ ONE—IN THE VILLAGE OF ABU MARD: 6:16 P.M. Azadeh picked up the bowl of rice and the bowl of horisht, thanked the headman's wife, and walked across the dirty, refuse-fouled snow to the hut that was set a little apart. Her face was pinched, her cough not good. She knocked, then went through the low doorway. "Hello, Johnny. How do you feel? Any better?"

"I'm fine," he said. But he wasn't.

The first night they had spent in a cave not far away, huddled together, shivering from the cold. "We can't stay here, Azadeh," he had said in the dawn. "We'll freeze to death. We'll have to try the base." They had gone through the snows and watched from hiding. They saw the two mechanics and even Nogger Lane from time to time—and the 206—but all over the base were armed men. Dayati, the base manager, had moved into Azadeh and Erikki's cabin—he, his wife and children. "Sons and daughters of dogs," Azadeh hissed, seeing the wife wearing a pair of her boots. "Perhaps we could sneak into the mechanics' huts. They'll hide us."

"They're escorted everywhere; I'll bet they've even guards at night. But who are the guards, Green Bands, the Khan's men, or who?"

"I don't recognize any of them, Johnny."

"They're after us," he said, feeling very low, the death of Gueng preying on him. Both Gueng and Tenzing had been with him since the beginning. And there was Rosemont. And now Azadeh. "Another night in the open and you'll have had it, we'll have had it."

"Our village, Johnny. Abu Mard. It's been in our family for more than a century. They're loyal, I know they are. We'd be safe there for a day or two."

"With a price on my head? And you? They'd send word to your father."

"I'd ask them not to. I'd say Soviets were trying to kidnap me and you were helping me. That's true. I'd say that we need to hide until my husband comes back—he's always been very popular, Johnny, his CASEVACs saved many lives over the years."

He looked at her, a dozen reasons against. "The village's on the road, almost right on the road an—"

"Yes, of course you're quite right and we'll do whatever you say, but it sprawls away into the forest. We could hide there—no one'd expect that."

He saw her tiredness. "How do you feel? How strong do you feel?"

"Not strong, but fine."

"We could hike out, go down the road a few miles—we'd have to skirt the roadblock, it's a lot less dangerous than the village. Eh?"

"I'd . . . I'd rather not. I could try." She hesitated, then said, "I'd rather not, not today. You go on. I'll wait. Erikki may come back today."

"And if he doesn't?"

"I don't know. You go on."

He looked back at the base. A nest of vipers. Suicide to go there. From where they were on a rise, he could see as far as the main road. Men still manned the roadblock—he presumed Green Bands and police—a line of traffic backed up and waiting to leave the area. No one'll give us a ride now, he thought, not unless it's for the reward. "You go to the village. I'll wait in the forest."

"Without you they'll just return me to my father—I know them, Johnny."

"Perhaps they'll betray you anyway."

"As God wants. But we could get some food and warmth, perhaps even a night's rest. In the dawn we could sneak away. Perhaps we could get a car or truck from them—the kalandar has an old Ford." She stifled a sneeze. Armed men were not far away. More than likely there were patrols out in the forest—coming here they had had to detour to avoid one. The village's madness, he thought. To get around the roadblock'll take hours in daylight, and by night—we can't stay outside another night.

"Let's go to the village," he said.

So they had gone yesterday and Mostafa, the kalandar, had listened to her story and kept his eyes away from Ross. News of their arrival had gone from mouth to mouth and in moments all the village knew and this news was added to the other, about the reward for the saboteur and kidnapper of the Khan's daughter. The kalandar had given Ross a one-room hut with dirt floor and old mildewed carpets. The hut was well away from the road, on the far edge of the village, and he noticed the steel-hard eyes and matted hair and stubbled beard—his carbine and kookri and ammunition-heavy knapsack. Azadeh he invited into his home. It was a two-room hovel. No electricity or running water. The joub was the toilet.

At dusk last night, hot food and a bottle of water had been brought to Ross by an old woman.

"Thank you," he said, his head aching and the fever already with him. "Where is Her Highness?" The woman shrugged. She was heavily lined, pockmarked, with brown stubs of teeth. "Please ask her to receive me."

Later he was sent for. In the headman's room, watched by the headman, his wife, some of his brood, and a few elders, he greeted Azadeh carefully—as a stranger might a highborn. She wore chador of course and knelt on carpets facing the door. Her face had a yellowish, unhealthy pallor, but he thought it might be from the light of the sputtering oil lamp. "Salaam, Highness, your health is good?"

"Salaam, Agha, yes, thank you, and yours?"

"There is a little fever I think." He saw her eyes flick up from the carpet momentarily. "I have medicine. Do you need any?"

"No. No, thank you."

With so many eyes and ears what he wanted to say was impossible. "Perhaps I may greet you tomorrow," he said. "Peace be upon you, Highness."

"And upon you."

It had taken him a long time to sleep. And her. With the dawn the village awoke, fires were stoked, goats milked, vegetable horisht set to stew —little to nourish it but a morsel of chicken, in some huts a piece of goat or sheep, the meat old, tough, and rancid. Bowls of rice but never enough. Food twice a day in good times, morning and before last light. Azadeh had money and she paid for their food. This did not go unnoticed. She asked that a whole chicken be put into tonight's horisht to be shared by the whole household, and she paid for it. This, too, did not go unnoticed.

Before last light she had said, "Now I will take food to him."

"But, Highness, it's not right for you to serve him," the kalandar's wife said. "I'll carry the bowls. We can go together if you wish."

"No, it's better if I go alone beca—"

"God protect us, Highness. Alone? To a man not your husband? Oh no, that would be unseemly, that would be very unseemly. Come, I will take it."

"Good, thank you. As God wants. Thank you. Last night he mentioned fever. It might be plague. I know how Infidels carry vile diseases that we are not used to. I only wished to save you probable agony. Thank you for sparing me."

Last night everyone in the room had seen the sheen of sweat on the Infidel's face. Everyone knew how vile Infidels were, most of them Satan worshipers and sorcerers. Almost everyone secretly believed that Azadeh had been bewitched, first by the Giant of the Knife, and now again by the saboteur. Silently the headman's wife had handed Azadeh the bowls and she had walked across the snow.

Now she watched him in the semidarkness of the room that had as window a hole in the adobe wall, no glass, just sacking covering most of it. The air was heavy with the smell of urine and waste from the joub outside.

"Eat, eat while it's hot. I can't stay long."

"You okay?" He had been lying under the single blanket, fully dressed, dozing, but now he sat cross-legged and alert. The fever had abated somewhat with the help of drugs from his survival kit but his stomach was upset. "You don't look so good."

She smiled. "Neither do you. I'm fine. Eat."

He was very hungry. The soup was thin but he knew that was better for his stomach. Another spasm started building but he held on and it went away. "You think we could sneak off?" he said between mouthfuls, trying to eat slowly.

"You could, I can't."

While he had been dozing all day gathering his strength, he had tried to make a plan. Once he had started to walk out of the village. A hundred eyes were on him, everyone watching. He went to the edge of the village then came back. But he had seen the old truck. "What about the truck?"

"I asked the headman. He said it was out of order. Whether he was lying or not I don't know."

"We can't stay here much longer. A patrol's bound to come here. Or your father will hear about us or be told. Our only hope is to run."

"Or to hijack the 206 with Nogger."

He looked at her. "With all those men there?"

"One of the children told me that they went back to Tabriz today."

"You're sure?"

"Not sure, Johnny." A wave of anxiety went over her. "But there's no reason for the child to lie. I, I used to teach here before I was married—I was the only teacher they had ever had and I know they liked me. The child said there's only one or two left there." Another chill swirled up and made her weak. So many lies, so many problems the last few weeks, she thought. Is it only weeks? So much terror since Rakoczy and the mullah burst in on Erikki and me after our sauna. Everything so hopeless now. Erikki, where are you? she wanted to scream, where are you?

He finished the soup and the rice and picked at the last grain, weighing the odds, trying to plan. She was kneeling opposite him and she saw his matted hair and filth, his exhaustion and gravity. "Poor Johnny," she murmured and touched him. "I haven't brought you much luck, have I?"

"Don't be silly. Not your fault—none of this is." He shook his head. "None of it. Listen, this's what we'll do: we'll stay here tonight, tomorrow after first light we'll walk out. We'll try the base—if that doesn't work then we'll hike out. You try to get the headman to help us by keeping his mouth shut, his wife too. The rest of the villagers should behave if he orders it, at least to give us a start. Promise them a big reward when things are normal again, and here . . ." He reached into his pack into the secret place, found the gold rupees, ten of them. "Give him five, keep the other five for emergency."

"But . . . but what about you?" she said, wide-eyed and filled with hope at so much potential pishkesh.

"I've ten more," he said, the lie coming easily. "Emergency funds, courtesy of Her Majesty's Government."

"Oh, Johnny, I think we've a chance now—this is so much money to them."

They both glanced at the window as a wind picked up and rustled the sacking that covered it. She got up and adjusted it as best she could. Not all the opening could be covered. "Never mind," he said. "Come and sit down." She obeyed, closer than before. "Here. Just in case." He handed her the grenade. "Just hold the lever down, pull the pin out, count three, and throw. Three, not four."

She nodded and pulled up her chador and carefully put the grenade into one of her ski-jacket pockets. Her tight ski pants were tucked into her boots. "Thanks. Now I feel better. Safer." Involuntarily, she touched him and wished she hadn't for she felt the fire. "I'd . . . I'd better go. I'll bring you food at first light. Then we'll leave."

He got up and opened the door for her. Outside it was dark. Neither saw the figure scuttle away from the window, but both felt eyes feeding on them from every side.

"What about Gueng, Johnny? Do you think he'll find us?"

"He'll be watching, wherever he is." He felt a spasm coming. " 'Night, sweet dreams."

"Sweet dreams."

They had always said it to each other in the olden time. Their eyes touched and their hearts and both of them were warmed and at the same time filled with foreboding. Then she turned, the darkness of her chador making her at once almost invisible. He saw the door of the headman's hut open and she went in and then the door closed. He heard a truck grinding up the road not far off, then a honking car that went past and soon faded away. A spasm came and it was too much so he squatted. The pain was big but little came out and he was thankful that Azadeh had gone. His left hand groped for some snow and he cleansed himself. Eyes were still watching him, all around. Bastards, he thought, then went back into the hut and sat on the crude straw mattress.

In the darkness he oiled the kookri. No need to sharpen it. He had done that earlier. Lights glinted off the blade. He slept with it out of its scabbard.

AT THE PALACE OF THE KHAN: 11:19 P.M. The doctor held the Khan's wrist and checked his pulse again. "You must have plenty of rest, Highness," he said worriedly, "and one of these pills every three hours."

"Every three hours . . . yes," Abdollah Khan said, his voice small and breathing bad. He was propped on cushions in the bed that was made up on deep carpets. Beside the bed was Najoud, his eldest daughter, thirty-five, and Aysha, his third wife, seventeen. Both women were white-faced. Two guards stood at the door and Ahmed knelt beside the doctor. "Now . . . now leave me."

"I'll come back at dawn with the ambulance an—"

"No ambulance! I stay here!" The Khan's face reddened, another pain went through his chest. They watched him, hardly breathing. When he could speak he said throatily, "I stay . . . here."

"But Highness, you've already had one heart attack, God be thanked just a mild one," the doctor said, his voice quavering. "There's no telling when you could have . . . I've no equipment here; you should have immediate treatment and observation."

"What . . . whatever you need, bring it here. Ahmed, see to it!"

"Yes Highness." Ahmed looked at the doctor.

The doctor put his stethoscope and blood pressure equipment into his old-fashioned bag. At the door he slipped his shoes on and went out. Najoud and Ahmed followed him. Aysha hesitated. She was tiny and had been married two years and had a son and a daughter. The Khan's face had an untoward pallor and his breath rasped heavily. She knelt closer and took his hand but he pulled it away angrily, rubbing his chest, cursing her. Her fear increased.

Outside in the hall, the doctor stopped. His face was old and lined, older than his age, his hair white. "Highness," he said to Najoud, "better he should be in hospital. Tabriz is not good enough. Tehran would be much better. He should be in Tehran though the trip there might . . . Tehran is better than here. His blood pressure's too high, it's been too high for years but, well, as God wants."

"Whatever you need we'll bring here," Ahmed said.

Angrily the doctor said, "Fool, I can't bring an operating theater and dispensary and aseptic surroundings!"

"He's going to die?" Najoud said, her eyes wide.

"In God's time, only in God's time. His pressure's much too high . . . I'm not a magician and we're so short of supplies. Have you any idea what caused the attack—was there a quarrel or anything?"

"No, no quarrel, but it was surely Azadeh. It was her again, that stepsister of mine." Najoud began wringing her hands. "It was her, running off with the saboteur yesterday morning, it wa—"

"What saboteur?" the doctor asked astonished.

"The saboteur everyone is looking for, the enemy of Iran. But I'm sure he didn't kidnap her, I'm sure she ran off with him—how could he kidnap her from inside the palace? She's the one who caused His Highness such rage—we've all been in terror since yesterday morning. . . ."

Stupid hag! Ahmed thought. The insane, roaring outburst was because of the men from Tehran, Hashemi Fazir and the Farsi-speaking Infidel, and what they demanded of my Master and what my Master had to agree to. Such a little thing, giving over to them a Soviet, a pretended friend who was an enemy, surely no cause to explode? Clever of my Master to set everything into motion: the day after tomorrow the burnt offering comes back over the border into the web and the two enemies from Tehran come back into the web. Soon my Master will decide and then I will act. Meanwhile, Azadeh and the saboteur are safely bottled in the village, at my Master's will—word sent to him by the headman the first moment. Few men on earth are as clever as Abdollah Khan and only God will decide when he should die, not this dog of a doctor. "Let us go on," he said. "Please excuse me, Highness, but we should fetch a nurse and drugs and some equipment. Doctor, we should hurry."

The door at the far end of the corridor opened. Aysha was even paler. "Ahmed, His Highness wants you for a moment."

When they were alone, Najoud caught the doctor by the sleeve and whispered, "How bad is His Highness? You must tell me the truth. I've got to know."

The doctor lifted his hands helplessly. "I don't know, I don't know. I've been expecting worse than this for . . . for a year or more. The attack was mild. The next could be massive or mild, in an hour or a year, I don't know."

Najoud had been in a panic ever since the Khan had collapsed a couple of hours before. If the Khan died, then Hakim, Azadeh's brother, was his legitimate heir—Najoud's own two brothers had died in infancy. Aysha's son was barely a year old. The Khan had no living brothers, so his heir should be Hakim. But Hakim was in disgrace and disinherited so there would have to be a regency. Her husband, Mahmud, was senior of the sons-in-law. He would be regent, unless the Khan ordered otherwise.

Why should he order otherwise? she thought, her stomach once more a bottomless pit. The Khan knows I can guide my husband and make us all strong. Aysha's son—pshaw, a sickly child, as sickly as the mother. As God wants, but infants die. He's not a threat, but Hakim—Hakim is.

She remembered going to the Khan when Azadeh had returned from school in Switzerland: "Father, I bring you bad tidings but you must know the truth. I overheard Hakim and Azadeh. Highness, she told him she'd been with child but with the help of a doctor had cast it out."

"What?"

"Yes . . . yes I heard her say it."

"Azadeh could not . . . Azadeh would not, could not do that!"

"Question her—I beg you do not say from where you heard it—ask her before God, question her, have a doctor examine her, but wait, that's not all. Against your wishes, Hakim's still determined to become a pianist and he told her he was going to run away, asking Azadeh to come with him to Paris, 'then you can marry your lover,' he said, but she said, Azadeh said, 'Father will bring you back, he'll force us back. He'll never permit us to go without his prior permission, never.' Then Hakim said, 'I will go. I'm not going to stay here and waste my life. I'm going!' Again she said, 'Father will never permit it, never.' 'Then better he's dead,' Hakim said and she said, 'I agree.' "

"I—I don't—believe it!"

Najoud remembered the face gone purple, and how terrified she had been. "Before God," she had said, "I heard them say it, Highness, before God. Then they said we must plan, we m—" She had quailed as he shouted at her, telling her to tell it exactly.

"Exactly he said, Hakim said, 'A little poison in his halvah, or in a drink, we can bribe a servant, perhaps we could bribe one of his guards to kill him or we could leave the gates open at night for assassins . . . there are a hundred ways for any one of a thousand enemies to do it for us, everyone hates him. We must think and be patient. . . .' "

It had been easy for her to weave her spell, deeper and deeper into the fabrication so that soon she was believing it—but not quite.

God will forgive me, she told herself confidently as she always told herself. God will forgive me. Azadeh and Hakim have always hated us, the rest of the family, wanted us dead, outcast, to take all our heritage unto themselves, they and their witch of a mother who cast an evil spell over Father to turn his face from us for so many years. Eight years he was under the spell —Azadeh this and Azadeh that, Hakim this and Hakim that. Eight years he dismissed us and our mother, his first wife, took no notice of me, carelessly married me to this clod, Mahmud, this foul-smelling, now impotent, vile, snoring clod, and so ruined my life. I hope my husband dies, eaten by worms, but not before he becomes Khan so my son will become Khan after him.

Father must get rid of Hakim before he dies. God keep him alive to do that—he must do it before he dies—and Azadeh must be humbled, cast out, destroyed too—even better, caught in her adultery with the saboteur, oh yes, then my revenge would be complete.

FRIDAY
February 23

NEAR TABRIZ ONE, AT THE VILLAGE OF ABU MARD: 6:17 A.M. In the dawn, the face of another Mahmud, the Islamic-Marxist mullah, was contorted with rage. "Have you lain with this man?" he shouted. "Before God have you lain with him?"

Azadeh was on her knees in front of him, panic-stricken. "You've no right to burst into th—"

"Have you lain with this man?"

"I . . . I am faithful to my . . . my husband," she gasped. It was only seconds ago that she and Ross had been sitting on the carpets in the hut, hastily eating the meal she had brought him, happy together, ready for immediate departure. The headman had gratefully and humbly accepted his pishkesh—four gold rupees to him and one she had secretly given to his wife—telling them to sneak out of the village by the forest side the moment they had finished eating, blessing her—then the door had burst open, aliens had rushed them, overpowering him and dragging them both into the open, shoving her at Mahmud's feet and battering Ross into submission. "I'm faithful, I swear it. I'm faithf—"

"Faithful? Why aren't you wearing chador?" he had shouted down at her, most of the village collected around them now, silent and afraid. Half a dozen armed men leaned on their weapons, two stood over Ross who was face downward in the snow, unconscious, blood trickling from his forehead.

"I was . . . I was wearing chador but I . . . I took it off while I was eat—"

"You took off your chador in a hut with the door closed eating with a stranger? What else had you taken off?"

"Nothing, nothing," she said in more panic, pulling her unzipped parka closer about her, "I was just eating and he's not a stranger but an old friend of mi . . . old friend of my husband," she corrected herself hastily but the slip had not gone unnoticed. "Abdollah Khan is my father and you have no r—"

"Old friend? If you're not guilty you've nothing to fear! Before God, have you lain with him? Swear it!"

"Kalandar, send for my father, send for him!" The kalandar did not move. All eyes were grinding into her. Helplessly she saw the blood on the snow, her Johnny groaning, coming around. "I swear by God I'm faithful to my husband!" she screamed. The cry went over them all and into Ross's mind and seared him awake.

"Answer the question, woman! Is it yes or no? In the Name of God, have you lain with him?" The mullah was standing over her like a diseased crow, the villagers waiting, everyone waiting, the trees and the wind waiting— even God.

Insha'Allah!

Her fear left her. In its place was hate. She stared back at this man Mahmud as she got up. "In the Name of God, I am and have always been faithful to my husband," she pronounced. "In the Name of God, yes, I loved this man, years upon years ago."

Her words made many that were there shudder and Ross was appalled that she had admitted it.

"Harlot! Loose woman! You openly admit yourself guilty. You will be punished accord—"

"No," Ross shouted over him. He dragged himself onto his knees and though the two mujhadin had guns at his head, he ignored them. "It was not the fault of Her Highness. I—I'm to blame, only me, only me!"

"You'll be punished, Infidel, never fear," Mahmud said, then turned to the villagers. "You all heard the harlot admit fornication, you all heard the

Infidel admit fornication. For her there is but one punishment—for the Infidel . . . what should happen to the Infidel?"

The villagers waited. The mullah was not their mullah, nor of their village, nor a real mullah but an Islamic-Marxist. He had come uninvited. No one knew why he had come here, only that he had appeared suddenly like the wrath of God with leftists—also not of their village. Not true Shi'as, only madmen. Hadn't the Imam said fifty times all such men were madmen who only paid lip service to God, secretly worshiping the Satan Marx-Lenin.

"Well? Should he share her punishment?"

No one answered him. The mullah and his men were armed.

Azadeh felt all eyes boring into her but she could no longer move or say anything. She stood there, knees trembling, the voices distant, even Ross's shouting, "You've no jurisdiction over me—or her. You defile God's name . . ." as one of the men standing over him gave him a brutal shove to send him sprawling then put a booted foot on his neck pinioning him. "Castrate him and be done with it," the man said and another said, "No, it was the woman who tempted him—didn't I see her lift her chador to him last night in the hut. Look at her now, tempting us all. Isn't the punishment for him a hundred lashes?"

Another said, "He put his hands on her, take off his hands."

"Good," Mahmud said. "First his hands, then the lash. Tie him up!"

Azadeh tried to cry out against this evil but no sound came out, the blood roaring in her ears now, her stomach heaving, her mind unhinged as they dragged her Johnny to his feet, fighting, kicking, to tie him spread-eagled between rafters that jutted from the hut—remembering the time she and Hakim were children and he, filled with bravado, had picked up a stone and thrown it at the cat, and the cat squealed as it rolled over and got up, now injured, and tried to crawl away, squealing all the time until a guard shot it, but now . . . now she knew no one would shoot her. She lurched at Mahmud with a scream, her nails out, but her strength failed her and she fainted.

Mahmud looked down at her. "Put her against that wall," he said to some of his men, "then bring her her chador." He turned and looked at the villagers. "Who is the butcher here? Who is the butcher of the village?" No one replied. His voice roughened. "Kalandar, who is your butcher?"

Quickly the headman pointed to a man in the crowd, a small man with rough clothes. "Abrim, Abrim is our butcher."

"Go and get your sharpest knife," Mahmud told him. "The rest of you collect stones."

Abrim went to do his bidding. As God wants, the others muttered to each other. "Have you ever seen a stoning?" someone asked. A very old woman said, "I saw one once. It was in Tabriz when I was a little girl." Her voice quavered. "The adulteress was the wife of a bazaari, yes, I remember she was the wife of a bazaari. Her lover was a bazaari too and they hacked off his head in front of the mosque, then the men stoned her. Women could throw stones too if they wanted but they didn't, I didn't see any woman do it. It took a long time, the stoning, and for years I heard the screams."

"Adultery is a great evil and must be punished, whoever the sinner, even *her*. The Koran says a hundred lashes for the man . . . the mullah is the lawgiver, not us," the kalandar said.

"But he's not a true mullah and the Imam has warned against their evil!"

"The mullah is the mullah, the law, the law," the kalandar said darkly, secretly wanting the Khan humbled and this woman who had taught new disturbing thoughts to their children destroyed. "Collect the stones."

Mahmud stood in the snow, ignoring the cold and the villagers and the saboteur who cursed and moaned and, frenzied, tried to fight out of his bonds, and the woman inert at the wall.

This morning, before dawn, coming to take over the base, he had heard about the saboteur and *her* being in the village. She of the sauna, he had thought, his anger gathering, she who had flaunted herself, the highborn whelp of the cursed Khan who pretends to be our patron but who has betrayed us and betrayed me, already engineering an assassination attempt on me last night, a burst of machine-gun fire outside the mosque after last prayer that killed many but not me. The Khan tried to have me murdered, me who am protected by the Sacred Word that Islam together with Marx-Lenin is the only way to help the world rise up.

He looked at her, seeing the long legs encased in blue ski pants, hair uncovered and flowing, breasts bulging against the blue and white ski jacket. Harlot, he thought, loathing her for tempting him. One of his men threw the chador over her. She moaned a little but did not come out of her stupor.

"I'm ready," the butcher said, fingering his knife.

"First the right hand," Mahmud said to his men. "Bind him above the wrists."

They bound strips of sacking ripped from the window tightly, villagers pressing forward to see better, and Ross used all his energy to stop his terror from bursting the dam, saw only the pockmarked face above the carving knife, the bedraggled mustache and beard, the eyes blank, the man's thumb testing the blade absently. Then his eyes focused. He saw Azadeh come out of her spell and he remembered.

"The grenade!" he shrieked. "Azadeh, the grenade!"

She heard him clearly and fumbled for it in her side pocket as he shrieked again and again, further startling the butcher, dragging everyone's attention to himself. The butcher came forward cursing him, took hold of his right hand firmly, fascinated by it, moved it a little this way and that, the knife poised, deciding where to slice through the sinews of the joint, giving Azadeh just enough time to pick herself up and hurtle across the small space to shove him in the back, sending him flying and the knife into the snow, then to turn on Mahmud, pull the pin out, and stand there trembling, the lever held in her small hand.

"Get away from him," she screamed. "Get away!"

Mahmud did not move. Everyone else scattered, trampling some, rushing for safety across the square, cursing and shouting.

"Quick, over here, Azadeh," Ross called out. *"Azadeh!"* She heard him through her mist and obeyed, backing toward him, watching Mahmud, flecks of foam at the corner of her mouth. Then Ross saw Mahmud turn and stalk off toward one of his men out of range and he groaned, knowing what would happen now. "Quick, pick up the knife and cut me loose," he said to distract her. "Don't let go of the lever—I'll watch them for you." Behind her he saw the mullah take the rifle from one of his men, cock it, and turn toward them. Now she had the butcher's knife and she reached for the bonds on his right hand and he knew the bullet would kill or wound her, the lever would fly off, four seconds of waiting, and then oblivion for both of them—but quick and clean and no obscenity. "I've always loved you, Azadeh," he whispered and smiled and she looked up, startled, and smiled back.

The rifle shot rang out, his heart stopped, then another and another, but they did not come from Mahmud but from the forest and now Mahmud was screaming and twisting on the snow. Then a voice followed the shots: "Allah-u Akbar! Death to all enemies of God! Death to all leftists, death to all enemies of the Imam!"

With a bellow of rage one of the mujhadin charged the forest and died. At once the rest fled, falling over themselves in their panic-stricken rush to hide. Within seconds the village square was empty but for the babbling howls of Mahmud, his turban no longer on his head. In the forest the leader of the four-man Tudeh assassination team who had tracked him since dawn silenced him with a burst of machine-gun fire, then the four of them retreated as silently as they had arrived.

Blankly Ross and Azadeh looked at the emptiness of the village. "It can't be . . . can't be . . ." she muttered, still deranged.

"Don't let go of the lever," he said hoarsely. "Don't let go of the lever. Quick, cut me loose . . . quick!"

The knife was very sharp. Her hands were trembling and slow and she cut him once but not badly. The moment he was free he grabbed the grenade, his hands tingling and hurting, but held the lever, began to breathe again. He staggered into the hut, found his kookri that had been mixed up in the blanket in the initial struggle, stuck it in its scabbard and picked up his carbine. At the doorway he stopped. "Azadeh, quick, get your chador and the pack and follow me." She stared at him. "Quick!"

She obeyed like an automaton, and he led her out of the village into the forest, grenade in his right hand, gun in the left. After a faltering run of a quarter of an hour, he stopped and listened. No one was following them. Azadeh was panting behind him. He saw she had the pack but had forgotten the chador. Her pale blue ski clothes showed clearly against the snow and trees. He hurried on again. She stumbled after him, beyond talking. Another hundred yards and still no trouble.

No place to stop yet. He went on, slower now, a violent ache in his side, near vomiting, grenade still ready, Azadeh flagging even more. He found the path that led to the back of the base. Still no pursuit. Near the rise, at the back of Erikki's cabin, he stopped, waiting for Azadeh, then his stomach heaved, he staggered and went down on his knees and vomited. Weakly, he got up and went up the rise to better cover. When Azadeh joined him she was laboring badly, her breath coming in great gulping pants. She slumped into the snow beside him, retching.

Down by the hangar he could see the 206, one of the mechanics washing it down. Good, he thought, perhaps it's being readied for a flight. Three armed revolutionaries were huddled on a nearby veranda under the overhang of a trailer in the lee of the small wind, smoking. No sign of life over the rest of the base, though chimney smoke came from Erikki's cabin and the one shared by the mechanics, and the cookhouse. He could see as far as the road. The roadblock was still there, men guarding it, some trucks and cars held up.

His eyes went back to the men on the veranda and he thought of Gueng and how his body had been tossed like a sack of old bones into the filth of the semi under their feet, perhaps these men, perhaps not. For a moment his head ached with the strength of his rage. He glanced back at Azadeh. She was over her spasm, still more or less in shock, not really seeing him, a dribble of saliva on her chin and a streak of vomit. With his sleeve he wiped her face. "We're fine now, rest awhile then we'll go on." She nodded and sank back on her arms, once more in her own private world. He returned his concentration to the base.

Ten minutes passed. Little change. Above, the cloud cover was a dirty blanket, snow heavy. Two of the armed men went into the office and he could see them from time to time through the windows. The third man paid little attention to the 206. No other movement. Then a cook came out of the cookhouse, urinated on the snow, and went back inside again. More time. Now one of the guards walked out of the office and trudged across the snow to the mechanics' trailer, an M16 slung over his shoulder. He opened the door and went inside. In a moment he came out again. With him was a tall European in flight gear and another man. Ross recognized the pilot Nogger Lane and the other mechanic. The mechanic said something to Lane, then waved and went back inside his trailer again. The guard and the pilot walked off toward the 206.

Everyone pegged, Ross thought, his heart fluttering. Awkwardly he checked his carbine, the grenade in his right hand inhibiting him, then put the last two spare magazines and the last grenade from his haversack into his side pocket. Suddenly fear swept into him and he wanted to run, oh, God help me, to run away, to hide, to weep, to be safe at home, away anywhere. . . .

"Azadeh, I'm going down there now," he forced himself to say. "Get ready to rush for the chopper when I wave or shout. Ready?" He saw her look at him and nod and mouth yes, but he wasn't sure if he had reached her. He said it again and smiled encouragingly. "Don't worry." She nodded mutely.

Then he loosened his kookri and went over the rise like a wild beast after food.

He slid behind Erikki's cabin, covered by the sauna. Sounds of children and a woman's voice inside. Dry mouth, grenade warm in his hand. Slinking from cover to cover, huge drums or piles of pipe and saws and logging spares, always closer to the office trailer. Peering around to see the guard and the pilot nearing the hangar, the man on the veranda idly watching them. The office door opened, another guard came out, and beside him a new man, older, bigger, clean-shaven, possibly European, wearing better quality clothes and armed with a Sten gun. On the thick leather belt around his waist was a scabbarded kookri.

Ross released the lever. It flew off. "One, two, three," and he stepped out of cover, hurled the grenade at the men on the veranda forty yards away, and ducked behind the tank again, already readying another.

They had seen him. For a moment they were stock-still, then as they dropped for cover the grenade exploded, blowing most of the veranda and overhang away, killing one of them, stunning another, and maiming the third. Instantly Ross rushed into the open, carbine leveled, the new grenade held tightly in his right hand, index finger on the trigger. There was no movement on the veranda, but down by the hangar door the mechanic and pilot dropped to the snow and put their arms over their heads in panic, the guard rushed for the hangar and for an instant was in the clear. Ross fired and missed, charged the hangar, noticed a back door, and diverted for it. He eased it open and leaped inside. The enemy was across the empty space, behind an engine, his gun trained on the other door. Ross blew his head off, the firing echoing off the corrugated iron walls, then ran for the other door. Through it he could see the mechanic and Nogger Lane hugging the snow near the 206. Still in cover, he called to them. "Quick! How many more hostiles're here?" No answer. "For Christ sake, answer me!"

Nogger Lane looked up, his face white. "Don't shoot, we're civilians, English—don't shoot!"

"How many more hostiles are here?"

"There . . . there were five . . . five . . . this one here and the rest in . . . in the office . . . I think in the office . . ."

Ross ran to the back door, dropped to the floor, and peered out at ground level. No movement. The office was fifty yards away—the only cover a detour around the truck. He sprang to his feet and charged for it. Bullets howled off the metal and then stopped. He had seen the automatic fire coming from a broken office window.

Beyond the truck was a little dead ground, and in the dead ground was a ditch that led within range. If they stay in cover they're mine. If they come out and they should, knowing I'm alone, the odds are theirs.

He slithered forward on his belly for the kill. Everything quiet, wind, birds, enemy. Everything waiting. In the ditch now. Progress slow. Getting near. Voices and a door creaking. Silence again. Another yard. Another. Now! He got his knees ready, dug his toes into the snow, eased the lever off the grenade, counted three, lurched to his feet, slipped but just managed to keep his balance, and hurled the grenade through the broken window, past the man standing there, gun pointing at him, and hit the snow again. The explosion stopped the burst of gunfire, almost blew out his own eardrums, and once again he was on his feet charging the trailer, firing as he went. He jumped over a corpse and went on in still firing. Suddenly his gun stopped and his stomach turned over, until he could jerk out the empty mag and slam in the new. He killed the machine gunner again and stopped.

Silence. Then a scream nearby. Cautiously he kicked the broken door away and went on to the veranda. The screamer was legless, demented, but still alive. Around his waist was the leather belt and the kookri that had been Gueng's. Fury blinded Ross, and he tore it out of the scabbard. "You got that at the roadblock?" he shouted in Farsi.

"Help me help me help me . . ." A paroxysm of some foreign language then, ". . . whoareyou who . . . help meeee . . ." The man continued screaming and mixed with it was, ". . . helpmehelpmeee yes I killed the saboteur . . . helpme . . ."

With a bloodcurdling scream Ross hacked downward and when his eyes cleared he was staring into the face of the head that he held up in his left hand. Revolted, he dropped it and turned away. For a moment he did not know where he was, then his mind cleared, his nostrils were filled with the stench of blood and cordite, he found himself in the remains of the trailer and looked around.

The base was frozen, but men were running toward it from the road-block. Near the chopper Lane and the mechanic were still motionless in the snow. He rushed for them, hugging cover.

Nogger Lane and the mechanic Arberry saw him coming and were panic-stricken—the stubble-bearded, matted-haired, wild-eyed maniac tribesman mujhadin or fedayeen who spoke perfect English, whose hands and sleeves were bloodstained from the head that only moments ago they had seen him hack off with a single stroke and a crazed scream, the bloody short sword-knife still in his hand, another in a scabbard, carbine in the other. They scrambled to their knees, hands up. "Don't kill us—we're friends, civilians, don't kill u—"

"Shut up! Get ready to take off. Quick!"

Nogger Lane was dumbfounded. "What?"

"For Christ's sake, hurry," Ross said angrily, infuriated by the look on their faces, completely oblivious of what he looked like. "You," he pointed at the mechanic with Gueng's kookri. "You, see that rise there?"

"Yes . . . yes, sir," Arberry croaked.

"Go up there fast as you can, there's a lady there, bring her down . . ." He stopped, seeing Azadeh come out of the forest edge and start running down the little hill toward them. "Forget that, go and get the other me-chanic, hurry for Christ's sake, the bastards from the roadblock'll be here any minute. Go on, hurry!" Arberry ran off, petrified but more petrified of the men he could see coming down the road. Ross whirled on Nogger Lane. "I told you to get started."

"Yes . . . yessir . . . that . . . that woman . . . that's not Azadeh, Erikki's Azadeh, is it?"

"Yes—I told you to start up!"

Nogger Lane never got a 206 into takeoff mode quicker, nor did the mechanics ever move faster. Azadeh still had a hundred yards to go and already the hostiles were too close. So Ross ducked under the whirling blades and got between her and them and emptied the magazine at them. Their heads went down and they scattered, and he threw the empty in their direction with a screaming curse. A few heads came up. Another burst and

another, conserving ammunition, kept them down, Azadeh close now but
slowing. Somehow she made a last effort and passed him, reeling drunkenly
for the backseat to be half pulled in by the mechanics. Ross fired another
short burst retreating, groped into the front seat, and they were airborne
and away.

KOWISS AIR BASE: 5:20 P.M. Starke picked up the card he had been dealt and looked at it. The ace of spades. He grunted, superstitious like most pilots, but just slid it importantly into his hand. The five of them were in his bungalow playing draw poker: Freddy Ayre, Doc Nutt, Pop Kelly, and Tom Lochart who had arrived late yesterday from Zagros Three with another load of spares, continuing the evacuation but too late to fly back. Because of the order forbidding flying today, Holy Day, he was grounded here until dawn tomorrow. There was a wood fire in the grate, the afternoon cold. In front of all of them were piles of rials, the biggest in front of Kelly, the smallest Doc Nutt's.

"How many cards, Pop?" Ayre asked.

"One," Kelly said without hesitation, discarded, and put the four he was keeping face downward on the table in front of him. He was a tall, thinnish man with a crumpled face, thin fair hair, ex-RAF, and in his early forties.

"Pop" was his nickname because he had seven children and another en route.

Ayre dealt the one card with a flourish. Kelly just stared at it for a moment, then, without looking at it, slowly mixed it with the others, then very carefully and elaborately picked up the hand, sneaked a look at the merest sliver of the top right corner, card by card, and sighed happily.

"Bullshit!" Ayre said and they all laughed. Except Lochart who stared moodily at his cards. Starke frowned, worried about him but very glad that he was here today. There was Gavallan's secret letter that John Hogg had brought on the 125 to discuss.

"1,000 rials for openers," Doc Nutt said and everyone looked at him. Normally he would bet 100 rials at the most.

Absently Lochart studied his hand, not interested in the game, his mind on Zagros—and Sharazad. The BBC last night had reported major clashes during the Women's Protest marches in Tehran, Isfahan, and Meshed with more marches scheduled for today and tomorrow. "Too rich for me," he said and threw in his cards.

"See you, Doc, and up a couple of thousand," Starke said and Doc Nutt's confidence vanished. Nutt had drawn two cards, Starke one, Ayre three.

Kelly looked at his straight, 4–5–6–7–8. "Your 2,000, Duke, and up 3,000!"

"Fold," Ayre said instantly, throwing away two pairs, kings and tens.

"Fold," Doc Nutt said with a sigh of relief, shocked with himself for being so rash initially and threw in the three queens he had been dealt, sure that Starke had filled a straight, flush or full house.

"Your 3,000, Pop, and up 30—thousand," Starke said sweetly, feeling very good inside. He had split a pair of sixes to keep four hearts, going for a flush. The ace of spades had made it a very busted flush but a winning hand if he could bluff Kelly to back off.

All eyes were on Kelly. The room was silent. Even Lochart was suddenly interested.

Starke waited patiently, guarding his face and hands, uneasy about the air of confidence surrounding Kelly and wondering what he would do if Kelly raised him again, knowing what Manuela'd say if she found out he was preparing to put a week's pay on a busted flush.

She'd bust a girdle for starters, he thought and smiled.

Kelly was sweating. He had seen Starke's sudden smile. He had caught him bluffing once but that was weeks ago and not for 30 thousand, only 4. I can't afford to lose a week's pay, still, the bugger could be bluffing. Something tells me old Duke's bluffing, and I could use an extra week's wages. Kelly rechecked his cards to make sure that his straight was a straight—of course it's a bloody straight for God's sake and Duke's bluffing! He felt his mouth begin to say, "I'll see your 30,000," but he stopped it and said instead, "Up yours, Duke," threw his cards in and everyone laughed. Except Starke. He picked up the pot, slid his cards into the deck, and shuffled them to make sure they could not be seen.

"I'll bet you were bluffing, Duke," Lochart said and grinned.

"Me? Me with a straight flush?" Starke said innocently amid jeers. He glanced at his watch. "I've got to do the rounds. Let's quit, continue after dinner, huh? Tom, you wanta come along?"

"Sure." Lochart put on his parka and followed Starke outside.

This was the best time of day for them in normal times—just before sundown, flying done, all the choppers washed and refueled ready for tomorrow, a drink to look forward to, time to read a little, write a few letters, listen to some music, eat, call home, then bed.

The base checked out fine. "Let's stroll, Tom," Starke said. "When're you going back to Tehran?"

"How about tonight?"

"Bad, huh?"

"Worse. I know Sharazad was on the Women's March even though I told her not to, then there's all the rest."

Last night Lochart had told him about her father, and all about the loss of HBC. Starke had been appalled, still was, and once more blessed his luck that he had not known when he had been taken by Hussain and his Green Bands for questioning.

"Mac'll have got hold of Sharazad by now, Tom. He'll make sure she's okay." When Lochart had arrived, they had got on to McIver on the HF, reception good for a change, and had asked him to see that she was safe. In a few minutes they would again have their one daily allowable radio link with Tehran HQ—"You're restricted but only until we're back to normal when you can call all you want—any day now," Major Changiz, the base commander, had said. And though they were monitored by the main tower across at the air force base, the link kept their sanity and gave an appearance of normality.

Starke said, "After Zagros Three's cleaned out Sunday and you're all here, why not take the 206, Monday, first thing? I'll fix it with Mac."

"Thanks, that'd be dandy." Now that his own base was closed down, Lochart was nominally under Starke's command.

"Have you thought of getting the hell out, taking the 212 instead of Scot? Once he's out of the Zagros he should be okay. Or even better, both of you going? I'll talk to Mac."

"Thanks but no, Sharazad can't leave her family just now."

They walked on awhile. Night was coming fast, cold but crisp, the air smelling heavily of gasoline from the huge refinery nearby that was still almost totally shut down and mostly dark, except for the tall stacks burning off oil vapor. On the base, lights were already on in most of their bungalows, hangars, and cookhouse—they had their own backup generators in case base power went out. Major Changiz had told Starke there was no chance the base generator system would be interfered with now: "The revolution is completely over, Captain, the Imam is in charge."

"And the leftists?"

"The Imam has ordered them eliminated, unless they conform to our Islamic state," Major Changiz had said, his voice hard and ominous. "Leftists, Kurds, Baha'is, aliens—any enemy. The Imam knows what to do."

Imam. It was the same at Starke's questioning in front of Hussain's komiteh. Almost as though he were semidivine, Starke had thought. Hussain had been the chief judge and prosecutor and the room, part of the mosque, crowded with hostile men of all ages, all Green Bands, five judges —no bystanders. "What do you know of the escape of the enemies of Islam from Isfahan by helicopter?"

"Nothing."

At once one of the other four judges, all young men, rough and hardly literate, said, "He's guilty of crimes against God and crimes against Iran as an exploiter for American Satanists. Guilty."

"No," Hussain said. "This is a court of law, Koranic law. He is here to answer questions, not yet for crimes, not yet. He is not accused of any crime. Captain, tell us everything you have heard about the Isfahan crime."

The air in the room had been fetid. Starke saw not a friendly face, yet all knew who he was, all knew about the battle against the fedayeen at Bandar Delam. His fear was a dull ache, knowing he was on his own now, at their mercy.

He took a breath and chose his words carefully. "In the Name of God the Compassionate, the Merciful," he said, starting as all the suras of the Koran begin, and an astonished stir went through the room. "I know nothing myself, I have witnessed nothing to do with it or been part of it. I was in Bandar Delam at the time. To my knowledge none of my people have had anything to do with it. I only know what Zataki of Abadan told me when he returned from Isfahan. Exactly he said: 'We heard that Tuesday some Shah supporters, all officers, fled south in a helicopter piloted by an American. God curse all Satanists.' That's all he said. That's all I know."

"You're a Satanist," one of the other judges interrupted triumphantly, "you're American. You're guilty."

"I am a person of the Book and I've already proved I'm no Satanist. If it wasn't for me many here would be dead."

"If we'd died at the base we'd be in Paradise now," a Green Band at the back of the room said angrily. "We were doing the Work of God. It was nothing to do with you, Infidel."

Shouts of agreement. Suddenly Starke let out a bellow of rage. "By God and the Prophet of God," he shouted, "I'm a person of the Book, and the Prophet gave us special privileges and protections!" He was shaking with rage now, his fear vanished, hating this kangaroo court and their blindness and stupidity and ignorance and bigotry. "The Koran says: 'Oh, People of the Book, overstep not the bounds of truth in your religion; neither follow the desires of those who have already gone astray and caused many others to stray from the evenness of the path.' I haven't," he ended harshly, bunching his fists, "and may God curse him who says otherwise."

Astonished, they all stared at him, even Hussain.

One of the judges broke the silence. "You . . . you quote the Koran? You read Arabic as well as speak Farsi?"

"No. No, I don't but th—"

"Then you had a teacher, a mullah?"

"No. No, I rea—"

"Then you're a sorcerer!" another shouted. "How can you know the Koran if you had no teacher nor read Arabic, the holy language of the Koran?"

"I read it in English, my own language."

Even greater astonishment and disbelief until Hussain spoke. "What he says is true. The Koran is translated into many foreign languages."

More astonishment. A young man peered at him myopically through cracked, thick-lensed glasses, his face pitted. "If it is translated into other languages, Excellency, then why isn't it in Farsi for us to read—if we could read?"

Hussain said, "The language of the Holy Koran is Arabic. To know the Holy Koran properly the Believer must read Arabic. Mullahs of all countries learn Arabic for this reason. The Prophet, whose Name be praised, was Arab. God spoke to him in that language for others to write down. To know the Holy Book truly it must be read as it was written." Hussain turned his black eyes on Starke. "A translation is always less than the original. Isn't it?"

Starke saw the curious expression. "Yes," he said, his intuition telling him to agree. "Yes, yes, it is. I would like to be able to read the original."

Another silence. The young man with glasses said, "If you know the

Koran so well that you can quote from it to us like a mullah, why aren't you Muslim, why aren't you a Believer?"

A rustle went through the room. Starke hesitated, almost in panic, not knowing how to answer but sure that the wrong answer would hang him. The silence grew, then he heard himself say, "Because God has not yet taken away the skin over my ears nor, not yet, opened my spirit," then added involuntarily, "I do not resist and I wait. I wait patiently."

The mood in the room changed. Now the silence was kind. Compassionate. Hussain said softly, "Go to the Imam and your waiting will be ended. The Imam would open your spirit to the glory of God. The Imam would open your spirit. I *know*, I've sat at the Imam's feet. I've heard the Imam preaching the Word, giving the Law, spreading the Calm of God." A sigh went through the room and now all concentrated on the mullah, watched his eyes and the light therein, heard the newness to his voice and the growing ecstasy therein—even Starke who felt chilled and at the same time elated. "Hasn't the Imam come to open the spirit of the world? Hasn't the Imam appeared among us to cleanse Islam of Evil and to spread Islam throughout the world, to carry the message of God . . . as has been promised? The Imam *is*."

The word hung in the room. They all understood. So did Starke. *Mahdi!* he thought, hiding his shock. Hussain's implying Khomeini's in reality the Mahdi, the legendary twelfth Imam who vanished centuries ago and Shi'as believe is just hidden from human sight—the Immortal One, promised by God to reappear some day to rule over a perfected world.

He saw them all staring at the mullah. Many nodding, tears running down the faces of others, all rapt and satisfied and not a disbeliever among them. Good God, he thought, dumbfounded, if Iranians give Khomeini that mantle there'll be no end to his power, there'll be twenty, thirty million men, women, and kids desperate to do his bidding, who'll rush happily to death at his merest whim—and why not? Mahdi would guarantee them a place in Heaven, guarantee it!

Someone said, "God is Great," others echoed it and they talked, one with another, Hussain leading them, Starke forgotten. At length they noticed him and they let him go, saying, "See the Imam, see and believe . . ."

Walking back to camp his feet had been strangely light, and he remembered now how the air had never tasted better, never had he been so full of the joy of life. Perhaps that's because I was so close to death, he thought. I was a dead man and somehow I was given back life. Why? And Tom, why did he escape Isfahan, Dez Dam, even HBC herself? Is there a reason? Or was it just luck?

* * *

And now in the dusk he watched Lochart, gravely concerned for him. Terrible about HBC, terrible about Sharazad's father, terrible that Tom and Sharazad are in a cauldron of no escape. Soon they'll both have to choose: exile together, probably never to return here—or to part, probably forever.

"Tom, there's something special. Very secret, just between us. Johnny Hogg brought a letter from Andy Gavallan." They were safely away from the base, strolling along the boundary road, skirting the eight-strand barbed-wire fence, and no fear of anyone overhearing. Even so he kept his voice down. "Basically Andy's mighty downbeat on our future here and says he's considering evacuating to cut his losses."

"No need for that," Lochart said quickly, a sudden bite in his voice. "Things'll get back to normal—they have to. Andy's got to sweat it out—we're sweating it out, so can he."

"He's sweating it out plenty, Tom. It's simple economics, you know that as well as any. We're not being paid for work done months ago, we've not enough work now for the birds and pilots here that he's paying out of Aberdeen, Iran's in a shambles, and we're getting a hard time all over."

"You mean because Zagros Three's been closed down there'll be a huge write-off on the books? Not my goddamn fault th—"

"Slow down, Tom. Andy's heard on the grapevine all foreign airplane companies, joint ventures or what the hell ever, particularly choppers, are going to be nationalized mighty damned soon."

Lochart was filled with a sudden hope. Wouldn't this give me a perfect excuse to stay? If they steal—nationalize—our birds they'll still need trained pilots, I can speak Farsi, I could train Iranians which's got to be their end plan and—and what about HBC? Back to HBC, he thought helplessly, always back to HBC. "How does he know, Duke?"

"Andy said it was an 'impeccable' source. What he's asking us—you, Scrag, Rudi, and me—is if he and Mac can come up with a workable plan, would we and however many pilots it takes fly all our birds into the Wild Blue across the Gulf?"

Lochart gaped at him. "Jesus, you mean just take off, no clearance no nothing?"

"Sure—but keep your voice down."

"He's crazy! How could we coordinate Lengeh, Bandar Delam, Kowiss, and Tehran—everyone'd have to go at the same time and the distances won't add up."

"Somehow they're gonna have to, Tom. Andy said it's that or close up."

"I don't believe it! The company's operating all over the world."

"He says if we lose Iran we're through."

"Easy for him," Lochart said bitterly. "It's just money. Easy to twist our arm when you're nice and safe and all you risk's money. He's saying if he just pulls personnel and leaves everything else, S-G's going belly-up?"

"Yes. That's what he's saying."

"I don't believe it."

Starke shrugged. Their ears caught the faint banshee wail and they turned and looked past their base to the far side of their part of the field. In the falling light they could just see Freddy Ayre with his bagpipes where, by common consent, he was allowed to practice. "Goddamn," Starke said sourly, "that noise drives me crazy."

Lochart ignored him. "Surely you're not going along with a goddamn hijack, because that's what it'll be! No way would I go along with that." He saw Starke shrug. "What do the others say?"

"They don't know yet and won't be asked yet. As I said this's between us at the moment." Starke glanced at his watch. "Almost time to call Mac." He saw a tremor go through Lochart. The lament of the bagpipes drifted on the wind. "How anyone can claim that's music, goddamned if I know," he said. "Andy's idea's worth considering, Tom. As an end plan."

Lochart did not answer him, feeling bad, the twilight bad, everything bad. Even the air smelled bad, polluted by the nearby refinery, and he wished he was back in Zagros, up near the stars where the air and the earth were not polluted, all of him desperate to be in Tehran where it was even more polluted—but she was there.

"Count me out," he said.

"Think about it, Tom."

"I have, I'm out, it's crazy, the whole idea. Soon as you think it out you'll see it's a mad dog scheme."

"Sure, old buddy." Starke wondered when his friend would realize that he, Lochart, of all of them, was counted in—one way or another.

U.S.S.R.

TURKEY

KHOI
TABRIZ

Caspian Sea

U.S.S.R.

MOUNT
SABALAN

BANDAR-E
PAHLAVI

QAZVIN

★ TEHRAN

IRAQ

AFGHANISTAN

BAGHDAD
★

IRAN

DEZ DAM

ZAGROS

•ISFAHAN

BANDAR DELAM

Shatt-
al-Arab
Estuary

ABADAN

•ZAGROS THREE

•KOWISS

MOUNTAINS

KUWAIT

KHARG

JELLET

Persian Gulf

LENGEH

Strait of
Hormuz

PAKISTAN

BAHRAIN

SIRL

SAUDI
ARABIA

AL SHARGAZ ○

Gulf of Oman

AT THE HOTEL INTERNATIONAL, AL SHARGAZ: 6:42 P.M.
"Could you do it, Scrag?" Gavallan said, sunset near.

"It'd be easy for me to sneak my five birds and men out of Lengeh,
Andy," Scragger said. "It'd have to be the right sort of day and we'd have to
slide under Kish radar but we could do it—if the lads wanted to be part of
the caper. But with all our spares too? No way, not possible."

"Would you do it, if it was possible?" Gavallan asked. He had arrived on
today's flight from London, all his business news from Aberdeen rotten—
Imperial Air putting on the pressure, undercutting him in the North Sea,
the oil companies squeezing him and Linbar calling a special board meeting
to investigate S-G's "possible" mismanagement. "Would you, Scrag?"

"Just me on my tod and everyone else safe and out? Like a shot."

"Would your lads do it?"

Scragger thought for a moment and sipped his beer. They were sitting at
a table on one of the immaculate terraces surrounding the swimming pool

of this, the newest of the hotels in the tiny sheikdom, other guests scattered around but none near, the air balmy and in the seventies with just enough breeze to tremble the palm fronds and promise a perfect evening. "Ed Vossi would." He grinned. "He's got enough Aussie larceny and Yankee get-up-and-go. Don't think Willi Neuchtreiter would. It'd be tough for him to break so many regs when it's not his tail and he's not threatened. Wot does Duke Starke say? And Tom Lochart and Rudi?"

"I don't know yet. I sent a letter to Duke via Johnny Hogg Wednesday."

"That's kind of dangerous, isn't it?"

"Yes and no. Johnny Hogg's a safe courier, but it's a big problem—to have safe communications. Tom Lochart'll soon be in Kowiss—you heard about Zagros?"

"Too right! They're all bonkers up in the mountains. What about old Rudi?"

"Don't know how to get to him safely yet. Maybe Mac'll have an idea. I'm on the 125 in the morning to Tehran and we're to talk at the airport. Then I'll come right back and I'm booked on the night flight to London."

"You're pushing it a bit, aren't you, old son?"

"I've a few problems, Scrag." Gavallan stared into his glass, absently swirling the whisky around the ice cubes. Other guests were going past. Three were girls, bikinied, golden skins, long black hair, towels casually around their shoulders. Scragger noticed them, sighed, then turned his attention back to Gavallan.

"Andy, I may have to take Kasigi back to Iran-Toda in a day or two—old Georges's been touching his toes since Kasigi agreed to pay him two dollars over spot. Kasigi thinks it'll go to twenty dollars a barrel by Christmas."

Gavallan's worry increased. "If it does it'll send a shock wave through every industrialized nation—inflation's going to soar again. I suppose if anyone'd know it'd be them." Earlier, the moment Scragger had mentioned Kasigi and Toda, he had reacted instantly, as Struan's supplied crews and leased many of the ships Toda built and were old associates. "Years ago I knew this Kasigi's boss, man called Hiro Toda. Did he ever mention it?"

"No, no, he never did. You knew him where? In Japan?"

"No, Hong Kong. Toda was doing business with Struan's—the company I used to work for—in those days it was Toda Shipping, shipbuilders mostly, not the huge conglomerate they are today." Gavallan's face hardened. "My family were Shanghai China traders from way back. Our company got more or less wiped out in the First World War, then we joined up with Struan's. My old man was at Nanking in '31 when the Japs raped it, and he got caught in Shanghai just after Pearl Harbor and never made it out of POW camp." He watched the reflections of his glass, his gloom increasing. "We lost a lot of good chums in Shanghai and Hong Kong. I can never forgive them for what they did in China, never will, but then, we have to move on, don't we? Have to bury the hatchet someday though you'd best keep your eye on the tooth marks."

"It's the same for me." Scragger shrugged. "Kasigi seems okay."

"Where is he now?"

"Kuwait. He's back tomorrow and I'm to take him to Lengeh for consultations in the morning."

"If you go to Iran-Toda, you think you might be able to get over to see Rudi? Maybe sound him out?"

"Too right. That's a good idea, Andy."

"When you see Kasigi, mention I know his chairman."

"Sure, sure I will. I could ask him if h—" He stopped, glanced over Gavallan's shoulder. "Look, Andy, now there's a sight for sore eyes!"

Gavallan looked around, westward. The sunset was unearthly—reds and purples and browns and golds painting the distant clouds, the sun almost three quarters under the horizon, bloodying the waters of the Gulf, the touch of wind flickering the candles on the starched tablecloths already laid for dinner on the dining terrace. "You're right, Scrag," he said at once. "It's the wrong time to be serious, it can wait. There's no sight in the world like a sunset."

"Eh?" Scragger was staring at him blankly. "For God's sake, I didn't mean the sunset—I meant the sheila."

Gavallan sighed. The sheila was Paula Giancani, just out of the pool below them, her bikini briefer than brief, the beads of water on her olive skin glistening and bejeweled by the sunset, now drying her legs and arms and back and now her legs again, putting on a gossamer swimming wrap, totally and joyously aware there was not a man within sight who did not appreciate her performance—or a woman who was not envious. "You're a horny bastard, Scrag."

Scragger laughed and thickened his accent. "It's me one joy in life, old cock! Cor', that Paula's one for the book."

Gavallan studied her. "Well, Italian girls generally have something extra special about them, but that young lady . . . she's not a stunner like Sharazad, and doesn't have Azadeh's exotic mystery, but I agree, Paula's something else."

Along with everyone else, they watched her walk through the tables, lust following, envy following, until she had vanished into the vast hotel lobby. They were all having dinner later, Paula, Genny, Manuela, Scragger, Gavallan, Sandor Petrofi, and John Hogg. Paula's Alitalia jumbo was again at Dubai, a few miles down the highway, waiting for clearance to go to Tehran

for another load of Italian nationals, and Genny McIver had met her by
chance shopping.

Scragger sighed. "Andy, old chap, I'd certainly like to give her one, no
doubt about it!"

"Wouldn't do you a bit of good, Scrag." Gavallan chuckled and ordered
another whisky and soda from a crisply dressed, smiling Pakistani waiter
who came instantly, some of the other guests already elegantly and expen-
sively dressed for a lovely evening, latest Paris fashions, much décolletage,
starched white dinner jackets—along with the expensive casual. Gavallan
wore well-cut tan tropicals, Scragger regulation uniform, short-sleeved white
shirt with epaulets and bars, black trousers and shoes. "Beer, Scrag?"

"No, thanks, mate. I'll nurse this and get ready for Pulsating Paula."

"Dreamer!" Gavallan turned back to the sunset, feeling better, put back
together by his old friend. The sun was almost under the horizon, never
more beautiful, reminding him of sunsets in China in the old days, sweep-
ing him back to Hong Kong and Kathy and Ian, laughter in the Great
House on the Peak, all the family fine and strong, their own house on a
promontory at Shek-o—when they were young and together, Melinda and
Scot still children, amahs padding about, sampans and junks and ships of all
sizes far below in the sunset on a safe sea.

The tip of the sun went under the sea. With great solemnity, Gavallan
quietly clapped his hands.

"Wot's that for, Andy?"

"Um? Oh, sorry, Scrag. In the old days we used to applaud the sun,
Kathy and I, the very second after it disappeared. To thank the sun for
being there and for the unique performance and for being alive to be able to
enjoy it—the last time ever you'd see that particular sunset. Like tonight.
You'll never see that one again." Gavallan sipped his whisky, watching the
afterglow. "The first person who introduced me to the idea was a wonderful
fellow, we became good friends—still are. Great man, his wife's crackerjack,
too. I'll tell you about them sometime." He turned his back to the west and
leaned forward and said softly, "Lengeh. You think it's possible?"

"Oh, yes—if it was just us at Lengeh. We'd still have to plan very careful,
Kish radar's more itchy than ever, but we could slip under her on the right
day. Big problem's that our Iranian ground crew and staff, along with our
presently friendly but zealous komiteh and our new unfriendly IranOil
joker, would know within minutes we'd done a bunk, they'd have to with all
birds up and away. At once they'd holler to IATC and they'd radio an all-
points alert to Dubai, Abu Dhabi, here—in fact from Oman through Saudi
and Kuwait up to Baghdad—telling them to impound us on arrival. Even if
we all got here . . . well, the old sheik's a great guy, liberal and a friend,

but hell, he couldn't go against Iran ATC when they were right—even if they were wrong. He couldn't pick a fight with Iran, he's got a good percentage of Shi'as among his Sunnis, not as bad as some on the Gulf, worse'n others."

Gavallan got up and walked to the edge of the terrace and looked down at the old city—once a great pearling port, pirate stronghold, and slave market, trading center and, like Sohar in Oman, called the Port of China. Since ancient times the Gulf was the golden sea link between the Mediterranean—then center of the world—and Asia. Seafaring Phoenician traders, who came from Oman originally, dominated this incredibly wealthy trade route, landing the goods of Asia and India at Shatt-al-Arab, thence by short caravan routes to their markets, eventually to carve their own seaborne Mediterranean empire, founding city-states like Carthage to threaten even Rome herself.

The old walled city was beautiful in the dying light, flat roofs, unspoiled and protected from modern buildings, the sheik's fort dominating it. Over the years Gavallan had come to know the old sheik and to admire him. The sheikdom was surrounded by the Emirates but was an independent, sovereign enclave barely twenty miles deep with seven miles of coastline. But inland and out to sea for a hundred miles up to Iranian waters, within easy drilling, was a pool of oil many billion barrels thick. So Al Shargaz had the old city and a separate new city with a dozen modern hotels and skyscrapers, and an airport that could just handle a jumbo. In riches nothing to compare with the Emirates, or Saudi, or Kuwait but enough for abundance in everything, if chosen wisely. The sheik was as wise as his Phoenician ancestors were worldly-wise, as fiercely independent, and though he himself could not read or write, his sons were graduates from the best universities on earth. He and his family and his tribe owned everything, his word was law, he was Sunni, not a fundamentalist, and tolerant with his foreign subjects and guests, provided they behaved.

"He also detests Khomeini and all fundamentalists, Scrag."

"Yes. But he still daren't pick a fight with Khomeini—that won't help us."

"It won't hurt us." Gavallan felt cleansed by the sunset. "I plan to hire a couple of jumbo freighters, get them here, and when our choppers arrive we strip rotors, stuff their bellies full, and blast off. Speed's the key—and planning."

Scragger whistled. "You really mean to do it?"

"I really mean to see if we *can* do it, Scrag, and what the odds are. This's the big one, if we lose all our Iranian choppers, equipment, and spares, we close. No insurance covers us and we're still liable to pay what we owe.

You're a partner, you can see the figures tonight. I brought them for you—and for Mac."

Scragger thought about his stake in the company, all the stake he had, and about Nell and his kids and their kids back in Sydney, and the station of Baldoon that had been the family sheep and cattle station for a century but was lost in the great drought, that he had had his eyes on for years and years and years to repossess for them.

"No need for me t'look at figures, Andy. If you say it's that bad, it's that bad." He was watching the patterns of the sky. "Tell you what, I'll take care of Lengeh if you can figure a plan and if the others're in. After dinner maybe we could talk logistics for an hour, and finish up over breakfast. Kasigi won't be back from Kuwait until 9:00 A.M. We'll figure her out."

"Thanks, Scrag." Gavallan clapped him on the shoulder, towering over him. "I'm damned glad you were here, damned glad you've been with us all these years. For the first time I think we've a chance and I'm not dreaming."

"One condition, old sport," Scragger added.

Gavallan was instantly on guard. "I can't square your medical if it's not up to scratch. There's no way th—"

"Do you mind?" Scragger was pained. "It's nothing to do with Dirty Duncan and my medical—that's going to be good till I'm seventy-three. No, the condition is at dinner you sit me next to Pulsating Paula, Genny on her other side, Manuela beside me, and that horny Hungarian Sandor way down the other end along with Johnny Hogg."

"Done!"

"Bonzer! Now don't you worry, mate, I've been sodded about by enough generals in five wars to've learned something. Time to change for dinner. Lengeh was getting boring and no doubt about it." He walked off, thin, straight, and sprightly.

Gavallan gave over his credit card to the smiling Pakistani waiter.

"No need for that, sahib, please just sign the bill," the man said. Then added softly, "If I might suggest, Effendi, when you pay, don't use American Express, it is the most expensive for the management."

Bemused, Gavallan left a tip and walked off.

On the other side of the terrace two men watched him leave. Both were well dressed and in their forties, one American, the other Middle Eastern. Both wore tiny hearing aids. The man who was Middle Eastern was toying with an old-fashioned fountain pen, and as Gavallan passed a well-dressed Arab and a very attractive young European girl in deep conversation, the man with the fountain pen became curious, pointed it at them and steadied it. At once both men could hear the voices in their earphones; "my dear, $500 U.S. is much more than market price," the man was saying.

"It depends what market forces concern you, my dear," she replied, her Middle-European accent pleasing, and they saw her smile gently. "The fee includes the very best silk underwear you wish to rip to pieces and the probe you require inserted at your moment of truth. Expertise is expertise and special services require special handling and if your schedule only permits between six and eight tomorrow evening—"

The voices vanished as the man turned the cap and put the pen on the tabletop with a wry smile. He was handsome and olive-skinned, an importer-exporter of fine carpets like generations of his forebears, American educated, his name Aaron ben Aaron—his main occupation major, Israeli Special Intelligence. "I'd never have figured Abu bin Talak as kinky," he said dryly.

The other man grunted. "They're all kinky. I wouldn't have figured the girl for a hooker."

Aaron's long fingers toyed with the pen, reluctant to let it go. "Great gadget, Glenn, saves so much time. Wish I'd had one years ago."

"KGB's got a new model out this year, good for a hundred yards' range." Glenn Wesson sipped his bourbon on the rocks. He was American, a long-time oil trader. Real profession, career CIA. "It's not as small as this but effective."

"Can you get us some?"

"Easier for you to do it. Just get your guys to ask Washington." They saw Gavallan disappear into the lobby. "Interesting."

"What'd'you think?" Aaron asked.

"That we could throw a British chopper company to the Khomeini wolves anytime we want—along with all their pilots. That'd make Talbot bust a gut and Robert Armstrong and all MI6 which isn't a bad idea." Wesson laughed softly. "Talbot needs a good shafting from time to time. What's the problem with S-G, you think they're an MI6 cover operation?"

"We're not sure what they're up to, Glenn. We suspect just the reverse, that's why I thought you should listen in. Too many coincidences. On the surface they're legit—yet they've a French pilot Sessonne who's sleeping with, and sponsoring, a well-connected PLO courier, Sayada Bertolin; they've a Finn, Erikki Yokkonen, closely associated with Abdollah Khan who's certainly a double agent leaning more to the KGB than our side and openly, violently anti-Jew; Yokkonen's very close to the Finnish Intelligence man, Christian Tollonen, who's suspect by definition, Yokkonen's family connections in Finland would position him to be a perfect deep-cover Soviet asset and we just got a buzz that he's up in the Sabalan with his 212, helping Soviets dismantle your covert radar sites all over."

"Jesus. You sure?"

"No—I said a buzz. But we're checking it out. Next, the Canadian Lochart: Lochart's married into a known anti-Zionist bazaari family, PLO agents are living in his apartment right now, h—"

"Yes, but we heard the pad was commandeered and don't forget he tried to help those pro-Shah, pro-Israel officers escape."

"Yes, but they got shot out of the skies, they're all dead and curiously he isn't. Valik and General Seladi would certainly have been in or near any cabinet-in-exile—we lost another two very important assets. Lochart's suspect, his wife and her family're pro-Khomeini which means anti-us." Aaron smiled sardonically. "Aren't we the great Satan after you? Next: the American Starke helps put down a fedayeen attack at Bandar Delam, gets very friendly with another rabid anti-Shah, anti-Israel zealot Zataki who—"

"Who?"

"An anti-Shah fighter, intellectual, Sunni Muslim who organized Abadan oil-field strikes, blew up three police stations, and now is heading up the Abadan Revolutionary Komiteh and not long for this earth. Drink?"

"Sure, thanks. Same. You mentioned Sayada Bertolin—we've had her tabbed too. You think she could be turned?"

"I wouldn't trust her. Best thing to do with her is just watch and see who she leads to. We're after her controller—can't peg him yet." Aaron ordered for Wesson and a vodka for himself. "Back to S-G. So Zataki's enemy. Starke speaks Farsi, like Lochart. Both keep bad company. Next Sandor Petrofi: Hungarian dissident with family still in Hungary, another potential KGB mole or at least a KGB tool. Rudi Lutz, German with close family over the Iron Curtain, always suspect, Neuchtreiter in Lengeh the same." He nodded to where Scragger had been. "The old man's just a trained killer, a mercenary to point at us, you, anyone with the same result. Gavallan? You should get your London people to tab him—don't forget he chose all the others, don't forget he's British—quite possibly his whole operation's a KGB cover an—"

"No way," Wesson said, suddenly irritated. Goddamn, he thought, why're these guys so paranoid—even old Aaron who's the best there is. "It's all too pat. No way."

"Why not? He could be fooling you. The British are past masters at it— like Philby, McLean, Blake, and all the rest."

"Like Crosse." Wesson's lips went into a thin line. "In that you're right, old buddy."

"Who?"

"Roger Crosse—ten-odd years back, Mister Spymaster, but buried and covered up with all the skill Limeys have—he's one of those from the Old Boys' Club, the foulest traitors of them all."

"Who was Crosse?"

"Armstrong's ex-boss and friend from Hong Kong Special Branch in the old days. Officially a minor deputy director of MI6 but really top of their cream operation, Special Intelligence, traitor, terminated by the KGB at his own request just before we were going to nail the bastard."

"You proved it? That they terminated him?"

"Sure. Poison dart from close range, SOP, that's what sent him onward. We had him cornered, no way he could get away like the others. We had him nailed, triple agent. At that time we'd a plant inside the Soviet embassy in London—guy called Brodnin. He gave us Crosse then disappeared, poor bastard, someone must've fingered him."

"God cursed British, they breed spies like lice."

"Not true, they've some great catchers too—we've all got traitors."

"We don't."

"Don't bet on it, Aaron," Wesson said sourly. "There're traitors all over —with all the leaks in Tehran before and since the Shah left, there's got to be another high-up traitor our side."

"Talbot or Armstrong?"

Wesson winced. "If it's either of them we should just quit."

"That's what the enemy wants you to do, quit and get to hell out of the Middle East. We can't, so we think differently," Aaron said, eyes dark and cold, face set, watching him carefully. "Talking of that, why should our old friend Colonel Hashemi Fazir get away with murdering the new SAVAMA hatchet man, General Janan?"

Wesson blanched. "Janan's dead? You're sure?"

"Car bomb, Monday night." Aaron's eyes narrowed. "Why so sorry? Was he one of yours?"

"Could have been. We, er, we were negotiating." Wesson hesitated, then sighed. "But Hashemi's still alive? I thought he was on the Revolutionary Komiteh's urgent condemned list."

"He was, not now. I heard this morning his name's off, his rank's confirmed, Inner Intelligence's reinstated—supposedly all approved by on high."

Aaron sipped his drink. "If he's back in favor, after all he did for the Shah and us, he's got to have a very high protector."

"Who?" Wesson saw the other shrug, eyes ranging the terraces. His smile vanished. "That could mean he's been working for the Ayatollah all the time."

"Perhaps." Aaron toyed with the fountain pen again. "Another curiosity. Tuesday Hashemi was seen getting on the S-G 125 at Tehran Airport with Armstrong; they went to Tabriz and were back in three hours-odd."

"I'll be goddamned!"

"What's that all add up to?"

"Jesus, I don't know—but I think we better find out." Wesson dropped his voice further. "One thing's certain, for Hashemi to get back in favor he's got to know where some very important bodies are buried, huh? Such information would be highly valuable . . . highly valuable, say to the Shah."

"Shah?" Aaron started to smile, stopped as he saw Wesson's expression. "You don't seriously figure the Shah's got a chance to come back?"

"Stranger things've happened, old buddy," Wesson said confidently and finished his drink. Why is it these guys don't understand what's going on in the world? he was thinking. It's time they smartened up, stopped being so one-track about Israel, the PLO, and the whole Middle East, and gave us room to maneuver. "Sure the Shah's gotta chance, though his son's a better bet—soon's Khomeini's dead and buried it'll be civil war, the army'll take over and they'll need a figurehead. Reza'd be a great constitutional monarch."

Aaron ben Aaron kept the disbelief off his face with difficulty, astounded that Wesson could still be so naive. After all the years you've been in Iran and the Gulf, he thought, how can you still misunderstand the explosive forces ripping Iran apart? If he had been a different man he would have cursed Wesson for the stupidity he represented, the hundreds of alarm signals disregarded, the hills of secret intelligence reports gathered with so much blood and cast aside unread, their years of pleading with politicians and generals and Intelligence—American and Iranian—warning of the gathering conflagration.

All to no avail. For years and years. The Will of God, he thought. God does not want it to be easy for us. Easy? In all history it's never once been easy for us. Never never never.

He saw Wesson watching him. "What?"

"You wait and see. Khomeini's an old man, he won't last the year. He's old and time's with us—you wait and see."

"I will." Aaron put aside his inclination to argue violently. "Meanwhile, the problem in hand: S-G could be a front for enemy cells. When you think about it, chopper pilots specializing in oil support'd be valuable assets for all kinds of sabotage if the going get worse."

"Sure. But Gavallan wants out of Iran. You heard him."

"Maybe he knew we were listening, or it's a ploy he's pulling."

"Come on, Aaron. I think he's kosher, and the rest of it's coincidence."
Wesson sighed. "Okay, I'll put a tab on him, and he won't shit without you knowing, but hell, old buddy, you guys see enemies under the bed, on the ceiling, and under the carpet."

"Why not? There're plenty around—known, unknown, active, or passive." Aaron was methodically watching around him, checking on newcomers, expecting enemies, aware of the multitude of enemy agents in Al Shargaz and the Gulf. And we know about enemies, here, outside in the old city and in the new city, up the road to Oman and down the road to Dubai and Baghdad and Damascus, to Moscow and Paris and London, across the sea to New York, south to both the Capes and north to the Arctic Circle, wherever there're people who're not Jews. Only a Jew not automatically suspect and even then, these days, you've got to be careful.

There're many among the Chosen who don't want Zion, don't want to go to war or pay for war, don't want to understand Israel hangs in the balance with the Shah, our only ally in the Middle East and sole OPEC supplier of oil for our tanks and planes cast aside, don't want to know our backs are to the Wailing Wall and we've to fight and die to protect our God-given land of Israel we repossessed with God's help at such cost!

He looked up at Wesson, liking him, forgiving him his faults, admiring him as a professional but sorry for him: he wasn't a Jew and therefore suspect. "I'm glad I was born a Jew, Glenn. It makes life so much easier."

"How?"

"You know where you stand."

AT DISCO TEX, HOTEL SHARGAZ: 11:52 P.M. Americans, British, and French dominated the room—some Japanese and other Asians. Europeans in the majority, many, many more men than women, their ages ranging between twenty-five and forty-five—the Gulf expat work force had to be young, strong, preferably unmarried, to survive the hard, celibate life. A few drunks, some noisy. Ugly and not so ugly, overweight and not so overweight, most of them lean, frustrated, and volcanic. A few Shargazi and others of the Gulf, but only the rich, the Westernized, the sophisticated, and men. Most of these sat on the upper level drinking soft drinks and ogling, and the few who danced on the small floor below danced with European women: secretaries, embassy personnel, airline staff, nurses, or other hotel staff—partners at a premium. No Shargazi or Arabian women were here.

Paula danced with Sandor Petrofi, Genny with Scragger, and Johnny Hogg was cheek to cheek with the girl who had been deep in conversation on the terrace, swaying at half tempo. "How long're you staying, Alexandra?" he murmured.

"Next week, only until next week. Then I must join my husband in Rio."

"Oh, but you're so young to be married! You're all alone till then?"

"Yes, alone, Johnny. It's sad, no?"

He did not reply, just held her a little tighter and blessed his luck that he had picked up the book she had dropped in the lobby. The strobe lights dazzled him for a moment, then he noticed Gavallan on the upper level, standing at the rail, grave and lost in thought, and again felt sorry for him. Earlier he had reluctantly arranged tomorrow's night flight to London for him, trying to persuade him to rest over a day. "I know how jet lag plays hell with you, sir."

"No problem, Johnny, thanks. Our takeoff for Tehran's still at 10:00 A.M.?"

"Yes, sir. Our clearance's still priority—and the charter onward to Tabriz."

"Let's hope that goes smoothly, just there and straight back."

John Hogg felt the girl's loins against him. "Will you have dinner tomorrow? I should be back sixish."

"Perhaps—but not before nine."

"Perfect."

Gavallan was looking down on the dancers, hardly seeing them, then turned and went down the stairs and outside onto the ground-floor terrace. The night was lovely, moon huge, no clouds. Around were acres of delicately floodlit, beautifully kept gardens within the encircling walls, some of the sprinklers on.

The Shargaz was the biggest hotel in the sheikdom, on one side the sea, the other the desert, its tower eighteen stories, with five restaurants, three bars, cocktail lounge, coffee shop, the disco, two swimming pools, saunas, steam rooms, tennis courts, health center, shopping mall with a dozen boutiques and antiques, an Aaron carpet shop, hairdressing salons, video library, bakery, electronics, telex office, typing pool, with, like all the modern European hotels, all rooms and suites air-conditioned, bathrooms and bidets *en suite*, twenty-four-hour room service—mostly smiling Pakistanis—same-day cleaners, instant pressing, a color TV in every room, in-house movies, stock market channel, and satellite distant dialing to every capital in the world.

True, Gavallan thought, but still a ghetto. And though the rulers of Al Shargaz and Dubai and Sharjah are liberal and tolerant so expats can drink in the hotels, can even buy liquor, though God help you if you resell any to a Muslim, our women can drive and shop and walk about, that's no guarantee it'll last. A few hundred yards away, Shargazi are living as they've lived for centuries, a few miles away over the border liquor's forbidden, a woman can't drive or be on the streets alone and has to cover her hair and arms and shoulders and wear loose pants, and over there in the real desert, people exist on a stratum of life that's pitiless.

A few years ago he had taken a Range Rover and a guide and, together with McIver and Genny and his new wife Maureen, had gone out into the desert to spend the night in one of the oases on the edge of Rub' al-Khali, the Empty Quarter. It had been a perfect spring day. Within minutes of their passing the airport, the road became a track that quickly petered out and they were grinding over the stony expanse under the bowl of sky. Picnic lunch, then on again, sometimes sandy, sometimes rocky, detouring in the wilderness where it never rained and nothing grew. Nothing. On again. When they stopped and turned the engine off, the silence came at them like a physical presence, the sun bore down, and space enveloped them.

That night was blue-black, stars enormous, tents fine and carpets soft, and even greater silence, greater space, so much space inconceivable. "I hate it, Andy," Maureen had whispered. "It frightens me to death."

"Me too. Don't know why but it does." Around the palm trees of the oasis, the desert went to every horizon, taunting and unearthly. "The immensity seems to suck the life out of you. Imagine what it's like in summer!"

She trembled. "It makes me feel less than a grain of sand. It's crushing me—somehow it's taken my balance away. Och, ay, laddie, once is enough for me. It's me for Scotland—London at a pinch—and never again."

And she had never come back. Like Scrag's Nell, he thought. Don't blame them. It's tough enough in the Gulf for men, but for women . . . He glanced around. Genny was coming out of the French windows, fanning herself, looking much younger than in Tehran. "Hello, Andy. You're the wise one, it's so stuffy in there, and the smoke, ugh!"

"Never was much of a dancer."

"The only time I get to dance is when Duncan's not with me. He's such a stick-in-the-mud." She hesitated. "On tomorrow's flight, do you think I co—"

"No," he said kindly. "Not yet. In a week or so—let the dust settle."

She nodded, not hiding her disappointment. "What did Scrag say?"

"Yes—if the others are in and it's feasible. We had a good talk and we're having breakfast." Gavallan put his arm around her and gave her a hug. "Don't worry about Mac, I'll make sure he's all right."

"I've another bottle of whisky for him, you don't mind, do you?"

"I'll put it in my briefcase—we're on notice by IATC not to have any booze as aircraft stores—no problem, I'll hand carry it."

"Then perhaps you'd better not, not this time." She found his gravity unsettling, so unusual in him. Poor Andy, anyone can see he's beside himself with worry. "Andy, can I make a suggestion?"

"Of course, Genny."

"Use this colonel and Roberts, no, Armstrong, the VIPs you've got to ferry to Tabriz. Why not ask them to route you back through Kowiss, say you need to pick up some engines for repair, eh? Then you can talk to Duke directly."

"Very good idea—go to the top of the class."

She reached up and gave him a sisterly kiss. "You're not bad yourself. Well, it's me back to the fray—haven't been so popular since the war." She laughed and so did he. "Night, Andy."

Gavallan went back to his hotel that was just down the road. He did not notice the men tailing him, nor that his room had been searched, his papers read, nor that now the room was bugged and the phone tapped.

SATURDAY
February 24

Map labels:
U.S.S.R. • U.S.S.R. • TURKEY • KHOI • TABRIZ • Caspian Sea • MOUNT SABALAN • BANDAR-E PAHLAVI • QAZVIN • TEHRAN • IRAQ • IRAN • BAGHDAD • ZAGROS • DEZ DAM • ISFAHAN • AFGHANISTAN • Shatt-al-Arab Estuary • ABADAN • BANDAR DELAM • ZAGROS THREE • KUWAIT • KOWISS • MOUNTAINS • KHARG • JELLET • Persian Gulf • LENGEH • Strait of Hormuz • PAKISTAN • BAHRAIN • SAUDI ARABIA • QATAR • SIRI • AL SHARGAZ • Gulf of Oman

CHAPTER 46

AT TEHRAN INTERNATIONAL AIRPORT: 11:58 A.M. The cabin door of the 125 closed behind Robert Armstrong and Colonel Hashemi Fazir. From the cockpit, John Hogg gave Gavallan and McIver, who stood on the tarmac beside his car, a thumbs-up and taxied away, outward bound for Tabriz. Gavallan had just arrived from Al Shargaz and this was the first moment he and McIver had been alone.

"What's up, Mac?" he said, the chill wind tugging at their winter clothes and billowing the snow around them.

"Trouble, Andy."

"I know that. Tell it to me quickly."

McIver leaned closer. "I've just heard we've barely a week, before we're grounded pending nationalization."

"What?" Gavallan was suddenly numb. "Talbot told you?"

"No, Armstrong, a few minutes ago when the colonel was in the loo and we were alone." McIver's face twisted. "The bastard told me with his smooth, put-on politeness, 'I wouldn't bet on more than ten days if I were you—a week'd be safe—and don't forget, Mr. McIver, a closed mouth catches no flies.' "

"My God, does he know we are planning something?" A gust speckled them with powdered snow.

"I don't know. I just don't know, Andy."

"What about HBC? Did he mention her?"

"No. When I asked about the papers, all he said was, 'They're safe.' "

"Did he say when we're to meet today?"

McIver shook his head. " 'If I'm back in time I'll be in touch.' Bastard." He jerked his car door open.

In turmoil Gavallan brushed off the excess snow and slid into the warmth. The windows were fogged up. McIver switched the defrost and fan to maximum, heat already at maximum, then pushed the music cassette home, jacked the sound up, turned it down again, cursing.

"What else's up, Mac?"

"Just about everything," McIver blurted out. "Erikki's been kidnapped by Soviets or the KGB and he's somewhere up near the Turkish border with his 212, doing Christ knows what—Nogger thinks he's being forced to help them clean out secret U.S. radar sites. Nogger, Azadeh, two of our mechanics and a British captain barely escaped from Tabriz with their lives, they got back yesterday and they're at my place at the moment—at least they were when I left this morning. My God, Andy, you should have seen the state they were in when they arrived. The captain was the same one who saved Charlie at Doshan Tappeh and whom Charlie dropped off at Bandar-e Pahlavi . . ."

"He what?"

"It was a secret op. He's a captain in the Gurkhas . . . name's Ross, John Ross, he and Azadeh were both pretty incoherent, Nogger too was pretty excited, and, at least they're safe now but . . ." McIver's voice became brittle. "Sorry to tell you we've lost a mechanic at Zagros, Effer Jordon, he was shot an—"

"Jesus Christ! Old Effer dead?"

"Yes . . . yes, I'm afraid so and your son was nicked . . . not badly," McIver added hastily as Gavallan blanched. "Scot's all right, he's okay an—"

"How badly?"

"Bullet through the fleshy part of the right shoulder. No bones touched, just a flesh wound—Jean-Luc said they've penicillin, a medic, the wound's clean. Scot won't be able to ferry the 212 out tomorrow to Al Shargaz so I

asked Jean-Luc to do it and take Scot with him, then come back to Tehran
on the next 125 flight and we'll get him back to Kowiss."

"What the hell happened?"

"I don't know exactly. I got a relayed message from Starke this morning
who'd just picked it up from Jean-Luc. It seems that terrorists are operating
in the Zagros, I suppose the same bunch that attacked Bellissima and Rosa,
they must've been hiding in ambush in the forests around our base. Effer
Jordon and Scot were loading spares into the 212 just after dawn this
morning and got sprayed. Poor old Effer got most of the bullets and Scot
just one . . ." Again McIver added hurriedly, seeing Gavallan's face,
"Jean-Luc assured me Scot's all right, Andy, honest to God!"

"I wasn't thinking just about Scot," Gavallan said heavily. "Effer's been
with us damn nearly since we started—hasn't he got three kids?"

"Yes, yes, he has. Terrible." McIver let in the clutch and eased the car
through the snow back toward their office. "They're all still at school, I
think."

"I'll do something about them soon as I get back. Go on about Zagros."

"Nothing much more. Tom Lochart wasn't there—he had to stay overnight at Kowiss Friday. Jean-Luc said they didn't see any of the attackers,
no one did, the shots just came out of the forest—the base's in chaos
anyway what with our birds working overtime, bringing men from all the
outlying rigs and ferrying them in batches to Shiraz, everyone pitching in to
clear out before the deadline tomorrow at sunset."

"Will they make it?"

"More or less. We'll get out all our oilers and our chaps, most of our
valuable spares and all choppers to Kowiss. The rig support equipment'll
have to be left but that's not our responsibility. God knows what'll happen
to the base and rigs without servicing."

"It'll all go back to wilderness."

"I agree, bloody stupid waste! Bloody stupid! I asked Colonel Fazir if
there was anything he could do. The bastard just smiled his thin rotten
smile and said it was hard enough to find out what the hell was going on at
the office next door in Tehran, let alone so far south. I asked him what
about the komiteh at the airport—could they help? He said no, that
komitehs have almost no liaison with anyone else, even in Tehran. To quote
him: 'Up in the Zagros among the half-civilized nomads and tribesmen,
unless you've guns, you're Iranian, preferably an ayatollah, you'd best do
what they say.' " McIver coughed and blew his nose irritably. "The bastard
wasn't laughing at us, Andy. Even so, he wasn't unhappy either."

Gavallan was in dismay, so many questions to ask and to be answered,
everything in jeopardy, here and at home. A week to doomsday? Thank

God that Scot . . . poor old Effer . . . Christ Almighty, Scot shot! Gloomily he looked out of the windshield and saw they were nearing the freight area. "Stop the car for a minute, Mac, better to talk in private, eh?"

"Sorry, yes, I'm not thinking too clearly."

"You're all right? I mean your health?"

"Oh, that's fine, if I get rid of this cough . . . It's just that . . . it's just that I'm afraid." McIver said it flat but the admission spiked through Gavallan. "I'm out of control, I've already lost one man, there's HBC still hanging over us, old Erikki's in danger, we're all in danger, S-G and everything we've worked for." He fiddled with the wheel. "Gen's fine?"

"Yes, yes, she is," Gavallan said patiently, concerned for him. This was the second time he had answered that question. McIver had asked him the moment he had come down the steps of the 125. "Genny's fine, Mac," he said, repeating what he had said earlier, "I've mail from her, she's talked to both Hamish and Sarah, both families're fine and young Angus has his first tooth. Everyone's well at home, all in good shape and I've a bottle of Loch Vay in my briefcase from her. She tried to talk her way past Johnny Hogg onto the 125—to stow away in the loo—even after I'd said no, so sorry." For the first time he saw a glimmer of a smile on McIver.

"Gen's ornery, no doubt about it. Glad she's there and not here, very glad, curious though how you miss 'em." McIver stared ahead. "Thanks, Andy."

"Nothing." Gavallan thought a moment. "Why get Jean-Luc to take the 212? Why not Tom Lochart? Wouldn't it be better to have him out?"

"Of course, but he won't leave Iran without Sharazad . . . there's another problem." The music on the tape went out and he turned it over and started it again. "I can't track her down. Tom was worried about her, asked me to go to her family's home near the bazaar which I did. Couldn't get an answer, didn't seem to be anyone there, Tom's sure she was on the Women's Protest March."

"Christ! We heard about the riots and arrests on the BBC—and attacks by nutters on some of the women. You think she's in jail?"

"I hope to God she isn't—you heard about her father? Oh, of course, I told you myself last time you were here, didn't I?" McIver wiped the windshield absently. "What would you like to do—wait here until the bird comes back?"

"No. Let's go into Tehran—do we have time?" Gavallan glanced at his watch. It read 12:25.

"Oh, yes. We've got a load of 'redundant' stores to put aboard. We'll have time if we leave now."

"Good. I'd like to see Azadeh and Nogger—and this man Ross—and particularly Talbot. We could go past the Bakravan house on the off chance. Eh?"

"Good idea. I'm glad you're here, Andy, very glad." He eased in the clutch, the wheels skidding.

"So'm I, Mac. Actually I've never been so down either."

McIver coughed and cleared his throat. "Home news is lousy?"

"Yes." Idly Gavallan wiped away the condensation from his side window with the back of his glove. "There's a special board meeting of Struan's Monday. I'll have to come up with answers about Iran. Damned nuisance!"

"Will Linbar be there?"

"Yes. That bugger's going to ruin the Noble House before he's through. Stupid to expand into South America when China's on the threshold of opening up."

McIver frowned at the new edge to Gavallan's voice but said nothing. For many years he had known of their rivalry and hatred, the circumstances of David MacStruan's death and everyone's surprise in Hong Kong that Linbar had achieved the top job. He still had many friends in the Colony who sent him clippings of the latest piece of gossip or rumor—the lifeblood of Hong Kong—about the Noble House and their rivals. But he never discussed them with his old friend.

"Sorry, Mac," Gavallan had said gruffly, "don't want to discuss those sort of things, or what goes on with Ian, Quillan, Linbar, or anyone else connected with Struan's. Officially I'm no longer with the Noble House. Let's leave it at that."

Fair enough, McIver had thought at the time and had continued to hold his peace. He glanced across at Gavallan. The years have been kind to Andy, he told himself, he's still as grand a looking man as ever—even with all the troubles. "Not to worry, Andy. Nothing you can't do."

"I wish I believed that right now, Mac. Seven days presents an enormous problem, doesn't it?"

"That's the understatement of the y—" McIver noticed his fuel gauge was on empty and he exploded: "Someone must've siphoned my tank while she was parked." He stopped and got out a moment and came back and slammed the door. "Bloody bastard broke the sodding lock. I'll have to fill up—fortunately we've still got a few five-gallon drums left and the underground tank's still half full of chopper fuel for emergencies." He lapsed into silence, his mind beset with Jordon and Zagros and HBC and seven days. Who do we lose next? Silently he began to curse and then he heard Genny's voice saying, We can do it if we want to, I know we can, I know we can . . .

Gavallan was thinking about his son. I won't rest easily until I see him with my own eyes. Tomorrow, with any luck. If Scot's not back before my plane to London, I'll cancel and go Sunday. And somehow I've got to see Talbot—maybe he can give me some help. My God, only seven days . . .

It took McIver no time to refuel, then he swung out of the airport into the traffic. A big USAF jet transport came low overhead in the landing pattern. "They're servicing about five jumbos a day, still with military controllers and 'supervising' Green Bands, everyone giving orders, countermanding them and no one listening anyway," McIver said. "BA's promised me three seats on every one of their flights for our nationals—with baggage. They hope to get a jumbo in every other day."

"What'd they want in return?"

"The crown jewels!" McIver said, trying to lighten their depression but the joke sounded flat. "No, nothing, Andy. The BA manager, Bill Shoesmith, is a great chap and doing a great job." He swung around the burned-out wreck of a bus that was on its side half across the road as though it were neatly parked. "The women are marching again today—rumor has it they are going to go on and on until Khomeini relents."

"If they stick together he'll have to."

"I don't know what to think these days." McIver drove on awhile then jerked a thumb out of the window at the pedestrians walking this way and that. "They seem to know all's well in the world. The mosques are packed, marches in support of Khomeini are multitudes, Green Bands're fighting the leftists fearlessly who fight back equally fearlessly." He coughed wheezily. "Our employees, well, they just give me the usual Iranian flattery and politeness and you never know what they're really thinking. Except you're sure they want us O-U-T!" He swerved onto the sidewalk to avoid a head-on collision with an oncoming car that was on the wrong side of the road, horn blaring, going much too fast for the snow conditions—then drove on again. "Bloody twit," he said. "If it wasn't for the fact I love old Lulu, I'd swap her for a beat-up half-track and have at the bloody lot of them!" He glanced at Gavallan and smiled. "Andy, I'm so glad you're here. Thanks. I feel better now. Sorry."

"No problem," Gavallan said calmly but inside he was churning. "What about Whirlwind?" he asked, not able to bottle it any longer.

"Well, whether it's seven days or seventy . . ." McIver swerved to avoid another accident neatly, returned the obscene gesture, and drove on again. "Let's pretend we're all agreed, and we could push the button if we wanted on D day, in seven days—no, Armstrong said best not to count on more than a week, so let's make it six, six days from today, Friday next—a Friday'd be best anyway, right?"

"Because it's their Holy Day, yes, my thought too."

"Then adapting what we've come up with—Charlie and me: Phase One: From today on we send out every expat and spare we can, every way we can, by the 125, by truck out to Iraq or Turkey, or as baggage and excess baggage by BA. Somehow I'll get Bill Shoesmith to increase our seat reservations and get priority of freight space. We've already got two of our 212s out 'for repair' and the Zagros one's due off tomorrow. We've five birds left here in Tehran, one 212, two 206s, and two Alouettes. We send the 212 and the Alouettes to Kowiss ostensibly to service Hotshot's request for choppers though why he wants them, God only knows—Duke says his birds are not all employed as it is. Anyway, we leave our two 206s here as camouflage."

"Leave them?"

"There's no way we get all our choppers out, Andy, whatever our lead time. Now, on D minus two, next Wednesday, the last of our headquarters staff—Charlie, Nogger, our remaining pilots and mechanics, and me—we get on the 125 Wednesday and flit the coop to Al Shargaz, unless of course we can get some of them out beforehand by BA. Don't forget we're supposed to be up to strength, one in for one out. Next we th—"

"What about papers, exit permits?"

"I'll try to get blanks from Ali Kia—I'll need some blank Swiss checks, he understands pishkesh but he's also a member of the board, very clever, hot and hungry, but not anxious to risk his skin. If we can't, then we'll just pishkesh our way onto the 125. Our excuse to the partners, Kia or whomever, when they discover we've gone is that you've called an urgent conference at Al Shargaz—it's a lame excuse but that's beside the point. That ends Phase One. If we're prevented from going, then that ends Whirlwind because we'd be used as hostages for the return of all birds, and I know you won't agree to expend us. Phase Two: we set up sh—"

"What about all your household things? And all those of the chaps who have apartments or houses in Tehran?"

"The company'll have to pay fair compensation—that should be part of Whirlwind's profit and loss. Agreed?"

"What'll that add up to, Mac?"

"Not a lot. We've no option but to pay compensation."

"Yes, yes, I agree."

"Phase Two: We set up shop at Al Shargaz by which time several things have happened. You've arranged for the 747 jumbo freighters to arrive at Al Shargaz the afternoon of D minus one. By then, Starke somehow has secretly cached enough forty-gallon drums on the shore to carry them across the Gulf. Someone else's cached more fuel on some godforsaken island off Saudi or the Emirates for Starke if he needs them, and for Rudi and his lads from Bandar Delam who definitely will. Scrag has no fuel problems. Mean-

while, you've arranged British registry for all birds we plan to 'export,' and
you've got permission to fly through Kuwait, Saudi, and Emirate airspace.
I'm in charge of Whirlwind's actual operation. At dawn on D day you say
to me go or no-go. If it's no-go, that's final. If it's go, I can abort the go
order if I think it's prudent, then that becomes final too. Agreed?"

"With two provisos, Mac: you consult with me before you abort, as I'll
consult with you before go or no-go, and second, if we can't make D day we
try again D plus one and D plus two."

"All right." McIver took a deep breath. "Phase Three: at dawn on D day,
or D plus one or D plus two—three days is the maximum I think we could
sweat out—we radio a code message which says 'Go!' The three bases
acknowledge and at once all escaping birds get airborne and head for Al
Shargaz. There's likely to be a four-hour difference between Scrag's arrivals
and the last ones, probably Duke's—if everything goes well. The moment
the birds land anywhere outside Iran we replace the Iranian registry numbers with British ones and that makes us partially legal. The moment they
land at Al Shargaz the 747s are loaded, and take off into the Wild Blue with
everyone aboard." McIver exhaled. "Simple."

Gavallan did not reply at once, sifting the plan, seeing the holes—the
vast expanse of dangers. "It's good, Mac."

"It isn't, Andy, it isn't good at all."

"I saw Scrag yesterday and we had a long talk. He says Whirlwind's
possible for him and he's in if it's a go. He said he'd sound out the others
over the weekend and let me know, but he was sure on the right day he
could get his birds and lads out."

McIver nodded but said nothing more, just drove on, the roads icy and
dangerous, twisting through the narrow streets to avoid the main highways
he knew would be congested. "We're not far from the bazaar now."

"Scrag said he might be able to get into Bandar Delam in the next few
days and see Rudi and sound him out—letters're too risky. By the way, he
gave me a note for you."

"What's it say, Andy?"

Gavallan reached into the back for his briefcase. He found the envelope
and put on reading glasses. "It's addressed: D. D. Captain McIver, Esq."

"I'll give him whatfor one day with his bloody 'Dirty Duncan,' " McIver
said. "Read it out."

Gavallan opened the envelope, pulled out the paper with another attached to it, and grunted. "The letter just says: 'Get stuffed.' Clipped to it's
a medical report . . ." He peered at it. ". . . signed by Dr. G. Gernin,
Australian Consulate, Al Shargaz. The old bastard's ringed cholesterol normal, blood pressure 130/85, sugar normal . . . everything's bloody normal

and there's a P.S. in Scrag's writing: 'I'm going to buzz you on me f'ing seventy-third birthday, old cock!' "

"I hope he does, the bugger, but he won't, time's not on his side. He'll m—" McIver braked cautiously. The street led out onto the square in front of the bazaar mosque but the exit was blocked by shouting men, many waving guns. There was no way to turn aside or detour, so McIver slowed and stopped. "It's the women again," he said catching sight of the surging demonstration beyond, cries and countercries growing in violence. Traffic on both sides of the street piled up with great suddenness, horns blaring angrily. There were no sidewalks, just the usual muck-filled joubs and banked snow, a few street stalls and pedestrians.

They were hemmed in on all sides. Bystanders began to join those ahead, pressing into the roadway around the cars and trucks. Among them were urchins and youths, and one made a rude sign at Gavallan through his side window, another of them kicked the fender, then another, and they all ran off laughing.

"Rotten little bastards." McIver could see them in the rearview mirror, other youths collecting around them. More men pushed past, more hostile looks, and a couple banged the sides carelessly with their firearms. Ahead the main part of the marching women, "Allah-u Akbarrrrr . . ." dominating, were passing the junction.

A sudden crash startled them as a stone slammed against the car, narrowly missing the window, then the whole car began to rock as urchins and youths swarmed around it, jumping on and off the bumpers, making more obscene gestures. McIver's rage exploded and he tore the door open, sending a couple of the youths sprawling, then jumped out and ripped into the pack that scattered at once. Gavallan got out equally fast, to charge those trying to overturn the car at the rear. He belted one and sent him flying. Most of the others retreated, slipping and shouting, amid curses from pedestrians, but two of the bigger youths rushed Gavallan from behind. He saw them coming and smashed one in the chest, slammed the other against a truck, stunning him, and the truck driver laughed and thumped the side of his cabin. McIver was breathing hard. On his side the youths were out of range, shouting obscenities.

"Look out, Mac!"

McIver ducked. The stone narrowly missed his head and smashed into the side of a truck, and the youths, ten or twelve of them, surged forward. There was nowhere for McIver to go so he stood his ground by the hood and Gavallan put his back to the car, also at bay. One of the youths darted at Gavallan with a piece of wood raised as a club while three others came at him from the side. He twisted away but the club caught the edge of his shoulder and he gasped, lunged at the youth, hit him in the face off balance, slipped, and sprawled in the snow. The rest came in for the kill. Suddenly he was not on the snow surrounded by hacking feet but being helped up. An armed Green Band was helping him, the youths cowering against the wall under the leveled gun of another, an elderly mullah nearby shouting at them in rage, pedestrians encircling them all. Blankly he saw McIver was also more or less unhurt near the front of the car, then the mullah came back to him and spoke to him in Farsi.

"Man zaban-e shoma ra khoob nami danam, Agha"—Sorry, I don't speak your language, Excellency—Gavallan croaked, his chest hurting him. The mullah, an old man with white beard and white turban and black robes, turned and shouted above the din at the watchers and people in other cars.

Reluctantly a driver nearby got out and came over and greeted the mullah deferentially, listened to him, then spoke to Gavallan in good though stilted English: "The mullah informs you that the youths were wrong to attack you, Agha, and have broken the law, and that clearly you were not breaking a law or provoking them."

Again he listened to the mullah a moment, then once more turned to Gavallan and McIver. "He wishes you to know that the Islamic Republic is obedient to the immutable laws of God. The youths broke the law which forbids attacking unarmed strangers peacefully going about their business." The man, bearded, middle-aged, his clothes threadbare, turned back to the mullah who now loudly addressed the crowd and the youths and there was widespread approval and agreement. "You are to witness that the law is upheld, the guilty punished and justice done at once. The punishment is fifty lashes, but first the youths will beg your forgiveness and the forgiveness of all others here."

In the midst of the uproar from the nearby demonstration, the terrified youths were shoved and kicked in front of McIver and Gavallan where they went down on their knees and abjectly begged forgiveness. Then they were herded back against the wall and thrashed with mule scourges readily offered by the interested and jeering crowd. The mullah, the two Green Bands, and others selected by the mullah enforced the law. Pitilessly.

"My God," Gavallan muttered, sickened.

The driver-translator said sharply, "This is Islam. Islam has one law for all people, one punishment for each crime, and justice immediate. The law is God's law, untouchable, everlasting, not like in your corrupt West where laws can be twisted and justice twisted and delayed for the benefit of lawyers who fatten on the twistings and corruptions and vilenesses or misfortunes of others . . ." Screams of some of the youths interrupted him.

"Those sons of dogs have no pride," the man said contemptuously, going back to his car.

When the punishment was over, the mullah gently admonished those youths who were still conscious, then dismissed them and went forward with his Green Bands. The crowd drifted away leaving McIver and Gavallan beside the car. Their attackers were now pathetic bundles of inert, bloodstained rags or moaning youths trying to drag themselves to their feet. Gavallan went forward to help one of them, but the youth scrambled away petrified so he stopped, then came back. The fenders were dented, there were deep scratches in the paintwork from stones the youths had used maliciously. McIver looked older than before. "Can't say they didn't deserve it, I suppose," Gavallan said.

"We'd've been trampled and very bloody hurt if the mullah hadn't come along," McIver said throatily, so glad that Genny had not been here. She'd have been punished by every lash they got, he thought, his chest and back aching from the blows. He pulled his eyes off his car, eased his shoulders painfully. Then he noticed the man who had translated for them in a nearby car still in the traffic jam and trudged painfully across the snow to him.

"Thanks, thanks for helping us, Agha," he said to him, shouting through the window and above the noise. The car was old and bent and four other men were crammed into the other seats.

The man rolled down the window. "The mullah asked for a translator, I was helping *him*, not you," he said, his lips curling. "If you had not come to Iran, those young fools would not have been tempted by your disgusting display of material wealth."

"Sorry, I just wanted to th—"

"And if it wasn't for your equally disgusting films and television that glorify your godless street gangs and rebellious classrooms that the Shah imported at the behest of his masters to corrupt our youth—my own son and own pupils included—those poor fools would be all correctly law-abiding. Better for you to leave before you too are caught breaking the law." He rolled up the window and, angrily, jabbed the horn.

AT LOCHART'S APARTMENT: 2:37 P.M. Her knuckles rapped a short code on the penthouse door. She was wearing a veil and dirt-stained chador.

A series of knocks answered her. Again she tapped four rapid and one slow. At once the door swung open a crack, Teymour was there with a gun in her face, and she laughed. "Don't you trust anyone, my darling?" she said in Arabic, Palestinian dialect.

"No, Sayada, not even you," he replied, and when he was sure she truly was Sayada Bertolin and alone, he opened the door wider, and she pulled away her veil and scarf and went into his arms. He kicked the door shut and relocked it. "Not even you." Then they kissed hungrily. "You're late."

"On time. You're early." Again she laughed and broke away and handed him the bag. "About half's there, I'll bring the rest tomorrow."

"Where did you leave the rest?"

"In a locker at the French Club." Sayada Bertolin put her chador aside and was transformed. She wore a padded ski jacket and warm cashmere turtleneck sweater and tartan skirt and thick socks and high fur boots, all of it couturier. "Where are the others?" she asked.

His eyes smiled. "I sent them out."

"Ah, love in the afternoon. When do they return?"

"Sunset."

"Perfect. First a shower—the water's still hot?"

"Oh, yes, and central heating's on, and the electric blanket. Such luxury! Lochart and his wife knew how to live, this's a veritable pasha's—what's the French word?—ah, yes, garçonnière."

Her laugh warmed him. "You've no idea what a pishkesh a hot shower is, my darling, so much nicer than a bath—let alone the rest." She sat on a chair to slip off her boots. "But it was old lecher Jared Bakravan, not Lochart, who knew how to live—originally this apartment was for a mistress."

"You?" he asked without malice.

"No, my darling, he required them young, very young. I'm mistress to no one, not even my husband. Sharazad told me. Old Jared knew how to live, a pity he didn't have more luck in his dying."

"He had served his purpose."

"That was no way for such a man. Stupid!"

"He was a notorious usurer and Shah supporter, even though he gave to Khomeini lavishly. He had offended the laws of God an—"

"The laws of zealots, my darling, zealots—as you and I break all sorts of laws, eh?" She got up and kissed him lightly, walked down the corridor on the lovely carpets, and went into Sharazad and Lochart's bedroom, across it into the luxurious mirrored bathroom, and turned on the shower, and stood there waiting for the water to heat up. "I always loved this apartment."

He leaned against the doorway. "My superiors thank you for suggesting it. How was the march?"

"Awful. Iranians are such animals, hurling abuse and filth at us, waving their penises at us, all because we want to be a little equal, want to dress as we want, to try to be beautiful for such a little time, we're young such a little time." Again she put her hand under the water, testing it. "Your Khomeini will have to relent."

He laughed. "Never—that's his strength. And only some are animals, Sayada, the rest know no better. Where's your civilized Palestinian tolerance?"

"Your men here have put it all into a squatting hole, Teymour. If you were a woman you'd understand." She tried the water again and felt the heat beginning. "It's time I went back to Beirut—I never feel clean here. I haven't felt clean in months."

"I'll be glad to get back too. The war here is over, but not in Palestine, Lebanon, or Jordan—they need trained fighters there. There are Jews to kill, the curse of Zion to cast out, and holy places to recapture."

"I'm glad you'll be back in Beirut," she said, her eyes inviting. "I've been told to go home too in a couple of weeks which suits me perfectly—then I can still be a marcher. The protest planned for Thursday's going to be the biggest ever!"

"I don't understand why you bother, Iran's not your problem and all your marches and protest meetings will achieve nothing."

"You're wrong—Khomeini's not a fool—I take part in the marches for the same reason I work for the PLO—for our home, for equality, equality for the women of Palestine . . . and yes, and for women everywhere." Her brown eyes were suddenly fiery and he had never seen her more beautiful. "Women are on the march, my darling, and by God of the Copts, the One God, and by your Marxist-Lenin you secretly admire, the day of man's dominance is over!"

"I agree," he said at once and laughed.

Abruptly she laughed with him. "You're a chauvinist—you who know differently." The temperature of the water was perfect. She took off her ski jacket. "Let's shower together."

"Good, tell me about the papers."

"Afterward." She undressed without shame and so did he, both aroused but patient, for they were confident lovers—lovers of three years, in Lebanon and Palestine and here in Tehran—and he soaped her and she soaped him and they toyed, one with another, their playing gradually more intimate and more sensuous and more erotic until she cried out and cried again, and then, the instant he was within they melded perfectly, ever more urgent now, one with another, imploding together—then later at peace together lying in the bed the electric blanket warming them.

"What's the time?" she said sleepily with a great sigh.

"Time for love."

Quietly she reached over and he jerked, unprepared, and retreated protesting, then caught her hand and held her closely. "Not yet, not even you, my love!" she said, content in his arms.

"Five minutes."

"Not for five hours, Teymour."

"One hour . . ."

"Two hours," she said smiling. "In two you'll be ready again but by then I won't be here—you'll have to bed one of your soldier whores." She stifled a yawn, then stretched as a cat would stretch. "Oh, Teymour, you're a wonderful lover, wonderful." Then her ears caught a sound. "Is that the shower?"

"Yes. I left it running. What luxury, eh?"

"Yes, yes, it is, but a waste."

She slid out of bed and closed the bathroom door, used the bidet, then went into the shower, and sang to herself as she washed her hair, then wrapped a fine towel around herself, dried her hair with an electric dryer and when she came back she expected to find him contentedly asleep. But he wasn't. He was lying in bed with his throat cut. The blanket that half covered him was soaked with blood, his severed genitals were neatly on the pillow beside him, and two men stood there watching her. Both were armed, their revolvers fitted with silencers. Through the open bedroom door she saw another man by the front door, on guard.

"Where're the rest of the papers?" one of the men said in curiously accented English, the revolver pointed at her.

"At . . . at the French Club."

"Where at the French Club?"

"In a locker." She had been too many years in the PLO undercover, and too versed in life to panic. Her heartbeat was slow and she was trying to decide what to do before she died. There was a knife in her handbag but she had left the handbag on the bedside table and now it was on the bed, the contents spilled out, and there was no knife. No weapon near at hand to help her. Nothing but time—at sunset the others came back. It was nowhere near sunset. "In the ladies' section," she added.

"Which locker?"

"I don't know—there are no numbers and it's the custom to give whatever you want kept safely to the woman attendant, you sign your name in the book which she initials, and she will give whatever it is back to you when you ask for it—but only to you."

The man glanced at the other one who nodded briefly. Both men were dark-haired and dark-eyed, mustached, and she could not place the accent.

They could be Iranian, Arab, or Jew—and from anywhere, from Egypt to Syria or south to Yemen. "Get dressed. If you try anything you will not go to hell painlessly like this man—we did not wake him first. Clear?"

"Yes." Sayada went back and began to dress. She did not try to hide. The man stood at the doorway and watched carefully, not her body but her hands. They're professionals, she thought, sickened.

"Where did you get the papers?"

"From someone called Ali. I've never seen him befo—"

"Stop!" The word cut like a razor though it was softly said. "The next time you lie to us I will slice off that beautiful nipple and make you eat it, Sayada Bertolin. One lie, to experiment, is forgiven. Never again. Go on."

Fear now gushed through her "The man's name was Abdollah bin Ali Saba, and this morning he went with me to the old tenement near the university. He led the way to the apartment and we searched where we had been told."

"Who told you?"

"The 'Voice.' The voice on the phone—I only know him as a voice. From . . . from time to time, he calls me with special instructions."

"How do you recognize him?"

"By his voice, and there is always a code." She pulled her sweater over her head and now she was dressed, except for her boots. The automatic with the silencer had never wavered. "The code is that he always mentions the previous day in some way or another in the first few minutes, whatever the day is."

"Go on."

"We searched under the floorboards and found the material—letters, files, and some books. I put them into my bag and went to the French Club and . . . and then, because the strap on the bag broke, I left half and came here."

"When did you meet the man, Dimitri Yazernov?"

"I never have, I was just told to go there with Abdollah and to make sure that no one was watching, to find the papers and to give them to Teymour."

"Why Teymour?"

"I did not ask. I never ask."

"Wise. What does—what did Teymour do?"

"I don't know, exactly, other than he's . . . he was an Iranian, trained as a Freedom Fighter by the PLO," she said.

"Which branch?"

"I don't know." Beyond the man she could see into the bedroom but she kept her eyes away from the bed and on this man who knew too much. From the questioning they could be agents of SAVAMA, KGB, CIA, MI6,

Israel, Jordan, Syria, Iraq, even one of the PLO extremist groups who did not acknowledge Arafat as leader—all of whom would like possession of the contents of the U.S. ambassador's safe.

"When does the Frenchman, your lover, return?"

"I don't know," she said at once, allowing her surprise to show.

"Where is he now?"

"At his base in the Zagros. It's called Zagros Three."

"Where is the pilot Lochart?"

"I think also at Zagros."

"When does he return here?"

"You mean here? This apartment? I don't think he'll ever return here."

"To Tehran?"

Her eyes strayed to the bedroom as much as she tried to resist and she saw Teymour. Her stomach revolted, she groped for the toilet and was violently sick. The man watched without emotion, satisfied that one of her barriers was broken. He was used to bodies reacting of their own volition to terror. Even so, his gun covered her and he watched carefully in case of a trick.

When the spasm had passed, she cleaned her mouth with a little water, trying to dominate her nausea, cursing Teymour for being so stupid as to send the others away. Stupid! she wanted to shriek, stupid when you're surrounded by enemies on the Right, or the Left, or in the Center—did it ever bother me before to make love when others were around, so long as the door was closed?

She leaned back against the basin, facing her nemesis.

"First we go to the French Club," he said. "You will get the rest of the material and give it to me. Clear?"

"Yes."

"From now on you will work for us. Secretly. You will work for us. Agreed?"

"Do I have a choice?"

"Yes. You can die. Badly." The man's lips thinned even more and his eyes became reptilian. "After you have died, a child by the name of Yassar Bialik will receive attention."

All color left her face.

"Ah, good! Then you remember your little son who lives with your uncle's family in Beirut's Street of the Flower Merchants?" The man stared at her, then demanded, "Well, do you?"

"Yes, yes, of course," she said, barely able to talk. Impossible for them to know about my darling Yassar, even my husband doesn't kn—

"What happened to the boy's father?"

"He . . . he was killed . . . he was . . . killed."

"Where?"

"In . . . the Golan Heights."

"Sad to lose a young husband just a few months married," the man said thinly. "How old were you then?"

"Sev . . . seventeen."

"Your memory does not fail you. Good. Now if you choose to work for us, you and your son and uncle and his family are safe. If you do not obey us perfectly, or if you try to betray us, or commit suicide, the boy Yassar will cease to be a man and cease to see. Clear?"

Helplessly she nodded, her face ashen.

"If we die, others will make sure we are avenged. Do not doubt it. Now, what's your choice?"

"I will serve you," and make my son safe and be avenged but how, how?

"Good, on the eyes and balls and cock of your son you will serve us?"

"Yes. Pl . . . please, who . . . who do I serve?"

Both men smiled. Without humor. "Never ask again or try to find out. We will tell you when it is necessary, if it is necessary. Clear?"

"Yes."

The man with the gun unscrewed the silencer and put it and the gun into his pocket. "We want to know immediately when either the Frenchman or Lochart return—you will make it your duty to find out—also how many helicopters they have here in Tehran and where. Clear?"

"Yes. How do I get in touch with you, please?"

"You will be given a phone number." The eyes flattened even more. "For yourself alone. Clear?"

"Yes."

"Where does Armstrong live? Robert Armstrong?"

"I don't know." Warning signals rushed through her. Rumor had it that Armstrong was a trained assassin employed by MI6.

"Who is George Telbot?"

"Talbot? He's an official in the British embassy."

"What official? What's his job?"

"I don't know, just an official."

"Are either of them your lovers?"

"No. They . . . they go to the French Club sometimes. Acquaintances."

"You will become Armstrong's mistress. Clear?"

"I . . . I will try."

"You have two weeks. Where is Lochart's wife?"

"I . . . I think at the Bakravan family house near the bazaar."

"You will make sure. And get a key to the front door." The man saw her eyes flicker and hid his amusement. *If that goes against your scruples, he thought, never mind. Soon you'll be eating shit with great joy if we wish it.* "Get your coat, we go at once."

Her knees were weak as she went across the bedroom, heading for the front door.

"Wait!" The man stuffed the contents back into her handbag and then, as an afterthought, carelessly wrapped that which was on the pillow in one of her paper tissues and put that also into the handbag. "To remind you to obey."

"No, please." Her tears flooded. "I can't . . . not that."

The man shoved the handbag into her hands. "Then get rid of it."

In misery she staggered back to the bathroom and threw it into the squatter and was very sick again, more than before.

"Hurry up!"

When she could make her legs work she faced him. "When the others . . . when they come back and find . . . if I'm not here they . . . they will know that . . . that I'm part of those who . . . who did this and . . ."

"Of course. Do you think we're fools? Do you think we're alone? The moment the four of them return they're dead and this place conflagrated."

AT McIVER'S APARTMENT: 4:20 P.M.   Ross said, "I don't know, Mr. Gavallan, I don't remember much after I left Azadeh on the hill and went into the base, more or less up to the time we got here." He was wearing one of Pettikin's uniform shirts and a black sweater and black trousers and black shoes and was shaved and neat, but his face showed his utter exhaustion. "But before that, everything happened as . . . as I told you."

"Terrible," Gavallan said. "But, thank God for you, Captain. But for you the others'd be dead. Without you they'd all be lost. Let's have a drink, it's so damned cold. We've some whisky." He motioned to Pettikin. "Charlie?"

Pettikin went to the sideboard. "Sure, Andy."

"I won't, thanks, Mr. McIver," Ross said.

"I'm afraid I will and the sun's not over the yardarm," McIver said.

"So will I," Gavallan said. The two of them had arrived not long ago, still shaken from their almost disaster and worried because at the Bakravan house they had used the iron door knocker again and again but to no avail. Then they had come here. Ross, dozing on the sofa, had almost leaped out of sleep when the front door opened, kookri threateningly in his hand.

"Sorry," he had said shakily, sheathing the weapon.

"That's all right," Gavallan had pretended, not over his fright. "I'm Andrew Gavallan. Hi, Charlie! Where's Azadeh?"

"She's still asleep in the spare bedroom," Pettikin answered.

"Sorry to make you jump," Gavallan had said. "What happened, Captain, at Tabriz?"

So Ross had told them, disjointedly, jumping back and forth until he had finished. Exploding out of heavy sleep had disoriented him. His head ached, everything ached, but he was glad to be telling what had happened, reconstructing everything, gradually filling in the blank parts, putting the pieces into place. Except Azadeh. No, I can't put her in place yet.

This morning when he had come out of a malevolent wake-sleep dream, he had been terrified, everything mixed up, jet engines and guns and stones and explosions and cold, and staring at his hands to make sure what was dream and what was real. Then he had seen a man peering at him and had cried out, "Where's Azadeh?"

"She's still asleep, Captain Ross, she's in the spare room down the hall," Pettikin had told him, calming him. "Remember me? Charlie Pettikin—Doshan Tappeh?"

Searching his memory. Things coming back slowly, hideous things. Big blanks, very big. Doshan Tappeh? What about Doshan Tappeh? Going there to hitch a chopper ride and . . .   "Ah, yes, Captain, how are you? Good to . . . to see you. She's asleep?"

"Yes, like a baby."

"Best thing, best thing for her to sleep," he had said, his brain still not working easily.

"First a cuppa. Then a bath and shave and I'll fix you up with some clothes and shaving gear. You're about my size. You hungry? We've eggs and some bread, the bread's a bit stale."

"Oh, thanks, no, no, I'm not hungry—you're very kind."

"I owe you one—no, at least ten. I'm damned pleased to see you. Listen, much as I'd like to know what happened . . . well, McIver's gone to the airport to pick up our boss, Andy Gavallan. They'll be back shortly, you'll have to tell them so I can find out then—so no questions till then, you must be exhausted."

"Thanks, yes it's . . . it's still all a bit . . . I can remember leaving Azadeh on the hill, then almost nothing, just flashes, dreamlike, until I woke a moment ago. How long have I been asleep?"

"You've been out for about sixteen hours. We, that's Nogger and our two mecs, half carried you both in here and then you both passed out. We put you and Azadeh to bed like babies—Mac and I. We undressed you, washed part of the muck off, carried you to bed—not too gently by the way—but you never woke up, either of you."

"She's all right? Azadeh?"

"Oh, yes. I checked her a couple of times but she's still flat out. What did . . . sorry, no questions! First a shave and bath. 'Fraid the water's barely warm but I've put the electric heater in the bathroom, it's not too bad. . . ."

Now Ross was watching Pettikin who was handing the whisky to McIver and to Gavallan. "Sure you won't, Captain?"

"No, no thanks." Without noticing it he felt his right wrist and rubbed it. His energy level was ebbing fast. Gavallan saw the man's tiredness and knew there was not much time. "About Erikki. You can't remember anything else to give us an idea where he might be?"

"Not any more than I've told you. Azadeh may be able to help—the Soviet's name was something like Certaga, the man Erikki was forced to work with up by the border—as I said they were using her as a threat and there was some complication about her father and a trip they were going to make together—sorry, I can't remember exactly. The other man, the one who was friends with Abdollah Khan was called Mzytryk, Petr Oleg." That reminded Ross about Vien Rosemont's code message for the Khan, but he decided that was none of Gavallan's business, nor about all the killing, nor about shoving the old man in front of the truck on the hill, nor that one day he would go back to the village and hack off the head of the butcher and the kalandar who, but for the grace of God or the spirits of the High Land, would have stoned her and mutilated him. He would do that after the debriefing when he saw Armstrong, or Talbot, or the American colonel, but before that he would ask them who had betrayed the operation at Mecca. Someone had. For a moment the thought of Rosemont and Tenzing and Gueng blinded him. When the mist cleared, he saw the clock on the mantelpiece. "I have to go to a building near the British embassy. Is that far from here?"

"No, we could take you if you like."

"Could that be now? Sorry, but I'm afraid I'll pass out again if I don't get with it."

Gavallan glanced at McIver. "Mac, let's go now . . . perhaps I can catch Talbot. We'll still have time to come back to see Azadeh, and Nogger if he's here."

"Good idea."

Gavallan got up and put on his heavy coat.

Pettikin said to Ross, "I'll lend you a coat and some gloves." He saw his eyes stray down the corridor. "Would you like me to wake Azadeh?"

"No, thanks. I'll . . . I'll just look in."

"It's the second door on the left."

They watched him go along the corridor, his walk noiseless and catlike, open the door noiselessly and stand there a moment and close it again. He collected his assault rifle and the two kookris, his and Gueng's. He thought a moment, then put his on the mantelpiece.

"In case I don't get back," he said, "tell her this's a gift, a gift for Erikki. For Erikki and her."

AT THE PALACE OF THE KHAN: 5:19 P.M. The kalandar of Abu Mard was on his knees and petrified. "No, no, Highness, I swear it was the mullah Mahmud who told us t—"

"He's not a real mullah, you son of a dog, everyone knows that! By God, you . . . you were going to stone my daughter?" the Khan shrieked, his face mottled, his breath coming in great pants, "*You* decided? *You* decided you were going to stone *my* daughter?"

"It was him, Highness," the kalandar whimpered, "it was the mullah who decided after questioning her and her admitting adultery with the saboteur . . ."

"You son of a dog! You aided and abetted that false mullah . . . Liar! Ahmed told me what happened!" The Khan propped himself on his bed pillows, a guard behind him, Ahmed and other guards close to the kalandar in front of him, Najoud, his eldest daughter, and Aysha, his young wife, seated to one side trying to hide their terror at his rage and petrified that he would turn on them. Kneeling beside the door still in his travel-stained clothes and filled with dread was Hakim, Azadeh's brother, who had just arrived and had been rushed here under guard in response to the Khan's summons, and who had listened with equal rage to Ahmed relating what had happened at the village.

"You son of a dog," the Khan shouted again, his mouth salivating. "You let . . . you let the dog of a saboteur escape . . . you let him drag my daughter off with him . . . you harbor the saboteur and then . . . then you dare to judge one of my—MY—family and would stone . . . without seeking my—MY—approval?"

"It was the mullah . . ." the kalandar cried out, repeating it again and again.

"Shut him up!"

Ahmed hit him hard on one of his ears, momentarily stunning him. Then dragged him roughly back onto his knees and hissed, "Say one more word and I'll cut your tongue out."

The Khan was trying to catch his breath. "Aysha, give me . . . give me one of those . . . those pills . . ." She scurried over, still on her knees, opened the bottle and put a pill into his mouth and wiped it for him. The Khan kept the pill under his tongue as the doctor had told him and in a moment the spasm passed, the thundering in his ears lessened, and the room stopped weaving. His bloodshot eyes went back onto the old man who was whimpering and shaking uncontrollably. "You son of a dog! So you dare to bite the hand that owns you—you, your butcher, and your festering village. Ibrim," the Khan said to one of the guards. "Take him back to Abu Mard and stone him, have the villagers stone him, *stone him*, then cut off the hands of the butcher."

Ibrim and another guard pulled the howling man to his feet, smashed him into silence, and opened the door, stopped as Hakim said harshly, "Then burn the village!"

The Khan looked at him, his eyes narrowed. "Yes, then burn the village," he echoed and kept his eyes on Hakim who looked back at him, trying to be brave. The door closed and now the quiet heightened, broken only by Abdollah's labored breathing. "Najoud, Aysha, leave!" he said.

Najoud hesitated, wanting to stay, wanting to hear sentence pronounced on Hakim, gloating that Azadeh had been caught in her adultery and was therefore due punishment whenever she was recaptured. Good, good, good. With Azadeh they both perish, Hakim and the Redhead of the Knife. "I will be within instant call, Highness," she said.

"You can go back to your quarters. Aysha—you wait at the end of the

corridor." Both women left. Ahmed closed the door contentedly, everything going as planned. The other two guards waited in silence.

The Khan shifted painfully, motioning to them. "Wait outside. Ahmed,
you stay." When they had gone and there were just the three of them in
the big, cold room he turned his gaze back to Hakim. "Burn the village, you
said. A good idea. But that doesn't excuse your treachery, or your sister's."

"Nothing excuses treachery against a father, Highness. But neither
Azadeh nor I have betrayed you or plotted against you."

"Liar! You heard Ahmed! She admitted fornicating with the saboteur,
she admitted it."

"She admitted 'loving' him, Highness, years and years ago. She swore
before God she had never committed adultery or betrayed her husband.
Never! In front of those dogs and sons of dogs and worse, that mullah of the
Left Hand, what should the daughter of a Khan say? Didn't she try to
protect your name in front of that godless mob of shit?"

"Still twisting words, still protecting the whore she became?"

Hakim's face went ashen. "Azadeh fell in love as Mother fell in love. If
she's a whore, then you whored my mother!"

Blood surged back into the Khan's face. *"How dare you say such a thing!"*

"It's true. You lay with her before you were married. Because she loved
you she let you secretly into her bedroom and so risked death. She risked
death because she loved you and you begged her. Didn't our mother persuade her father to accept you, and persuade your father to allow *you* to
marry her, instead of your older brother who wanted her as a second wife
for himself?" Hakim's voice broke, remembering her in her dying, him
seven, Azadeh six, not understanding very much, only that she was in terrible pain from something called "tumor" and outside, in the courtyard, their
father Abdollah beset with grief. "Didn't she always stand up for you
against your father and your older brother and then, when your brother was
killed and you became heir, didn't she heal the breach with your father?"

"You can't . . . can't know such things, you were . . . you were too
young!"

"Old Nanny Fatemeh told us, she told us before she died, she told us
everything she could remember. . . ."

The Khan was hardly listening, remembering too, remembering his
brother's hunting accident he had so deftly engineered—old Nanny might
have known about that too and if she did then Hakim knows and Azadeh
knows, all the more reason to silence them. Remembering, too, all the
magic times he had had with Napthala the Fair, before and after marriage
and during all the days until the beginning of the pain. They had been
married not even one year when Hakim was born, two when Azadeh ap-

peared, Napthala just sixteen then, tiny, physically a pattern of Aysha but a thousand times more beautiful, her long hair like spun gold. Five more heavenly years, no more children, but that never mattered, hadn't he a son at long last, strong and upright—where his three sons from his first wife had all been born sickly, soon to die, his four daughters ugly and squabbling. Wasn't his wife still only twenty-two, in good health, as strong and as wonderful as the two children she had already birthed? Plenty of time for more sons.

Then the pain beginning. And the agony. No help from all the doctors in Tehran.

Insha'Allah, they said.

No relief except drugs, ever more strong as she wasted away. God grant her the peace of Paradise and let me find her there.

He was watching Hakim, seeing the pattern of Azadeh who was a pattern of the mother, listening to him running on: "Azadeh only fell in love, Highness. If she loved that man, can't you forgive her? Wasn't she only sixteen and banished to school in Switzerland as later I was banished to Khoi?"

"Because you were both treacherous, ungrateful, and poisonous!" the Khan shouted, his ears beginning to thunder again. "Get out! You're to . . . to stay away from all others, under guard, until I send for you. Ahmed, see to it, then come back here."

Hakim got up, near tears, knowing what was going to happen and powerless to prevent it. He stumbled out, Ahmed gave the necessary orders to the guards and came back into the room. Now the Khan's eyes were closed, his face very gray, his breathing more labored than before. Please God do not let him die yet, Ahmed prayed.

The Khan opened his eyes and focused. "I have to decide about him, Ahmed. Quickly."

"Yes, Highness," his counselor began, choosing his words carefully, "you have but two sons, Hakim and the babe. If Hakim were to die or," he smiled strangely, "happened to become sightless and crippled, then Mahmud, husband of Her Highness Najoud will be regent unt—"

"That fool? Our lands and power would be lost within a year!" Patches of redness flared in the Khan's face and he was finding it increasingly difficult to think clearly. "Give me another pill."

Ahmed obeyed and gave him water to drink, gentling him. "You're in God's hands, you will recover, don't worry."

"Don't worry?" the Khan muttered, pain in his chest. "The Will of God the mullah died in time . . . strange. Petr Oleg kept his bargain . . . though he . . . the mullah died too fast . . . too fast."

"Yes, Highness."

In time the spasm again passed. "Wh . . . what's your advice . . . about Hakim?"

Ahmed pretended to think a moment. "Your son Hakim is a good Muslim, he could be trained, he has managed your affairs in Khoi well, and has not fled as perhaps he could have done. He is not a violent man—except to protect his sister, eh? But that's very important, for therein lies his key." He came closer and said softly, "Decree him your heir, High—"

"Never!"

"Providing he swears by God to guard his young brother as he would his sister, providing further his sister returns at once of her own will to Tabriz. In truth, Highness, you have no real evidence against them, only hearsay. Entrust me to find out the truth of him and of her—and to report secretly to you."

The Khan was concentrating, listening carefully, though the effort was taxing him. "Ah, the brother's the bait to snare the sister—as she was the bait to snare the husband?"

"As they're both bait for the other! Yes, Highness, of course you thought of it before me. In return for giving the brother your favor, she must swear before God to stay here to help him."

"She'll do that, oh, yes, she'll do that!"

"Then they'll both be within your reach and you can toy with them at your pleasure, giving and withholding at your whim, whether they're guilty or not."

"They're guilty."

"If they're guilty, and I will know quickly if you give me complete authority to investigate, then it's God's will that they will die slowly, that you decree Fazulia's husband to be Khan after you, not much better than Mahmud. If they're not guilty, then let Hakim remain heir, providing she stays. And if it were to happen, again at God's will, that she is a widow, she'd even betroth him whom you choose, Highness, to keep Hakim your heir—even a Soviet, should he escape the trap, no?"

For the first time today, the Khan smiled. This morning when Armstrong and Colonel Hashemi Fazir had arrived to take possession of Petr Oleg Mzytryk, they had pretended to be suitably concerned about the Khan's health as he had pretended outwardly to be sicker than he had felt at that time. He had kept his voice wan and hesitant and very low so they both had had to lean forward to hear him. "Petr Oleg is coming here today. I was going to meet him but I asked him to come here because of my . . . because I'm sick. I sent him word to come here and he should be at the border at sunset. At Julfa. If you go at once you'll be in plenty of time . . .

he sneaks over the border in a small Soviet helicopter gunship and lands near a side road off the Julfa–Tabriz road where his car is waiting for him . . . no chance to miss the turning, it's the only one . . . a few kilometers north of the city . . . it's the only side road, desolate country, soon little more than a track. How you . . . how you take him is your affair and . . . and as I cannot be present, you will give me a tape of the . . . the investigation?"

"Yes, Highness," Hashemi had said. "How would you advise us to take him?"

"Choke the road both sides of the turnoff with a couple of old, heavily laden farm trucks . . . firewood or crates of fish . . . the road's narrow and twisting and potholed and heavy with traffic, so an ambush should be easy. But . . . but be careful, there're always Tudeh cars to run interference for him, he's a wise man and fearless . . . there's a poison capsule in his lapel."

"Which one?"

"I don't know . . . I don't know. He will land near sunset. You can't miss the turnoff, it's the only one. . . ."

Abdollah Khan sighed, lost in his thoughts. Many times he had been picked up by the same helicopter to go to the dacha at Tbilisi. Many good times there, the food lavish, the women young and accommodating, full-lipped and hungry to please—then, if he was lucky, Vertinskya, the hellcat, for further entertainment.

He saw Ahmed watching him. "I hope Petr escapes the trap. Yes, it would be good for him to . . . to have her." Tiredness swamped him. "I'll sleep now. Send my guard back and after I've eaten tonight, assemble my 'devoted' family here and we will do as you suggest." His smile was cynical. "It's wise to have no illusions."

"Yes, Highness." Ahmed got to his feet. The Khan envied him his lithe and powerful body.

"Wait, there was something . . . something else." The Khan thought a moment, the process strangely tiring. "Ah, yes, where's Redhead of the Knife?"

"With Cimtarga, up near the border, Highness. Cimtarga said they might be away for a few days. They left Tuesday night."

"Tuesday? What's today?"

"Saturday, Highness," Ahmed replied, hiding his concern.

"Ah, yes, Saturday." Another wave of tiredness. His face felt strange and he lifted his hand to rub it but found the effort too much. "Ahmed, find out where he is. If anything happens . . . if I have another attack and I'm

. . . well, see that . . . that I'm taken to Tehran, to the International Hospital, at once. At once. Understand?"

"Yes, Highness."

"Find out where he is and . . . and for the next few days keep him close by . . . overrule Cimtarga. Keep He of the Knife close by."

"Yes, Highness."

When the guard came back into the room, the Khan closed his eyes and felt himself sinking into the depths. "There is no other God but God . . ." he muttered, very afraid.

NEAR THE NORTH BORDER, EAST OF JULFA: 6:05 P.M.

It was near sunset and Erikki's 212 was under a crude, hastily constructed lean-to, the roof already a foot deep in snow from the storm last night, and he knew much more exposure in subzero weather would ruin her. "Can't you give me blankets or straw or something to keep her warm?" he had asked Sheik Bayazid the moment they had arrived back from Rezaiyeh with the body of the old woman, the chieftain, two days ago. "The chopper needs warmth."

"We do not have enough for the living."

"If she freezes she won't work," he had said, fretting that the Sheik would not allow him to leave at once for Tabriz, barely sixty miles away— worried sick about Azadeh and wondering what had happened to Ross and Gueng. "If she won't work, how are we going to get out of these mountains?"

Grudgingly, the Sheik had ordered his people to construct the lean-to and had given him some goat- and sheepskins that he had used where he thought they would do the most good. Just after dawn yesterday he had tried to leave. To his total dismay Bayazid had told him that he and the 212 were to be ransomed.

"You can be patient, Captain, and free to walk our village with a calm guard, to tinker with your airplane," Bayazid had said curtly, "or you can be impatient and angry and you will be bound up and tethered as a wild beast. I seek no trouble, Captain, want none, or argument. We seek ransom from Abdollah Khan."

"But I've told you he hates me and won't help me to be rans—"

"If he says no, we seek ransom elsewhere. From your company in Tehran, or your government—perhaps your Soviet employers. Meanwhile, you stay here as guest, eating as we eat, sleeping as we sleep, sharing equally. Or bound and tethered and hungry. Either way you stay until ransom is paid."

"But that might take months an—"

"Insha'Allah!"

All day yesterday and half the night Erikki had tried to think of a way out of the trap. They had taken his grenade but left him his knife. But his guards were watchful and constant. In these deep snows, it would be almost impossible for him in flying boots and without winter gear to get down to the valley below, and even then he was in hostile country. Tabriz was barely thirty minutes away by 212, but by foot?

"More snow tonight, Captain."

Erikki looked around. Bayazid was a pace away and he had not heard him approach. "Yes, and a few more days in this weather and my bird, my airplane, won't fly—the battery'll be dead and most of the instruments wrecked. I have to start her up to charge the battery and warm her pots, have to. Who's going to ransom a wrecked 212 out of these hills?"

Bayazid thought a moment. "For how long must engines turn?"

"Ten minutes a day—absolute minimum."

"All right. Just after full dark, each day you may do it, but first you ask me. We help you drag her—why is it 'she,' not an 'it' or a 'he'?"

Erikki frowned. "I don't know. Ships are always 'she'—this is a ship of the sky." He shrugged.

"Very well. We help you drag her into open and you start her up and while her engines running there will be five guns within five feet, should you be tempted."

Erikki laughed. "Then I won't be tempted."

"Good." Bayazid smiled. He was a handsome man though his teeth were bad.

"When do you send word to the Khan?"

"It's already gone. In these snows it takes a day to get down to road, even on horseback, but not long to reach Tabriz. If the Khan replies favorably, at once, perhaps we hear tomorrow, perhaps the day after, depending on the snows."

"Perhaps never. How long will you wait?"

"Are all people from the Far North so impatient?"

Erikki's chin jutted. "The ancient gods were very impatient when they were held against their will—they passed it on to us. It's bad to be held against your will, very bad."

"We are a poor people, at war. We must take what the One God gives us. To be ransomed is an ancient custom." He smiled thinly. "We learned from Saladin to be chivalrous with our captives, unlike many Christians. Christians are not known for their chivalry. We are treat—" His ears were sharper than Erikki's and so were his eyes. "There, down in the valley!"

Now Erikki heard the engine also. It took him a moment to pick out the low-flying camouflaged helicopter approaching from the north. "A Kajychokiv 16. Close-support Soviet army gunship . . . what's she doing?"

"Heading for Julfa." The Sheik spat on the ground. "Those sons of dogs come and go as they please."

"Do many sneak in now?"

"Not many—but one is too many."

NEAR THE JULFA TURNOFF: 6:15 P.M. The winding side road through the forest was snow heavy and not plowed. A few cart and truck tracks and those made by the old four-wheel-drive Chevy that was parked under some pines near the open space, a few yards off the main road. Through their binoculars Armstrong and Hashemi could see two men in warm coats and gloves sitting in the front seat, the windows open, listening intently.

"He hasn't much time," Armstrong muttered.

"Perhaps he's not coming after all." They had been watching for half an hour from a slight rise among the trees overlooking the landing area. Their car and the rest of Hashemi's men were parked discreetly on the main road below and behind them. It was very quiet, little wind. Some birds went overhead, cawing plaintively.

"Hallelujah!" Armstrong whispered, his excitement picking up. One man had opened the side door and got out. Now he was looking into the northern sky. The driver started the engine. Then, over it, they heard the incoming chopper, saw her slip over the rise and fall into the valley, hugging the treetops, her piston engine throttled back nicely. She made a perfect landing in a billowing cloud of snow. They could see the pilot and another man beside him. The passenger, a small man, got out and went to meet the other. Armstrong cursed.

"You recognize him, Robert?"

"No. That's not Suslev—Petr Oleg Mzytryk. I'm certain." Armstrong was bitterly disappointed.

"Facial surgery?"

"No, nothing like that. He was a big bugger, heavyset, tall as I am." They watched as he met the other, then handed over something.

"Was that a letter? What did he give him, Robert?"

"Looked like a package, could be a letter." Armstrong muttered another curse, concentrating on their lips.

"What're they saying?" Hashemi knew Armstrong could lip-read.

"I don't know—it's not Farsi, or English."

Hashemi swore and refocused his already perfectly focused binoculars.

"It looked like a letter to me." The man spoke a few more words then went back to the chopper. At once the pilot put on power and swirled away. The other man then trudged back to the Chevy.

"Now what?" Hashemi said exasperated.

Armstrong watched the man walking toward the car. "Two options: intercept the car as planned and find out what 'it' is, providing we could neutralize those two bastards before they destroyed 'it'—but that'd blow that we know the arrival point for Mister Big—or just tail them, presuming it's a message for the Khan giving a new date." He was over his disappointment that Mzytryk had avoided the trap. You must have the luck in our game, he reminded himself. Never mind, next time we'll get him and he'll lead us to our traitor, to the fourth and fifth and sixth man and I'll piss on their graves and Suslev's—or whatever Petr Oleg Mzytryk calls himself—if the luck's with me. "We needn't even tail them—he'll go straight to the Khan."

"Why?"

"Because he's a vital pivot in Azerbaijan, either for the Soviets or against them, so they'd want to find out firsthand just how bad his heart is—and who he's chosen as regent till the babe comes of age, or more likely is levitated. Doesn't the power go with the title, along with the lands and the wealth?"

"And the secret, numbered Swiss bank accounts—all the more reason to come at once."

"Yes, but don't forget something serious might have happened in Tbilisi to make for the delay—Soviets're just as pissed off and anxious as we are about Iran."

They saw the man climb back into the Chevy and begin talking volubly. The driver let in the clutch and turned back for the main road. "Let's get back to our car."

The way back down the rise was fairly easy going, traffic heavy on the Julfa–Tabriz road below, a few headlights already on and no way for their prey to escape the ambush if they decided to stage it. "Hashemi, another possibility's that Mzytryk could have found out in the nick that he's been betrayed by his son, and he's sent a warning to the Khan whose cover would also have been blown. Don't forget we still haven't found out what happened to Rakoczy since your late departed friend General Janan let him go."

"That dog'd never do it on his own," Hashemi said with a twisted smile, remembering his vast joy when he had touched the transmit button and had seen the resultant car bomb explosion obliterate that enemy, along with his house, his future, and his past. "That would be ordered by Abrim Pahmudi."

"Why?"

Hashemi veiled his eyes and glanced at Armstrong but read no hidden guile therein. You know too many secrets, Robert, know about the Rakoczy tapes, and worst of all about my Group Four and that I assisted Janan into hell—where the Khan will soon join him, as Talbot's due to in a couple of days, and you, my old friend, at my leisure. Should I tell you Pahmudi has ordered Talbot punished for his crimes against Iran? Should I tell you I'm happy to oblige? For years I've wanted Talbot removed but've never dared to go against him alone. Now Pahmudi is to blame, may God burn him, and another irritant will be out of my way. Ah, yes, and Pahmudi himself this coming week—but you, Robert, you're the chosen assassin for that, probably to perish. Pahmudi's not worth one of my real assassins.

He chortled to himself, trudging down the hill, not feeling the cold, not worried about Mzytryk's nonappearance. I've more important worries, he was thinking. At all costs I've got to protect my Group Four assassins—my guarantee for an earthly paradise with power over even Khomeini himself.

"Pahmudi's the only one who could have ordered Rakoczy's release," he said. "Soon I'll find out why and where he is. He's either in the Soviet embassy, a Soviet safe house, or in a SAVAMA interrogation dungeon."

"Or safely out of the country by now."

"Then he's safely dead—the KGB don't tolerate traitors." Hashemi smiled sardonically. "What's your bet?"

For a moment Armstrong did not answer, thrown by the question that was unusual for Hashemi who disapproved of gambling, as he did. Now. The last time he had bet was in Hong Kong in '63 with bribe money that had been put into his desk drawer when he was a superintendent, CID. Forty thousand Hong Kong dollars—about seven thousand U.S. then. Against all his principles, he had taken the *heung yau*, the Fragrant Grease as it was called there, out of the drawer and, at the races that afternoon, had bet it all on the nose of a horse called Pilot Fish, all in one insane attempt to recoup his gambling losses—horses and the stock market.

This was the first bribe money he had ever taken in eighteen years in the force though it was always readily available in abundance. That afternoon he had won heavily and had replaced the money before the police sergeant giver had noticed it had been touched—with more than enough left over for his debts. Even so he had been disgusted with himself and appalled at his stupidity. He had never bet again, nor touched *heung yau* again though the opportunity was always there. "You're a bloody fool, Robert," some of his peers would say, "no harm in a little dolly money for retirement."

Retirement? What retirement? Christ, twenty years a copper in Hong Kong on the straight and narrow, eleven years here, equally so, helping these bloodthirsty twits, and it's all up the bloody spout. Thank God I've only me to worry about, no wife now or kids or close relations, just me. Still, if I get bloody Suslev who'll lead me to one of our high-up murdering bloody traitors, it'll all have been worth it.

"Like you, I'm not a betting men, Hashemi, but if I was . . ." He stopped and offered his packet of cigarettes and they lit up gratefully. The smoke mixed with the cold air and showed clear in the falling light. "If I was, I'd say it was odds-on that Rakoczy was your Pahmudi's pishkesh to some Soviet VIP, just to play it safe."

Hashemi laughed. "You're becoming more Iranian every day. I'll have to be more careful." They were almost to the car now and his assistant got out to open the rear door for him. "We'll go straight to the Khan, Robert."

"What about the Chevy?"

"We'll leave others to tail it, I want to get to the Khan first." The colonel's face darkened. "Just to make sure that traitor's more on our side than theirs."

AT KOWISS AIR BASE: 6:35 P.M. Starke stared at Gavallan in total shock. "Whirlwind in six days?"

" 'Fraid so, Duke." Gavallan unzipped his parka and put his hat on the hall stand. "Wanted to tell you myself—sorry, but there it is." The two men were in Starke's bungalow, and he had stationed Freddy Ayre outside to make sure they were not overheard. "I heard this morning all our birds are going to be grounded, pending nationalization. We've six safe days to plan and execute Whirlwind—if we do it. That makes it next Friday. On Saturday we're on borrowed time."

"Jesus." Absently Starke unzipped his flight jacket and clomped over to the sideboard, his flying boots leaving a little trail of snow and water droplets on the carpet. At the back of the bottom drawer was his last bottle of beer. He nipped the top off, poured half into a glass and gave it to Gavallan. "Health," he said, drinking from the bottle, and sat on the sofa.

"Health."

"Who's in, Andy?"

"Scrag. Don't know yet about the rest of his lads but I'll know tomorrow. Mac's come up with a schedule and an overall three-phase plan that's full of holes but possible. Let's say it's possible. What about you and your lads?"

"What's Mac's plan?"

Gavallan told him.

"You're right, Andy. It's full of holes."

"If you were to do a bunk, how'd you plan it from here—you've got the longest distances and the most difficulty."

Starke went over to the flight map on the wall and pointed at a line that went from Kowiss to a cross a few miles out in the Gulf, indicating a rig. "This rig's called Flotsam, one of our regulars," he said, and Gavallan noticed how tight his voice had become. "It takes us about twenty minutes to reach the coast and another ten to get to the rig. I'd cache fuel on the shore near that bearing. I think it could be done without causing too much suspicion; it's just sand dunes and no huts within miles and a lot of us used to picnic there. An 'emergency' landing to safety-check flotation gear before going out to sea shouldn't get radar too itchy though they get worse every day. We'd have to cache two forty-gallon drums per chopper to get us across the Gulf and we'd have to refuel in flight by hand."

It was almost dusk. Windows looked out on the runway and beyond it to the air force base. The 125, with priority clearance onward to Al Shargaz, was parked on the apron, waiting for the fuel truck to arrive. Officious, nervous Green Bands surrounded her. Refueling was not really necessary but Gavallan had told John Hogg to request it anyway to give him more time with Starke. The other two passengers, Arberry and Dibble, being sent on leave after their escape from Tabriz—and crammed between a full load of crates of spares hastily packed and marked in English and Farsi: FOR IMMEDIATE REPAIR AND RETURN TO TEHRAN—were not allowed to land, even to stretch their legs. Nor the pilots, except to ground-check and to supervise the fueling when the truck arrived.

"You'd head for Kuwait?" Gavallan asked, breaking the silence.

"Sure. Kuwait'd be our best bet, Andy. We'd have to refuel in Kuwait, then work our way down the coast to Al Shargaz. If it was up to me I guess I'd park more fuel against an emergency." Starke pinpointed a tiny speck of an island off Saudi. "Here'd be good—best to stay offshore Saudi, no telling what they'd do." Queasily he stared at all the distances. "The island's called Jellet, the Toad, which's what it looks like. No huts, no nothing, but great fishing. Manuela and I went out there once or twice when I was stationed at Bahrain. I'd park fuel there."

He took off his flight cap and wiped the droplets off his forehead then put his cap back on again, his face more etched and tired than usual, all flights more harassed than usual, canceled then reordered, and canceled again, Esvandiary more foul than usual, everyone edgy and irritable, no mail or contact with home for weeks, most of his people, including himself, overdue leave and replacement. Then there's the added problems of the incoming Zagros Three personnel and airplanes and what to do with old Effer Jordon's body when it arrives tomorrow. That had been Starke's first question when he had met Gavallan at the 125 steps.

"I've got that in hand, Duke," Gavallan had said heavily, the wind ten knots and chill. "I've got ATC's permission for the 125 to come back tomorrow afternoon to pick up the coffin. I'll ship it back to England on the first available flight. Terrible. I'll see his wife as soon as I get back and do what I can."

"Lousy luck—thank God young Scot's okay, huh?"

"Yes, but lousy that anyone got hurt, lousy." What if it was Scot's corpse and Scot's coffin? Gavallan was thinking again, the question never ending. What if it had been Scot, could you still compartmentalize the murder so easily? No, of course not. All you can do is bless your joss this time and do the best you can—just do the best you can. "Curiously, Tehran ATC and the airport komiteh were as shocked as we were, and very helpful. Let's go and chat—I've not much time. Here's mail for some of the lads and one from Manuela. She's fine, Duke. She said not to worry. Kids're fine and want to stay in Texas. Your folks're fine too—she asked me to tell you first thing when I caught up with you . . ."

Then Gavallan had delivered the bombshell of six days and now Starke's mind was in a fog. "With Zagros's birds here, I'll have three 212s, one Alouette, and three 206s plus a load of spares. Nine pilots, including Tom Lochart and Jean-Luc, and twelve mechanics. That's way too many for a caper like Whirlwind, Andy."

"I know." Gavallan looked out the window. The fueling truck was lumbering alongside the 125 and he saw Johnny Hogg come down the steps. "How long will she take to refuel?"

"If Johnny doesn't hurry them up, three quarters of an hour, easy."

"Not much time to make a plan," Gavallan said. He looked back at the map. "But then there'd never be enough. Is there a rig near that bearing that's empty—still closed down?"

"Dozens. There're dozens that're still as the strikers left them months ago—doors welded closed, crazy, huh? Why?"

"Scrag said one of them might be an ideal spot to park gasoline and refuel."

Starke frowned. "Not in our area, Andy. He's got some big platforms—

ours're little bitty ones mostly. We've none that could take more than one chopper at a time, and we sure as hell wouldn't want to wait around. What'd old Scrag say?"

Gavallan told him.

"You think he'll get to go see Rudi?"

"He said in the next few days. I can't wait that long now. Could you find an excuse to get down to Bandar Delam?"

Starke's eyes narrowed. "Sure. Maybe we could send a couple of our birds there an' say we're redeploying them—even better, tell Hotshot we're putting 'em on loan for a week. We can still get occasional clearances—so long as that sonofabitch's out of the way."

Gavallan sipped the beer, making it last. "We can't operate any longer in Iran. Poor old Jordon should never have happened, and I'm damned sorry I didn't order an evacuation weeks ago. Damned sorry."

"He wasn't your fault, Andy."

"In a way he was. In any event we have to pull out. With or without our planes. We have to try to salvage what we can—without risking personnel."

"Any caper's going to be goddamn risky, Andy." Starke's voice was gentle.

"I know. I'd like you to ask your lads if they'd be part of Whirlwind."

"There's no way we could get out all our choppers. No way."

"I know, so I propose we concentrate on our 212s only." Gavallan saw Starke look at him with more interest. "Mac agreed. Could you fly your three out?"

Starke thought a moment. "Two's max that I could handle—we'd need two pilots, with say one mechanic per chopper for emergencies and some extra hands to handle the spare drums or in-flight refuel—that'd be minimum. It'd be tricky but if we got lucky . . ." He whistled tonelessly, "Maybe we could send the other 212 to Rudi at Bandar Delam? Sure, why the hell not? I'd tell Hotshot she's on loan for ten days. You could send me a confirm telex asking for the transfer. But hell, Andy, we'd still have three pilots here an—"

The interbase phone rang. "Goddamn," he said irritably, getting up and going over to it. "I'm so used to having the phones out, every time one rings I jump like a scalded cat expecting Armageddon. Hello, this's Starke. Yeah?"

Gavallan watched Starke, tall, lean, and so strong. Wish I was as strong, he thought.

"Ah, thanks," Starke was saying. "Okay . . . sure, thanks, Sergeant. Who? . . . Sure, put him on." Gavallan noticed the change in the voice and his attention increased. "Evening . . . No, we can't, not now. . . .

NO! We can't! Not now, we're busy." He put the phone down with a muttered "sonofabitch." "Hotshot, wanting to see us. 'I want you both over in my office at once!' Asshole!" He sipped some beer and felt better. "It was also Wazari in the tower reporting the last of our birds has just touched down."

"Who?"

"Pop Kelly, he's been on the Flotsam run, ferrying a few oilers from rig to rig—they're way down in strength, except in fat-ass komitehs who're more concerned with prayer meetings and kangaroo courts than pumping oil." He shivered. "I tell you, Andy, the komitehs are Satan-sponsored." Gavallan noted the word but said nothing as Starke continued, "They're the pits."

"Yes. Azadeh nearly got killed—by stoning."

"What?"

Gavallan told him about the village and her escape from the village. "We still don't know where the hell old Erikki is—I saw her before I left and she was . . . glazed is about the only word, still not over the shock."

Starke's face became even grimmer. With an effort he shook off his anger. "Say we can get the 212s out, what about the guys? We've still three pilots and maybe ten mecs to get out before the caper, what about them? And what about all the spares? We'd be leaving three 206s and the Alouette . . . and what about all our household bits and pieces, our bank accounts, apartments in Tehran, photos, and all the kids' stuff—hell, not just ours but all the other guys', the ones we got out in the exodus? If we shove off, everything'll be lost. Everything."

"The company'll reimburse everyone. I can't do the bric-a-brac but we'll pay bank accounts and cover the rest. Most're minimal as most of you keep your funds in England and draw on them as you need them. For the last few months—certainly since the banks went on strike—we've been crediting all pay and allowances in Aberdeen. We'll pay to replace furniture and personal stuff. Seems to me we can't get most of it out anyway—ports are still clogged, practically no truckers, railways aren't working, air freight almost nonexistent. Everyone'll be reimbursed."

Starke nodded slowly. He finished his beer to the dregs. "Even if we get the 212s out, you're going to take a bath."

Gavallan said patiently, "No. Add it up for yourself. Each 212's worth $1 million, each 206 $150,000, an Alouette $500,000. We've twelve 212s in Iran. If we could get them out we'd be okay, still in business, and I could absorb Iran's losses. Just. Business's booming and twelve 212s would keep us going. Any spares we could get out'd be an extra bonus—again we could concentrate on 212 spares only. With our 212s we're in business."

He tried to maintain his confidence, but it was waning. So many hurdles to jump, mountains to scale, gorges to cross. Yes, but don't forget that a journey of ten thousand leagues begins with one step. Be a little Chinese, he told himself. Remember your childhood in Shanghai and old Nanny Ah Soong and how she taught you about joss—part luck, part karma: "Joss is joss, young Master, good or bad. Sometimes you can pray for good joss and get it, sometimes not. But *ayeeyah*, don't trust the gods too far—gods are like people. They sleep, go out to lunch, get drunk, forget what they're supposed to do, lie, and promise, and lie again. Pray all you want but don't depend on gods—only yourself and your family and even with them depend on yourself. Remember gods don't like people, young Master, because people remind them of themselves. . . ."

"Of course we'll get the lads out, every last one. Meanwhile, would you ask for volunteers to fly out your two birds if, *if* I push the button on Whirlwind?"

Starke glanced back at the map. Then he said, "Sure. It'll be me and either Freddy or Pop Kelly—the other guy can take the 212 to Rudi and join him in his plan, they've not so far to go." He smiled wryly. "Okay?"

"Thanks," Gavallan said, feeling very good inside. "Thanks. Did you mention Whirlwind to Tom Lochart when he was here?"

"Sure. He said to count him out, Andy."

"Oh." The good feeling vanished. "Then that's it. If he stays we can't go forward."

"He's a 'go,' Andy, whether he likes it or not," Starke said compassionately. "He's committed—with or without Sharazad. That's the tough part, with or without. He can't escape HBC, Valik, and Isfahan."

After a moment Gavallan said, "I suppose you're right. Unfair, isn't it?"

"Yes. Tom's all right, he'll understand eventually. I'm not so sure about Sharazad."

"Mac and I tried to see her in Tehran. We went to the Bakravan house and knocked for ten minutes. No answer. Mac went yesterday too. Maybe they're just not answering the door."

"Not like Iranians." Starke took off his flight jacket and hung it up in the small hall. "Soon as Tom gets back here tomorrow, I'll send him to Tehran if there's enough daylight left—latest, Monday morning. I was going to clear it with Mac tonight on our regular call."

"Good idea." Gavallan went on to the next problem. "Damned if I know what to do about Erikki either. I saw Talbot and he said he'd see what he could do, then I went to the Finnish embassy and saw a first secretary called Tollonen and told him too. He seemed very concerned—and just as helpless. 'That's rather a wild country and the border's as fluid as the rebellion,

insurrection, or fighting that's going on there. If the KGB's involved . . .'
He left it hanging, Duke, just like that. 'If the KGB's involved . . .' "

"What about Azadeh, can't her daddy, the Khan, help?"

"Seems they all had a huge row. She was very shook. I asked her to forget
her Iranian papers and get on the 125 and wait for Erikki in Al Shargaz, but
that went down like a lead balloon. She won't move till Erikki reappears. I
pointed out the Khan's a law unto himself—he can reach into Tehran and
kidnap her back too easily if he wants. She said, 'Insha'Allah.' "

"Erikki'll be okay. I'd bet on that." Starke was confident. "His ancient
gods'll guard him."

"Hope so." Gavallan had kept his parka on. Even so he was still feeling
cold. Out of the window he could see the fueling still continuing. "How
about a cuppa before I leave?"

"Sure." Starke went to the kitchen. Above the sink was a mirror and over
the butane stove opposite was an old, worn needlepoint mounted in frame
that a friend in Falls Church had given to Manuela as a wedding present:
SCREW HOME COOKING. He smiled, remembering how they had laughed
when they had got it, then noticed the reflection of Gavallan in the mirror
brooding at the map. I must be crazy, he thought, zeroing back to six days
and two choppers. How the hell're we gonna clean out the base and still
keep ourselves in one piece 'cause Andy's right that one way or another
we're finished here. I must be crazy to volunteer. But what the hell? You
can't ask one of your guys to volunteer if you don't do it yourself. Yeah,
bu—

There was a knock on the front door and it opened immediately. Freddy
Ayre said softly, "Hotshot's heading this way with a Green Band."

"Come on in, Freddy, and shut the door," Starke said. They waited in
silence. An imperious knock. He opened the door, saw the arrogant sneer
on Esvandiary, instantly recognizing the young Green Band as one of the
mullah Hussain's men and also a member of the komiteh at his questioning.
"Salaam," he said politely.

"Salaam, Agha," the Green Band said with a shy smile. He had thick,
cracked glasses and threadbare clothes and an M16.

Abruptly, Starke's mind went into overload and he heard himself say,
"Mr. Gavallan, I think you know Hotshot."

"My name's Esvandiary—Mr. Esvandiary!" the man said angrily. "How
many times do you have to be told? Gavallan, it would help your operation
greatly to get rid of this man before we throw him out as an undesirable!"

Gavallan flushed at the rudeness. "Now just a minute, Captain Starke's
the best capt—"

"You're Hotshot, you're also a sonofabitch," Starke exploded, bunching his fists, suddenly so dangerous that Ayre and Gavallan were aghast, Esvandiary backed off a foot, and the young Green Band gaped. "You've always been Hotshot and I'd call you Esvandiary or whatever goddamn name you want but for what you did to *Captain* Ayre. You're a sonofabitch with no balls and need pasting and before you're very much older you're gonna get it!"

"I'll have you before the komiteh tom—"

"You're a yellow-bellied eater of camel dung, so go blow it outta your ass." Contemptuously Starke turned to the Green Band who was still gaping at him, and without missing a beat, switched to Farsi, his voice now polite and deferential. "Excellency, I told this dog," he jerked his thumb rudely at Esvandiary, "that he is an eater of camel dung, with no courage, who needs *men* with guns to protect him while he orders other *men* to beat and threaten unarmed peaceful members of my tribe against the law, who will not . . ."

Choked with rage, Esvandiary tried to interrupt but Starke overrode him, ". . . who will not stand against me as a man—with knife or sword or gun or fist—according to custom among the Bedouin to avoid a family blood feud, and according to my custom also."

"Blood feud? You've gone mad! In the Name of God, what blood feud? Blood feuds're against the law . . ." Esvandiary shouted and continued the tirade, Gavallan and Ayre watching helplessly, not understanding Farsi and completely thrown by Starke's outburst.

But the young Green Band closed his ears to Esvandiary, then held up his hand, still awed by Starke and his knowledge and not a little envious. "Please, Excellency Esvandiary," he said, his eyes magnified by the thickness of the old, cracked lenses, and when there was quiet he said to Starke, "You claim the ancient right of blood feud against this man?"

Starke could feel his heart pumping, and he heard himself say firmly, "Yes," knowing it was a dangerous gamble but he had to take it, "yes."

"How can an Infidel claim such a right?" Esvandiary said furiously. "This is not the Saudi desert, our laws forbid blo—"

"I claim that right!"

"As God wants," the Green Band said and looked at Esvandiary. "Perhaps this man is not an Infidel, not truly. This man can claim what he likes, Excellency."

"Are you mad? Of course he's an Infidel and don't you know blood feuds're against the law. You fool, it's against the law, it's ag—"

"You're not a mullah!" the youth said, angry now. "You're not a mullah to say what is the law and what isn't! Shut your mouth! I'm no illiterate peasant, I can read and write and I'm a member of the komiteh to keep the peace here and now you threaten the peace." He glared at Esvandiary who once more backed off. "I will ask the komiteh and mullah Hussain," he said to Starke. "There is little chance that they would agree but . . . as God wants. I agree the law is the law and that a man does not need other men with guns to beat unarmed innocents against the law—or even to punish the evil, however evil, only the strength of God. I leave you to God." He turned to go.

"A moment, Agha," Starke said. He reached over and took a spare parka that hung on a hook beside the still-open door. "Here," he said, offering the coat, "please accept this small gift."

"I could not possibly do that," the youth said, eyes wide and filled with longing.

"Please, Excellency, it is so insignificant that it hardly bears noticing."

Esvandiary began to say something but stopped as the youth looked over at him, then again turned his attention to Starke. "I could not possibly accept it—it is so rich and I could not possibly accept it from His Excellency."

"Please," Starke said patiently, continuing the formality, then at length held the coat up for the youth to slip on.

"Well, if you insist . . ." the youth said, pretending reluctance. He gave Ayre the M16 while he slipped into the coat, the others not knowing quite what was going on, except Esvandiary who watched and waited, swearing revenge. "It is wonderful," the youth said, zipping it up, feeling warm for the first time in many months. Never in all his life had he had such a coat. "Thank you, Agha." He saw the look on Esvandiary's face and his disgust for him increased—wasn't he just accepting pishkesh as was his right? "I shall try to persuade the komiteh to grant the right His Excellency asks," he said, then contentedly went off into the gloaming.

At once Starke whirled on Esvandiary. "Now what the hell did you want?"

"Many pilots' licenses and resident permits're out of date an—"

"No British or American pilot's license's out of date—only Iranian and they're automatic if the others are okay! Of course they're out of date! Haven't your offices been closed for months—pull your head out of your ass!"

Esvandiary went beet red and the moment he started to reply, Starke turned his back on him and looked directly at Gavallan for the first time. "It's clearly impossible to operate here any longer, Mr. Gavallan—you've seen it for yourself now, we're harassed, Freddy here was beaten, we're overruled, and there's no way we can work with this sort of crap. I think you should close down the base for a couple of months. At once!" he added.

Gavallan suddenly understood. "I agree," he said and grabbed the initiative. Starke sighed with relief, pushed past, and sat down with pretended sullenness, heart racing in his chest. "I'm closing the base at once. We'll send all our choppers and personnel elsewhere. Freddy, get five men overdue leave and put them aboard the 125 right now with their luggage, *right now* an—"

"You can't close down the base," Esvandiary snarled. "Nor can y—"

"It's closed, by God," Gavallan said, working himself into a towering rage. "They're my aircraft and my personnel and we're not going to suffer all this harassment and beating. Freddy, who's overdue leave?"

Blankly Ayre began to give names and Esvandiary was in shock. To close down the base did not suit him at all. Wasn't Minister Ali Kia visiting here on Thursday and wasn't he then going to offer him an extraordinary pishkesh? If the base was closed that would ruin all his plans.

"You can't take our helicopters out of this area without my approval," he shouted. "They're Iranian property!"

"They're the property of the joint venture when they're paid for," Gavallan shouted back, more than a little imposing in rage. "I'm going to complain to higher authority you're interfering with the Imam's direct order to get production back to normal. You are! Y—"

"You're forbidden to close down. I'll have the komiteh put Starke in jail for mutiny if y—"

"Balderdash! Starke, I'm ordering you to close the base down. Hotshot, you seem to forget we're well connected. I'll complain directly to Minister Ali Kia. He's adviser to our board now and he'll deal with you and IranOil!"

Esvandiary blanched. "Minister Kia's on . . . on the . . . on the board?"

"Yes, yes, he is." For a split second Gavallan was nonplussed. He had used Kia's name as the only one he knew in the present government and was astonished at the impact it had had on Esvandiary. But hardly missing a beat, he pressed home his advantage. "My close friend Ali Kia will deal with all this! And with you. You're a traitor to Iran! Freddy, get five men aboard the 125 right now! And Starke, send every aircraft we have to Bandar Delam at first light—at first light!"

"Yessir!"

"Wait," Esvandiary said, seeing his whole plan in ruins. "There's no need to close down the base, Mr. Gavallan. There may have been misunderstandings, mostly due to Petrofi and that man Zataki. I wasn't responsible for that beating, it wasn't me!" He forced his voice to be reasonable but inside he wanted to shout with rage and see them all in jail, flogged and screaming for mercy they would never get. "No reason to close the base down, Mr. Gavallan. Flying can stay normal!"

"It's closed," Gavallan said imperiously and glanced at Starke for guidance. "Much as I'm against it."

"Yessir. You're right." Starke was very deferential. "Of course you can close the base. We can redeploy the choppers or mothball them. Bandar Delam needs an immediate 212 for . . . for the Iran-Toda contract. Perhaps we could send 'em one of ours, and close down the rest."

Esvandiary said quickly, "Mr. Gavallan, work is getting more normal every day. The revolution is successful and over, the Imam in charge. The komitehs . . . the komitehs'll soon disappear. There'll be all the Guerney contracts to service, double the number of 212s needed. As to overdue license renewals—Insha'Allah! We will wait thirty days. No need to close operations. No need to be hasty, Mr. Gavallan, you've been on this base a long time, you've a big investment here an—"

"I know what our investment is," Gavallan snapped with real anger, hating the unctuous undercurrent. "Very well, Captain Starke, I'll take your advice and by God you'd better be right. Put two men on the 125 tonight, their replacements will be back next week. Send the 212 to Bandar Delam tomorrow—how long is she to be on loan?"

"Six days, sir, back next Sunday."

Gavallan said to Esvandiary, "She'll come back, pending an improved situation here."

"The 212 is ours . . . the 212 is the base's equipment, Mr. Gavallan," Esvandiary corrected himself quickly. "We carry it on our manifests. It will have to come back. As to personnel, the rule is that incoming pilots and mechanics arrive first to replace those going on leave an—"

"Then we're going to bend the rules—Mister Esvandiary—or I close the base now," Gavallan said curtly and held on to his hope. "Starke, put two men on the plane tonight, all but a skeleton staff on the Thursday flight, and we'll send her back with full replacements on Friday, pending the situation coming back to normal."

Starke saw Esvandiary's rage returning so he said quickly, "We're not allowed to fly on Holy Day, sir. The full crew should come first thing Saturday morning." He glanced at Esvandiary. "Don't you agree?"

For a moment Esvandiary thought he was going to explode, his pent-up rage almost overcoming his resolve. "If you . . . if you apologize—for the foul names and your foul manners."

There was a big silence, the door still open, the room chill, but Starke felt the sweat on his back as he weighed his answer. They had achieved so much —if Whirlwind was to come to pass—but Esvandiary was no fool and a quick acquiescence would make him suspicious, as a refusal might jeopardize their gains. "I apologize for nothing—but I will call you Mr. Esvandiary in future," he said.

Without a word Esvandiary turned on his heel and stormed off. Starke closed the door, his shirt under his sweater sticking to him.

"What the hell was all that about, Duke?" Ayre said angrily. "Are you bonkers?"

"Just a moment, Freddy," Gavallan said. "Duke, will Hotshot go along with it?"

"I . . . I don't know." Starke sat down, his knees trembling. "Jesus."

"If he does . . . if he does . . . Duke, you were brilliant! It was a brilliant idea, brilliant."

"You caught the ball, Andy, you made the touchdown."

"If it is a touchdown." Gavallan wiped the sweat off his own brow. He began to explain to Ayre, stopped as the phone rang.

"Hello? This's Starke . . . Sure, hang on . . . Andy, it's the tower. McIver's on the HF for you. Wazari asks if you want to go over right away or call him back—McIver says to tell you he's gotten a message from a guy called Avisyard."

In the control room, Gavallan touched the send switch, almost sick with worry, Wazari watching him, another English-speaking Green Band as attentive. "Yes, Captain McIver?"

"Evening, Mr. Gavallan, glad I caught you." McIver's voice was heavy with static and noncommittal. "How do you read?"

"Three by five, Captain McIver, go ahead."

"I've just got a telex from Liz Chen. It says: 'Please forward to Mr. Gavallan the following telex, dated 25 Feb., just arrived: "Your request is approved, [signed] Masson Avisyard." A copy has gone to Al Shargaz.' Message ends."

For a moment Gavallan did not believe his ears. "Approved?"

"Yes. I repeat: 'Your request is approved.' Telex's signed Masson Avisyard. What should I reply?"

Gavallan was hard put to keep the glow off his face. Masson was the name of his friend in the Aviation Registration Office in London and the "request" was to put all their Iranian-based helicopters temporarily back onto British registry. "Just acknowledge it, Captain McIver."

"We can proceed with planning."

"Yes. I agree. I'm off in a couple of minutes, is there anything else?"

"Not for the moment—just routine. I'll bring Captain Starke up to date tonight at our regular time. Very glad about Masson, happy landings."

"Thanks, Mac, and you." Gavallan clicked off the switch and handed the mike back to young Sergeant Wazari. He had noticed the bad bruising, broken nose, and that some of his teeth were missing. But he said nothing. What was there to say, "Thank you, Sergeant?"

Wazari motioned out of the windows at the apron below where the refueling crew had started winding in the long hoses. "She's all gassed, s—" He just stopped the automatic "sir." "We've, er, we've no runway lights operating so you'd best be aboard soon as possible."

"Thank you." Gavallan felt almost light-headed as he walked for the stairs. The interbase HF crackled into life. "This's the base commander. Put Mr. Gavallan on."

At once Wazari clicked the send switch. "Yessir." Nervously he handed the mike to Gavallan whose caution had soared. "He's Maj—sorry, he's now Colonel Changiz."

"Yes, Colonel? Andrew Gavallan."

"Aliens are forbidden to use the HF for code messages—who is Masson Avisyard?"

"A design engineer," Gavallan said. It was the first thought that came into his head. Watch yourself, this bastard's clever. "I certainly wasn't tr—"

"What was your 'request' and who is . . ." There was a slight pause and muffled voices. ". . . who is Liz Chen?"

"Liz Chen is my secretary, Colonel. My request was to . . ." To what? he wanted to shout, then all at once the answer came to him. ". . . to confine seating to a configuration six rows of two seats either side of a gangway of a new chopper, the X63. The manufacturers wanted a different configuration but our engineers believe that this six by four would enhance safety and make for speedy exit in case of emergency. It would also save money and m—"

"Yes, very well," the colonel interrupted him testily. "I repeat, the HF is not to be used except with prior approval until the emergency is over, and certainly not for code. Your refueling is completed, you're cleared for immediate takeoff. Tomorrow's landing to pick up the body of the Zagros casualty is not approved. EchoTangoLimaLima may land Monday between 1100 and 1200, subject to confirm by HQ that will be sent to Kish radar. Good night."

"But we already have Tehran's formal approval, sir. My pilot gave it to your landing chief the moment he arrived."

The colonel's voice hardened even more: "The Monday clearance is subject to confirmation by Iran Air Force HQ. *Iran Air Force HQ.* This is an Iran Air Force base, you are subject to Iran Air Force regulation and discipline and will abide by Iran Air Force regulations and discipline. Do you understand?"

After a pause, Gavallan said, "Yes, sir, I understand, but we're a civilian oper—"

"You're in Iran, on an Iran Air Force base and therefore subject to Iran Air Force regulations and discipline." The channel went dead. Nervously Wazari tidied his already meticulous desk.

SUNDAY
February 25

ZAGROS—RIG BELLISSIMA: 11:05 A.M. In the biting cold Tom Lochart watched Jesper Almqvist, the down-hole expert, handle the big plug that now was suspended by a wire over the exposed drilling hole. All around was the burned-out wreckage of the rig and trailers from the terrorist firebomb attack, already half buried in new snow.

"Lower away," the young Swede shouted. At once his assistant in the small, self-contained cabin started the winch. Awkwardly fighting the wind, Jesper guided the plug down into the well's metal casing. The plug consisted of an explosive charge over two metal half cups fixed around a rubber sealing ring. Lochart could see how tired both men were. This was the fourteenth well they had capped over the last three days, still five more to go, the sunset deadline only seven hours away, each well a two- to three-hour job in good conditions—once they were on site.

"Sonofabitching conditions," Lochart muttered, equally weary. Too many flying hours since the Green Band of the komiteh had decreed the deadline, too many problems: scrambling to close down the whole field with its eleven sites, rushing to Shiraz to fetch Jesper, airlifting crews to Shiraz from dawn to dusk, spares to Kowiss—deciding what to take and what to leave, impossible to do everything at such short notice. Then the death of Jordon and Scot being clipped.

"That's it, hold her there!" Jesper shouted, then hurried back through the snow to the cabin. Lochart watched him check the depth gauge, then stab a button. There was a muffled explosion. A puff of smoke came out of the drill hole. At once his assistant winched in the remains of the wire as Jesper went back, fought the pipe rams closed over the drill hole, and it was done—"The explosive charge blows the two cups together," Jesper had explained earlier; "this forces the rubber seal against the steel casing and she's capped, the seal good for a couple of years. When you want to open her, we come back and with another special tool drill out the plug and she's as good as new. Maybe."

He wiped his face with his sleeve. "Let's get the hell out, Tom!" He trudged back to the cabin, turned the main electric switch off, stuffed all the computer printouts into a briefcase, closed and locked the door.

"What about all the gear?"

"It stays. The cabin's okay. Let's get aboard, I'm frozen to hell." Jesper headed for the 206 that was parked on the helipad. "Soon as I get back to Shiraz I'll see IranOil and get 'em to get us permission to come back and pick the cabin up, along with the others. Eleven cabins're one hell of an investment to leave lying around and not working. Weatherwise they're good for a year, locked up. They're designed to take a lot of weather beating, though not vandalizing." He motioned to the wreckage around them. "Stupid!"

"Yes."

"Stupid! Tom, you should've seen the IranOil execs when I told them you'd been ordered out and Mr. Sera was closing down the field." Jesper grinned, fair hair, blue eyes. "They screamed like slitted pigs and swore there were no komiteh orders to stop production."

"I still don't see why they didn't come back with you and overrule the bastards here."

"I invited them and they said next week. This's Iran, they'll never come." He looked back at the site. "That well alone's worth sixteen thousand barrels a day." He got into the left seat beside Lochart, his assistant, a taciturn Breton, clambered into the back and pulled the door closed. Lochart started up, heat to maximum.

"Next, Rig Maria, okay?"

Jesper thought a moment. "Better leave her till last. Rig Rosa's more important." He stifled another yawn. "We've two producers to cap there and the one still drilling. Poor bastards haven't had time to tip out about seven thousand feet of pipe so we'll have to plug her with it all in. Sonofa-beetching waste." He clipped his seat belt on and huddled closer to the heat fan.

"What happens then?"

"Routine." The young man laughed. "When you want to open her up, we core the plug, then start fishing the pipe out piece by piece. Slow, tedious, and expensive." Another huge yawn. He closed his eyes and was almost instantly asleep.

Mimmo Sera met the 206 at Rig Rosa. A 212 was also on the pad, engine idling, Jean-Luc at the controls, men loading luggage and getting aboard. "*Buon giorno*, Tom."

"Hi, Mimmo. How'd it go?" Lochart waved a greeting to Jean-Luc.

"These are the last of my men except for a roustabout to help Jesper." Mimmo Sera was bleary with fatigue. "There was no time to tip pipe out of Three."

"No problem—we'll cap her as is."

"*Sì*." A tired smile. "Think of all the money you'll make tipping it out."

Jesper laughed. "Seven thousand, eight hundred and sixty feet at—maybe we'll make you a special price."

Good-naturedly the older man made an expressive Italian gesture.

Lochart said, "I'll leave you two to it. When do you want me to come back for you?"

Jesper looked at his watch. It was near noon. "Come for us at four-thirty. Okay?"

"Four-thirty on the dot. Sunset's at six-thirty-seven." Lochart went over to the 212.

Jean-Luc was muffled against the cold but still managed to look elegant. "I'll take this batch direct Shiraz—they're the last—except for Mimmo and your crew."

"Good. How's it below?"

"Chaos." Jean-Luc swore with great passion. "I smell disaster, more di-saster."

"You expect disaster all the time—except when you're bedding. Not to worry, Jean-Luc."

"Of course to worry." Jean-Luc watched the loading for a moment—almost completed now, suitcases, knapsacks, two dogs, two cats, with a full load of men waiting impatiently—then turned back, lowered his voice, and said seriously, "Tom, the sooner we're out of Iran the better."

"No. Zagros's just an isolated case. Anyway, I'm still hoping Iran works out." HBC swirled up into the front of Lochart's brain, and Sharazad, and Whirlwind. He had told no one here about Whirlwind and his talk with Starke: "I'll leave that to you, Duke," he had said just before he left. "You can put the case better than me—I'm totally against it."

"Sure. That's your privilege. Mac approved your trip to Tehran Monday."

"Thanks. Has he seen Sharazad yet?"

"No, Tom, not yet."

Where the hell is she? he thought, another twinge going through him. "I'll see you at the base, Jean-Luc. Have a safe trip."

"Make sure Scot and Rodrigues are ready when I get back. I'll have to do a quick turnaround if I'm to get to Al Shargaz tonight." The cabin door slammed shut, Jean-Luc glanced around, and got the thumbs-up. He acknowledged, then turned back again. "I'm off—make sure Scot slips aboard quietly, eh? I don't want to get shot out of the skies—I still say Scot was their target, no one else."

Lochart nodded bleakly, headed for his 206.

He had been en route back from Kowiss when the dawn disaster had happened yesterday. Jean-Luc was getting up at the time and, by chance, had been looking out of his window. "The two of them, Jordon and Scot, were very close together, carrying spares between them, loading HIW," he had told Lochart as soon as he had landed. "I didn't see the first shots, just heard them, but I saw Jordon stagger and cry out, hit in the head, and Scot look off toward the trees at the back of the hangar. Then Scot bent down and tried to help Jordon—I've seen enough men shot to know poor Effer was dead before he touched the snow. Then there were more shots, three or four, but it wasn't a machine gun, more like an M16 on automatic. This time Scot got one in the shoulder and it spun him around and he fell into the snow beside Jordon, half covered by him—Jordon between him and the trees. Then the bullets started pumping again . . . at Scot, Tom, I'm sure of it."

"How can you be sure, Jean-Luc?"

"I'm certain. Effer was directly in the line of fire, directly, and took them all—the attackers weren't spraying the base, just aiming at Scot. I grabbed my Very pistol and charged out, saw no one, but fired anyway in the general direction of the trees. When I got to Scot, he had the shakes and Jordon was a mess, hit perhaps eight times. We got Scot to the medic—he's all right, Tom, shoulder wound, I watched him patched myself, wound's clean and the bullet went right through."

Lochart had gone at once to see Scot in the trailer room they called the infirmary. Kevin O'Sweeney, the medic, said, "He's okay, Captain."

"Yes," Scot echoed, his face white and still in shock. "Really okay, Tom."

"Let me talk to Scot a moment, Kevin." When they were alone he said quietly, "What happened while I was away, Scot, you see Nitchak Khan? Anyone from the village?"

"No. No one."

"And you told no one about what happened in the square?"

"No, no, not at all. Why, what's all this about, Tom?"

"Jean-Luc thinks you were the target, not Jordon or the base, just you."

"Oh, Christ! Old Effer bought it because of me?"

Lochart remembered how distraught Scot had been. The base had been filled with gloom, everyone still working frantically, boxing spares, loading the two 212s, the 206, and the Alouette for today, last day at Zagros. The only bright spot yesterday was dinner—a barbecued haunch of fresh wild goat that Jean-Luc had cooked with plenty of delicious Iranian rice and horisht.

"Great barbecue, Jean-Luc," he had said.

"Without French garlic and my skill this would taste like old English mutton, ugh!"

"The cook buy it in the village?"

"No, it was a gift. Young Darius—the one who speaks English—he brought us the whole carcass on Friday as a gift from Nitchak's wife."

Abruptly the meat in Lochart's mouth tasted foul. "His wife?"

"*Oui.* Young Darius said she'd shot it that morning. *Mon Dieu,* I didn't know she was a hunter, did you? What's the matter, Tom?"

"It was a gift to whom?"

Jean-Luc frowned. "To me and to the base . . . actually Darius said, 'This is from the kalandaran for the base and to give thanks for France's help to the Imam, may God protect him.' Why?"

"Nothing," Lochart had said but later he had taken Scot aside. "Were you there when Darius delivered the goat?"

"Yes, yes, I was. I happened to be in the office and just thanked him an—" The color had left Scot's face. "Now that I think of it, Darius said as he was leaving, 'It's fortunate that the kalandaran is a great shot, isn't it?' I think I said, 'Yes, fantastic.' That'd be a dead giveaway, wouldn't it?"

"Yes—if you add it to my slip which now, now I think's got to be a deliberate trap. I was trapped too, so now Nitchak's got to know there're two of us who could be witnesses against the village."

Last night and all today Lochart had been wondering what to do, how to get Scot and himself out, and he still had no solution.

Absently he climbed into the 206, waited until Jean-Luc was clear, and took off. Now he was flying over the Ravine of the Broken Camels. The road that led to the village was still buried under tons of snow the avalanche had brought. They'll never dig that out, he thought. On the rolling plateau he could see herds of goats and sheep with their shepherds. Ahead was Yazdek village. He skirted it. The schoolhouse was a scar in the earth, black amid the whiteness. Some villagers were in the square and they looked up briefly then went about their business. I won't be sorry to leave, he thought. Not with Jordon murdered here. Zagros Three'll never be the same.

The base was in chaos, men milling about—the last of those brought from other rigs and due to go to Shiraz, thence out of Iran. Cursing, exhausted mechanics were still packing spares, piling boxes and luggage for transshipment to Kowiss. Before he could get out of the cockpit, the refueling tender arrived with Freddy Ayre jauntily sitting on the hood. Yesterday, at Starke's suggestion, Lochart had brought Ayre and another pilot, Claus Schwartenegger, to substitute for Scot. "I'll take her now, Tom," Ayre said. "You go and eat."

"Thanks, Freddy. How'd it go?"

"Ropy. Claus's taken another load of spares to Kowiss and he'll be back in good time for the last one. Come sunset I'll take the Alouette, she's loaded to the gills and a bit more. What d'you want to fly out?"

"The 212—I'll have Jordon aboard. Claus can take the 206. You're off to Shiraz?"

"Yes. We've still got ten bods to get there—I was, er, thinking of taking five passengers instead of four for two trips. Eh?"

"If they're small enough—no luggage—and so long as I don't see you. Okay?"

Ayre laughed, the cold making his bruises more livid. "They're all so anxious I don't think they care much about luggage—one of the guys from Rig Maria said they heard shooting nearby."

"One of the villagers hunting, probably." The specter of the huntress with her high-powered rifle or for that matter any of the Kash'kai—all expert marksmen—filled him with dread. We're so goddamn helpless, he thought, but kept it off his face. "Have a safe trip, Freddy." He went to the cookhouse and got some hot horisht.

"Agha," the cook said nervously, the other four helpers crowding around. "We're due two months' pay—what's going to happen to our pay and to us?"

"I've already told you, Ali. We'll take you back to Shiraz where you came from. This afternoon. We pay you off there and as soon as I can I'll send you the month's severance pay we owe you. You keep in touch through IranOil as usual. When we come back you get your jobs back."

"Thank you, Agha." The cook had been with them for a year. He was a thin, pale man with stomach ulcers. "I don't want to stay among these barbarians," he said nervously. "When this afternoon?"

"Before sunset. At four o'clock you start cleaning up and get everything neat and tidy."

"But, Agha, what's the point of that? The moment we leave, the lice-covered Yazdeks will come and steal everything."

"I know," Lochart said wearily. "But you will leave everything neat and tidy and I will lock the door and maybe they won't."

"As God wants, Agha. But they will."

Lochart finished his meal and went to the office. Scot Gavallan was there, face drawn, arm painfully in a sling. The door opened. Rod Rodrigues came in, dark rings around his eyes, his face pasty. "Hi, Tom, you haven't forgotten, huh?" he asked anxiously. "I'm not on the manifest."

"No problem. Scot, Rod's going with HJX. He's going with you and Jean-Luc to Al Shargaz."

"Great, but I'm fine, Tom. I think I'd rather go to Kowiss."

"For Christ's sake, you're out to Al Shargaz and that's the end of it!"

Scot flushed at the anger. "Yes. All right, Tom." He walked out.

Rodrigues broke the silence. "Tom, what you want we send with HJX?"

"How the hell do I know, for Ch—" Lochart stopped. "Sorry, I'm getting tired. Sorry."

"No sweat, Tom, so're we all. Maybe we send her empty, huh?"

With an effort Lochart put away his fatigue. "No, put the spare engine aboard—and any other 212 spares to make up the load."

"Sure. That'd be good. Maybe y—" The door opened and Scot came back in quickly. "Nitchak Khan! Look out the window!"

Twenty or more men were coming up the track from the village. All were armed. Others were already spreading out over the base, Nitchak Khan heading for the office trailer. Lochart went to the back window, jerked it open. "Scot, go to my hut, keep away from the windows, don't let 'em see you and don't move until I come get you. Hurry!"

Awkwardly Scot climbed out and rushed off. Lochart pulled the window closed.

The door opened. Lochart got up. "Salaam, Kalandar."

"Salaam. Strangers have been seen in the forests nearby. The terrorists must be back so I have come to protect you." Nitchak Khan's eyes were hard. "As God wants, but I would regret it if there were more deaths before you leave. We will be here until sunset." He left.

"What'd he say?" Rodrigues asked, not understanding Farsi.

Lochart told him and saw him tremble. "No problem, Rod," he said, covering his own fear. There was no way they could take off or land without being over forest, low, slow, and in sitting-duck range. Terrorists? Bullshit! Nitchak knows about Scot, knows about me, and I'll bet my life he's got marksmen planted all around, and if he's here till sunset there's no way to sneak off, he'll know which chopper we're on. Insha'Allah. Insha'Allah, but meanwhile what the hell're you going to do?

"Nitchak Khan knows the countryside," he said easily, not wanting to panic Rod, enough fear on the base already without adding to it. "He'll protect us, Rod—if they're there. Is the spare engine crated?"

"Huh? Sure, Tom, sure, she's crated."

"You take care of the loading. I'll see you later. No sweat."

For a long time Lochart stared at the wall. When it was time to return to Rig Rosa, Lochart went to find Nitchak Khan. "You will want to see that Rig Rosa's been closed down properly, Kalandar, isn't it on your land?" he said, and though the old man was reluctant, to his great relief he managed to persuade him with flattery to accompany him. With the Khan aboard, Lochart knew he would be safe for the time being.

So far so good, he thought. I'll have to be the last away. Until we're well away, Scot and I, I have to be very clever. Too much to lose now: Scot, the lads, Sharazad, everything.

AT RIG ROSA: 5:00 P.M. Jesper was driving their unit truck fast along the path through the pines that led to the last well to be capped. Beside him was Mimmo Sera, the roustabout and his assistant were in the back, and he was humming to himself, mostly to keep awake. The plateau was large, almost half a mile between wells, the countryside beautiful and wild.

"We're overdue," Mimmo said wearily, looking at the lowering sun. *"Stronzo!"*

"We'll give it a go," Jesper said. In the side pocket was the last of the energy-giving chocolate bars. The two men shared it. "This looks a lot like Sweden," Jesper said, skidding a bend, the speed exhilarating him.

"Never been to Sweden. There she is," Mimmo said. The well was in a clearing, already on stream and producing about 12,000 barrels daily, the whole field immensely rich. Over the well was a giant column of valves and pipes, called the Christmas Tree, that connected it to the main pipeline. "This was the first we drilled here," he said absently. "Before your time."

When Jesper switched the engine off, the silence was eerie, no pumps needed here to bring the oil to the surface—abundant gas pressure trapped in the oil dome thousands of feet below did that for them and would do so for years yet. "We've no time to cap it properly, Mr. Sera—unless you want to overstay our welcome."

The older man shook his head, pulled his woolen cap down over his ears. "How long will the valves hold?"

Jesper shrugged. "Should be as long as you want—but unattended or inspected from time to time? Don't know. Indefinitely—unless we get a gas surge—or one of the valves or seals're faulty."

"*Stronzo!*"

"*Stronzo,*" Jesper said agreeably, motioned to his assistant and the roustabout and went forward. "We'll just shut it down, no capping." The snow crunched underfoot. Wind rustled the treetops and then they heard the incoming engine of the chopper back from the base. "Let's get with it."

They were hidden from the helipad and main buildings of Rosa, half a mile away. Irritably, Mimmo lit a cigarette and leaned against the hood and watched the three men work diligently, fighting the valves, some stuck, then fetching the huge wrench to unglue them, then the bullet ricocheted off the Christmas Tree and the following crackkkkkkkkk echoed through the forest. All of them froze. They waited. Nothing.

"You see where it came from?" Jesper muttered. No one answered him. Again they waited. Nothing. "Let's finish," he said and again put his weight onto the wrench. The others came forward to help. At once there was another shot and the bullet went through the windshield of the truck, tore a hole in the cabin wall, and ripped a computer screen and some electrical gear apart before going out the other side. Silence.

No movement anywhere. Just wind and a little snow falling, disturbed by the wind. Sound of the chopper jets shrieking now in the landing flare.

Mimmo Sera shouted out in Farsi, "We just shut down the well, Excellencies, to make it safe. We shut it down and then we leave." Again they waited. No answer. Again, "We only make the well safe! Safe for Iran—not for us! For Iran and the Imam—it's your oil not ours!"

Waiting again and never a sound but the sounds of the forest. Branches crackling. Somewhere far off an animal cried. "Mamma mia," Mimmo said, his voice hoarse from shouting, then walked over and picked up the wrench and the bullet sang past his face so close he felt its wake. His shock was sudden and vast. The wrench slipped from his gloves. "Everyone in the truck. We leave."

He backed away and got into the front seat. The others followed. Except Jesper. He retrieved the wrench and when he saw the havoc the errant bullet had caused in *his* cabin, to *his* equipment, his face closed, his anger exploded, and he hurled the wrench impotently at the forest with a curse and stood there a moment, feet slightly apart, knowing he was an easy target but suddenly not caring. *"Förbannades shitdjävlarrrrrr!"*

"Get in the car," Mimmo called out.

"Förbannades shitdjävlar," Jesper muttered, the Swedish obscenity pleasing him, then got into the driver's seat. The truck went back the way it had come and when it was out of sight a fusillade of bullets from both sides of the forest slammed into the Christmas Tree, denting parts of the metal, screaming away into the snow or sky. Then silence. Then someone laughed and called out, "Allahhhh-u Akbarrr . . ."

The cry echoed. Then died away.

AT ZAGROS THREE: 6:38 P.M. The sun touched the horizon. Last of the spares and luggage being put aboard. All four choppers were lined up, two 212s, the 206, and the Alouette, pilots ready, Jean-Luc stomping up and down—departures delayed by Nitchak Khan who had, earlier, arbitrarily ordered all aircraft to leave together which had made it impossible for Jean-Luc to make Al Shargaz, only Shiraz, there to overnight as night flying was forbidden in Iranian skies.

"Explain to him again, Tom," Jean-Luc said angrily.

"He's already told you no, told me no, so it's no and it's too goddamn late anyway! You all set, Freddy?"

"Yes," Ayre called out irritably. "We've been waiting an hour or more!"

Grimly Lochart headed for Nitchak Khan who had heard the anger and irritation and saw with secret delight the discomfiture of the strangers. Standing beside Nitchak Khan was the Green Band Lochart presumed was from the komiteh, and a few villagers. The rest had drifted away during the afternoon. Into the forest, he thought, his mouth dry. "Kalandar, we are almost ready."

"As God wants."

Lochart called out, "Freddy, last load, now!" He took off his peaked cap and the others did likewise as Ayre, Rodrigues, and two mechanics carried the makeshift coffin out of the hangar across the snow and carefully loaded it into Jean-Luc's 212. When it was done, Lochart stepped aside. "Shiraz party board." He shook hands with Mimmo, Jesper, the roustabout, and Jesper's assistant as they climbed aboard, settling themselves amid the luggage, spares, and coffin. Uneasily Mimmo Sera and his Italian roustabout crossed themselves, then locked their seat belts.

Jean-Luc climbed into the pilot's seat, Rodrigues beside him. Lochart turned back to the rest of the men. "All aboard!"

Watched carefully by Nitchak Khan and the Green Band, the remainder went aboard, Ayre flying the Alouette, Claus Schwartenegger the 206, all seats full, tanks full, cargo belly full, external skid carriers lashed with spare rotor blades. Lochart's 212 was crammed and over maximum: "By the time we get to Kowiss we'll've used a lot of fuel so we'll be legal—anyway it's downhill all the way," he had told all pilots when he had briefed them earlier.

Now he stood alone on the snow of Zagros Three, everyone else belted in and doors closed. "Start up!" he ordered, his tension mounting. He had told Nitchak Khan he had decided to act as takeoff master.

Nitchak Khan and the Green Band came up to Lochart. "The young pilot, the one who was wounded, where is he?"

"Who? Oh, Scot? If he's not here, he's in Shiraz, Kalandar," Lochart said and saw anger rush into the old man's face and the Green Band's mouth drop open. "Why?"

"That's not possible!" the Green Band said.

"I didn't see him board so he must have gone on an earlier flight . . ." Lochart had to raise his voice over the growing scream of the jets, all engines now up to speed, ". . . on an earlier flight when we were at Rig Rosa and Maria, Kalandar. Why?"

"That's not possible, Kalandar," the Green Band repeated, frightened, as the old man turned on him. "I was watching carefully!"

Lochart ducked under the whirling blades and went to the pilot's window of Jean-Luc's 212, taking out a thick white envelope. "Here, Jean-Luc, *bonne chance*," he said and gave it to him. "Take off!" For an instant he saw the glimmer of a smile before he hurried to safety, Jean-Luc shoved on maximum power for a quick takeoff, and she lifted and trundled away, the wash from the blades ripping at his clothes and those of the villagers, the jets drowning out what Nitchak Khan was shouting.

Simultaneously—also by prearrangement—Ayre and Schwartenegger gunned their engines, easing away from each other before lumbering in a slow labored climb for the trees. Lochart held on to his hope and then the furious Green Band caught him by the sleeve and pulled him around.

"You lied," the man was shouting, "you lied to the kalandar—the young pilot did not leave earlier! I would have seen him, I watched carefully—tell the kalandar you lied!"

Abruptly Lochart ripped his sleeve away from the young man, knowing that every second meant a few more feet of altitude, a few more yards to safety. "Why should I lie? If the young pilot's not in Shiraz then he's still here! Search the camp, search my airplane—come on, first let us search my airplane!" He stalked off toward his 212 and stood at the open door, from the corners of his eyes seeing Jean-Luc's 212 now over the tree line, Ayre so overloaded barely making it, and the 206 still climbing. "In all the Names of God, let's search," he said, willing their attention onto him and away from the escaping choppers, willing them not to search his airplane but the camp itself. "How can a man hide here? Impossible. What about the office or the trailers, perhaps he's hiding . . ."

The Green Band pulled the gun off his shoulder and aimed at him. "Tell the kalandar you lied or you die!"

With hardly any effort, Nitchak Khan angrily ripped the gun out of the youth's hands and threw it into the snow. "I'm the law in Zagros—not you! Go back to the village!" Filled with fear, the Green Band obeyed instantly.

The villagers waited and watched. Nitchak Khan's face was graven and his small eyes went from chopper to chopper. They were away now, but not yet out of range of those he had posted around the base—to fire only on his signal, only his. One of the smaller choppers was banking, still climbing as fast as possible, coming around in a big circle. To watch us, Nitchak Khan thought, to watch what happens next. As God wants.

"Dangerous to shoot down the sky machines," his wife had said. "That will bring wrath down upon us."

"Terrorists will do that—we will not. The young pilot saw us, and the Farsi-speaking kalandar pilot knows. They must not escape. Terrorists have no mercy, they care nothing for law and order, and how can their existence be disproved? Aren't these mountains ancient havens for brigands? Haven't we chased these terrorists to the limit of our power? What could we do to prevent the tragedy—nothing."

And now before him was the last of the Infidels, his main enemy, the one who had cheated him and lied and whisked the other devil away. At least this one will not escape, he thought. The barest tip of the sun was just above the horizon. As he watched, it vanished. "Peace be with you, pilot."

"And with you, Kalandar, God watch you," Lochart said thinly. "That envelope I gave to my French pilot. You saw me give it to him?"

"Yes, yes, I saw it."

"That was a letter addressed to the Revolutionary Komiteh in Shiraz, with a copy to the Iranian kalandar in Dubai across the Great Sea, signed by the young pilot, witnessed by me, telling exactly what occurred in the village square, what was done by whom, to whom, who was shot, the number of men bound in the Green Band truck before it went into the Ravine of the Broken Camels, the manner of Nasiri's murder, your terr—"

"Lies, all lies! By the Prophet what is this word murder? Murder? That is for bandits. The man died—as God wants," the old man said sullenly, aware of the villagers gaping at Lochart. "He was a known supporter of the Satanic Shah who surely you will meet in hell soon."

"Perhaps, perhaps not. Perhaps my loyal servant who was murdered here by cowardly sons of dogs has already told the One God and the One God knows who is telling the truth!"

"He was not Muslim, he did not serve Islam an—"

"But he was a Christian and Christians serve the One God and my tribesman was murdered by cowards from ambush, sons of dogs with no courage who shot from ambush—surely eaters of shit and men of the Left Hand and accursed! It's true he was murdered like the other Christian at the rig. By God and the Prophet of God, their deaths will be avenged!"

Nitchak Khan shrugged. "Terrorists," he blustered, very afraid, "terrorists did that, of course it was terrorists! As to the letter it's all lies, lies, the pilot was liar, we all know what happened in the village. It's all lies what he said."

"All the more reason that the letter should not be delivered." Lochart was choosing his words very carefully. "Therefore please protect me from the 'terrorists' as I fly away. Only I can prevent the letter being delivered." His heart was beating heavily as he saw the old man take out a cigarette, weighing the pros and cons, and light the cigarette with Jordon's lighter and he wondered again how he could have vengeance for Jordon's murder, still an unresolved part of the plan that so far had worked perfectly: his taking the too vigilant Nitchak Khan away, Scot Gavallan sneaking into the makeshift coffin to be carried aboard Jean-Luc's 212, Jordon's shrouded body already put into the long crate that once housed tail rotors to be loaded into his 212, then the letter and the three choppers flying off together, all perfectly as planned.

And now it was time to finish. Ayre in the Alouette circled overhead in station, well out of range. "Salaam, Kalandar, God's justice be with you," he said and headed for his cockpit.

"I have no control over terrorists!" And when Lochart did not stop, Nitchak Khan shouted louder, "Why would you stop delivery of the lies, eh?"

Lochart got into the cockpit, wanting to be away, hating this place now and the old man. "Because, before God, I deplore lies."

"Before God, you would stop the delivery of these lies?"

"Before God I will see that letter burned. God's justice be with you, Kalandar, and with Yazdek." He pressed the starter. The first jet fired up. Above him the blades began to turn. More switches. Now the second engine caught and all the time he was watching the old man. Rot in hell, old man, he thought, Jordon's blood's on your head, and Gianni's, I'm sure of it though I'll never prove it. Perhaps mine too.

Waiting. Now all needles in the Green. Lift-off.

Nitchak Khan watched the chopper shudder into the air, hesitate, then turn slowly and begin to leave. So easy to raise my hand, he thought, and so soon the Infidel and that howling monster become a funeral pyre falling out of the sky, and as to the letter, lies, all lies.

Two men dead? All know that it's their own fault they're dead. Did we invite them here? No, they came to exploit our land. If they had not come here they would still be alive and waiting for the hell that inevitably is their due.

His eyes never left the air machine. There was plenty of time yet. He smoked slowly, enjoying the cigarette greatly, enjoying the knowledge that he could terminate such a great machine just by raising his hand. But he did not. He remembered the advice of the kalandaran and lit another cigarette from the stub and smoked that, waiting patiently. Soon the hateful sound of the engines was distant, fading quickly, and then, overhead, he saw the smaller air machine break off circling and also head south and west.

When all Infidel sound had quite gone he judged that peace had once more come to his Zagros. "Fire the base," he said to the others. Soon the flames were high. Without regret he cast the lighter into the flames and, contentedly, he strolled home.

MONDAY
February 26

U.S.S.R.

Caspian Sea

U.S.S.R.

TURKEY

KHOI
TABRIZ

MOUNT
SABALAN

BANDAR-E
PAHLAVI

QAZVIN

★ TEHRAN

IRAQ

BAGHDAD

DEZ DAM

ZAGROS

•ISFAHAN

IRAN

AFGHANISTAN

BANDAR DELAM

Shatt-
al-Arab
Estuary

ABADAN

•ZAGROS THREE

KUWAIT

KOWISS

MOUNTAINS

KHARG

JELLET

Persian Gulf

LENGEH

Strait of
Hormuz

PAKISTAN

BAHRAIN

SAUDI
ARABIA

QATAR

SIRI

Gulf of Oman

AL SHARGAZ

NEAR BANDAR DELAM AIR BASE: 9:16 A.M.   In torrential rain
the Subaru station wagon with the Iran-Toda insignia on the doors hurried
along the road, windshield wipers full speed, the road potholed and water-
logged in parts, the driver Iranian. Scragger sat uneasily beside him, his seat
belt tight, and in the back a Japanese radio mechanic hung on as best he
could. Ahead through the heavy rain splats, Scragger saw an old bus hog-
ging most of the road and, not far away, oncoming traffic.

"Minoru, tell him to slow down. Again," he said. "He's witless."

The young Japanese leaned forward and spoke sharply in Farsi, and the
driver nodded benignly and paid no attention, jabbed his palm on the horn,
and kept it there as he swerved out almost onto the other shoulder, overtaking the bus, accelerated when he should have braked, skidded, recovered,
and just made the narrowing gap between the bus and the oncoming car, all
three vehicles with their horns shrieking.

Scragger muttered another curse. Beaming, the driver, a young bearded

man, took his attention off the road and said something in Farsi, bouncing
through a large pothole in a shower of water. Minoru interpreted: "He says
with the Help of God we'll be at the airfield in a few minutes, Captain
Scragger."

"With the Help of God we'll be there in one piece and not fifty."
Scragger would have preferred to drive but it had not been allowed, nor
were any Iran-Toda personnel allowed to drive themselves. "We've found it
to be good policy, Captain Scragger, the roads and the rules and Iranians
being what they are," Watanabe, the engineer in charge, had said. "But
Mohammed is one of our best drivers and very reliable. See you this evening."

To Scragger's relief he saw the airfield ahead. Green Bands guarded the
gate. The driver paid them no attention, just barreled through and pulled
up in a shower of water outside the two-story office building. "Allah-u
Akbar," he said proudly.

Scragger exhaled. "Allah-u Akbar it is," he said, unlocked his seat belt,
readying his umbrella as he looked around, his first time here. Big apron and
small tower, some windows smashed, others boarded up, the two-story office
building derelict with more broken windows, S-G company trailers, good
hangars now closed against the storm, with bullet holes all over and in the
walls of the trailers. He whistled, remembering being told about the fight
here between the Green Bands and the mujhadin. Must've been a lot worse
than Duke let on, he thought.

Two Royal Iran Air twin jet passenger airplanes were parked haphazardly
—the "Royal" now crudely slashed out with black paint—tires flat, cockpit
windows smashed, and left to rot. "Bloody sacrilege," he muttered, seeing
the rain pouring into the cockpits.

"Minoru, me son, tell Mohammed here not to move a muscle till we're
ready to leave, okay?"

Minoru did as he was asked, then followed Scragger out into the rain.
Scragger stood beside the car, not knowing where to go. Then one of the
trailer doors opened.

"*Mein Gott,* Scrag! I thought it was you—what the hell're you doing
here?" It was Rudi Lutz, beaming. Then he saw Starke join Rudi and his
heart picked up.

"Hi, me sons!" He shook hands warmly with both of them, all three
talking together for a moment. "Well, Duke, this's a pleasant surprise!"

"What the hell're you doing here, Scrag?"

"First things first, me son. This's Minoru Fuyama, radio mec with Iran-
Toda. My UHF was acting up on the way in—I'm on a beaut charter from
Lengeh. Minoru's pulled the box and it's in the car, can you replace her?"

"No problem. Come along, Mr. Fuyama." Rudi went next door to find Fowler Joines to make the arrangements.

"I'm damn glad to see you, Scrag—lots to talk about," Starke said.

"Like weather problems and whirlwinds?"

"Yes, yes, I'd say the weather's been on my mind a lot." Starke seemed older, his eyes ranging the base, the downpour even heavier than before, the day warm and tacky.

"I saw Manuela at Al Shargaz, she's same as usual, pretty as a picture—anxious, but okay."

Rudi rejoined them, splashing through the rain, and led the way back into his office trailer. "You won't be flying in this mess, Scrag. Would you like a beer?"

"No thanks, mate, but I'd love a cuppa." Scragger said it automatically though his thirst for a cool beer was monumental. But ever since his first medical with Dr. Nutt just after he had sold Sheik Aviation to Gavallan, and Dr. Nutt had said, "Scrag, unless you quit smoking and cut down on the beer you'll be grounded in a couple of years," he had been extra careful. Too bloody right, he thought. No fags, no booze, no food, and plenty of sheilas. "You still have supplies, Rudi? At Lengeh it's getting rough 'cept for de Plessey and his wine."

"I got some off a tanker that's tied up down at the port," Rudi called back from the small kitchen, putting on the kettle. "CASEVAC, seaman with his head and face smashed up. The captain said he'd had a fall but it looked more like a bad fight. Not surprisingly really, the ship's been stuck at anchor for three months. *Mein Gott*, Scrag, did you see the pileup in the port when you came in? Must be a hundred ships waiting to unload, or to take on oil."

"Same at Kharg and all along the coast, Rudi, everywhere's clogged. Wharfs sky-high with crates, bales, an' Gawd knows what, all left rotting in the sun or rain. Enough of that, wot're you doing here, Duke?"

"I ferried a 212 from Kowiss yesterday. But for the weather I'd've left at dawn—glad I didn't now."

Scragger heard the caution in the voice and looked around. No one listening that he could see. "Problem?" He saw Starke shake his head. Rudi turned on the music cassette. Wagner. Scragger hated Wagner. "Wot's up?"

"Just cautious—these damn walls are too thin—and I caught one of the staff eavesdropping. I think most of them are spies. Then we've a new base manager, Numir, Nasty Numi we call him. He's off today, otherwise you'd be explaining why you're here in triplicate." Rudi made his voice lower.

"There are whirlwinds to talk about. But what are you doing here, Scrag? Why didn't you call us?"

"Came into Iran-Toda yesterday on a charter for a guy called Kasigi who's the big buyer of Siri crude and a bigwig with Iran-Toda—old Georges de Plessey arranged it. I'm here for today, leave tomorrow early. Andy asked me to see you to sound you out and this was as soon as I could make it. I couldn't raise you on the UHF coming in—could've been the storm, I just snuck in in time. Couldn't get permission to fly over here, so I pulled a wire off the pot just in case and 'urgently needed a repair.' Duke, Andy told you wot we talked about in Al Shargaz?"

"Yes, yes, he did. And you better know there's a new twist. Andy's been told we're being grounded pending nationalization and we've only five days —five safe days only. If we're to do it, at the latest it should be Friday."

"Jesus H. Christ!" Scragger felt his chest tighten. "Duke, there's no way I can get ready by Friday."

"Andy says we take out 212s only."

"Eh?"

Starke explained what had happened at Kowiss and what, hopefully, would happen "if Andy pushes the go."

"Come off it—not if, when. Andy has to. The question is, do we stick our necks out?"

Starke laughed. "You already have. I said I'm in if everyone else is—with two 212s it's possible for me, and now that . . . well, now that our birds're back on British registry once we're out, that makes it legit."

"The hell it does," Rudi said. "It's just not legal. I told you last night and Pop Kelly agreed. Scrag, how're—"

"Pop's here?"

"Sure," Starke said. "He came down with me." He explained why, then added, "Hotshot approved the 'loan,' we got two guys out on the 125 and the rest scheduled for Thursday but I'm not so sure about that. Colonel Changiz said in future all personnel movements're to be approved by him, not just by Hotshot."

"How're you getting back?"

"I'll take a 206." Starke looked out of the window at the rain. "Goddamn front!"

"She'll be through by tonight, Duke," Scragger said confidently.

Rudi said, "How're you going to get your men out, Scrag? *Hein?*"

"If it's just my two 212s, that makes it much easier. Much." Scragger saw Rudi quaff some of his ice-cold beer, the beads on the can glistening, and his thirst increased. "Friday'd be a good day for a caper because Iranians'll be at prayer meetings or whatever."

"I'm not so sure, Scrag," Rudi said. "Friday they still man the radar—they'll have to know something's up with my four birds charging across the Gulf, let alone your three and Duke's two. Abadan's itchy as all hell about choppers—particularly after HBC."

"There been any more inquiries about her, Rudi?"

"Yes. Last week Abbasi came by, he's the pilot who blew her out of the sky. Same questions, nothing more."

"Does he know his brother was HBC's pilot?"

"Not yet, Scrag."

"Tom Lochart was bloody lucky. Bloody lucky."

"We've all been 'bloody lucky.' So far," Starke said. "Except Erikki." He brought Scragger up to date with the little they knew.

"Christ, wot next? How're we going to do Whirlwind with him still in Iran?"

"We can't Scrag—that's what I think," Rudi said. "We can't leave him."

"That's right but maybe . . ." Starke drank some coffee, his own anxiety making him feel a little bilious. "Maybe Andy won't push the button. Meanwhile we hope to God Erikki gets away, or is let go before Friday. Then Andy can. Shit, if it was up to me, just me, goddamned if I'd risk Whirlwind."

"Nor me." Rudi was equally queasy.

"If they were all your planes and your company and your future, bet you would. Know I would." Scragger beamed. "Me, I'm for Whirlwind. I got to be for it, sport, no bloody company'll employ me at my age so I bloody have to keep Dirty Dunc and Andy the Gav in biz if I'm to keep flying." The kettle began singing. He got up. "I'll make it, Rudi. Wot about you? You in or out?"

"Me, I'm in if you two are, and if it's a possible—but I like it not a bit and I'm telling you straight I'll only lead my four out if *I* really think we've a chance. We talked to the other pilots last night, Scrag. Marc Dubois and Pop Kelly said they'd have a go, Block and Forsyth said thanks, but no thanks, so we've three pilots for four 212s. I've asked Andy to send me a volunteer." Rudi mirrored his disquiet. "But *reissen mit scheissen!* I'll have four to get airborne somehow, all at the same time, when we're supposed to have start-up clearance—with Green Bands all over the base, our radio op Jahan no idiot, and then there's Nasty Numi . . ." His eyebrows soared.

"You've no problem, old cock," Scragger said airily. "Tell 'em you're going to do a flyby victory salute for Khomeini over Abadan!"

"Up yours, Scrag!" The music ended and Rudi turned the tape over. Then his face hardened. "But I agree with you that Andy *will* push the button and the when's Friday. Me, I say if one of us aborts we all abort—agreed?"

Scragger broke the silence. "If Andy says go, I go. I have to."

BANDAR DELAM PORT: 3:17 P.M. Scragger's station wagon turned off a main road in the sprawling, noisy town into a lesser road, cut down it, then turned into a square in front of a mosque, Mohammed driving as usual, his finger on the horn almost constantly. The rain had lessened appreciably but the day was still miserable. In the backseat Minoru dozed, cradling the replacement radio. Scragger was absently staring ahead, so much to think about, plans, codes, and what about Erikki? Poor old bugger! But if anyone can make it he will. Swear to God old Erikki'll make it somehow. Say he doesn't or Andy doesn't push go, wot you going to do for a job? I'll worry about that next week.

He did not see the police car come charging out of a side turning, skid on the slippery surface, and smash into the back of them. There was no way that Mohammed could have avoided the accident, and the speed of the police car, added to his own, hurtled them broadside across the road into a street stall and the crowds, killing one old woman, decapitating another, and injuring many as the wheels fell into the joub, the momentum rolling the car over to smash it against the high walls with a howling screech of metal.

Instinctively Scragger had put his hands over his face but the final crash bashed his head against the side, stunning him momentarily, the seat belt saving him from real damage. The driver had gone through the windshield and now was half in and half out of the car, badly injured. In the back, the seat had protected Minoru and he was the first to recover, the radio still protectively in his lap. Amid the screams and pandemonium he fought his door open and scrambled out, covered by the melee of pedestrians and injured, unnoticed as a passenger, Japanese from Iran-Toda normal in the streets here.

At that moment the occupants of the police car that now was swiveled half across the road—its front crumpled—ran over. The police shoved their way up to the station wagon, took one look at the driver then pulled the side door open and hauled Scragger out.

Angry shouts of "Amerikan!" and more screams and noise, Scragger still half stunned. "Tha . . . thanks, I'm . . . I'm okay . . ." but they held him firmly, shouting at him.

"For Christ's sake . . ." he gasped, "I wasn't driving . . . what the hell happ—" Around him was a tumult of Farsi and panic and anger and one of the police snapped handcuffs on him and then they dragged him roughly to the other car, pushed him into the backseat and got in, still cursing him. The driver started up.

On the other side of the road, Minoru was futilely trying to push through the crowd to help Scragger. He stopped, crestfallen, as the car hurtled away down the street.

CHAPTER 51

NEAR DOSHAN TAPPEH: 3:30 P.M. McIver was driving along the empty perimeter road outside the barbed-wire fence of the military airfield. The fenders were badly bent and there were many more dents than before. One headlight was cracked and roughly taped, the red glass of one taillight missing, but the engine still sounded sweet and her snow tires were firm on the surface. Snow banked the roadway. No sun came through the overcast that was barely twelve hundred feet and obscured all but the foot-hills of the northern mountains. It was cold and he was late.

On the inside of his windshield was a big green permit and, seeing it, the motley group of Green Band and air force guards stationed near the gate waved him through, then crowded back around the open fire to warm themselves. He headed for the S-G hangar. Before he could reach it, Tom Lochart came out of a side door to intercept him.

"Hi Mac," he said, getting in quickly. He was wearing flight gear and carried his flight bag and had just flown in from Kowiss. "How's Sharazad?"

"Sorry to take so long, traffic was terrible."

"Have you seen her?"

"No, not yet. Sorry." He saw Lochart's immediate tension. "I went again early this morning. A servant answered the door but didn't seem to understand me—I'll get you there as soon as I can." He let in the clutch and turned for the gate. "How was Zagros?"

"Rotten, I'll fill you in on that in a second," Lochart said hurriedly. "Before we can leave we've got to report to the base commander."

"Oh? Why?" McIver put on the brake.

"They didn't say. They left a message with the clerk that when you came in today to report to base commander. Any problems?"

"Not that I know of." McIver let in the clutch and swung around. Now what? he thought, holding down his anxiety.

"Could it be HBC?"

"Let's hope not."

"What happened to Lulu? You have a prang?"

"No, just some street vandals," McIver said, his mind on HBC.

"Every day it gets rougher. Any news of Erikki?"

"Nothing. He's just vanished. Azadeh sits by the phone all day in the office."

"She's still staying with you?"

"No, she went back to her own apartment on Saturday." McIver was heading for the buildings on the other side of the runway. "Tell me about Zagros." He listened without comment until Lochart had finished. "Awful, just awful!"

"Yes, but Nitchak Khan didn't give the signal to shoot us down. If he had he'd've gotten away with it. Goddamn hard to break the 'terrorist' story. Anyway, when we got to Kowiss, Duke and Andy had had a fracas with Hotshot." Lochart told him about that. "But the ruse seems to be working; yesterday Duke and Pop ferried the 212 to Rudi and this morning EchoTangoLimaLima came in for Jordon's body."

"Terrible. Feel very responsible for old Effer."

"Guess we all do." Ahead they could see the HQ building with sentries outside it. "We all turned out and put the coffin aboard, young Freddy played a lament on the pipes, not much else we could do. Curiously Colonel Changiz sent an air force honor guard and gave us a proper coffin. Iranians're strange, so strange. They seemed genuinely sorry." Lochart was talking automatically, sick with anxiety at the delays—having to wait at Kowiss, then flying here and ATC harassing him, then no transport and waiting interminably for McIver to arrive and now another delay. What's happened to Sharazad?

They were near the office building that housed the base commander's suite and officers' mess where they both had spent many good times in the past. Doshan Tappeh had been an elite base—the Shah had kept some of his private jet fleet and his Fokker Friendship here. Now the walls of the two-story building were scored by bullets and broken here and there by shellfire, most windows out, a few boarded up. Outside a few Green Bands and slovenly airmen lolled around as sentries.

"Peace be with you! Excellency McIver and Lochart to see the camp commandant," Lochart said in Farsi. One of the Green Bands waved them into the building. "Where is the office, please?"

"Inside."

They walked up the steps toward the main door, the air heavy with the smell of fire and cordite and drains. Just as they reached the top step, the main door slammed open and a mullah with some Green Bands hurried out, dragging two young air force officers between them, their hands bound and uniforms torn and filthy. Lochart gasped, recognizing one of them. "Karim!" he burst out and now McIver recognized the youth also—Karim Peshadi, Sharazad's adored cousin, the man he had asked to try to retrieve HBC's clearance from the tower.

"Tom! In the Name of God tell them I'm not a spy or traitor," Karim shouted, in English. "Tom, tell them!"

"Excellency," Lochart said in Farsi to the mullah, "surely there's some mistake. This man is Pilot Captain Peshadi, a loyal helper of the Ayatollah, a supp—"

"Who're you, Excellency?" asked the mullah, dark-eyed, short, stocky. "American?"

"My name is Lochart, Excellency, Canadian, a pilot for IranOil, and this is the leader of our company across the airfield, Captain McIver, an—"

"How do you know this traitor?"

"Excellency, I'm sure there's a mistake, he can't possibly be a traitor, I know him because he is a cousin of my wife and the so—"

"Your wife is Iranian?"

"Yes, Excell—"

"You are Muslim?"

"No, Excellen—"

"Better then she divorces and so saves her soul from pollution. As God wants. There's no mistake about these traitors—mind your own business, Excellency." The mullah motioned to the Green Bands. At once they went on down the steps, half carrying, half dragging the two young officers who shouted and protested their innocence, then he turned back for the main door.

"Excellency," Lochart called out urgently, catching up to him. "Please, in the Name of the One God, I know that young man to be loyal to the Imam, a good Muslim, a patriot of Iran, I know for a fact that he was one of those who went against the Immortals here at Doshan Tappeh and helped the revolu—"

"Stop!" The mullah's eyes hardened even more. "This is not your affair, foreigner. No longer do foreigners or foreign laws or a foreign-dominated Shah rule us. You are not Iranian, nor a judge, nor a lawgiver. Those men were tried and judged."

"I beg your patience, Excellency, there must be some mistake, there mus—" Lochart whirled as a volley of rifle shots exploded nearby. The sentries below were staring across the road at some barracks and buildings. From his position atop the steps he could not see what they saw. Then the Green Bands reappeared from behind one of the barracks, shouldering their arms. They trooped back up the steps. The mullah motioned them back inside.

"The law is the law," the mullah said, watching Lochart. "Heresy must be removed. Since you know his family you can tell them to beg forgiveness of God for harboring such a son."

"What was he supposed to have been guilty of?"

"Not 'supposed,' Excellency," the mullah said, an angry edge creeping into his voice. "Karim Peshadi openly admitted stealing a truck and leaving the base without permission, openly admitted joining forbidden demonstrations, openly declared against our forthcoming absolute Islamic state, openly opposed the abolition of the anti-Islamic Marriage Act, openly advocated acts contrary to Islamic law, was caught in suspected acts of sabotage, openly decried the total absoluteness of the Koran, openly defied the Imam's right to be *faqira*—he who is above the law and final arbiter of the law." He pulled his robes closer about him against the cold. "Peace be with you." He went back into the building.

For a moment Lochart could not speak. Then he explained to McIver what had been said. " 'Suspected acts of sabotage,' Tom? Was he caught in the tower?"

"What does it matter?" Lochart said bitterly. "Karim's dead—for crimes against God."

"No, laddie," McIver said kindly, "not against God, against their version of truth spoken in the Name of the God they will never know." He squared his shoulders and led the way inside the building. At length they found the base commander's office and were ushered in.

Behind the desk was a major. The mullah sat beside him. Above them, the only decoration in the small untidy room was a big photograph of

Khomeini. "I'm Major Betami, Mr. McIver," the man said crisply in English. "This is the mullah Tehrani." Then he glanced at Lochart and switched to Farsi. "As His Excellency Tehrani does not speak English, you will interpret for me. Your name, please."

"Lochart, Captain Lochart."

"Please sit down, both of you. His Excellency says you are married to an Iranian. What was her maiden name?"

Lochart's eyes hardened. "My private life is my private life, Excellency."

"Not for a foreign helicopter pilot in the middle of our Islamic revolution against foreign domination," the major said angrily, "nor one who knows traitors to the state. Do you have something to hide, Captain?"

"No, no, of course not."

"Then please answer the question."

"Are you police? By what authority do y—"

The mullah said, "I am a member of the Doshan Tappeh komiteh—you prefer to be summoned officially? Now? This minute?"

"I prefer not to be questioned about my private life."

"If you have nothing to hide you can answer the question. Please choose."

"Bakravan." Lochart saw the name register on both men. His stomach became even more queasy.

"Jared Bakravan—the bazaari moneylender? One of his daughters?"

"Yes."

"Her name, please."

Lochart held on to his blinding rage, compounded by Karim's murder. It *is* murder, he wanted to shout, whatever you say. "Her Excellency, Sharazad."

McIver had been watching intently. "What's all this about, Tom?"

"Nothing. Nothing, I'll tell you later."

The major made a note on a piece of paper. "What is your relationship to the traitor Karim Peshadi?"

"I've known him for about two years, he was one of my student pilots. He's my wife's first cousin—was my wife's first cousin—and I can only repeat it's inconceivable that he would be a traitor to Iran or Islam."

The major made another note on the pad, the pen scratching loudly. "Where are you staying, Captain?"

"I . . . I'm not sure. I was staying at the Bakravan house near the bazaar. Our . . . our apartment was commandeered."

The silence gathered in the room, making it claustrophobic. The major finished writing then picked up a page of notes and looked directly at

McIver. "First, no foreign helicopters may be moved in or out of Tehran airspace without air force HQ clearance."

Lochart translated and McIver nodded noncommittally. This was nothing new, except that the komiteh at Tehran International Airport had just issued official written instructions on behalf of the all-powerful Revolutionary Komiteh that the komiteh alone could authorize and grant such clearances. McIver had got permission to send out his remaining 212 and one of his Alouettes to Kowiss "on temporary loan" just in time, he thought grimly, concentrating on the major, but wondering what the sharp Farsi exchange with Lochart had been all about.

"Second: we require a complete list of all helicopters under your present control, where they are in Iran, their engine numbers, and the amount and type of spares you are carrying per helicopter."

Lochart saw McIver's eyes widen, his own mind locked into Sharazad and why they wanted to know where he lived and her relationship with Karim, hardly listening to the words as he translated back and forth. "Captain McIver says: 'Very well. It will take me a little time, because of communications, but I will get it for you as soon as possible.'"

"I would like it tomorrow."

"If I can get it by then, Excellency, rest assured you will have it. You will have it as soon as possible."

"Third: all your helicopters in the Tehran area will be assembled here starting tomorrow, and from now on will operate only out of here."

"I will certainly inform my superiors in IranOil of your request, Major. Instantly."

The major's face hardened. "The air force is the arbiter of this."

"Of course. I will inform my superiors at once. Was that all, Major?"

The mullah said, "About the helicopter." He referred to a note on the desk in front of him. "HBC. We w—"

"HBC!" McIver allowed his panic to explode into a righteous anger that Lochart had a hard time keeping up with: "Security's the responsibility of the air force on the base and how they could have been so lax to allow HBC to be hijacked I don't know! Time and again I've complained about laxness, sentries never appearing, no guards at night. A million dollars of theft! Irreplaceable! I am instituting a claim against the air force for negligence an—"

"It wasn't our fault," the major began angrily, but McIver paid no attention and continued the offensive, allowing him no opening, nor did Lochart, who turned McIver's tirade into apt Iranian words and phrases for an even more slashing attack on air force perfidy.

". . . unbelievable negligence—I might even say deliberate treachery and collusion by other officers—to allow some unknown American to get into our hangar under the very noses of our supposed guardians, to be given clearance to fly off by our supposed protectors, and then allowed to do damage to the great Iranian state! Unforgivable! Of course it was treachery and preplanned by 'persons unknown holding officer rank,' and I must ins—"

"How dare you imply th—"

"Of course it must have been with air force officer collusion—who controls the base? Who controls the airwaves, who sits in the tower? We hold the air force responsible and I'm registering the complaint to the highest level of IranOil demanding restitution and . . . and next week, next week I will apply for redress to the illustrious Revolutionary Komiteh and the Imam himself, may God protect him! Now, Excellency, if you will excuse us we will go about our business. Peace be with you!"

McIver went for the door, Lochart following, both men overloaded with adrenaline, McIver feeling terrible, his chest aching.

"Wait!" the mullah ordered.

"Yes, Excellency?"

"How do you explain that the traitor Valik—who 'happens' to be a partner of your company and kinsman of the usurer and Shah supporter Bakravan—arrived in Isfahan in this helicopter to pick up other traitors, one of whom was General Seladi, another kinsman of Jared Bakravan—father-in-law to one of your senior pilots?"

Lochart's mouth was very dry as he spoke the doom-filled words but McIver did not hesitate and came back to the attack. "I did not appoint General Valik to our board, he was appointed by high-up Iranians according to your then current law—we did not seek Iranian partners, it was Iranian law that we had to have them, they were forced upon us. Nothing to do with me. As to the rest, Insha'Allah—the Will of God!" Heart thundering, he opened the door and stalked off. Lochart finished translating. "Salaam." He followed.

"You've not heard the last of this," the major shouted after him.

NEAR THE UNIVERSITY: 6:07 P.M. They were lying side by side on soft carpets in front of the wood fire that burned merrily in the pleasant room. Sharazad and Ibrahim Kyabi. They were not touching, just watching the fire, listening to the good, modern music from the cassette player, lost in thought, each too aware of the other.

"Thou, gift of the Universe," he murmured, "thou of the ruby lips and breath like wine, thou, tongue of Heaven . . ."

"Oh, Ibrahim," she laughed. "What is this 'tongue of Heaven'?"

He raised himself onto an elbow and looked down at her, blessing fate that had allowed him to save her from the insane zealot at the Women's March, the same fate that would soon guide him to Kowiss to revenge his father's murder. "I was quoting the *Rubáiyát*," he said, smiling at her.

"I don't believe a word of it! I think you made it up." She returned his smile, then shielded her eyes from the glow of his love by looking again at the embers.

After the first Protest March, now six days ago, long into that evening they had talked together, discussing the revolution and finding common cause in the murder of her father and his father, both of them children of loneliness now, their mothers not understanding, only weeping and Insha'Allah and never the need for revenge. Their lives turned upside down like their country, Ibrahim no longer a Believer—only in the strength and purpose of the People—her belief shaken, questioning for the first time, wondering how God could permit such evil and all the other evils that had come to pass, the corruption of the land and its spirit. "I agree, Ibrahim, you're right. We haven't rid ourselves of one despot to acquire another! You're right, the despotism of the mullahs daily becomes more clear," she had said. "But why does Khomeini oppose the rights that the Shah gave to us, reasonable rights?"

"They're your inalienable rights as a human being, not the Shah's to give, or anyone's—like your body's your own, not a 'field to be plowed.' "

"But why is the Imam opposed?"

"He's not an Imam, Sharazad, just an ayatollah, a man and a fanatic. It's because he's doing what priests have always done throughout history: he's using his version of religion to drug the people into senselessness, to keep them dependent, uneducated, to secure mullahs in power. Doesn't he want only mullahs responsible for education? Doesn't he claim mullahs alone understand 'the law,' study 'the law,' have the knowledge of 'the law'? As if they alone have *all* knowledge!"

"I never thought of it like that, I accepted so much, so very much. But you're right, Ibrahim, you make everything so clear to me. You're right, mullahs believe only what's in the Koran—as if what was correct for the days of the Prophet, peace be upon him, should apply today! I refuse to be a chattel without the vote and the right to choose . . ."

Finding so many common grounds of thought, he a modern, university trained, she wanting to be modern but unsure of her way. Sharing secrets and longings, understanding each other instantly, using the same nuances, belonging to the same heritage—he so very much like Karim in speech and looks they could be brothers.

That night she had slept blissfully and the next morning slipped out early to meet him again, drinking coffee in a little café, she chadored for safety and secrecy, laughing so much together, for no reason or every reason, serious sometimes. Both aware of the currents, no need to speak them. Then the second Protest March, bigger than the first, better and with little opposition.

"When do you have to be back, Sharazad?"

"I, I told Mother I would be late, that I'd visit a friend on the other side of the city."

"I'll take you there now, quickly, and you can leave quickly and then, if you like we could talk some more, or even better I've a friend who has an apartment and some wonderful records . . ."

That was five days ago. Sometimes his friend, another Tudeh student leader, would be here, sometimes other students, young men and women, not all of them Communist—new ideas, free exchange, heady ideas of life and love and living free. Occasionally they were alone. Heavenly days, marching and talking and laughing and listening to records and peace-filled nights at home near the bazaar.

Yesterday victory. Khomeini had relented, publicly, saying that women were not forced to wear chador, provided they covered their hair and dressed modestly. Last night celebrating, dancing with joy in the apartment, all of them young, embracing and then going home again. But last night her sleep had been all about him and her together. Erotic. Lying there half asleep this morning, afraid yet so excited.

The cassette ended. It was one of the Carpenters, slow, romantic. He turned it and now the other side was even better. Dare I? she asked herself dreamily, feeling his eyes on her. Through a crack in the curtains she could see that the sky was darkening. "It's almost time to go," she said, not moving, a throb in her voice.

"Jari can wait," he said tenderly. Jari, her maid, was party to their secret visits. "Better no one knows," he had said on the second day. "Even her."

"She has to know, Ibrahim, or I can never get out alone, never see you. I've nothing to hide but I am married and it's . . ." No need to articulate "dangerous." Every moment they were alone screamed danger.

So he had shrugged and petitioned fate to protect her, as he did now. "Jari can wait."

"Yes, yes, she can, but first we've got to do some errands and my dear brother Meshang won't—tonight I have to have dinner with him and Zarah."

Ibrahim was startled. "What's he want? He doesn't suspect you?"

"Oh, no, it's just family, just that." Languorously she looked at him.

"What about your business in Kowiss? Will you wait another day or will you go tomorrow?"

"It's not urgent," he said carelessly. He had delayed and delayed even though his Tudeh controller had said that every extra day he stayed in Tehran was dangerous: "Have you forgotten what happened to Comrade Yazernov? We hear Inner Intelligence was involved! They must have spotted you going into the building with him, or coming out of it."

"I've shaved off my beard, I've not gone home, and I'm avoiding the university. By the way, comrade, it's better we don't meet for a day or two —I think I'm being followed." He smiled to himself, remembering the alacrity with which the other man, an old-time Tudeh supporter, had vanished around the street corner.

"Why the smile, my darling?"

"Nothing. I love you, Sharazad," he said simply and cupped her breast as he kissed her.

She kissed him back but not completely. His passion grew, and hers, though she tried to hold back, his hands caressing her, fire in their wake.

"I love you, Sharazad . . . love me."

She did not wish to pull away from the heat, or his hands, or the pressure of his limbs, or the thunder of her heart. But she did. "Not now, my darling," she murmured and gained a breathing space and then, when the thunder lessened, she looked up at him, searching his eyes. She saw disappointment but no anger. "I'm . . . I'm not ready, not for love, not now . . ."

"Love happens. I've loved you from the first moment. You're safe, Sharazad, your love will be safe with me."

"I know, oh, yes, I know that. I . . ." She frowned, not understanding herself, only that now was wrong. "I have to be sure of what I'm doing. Now I'm not."

He debated with himself, then leaned down and kissed her, not forcing the kiss on her—quite confident that soon they would be lovers. Tomorrow. Or the next day. "You're wise as always," he said. "Tomorrow we will have the apartment to ourselves. I promise. Let's meet as usual, coffee at the usual place." He got up, and helped her up. She held on to him and thanked him and kissed him and he unlocked the front door. Silently she wrapped the chador around her, blew him another kiss, and left, perfume in her wake. Then that too vanished.

With the door relocked he went back and put on his shoes, the ache still present. Thoughtfully he picked up his M16 that stood in the corner of the room, checked the action and the magazine. Away from her spell he had no illusions about the danger or the realities of his life—and early death. His excitement quickened.

Death, he thought. Martyrdom. Giving my life for a just cause, freely embracing death, welcoming it. Oh, I will, I will. I can't lead an army like the Lord of the Martyrs, but I can revolt against Satanists calling themselves mullahs and extract revenge on the mullah Hussain of Kowiss for murdering my father in the name of false gods, and for desecrating the Revolution of the People!

He felt his ecstasy growing. Like the other. Stronger than the other.

I love her with all my soul but I should go tomorrow. I don't need a team with me, alone it would be safer. I can easily catch a bus. I should go tomorrow. I should but I can't, I can't, not yet. After we've made love . . .

AL SHARGAZ AIRPORT: 6:17 P.M. Almost eight hundred miles away, southeast across the Gulf, Gavallan was standing at the heliport watching the 212 coming in to land. The evening was balmy, the sun on the horizon. Now he could see Jean-Luc at the controls with one of the other pilots beside him, not Scot as he had first thought and expected. His anxiety increased. He waved and then, as the skids touched, impatiently went forward to the cabin door. It swung open. He saw Scot unbuckling one-handed, his other arm in a sling, his face stretched and pale but in one piece. "Oh, my son," he said, heart pounding with relief, wanting to rush forward and hug him but standing back and waiting until Scot had walked down the steps and was there on the tarmac beside him.

"Oh, laddie, I was so worried . . ."

"Not to worry, Dad. I'm fine, just fine." Scot held his good arm tightly around his father's shoulders, the reassuring contact so necessary to both of them, oblivious of the others. "Christ, I'm so happy to see you. I thought you were due in London today."

"I was. I'm on the red-eye in an hour." Now I am, Gavallan was thinking, now that you're here and safe. "I'll be there first thing." He brushed a tear away, pretending it was dust, and pointed at a car nearby. Genny was at the wheel. "Don't want to fuss you but Genny'll take you to the hospital right away, just X ray, Scot, it's all arranged. No fuss, promise—you've a room booked next door to mine at the hotel. All right?"

"All right, Dad. I, er, I . . . I could use an aspirin. I admit I feel lousy— the ride was bumpy to hell. I, er, I . . . you're on the red-eye? When're you back?"

"Soon as I can. In a day or so. I'll call you tomorrow, all right?"

Scot hesitated, his face twisting. "Could you . . . perhaps . . . perhaps you could come with me—I can fill you in about Zagros, would you have time?"

"Of course. It was bad?"

"No and yes. We all got out—except Jordon—but he was shot because of me, Dad, he was . . ." Tears filled Scot's eyes though his voice stayed controlled and firm. "Can't do anything about it . . . can't." He wiped the tears away and mumbled a curse and hung on with his good hand. "Can't do anything . . . don't, don't know how to . . ."

"Not your fault, Scot," Gavallan said, torn by his son's despair, frightened for him. "Come along, we'll . . . let's get you started." He called out to Jean-Luc, "I'm taking Scot off for X ray, be back right away."

TEHRAN—AT McIVER'S APARTMENT: 6:35 P.M. In candlelight, Charlie Pettikin and Paula were sitting at the dining table, clinking wine-filled glasses with Sayada Bertolin, a large bottle of Chianti open, plates with two big salamis, one partially eaten, a huge slice of dolce latte cheese as yet untouched, and two fresh French baguettes that Sayada had brought from the French Club, one mostly gone: "There may be a war on," she had said with forced gaiety when she had arrived uninvited, half an hour ago, "but whatever happens, the French must have proper bread."

"Vive la France, and *viva l'Italia,"* Pettikin had said, reluctantly inviting her in, not wanting to share Paula with anyone. Since Paula had terminated any interest in Nogger Lane, he had rushed into the breech, hoping against hope. "Paula came in on this afternoon's Alitalia flight, smuggled in all the swag at the risk of her life and—and doesn't she look superissssssima?"

Paula laughed. "It's the dolce latte, Sayada; Charlie told me it was his favorite."

"Isn't it the best cheese on earth? Isn't everything Italian the best on earth?"

Paula brought out the corkscrew and handed it to him, her green-flecked eyes sending more shivers down his spine. "For you, *caro!"*

"Magnifico! Are all young ladies of Alitalia as thoughtful, brave, beautiful, efficient, tender, sweet-smelling, loving, and, er, cinematic?"

"Of course."

"Join the feast, Sayada," he had said. When she came closer into the light he saw her properly, noticing the strangeness to her. "You all right?"

"Oh, yes, it's, it's nothing." Sayada was glad for the candlelight to hide behind. "I, er, thanks I won't stay, I . . . I just miss Jean-Luc, wanted to find out when he's back, I thought you could use the baguettes."

"Delighted you arrived—we haven't had a decent loaf for weeks, thanks, but stay anyway. Mac's gone to Doshan Tappeh to pick up Tom. Tom'll know about Jean-Luc—they should be back any moment."

"How's Zagros?"

"We've had to close it down." As he busied himself getting glasses and setting up the table, Paula helping and doing most of it, he told them why, and about the terrorist attack on Rig Bellissima, Gianni's being killed, then later, Jordon, and Scot Gavallan being wounded. "Bloody business, but there you are."

"Terrible," Paula said. "That explains why we're routed back through Shiraz with instructions to keep fifty seats open. Must be for our nationals from the Zagros."

"What rotten luck," Sayada said, wondering if she should pass that information on. To *them*—and *him*. The Voice had called yesterday, early, asking what time she had left Teymour on Saturday. "About five, perhaps five-fifteen, why?"

"The cursed building caught fire just after dark—somewhere on the third floor, trapping the two above. The whole building's gutted, many people killed, and there's no sign of Teymour or the others. Of course the fire department was too late . . ."

No problem to find real tears and to let her agony pour out. Later in the day the Voice had called again: "Did you give Teymour the papers?"

"Yes . . . yes, yes, I did."

There had been a muffled curse. "Be at the French Club tomorrow afternoon. I will leave instructions in your box." But there was no message so she had wheedled the loaves from the kitchen and had come here—nowhere else to go and still very frightened.

"So sad," Paula was saying.

"Yes, but enough of that," Pettikin said, cursing himself for telling them —none of their problem, he thought. "Let's eat, drink, and be merry."

"For tomorrow we die?" Sayada said.

"No." Pettikin raised his glass, beamed at Paula. "For tomorrow we live. Health!" He touched glasses with her, then Sayada, and he thought what a smashing pair they make but Paula's far and away the most . . .

Sayada was thinking: Charlie's in love with this siren harpy who'll consume him at her whim and spew out the remains with hardly a belch, but why do *they*—my new masters, whoever they are—why do *they* want to know about Jean-Luc and Tom and want mè to be Armstrong's mistress and how do they know about my son, God curse *them*.

Paula was thinking: I hate this shit-roll of a city where everyone's so gloomy and doom-ridden and downbeat like this poor woman who's obviously got the usual man trouble, when there's Rome and sunshine and Italy and the sweet life to become drunk with, wine and laughter and love to be enjoyed, children to bear with a husband to cherish but only so long as the devil behaves—why are all men rotten and why do I like this man Charlie who is too old and yet not, too poor and yet not, too masculine and yet . . .

"*Alora*," she said, the wine making her lips more juicy, "Charlie, *amore*, we must meet in Rome. Tehran is so . . . so depression, *scusa*, depressing."

"Not when you're around," he said.

Sayada saw them smiling at each other, and envied them. "I think I'll come back later," she said, getting up. Before Pettikin could say anything, a key turned in the lock and McIver came in.

"Oh, hello," he said, trying to throw off his weariness. "Hi, Paula, hi, Sayada—this is a pleasant surprise." Then he noticed the table. "What's this, Christmas?" He took off his heavy coat and gloves.

"Paula brought it—and Sayada the bread. Where's Tom?" Pettikin asked, immediately sensing something was wrong.

"I dropped him off at Bakravan's, near the bazaar."

"How is she?" Sayada asked. "I haven't seen her since . . . since the day of the march, the first march."

"Don't know, lassie, I just dropped him off and came on." McIver accepted a glass of wine, returned Pettikin's look levelly. "Traffic was rotten. Took me an hour to get here. Health! Paula, you're a sight for sore eyes. You staying tonight?"

"If that's all right? I'm off early in the morning, no need for transport, *caro*, one of the crew dropped me off and will pick me up. Genny said I could use the spare room—she thought it might need a spring clean but it looks fine." Paula got up and both men, unknowingly, were instantly magnetized by the sensuousness of her movements. Sayada cursed her, envying her, wondering what it was, certainly not the uniform that was quite severe though beautifully tailored, knowing that she herself was far more beautiful, far better dressed—but not in the same race. Cow!

Paula reached into her handbag and found the two letters and gave them to McIver. "One from Genny and one from Andy."

"Thanks, thanks very much," McIver said.

"I was just going, Mac," Sayada said. "Just wanted to ask when Jean-Luc'll be back."

"Probably on Wednesday—he's ferrying a 212 to Al Shargaz. He should be there today and back Wednesday." McIver glanced at the letters. "No need to go, Sayada . . . excuse me a second."

He sat down in the easy chair by the electric fire that was at half power, switched on a nearby lamp. The light took away much of the romance of the room. Gavallan's letter read: "Hi, Mac, this in a hurry, courtesy of the fairest of them all! I'm waiting for Scot. Then red-eyeing it to London tonight, if he's all right, but I'll be back in two days, three at the most. Finessed Duke out of Kowiss down to Rudi in case Scrag's delayed—he should be back Tuesday. Kowiss is very dicey—I had a big run-in with Hotshot—so's Zagros. Have just talked to Masson from here and that's fact. So I'm pushing the button for planning. It's pushed. See you Wednesday. Give Paula a hug for me and Genny says don't you bloody dare!"

He stared at the letter, then sat back a moment, half listening to a story Paula was telling about their incoming flight to Tehran. So the button's pushed. Don't delude yourself, Andy, I knew you'd push it from the first moment—that's why I said, All right, provided I can abort Whirlwind if I think it's too risky and my decision's final. I think you must push the button all the way—you've no alternative if you want to survive.

The wine tasted very good. He finished the glass, then opened Genny's letter. It was just news about home and the kids, all of them healthy and in place, but he knew her too well not to read the underlying concern: "Don't worry, Duncan, and don't sweat out winds, any winds. And don't think I plan on a rose-covered cottage in England. It's us for the Casbah and me for a yashmak and I'm practicing belly dancing so you'd better hurry. Luv, Gen."

McIver smiled to himself, got up, and poured himself some wine, calmer now. "Here's to women, bless 'em." He touched glasses with Pettikin. "Smashing wine, Paula. Andy sends you a hug . . ." At once she smiled and reached over and touched him and he felt the current rush up his arm. What the hell is it about her? he asked himself, unsettled, and quickly said to Sayada, "He'd send one to you too if he knew you were here." A candle on the mantelpiece was guttering. "I'll get it. Any messages?"

"One from Talbot. He's doing all he can to find Erikki. Duke's delayed at Bandar Delam by a storm but he should be back at Kowiss tomorrow."

"And Azadeh?"

"She's better today. Paula and I walked her home. She's okay, Mac. You better have something to eat, there's bugger all for dinner."

Sayada said, "How about dining at the French Club? The food's still passable."

"I'd love to," Paula said brightly and Pettikin cursed. "What a wonderful idea, Sayada! Charlie?"

"Wonderful. Mac?"

"Sure, if it's my treat and you don't mind an early night." McIver held his glass up to the light, admiring the color of the wine. "Charlie, I want you to take the 212 to Kowiss bright and early, Nogger'll take the Alouette —you can help Duke out for a couple of days. I'll send Shoesmith in a 206 to bring you back Saturday. All right?"

"Sure," Pettikin said, wondering why the change of plan that had been for McIver, Nogger, and him to get aboard the Wednesday flight, two other pilots to go to Kowiss tomorrow. Why? Must be Andy's letter. Whirlwind? Is Mac aborting?

IN THE SLUMS OF JALEH: 6:50 P.M.   The old car stopped in the alleyway. A man got out of the side door and looked around. The alley was deserted, high walls, a joub to one side that long ago was buried under snow and refuse. Across from where the car had stopped, dimly seen in the reflection from the headlights, was a broken-down square. The man tapped on the roof. The headlights were doused. The driver got out and went to help the other man who had opened the trunk. Together they carried the body, wrapped and bound in a dark blanket, across the square.

"Wait a moment," the driver said in Russian. He took out his flashlight and switched it on briefly. The circle of light found the opening in the far wall they sought.

"Good," the other said and they went through it, then once more stopped to get their bearings. Now they were in a cemetery, old, almost derelict. The light went from gravestone to gravestone—some of the writing Russian, some in Roman letters—to find the open grave, newly dug. A shovel stood upright in the mound of earth.

They went and stood on the lip. The taller man, the driver, said, "Ready?"

"Yes." They let the body fall into the hole. The driver shone the light onto it. "Straighten him up."

"He won't give a shit," the other man said and took up the shovel. He was broad-shouldered and strong and he began to fill the grave. The driver lit a cigarette, irritably threw the match into the grave. "Maybe you should say a prayer for him."

The other laughed. "Marx-Lenin wouldn't approve—nor old Stalin."

"That mother fornicator—may he rot!"

"Look what he did for Mother Russia! He made us an empire, the biggest in the world, he screwed the British, outsmarted the Americans, built the biggest and best army, navy, air force, and made the KGB all powerful."

"For damn near every rouble we've got and twenty million lives. Russian lives."

"Expendables! Scum, fools, the dregs, plenty more where they came from." The man was sweating now and he gave the shovel to the other. "What the hell's the matter with you anyway—you've been pissed off all day."

"Tired, I'm just tired. Sorry."

"Everyone's tired. You need a few days off. Apply for Al Shargaz—I had a great three days, didn't want to come back. I've applied for a transfer there—we've quite an operation now, growing every day, the Israelis have stepped up their ops too—so've the CIA. What's happened since I was away?"

"Azerbaijan's warming up nicely. There's a rumor old Abdollah Khan's dying or dead."

"The Section 16/a?"

"No, heart attack. Everything else's normal. You really had a good time?"

The other laughed. "There's an Intourist secretary who's very accommodating." He scratched his scrotum at the thought. "Who is this poor sod anyway?"

"His name wasn't listed," the driver said.

"Never is. So who was he?"

"Agent called Yazernov, Dimitri Yazernov."

"Means nothing to me. To you?"

"He was an agent from Disinformation on the university detail; I worked with him for a short time, a year back. Smartass, university type, full of ideological bullshit. It seems he was caught by Inner Intelligence and interrogated seriously."

"Bastards! They killed him, eh?"

"No." The taller man stopped shoveling a moment and looked around. No chance of them being overheard and while he did not believe in ghosts or God or anything but the Party and the KGB—the spearhead of the Party —he did not like this place. He lowered his voice. "When he was sprung, almost a week ago, he was in bad shape, unconscious, should never've been moved, not in his state. SAVAMA got him away from Inner Intelligence— the director thinks SAVAMA worked him over too before handing him back." He leaned on the shovel a moment. "SAVAMA gave him to us with the report that they thought he'd been cleared out through the third level. The director said to find out who he was fast, if he had other secret clearances, or was an internal spy or a plant from higher up, and what the hell he'd told them—who the hell he was. He's not carried on our files as anything other than an agent on the university detail." He wiped the sweat off his forehead and began shoveling again. "I heard the team waited and waited for him to regain consciousness, then today gave up waiting and tried to wake him up."

"A mistake? Someone gave him too much?"

"Who knows—the poor sod's dead."

"That's the one thing that scares me," the other said with a shiver. "Getting fed too much. Nothing you can do about it. He never woke up? Never said anything?"

"No. Not a damned thing. The shit's that he was caught at all. It was his own fault—the mother was working on his own."

The other cursed. "How'd he get away with that?"

"Buggered if I know! I remember him as one of those who think they know it all and sneer at the Book. Smart? Bullshit! These bastards cause more trouble than they're worth." The taller man worked strongly and steadily. When he was tired the other took a turn.

Soon the grave was filled. The man patted the earth flat, his breathing heavy. "If this mother got himself caught, why're we taking all this trouble, then?"

"If the body can't be repatriated, a comrade's entitled to be buried properly, that's in the Book. This's a Russian cemetery, isn't it?"

"Sure, of course it is, but damned if I'd like to be buried here." The man wiped the dirt off his hands then turned and relieved himself on the nearest gravestone.

The taller man was working a gravestone loose. "Give me a hand." Together they lifted the stone and replanted it at the head of the grave they had just filled.

Damn the young bastard for dying, he thought, cursing him. Not my fault he died. He should've withstood the dose. Sodding doctors! They're supposed to know! We had no option, the bastard was sinking anyway and there were too many questions to be answered, like what was so important about him that that archbastard Hashemi Fazir did the interrogation himself, along with that sonofabitch Armstrong? Those two high-flying professionals don't waste their time on small fry. And why did Yazernov say "Fedor . . ." just before he croaked? What's the significance of that?

"Let's go home," the other man said. "This place's foul and it stinks, it stinks worse than normal." He took the shovel and trudged off into the night.

Just then the writing on the stone caught the driver's eye but it was too dark to read. He switched on the light momentarily. The writing said, "Count Alexi Pokenov, Plenipotentiary to Shah Nasiru'd Din, 1830–1862."

Yazernov'd like that, he thought, his smile twisted.

AT THE BAKRAVAN HOUSE, NEAR THE BAZAAR: 7:15

P.M. The outer door in the wall swung open. "Salaam, Highness." The servant watched Sharazad as she swept past happily, followed by Jari, into the forecourt and pulled the chador off and was now shaking her hair and puffing it with her fingertips more comfortably. "The . . . your husband's back, Highness; he came back just after sunset."

For a moment Sharazad was frozen in the light of the oil lamps that flickered in the snow-covered courtyard leading to the front door.

Then it's over, she was thinking. Over before it began. It almost began today, I was ready and yet not . . . and now, now I'm saved from . . . from my lust—was it lust or love, was that what I was trying to decide? I don't know, I don't know but . . . but tomorrow I'll see him a last time, I have to see him once more, have to, just . . . just once more . . . just to say good-bye. . . .

Tears filled her eyes and she ran into the house and into the rooms and salons and up the stairs and into their suite and into his arms. "Oh, Tommyyyyyy, you've been away such a long time!"

"Oh, I've missed you, where have you . . . Don't cry, my darling, there's no need to cry. . . ."

His arms were around her and she caught the faint, familiar oil-gasoline smell that came from his flight clothes hanging on a peg. She saw his gravity. HBC flared into her head but she put it all away and, not giving him a second, she stood on tiptoe, kissed him, and said in a rush, "I've such wonderful news, I'm with child, oh, yes, it's true and I've seen a doctor and tomorrow I'll get the result of the test but I *know*!" Her smile was vast and true. "Oh, Tommy," she continued in the same rush, feeling his arms tighten even more, "will you marry me, please please please?"

"But we are mar—"

"Say it, oh, please, please say it!" She looked up and saw he was still pale and smiling only a very little but that was enough for the moment, and she heard him say, Of course I'll marry you. "No, say it properly, I marry you, Sharazad Bakravan. I marry you I marry you I marry you," then hearing him say it and that made everything perfect. "Perfect," she burst out and hugged him back, then pushed away and ran over to the mirror to repair her makeup. She caught sight of Lochart in the mirror, his face so severe, unsettled. "What is it?"

"You're sure, sure about the child?"

She laughed. "Oh, I'm sure, but the doctor needs proof, husbands need proof. Isn't it wonderful?"

"Yes . . . yes, it is." He put his hands on her shoulders. "I love you!"

In her head she heard the other I love you that had been said with such passion and longing, and she thought how strange that though her husband's love was sure and proven, Ibrahim's was not—yet Ibrahim's was without reservation whereas, even after her wonderful news, her husband frowned at her.

"The year and a day have gone, Tommy, the year and a day you wanted," she said gently and got up from the dressing table, put her hands around his neck, smiling up at him, knowing that it was up to her to help him: "Foreigners aren't like us, Princess," Jari had said, "their reactions are different, training different, but don't worry, just be your own delightful self and he will be clay in your hands. . . ." Tommy'll be the best father ever, she promised herself, irrepressibly happy that she had not melted this afternoon, that she had made her announcement, and now they would live happily ever after. "We will, Tommy, won't we?"

"What?"

"Live happily ever after."

For a moment her joy obliterated his misery about Karim Peshadi and about what to do and how to do it. He caught her up in his arms and sat in the deep chair, cradling her. "Oh, yes. Oh, yes, we will. There's so much to talk ab—" Jari's knock on the door interrupted him.

"Come in, Jari."

"Please excuse me, Excellency, but His Excellency Meshang and Her Highness have arrived and are waiting to have the pleasure of seeing you both when convenient."

"Tell His Excellency we'll be there as soon as we've changed." Lochart did not notice Jari's relief as Sharazad nodded and beamed at her.

"I'll run your bath, Highness," Jari said and went into the bathroom. "Isn't it wonderful about Her Highness, Excellency? Oh, many congratulations, Excellency, many congratulations . . ."

"Thank you, Jari," Lochart said, not listening to her, thinking about the child to be, and Sharazad, lost in worry and happiness. So complicated now, so difficult.

"Not difficult," Meshang said after dinner.

Conversation had been boring with Meshang dominating it as he always did now that he was head of the household, Sharazad and Zarah hardly talking, Lochart saying little—no point in mentioning Zagros as Meshang had always been totally disinterested in his opinions or what he did. Twice he had almost blurted out about Karim—no reason to tell them yet, he had thought, hiding his despair. Why be the bearer of bad tidings?

"You don't find life in Tehran difficult now?" he said. Meshang had been moaning about all the new regulations implanted on the bazaar.

"Life is always difficult," Meshang said, "but if you're Iranian, a trained bazaari, with care and understanding, with hard work and logic, even the Revolutionary Komiteh can be curbed—we've always curbed tax collectors and overloads, shahs, commissars, or Yankee and British pashas."

"I'm glad to hear it, very glad."

"And I'm very glad you're back, I've been wanting to talk to you," Meshang said. "My sister has told you about the child to be?"

"Yes, yes, she has. Isn't it wonderful?"

"Yes, yes, it is. God be praised. What are your plans?"

"How do you mean?"

"Where are you going to live? How are you going to pay for everything now?"

The silence was vast. "We'll manage," Lochart began. "I int—"

"I don't see how you can, logically. I've been going through last year's bills an—" Meshang stopped as Zarah got up.

"I don't think this is a good time to talk about bills," she said, her face suddenly white, Sharazad's equally so.

"Well, I do," Meshang said harshly. "How's my sister going to survive? Sit down, Zarah, and listen! Sit down! And when I say you will not go on a protest march or anything else in future you will obey or I'll whip you! *Sit down!*" Zarah obeyed, shocked at his bad manners and violence. Sharazad was stunned, her world collapsing. She saw her brother turn on Lochart. "Now, Captain, your bills for the last year, the bills paid by my father, not counting the ones still owing and due, are substantially more than your salary. Is that true?"

Sharazad's face was burning with shame and anger and before Lochart could answer she said quickly in her most honeyed voice, "Darling Meshang, you're quite right to be concerned about us but the apar—"

"Kindly keep quiet! I have to ask your husband, not you, it's his problem, not yours. Well, Cap—"

"But darling Mesh—"

"Keep quiet! Well, Captain, is it true or isn't it?"

"Yes, it's true," Lochart replied, desperately seeking a way out of the abyss. "But you'll remember His Excellency gave me the apartment, in fact the building, and the other rents paid the bills and the rest was for an allowance to give to Sharazad for which I was eternally grateful. As to the future, I'll take care of Sharazad, of course I will."

"With what? I've read your divorce settlement and it's clear that with the payments you make to your previous wife and child there's little chance you can keep my sister out of penury."

Lochart was choked with rage. Sharazad shifted in her chair and Lochart saw her fear and dominated his urge to smash Meshang into the table. "It's all right, Sharazad. Your brother has the right to ask. That's fair, he has the right." He read the smugness under the etched handsome face and knew that the fight was joined. "We'll manage, Meshang, I'll manage. Our apartment, it won't be commandeered forever, or we can take another. We'll m—"

"There is no apartment, or building. It burned down on Saturday. It's all gone, everything."

They gaped at him, Sharazad the most shocked. "Oh, Meshang, you're sure? Why didn't you tell me? Wh—"

"Is your property so abundant you don't check it from time to time? It's gone, all of it!"

"Oh, Christ!" Lochart muttered.

"Better you don't blaspheme," Meshang said, finding it hard not to gloat openly. "So there's no apartment, no building, nothing left. Insha'Allah. Now, now how do you intend to pay your bills?"

"Insurance!" Lochart burst out. "There's got to be in—"

A bellow of laughter drowned him, Sharazad knocked over a glass of water that no one noticed. "You think insurance will be paid?" Meshang jeered. "Now? Even if there was any? You've taken leave of all your senses, there is no insurance, there never was. So, Captain: many debts, no money, no capital, no building—not that it was even legally yours, merely a face-saving way my father arranged to provide you with the means to look after Sharazad." He picked up a piece of halvah and popped it into his mouth. "So what do you propose?"

"I'll manage."

"How, please tell me—and Sharazad, of course, she has the right, the legal right to know. How?"

Sharazad muttered, "I've jewelry, Tommy, I can sell that."

Cruelly Meshang left the words hanging in the air over the table, delighted that Lochart was at bay, humiliated, stripped naked. Filthy Infidel! If it wasn't for the Locharts in our world, the rapacious foreigners, exploiters of Iran, we'd be free of Khomeini and his mullahs, my father would still be alive, Sharazad married properly. "Well?"

"What do you suggest?" Lochart said, no way out of the trap.

"What do *you* suggest?"

"I don't know."

"Meanwhile you've no house, very substantial bills, and soon you'll be jobless—I doubt if your company will be allowed to operate here very much longer; quite correctly foreign companies are persona non grata." Meshang was delighted that he had remembered the Latin phrase, "no longer needed, wanted, or necessary."

"If that happens I'll resign and apply to fly choppers for Iranian companies. They'll need pilots immediately. I can speak Farsi, I'm an expert pilot
and trainer. Khomeini . . . the Imam wants oil production brought back
to normal immediately, so of course they'll need trained pilots."

Meshang laughed to himself. Yesterday Minister Ali Kia had come to the
bazaar, correctly humble and anxious to please, bringing an exquisite
pishkesh—wasn't his annual "consulting fee" due for renewal soon?—and
had told him of his plans to acquire all partnership airplanes and freeze all
bank accounts. "We'll have no problem to get all the mercenaries we need
to fly *our* helicopters, Excellency Meshang," Kia had said. "They'll flock to
us at half their normal salaries."

Yes, they will, but not you, temporary husband of my sister, not even for
a tenth salary. "I suggest you be more practical." Meshang examined his
beautifully manicured nails that this afternoon had fondled the fourteen-
year-old Ali Kia had given him: "the first of many, Excellency!" Lovely
white Circassian skin, the temporary marriage for this afternoon that he
had gladly extended for the week so easily arranged. "The present rulers of
Iran are xenophobic, particularly about Americans."

"I'm Canadian."

"I doubt if that matters. It's logical to presume you won't be permitted
to stay." He looked sharply at Sharazad, "Or to return."

"Surmise," Lochart said through his teeth, seeing the look on her face.

"Captain, my late father's charity can no longer be supported—times are
hard. I want to know how you intend to support my sister and her forthcoming child, where you intend to live and how."

Abruptly Lochart got up, startling everyone else. "You've made your
point, clearly, Excellency Meshang. I'll answer you tomorrow."

"I want an answer now."

Lochart's face closed. "First I'll talk to my wife and then I'll talk to you
tomorrow. Come on, Sharazad." He stalked out. In tears she stumbled after
him and closed the door.

Meshang smiled sardonically, picked up another sweet, and began to eat
it.

Zarah exhaled, enraged. "What in the Name of G—"

He reached over and smashed her openhanded around the face. "Shut
up!" he shouted. It was not the first time he had hit her but never before
with such violence. "Shut up or I'll divorce you! I'll divorce you, you hear?
I'm going to take another wife anyway—someone young, not dry and an old
nagging hag like you. Don't you understand Sharazad's in danger, we're all
in danger because of that man? Go beg God's forgiveness for your foul
manners! Get out!" She fled. He hurled a cup after her.

IN THE NORTHERN SUBURBS: 9:14 P.M. Azadeh drove the small, badly dented car fast along the street that was lined with fine houses and apartment buildings—most of them dark, a few vandalized—headlights carelessly on bright, dazzling the oncoming traffic, her horn blaring. She braked, skidded as she cut dangerously across the traffic, narrowly avoiding an accident, and headed into the garage of one of the buildings with a screech of rubber.

The garage was dark. In the side pocket was a flashlight. She turned it on, got out, and locked the car. Her coat was well cut and warm, skirt and boots and fur mits and hat, her hair flowing. On the other side of the garage was a staircase and a switch for the lights. When she tried it, the nearest bulb sparked and died. She went up the stairs heavily. Four apartments on each landing. The apartment that her father had lent her and Erikki was on the third landing, facing the street. Today was Monday. She had been here since Saturday. "It's not risky, Mac," she had said when she announced she was going and he had tried to persuade her to remain in his apartment, "but if my father wants me back in Tabriz, staying here with you won't help me at all. In the apartment I've a phone, I'm only half a mile away and can walk it easily, I've clothes there and a servant. I'll check every day and come into the office and wait, that's all I can do."

She had not said that she preferred to be away from him and Charlie Pettikin. I like them both dearly, she thought, but they're rather old and pedantic and nothing like Erikki. Or Johnny. Ah, Johnny, what to do about you, dare I see you again?

The third landing was dark but she had the flashlight and found her key, put it in the lock, felt eyes on her, and whirled in fright. The swarthy, unshaven lout had his pants open and he waved his stiff penis at her. "I've been waiting for you, princess of all whores, and God curse me if it's not ready for you front or back or sideways . . ." He came forward mouthing obscenities and she backed against the door in momentary terror, grabbed the key, turned it, and flung the door open.

The Doberman guard dog was there. The man froze. An ominous growl, then the dog charged. In panic the man screamed and tried to beat the dog off, then took to his heels down the steps, the dog growling and snarling and ripping at his legs and back, tearing his clothes, and Azadeh shouted after him, "Now show it to me!"

"Oh, Highness, I didn't hear you knock, what's going on?" the old man-servant called out, rushing from the kitchen area.

Angrily she wiped the perspiration off her face and told him. "God curse you, Ali, I've told you twenty times to meet me downstairs with the dog. I'm on time, I'm always on time. Have you no brains?"

The old man apologized but a rough voice behind her cut him short. "Go and get the dog!" She looked around. Her stomach twisted.

"Good evening, Highness." It was Ahmed Dursak, tall, bearded, chilling, standing in the doorway of the living room. Insha'Allah, she thought. The waiting is over and now it begins again. "Good evening, Ahmed."

"Highness, please excuse me, I didn't realize about people in Tehran or I would have waited downstairs myself. Ali, get the dog!"

Afraid and still mumbling apologies, the servant scuttled down the stairs. Ahmed closed the door and watched Azadeh use the heel fork to take off her boots, slip her small feet into curved Turkish slippers. She went past him into the comfortable, Western-style living room and sat down, her heart thumping. A fire flickered in the grate. Priceless carpets, others used as wall hangings. Beside her was a small table. On the table was the kookri that Ross had left her. "You have news of my father and my husband?"

"His Highness the Khan is ill, very ill an—"

"What illness?" Azadeh asked, at once genuinely concerned.

"A heart attack."

"God protect him—when did this happen?"

"On Thursday last." He read her thought. "That was the day you and . . . and the saboteur were in the village of Abu Mard. Wasn't it?"

"I suppose so. The last few days have been very confused," she said icily. "How is my father?"

"The attack on Thursday was mild, thanks be to God. Just before midnight Saturday he had another. Much worse." He watched her.

"How much worse? Please don't play with me! Tell me everything at once!"

"Ah, so sorry, Highness, I did not mean to toy with you." He kept his voice polite and his eyes off her legs, admiring her fire and pride and wanting to toy with her very much. "The doctor called it a stroke and now the left side of His Highness is partially paralyzed; he can still talk—with some difficulty—but his mind is as strong as ever. The doctor said he would recover much quicker in Tehran but the journey is not possible yet."

"He will recover?" she asked.

"I don't know, Highness. As God wants. To me he seems very sick. The doctor, I don't think much of him, all he said was His Highness's chances would be better if he was here in Tehran."

"Then bring him here as soon as possible."

"I will, Highness, never fear. Meanwhile I have a message for you. The Khan, your father, says, 'I wish to see you. At once. I do not know how long I will live but certain arrangements must be made and confirmed. Your brother is with me now and—' "

"God protect him," Azadeh burst out. "Is my father reconciled with Hakim?"

"His Highness has made him his heir. But pl—"

"Oh, that's wonderful, wonderful, God be praised! But h—"

"Please be patient and let me finish his message: 'Your brother Hakim is with me now and I have made him my heir, subject to certain conditions, from you and from him.'" Ahmed hesitated and Azadeh wanted to rush into the gap, her happiness brimming and her caution brimming. Her pride stopped her.

"'It is therefore necessary that you return with Ahmed at once.' That is the end of the message, Highness."

The front door opened. Ali relocked it and unleashed the dog. At once the dog loped into the living room and put his head in Azadeh's lap. "Well done, Reza," she said petting him, welcoming the moment to collect her wits. "Sit. Go on, sit! Sit!" Happily the dog obeyed, then lay at her feet, watching the door and watching Ahmed who stood near the other sofa. Absently her hand played with the hilt of the kookri, its touch giving her reassurance. Obliquely Ahmed was conscious of it and its implications. "Before God you have told me the truth?"

"Yes, Highness. Before God."

"Then we will go at once." She got up. "You came by car?"

"Yes, Highness. I brought the limousine and chauffeur. But there's a little more news—good and bad. A ransom note came to His Highness. His Excellency your husband is in the hands of bandits, tribesmen . . ." She tried to maintain her composure, her knees suddenly weak. ". . . somewhere near the Soviet border. Both him and his helicopter. It seems that these . . . these bandits claim to be Kurds but the Khan doubts it. They surprised the Soviet Cimtarga and his men and killed them all, capturing His Excellency and the helicopter, early Thursday they claimed. Then they flew to Rezaiyeh where he was seen and appeared unharmed before flying off again."

"Praise be to God," was all her pride allowed herself. "Is my husband ransomed?"

"The ransom note arrived late on Saturday, through intermediaries. As soon as His Highness regained consciousness yesterday he gave me the message for you and sent me here to fetch you."

She heard the "fetch" and knew its seriousness but Ahmed made nothing of it openly and reached into his pocket. "His Highness Hakim gave me this for you." He handed her the sealed envelope. She ripped it open, startling the dog. The note was in Hakim's handwriting: "My darling, His Highness has made me his heir and reinstated both of us, subject to conditions, wonderful conditions, easy to agree. Hurry back, he's very ill, and he will not deal with the ransom until he sees you. Salaam."

Swamped with happiness she hurried out, packed a bag in almost no time, scribbled a note for McIver, telling Ali to deliver it tomorrow. As an afterthought she picked up the kookri and walked out, cradling it. Ahmed said nothing, just followed her.

TUESDAY
February 27

BANDAR DELAM: 8:15 A.M. Kasigi was hurrying after the grim-faced police officer through the drab crowded corridors of the hospital—the radio mechanic, Minoru, a few paces behind him. Sick and wounded men and women and children were on stretchers or chairs or standing or simply lying on the floor, waiting for someone to help them, the very sick mixed with the lightly sick, a few relieving themselves, a few eating and drinking provisions brought by their visiting relatives who abounded—and all who could, complained loudly. Harassed nurses and doctors went in and out of rooms, all medical women dressed in chador except a few British, Queen Alexandra nurses whose severe headdress was almost the equivalent and acceptable.

Eventually the policeman found the door he sought and pushed his way into the crowded ward. Beds lined both sides with another row in the middle, all occupied by men patients—their visiting families chattering or complaining, children playing, and over in one corner, an old woman cooking on a portable stove.

Scragger had one wrist and one ankle handcuffed to an old iron bedstead. He was lying on a straw mattress in his clothes and shoes, a bandage around his head, unshaven and dirty. When he saw Kasigi and Minoru behind the policeman his eyes lit up. "Hello, mates," he said, his voice raw.

"How are you, Captain?" Kasigi said, appalled by the handcuffs.

"If I could get free I'd be fine."

Irritably the policeman interrupted loudly in Farsi for the benefit of the watchers, "This is the man you wanted to see?"

"Yes, Excellency," Minoru said for Kasigi.

"So now you've seen him. You can report to your government or whomever you wish that clearly he's been given treatment. He will be tried by the traffic komiteh." Pompously he turned to go.

"But the captain pilot wasn't the driver," Kasigi said patiently in English, Minoru translating for him, having said it for most of the night and since dawn this morning to various policemen of various ranks, always getting varying degrees of the same answer: "If the foreigner wasn't in Iran the accident would never have happened, of course he's responsible."

"It doesn't matter he wasn't the driver, he's still responsible!" the policeman said angrily, his voice echoing off the walls. "How many times must you be told? He was in charge of the car. He ordered it. If he hadn't ordered it the accident would never have happened, people were killed and injured, of course he's responsible!"

"But, I repeat, my assistant here was an eyewitness and will give evidence that the accident was caused by the other car."

"Lies in front of the komiteh will be dealt with seriously," the man said darkly, one of those who had been in the police car.

"Not lies, Agha. There are other witnesses," Kasigi said, not that he had any, his voice sharpening. "I insist this man be released. He's an employee of my government which has invested billions of dollars in our Iran-Toda petrochemical plant, to the benefit of Iran and particularly all people in Bandar Delam. Unless he is released at once, at once, I will order all Japanese out and cease all work!" His biliousness increased, for he did not have the authority, nor would he issue such orders. "Everything will stop!"

"By the Prophet, we're no longer subject to foreign blackmail," the man blustered and turned away. "You'll have to discuss this with the komiteh!"

"Unless he's released at once, all work ceases and there'll be no more jobs. None!" As Minoru translated, Kasigi noticed a difference in the silence and the mood of those around. And even in the police officer himself, nastily aware that all eyes were on him and sensing the sudden hostility.

One youth nearby wearing a green band on his grimy pajamas said thickly, "You want to jeopardize our jobs, eh? Who're you? How do we know you're not a Shah man? Have you been cleared by the komiteh?"

"Of course I have! By the One God I've been for the Imam for years!" the man replied angrily but a wave of fear went through him. "I helped the revolution, everyone knows. You," he pointed at Kasigi, silently cursing him for causing all this trouble, "you follow me!" He pushed a way through the onlookers.

"I'll be back, Captain Scragger, don't worry." Kasigi and Minoru rushed off in pursuit.

The police officer led the way down a flight of stairs and along a corridor and down other stairs, all of them crowded. Kasigi's nervousness increased as they descended deeper into the hospital. Now the man opened the door with a notice in Farsi on it.

Kasigi broke out in a cold sweat. They were in the morgue. Marble slabs with bodies covered with grimy sheets. Many of them. Odor of chemicals and dried blood and offal and excrement. "Here!" the police officer said and tore back a sheet. Beneath it was the headless corpse of a woman. Her head was obscenely near the trunk, eyes open. "Your car caused her death, what about her and her family?" Kasigi heard the "your" and a freezing current went through him. "And here!" He ripped away another sheet. A badly mashed woman, unrecognizable. "Well?"

"We're . . . we're deeply sorry of course . . . of course we're deeply sorry that anyone was hurt, deeply sorry, but that is karma, Insha'Allah, not our fault or the fault of the pilot upstairs." Kasigi was hard put to hold his nausea down. "Deeply sorry."

Minoru translated, the police officer leaning insolently against the slab. Then he replied and the young Japanese's eyes widened: "He says, he says the bail, the fine to release Mr. Scragger immediately is 1 million rials. At once. What the komiteh decides is nothing to do with him."

One million rials was about $12,000. "That's not possible, but we could certainly pay 100,000 rials within the hour."

"A million," the man shouted. He grabbed the woman's head by the hair and held it up to Kasigi who had to force himself to stand erect. "What about her children who are now condemned forever to be motherless? Don't they deserve compensation? Eh?"

"There's . . . there's not that amount of cash in . . . in the whole plant, so sorry."

The policeman swore and continued to haggle but then the door opened. Orderlies with a trolley and another body came in, eyeing them curiously. Abruptly the policeman said, "Very well. We will go to your office at once."

They went and got the last amount Kasigi had offered, 250,000 rials—about $3,000—but no receipt, only a verbal agreement that Scragger could leave. Not trusting the man, Kasigi gave him half in the office and put the rest into an envelope that he kept in his pocket. They returned to the hospital. There he waited in the car while Minoru and the man went inside. The waiting seemed interminable but finally Minoru and Scragger came down the steps with the policeman. Kasigi got out and gave the policeman the envelope. The man cursed all foreigners and went away truculently.

"So," Kasigi said and smiled at Scragger. They shook hands, Scragger thanking him profusely, apologizing for all the trouble, both men cursing fate, blessing it, getting into the car quickly. The Iranian chauffeur swerved out into the traffic, swore loudly at an overtaking car that had the right of way and almost collided with him, jabbing the horn.

"Tell him to slow down, Minoru," Kasigi said. Minoru obeyed and the driver nodded and smiled and obeyed. The slowdown lasted a few seconds.

"Are you all right, Captain?"

"Oh, yes. Headache's a beaut but okay. The worst was wanting to pee."

"What?"

"The bastards kept me handcuffed to the bed and wouldn't let me get to the loo. I just couldn't do it in my pants, or in the bed, and it wasn't till early this morning a nurse brought me a bottle. Christ, I thought my bladder was bust." Scragger rubbed the tiredness out of his eyes. "No problem, old sport. I owe you one. Plus the ransom! How much was it?"

"Nothing, nothing to you. We have a fund for these hazards."

"It's no problem, Andy Gavallan'll pay—oh, that reminds me, he said he knew your boss some years ago, Toda, Hiro Toda."

"*Ah so desu ka?*" Kasigi was genuinely surprised. "Gavallan has choppers in Japan?"

"Oh, no. It was when he was a China trader, out of Hong Kong, when he was working for Struan's." The name sent a warning bolt through Kasigi that he kept bottled. "You ever heard of them?"

"Yes, a fine company. Toda's do, or did business with Struan's," Kasigi said smoothly, but he docketed the information for future consideration—wasn't it Linbar Struan who unilaterally canceled five ship-leasing contracts two years ago that almost broke us? Perhaps Gavallan could be an instrument to recoup, one way or another. "Sorry you had such a bad time."

"Not your fault, cobber. But Andy'd want to pay the ransom. Wot'd they stick us for?"

"It was very modest. Please, let it be a gift—you saved my ship."

After a pause Scragger said, "Then I owe you two, old sport."

"We selected the driver—it was our fault."

"Where is he, where's Mohammed?"

"So sorry, he's dead."

Scragger swore. "It wasn't his fault, it wasn't at all."

"Yes, yes, I know. We have given his family compensation, and we will do the same for the victims." Kasigi was trying to read how shaken Scragger was, wanting to know very much when he would be fit to fly, and greatly irritated with the day's delay. It was imperative to get back to Al Shargaz as soon as possible, thence home to Japan. His work here was finished. Chief Engineer Watanabe was now totally on his side, the copies of his private reports would cement his own corporate position and enormously help him —and Hiro Toda—to reopen the possibility of persuading the government to declare Iran-Toda a National Project.

Not possibility, certainty! he thought, more confident than he had ever been. We'll be saved from bankruptcy, we'll bury our enemies, the Mitsuwari and Gyokotomo, and gain nothing but face ourselves—and profit, vast profit! Oh, yes. And the added piece of good fortune, Kasigi allowed himself a cynical smile, the explosively important copy of dead Chief Engineer Kasusaka's private report to Gyokotomo, dated and signed, that Watanabe had miraculously "found" in a forgotten file while I was in Al Shargaz! I'll have to be very careful how I use it, oh, very careful indeed, but it makes it all the more important that I get home as soon as possible.

The streets and alleys were clogged with traffic. Above, the sky was still overcast but the storm had passed through and he knew the weather was flyable. Ah, I wish I had my own airplane, he thought. Say a Lear jet. The reward for all my work here should be substantial.

He let himself drift happily, enjoying his sense of achievement and power. "It looks like we will be able to begin construction very soon now, Captain."

"Oh?"

"Yes. The head of the new komiteh assured us of their cooperation. It seems he knows one of your pilots, a Captain Starke—his name's Zataki."

Scragger glanced at him sharply. "He's the one Duke, Duke Starke, saved from the leftists and flew to Kowiss. If I were you, cobber, I'd, er, watch him." He told Kasigi how volatile the man was. "He's a right madman."

"He didn't give that appearance, not at all. Curious—Iranians are very . . . very curious. But more important, how are you feeling?"

"I'm bonzer now." Scragger exaggerated blithely. Yesterday and all night had been very bad, all the cursing and shouting and being handcuffed, not being able to make anyone understand, surrounded by hostility, eyes everywhere. Lost. And afraid. The pain increasing. Time agonizingly slow, hope fading, sure that Minoru was injured or dead along with the driver so that no one would know where he was or what had happened.

"Nothing that a good cup of tea won't cure. If you'd like to leave at once, I'm okay. Just a quick bath and shave and cuppa and some grub and we'll be on our merry way."

"Excellent. Then we'll leave the moment you're ready—Minoru has installed the radio and checked it."

All the way to the refinery and during the flight back to Lengeh, Kasigi was in very good spirits. Near Kharg they thought they spotted the huge hammerhead shark Scragger had once mentioned. They kept low and close inshore, the clouds still low and heavy, nimbus here and there with an occasional flash of lightning menacing them but not badly, only a little bumpy now and then. Radar surveillance and clearances were efficient and immediate which increased Scragger's foreboding. Two days to Whirlwind, not counting today, was in the forefront of his mind. Losing a day makes it all the more hairy, he thought anxiously. Wot's happened since I was away?

Well past Kharg he landed to refuel and take a break. His stomach still ached nastily and he noticed a little blood in his urine. Nothing to worry about, he told himself. Sure to be a little hemorrhage after an accident like that. Shit in a bucket but I was lucky!

They were on a sandbank, finishing a packed lunch—cold rice and pieces of fish and pickles. Scragger had a big hunk of Iranian bread he had scrounged from the spotless cookhouse and lots of cold yakatori chicken and soy sauce that he enjoyed very much. Kasigi was sipping Japanese beer that Scragger had refused: "Thanks, but drinking and driving don't mix."

Kasigi ate sparingly, Scragger hungrily and quickly. "Good grub," he said. "Soon as you're ready we'd better get on."

"I'm finished." Soon they were airborne again. "Will there be time to get me on to Al Shargaz or Dubai today?"

"Not if we go to Lengeh." Scragger adjusted his headset slightly. "Tell you wot, when we get into Kish Traffic Control I'll ask if I can divert to Bahrain. You could pick up an international or local flight there. We'll need to refuel at Lavan but they'll approve that if they agree. As I said, I owe you a couple."

"You owe us nothing." Kasigi smiled to himself. "At the komiteh meeting yesterday, this man Zataki asked how soon we'd have our chopper fleet up to strength. I promised immediate action. As you know Guerney no longer services us. What I'd like is three of your 212s and two 206s for the next three months, a year-long contract to be negotiated then, depending on our needs, renewable annually—with you in charge. Would that be possible?"

Scragger hesitated, not knowing how to reply. Normally such an offer would send glad tiding bells ringing all the way to Aberdeen, Gavallan would be on the phone personally, and everyone would be in for a huge bonus. But with Whirlwind scheduled, Guerney out of the picture, and no one else available, there was no way to help Kasigi. "When, er, when would you need the birds to start?" he asked to give himself time to think.

"Immediately," Kasigi continued blithely, watching a tanker below. "I guaranteed Zataki and the komiteh that if they cooperated we'd start up at once. Tomorrow or the next day at the latest. Perhaps you could ask your head office temporarily to divert some of the 212s stationed at Bandar Delam and not being used to capacity. Yes?"

"I'll certainly ask, as soon as we land."

"For a week or so we'll need a temporary air link with Kuwait to pick up and replace crews from Japan—Zataki said their komiteh'd arrange with the Abadan airport komiteh today to open it for us, certainly by the end of the week. . . ."

Scragger was only half listening to the confident plans of this man who had befriended him, without whom he would still be handcuffed to the bed. His choice was simple: you tell him about Whirlwind or you leave him in the shit. But if you tell him you betray a bigger trust, a long-term trust. Kasigi might let Whirlwind slip. He's bound to tell de Plessey. The question is how far can I trust him—and de Plessey?

Greatly unsettled he glanced out of his window and rechecked his position. "Sorry to interrupt but I've got to report in." He pressed the send button: "Kish radar, this is HotelSierraTango, do you read?"

"HST, Kish radar, we read you four by five, go ahead."

"HST on charter from Iran-Toda inbound to home base in Lengeh, approaching Lavan at one thousand, one passenger aboard. Request permission to refuel at Lavan and divert to Bahrain to drop my passenger who has urgent business on behalf of Iran."

"Request refused, maintain one thousand and present heading."

"My passenger is Japanese, head of Iran-Toda, and urgently needs to consult his Japanese government on behalf of the Iran government's wish to resume immediate operations. Request special consideration in this instance."

"Request refused. No trans-Gulf flights are authorized without a twenty-four-hour notice. Turn to 095 degrees for direct Lengeh, report abeam Kish, not overhead Kish. Do you copy?"

Scragger glanced at Kasigi who could also hear the exchange. "Sorry, mate." He eased onto the new heading. "HST copies. Request clearance for Al Shargaz at dawn tomorrow with one passenger."

"Standby One." Static cracked in their earphones. To starboard the sea bridge of tankers continued, inbound and outbound, from or to the Gulf terminals of Saudi, the Emirates, Abu Dhabi, Bahrain, Kuwait, and Iraq. None were loading at Kharg or Abadan where normally a dozen would be serviced with another dozen waiting. Now there were only the swarms of ships waiting, some over two months. The sky was still overcast and nasty. "HST, this is Kish. In this instance your request is approved to go from Lengeh to Al Shargaz, tomorrow Wednesday twenty-eighth, noon departure. Until further notice all, repeat, all trans-Gulf flights will require a twenty-four-hour notice, and all, repeat, all engine starts require clearance. Do you copy?"

Scragger swore, then acknowledged.

"What is it?" Kasigi asked.

"We've never had to get clearance to start engines before. The bastards are really getting touchy." Scragger was thinking about Friday and his two 212s to start up and Kish too nosy and too efficient. "Crummy lot!"

"Yes. Will you be able to head up our chopper requirements?"

"There're lots of better guys than me."

"Ah, so sorry, but it would be important to me. I would know that the operation would be in good hands."

Again Scragger hesitated. "Thanks, if I could, I would, sure, sure I would."

"Then it's settled. I'll formally apply to your Mr. Gavallan." Kasigi glanced at Scragger. Something's changed, he thought. What? Now that I think of it, the pilot didn't react with the amount of enthusiasm I would have forecast when I announced the deal—he certainly would understand the value of the contract he's being offered. What's he hiding? "Could you contact Bandar Delam through your base at Kowiss to ask them about supplying us with at least one 212 tomorrow?" he asked, beginning to probe.

"Yes, yes, of course . . . soon as we arrive."

Ah, Kasigi thought, having watched and listened very carefully, I was right, something's very definitely different now. The friendliness is gone. Why? I've certainly not said anything to offend him. It can't be the deal—that's too good for any chopper company. His health? "Are you feeling all right?"

"Oh, fine, old sport, I'm fine."

Ah, the smile was real that time and the voice as usual. Then it has to be something to do with the choppers. "If I don't have your help, it will make things very difficult for me."

"Yes, I know. Me, I'd like to help you all I can."

Ah, the smile vanished and the voice became serious again. Why? And why the "me, I'd like to help" as though he would help but is forbidden to help by someone else. Gavallan? Could it be he knows that Gavallan, because of Struan's, wouldn't help us?

For a long time Kasigi considered all manner of permutations but could not come up with a satisfactory answer. Then he fell back on the one, almost infallible, ploy to use with a foreigner such as this one.

"My friend," he said, using his most sincere voice, "I know something's the matter, please tell me what it is?" Seeing Scragger's face become even more solemn, he added the coup de grace. "You can tell me, you can trust me, I really am your friend."

"Yes . . . yes, I know that, mate."

Kasigi watched Scragger's face and waited, watched the fish wriggling on the hook that was held by a line so thin and so strong that stretched back to a broken rotor blade, a handshake, shared danger aboard the *Rikumaru*, shared war service, and common reverence for dead comrades. So many of us dead, so young. Yes, he thought with a sudden anger, but if we'd had a tenth of their airplanes, their armaments and their ships and a twentieth part of their oil and raw materials we would have been invincible and the emperor would never have had to terminate the war as *he* did. We'd have been invincible—but for the bomb, the two bombs. All gods torment for all eternity those who invented the bomb that broke *his* will that took preference over ours. "What is it?"

"I, er, can't tell you, just yet—sorry."

Danger signals went through Kasigi. "Why, my friend? I assure you, you can trust me," he said soothingly.

"Yes . . . yes, but it's not just up to me. In Al Shargaz, tomorrow, bear with me, will you?"

"If it's that important, I should know now, shouldn't I?" Again Kasigi waited. He knew the value of waiting and of silence at a time like this. No need to remind the other man of the "I owe you two." Yet.

Scragger was remembering. At Bandar Delam, Kasigi saved my bloody neck and no doubt about that. Aboard his ship at Siri he proved he's got balls and today he's proved a good friend, he needn't've gone to all that trouble so fast, tomorrow or the next day wouldn't have mattered to him.

His eyes were scanning the instruments and the outside and he saw no dangers within or without, Kish coming up soon to starboard and he glanced across at Kasigi. Kasigi was staring ahead, his strong, good-looking face set, frowning slightly. Shit, old sport, if you don't perform, Zataki's likely to go berserk! But you can't perform. You can't, old sport, and it's so hard to see you just sitting there, not reminding me wot I owe you. "Kish, this is HST. Abeam Kish, steady at one thousand."

"Kish. Maintain one thousand. You have traffic due east at ten thousand."

"I have them in sight." They were two fighters. He pointed for Kasigi who had not seen them. "They're F14s, probably out of Bandar Abbas," he said. Kasigi did not reply, just nodded, and this made Scragger feel worse. The minutes passed. Droning onward.

Then Scragger decided, hating having to do it. "Sorry," he said gruffly, "but you'll have to wait until Al Shargaz. Andy Gavallan can help, I can't."

"He can help? In what way? What's the trouble?"

After a pause Scragger said, "If anyone can help, he can. Let's leave it at that, cobber."

Kasigi heard the finality but dismissed it and let the matter rest for a moment, his mind abuzz with fresh danger signals. That Scragger had not fallen into his trap and told him the secret made him respect the man more. But that doesn't forgive him, he thought, his fury building. He's told me enough to forewarn me, now it's up to me to find out the rest. So Gavallan's the key? To what?

Kasigi felt his head about to burst. Haven't I promised that madman Zataki we would be in business at once? How dare these men jeopardize our whole project—our *National* Project. Without choppers we can't start! It's tantamount to treason against Japan! What is it they're planning?

With a great effort he kept his face bland. "I'll certainly see Gavallan as soon as possible, and let's hope you'll head up our new operation, eh?"

"Whatever Andy Gavallan says, it's up to him."

Don't be too sure, Kasigi was thinking, because whatever happens I will have choppers, at once—yours, Guerney's, I don't care whose. But by my samurai ancestors, the Iran-Toda will not be put to further risk! It will not! *Nor will I!*

Inside the map:

U.S.S.R.
Caspian Sea
U.S.S.R.

TURKEY
KHOI
TABRIZ
MOUNT SABALAN
BANDAR-E PAHLAVI
QAZVIN
★ TEHRAN

IRAQ
BAGHDAD
ZAGROS
DEZ DAM
• ISFAHAN

IRAN

AFGHANISTAN

BANDAR DELAM
Shatt-al-Arab Estuary
ABADAN
• ZAGROS THREE
• KOWISS
MOUNTAINS

KUWAIT
KHARG
JELLET
Persian Gulf
LENGEH
Strait of Hormuz
PAKISTAN

BAHRAIN
SAUDI ARABIA
QATAR
SÎRI
Gulf of Oman
AL SHARGAZ

CHAPTER
53

TABRIZ—AT THE KHAN'S PALACE: 10:50 A.M. Azadeh followed Ahmed into the Western-style room and over to the four-poster bed, and now that she was again within the walls she felt her skin crawling with fear. Sitting near the bed was a nurse in a starched white uniform, a book half open in her lap, watching them curiously through her glasses. Musty brocade curtains covered the windows against drafts. Lights were dimmed. And the stench of an old man hung in the air.

The Khan's eyes were closed, his face pasty and breathing strangled, his arm connected to a saline drip that stood beside the bed. Half asleep in a chair nearby was Aysha, curled up and tiny, her hair disheveled and her face tear-stained. Azadeh smiled at her tentatively, sorry for her, then said to the nurse in a voice not her own, "How is His Highness, please?"

"Fair. But he mustn't have any excitement, or be disturbed," the nurse said softly in hesitant Turkish. Azadeh looked at her and saw that she was European, in her fifties, dyed brown hair, a red cross on her sleeve.

"Oh, you're English, or French?"

"Scots," the woman replied in English with obvious relief, her accent slight. She kept her voice down, watching the Khan. "I'm Sister Bain from the Tabriz Hospital and the patient is doing as well as can be expected—considering he will no' do as he's told. And who might you be, please?"

"I'm his daughter, Azadeh. I've just arrived from Tehran—he sent for me. We've . . . we've traveled all night."

"Ah, yes," she said, surprised that someone so beautiful could have been created by a man so ugly. "If I might suggest, lassie, it would be better to leave him sleeping. As soon as he wakes I'll tell him you're here and send for you. Better he sleeps."

Ahmed said irritably, "Please, where's His Highness's guard?"

"There's no need for armed men in a sickroom. I sent him away."

"There will always be a guard here unless the Khan orders him out or I order him out." Angrily Ahmed turned and left.

Azadeh said, "It's just a custom, Sister."

"Aye, very well. But that's another custom we can do without."

Azadeh looked back at her father, hardly recognizing him, trying to stop the terror that possessed her. Even like that, she thought, even like that he can still destroy us, Hakim and me—he still has his running dog Ahmed. "Please, really, how is he?"

The lines on the nurse's face creased even more. "We're doing all we can."

"Would it be better for him to be in Tehran?"

"Aye, if he has another stroke, yes, it would." Sister Bain took his pulse as she talked. "But I wouldna recommend moving him, not at all, not yet." She made a notation on a chart and then glanced at Aysha. "You could tell the lady there's no need to stay, she should get some proper rest too, poor child."

"Sorry, I may not interfere. Sorry, but that's a custom too. Is . . . is it likely he'll have another stroke?"

"You never know, lassie, that's up to God. We hope for the best." They looked around as the door opened. Hakim stood there beaming. Azadeh's eyes lit up and she said to the nurse, "Please call me the instant His Highness awakes," then hurried across the room, out into the corridor, closed the door, and hugged him. "Oh, Hakim, my darling, it's been such a long time," she said breathlessly. "Oh, is it really true?"

"Yes, yes, it is but how did . . ." Hakim stopped, hearing footsteps. Ahmed and a guard turned into the corridor and came up to them. "I'm glad you're back, Ahmed," he said politely. "His Highness will be happy too."

"Thank you, Highness. Has anything happened in my absence?"

"No, except that Colonel Fazir came this morning to see Father."

Ahmed was chilled. "Was he allowed in?"

"No. You left instructions no one was to be admitted without His Highness's personal permission; he was asleep at the time and he's been asleep most of the day—I check every hour and the nurse says he's unchanged."

"Good. Thank you. Did the colonel leave a message?"

"Only that he was going to Julfa today as arranged with his 'associate.' Does that mean anything to you?"

"No, Highness," Ahmed lied blandly. He glanced from one to the other but before he could say anything, Hakim said, "We'll be in the Blue Salon; please summon us the moment my father awakens."

Ahmed watched them go arm in arm down the corridor, the young man tall and handsome, the sister willowy and desirable. Traitors? Not much time to get the proof, he thought. He went back into the sickroom and saw the pallor of the Khan, his nostrils rebelling against the smell. He squatted on his haunches, careless of the disapproving nurse, and began his vigil.

What did that son of a dog Fazir want? he asked himself. Saturday evening when Hashemi Fazir and Armstrong had come back from Julfa without Mzytryk, Fazir had angrily demanded to see the Khan. Ahmed had been present when the Khan had seen them, declared himself as mystified as they that Mzytryk was not with the helicopter. "Come back tomorrow— if the man brings me a letter you can see it," the Khan had said.

"Thank you, but we will wait—the Chevy can't be far behind us."

So they had waited, the Khan seething but unable to do anything, Hashemi's men spread around the palace in ambush. An hour later the Chevy had arrived. He himself had admitted the chauffeur while Hashemi and the Farsi-speaking Infidel hid in the room next door. "I have a private message for His Highness," the Soviet had said.

In the sickroom the Soviet said, "Highness, I'm to give it to you when you're alone."

"Give it to me now. Ahmed is my most trusted counselor. Give it to me!" Reluctantly the man obeyed and Ahmed remembered the sudden flush that had rushed into the Khan's face the moment he began to read it.

"There is an answer?" the Soviet had said truculently.

Choked with rage the Khan had shaken his head and dismissed the man and had handed Ahmed the letter. It read: "My friend, I was shocked to hear about your illness and would be with you now but I have to stay here on urgent matters. I have bad news for you: it may be that you and your spy ring are betrayed to Inner Intelligence or SAVAMA—did you know that turncoat Abrim Pahmudi now heads this new version of SAVAK? If you're betrayed to Pahmudi, be prepared to defect at once or you'll quickly see the inside of a torture chamber. I have alerted our people to help you if necessary. If it appears safe, I will arrive Tuesday at dusk. Good luck."

The Khan had had no option but to show the message to the two men. "Is it true? About Pahmudi?"

"Yes. He's an old friend of yours, isn't he?" Fazir had said, taunting him.

"No . . . no he is not. Get out!"

"Certainly, Highness. Meanwhile this palace is under surveillance. There's no need to defect. Please do nothing to interfere with Mzytryk's arrival on Tuesday, do nothing to encourage any more revolt in Azerbaijan. As to Pahmudi and SAVAMA, they can do nothing here without my approval. I'm the law in Tabriz now. Obey and I'll protect you, disobey and you'll be his pishkesh!"

Then the two men had left, and the Khan had exploded with rage, more angry than Ahmed had ever seen him. The paroxysm became worse and worse then suddenly it ceased, the Khan was lying on the floor, and he was looking down on him, expecting to see him dead but he was not. Just a waxen pallor and twitching, breathing choked.

"As God wants," Ahmed muttered, not wanting to relive that night.

IN THE BLUE SALON: 11:15 A.M. When they were quite alone, Hakim swung Azadeh off her feet. "Oh, it's wonderful wonderful wonderful to see you again. . . ." she began, but he whispered, "Keep your voice down, Azadeh, there are ears everywhere and someone's sure to misinterpret everything and lie again."

"Najoud? May she be cursed forever an—"

"Shushhhh, darling, she can't hurt us now. I'm the heir, officially."

"Oh, tell me what happened, tell me everything!"

They sat on the long cushion sofa and Hakim could hardly get the words out fast enough. "First about Erikki: the ransom is 10 million rials, for him and the 212 an—"

"Father can bargain that down and pay, he can certainly pay, then find them and have them torn apart."

"Yes, yes, of course he can and he told me in front of Ahmed as soon as you're back he'll start and it's true he's made me his heir provided I swear by God to cherish little Hassan as I would cherish you—of course I did that happily at once—and said that you would also swear by God to do the same, that we would both swear to remain in Tabriz, me to learn how to follow him and you to be here to help me and oh we're going to be so happy!"

"That's all we have to do?" she asked incredulously.

"Yes, yes, that's all—he made me his heir in front of all the family—they looked as though they would die but that doesn't matter, Father named the conditions in front of them, I agreed at once, of course, as you will—why shouldn't we?"

"Of course, of course—anything! God is watching over us!" Again she embraced him, burying her face into his shoulder so that the tears of joy would be dried away. All the way back from Tehran, the journey rotten and Ahmed uncommunicative, she had been terrified what the "conditions" would be. But now? "It's unbelievable, Hakim, it's like magic! Of course we'll cherish little Hassan and you'll pass the Khanate on to him or his successors if that's Father's wish. God protect us and protect him and Erikki, and Erikki can fly as much as he likes—why shouldn't he? Oh, it's going to be wonderful." She dried her eyes. "Oh, I must look awful."

"You look wonderful. Now tell me what happened to you—I know only that you were caught in the village with . . . with the British saboteur and then somehow escaped."

"It was another miracle, only with the help of God, Hakim, but at the time terrible, that vile mullah—I can't remember how we got out only what Johnny . . . what Johnny told me. My Johnny Brighteyes, Hakim."

His eyes widened. "Johnny from Switzerland?"

"Yes. Yes it was him; he was the British officer."

"But how . . . It seems impossible."

"He saved my life, Hakim, and oh, there's so much to tell."

"When Father heard about the village he . . . you know the mullah was shot by Green Bands, don't you?"

"I don't remember it but Johnny told me."

"When Father heard about the village he had Ahmed drag the kalandar here, questioned him, then sent him back, had him stoned, the hands of the butcher cut off, and then the village burned. Burning the village was my idea—those dogs!"

Azadeh was greatly shocked. The whole village was too terrible a vengeance.

But Hakim allowed nothing to interrupt his euphoria. "Azadeh, Father's taken off the guard and I can go where I like—I even took a car and went into Tabriz today alone. Everyone treats me as heir, all the family, even Najoud, though I know she's gnashing her teeth and has to be guarded against. It's . . . it's not what I expected." He told her how he had been almost dragged from Khoi, expecting to be killed, or mutilated. "Don't you remember when I was banished, he cursed me and swore Shah Abbas knew how to deal with traitorous sons?"

She trembled, recollecting that nightmare, the curses and rage and so unfair, both of them innocent. "What made him change? Why should he change toward you, toward us?"

"The Will of God. God's opened his eyes. He has to know he's near death and must make provision . . . he's, he's the Khan. Perhaps he's frightened and wants to make amends. We were guilty of nothing against him. What does the reason matter? I don't care. We're free of the yoke at long last, free."

IN THE SICKROOM: 11:16 A.M.   The Khan's eyes opened. Without moving his head he looked to his limits. Ahmed, Aysha, and the guard. No nurse. Then he centered on Ahmed who was sitting on the floor. "You brought her?" He stammered the words with difficulty.

"Yes, Highness. A few minutes ago."

The nurse came into his field of vision. "How do you feel, Excellency?" she said in English as he had ordered her, telling her her Turkish was vile.

"S'ame."

"Let me make you more comfortable." With great tenderness and care—and strength—she lifted him and straightened the pillows and bed. "Do you need a bottle, Excellency?"

The Khan thought about that. "Yes."

She administered it and he felt befouled that it was done by an Infidel woman, but since she had arrived he had learned she was tremendously efficient, very wise and very good, the best in Tabriz, Ahmed had seen to that—so superior to Aysha who had proved to be totally useless. He saw Aysha smile at him tentatively, big eyes, frightened eyes. I wonder if I'll ever thrust it in again, up to its hilt, stiff as bone, like the first time, her tears and writhing improving the act, momentarily.

"Excellency?"

He accepted the pill and the sip of water and was glad for the cool of the nurse's hands that guided the glass. Then he saw Ahmed again and he smiled at him, glad his confidant was back. "Good jour'ney?"

"Yes, Highness."

"Will'ingly? Or with for'ce?"

Ahmed smiled. "It was as you planned, Highness. Willingly. Just as you planned."

"I dinna think you should talk so much, Excellency," the nurse said.

"Go aw'ay."

She patted his shoulder kindly. "Would you like some food, perhaps a little horisht?"

"Halvah."

"The doctor said sweets were not good for you."

"Halvah!"

Sister Bain sighed. The doctor had forbidden them and then added, "But if he insists you can give him them, as many as he wants, what does it matter now? Insha'Allah." She found them and popped one into his mouth and wiped the saliva away, and he chewed it with relish, nutty but smooth and oh so sweet.

"Your daughter's arrived from Tehran, Excellency," she said. "She asked me to tell her the moment you awoke."

Abdollah Khan was finding talking very strange. He would try to say the sentences, but his mouth did not open when it was supposed to open and the words stayed in his mind for a long time and then, when a simple form of what he wanted to say came out, the words were not well formed though they should have been. But why? I'm not doing anything differently than before. Before what? I don't remember, only a massive blackness and blood roaring and possessed by red-hot needles and not being able to breathe.

I can breathe now and hear perfectly and see perfectly and my mind's working perfectly and filled with plans as good as ever. It's just getting it all out. "Ho'w?"

"What, Excellency?"

Again the waiting. "How ta'lk better?"

"Ah," she said, understanding at once, her experience of strokes great. "Dinna worry, you'll find it just a wee bit difficult at first. As you get better, you'll regain all your control. You must rest as much as you can, that's very important. Rest and medicine, and patience, and you'll be as good as ever. All right?"

"Y'es."

"Would you like me to send for your daughter? She was very anxious to see you, such a pretty girl."

Waiting. "Late'r. See late'r. Go 'way, everyone . . . not Ahm'd."

Sister Bain hesitated, then again patted his hand kindly. "I'll give you ten minutes—if you promise to rest afterward. All right?"

"Y'es."

When they were alone Ahmed went closer to the bed. "Yes, Highness?"

"Wh'at time?"

Ahmed glanced at his wristwatch. It was gold and ornate and he admired it very much. "It's almost eleven-thirty on Tuesday."

"Pe'tr?"

"I don't know, Highness." Ahmed told him what Hakim had related. "If Petr comes today to Julfa, Fazir will be waiting for him."

"Insha'Allah. Az'deh?"

"She was genuinely worried about your health and agreed to come here at once. A moment ago I saw her together with your son. I'm sure she will agree to anything to protect him—as he will to protect her." Ahmed was trying to say everything clearly and concisely, not wanting to tire him. "What do you want me to do?"

"Ev'thing." Everything I've discussed with you and a little more, the Khan thought with relish, his excitement picking up: Now that Azadeh's back, cut the throat of the ransom messenger so the tribesmen in fury will do the same to the pilot; find out if those whelps're traitors by whatever means you want, and if they are, take out Hakim's eyes and send her north to Petr. If they're not, cut up Najoud slowly and keep them close-confined here, until the pilot's dead by whatever means, then send her north. And Pahmudi! Now I'm putting a price on his head that would tempt even Satan. Ahmed, offer it first to Fazir and tell him I want vengeance, I want Pahmudi racked, poisoned, cut up, mutilated, castrated . . .

His heart began creaking, palpitating, and he lifted his hand to rub his chest but his hand did not move. Not an inch. Even now as he looked down at it lying on the bedspread, willing it to move, there was no motion. Nothing. Nor feeling. Neither in his hand nor in his arm. Fear gushed through him.

Don't be afraid, the nurse said, he reminded himself desperately, sound of waves roaring in his ears. You've had a stroke, that's all, not a bad one the doctor said and he said many people have strokes. Old Komargi had one a year or so ago and he's still alive and active and claims he can still bed his young wife. With modern treatment . . . you're a good Muslim and you'll go to Paradise so there's nothing to fear, nothing to fear, nothing to fear . . . nothing to fear, if I die I go to Paradise. . . .

I don't want to die, he shrieked. I don't want to die, he shrieked again, but it was only in his head and no sound came out.

"What is it, Highness?"

He saw Ahmed's anxiety and that calmed him a little. God be thanked for Ahmed. I can trust Ahmed, he thought, sweat pouring out of him. Now what do I want him to do? "Fam'ly, all he're later. First Az'deh, H'kim, Naj'oud—under's'd?"

"Yes, Highness. To confirm the succession?"

"Y'es."

"I have your permission to question Her Highness?"

He nodded, his eyelids leaden, waiting for the pain in his chest to lessen. While he waited he moved his legs, feeling pins and needles in his feet. But nothing moved, not the first time, only the second, and only then with an effort. Terror rushed back into him. In panic he changed his mind: "Pay

ran'som quick'ly, get pil'ot here, Erikki here, me to Teh'ran. Under'stand?"
He saw Ahmed nod. "Quickly," he mouthed and motioned him to go but
his left hand still did not move. Terrified he tried his right hand and it
worked, not easily, but it moved. Part of his panic subsided. "Pay ran'som
no'w—kee'p secr't. Get nur'se."

AT THE JULFA TURNOFF: 6:25 P.M. Hashemi Fazir and Armstrong were once more in ambush under the snow-laden trees. Below the
Chevy waited, lights off, windows open, two men in the front seat, just as
before. Down the slope behind them both sides of the Julfa–Tabriz road
were primed for the intercept with half a hundred paramilitary poised. The
sun had vanished over the mountains and now the sky was blackening
perceptibly.

"He's not got much more time," Hashemi muttered again.

"He arrived at dusk last time. It's not dusk yet."

"Piss on him and his ancestors—I'm chilled to the bone."

"Not long now, Hashemi, old chap!" If it was up to him, Armstrong
knew he would wait forever to catch Mzytryk, alias Suslev, alias Brodnin.
He had offered to wait in Tabriz after the debacle on Saturday: "Leave me
the men, Hashemi, I'll lead the ambush Tuesday. You go back to Tehran,
I'll wait here and get him and bring him to you."

"No, I'll leave at once and be back early Tuesday. You can stay here."

"Here" was a safe house, an apartment overlooking the Blue Mosque,
warm and stocked with whisky. "You really meant what you said to Abdollah Khan, Hashemi, that now you're the law here and SAVAMA and
Pahmudi are powerless without your support?"

"Yes, oh, yes."

"Pahmudi really got under Abdollah's skin. What's that all about?"

"Pahmudi had Abdollah banned from Tehran."

"Christ! Why?"

"Old enmity, goes back years. Ever since Abdollah became Khan in '53,
he truculently advised various prime ministers and court officials to be cautious over political reforms and so-called modernizations. Pahmudi, the
well-bred, European-trained intellectual, despised him, was always against
him, always blocking him from private access to the Shah. Unfortunately
for the Shah, Pahmudi had the Shah's ear."

"To betray him in the end."

"Oh, yes, Robert, perhaps even from the beginning. The first time
Abdollah Khan and Pahmudi clashed openly was in '63 over the Shah's
proposed reforms, giving the women the vote, giving the voting franchise to

non-Muslims and allowing non-Muslims to be elected to the Majlis. Of course Abdollah, along with every thinking Iranian, knew this would bring an immediate outcry from all religious leaders, particularly Khomeini who was just getting into his stride then."

"Almost unbelievable that no one could get to the Shah," Armstrong had said, "to warn him."

"Many did, but no one with enough influence. Most of us agreed with Khomeini, openly or secretly. I did. Abdollah lost round after round with Pahmudi—against all our advice the Shah changed the calendar from the Islamic one as sacred to Muslims as B.C. and A.D. are to Christians and tried to force a phony counting back to Cyrus the Great . . . of course that blew the minds of all Muslims, and after near revolution it was withdrawn . . ." Hashemi finished his drink and poured another. "Then, publicly, Pahmudi told Abdollah to piss off, literally—I have it all documented— taunted him that he was stupid, behind the times, living in the Dark Ages, 'Is it any wonder coming from Azerbaijan,' and to stay out of Tehran until he was summoned or he would be arrested. Worse he jeered at him, at a major function, and had thinly veiled cartoons published in the press."

"I never took Pahmudi for that much of a fool," Armstrong said to encourage him to continue, wondering if he would make a slip and reveal something of value.

"Thank God he is—and why his days are numbered."

Armstrong remembered the strange confidence that had pervaded Hashemi and how unsettled he had been. The feeling had stayed with him all during the waiting for Hashemi to return to Tabriz, unwise to wander the streets that were still filled with rival mobs trying to possess them. During the day the police and loyalist army maintained the peace in the name of the Ayatollah—at night, it was difficult if not impossible to stop small groups of fanatics bent on violence from terrorizing parts of the city: "We can still stamp them out, easily, if that old devil Abdollah will help us," Hashemi had said angrily.

"Abdollah Khan still has so much power, even like that, half dead?"

"Oh, yes, he's still hereditary chief of a vast tribe—his wealth, hidden and real, would rival a shah's, not Mohammed Reza Shah's but certainly his father's."

"He's going to die soon. What then?"

"His heir'll have the same power—presuming that poor sonofabitch Hakim stays alive to use it. Did I tell you he's made him heir?"

"No. What's strange about that?"

"Hakim is his eldest son who's been banished to Khoi for years in disgrace. He's been brought back and reinstated."

"Why? Why was he banished?"

"The usual—he was caught plotting to send his father on—as Abdollah did his father."

"You're sure?"

"No, but curiously Abdollah's father died at your Mzytryk's dacha in Tbilisi." Hashemi smiled sardonically at the effect of his information. "Of apoplexy."

"How long have you known?"

"Long enough. We'll ask your Mzytryk if it's true when we catch him. We will catch him, though it'd certainly be easier with Abdollah alive." Hashemi became grimmer. "I hope he stays alive long enough to order support for us to stop the war. Then he can rot. I hate that vile old man for double-dealing and double-crossing and using us all for his own purposes, that's why I taunted him with Pahmudi. Sure I hate him, even so I'd never deliver him to Pahmudi, he's too much of a patriot in his own vile way. Well I'm off to Tehran, Robert, you know where to find me. You'd like company for your bed?"

"Just hot and cold running water."

"You should experiment a little, try a boy for a change. Oh, for the love of God don't be so embarrassed. There're so many times you disappoint me, I don't know why I'm so patient with you."

"Thanks."

"You English're all so depraved and twisted about sex, too many of you overt or covert homosexuals which the rest of you find disgusting and sinful and vile in the extreme, against the laws of God—which it isn't. And yet in Arabia where connection between men is historically normal and ordinary —because by law it's hands off a woman unless you're married to her or else —homosexuality as you understand it is unknown. So a man prefers sodomy, so what? That doesn't interfere with his masculinity here. Give yourself a new experience—life is short, Robert. Meanwhile, she'll be here to use if you wish. Don't insult me by paying her."

"She" had been Caucasian, Christian, attractive, and he had partaken of her without need or passion, for politeness, and had thanked her and let her sleep in the bed and stay the next day, to clean and cook and entertain him and then, before he awoke this morning, she had vanished.

Now Armstrong looked up into the western sky. It was much darker than before, the light going fast. They waited another half an hour.

"The pilot won't be able to see to land now, Robert. Let's leave."

"The Chevy hasn't moved yet." Armstrong took out his automatic and checked the action. "I'll leave when the Chevy leaves. Okay?"

The thickset Iranian stared at him, his face hard. "There'll be a car below, parked facing Tabriz. It'll take you to our safe house. Wait for me there—I'm going back to Tehran now; there are some important things that cannot wait, more important than this son of a dog—I think he knows we're on to him."

"When will you be back here?"

"Tomorrow—there's still the problem of the Khan." He stomped off into the darkness, cursing.

Armstrong watched him go, glad to be alone. Hashemi was becoming more and more difficult, more dangerous than usual, ready to explode, nerves too taut, too taut for a head of Inner Intelligence with so much power and a private band of trained assassins in secret. Robert, it's time to begin a bailout. I can't, I can't, not yet. Come on, Mzytryk, there's plenty of moonlight to land with, for God's sake.

Just after ten o'clock the Chevy's lights came on. The two men wound up the windows and drove away into the night. Carefully Armstrong lit a cigarette, his gloved hand cupping the tiny flame against the wind. The smoke pleased him greatly. When he had finished he threw the stub into the snow and stubbed it out. Then he too left.

NEAR THE IRAN-SOVIET BORDER: 11:05 P.M.   Erikki was pretending to sleep in the small, crude hut, his chin stubbled. A wick, floating in oil in an old chipped clay cup, was guttering and cast strange shadows. Embers in the rough stone fireplace glowed in the drafts. His eyes opened and he looked around. No one else was in the hut. Noiselessly he slid from under the blankets and animal skins. He was fully dressed. He put on his boots, made sure his knife was under his belt and went to the door, opened it softly.

For a moment he stood there, listening, head slightly on one side. Layers of high clouds misted the moon and the wind moved the lightest of the pine branches. The village was quiet under its coverlet of snow. No guards that he could see. No movement near the lean-to where the 212 was parked. Moving as a hunter would move, he skirted the huts and headed for the lean-to.

The 212 was bedded down, skins and blankets where they were most needed, all the doors closed. Through a side window of the cabin he could see two tribesmen rolled up in blankets sprawled full length on the seats, snoring. Rifles beside them. He eased forward slightly. The guard in the cockpit was cradling his gun, wide awake. He had not yet seen Erikki. Quiet footsteps approaching, the smell of goat and sheep and stale tobacco preceding them.

"What is it, pilot?" the young Sheik Bayazid asked softly.

"I don't know."

Now the guard heard them and he peered out of the cockpit window, greeted his leader, and asked what was the matter. Bayazid replied, "Nothing," waved him back on guard and searched the night thoughtfully. In the few days the stranger had been in the village he had come to like him and respect him, as a man and as a hunter. Today he had taken him into the forest, to test him, and then as a further test and for his own pleasure he had given him a rifle. Erikki's first shot killed a distant, difficult mountain goat as cleanly as he could have done. Giving the rifle was exciting, wondering what the stranger would do, if he would, foolishly, try to turn it on him or even more foolishly take off into the trees where they could hunt him with great enjoyment. But the Redhead of the Knife had just hunted and kept his thoughts to himself, though they could all sense the violence simmering.

"You felt something—danger?" he asked.

"I don't know." Erikki looked out at the night and all around. No sounds other than the wind, a few night animals hunting, nothing untoward. Even so he was unsettled. "Still no news?"

"No, nothing more." This afternoon one of the two messengers had returned. "The Khan is very sick, near death," the man had said. "But he promises an answer soon."

Bayazid had reported all this faithfully to Erikki. "Pilot, be patient," he said, not wanting trouble.

"What's the Khan sick with?"

"Sick—the messenger said they'd been told he was sick, very sick. Sick!"

"If he dies, what then?"

"His heir will pay—or not pay. Insha'Allah." The Sheik eased the weight of his assault rifle on his shoulder. "Come into the lee, it's cold." From the edge of the hut now they could see down into the valley. Calm and quiet, a few specks of headlights from time to time on the road far, far below.

Barely thirty minutes from the palace and Azadeh, Erikki was thinking. And no way to escape.

Every time he started engines to recharge his batteries and circulate the oil, five guns were pointing at him. At odd times he would stroll to the edge of the village or, like tonight, he would get up, ready to run and chance it on foot but never an opportunity, guards too alert. During the hunting today he had been sorely tempted to try to break out, useless of course, knowing they were just playing with him.

"It's nothing, pilot, go back to sleep," Bayazid said. "Perhaps there'll be good news tomorrow. As God wants."

Erikki said nothing, his eyes raking the darkness, unable to be rid of his foreboding. Perhaps Azadeh's in danger or perhaps . . . or perhaps it's nothing and I'm just going mad with the waiting and the worry and what's going on? Did Ross and the soldier make a break for it and what about Petr *matyeryebyets* Mzytryk and Abdollah? "As God wants, yes, I agree, but *I* want to leave. The time has come."

The younger man smiled, showing his broken teeth. "Then I will have to tie you up."

Erikki smiled back, as mirthlessly. "I'll wait tomorrow and tomorrow night, then the next dawn I leave."

"No."

"It will be better for you and better for me. We can go to the palace with your tribesmen, I can lan—"

"No. We wait."

"I can land in the courtyard, and I'll talk to him and you'll get the ransom and th—"

"No. We wait. We wait here. It's not safe there."

"Either we leave together or I leave alone."

The Sheik shrugged. "You have been warned, pilot."

AT THE PALACE OF THE KHAN: 11:38 P.M. Ahmed drove Najoud and her husband Mahmud down the corridor before him like cattle. Both were tousled and still in their bedclothes, both petrified, Najoud in tears, two guards behind them. Ahmed still had his knife out. Half an hour ago he had rushed into their quarters with the guards, dragged them out of their carpet beds, saying the Khan at long last knew they'd lied about Hakim and Azadeh plotting against him, because tonight one of the servants admitted he had overheard the same conversation and nothing wrong had been said.

"Lies," Najoud gasped, pressed against the carpet bed, half blinded by the flashlight that one of the guards directed at her face, the other guard holding a gun at Mahmud's head, "all lies . . ."

Ahmed slid out his knife, needle sharp, and poised it under her left eye. "Not lies, Highness! You perjured yourself to the Khan, *before God*, so I am here at the Khan's orders to take out your sight." He touched her skin with the point and she cried out, "No please I beg you I beg you please don't . . . wait wait . . ."

"You admit lying?"

"No. I never lied. Let me see my father he'd never order this without seeing me fir—"

"You'll never *see* him again! Why should he see you? You lied before and you'll lie again!"

"I . . . I never lied never lied . . ."

His lips twisted into a smile. For all these years he had known she had lied. It had mattered nothing to him. But now it did. "You lied, *in the Name of God.*" The point pricked the skin. The panic-stricken woman tried to scream but he held his other hand over her mouth and he was tempted to press the extra half inch, then out and in again the other side and out and all finished, finished forever. "Liar!"

"Mercy," she croaked, "mercy, in the Name of God . . ."

He relaxed his grip but not the point of the knife. "I cannot grant you mercy. Beg the mercy of God, the Khan has sentenced you!"

"Wait . . . wait," she said frantically, sensing his muscles tensing for the probe, "please . . . let me go to the Khan . . . let me ask his mercy I'm his daugh—"

"You admit you lied?"

She hesitated, eyes fluttering with panic along with her heart. At once the knife point went in a fraction and she gasped out, "I admit . . . I admit I exagg—"

"In God's name, did you lie or didn't you?" Ahmed snarled.

"Yes . . . yes . . . yes I did . . . please let me see my father . . . please." The tears were pouring out and he hesitated, pretending to be unsure of himself, then glared at her husband who lay on the carpet nearby quivering with terror. "You're guilty too!"

"I knew nothing about this, nothing," Mahmud stuttered, "nothing at all, I've never lied to the Khan never never I knew nothing . . ."

Ahmed shoved them both ahead of him. Guards opened the door of the sickroom. Azadeh and Hakim and Aysha were there, summoned at a moment's notice, in nightclothes, all frightened, the nurse equally, the Khan awake and brooding, his eyes bloodshot. Najoud went down on her knees and blurted out that she had exaggerated about Hakim and Azadeh and when Ahmed came closer she suddenly broke, "I lied I lied I lied please forgive me Father please forgive me . . . forgive me . . . mercy . . . mercy . . ." in a mumbling gibberish. Mahmud too was moaning and crying, saying he knew nothing about this or he would have spoken up, of course he would have, before God, of course he would, both of them begging for mercy—everyone knowing there would be none.

The Khan cleared his throat noisily. Silence. All eyes on him. His mouth worked but no sound came out. Both the nurse and Ahmed came closer. "Ah'med stay an'd Hakim, Aza'deh . . . res't go—*them* un'der gu'ard."

"Highness," the nurse said gently, "can it no' wait until tomorrow? You've tired yourself very much. Please, please make it tomorrow."

The Khan shook his head. "N'ow."

The nurse was very tired. "I dinna accept any responsibility, Excellency Ahmed. Please make it as short as possible." Exasperated, she walked out. Two guards pulled Najoud and Mahmud to their feet and dragged them away. Aysha followed shakily. For a moment the Khan closed his eyes, gathering his strength. Now only his heavy, throttled breathing broke the silence. Ahmed and Hakim and Azadeh waited. Twenty minutes passed. The Khan opened his eyes. For him the time had been only seconds. "My so'n, trus't Ahmed as fir'st confid'ant."

"Yes, Father."

"Swea'r by G'd, bo'th of you."

He listened carefully as they both chorused, "I swear by God I will trust Ahmed as first confidant." Earlier they had both sworn before all the family the same thing and everything else he required of them: to cherish and guard little Hassan; for Hakim to make Hassan his heir; for the two of them to stay in Tabriz, Azadeh to stay at least two years in Iran without leaving: "This way, Highness," Ahmed had explained earlier, "no alien outside influence, like that of her husband, could spirit her away before she's sent north, whether guilty or innocent."

That's wise, the Khan thought, disgusted with Hakim—and Azadeh— that they had allowed Najoud's perjury to be buried for so many years and to let it go unpunished for so many years—loathing Najoud and Mahmud for being so weak. No courage, no strength. Well, Hakim'll learn and she'll learn. If only I had more time . . .

"Aza'deh."

"Yes, Father?"

"Naj'oud. Wh'at punish'ment?"

She hesitated, frightened again, knowing how his mind worked, feeling the trap close on her. "Banishment. Banish her and her husband and family."

Fool, you'll never breed a Khan of the Gorgons, he thought, but he was too tired to say it so he just nodded and motioned her to leave. Before she left, Azadeh went to the bed and bent and kissed her father's hand. "Be merciful, please be merciful, Father." She forced a smile, touched him again, and then she left.

He watched her close the door. "Hak'im?"

Hakim also had detected the trap and was petrified of displeasing his father, wanting vengeance but not the malevolent sentence the Khan would pronounce. "Internal banishment forever, penniless," he said. "Let them earn their own bread in future and expel them from the tribe."

A little better, thought Abdollah. Normally that would be a terrible punishment. But not if you're a Khan and them a perpetual hazard. Again he moved his hand in dismissal. Like Azadeh, Hakim kissed his father's hand and wished a good night's sleep.

When they were alone, Abdollah said, "Ah'med?"

"Tomorrow banish them to the wastelands north of Meshed, penniless, with guards. In a year and a day when they're sure they've escaped with their lives, when they've got some business going or house or hut, burn it and put them to death—and their three children."

He smiled. "G'ood, do i't."

"Yes, Highness." Ahmed smiled back at him, very satisfied.

"Now sl'eep."

"Sleep well, Highness." Ahmed saw the eyelids close and the face fall apart. In seconds the sick man was snoring badly.

Ahmed knew he had to be most careful now. Quietly he opened the door. Hakim and Azadeh were waiting in the corridor with the nurse. Worriedly, the nurse went past him, took the Khan's pulse, peering at him closely.

"Is he all right?" Azadeh asked from the doorway.

"Who can say, lassie? He's tired himself, tired himself badly. Best you all leave now."

Nervously Hakim turned to Ahmed, "What did he decide?"

"Banished to the lands north of Meshed at first light tomorrow, penniless and expelled from the tribe. He will tell you himself tomorrow, Highness."

"As God wants." Azadeh was greatly relieved that worse had not been ordered. Hakim was glowing that his advice had been taken. "My sister and I, we, er, we don't know how to thank you for helping us, Ahmed, and, well, for bringing the truth out at long last."

"Thank you, Highness, but I only obeyed the Khan. When the time comes I will serve you as I serve His Highness, he made me swear it. Good night." Ahmed smiled to himself and closed the door and went back to the bed. "How is he?"

"No' so good, Agha." Her back was aching and she was sick with tiredness. "I must have a replacement tomorrow. We should have two nurses and a sister in charge. Sorry, but I canna continue alone."

"Whatever you want you will have, provided you stay. His Highness appreciates your care of him. If you like I will watch him for an hour or two. There's a sofa in the next room and I can call you in case anything happens."

"Oh, that's very kind of you, I'm sure. Thank you, I could use a wee rest, but call me if he wakes, and anyway in two hours."

He saw her into the next room, told the guard to relieve him in three hours and dismissed him, then began a vigil. Half an hour later he quietly peered in at her. She was deeply asleep. He came back into the sickroom and locked the door, took a deep breath, tousled his hair and rushed for the bed, shaking the Khan roughly. "Highness," he hissed as though in panic, "wake up, wake up!"

The Khan clawed his way out of leaden sleep, not knowing where he was or what had happened or if he was nightmaring again. "Wh'at . . . wh'at . . ." Then his eyes focused and he saw Ahmed, seemingly terrified which was unheard of. His spirit shuddered. "Wh'a—"

"Quick, you've got to get up, Pahmudi's downstairs, Abrim Pahmudi with SAVAMA torturers, they've come for you," Ahmed panted; "someone opened the door to them, you're betrayed, a traitor betrayed you to him, Hashemi Fazir's given you to Pahmudi and SAVAMA as a pishkesh, quick, get up, they've overpowered all the guards and they're coming to take you away . . ." He saw the Khan's gaping horror, the bulging eyes, and he rushed on: "There're too many to stop! Quick, you've got to escape . . ."

Deftly he unclipped the saline drip and tore the bedclothes back, started to help the frantic man to get up, abruptly shoved him back, and stared at the door. "Too late," he gasped, "listen, here they come, here they come, Pahmudi at the head, here they come!"

Chest heaving, the Khan thought he could hear their footsteps, could see Pahmudi, could see his thin gloating face and the instruments of torture in the corridor outside, knowing there would be no mercy and they would keep him alive to howl his life away. Demented he shouted at Ahmed, Quick, help me. I can get to the window, we can climb down if you help me! In the Name of God, Ahmedddddddd . . . but he could not make the words come out. Again he tried but still his mouth did not coordinate with his brain, his neck muscles stretched with effort, the veins overloaded.

It seemed forever he was screaming and shouting at Ahmed who just stood watching the door, not helping him, footsteps coming closer and closer. "He'lp," he managed to gasp, fighting to get out of bed, the sheets and coverlet weighing him down, restricting him, drowning him, chest pains growing and growing, monstrous now like the noise.

"There's no escape, they're here, I've got to let them in!"

At the limit of his terror he saw Ahmed start for the door. With the remains of his strength he shouted at him to stop but all that happened was a strangled croak. Then he felt something twist in his brain and something else snap. A spark leaped across the wires of his mind. Pain ceased, sound ceased. He saw Ahmed's smile. His ears heard the quiet of the corridor and silence of the palace and he knew that he was truly betrayed. With a last, all-embracing effort, he lunged for Ahmed, the fires in his head lighting his way down into the funnel, red and warm and liquid, and there, at the nadir, he blew out all the fire and possessed the darkness.

Ahmed made sure the Khan was dead, glad that he had not had to use the pillow to smother him. Hastily he reconnected the saline drip, checked that there were no telltale leaks, partially straightened the bed, and then, with great care, examined the room. Nothing to give him away that he could see. His breathing was heavy, his head throbbing, and his exhilaration immense. A second check, then he walked over to the door, quietly unlocked it, noiselessly returned to the bed. The Khan was lying sightlessly against the pillows, blood hemorrhaged from his nose and mouth.

"Highness!" he bellowed. "Highness . . ." then leaned forward and grabbed him for a moment, released him, and rushed across the room, tore open the door. "Nurse!" he shouted and rushed into the next room, grabbed the woman out of her deep sleep and half carried, half dragged her back to the Khan.

"Oh, my God," she muttered, weak with relief that it had not happened while she was alone, perhaps to be blamed by this knife-wielding, violent bodyguard or these mad people, screaming and raving. Sickly awake now, she wiped her brow and pushed her hair into shape, feeling naked without her headdress. Quickly she did what she had to and closed his eyes, her ears hearing Ahmed moaning and grief-stricken. "Nothing anyone could do, Agha," she was saying. "It could have happened any time. He was in a great deal of pain, his time had come, better this way, better than living as a vegetable."

"Yes . . . yes, I suppose so." Ahmed's tears were real. Tears of relief. "Insha'Allah. Insha'Allah."

"What happened?"

"I . . . I was dozing and he just . . . just gasped and started to bleed from his nose and mouth." Ahmed wiped some of the tears away, letting his voice break. "I grabbed him as he was falling out of bed and then . . . then I don't know I . . . he just collapsed and . . . and I came running for you."

"Dinna worry, Agha, nothing anyone could do. Sometimes it's sudden and quick, sometimes not. Better to be quick, that's a blessing." She sighed and straightened her uniform, glad it was over and now she could leave this place. "He, er, he should be cleaned before the others are summoned."

"Yes. Please let me help, I wish to help."

Ahmed helped her sponge away the blood and make him presentable and all the time he was planning: Najoud and Mahmud to be banished before noon, the rest of their punishment a year and a day from now; find out if Fazir caught Petr Oleg; make sure the ransom messenger's throat was cut this afternoon as he had ordered in the Khan's name.

Fool, he said to the corpse, fool to think I'd arrange to pay ransom to bring back the pilot to fly you to Tehran to save your life. Why save a life for a few more days or a month? Dangerous to be sick and helpless with your sickness, minds become deranged, oh, yes, the doctor told me what to expect, losing more of your mind, more vindictive than ever, more danger- ous than ever, dangerous enough to perhaps turn on me! But now, now the succession is safe, I can dominate the whelp and with the help of God marry Azadeh. Or send her north—her hole's like any other.

The nurse watched Ahmed from time to time, his deft strong hands and their gentleness, for the first time glad of his presence and not afraid of him, now watching him combing the beard. People are so strange, she thought. He must have loved this evil old man very much.

WEDNESDAY
February 28

TEHRAN: 6:55 A.M. McIver continued sorting through the files and papers he had taken from the big office safe, putting only those that were vital into his briefcase. He had been at it since five-thirty this morning and now his head ached, his back ached, and the briefcase was almost full. So much more I should be taking, he thought, working as fast as he could. In an hour, perhaps less, his Iranian staff would arrive, and he would have to stop.

Bloody people, he thought irritably, never here when we wanted them but now for the last few days, can't get rid of them, like bloody limpets: "Oh, no, Excellency, please allow me to lock up for you, I beg you for the privilege . . ." or "Oh, no, Excellency, I'll open the office for you, I insist, that is not the job of Your Excellency." Maybe I'm getting paranoid, but it's just as though they're spies, ordered in to watch us, the partners more nosy than ever. Almost as though someone's on to us.

And yet, so far—touch wood—everything's working like a well-tuned jet:

us out by noon today or a little after; already Rudi's poised for Friday with all of his extra bods and a whole load of spares already out of Bandar Delam by road to Abadan where a BA Trident snuck in, cleared by Duke's friend Zataki to evacuate British oilers; at Kowiss, by now Duke should have cached the extra fuel, all his lads still cleared to leave tomorrow on the 125 —touch more wood—already three truckloads of spares out to Bushire for transshipment to Al Shargaz; Hotshot, Colonel Changiz, and that damned mullah, Hussain, still behaving themselves, fifty times touch wood; at Lengeh Scrag'll be having no problems, plenty of coastal ships available for his spares and nothing more to do but wait for D—no, not D day—W day.

Only bad spot, Azadeh. And Erikki. Why the devil didn't she tell me before leaving on a wild-goose chase after poor old Erikki? My God, she escapes Tabriz with the skin of her skin and then goes and puts her pretty little head back in it. Women! They're all crazy. Ransom? Balls! I'll bet it's another trap set by her father, the rotten old bastard. At the same time, it's just as Tom Lochart said: She would have gone anyway, Mac, and would you have told her about Whirlwind?

His stomach began churning. Even if the rest of us get out there's still the problem of Erikki and Azadeh. Then there's poor old Tom and Sharazad. How the hell can we get those four to safety? Must come up with something. We've two more days, perhaps by th—

He whirled, startled, not having heard the door open. His chief clerk, Gorani, stood in the doorway, tall and balding, a devout Shi'ite, a good man who had been with them for many years. "Salaam, Agha."

"Salaam. You're early." McIver saw the man's open surprise at all the mess—normally McIver was meticulously tidy—and felt as though he'd been caught with his hand in the chocolate box.

"As God wants, Agha. The Imam's ordered normality and everyone to work hard for the success of the revolution. Can I help?"

"Well, er, no, no, thank you, I, er, I'm just in a hurry. I've lots to do today, I'm off to the embassy." McIver knew his voice was running away from him but he was unable to stop it. "I've, er, appointments all day and must be at the airport by noon. I have to do some homework for the Doshan Tappeh komiteh. I won't come back to the office from the airport so you can close early, take the afternoon off—in fact you can take the day off."

"Oh, thank you, Agha, but the office should remain open until the us—"

"No, we'll close for the day when I leave. I'll go straight home and be there if I'm needed. Please come back in ten minutes, I want to send some telexes."

"Yes, Agha, certainly, Agha." The man left.

McIver hated the twistings of the truth. What's going to happen to Gorani? he asked himself again, to him and all the rest of our people all over Iran, some of them fine, them and their families?

Unsettled, he finished as best he could. There were 100,000 rials in the cashbox. He left the notes, relocked the safe, and sent some inconsequential telexes. The main one he had sent at five-thirty this morning to Al Shargaz with a copy to Aberdeen in case Gavallan had been delayed: "Air freighting the five crates of parts to Al Shargaz for repairs as planned." Translated, the code meant that Nogger, Pettikin and he, and the last two mechanics he had not yet been able to get out of Tehran, were readying to board the 125 today, as planned, and it was still all systems go.

"Which crates are these, Agha?" Somehow Gorani had found the copies of the telex.

"They're from Kowiss, they'll go on the 125 next week."

"Oh, very well. I'll check it for you. Before you go, could you please tell me when does our 212 return? The one we lent to Kowiss."

"Next week, why?"

"Excellency Minister and Board Director Ali Kia wanted to know, Agha."

McIver was instantly chilled. "Oh? Why?"

"He probably has a charter for it, Agha. His assistant came here last night, after you had left, and he asked me. Minister Kia also wanted a progress report today of our three 212s sent out for repairs. I, er, I said I would have it today—he's coming this morning so I can't close the office."

They had never discussed the three aircraft, or the peculiarly great number of spares they had been sending out by truck, car, or as personal baggage —no aircraft space for freight. It was more than possible that Gorani would know the 212s did not need repair. He shrugged and hoped for the best. "They'll be ready as planned. Leave a note on the door."

"Oh, but that would be very impolite. I will relay that message. He said he would return before noon prayer and particularly asked for an appointment with you. He has a very private message from Minister Kia."

"Well, I'm going to the embassy." McIver debated a moment. "I'll be back as soon as I can." Irritably he picked up the briefcase and hurried down the stairs, cursing Ali Kia and then adding a curse for Ali Baba too.

Ali Baba—so named because he reminded McIver of the Forty Thieves —was the wheedling half of their live-in couple who had been with them for two years but had vanished at the beginning of the troubles. Yesterday at dawn Ali Baba came back, beaming and acting as though he had just been away for the weekend instead of almost five months, happily insisting he take their old room back: "Oh, most definitely, Agha, the home has to be most clean and prepared for the return of Her Highness; next week my wife will be here to do that but meanwhile I bring you tea-toast in a most instant as you ever liked. May I be sacrificed for you but I bargained mightily today for fresh bread and milk from the market at the oh so reasonable best price for me only, but the robbers charge five times last year's, so sad, but please give me the money now, and as most soon as the bank is opened you can pay me my mucroscupic back salary . . ."

Bloody Ali Baba, the revolution hasn't changed him a bit. "Microscopic"? It's still one loaf for us and five for him, but never mind, it was fine to have tea and toast in bed—but not the day before we sneak out. How the hell are Charlie and I going to get our baggage out without him smelling the proverbial rat?

In the garage he unlocked his car. "Lulu, old girl," he said, "sorry, there's bugger all I can do about it, it's time for the Big Parting. Don't quite know how I'm going to do it, but I'm not leaving you as a burnt offering or for some bloody Iranian to rape."

Talbot was waiting for him in a spacious, elegant office. "My dear Mr. McIver, you're bright and early, I heard all the adventures of young Ross— my word we were all very lucky, don't you think?"

"Yes, yes, we were, how is he?"

"Getting over it. Good man, did a hell of a good job. I'm seeing him for lunch and we're getting him out on today's BA flight—just in case he's been spotted, can't be too careful. Any news of Erikki? We've had some inquiries from the Finnish embassy asking for help."

McIver told him about Azadeh's note. "Bloody ridiculous."

Talbot steepled his fingers. "Ransom doesn't sound too good. There's, er, there's a rumor the Khan's very sick indeed. Stroke."

McIver frowned. "Would that help or hurt Azadeh and Erikki?"

"I don't know. If he does pop off, well, it'll certainly change the balance of power in Azerbaijan for a while, which will certainly encourage our misguided friends north of the border to agitate more than usual, which'll cause Carter and his powers-that-be to fart more dust."

"What the devil's he doing now?"

"Nothing, old boy, sweet Fanny Adams—that's the trouble. He scattered his peanuts and scarpered."

"Anything more on us being nationalized—Armstrong said it's imminent."

"It might well be you'll lose positive control of your aircraft imminently," Talbot said with studied care and McIver's attention zeroed. "It, er, might be more of a personal acquisition by interested parties."

"You mean Ali Kia and the partners?"

Talbot shrugged. "Ours not to reason why, eh?"

"This is official?"

"My dear chap, good Lord, no!" Talbot was quite shocked. "Just a personal observation, off the record. What can I do for you?"

"Off the record, on Andy Gavallan's instructions, all right?"

"Let's have it on the record."

McIver saw the slightly pink humorless face and got up, relieved. "No way, Mr. Talbot. It was Andy's idea to keep you in the picture, not mine."

Talbot sighed with practiced eloquence. "Very well, off the record."

McIver sat. "We're, er, we're transferring our HQ to Al Shargaz today."

"Very wise. So?"

"We're going today. All remaining expat personnel. On our 125."

"Very wise. So?"

"We're, er, we're closing down all operations in Iran. On Friday."

Talbot sighed wearily. "Without personnel I'd say that's axiomatic. So?"

McIver was finding it very hard to say what he wanted to say. "We, er, we're taking our aircraft out on Friday—this Friday."

"Bless my soul," Talbot said in open admiration. "Congratulations! How on earth did you twist that rotter Kia's arm to get the permits? You must've promised him a life membership at the Royal Box at Ascot!"

"Er, no, no, we didn't. We decided not to apply for exit permits, waste of time." McIver got up. "Well, see you soo—"

Talbot's face almost fell off his face. "No permits?"

"No. You know yourself our birds're going to be nicked, nationalized, taken over, whatever you want to call it, there's no way we could get exit permits so we're just going." McIver added airily, "Friday we flit the coop."

"Oh, my word!" Talbot was shaking his head vigorously, his fingers toying with a file on his desk. "Bless my soul, very very un-bloody-wise."

"There isn't any alternative. Well, Mr. Talbot, that's all, have a nice day. Andy wanted to forewarn you so you could . . . so you could do whatever you want to do."

"What the hell is that?" Talbot exploded.

"How the hell do I know?" McIver was equally exasperated. "You're supposed to protect your nationals."

"But y—"

"I'm just not going to be put out of business and that's the end of it!"

Talbot's fingers drummed nervously. "I think I need a cup of tea." He clicked on the intercom. "Celia, two cups of the best and I think you better insert a modest amount of Nelson's Blood into the brew."

"Yes, Mr. Talbot," the adenoidal voice said and sneezed.

"Bless you," Talbot said automatically. His fingers stopped drumming and he smiled sweetly at McIver. "I'm awfully glad you didn't tell me anything about anything, old boy."

"So'm I."

"Rest assured, should I ever hear that you're in pokey doing—what's the expression? Ah, yes, 'doing porridge'—I shall be glad to visit you on behalf of Her Majesty's Government and attempt to extricate you from the errors of your ways." Talbot's eyebrows went off his forehead. "Grand larceny! Bless my soul, but jolly good luck, old boy."

IN AZADEH'S APARTMENT: 8:10 A.M. The old maidservant carried the heavy silver breakfast tray along the corridor—four boiled eggs, toast and butter and marmalade, two exquisite coffee cups, steaming coffeepot, and the finest Egyptian cotton napkins. She put the tray down and knocked.

"Come in."

"Good morning, Highness. Salaam."

"Salaam," Sharazad said dully. She was propped against the many pillows of the carpet bed, her face puffy from tears. The bathroom door was ajar, sound of water running. "You can put it here, on the bed."

"Yes, Highness." The old woman obeyed. With a sidelong glance at the bathroom, she left silently.

"Breakfast, Tommy," Sharazad called out, trying to sound bright. No answer. She half shrugged to herself, sniffed a little, more tears not far away, then looked up as Lochart came back into the bedroom. He was shaved and dressed in winter flying gear—boots, trousers, shirt, and heavy sweater. "Coffee?" she asked with a tentative smile, hating his set face and the air of disapproval that he wore.

"In a minute," he said without enthusiasm. "Thank you."

"I . . . I ordered everything just as you like it."

"Looks good—don't wait for me." He went over to the bureau and began to tie his tie.

"It really was wonderful of Azadeh to lend us the apartment while she's away, wasn't it? So much nicer than home."

Lochart looked at her in the mirror. "You didn't say that at the time."

"Oh, Tommy, of course you're right but please don't let's quarrel."

"I'm not. I've said it all and so have you." I've had that, he thought, anguished, knowing she was as miserable as he was but unable to do anything about it. When Meshang had challenged him in front of her and Zarah, two nights ago, the nightmare had begun that continued even now, tearing them apart, bringing him to the edge of madness. Two days and nights of broken tears and him saying over and over, "No need to worry, we'll manage somehow, Sharazad," and then discussing the future. What future? he asked his reflection, once more wanting to explode.

"Here's your coffee, darling Tommy."

Glumly he took it, sat on a chair facing her, not looking at her. The coffee was hot and excellent but it did not take away the foul taste in his mouth, so he left it almost untouched and got up and went for his flight jacket. Thank God I've today's ferry to Kowiss, he thought. Goddamn everything!

"When do I see you, darling, when do you come back?"

He watched himself shrug, hating himself, wanting to take her in his arms and tell her the depth of his love but he had been through that agony four times in the last two days and she was still as relentless and inflexible as her brother: "Leave Iran? Leave home forever?" she had cried out. "Oh, I can't, I can't!"

"But it won't be forever, Sharazad. We'll spend some time in Al Shargaz then go to England, you'll love England and Scotland and Aberd—"

"But Meshang says th—"

"Screw Meshang!" he had shouted and saw the fear in her and that only served to whip his anger into a frenzy. "Meshang's not God Almighty, for Christ's sake! What the goddamn hell does he know?" and she had sobbed like a terrified child, cowering away from him. "Oh, Sharazad, I'm so sorry . . ." Taking her into his arms, almost crooning his love to her, she safe in his arms.

"Tommy, listen, my darling, you were right and I was wrong, it was my fault, but I know what to do, tomorrow I'll go and see Meshang, I'll persuade him to give us an allowance and . . . what's the matter?"

"You haven't heard a goddamned word I've said."

"Oh, but I have, yes, indeed, I listened very carefully, please don't be angry again, you're right of course to be angry but I list—"

Flaring back: "Didn't you hear what Meshang said? We've no money— the money's finished, the building's finished, he has total control over the family money, total, and unless you obey him and not me you'll get nothing more. But that's not important, I can make enough for us! I can! The point is we have to leave Tehran. Leave for . . . for a little while."

"But I haven't any papers, I haven't, Tommy, and can't get any yet and Meshang's right when he says if I leave without papers they'll never let me back, never, never."

More tears and more arguing, not being able to get through to her, more tears, then going to bed, trying to sleep, no sleep for either of them. "You can stay here, Tommy. Why can't you stay here, Tommy?"

"Oh, for Christ's sake, Sharazad, Meshang made that very clear. I'm not wanted and foreigners are out. We'll go somewhere else. Nigeria, or Aberdeen, somewhere else. Pack a suitcase. You'll get on the 125 and we'll meet at Al Shargaz—you've a Canadian passport. You're Canadian!"

"But I can't leave without papers," she wailed and sobbed and the same arguments, over and over, and more tears.

Then, yesterday morning, hating himself, he had put aside his pride and had gone to the bazaar to reason with Meshang, to get him to relent—all that he was going to say painstakingly worked out. But he had come up against a wall as high as the sky. And worse.

"My father held a controlling interest in the IHC partnership, which of course I inherit."

"Oh, that's wonderful, that makes all the difference, Meshang."

"It makes no difference at all. The point is how do you intend to pay your debts, pay your ex-wife, and pay for my sister and her child without a very great infusion of charity?"

"A job's not charity, Meshang, it's not charity. It could be mightily profitable for both of us. I'm not suggesting a partnership, anything like that, I'd work for you. You don't know the helicopter business, I do, inside out. I could run the new partnership for you, make it instantly profitable. I know pilots and how to operate. I know all of Iran, most of the fields. That would solve everything for both of us. I'd work like hell to protect the family interests, we'd stay in Tehran, Sharazad could have the baby here an—"

"The Islamic state will require Iranian pilots only, Minister Kia assures me. One hundred percent."

Sudden understanding. His universe abruptly ripped asunder. "Ah, now I get it, no exceptions, eh, particularly me?"

He had seen Meshang shrug disdainfully. "I'm very busy. To be blunt, you cannot stay in Iran. You've no future in Iran. Out of Iran Sharazad has no future of any value with you and she will never permanently exile herself —which will happen if she goes without my permission and without proper papers. Therefore you must divorce."

"No."

"Send Sharazad back from the Khan's apartment this afternoon—more charity by the way—and leave Tehran immediately. Your marriage wasn't Muslim so it's unimportant—the Canadian civil ceremony will be annulled."

"Sharazad will never agree."

"Oh? Be at my house at 6:00 P.M. and we will make final this matter. After you've left I'll settle your Iranian debts—I cannot have bad debts hanging over our good name. 6:00 P.M. sharp. Good morning."

Not remembering how he got back to the apartment but telling her and more tears and then to the Bakravan house that evening and Meshang repeating what he had said, infuriated with Sharazad's abject begging: "Don't be ridiculous, Sharazad! Stop howling, this is for your own good, your son's good, and the family's good. If you leave on a Canadian passport without proper Iranian papers you'll never be allowed back. Live in Aberdeen? God protect you, you'd die of cold in a month and so would your son. . . . Nanny Jari won't go with you, not that he could pay for her; she's not mad, she won't leave Iran and her family forever. You'll never see us again, think of that . . . think of your son . . ." over and over until Sharazad was reduced to incoherence and Lochart to pulp.

"Tommy."

This brought him out of his reverie. "Yes?" he asked, hearing the old tone to her voice.

"Thou, art thou leaving me forever?" she said in Farsi.

"I can't stay in Iran," he said, at peace now, the "thou" helping so very much. "When we're closed down there's no job for me here, I've no money, and even if the place hadn't burned down . . . well, I was never one for handouts." His eyes were without guile. "Meshang's right about a lot of things: there wouldn't be much of a life with me and you're right to stay, certainly without papers it'd be dangerous to leave, and you've to think of the child, I know that. There's also . . . no, let me finish," he said kindly, stopping her. "There's also HBC." This reminded him about her cousin, Karim. Another horror yet to arrive. Poor Sharazad . . .

"Thou, art thou leaving me forever?"

"I'm leaving today for Kowiss. I'll be there a few days then I'll go to Al Shargaz. I'll wait there, I'll wait a month. This will give you time to think it through, what you want. A letter or telex care of Al Shargaz Airport will find me. If you want to join me, the Canadian embassy'll arrange it at once, priority, I've already fixed that . . . and of course I'll keep in touch."

"Through Mac?"

"Through him or somehow."

"Thou, art thou divorcing me?"

"No, never. If you want that or . . . let me put it another way, if you think it's necessary to protect our child, or for whatever reason, then whatever you want I will do."

The silence grew and she watched him, a strange look in her huge dark eyes, somehow older than before and yet so much younger and more frail, the translucent nightgown enhancing the sheen of her golden skin, her hair flowing around her shoulders and breasts.

Lochart was consumed with helplessness, dying inside, wanting to stay, knowing there was no longer any reason to stay. It's all been said and now it's up to her. If I was her I wouldn't hesitate, I'd divorce, I'd've never have married in the first place. "Thou," he said in Farsi, "fare thee well, Beloved."

"And thee, Beloved."

He picked up his jacket and left. In a moment she heard the front door close. For a long time she stared after him, then, thoughtfully, poured some coffee and sipped it, hot and strong and sweet and life-giving.

As God wants, she told herself, at peace now. Either he will come back or he will not come back. Either Meshang will relent or he will not relent. Either way I must be strong and eat for two and think good thoughts while I build my son.

She decapitated the first of the eggs. It was perfectly cooked and tasted delicious.

AT McIVER'S APARTMENT: 11:50 A.M. Pettikin came into the living room carrying a suitcase and was surprised to see the servant, Ali Baba, tentatively polishing the sideboard. "I didn't hear you come back. I thought I'd given you the day off," he said irritably, putting down the suitcase.

"Oh, yes, Agha, but there is most much to do, the place she is filth-filled and the kitchen . . ." His lush brown eyebrows rose to heaven.

"Yes, yes, that's true but you can start in tomorrow." Pettikin saw him looking at the suitcase and swore. Directly after breakfast he had sent Ali Baba off for the day with instructions to be back at midnight, which normally would mean that he would not come back until the next morning. "Now off you go."

"Yes, Agha, you are going on holiday or on the leaves?"

"No, I'm, er, I'm going to stay with one of the pilots for a few days, so make sure my room's cleaned tomorrow. Oh, yes, and you better give me your key, I've misplaced mine." Pettikin held out his hand, cursing himself for not thinking of it before. With curious reluctance, Ali Baba gave it to him. "Captain McIver wants the place to himself, he has work to do and doesn't want to be disturbed. See you soon, good-bye!"

"But, Agha . . ."

"Good-bye!" He made sure Ali Baba had his coat, opened the door, half shoved him out, and closed it again. Nervously he glanced again at his watch. Almost noon and still no McIver and they were supposed to be at the airport by now. He went into the bedroom, reached into the cupboard for the other suitcase, also packed, then came back and put it beside the other one, near the front door.

Two small cases and a carryall, he thought. Not much to show for all the years in Iran. Never mind, I prefer to travel light and perhaps this time I can get lucky and make more money or start a business on the side and then there's Paula. How in the hell can I afford to get married again? Married? Are you mad? An affair's about all you could manage. Yes, but God damn, I'd like to marry her an—

The phone rang and he almost jumped out of himself, so unused to its ringing. He picked it up, his heart pounding. "Hello?"

"Charlie? It's me, Mac, thank God the bloody thing's working, tried it on the off chance. I've been delayed."

"You've a problem?"

"Don't know, Charlie, but I've got to go and see Ali Kia—bastard's sent his bloody assistant and a Green Band to fetch me."

"What the hell does Kia want?" Outside, all over the city, muezzins began calling the Faithful to noon prayer, distracting him.

"Don't know. The appointment's in half an hour. You'd better go on out to the airport and I'll get there as soon as I can. Get Johnny Hogg to delay."

"Okay, Mac. What about your gear, is it in the office?"

"I snuck it out early this morning while Ali Baba was snoring, and it's in Lulu's boot. Charlie, there's one of Genny's needlepoints in the kitchen, 'Down with cornbeef pie.' Stick it in your suitcase for me, will you? She'd have my guts for garters if I forgot that. If I've time I'll come back and make sure everything's okay."

"Do I shut the gas off, or electricity?"

"Christ, I don't know. Leave it, okay?"

"All right. You sure you don't want me to wait?" he asked, the metallic, loudspeaker voices of muezzins adding to his disquiet. "I don't mind waiting. Might be better, Mac."

"No, you go on out. I'll be there right smartly. 'Bye."

" 'Bye." Pettikin frowned, then, having a dialing tone, he dialed their office at the airport. To his astonishment the connection went through.

"Iran Helicopters, hello?"

He recognized the voice of their freight manager. "Morning, Adwani, this's Captain Pettikin. Has the 125 come in yet?"

"Ah, Captain, yes it's in the pattern and should be landing any minute."

"Is Captain Lane there?"

"Yes, just a moment please . . ."

Pettikin waited, wondering about Kia.

"Hello, Charlie, Nogger here—you've friends in high places?"

"No, the phone just started working. Can you talk privately?"

"No. Not possible. What's cooking?"

"I'm still at the flat. Mac's been delayed—he's got to go and see Ali Kia. I'm on my way to the airport now and he'll come directly from Kia's office. Are you ready to load?"

"Yes, Charlie, we're sending the engines for repairs and reconditioning as Captain McIver ordered. Everything as ordered."

"Good, are the two mecs there?"

"Yes. Both those spares are also ready for shipping."

"Good. No problem that you can see?"

"Not yet, old chum."

"See you." Pettikin hung up. He packed the needlepoint and looked around the apartment a last time, now curiously saddened. Good times and bad times but the best when Paula was staying. Out of the window he noticed distant smoke over Jaleh and now as the muezzins' voices died away, the usual sporadic gunfire. "The hell with all of them," he muttered. He got up and went out with his luggage and locked the door carefully. As he drove out of the garage he saw Ali Baba duck back into a doorway across the road. With him were two other men he had never seen before. What the hell's that bugger up to? he thought uneasily.

AT THE MINISTRY OF TRANSPORT: 1:07 P.M. The huge room was freezing in spite of a log fire, and Minister Ali Kia wore a heavy, expensive Astrakhan overcoat with a hat to match, and he was angry. "I repeat, I need transport to Kowiss tomorrow and I require you to accompany me."

"Can't tomorrow, sorry," McIver said, keeping his nervousness off his face with difficulty. "I'd be glad to join you next week. Say Monday an—"

"I'm astonished that after all the 'cooperation' I've given you it's necessary even to argue! Tomorrow, Captain, or . . . or I shall cancel all clearances for our 125—in fact, I'll hold it on the ground today, impound it today pending investigations!"

McIver was standing in front of the vast desk, Kia sitting behind it in a big carved chair that dwarfed him. "Could you make it today, Excellency? We've an Alouette to ferry to Kowiss. Captain Lochart's leav—"

"Tomorrow. Not today." Kia flushed even more. "As ranking board director you are ordered: you *will* come with me, we *will* leave at ten o'clock. Do you understand?"

McIver nodded bleakly, trying to figure a way out of the trap. Then pieces of a tentative plan fell into place. "Where do you want to meet?"

"Where's the helicopter?"

"Doshan Tappeh. We'll need a clearance. Unfortunately there's a Major Delami there, along with a mullah, and both're rather difficult, so I don't see how we can do it."

Kia's face darkened even more. "The PM's given new orders about mullahs and interference with the legal government and the Imam agrees wholeheartedly. They both better behave. I will see you at ten tomorrow an—"

At that moment there was a large explosion outside. They rushed to the window but could see only a cloud of smoke billowing into the cold sky from around the bend in the road. "Sounded like another car bomb," McIver said queasily. Over the last few days there had been a number of assassination attempts and car bomb attacks by left-wing extremists, mostly on high-ranking ayatollahs in the government.

"Filthy terrorists, may God burn their fathers, and them!" Kia was clearly frightened, which pleased McIver.

"The price of fame, Minister," he said, his voice heavy with concern. "Those in high places, important people like you, are obvious targets."

"Yes . . . yes . . . we know, we know. Filthy terrorists . . ."

McIver smiled all the way back to his car. So Kia wants to go to Kowiss. I'll see he bloody gets to Kowiss and Whirlwind continues as planned.

Around the corner, the main road ahead was partially blocked with debris, a car still on fire, others smoldering, and a hole in the roadbed where the parked car bomb had exploded, blowing out the front of a restaurant and the shuttered foreign bank beside it, glass from them and other shop windows scattered everywhere. Many injured, dead or dying. Agony and panic and the stink of burning rubber.

Traffic was jammed both ways. There was nothing to do but wait. After half an hour an ambulance arrived, some Green Bands, and a mullah began directing traffic. In time McIver was waved forward, cursed forward. Easing past the wreckage, all traffic enraged and blaring, he did not notice the headless body of Talbot half buried under the restaurant debris, nor recognize Ross dressed in civvies, lying unconscious nearby, half against the wall, his coat ripped, blood seeping from his nose and ears.

AL SHARGAZ AIRPORT FOYER—ACROSS THE GULF: 2:05 P.M. Scot Gavallan was among the crowd waiting outside the Custom and Immigration area, his right arm in a sling. From the loudspeaker came air traffic announcements in Arabic and English, and the big arrival and departure board clattered, fixing schedules and boarding gates, the whole terminal thriving. He saw his father come through the green door, his face lit up, and he went forward to intercept him. "Hi, Dad!"

"Oh, Scot, laddie!" Gavallan said happily and hugged him back but carefully, because of his shoulder. "How are you?"

"I'm fine, Dad, really. I told you, I'm fine now."

"Yes, I can see that." Since Gavallan had left on Monday he had spoken to his son by phone many times. But talking on the phone's not the same, he thought. "I—I was so worried . . ."

Gavallan had not wanted to leave at all but the English doctor at the hospital had assured him Scot was all right, and there were urgent business problems in England and the postponed board meeting to deal with. "The X rays show no bone damage, Mr. Gavallan. The bullet's gone through part of the muscle, the wound nasty but repairable." To Scot the doctor had said: "It'll ache a lot and you won't be flying for two months or more. As to the tears . . . no need to worry either. It's just a fairly normal reaction to a gunshot wound. The flight from Zagros didn't help—you escaped in a coffin, you say? That's enough to give you the heebie-jeebies, let alone being shot. It would me. We'll keep you overnight."

"Is that necessary, Doctor? I'm . . . I'm feeling much better . . ." Scot had got up, his knees had given way on him, and he would have fallen if Gavallan had not been ready to catch him.

"First we have to fix you up. A good sleep and he'll be as right as rain, Mr. Gavallan, promise you." The doctor gave Scot a sedative and Gavallan had stayed with him, reassuring him about Jordon's death. "If anyone's responsible, it's me, Scot. If I'd ordered an evacuation before the Shah left, Jordon'd still be alive."

"No, that's not right, Dad . . . the bullets were meant for me . . ."

Gavallan had waited until he was asleep. By this time he had missed his connection but just caught the midnight flight and was in London in good time.

"What the hell's going to happen in Iran?" Linbar had asked without preamble.

"What about the others?" Gavallan had said tightly. Only one other director was in the room, Paul Choy, nicknamed "Profitable," who had flown in from Hong Kong. Gavallan respected him greatly for his business acumen—the only cloud between them Choy's close involvement at David MacStruan's accidental death and Linbar's subsequent succession. "We should wait for them, don't you think?"

"No one else is coming," Linbar rapped. "I canceled them and don't need them. I'm taipan and can do whatever I like. Wh—"

"Not with S-G Helicopters, you can't." Tightly Gavallan looked across at Choy. "I propose we postpone."

"Sure we can," Profitable Choy said easily, "but hell, Andy, I came in special and the three of us can constitute a quorum, if we want to vote it."

"I vote it," Linbar said. "What the hell're you afraid of?"

"Nothing. Bu—"

"Good. Then we've a quorum. Now what about Iran?"

Gavallan held on to his temper. "Friday's D day, weather permitting. Whirlwind's set up as best we can."

"I'm sure of that, Andy." Profitable Choy's smile was friendly. "Linbar says you plan only to try to get 212s out?" He was a good-looking, immensely wealthy man in his late thirties, a director of Struan's and many of its subsidiary boards for a number of years, who had major interests outside of Struan's, in shipping, pharmaceutical manufacturing in Hong Kong and Japan, and in the Chinese Stock Exchange. "What about our 206s and Alouettes?"

"We have to leave them—can't possibly fly them out. No way." A silence followed his explanation.

Paul Choy said, "What's the final Whirlwind plan?"

"Friday at 7:00 A.M., weather permitting, I radio the code that Whirlwind's a go. All flights get airborne. We'll have four 212s positioned at Bandar Delam under Rudi, they'll head for Bahrain, refuel, then on to Al Shargaz; our two 212s at Kowiss have to refuel on the coast then head for Kuwait for more fuel, then to Jellet—that's a small island off Saudi where we've cached fuel—then on to Bahrain and Al Shargaz. The three at Lengeh under Scragger shouldn't have any problem, they just head for Al Shargaz direct. Erikki gets out through Turkey. As soon as they arrive we start stripping them for loading into the 747s I've already chartered and get out as fast as possible."

"What odds're you giving on not losing a man or a chopper?" Profitable Choy asked, his eyes suddenly hard. He was a famous gambler and racehorse owner and a steward of Hong Kong's Jockey Club. Rumor had it he was also a member of Macao's gambling syndicate.

"I'm not a betting man. But the chances are good—otherwise I wouldn't even contemplate it. McIver's already managed to get three 212s out, that's a saving of better than $3 million. If we get all our 212s out and most of the spares S-G'll be in good shape."

"Rotten shape," Linbar said curtly.

"Better shape than Struan's will be this year."

Linbar flushed. "You should have been prepared for this catastrophe, you and bloody McIver. Any fool could see the Shah was on his last legs."

"Enough of this, Linbar," Gavallan snapped. "I didn't come back to quarrel, just to report, so let's finish and I can get my plane back. What else, Profitable?"

"Andy, even if you get 'em out what about Imperial undercutting you in the North Sea, taking twenty-odd contracts from you—then there's your commitment for the six X63s?"

"A bloody stupid and ill-timed decision," Linbar said.

Gavallan dragged his eyes off Linbar and concentrated. Choy had the right to ask and he had nothing to hide. "So long as I've my 212s I can get back to normal; there's a huge amount of work for them. I'll start dealing with Imperial next week—I know I'll get some of the contracts back. The rest of the world's frantic for oil, so ExTex will come around with the new Saudi, Nigerian, and Malaysian contracts, and when they get our report on the X63 they'll double their business with us—and so will all the other majors. We'll be able to give them better than ever service, more safety in all weather conditions, at less cost per mile per passenger. The market's great, soon China'll open up an—"

"Pipe dream," Linbar said. "You and bloody Dunross have your heads in the clouds."

"China'll never be any good for us," Profitable Choy said, his eyes curious. "I agree with Linbar."

"I don't." Gavallan noticed something odd about Choy but his rage took him onward. "We'll wait on that one. China has to have oil somewhere, in abundance. To finalize, I'm in good shape, great shape, last year profits were up fifty percent and this year we're the same if not better. Next week I'll b—"

Linbar interrupted. "Next week you'll be out of business."

"This weekend will tell it one way or another." Gavallan's chin came out. "I propose we reconvene on Monday next. That'll give me time to get back."

"Paul and I return to Hong Kong on Sunday. We'll reconvene there."

"That's not possible for me an—"

"Then we will have to get on without you." Linbar's temper broke. "If Whirlwind fails you're finished, S-G Helicopters will be liquidated, a new company, North Sea Helicopters, already formed by the way, will acquire the assets, and I doubt if we'll pay half a cent on the dollar."

Gavallan flushed. "That's bloody robbery!"

"Just the price of failure! By God if S-G goes down you're finished and none too soon for me, and if you can't afford to buy your own plane ticket to board meetings you won't be missed."

Gavallan was beside himself with suppressed rage, but he held on. Then at a sudden thought, he looked across at Profitable Choy. "If Whirlwind's a success, will you help me finance a Struan buy-out?"

Before Choy could answer Linbar bellowed, "Our controlling interest's not for sale."

"Maybe it should be, Linbar," Profitable Choy said thoughtfully. "That way maybe you ease out of the hole you're in. Why not unload an irritant—you two guys hack all the time and for what? Why not call it a day, huh?"

Linbar said tightly, "Would you finance the buy-out?"

"Maybe. Yeah, maybe, but only if you agreed, Linbar, only then. This's a family matter."

"I'll never agree, Profitable." Linbar's face twisted and he glared at Gavallan. "I want to see you rot—you and bloody Dunross!"

Gavallan got up. "I'll see you at the next meeting of the Inner Office. We'll see what they say."

"They'll do what I tell them to do. I'm taipan. By the way, I'm making Profitable a member."

"You can't, it's against Dirk's rules." Dirk Struan, founder of the company, had set down that members of the Inner Office could only be family, however loosely connected, and Christian. "You swore by God to uphold them."

"The hell with Dirk's rules," Linbar slammed back at him; "you're not party to all of them or to Dirk's legacy, only a taipan is, by God, and what I swore to uphold's my own business. You think you're so goddamned clever, you're not! Profitable's become Episcopalian, last year he was divorced, and soon he's going to marry into the family, one of my nieces, with my blessing —he'll be more family than you!" He laughed uproariously.

Gavallan did not. Nor did Profitable Choy. They watched each other, the die cast now. "I didn't know you were divorced," Gavallan said. "I should congratulate you on . . . on your new life and appointment."

"Yeah, thanks," was all his enemy said.

In the Al Shargaz airport, Scot bent down to pick up his father's suitcase, other passengers bustling past, but Gavallan said, "Thanks, Scot, I can manage." He picked it up. "I could use a shower and a couple of hours' sleep. Hate flying at night."

"Genny's got the car outside." Scot had noticed his father's tiredness from the first moment. "You had a rough time back home?"

"No, no, not at all. So glad you're okay. What's new here?"

"Everything's terrific, Dad, going according to plan. Like clockwork."

IN TEHRAN'S NORTHERN SUBURBS: 2:35 P.M. Jean-Luc, debonair as always in his tailored flying gear and custom-made boots, got out of the taxi. As promised, he took out the hundred-dollar bill and carefully tore it in half. *"Voilà!"*

The driver examined his half of the note closely. "Only one hour, Agha? In God's name, Agha, no more?"

"One hour and a half, as we agreed, then straight back to the airport. I'll have some luggage."

"Insha'Allah." The driver looked around nervously. "I can't wait here— too many eyes. One hour and half hour. I around corner, there!" He pointed ahead, then drove off.

Jean-Luc went up the stairs and unlocked the door of Apartment 4a that overlooked the tree-lined road and faced south. This was *his* pad, though his wife, Marie-Christene, had found it and arranged it for him and stayed here on her rare visits. One bedroom with a big low double bed, well-equipped kitchen, living room with a deep sofa, good hi-fi and record player: "To beguile your lady friends, *chéri*, so long as you don't import one into France!"

"Me, *chérie*? Me, I'm a lover not an importer!"

He smiled to himself, glad to be home and only a little irritated that he had to leave so much—the hi-fi was the best, the records wonderful, the sofa seductive, the bed oh so resilient, the wine so painstakingly smuggled in, and then there were his kitchen utensils. *"Espèce de con,"* he said out loud and went into the bedroom and tried the phone. It wasn't working.

He took a suitcase out of the neat wall bureau and started packing, quickly and efficiently, for he had given it much thought. First his favorite knives and omelette pan, then six bottles of the very best wines, the remaining forty-odd bottles would stay for the new tenant, a temporary tenant in case he ever came back, who was renting the whole place from him from tomorrow—with payment in good French francs, monthly in advance into Switzerland, with another good cash deposit for breakages, also in advance.

The deal had been simmering since before he went on Christmas leave. While everyone else wore blinkers, he chortled, I was ahead of the game. But then of course I have an extreme advantage over the others. I'm French.

Happily he continued packing. The new owner was also French, an elderly friend in the embassy who for weeks had desperately needed an imme-

diate, well-equipped *garçonnière* for his teenage Georgian-Circassian mistress who was swearing to leave him unless he delivered: "Jean-Luc, my
dearest friend, let me rent it for a year, six months, three—I tell you em-
phatically, soon the only Europeans resident here will be diplomats. Tell no
one else, but I have it on the highest authority from our inside contact with
Khomeini in Neauphle-le-Château! Frankly we know everything that's going on—aren't many of his closest associates French speaking and French
university trained? Please, I beg you, I simply have to satisfy the light of my
life."

My poor old friend, Jean-Luc thought sadly. Thank God I'll never have
to kowtow to any woman—how lucky Marie-Christene is that she's married
to me who can wisely guard her fortune!

The last items he packed were his flight instruments and half a dozen
pairs of sunglasses. All his clothes he had put away in one locked cupboard.
Of course I shall be reimbursed by the company and buy new ones. Who
needs old clothes?

Now he was finished, everything neat and tidy. He looked at the clock. It
had taken him only twenty-two minutes. Perfect. The La Doucette in the
freezer was cool, the freezer still working in spite of the electricity cuts. He
opened the bottle and tried it. Perfect. Three minutes later the door
knocker sounded. Perfect.

"Sayada, *chérie*, how beautiful you are," he said warmly and kissed her,
but he was thinking, you don't look good at all, tired and weary. "How are
you, *chérie*?"

"I've had a chill, nothing to worry about," she said. This morning she
had seen her worry lines and the dark rings in her mirror and knew Jean-
Luc would notice. "Nothing serious and I'm over it now. And you, *chéri*?"

"Today fine, tomorrow?" He shrugged, helped her off with her coat,
lifted her easily into his arms and sank into the embrace of the sofa. She was
very beautiful and he was saddened to leave her. And Iran. Like Algiers, he
thought.

"What're you thinking about, Jean-Luc?"

" '63, being shoved out of Algiers. Just like Iran in a way, we're being
forced out the same." He felt her stir in his arms. "What is it?"

"The world's so awful sometimes." Sayada had told him nothing about
her real life. "So unfair," she said sickened, remembering the '67 war in
Gaza and the death of her parents, then fleeing—her story much like his—
remembering more the catastrophe of Teymour's murder and *them*. Nausea
swept into her as she pictured little Yassar and what they would do to her
son if she misbehaved. If only I could find out who *they* are . . .

Jean-Luc was pouring the wine that he had put on the table in front of them. "Bad to be serious, *chérie*. We've not much time. *Santé!*"

The wine tasted cool and delicate and of spring. "How much time? Aren't you staying?"

"I must leave in an hour."

"For Zagros?"

"No, *chérie*, for the airport, then Kowiss."

"When will you be back?"

"I won't," he said and felt her stiffen. But he held her firmly and, in a moment, she relaxed again, and he continued—never a reason not to trust her implicitly. "Between us, Kowiss is temporary, very. We're pulling out of Iran, the whole company—it's obvious we're not wanted, we can't operate freely anymore, the company's not being paid. We've been tossed out of the Zagros . . . one of our mechanics was killed by terrorists a few days ago and young Scot Gavallan missed getting killed by a millimeter. So we're pulling out. *C'est fini.*"

"When?"

"Soon. I don't know exactly."

"I'll . . . I will miss . . . will miss you, Jean-Luc," she said and nestled closer.

"And I'll miss you, *chérie*," he said gently, noticing the silent tears now flooding her cheeks. "How long are you staying in Tehran?"

"I don't know." She kept the misery out of her voice. "I'll give you an address in Beirut, they'll know where to find me."

"You can find me through Aberdeen."

They sat there on the sofa, she lying in his arms, the clock on the mantelpiece over the fireplace ticking, normally so soft but now so loud, both of them conscious of the time that passed and the ending that had occurred—not of their volition.

"Let's make love," she murmured, not wanting to but knowing that bed was expected of her.

"No," he said gallantly, pretending to be strong for both of them, knowing that bed was expected of him and then they would get dressed and be French and sensible about the ending of their affair. His eyes strayed to the clock. Forty-three minutes left.

"You don't want me?"

"More than ever." His hand cupped her breast and his lips brushed her neck, her perfume light and pleasing, ready to begin.

"I'm glad," she murmured in the same sweet voice, "and so glad that you said no. I want you for hours, my darling, not for a few minutes—not now. It would spoil everything to hurry."

For a moment he was nonplussed, not expecting that gambit in the game they played. But now that it was said he was glad too. How brave of her to forgo such pleasure, he thought, loving her deeply. Much better to remember the great times than to thrash around hurriedly. It certainly saves me a great deal of sweat and effort and I didn't check if there's any hot water. Now we can sit and chat and enjoy the wine, weep a little and be happy. "Yes, I agree. For me too." Again his lips brushed her neck. He felt her tremble and for a moment he was tempted to inflame her. But decided not to. Poor baby, why torment her?

"How are you all leaving, my darling?"

"We'll fly out together. Wine?"

"Yes, yes, please, it's so good." She sipped the wine, dried her cheeks, and chatted with him, probing this extraordinary "pullout." Both *they* and the Voice will find all this very interesting, perhaps even bring me to discover who *they* are. Until I know I can't protect my son. Oh, God, help me to corner them.

"I love you so much, *chéri*," she said.

AT TEHRAN AIRPORT: 6:05 P.M. Johnny Hogg, Pettikin, and Nogger stared at McIver blankly. "You're staying—you're not leaving with us?" Pettikin stuttered.

"No. I told you," McIver said briskly. "I've got to accompany Kia to Kowiss tomorrow." They were beside his car in their parking lot, away from alien ears, the 125 on the apron, laborers loading the last few crates, the inevitable group of Green Band guards watching. And a mullah.

"The mullah's one we've never seen before," Nogger said nervously, like all of them trying to hide it.

"Good. Is everyone else ready to board?"

"Yes, Mac, except Jean-Luc." Pettikin was very unsettled. "Don't you think you'd better chance leaving Kia?"

"That'd really be crazy, Charlie. Nothing to worry about. You can set up everything at Al Shargaz Airport with Andy. I'll be there tomorrow. I'll get on the 125 tomorrow at Kowiss with the rest of the lads."

"But for God's sake they're all cleared, you're not," Nogger said.

"For God's sake, Nogger, none of us're cleared from here, for God's sake," McIver added with a laugh. "How the hell will we be sure of our Kowiss lads until they're airborne and out of Iran airspace? Nothing to worry about. First things first, we've got to get this part of the show in the air." He glanced at the taxi skidding to a stop. Jean-Luc got out, gave the driver the other half of the note, and strolled over carrying a suitcase.

"Alors, mes amis," he said with a contented smile. *"Ça marche?"*

McIver sighed. "Jolly sporting of you to advertise you're going on a holiday, Jean-Luc."

"What?"

"Never mind." McIver liked Jean-Luc, for his ability, his cooking, and single-mindedness. When Gavallan had told Jean-Luc about Whirlwind, Jean-Luc had said at once, "Me, I will certainly fly out one of the Kowiss 212s—providing I can be on the Wednesday flight to Tehran and go into Tehran for a couple of hours."

"To do what?"

"Mon Dieu, you Anglais! To say *adieu* to the Imam perhaps?"

McIver grinned at the Frenchman. "How was Tehran?"

"Magnifique!" Jean-Luc grinned back, and thought, I haven't seen Mac so young in years. Who's the lady? *"Et toi, mon vieux?"*

"Good." Behind him, McIver saw Jones, the copilot, come down the steps two at a time, heading for them. Now there were no more crates left on the tarmac and their Iranian ground crew were all strolling back to the office. "You all set aboard?"

"All set, Captain, except for passengers," Jones said, matter of fact. "ATC's getting itchy and says we're overdue. Quick as you can, all right?"

"You're still cleared for a stop at Kowiss?"

"Yes, no problem."

McIver took a deep breath. "All right, here we go, just as we planned, except I'll take the papers, Johnny." Johnny Hogg handed them to him and the three of them, McIver, Hogg, and Jones, went ahead, straight to the mullah, hoping to distract him. By prearrangement the two mechanics were already aboard, ostensibly loaders. "Good day, Agha," McIver said, and ostentatiously handed the mullah the manifest, their position blocking a direct view of the steps. Nogger, Pettikin, and Jean-Luc went up them nimbly to vanish inside.

The mullah leafed through the manifest, clearly not accustomed to it. "Good. Now inspect," he said, his accent thick.

"No need for that, Agha, ev—" McIver stopped. The mullah and the two guards were already going for the steps. "Soon as you're aboard, start engines, Johnny," he said softly and followed.

The cabin was piled with crates, the passengers already seated, seat belts fastened. All eyes studiously avoided the mullah. The mullah stared at them. "Who men?"

McIver said brightly, "Crews for replacements, Agha." His excitement picked up as the engines began to howl. He motioned haphazardly at Jean-

Luc. "Pilot for Kowiss replacement, Agha," then more hurriedly, "Tower komiteh wants the aircraft to leave now. Hurry, all right?"

"What in crates?" The mullah looked at the cockpit as Johnny Hogg called out in perfect Farsi, "Sorry to interrupt, Excellency, as God wants, but the tower orders us to take off at once. With your permission, please?"

"Yes, yes, of course, Excellency Pilot." The mullah smiled. "Your Farsi is very good, Excellency."

"Thank you, Excellency, God keep you, and His blessings on the Imam."

"Thank you, Excellency Pilot, God keep you." The mullah left.

On his way out McIver leaned into the cockpit. "What was that all about, Johnny? I didn't know you spoke Farsi."

"I don't," Hogg told him dryly—and what he had said to the mullah. "I just learned that phrase, thought it might come in handy."

McIver smiled. "Go to the top of the class!" Then he dropped his voice. "When you get to Kowiss get Duke to arrange with Hotshot, however he can, to pull the lads' ferry forward, early as possible in the morning. I don't want Kia there when they take off—get 'em out early however he can. Okay?"

"Yes, of course, I'd forgotten that. Very wise."

"Have a safe flight—see you in Al Shargaz." From the tarmac he gave them a beaming thumbs-up as they taxied away.

The second they were airborne, Nogger exploded, with a cheer, "We did it!" that everyone echoed, except Jean-Luc who crossed himself superstitiously and Pettikin touched wood. *"Merde,"* Jean-Luc called out. "Save your cheers, Nogger, you may be grounded in Kowiss. Save your cheers for Friday, too much dust to blow across the Gulf between now and then!"

"Right you are, Jean-Luc," Pettikin said, sitting in the window seat beside him, watching the airport receding. "Mac was in good humor. Haven't seen him that happy for months and he was pissed off this morning. Curious how people can change."

"Yes, curious. Me, I would be very pissed off indeed to have such a change of plan." Jean-Luc was getting himself comfortable and sat back, his mind on Sayada and their parting that had been significant and sweet sorrow. He glanced at Pettikin and saw the heavy frown. "What?"

"I suddenly wondered how Mac's getting to Kowiss."

"By chopper, of course. There're two 206s and an Alouette left."

"Tom ferried the Alouette to Kowiss today, and there aren't any pilots left."

"So he is going by car, of course. Why?"

"You don't think he'd be crazy enough to fly Kia himself, do you?"

"Are you mad? Of course not, he's not that cr—" Jean-Luc's eyebrows soared. *"Merde,* he's that crazy."

AT INNER INTELLIGENCE HQ: 6:30 P.M. Hashemi Fazir stood at the window of his vast office, looking out over the roofs of the city and the minarets, huge mosque domes among the modern tall high-rise hotels and buildings, the last of the muezzins' sunset calls dying away. A few more city lights on than usual. Distant gunfire. "Sons of dogs," he muttered, then, without turning added sharply, "That's all she said?"

"Yes, Excellency. 'In a few days.' She said she was 'fairly sure' the Frenchman did not know exactly when they were leaving."

"She should have made sure. Careless. Careless agents are dangerous. Only 212s, eh?"

"Yes, she was sure about that. I agree she's careless and should be punished."

Hashemi heard the malicious pleasure in the voice but did not let it disturb his good humor, just let his mind wander, deciding what to do about Sayada Bertolin and her information. He was very pleased with himself.

Today had been excellent. One of his secret associates had been appointed number two to Abrim Pahmudi in SAVAMA. At noon a telex from Tabriz had confirmed the death of Abdollah Khan. Immediately he had telexed back to arrange a private appointment tomorrow with Hakim Khan and requisitioned one of SAVAMA's light, twin-engined airplanes. Talbot's assist into hell had gone perfectly, and he had found no traces of the men responsible—a Group Four team—when he had inspected the bomb area, for, of course, he had been instantly summoned. Those nearby had seen no one park the car: "One moment there was God's peace, the next Satan's rage."

An hour ago Abrim Pahmudi had called personally, ostensibly to congratulate him. But he had avoided the trap and had carefully denied the explosion had anything to do with him—better not to draw attention to the similarity with the first car bomb that blew General Janan to pieces, better to keep Pahmudi guessing and off guard and under pressure. He had hid his laughter and said gravely, "As God wants, Excellency, but clearly this was another cursed leftist terrorist attack. Talbot wasn't the target though his convenient demise certainly eliminates that problem. Sorry to tell you but the attack was again against the favored of the Imam." Blaming terrorists and claiming the attack was against the ayatollahs and mullahs who frequented the restaurant would frighten them and it nicely led the trail away from Talbot and so would avoid possible British retaliation—certainly from

Robert Armstrong if he ever found out—and so squashed several scorpions with one stone.

Hashemi turned and looked at the sharp-faced man, Suliman al Wiali, the Group Four team leader who had planted today's car bomb—the same man who had caught Sayada Bertolin in Teymour's bedroom. "In a few minutes I'm leaving for Tabriz. I'll be back tomorrow or the next day. A tall Englishman, Robert Armstrong, will be with me. Assign one of your men to follow him, make sure the man knows where Armstrong lives, then have him finish him off somewhere in the streets, after dark. Don't do it yourself."

"Yes, Excellency. When?"

Hashemi thought through his plan again and could find no flaw. "Holy Day."

"This is the same man you wanted the Sayada woman to fornicate with?"

"Yes. But now I've changed my mind." Robert's no longer of any value, he thought. More than that, his time has come.

"Do you have any other work for her, Excellency?"

"No. We've broken the Teymour ring."

"As God wants. May I make a suggestion?"

Hashemi studied him. Suliman was his most efficient, trustworthy, and deadly Group Four leader with a cover job as a minor agent for Inner Intelligence reporting directly to him. Suliman claimed that originally he came from the Shrift Mountains north of Beirut before his family was murdered and he was driven out by Christian militiamen, and Hashemi had inducted him five years ago after bribing him out of a Syrian prison where he had been condemned to death for murder and banditry on both sides of the borders, his sole defense: "I only killed Jews and Infidels as God ordered, so I do God's work. I am an Avenger."

"What suggestion?" he asked.

"She's an ordinary PLO courier, not a very good one and in her present state dangerous and a possible threat—easy to be subverted by Jews or CIAs and used against us. Like good farmers we should plant seeds where we can to reap a future crop." Suliman smiled. "You're a wise farmer, Excellency. My suggestion is I tell her it's time to go back to Beirut, that we, the two of us who caught her in her harlotry, now want her to work for us there. We let her overhear us talking privately—and we pretend to be part of a cell of Christian militiamen from southern Lebanon, acting under Israeli orders for their CIA masters." The man laughed quietly, seeing his employer's surprise.

"And then?"

"What would turn a lukewarm, anti-Israeli, Palestinian Copt into a permanent, fanatic hellcat bent on vengeance?"

Hashemi looked at him. "What?"

"Say *some* of these same 'Christian militiamen, acting under Israeli orders for their CIA masters,' maliciously, openly hurt her child, hurt him badly, the day before she arrived back, then vanished—wouldn't that make her a fiendish enemy of our enemies?"

Hashemi lit a cigarette to hide his disgust. "I agree only that her usefulness is over," he said and saw a flash of irritation.

"What value has her child, and what future?" Suliman said scornfully. "With such a mother and living with Christian relatives he will remain Christian and go to hell."

"Israel is our ally. Stay out of Middle Eastern affairs or they will eat you up. It's forbidden!"

"If you say it is forbidden it is forbidden, Master." Suliman bowed and nodded agreement. "On the head of my children."

"Good. You did very well today. Thank you." He went to the safe and took a bundle of used dollars off the stacks there. He saw Suliman's face light up. "Here's a bonus for you and your men."

"Thank you, thank you, Excellency, God protect you! The man Armstrong may be considered dead." Very gratefully, Suliman bowed again and left.

Now that he was alone Hashemi unlocked a drawer and poured himself a whisky. A thousand dollars is a fortune to Suliman and his three men, but a wise investment, he thought contentedly. Oh, yes. Glad I decided about Robert. Robert knows too much, suspects too much—wasn't it he who named my teams? "Group Four teams must be used for good and not evil, Hashemi," he had said in that know-all voice of his. "I just caution you, their power could be heady and backfire on you. Remember the Old Man of the Mountains. Eh?"

Hashemi had laughed to cover his shock that Armstrong had read his most secret heart. "What have al-Sabbah and his assassins to do with me? We're living in the twentieth century and I'm not a religious fanatic. More important, Robert, I don't have a Castle Alamut!"

"There's still hashish—and better."

"I don't want addicts or assassins, just men I can trust."

Assassin was derived from *hashshashin,* they who take hashish. Legend told that in the eleventh century at Alamut—Hasan ibn al-Sabbah's impregnable fortress in the mountains near Qazvin—he had had secret gardens made just like the Gardens of Paradise described in the Koran, where wine and honey flowed from fountains and beautiful, compliant maidens lay. Here hashish-drugged devotees would be secretly introduced and given a foretaste of the promised, eternal, and erotic bliss that awaited them in Paradise after death. Then, in a day or two or three, the "Blessed One" would be brought "back to earth," to be guaranteed quick passage back—in return for absolute obedience to his will.

From Alamut, Hasan ibn al-Sabbah's fanatical band of simple-minded, hashish-taking zealots—the Assassins—terrorized Persia, soon to reach into most of the Middle East. This continued for almost two centuries. Until 1256. Then a grandson of Genghiz Khan, Hulugu Khan, came down into Persia and set his hordes against Alamut, tore it stone by stone from its mountain peaks, and stamped the Assassins into the dust.

Hashemi's lips were in a thin line. Ah, Robert, how did you pierce the veil to see my secret plan: to modernize al-Sabbah's idea, so easy to do now that the Shah has gone and the land's in ferment. So easy with psychedelic drugs, hallucinogens, and a never-ending pool of simple-minded zealots already imbued with the wish for martyrdom, who just have to be guided and pointed in the right direction—to remove whomever I choose. Like Janan and Talbot. Like you!

But what carrion I have to deal with for the greater glory of my fief. How can people be so cruel? How can they openly enjoy such wanton cruelty, like cutting off that man's genitals, like contemplating hurting a child? Is it just because they're of the Middle East, live in the Middle East, and belong nowhere else? How terrible that they can't learn from us, can't benefit from our ancient civilization. The Empire of Cyrus and Darius must come to pass again, by God—in that the Shah was right. My assassins will lead the way, even to Jerusalem.

He sipped his whisky, very pleased with his day's work. It tasted very good. He preferred it without ice.

THURSDAY
March 1

IN THE VILLAGE NEAR THE NORTH BORDER: 5:30 A.M.

In the light of false dawn, Erikki pulled on his boots. Now on with his flight
jacket, the soft, well-worn leather rustling, knife out of the scabbard and
into his sleeve. He eased the hut door open. The village was sleeping under
its snow coverlet. No guards that he could see. The chopper's lean-to was
also quiet but he knew she would still be too well guarded to try. Various
times during the day and night he had experimented. Each time the cabin
and cockpit guards had just smiled at him, alert and polite. No way he could
fight through the three of them and take off. His only chance by foot, and
he had been planning it ever since he had had the confrontation with Sheik
Bayazid the day before yesterday.

His senses reached out into the darkness. The stars were hidden by thin
clouds. Now! Surefooted he slid out of the door and along the line of huts,
making for the trees, and then he was enmeshed in the net that seemed to
appear out of the sky and he was fighting for his life.

Four tribesmen were on the ends of the net used for trapping and curbing wild goats. Skillfully they wound it around him, tighter and tighter, and though he bellowed with rage and his immense strength ripped some of the ropes asunder, soon he was helplessly thrashing in the snow. For a moment he lay there panting, then again tried to break his bonds, the feeling of impotence making him howl. But the more he fought the ropes, the more they seemed to knot tighter. Finally he stopped fighting and lay back, trying to catch his breath, and looked around. He was surrounded. All the village was awake, dressed, and armed. Obviously they had been waiting for him. Never had he seen or felt so much hatred.

It took five men to lift him and half carry, half drag him into the meeting hut and throw him roughly on the dirt floor in front of the Sheik Bayazid who sat cross-legged on skins in his place of honor near the fire. The hut was large, smoke blackened, and filled with tribesmen.

"So," the Sheik said. "So you dare to disobey me?"

Erikki lay still, gathering his strength. What was there to say?

"In the night one of my men came back from the Khan." Bayazid was shaking with fury. "Yesterday afternoon, on the Khan's orders, my messenger's throat was cut against all the laws of chivalry! What do you say to that? His throat cut like a dog! Like a dog!"

"I . . . I can't believe the Khan would do that," Erikki said helplessly. "I can't believe it."

"In all the Names of God, his throat was cut. He's dead and we're dishonored. All of us, me! Disgraced, because of you!"

"The Khan's a devil. I'm sorry but I'm no—"

"We treated with the Khan honorably, and you honorably, you were spoils of war won from the Khan's enemies and ours, you're married to his daughter and he's rich with more bags of gold than a goat has hairs. What's 10 million rials to him? A piece of goat's shit. Worse, he's taken away our honor. God's death on him!"

A murmur went through those who watched and waited, not understanding the English but hearing the jagged barbs of anger.

Again the hissing venom: "Insha'Allah! Now we release you as you want, on foot, and then we will hunt you. We will not kill you with bullets, nor will you see the sunset, and your head will be a Khan's gift." The Sheik repeated the punishment in his own tongue and waved his hand. Men surged forward.

"Wait, wait!" Erikki shouted as his fear thrust an idea at him.

"You wish to beg for mercy?" Bayazid said contemptuously. "I thought you were a man—that's why I didn't order your throat cut while you sleep."

"Not mercy, vengeance!" Then Erikki roared, "Vengeance!" There was an astonished silence. "For you and for me! Don't you deserve vengeance for such dishonor?"

The younger man hesitated. "What trickery is this?"

"I can help you regain your honor—I alone. Let us sack the palace of the Khan and both be revenged on him," Erikki prayed to his ancient gods to make his tongue golden.

"Are you mad?"

"The Khan is my enemy more than yours, why else would he disgrace both of us if not to infuriate you against me? I know the palace. I can get you and fifteen armed men into the forecourt in a split second an—"

"Madness," the Sheik scoffed. "Should we throw our lives away like hashish-infected fools? The Khan has too many guards."

"Fifty-three on call within the walls, no more than four or five on duty at any one time. Are your fighters so weak they can't deal with fifty-three? We have surprise on our side. A sudden commando attack from the sky, a relentless charge to avenge your honor—I could get you in and out the same way in minutes. Abdollah Khan's sick, very sick, guards won't be prepared, nor the household. I know the way in, where he sleeps, everything. . . ."

Erikki heard his voice pick up excitement, knowing it could be done: the violent flare over the walls and sudden touchdown, jumping out, leading the way up the steps and in, up the staircase onto the landing, down the corridor, knocking aside Ahmed and whoever stood in the way, into the Khan's room, then stepping aside for Bayazid and his men to do what they wanted, somehow getting to the north wing and Azadeh and saving her, and if she was not there or hurt, then killing and killing, the Khan, guards, these men, everyone.

His plan possessed him now. "Wouldn't your name last a thousand years because of your daring? Sheik Bayazid, he who dared to humble, to challenge the Khan of all the Gorgons inside his lair for a matter of honor? Wouldn't minstrels sing songs about you forever at the campfires of all the Kurds? Isn't that what Saladin the Kurd would do?"

He saw the eyes in the firelight glowing differently now, saw Bayazid hesitate, the silence growing, heard him talk softly to his people—then one man laughed and called out something that others echoed and then, with one voice, they roared approval.

Willing hands cut him loose. Men fought viciously for the privilege of being on the raid. Erikki's fingers trembled as he pressed Engine Start. The first of the jets exploded into life.

IN THE PALACE OF THE KHAN: 6:35 A.M. Hakim came out of sleep violently. His bodyguard near the door was startled. "What is it, Highness?"

"Nothing, nothing, Ishtar, I was . . . I was just dreaming." Now that he was wide awake, Hakim lay back and stretched luxuriously, eager for the new day. "Bring me coffee. After my bath, breakfast here—and ask my sister to join me."

"Yes, Highness, at once."

His bodyguard left him. Again he stretched his taut body. Dawn was murky. The room ornate and vast and drafty and chilly but the bedroom of the Khan. In the huge fireplace a fire burned brightly fed by the guard through the night, no one else allowed in, the guard chosen by him personally from the fifty-three within the palace, pending a decision about their future. Where to find those to be trusted, he asked himself, then got out of bed, wrapping the warm brocade dressing gown tighter—one of a half a hundred that he had found in the wardrobe—faced Mecca and the open Koran in the ornately tiled niche, knelt, and said the first prayer of the day. When he had finished he stayed there, his eyes on the ancient Koran, immense, bejeweled, hand-calligraphed, and without price, the Gorgon Khan's Koran—*his* Koran. So much to thank God for, he thought, so much still to learn, so much still to do—but a wonderful beginning already made.

Not long after midnight yesterday, before all the assembled family in the house, he had taken the carved emerald and gold ring—symbol of the ancient khanate—from the index finger of his father's right hand and put it on his own. He had had to fight the ring over a roll of fat and close his nostrils to the stink of death that hung in the room. His excitement had overcome his revulsion, and now he was truly Khan. Then all the family present knelt and kissed his ringed hand, swearing allegiance, Azadeh proudly first, next Aysha trembling and frightened, then the others, Najoud and Mahmud outwardly abject, secretly blessing God for the reprieve.

Then downstairs in the Great Room with Azadeh standing behind him, Ahmed and the bodyguards also swore allegiance—the rest of the far-flung family would come later, along with other tribal leaders, personal and household staff and servants. At once he had given orders for the funeral and then he allowed his eyes to see Najoud. "So."

"Highness," Najoud said unctuously, "with all our hearts, before God, we congratulate you, and swear to serve you to the limits of our power."

"Thank you, Najoud," he had said. "Thank you. Ahmed, what was the Khan's sentence decreed on my sister and her family before he died?" Tension in the Great Room was sudden.

"Banishment, penniless to the wastelands north of Meshed, Highness, under guard—at once."

"I regret, Najoud, you and all your family will leave at dawn as decreed."

He remembered how her face had gone ashen and Mahmud's ashen and she had stammered, "But, Highness, now you are Khan, your word is our law. I did not expect . . . you're Khan now."

"But the Khan, our father, gave the order when he was the law, Najoud. It is not correct to overrule him."

"But you're the law now," Najoud had said with a sickly smile. "You do what's right."

"With God's help I will certainly try, Najoud. But I can't overrule my father on his deathbed."

"But, Highness . . ." Najoud had come closer. "Please, may . . . may we discuss this in private?"

"Better here before the family, Najoud. What did you want to say?"

She had hesitated and come even closer and he felt Ahmed tense and saw his knife hand ready, and the hair on his neck stiffened. "Just because Ahmed *says* that the Khan gave such an order doesn't mean that it . . . does it?" Najoud had tried to whisper but her words echoed off the walls.

Breath sighed out of Ahmed's lips. "May God burn me forever if I lied."

"I know you didn't, Ahmed," Hakim had said sadly. "Wasn't I there when the Khan decided? I was there, Najoud, so was Her Highness, my sister, I regret th—"

"But you can be mercifulll!" Najoud had cried out. "Please, please be merciful!"

"Oh, but I am, Najoud. I forgive you. But the punishment was for lying in the Name of God," he had said gravely, "not punishment for lying about my sister and me, causing us years of grief, losing us our father's love. Of course we forgive you that, don't we, Azadeh?"

"Yes, yes, that is forgiven."

"That is forgiven openly. But lying in the Name of God? The Khan made a decree. I cannot go against it."

Mahmud burst out over her pleadings, "I knew nothing about this, Highness, nothing, I swear before God, I believed her lies. I divorce her formally for being a traitor to you, I never knew anything about her lies!"

In the Great Room everyone watched them both grovel, some loathing them, some despising them for failing when they had had the power. "At dawn, Mahmud, you are banished, you and your family," he had said so sadly, "penniless, under guard . . . pending my pleasure. As to divorce it is forbidden in my house. If you wish to do that north of Meshed . . . In-sha'Allah. You are still banished there, pending my pleasure. . . ."

* * *

Oh, you were perfect, Hakim, he told himself delightedly, for of course everyone knew this was your first test. You were perfect! Never once did you gloat openly or reveal your true purpose, never once did you raise your voice, keeping calm and gentle and grave as though you really were sad with your father's sentence but, rightly, unable to overrule it. And the benign, sweet promise of "pending my pleasure"? My pleasure's that you're all banished forever and if I hear one tiny threat of a plot, I will snuff you all out as quickly as an old candle. By God and the Prophet, on whose Name be praised, I'll make the ghost of my father proud of this Khan of all the Gorgons—may he be in hell for believing such wanton lies of an evil old hag.

So much to thank God for, he thought, mesmerized by the firelight flickering in the Koran's jewels. Didn't all the years of banishment teach you secretiveness, deception, and patience? Now you've your power to cement, Azerbaijan to defend, a world to conquer, wives to find, sons to breed, and a lineage to begin. May Najoud and her whelps rot!

At dawn he had "regretfully" gone with Ahmed to witness their departure. Wistfully he had insisted that none of the rest of the family see them off. "Why increase their sorrow and mine?" There, on his exact instructions, he had watched Ahmed and guards tear through their mountains of bags, removing anything of value until there was but one suitcase each for them and their three children who watched, petrified.

"Your jewelry, woman," Ahmed had said.

"You've taken everything, everything . . . please, Hakim . . . Highness, please . . ." Najoud sobbed. Her special jewel satchel, secreted in a pocket of her suitcase, had already been added to the pile of valuables. Abruptly Ahmed reached out and ripped off her pendant and tore the neck of her dress open. A dozen necklaces weighed her down, diamonds, rubies, emeralds, and sapphires.

"Where did you get these?" Hakim had said, astonished.

"They're . . . they're my . . . my mother's and mine I bought over the ye—" Najoud stopped as Ahmed's knife came out. "All right . . . all right . . ." Frantically she pulled the necklaces over her head, unfastened the rest, and gave them to him. "Now you have everyth—"

"Your rings!"

"But, Highness, leave me someth—" She screamed as Ahmed impatiently grabbed a finger to cut it off with the ring still on it, but she pulled away, tore the rings off and also the bracelets secreted up her sleeve, howling with grief, and threw them on the floor. "Now you've everything. . . ."

"Now pick them up and hand them to His Highness, on your knees!"

Ahmed hissed, and when she did not obey instantly, he grabbed her by the hair and shoved her face on the floor, and now she was groveling and obeying.

Ah, that was a feast, Hakim thought, reliving every second of their humiliation. After they're dead, God will burn them.

He made another obeisance, put God away until next prayer at noon, and jumped up, brimming with energy. A maid was on her knees pouring the coffee, and he saw the fear in her eyes and was very pleased. The moment he became Khan, he had known it was vital to work quickly to take over the reins of power. Yesterday morning he had inspected the palace. The kitchen was not clean enough for him, so he had had the chef beaten senseless and put outside the walls, then promoted the second chef in his place with dire warnings. Four guards were banished for oversleeping, two maids whipped for slovenliness. "But, Hakim, my darling," Azadeh had said when they were alone, "surely there was no need to beat them?"

"In a day or two there won't be," he had told her. "Meanwhile the palace *will* change to the way I want it."

"Of course you know best, my darling. What about the ransom?"

"Ah, yes, at once." He had sent for Ahmed.

"I regret, Highness, the Khan your father ordered the messenger's throat cut yesterday afternoon."

Both he and Azadeh had been appalled. "But that's terrible! What can be done now?" she had cried out.

Ahmed said, "I will try to contact the tribesmen—perhaps, because now the Khan your father is dead they will . . . they will treat with you newly. I will try."

Sitting there in the Khan's place, Hakim had seen Ahmed's suave confidence and realized the trap he was in. Fear swept up from his bowels. His fingers were toying with the emerald ring on his finger. "Azadeh, come back in half an hour, please."

"Of course," she said obediently, and when he was alone with Ahmed, he said, "What arms do you carry?"

"A knife and an automatic, Highness."

"Give them to me." He remembered how his heart had throbbed and there was an unusual dryness in his mouth but this had had to be done and done alone. Ahmed had hesitated then obeyed, clearly not pleased to be disarmed. But Hakim had pretended not to notice, just examined the action of the gun and cocked it thoughtfully. "Now listen carefully, Counselor: you won't *try* to contact the tribesmen, you will do it very quickly and you will make arrangements to have my sister's husband returned safely—on your head, by God and the Prophet of God!"

"I—of course, Highness." Ahmed tried to keep the anger off his face.

Lazily Hakim pointed the gun at his head, sighting down it. "I swore by God to treat you as first counselor and I will—while you live." His smile twisted. "Even if you happen to be crippled, perhaps emasculated, even blinded by your enemies. Do you have enemies, Ahmed Dursak the Turkoman?"

Ahmed laughed, at ease now, pleased with the *man* who had become Khan and not the whelp that he had imagined—so much easier to deal with a man, he thought, his confidence returning. "Many, Highness, many. Isn't it custom to measure the quality of a man by the importance of his enemies? Insha'Allah! I didn't know you knew how to handle guns."

"There are many things you don't know about me, Ahmed," he had said with grim satisfaction, an important victory gained. He had handed him back the knife, but not the automatic. "I'll keep this as pishkesh. For a year and a day don't come into my presence armed."

"Then how can I protect you, Highness?"

"With wisdom." He had allowed a small measure of the violence he had kept pent up for years to show. "You have to prove yourself. To me. To me alone. What pleased my father won't necessarily please me. This is a new era, with new opportunities, new dangers. Remember, by God, the blood of my father rests easily in my veins."

The remainder of the day and well into the evening he had received men of importance from Tabriz and Azerbaijan and asked questions of them, about the insurrection and the leftists, the mujhadin, and fedayeen and other factions. Bazaaris had arrived and mullahs and two ayatollahs, local army commanders and his cousin, the chief of police, and he had confirmed the man's appointment. All of them had brought suitable pishkesh.

And so they should, he thought, very satisfied, remembering their contempt in the past when his fortune had been zero and his banishment to Khoi common knowledge. Their contempt will be very costly to every last one . . .

"Your bath is ready, Highness, and Ahmed's waiting outside."

"Bring him in, Ishtar. You stay." He watched the door open. Ahmed was tired and crumpled.

"Salaam, Highness."

"What about the ransom?"

"Late last night I found the tribesmen. There were two of them. I explained that Abdollah Khan was dead and the new Khan had ordered me to give them half the ransom asked at once as a measure of faith, promising them the remainder when the pilot is safely back. I sent them north in one of our cars with a trusted driver and another car to follow secretly."

"Do you know who they are, where their village is?"

"They told me they were Kurds, one named Ishmud, the other Alilah, their chief al-Drah and their village was called Broken Tree in the mountains north of Khoi—I'm sure all lies, Highness, and they're not Kurds though they claim to be. I'd say they were just tribesmen, bandits mostly."

"Good. Where did you get the money to pay them?"

"The Khan, your father, put twenty million rials into my safekeeping against emergencies."

"Bring the balance to me before sunset."

"Yes, Highness."

"Are you armed?"

Ahmed was startled. "Only with my knife, Highness."

"Give it to me," he said, hiding his pleasure that Ahmed had fallen into the trap he had set for him, accepting the knife, hilt first. "Didn't I tell you not to come into my presence armed for a year and a day?"

"But as . . . you gave my knife back to me I thought . . . I thought the knife . . ." Ahmed stopped, seeing Hakim standing in front of him, knife held correctly, eyes dark and hard and the pattern of the father. Behind him, the guard Ishtar watched openmouthed. The hackles on Ahmed's neck twisted. "Please excuse me, Highness, I thought I had your permission," he said in real fear.

For a moment Hakim Khan just stared at Ahmed, the knife poised in his hand, then he slashed upward. With great skill only the point of the blade went through Ahmed's coat, touched the skin but only enough to score it then came out again in perfect position for the final blow. But Hakim did not make it, though he wanted to see blood flow and this a good time, but not the perfect time. He still had need of Ahmed.

"I give you back your . . . your body." He chose the word and all it implied with great deliberation. "Intact, just—this—once."

"Yes, Highness, thank you, Highness," Ahmed muttered, astonished that he was still alive, and went down on his knees. "I . . . it will never happen again."

"No, it won't. Stay there. Wait outside, Ishtar." Hakim Khan sat back on the cushions and toyed with the knife, waiting for the adrenaline to subside, remembering that vengeance was a dish best eaten cold. "Tell me everything you know about the Soviet, this man called Mzytryk: what holds he had over my father, my father over him."

Ahmed obeyed. He told him what Hashemi Fazir had said in the 125, what the Khan had told him in secret over the years, about the dacha near Tbilisi that he too had visited, how the Khan contacted Mzytryk, their code words, what Hashemi Fazir had said and threatened, what was in Mzytryk's letter, what he had overheard and what he had witnessed a few days ago.

The air hissed out of Hakim's mouth. "My father was going to take my sister to . . . he was going to take her to this dacha and give her to Mzytryk?"

"Yes, Highness, he even ordered me to send her north if . . . if he had to leave here for hospital in Tehran."

"Send for Mzytryk. Urgently. Ahmed, do it now. At once."

"Yes, Highness," Ahmed said and trembled at the contained violence. "Best, at the same time, best to remind him of his promises to Abdollah Khan, that you expect them fulfilled."

"Good, very good. You've told me everything?"

"Everything I can remember now," Ahmed told him sincerely. "There must be other things—in time I can tell you all manner of secrets, Khan of all the Gorgons, and I swear again before God to serve you faithfully." I'll tell you everything, he thought fervently, except the manner of the Khan's death and that now, more than ever, I want Azadeh as wife. Some way I will make you agree—she'll be my only real protection against you, spawn of Satan!

JUST OUTSIDE TABRIZ: 7:20 A.M.   Erikki's 212 came over the rise of the forest, inbound at max revs. All the way Erikki had been at treetop level, avoiding roads and airfields and towns and villages, his mind riveted on Azadeh and vengeance against Abdollah Khan, all else forgotten. Now, suddenly ahead, the city was rushing toward them. As suddenly a vast unease washed over him.

"Where's the palace, pilot?" Sheik Bayazid shouted gleefully. "Where is it?"

"Over the ridge, Agha," he said into the boom mike, part of him wanting to add, We'd better rethink this, decide if the attack's wise, the other part shouting, This's the only chance you've got, Erikki, you can't change plans, but how in the hell're you going to escape with Azadeh from the palace and from this bunch of maniacs? "Tell your men to fasten their seat belts, to wait until the skids touch down, not to take off their safety catches until they're on the ground, and then to spread out, tell two of them to guard the chopper and protect it with their lives. I'll count down from ten for the landing and . . . and I'll lead."

"Where's the palace, I can't see it."

"Over the ridge, a minute away—tell them!" The trees were blurring as he went closer to them, his eyes on the col in the mountain ridge, horizon twisting. "I want a gun," he said, sick with anticipation.

Bayazid bared his teeth. "No gun until we possess the palace."

"Then I won't need one," he said with a curse. "I've got to ha—"

"You can trust me, you have to. Where's this palace of the Gorgons?"

"There!" Erikki pointed to the ridge just above them. "Ten . . . nine . . . eight . . ."

He had decided to come in from the east, partially covered by the forests, city well to his right, the col protecting him. Fifty yards to go. His stomach tightened.

The rocks hurtled at them. He felt more than saw Bayazid cry out and hold up his hands to protect himself against the inevitable crash, then Erikki slid through the col and swung down, straight for the walls. At the exact last moment he cut all power, hauled the chopper up over the wall with inches to spare, flaring into an emergency stop procedure, banked slightly for the forecourt, and let her fall out of the air, cushioned the fall perfectly, and set down on the tiles to skid forward a few yards with a screech, then stop. His right hand jerked the circuit breakers out, his left unsnapped the seat belt and shoved the door open, and he was still easily first on the ground and rushing for the front steps. Behind him Bayazid was now following, the cabin doors open and men pouring out, falling over one another in their excitement, the rotor still turning but the engines dying.

As he reached the front door and swung it open, servants and an astonished guard came running up to see what all the commotion was about. Erikki tore the assault rifle out of his hands, knocked him unconscious. The servants scattered and fled, a few recognizing him. For the moment the corridor ahead was clear. "Come on!" he shouted, then as Bayazid and some of the others joined him, rushed down the hallway and up the staircase toward the landing. A guard poked his head over the banister, leveled his gun, but a tribesman peppered him. Erikki jumped over the body and rushed the corridor.

A door opened ahead. Another guard came out, gun blazing. Erikki felt bullets slice through his parka but he was untouched. Bayazid blew the man against the doorjamb, and together they charged toward the Khan's room. Once there Erikki kicked the door open. Sustained gunfire came at him, missed him and the Sheik but caught the man next to him and spun the man around. The others scattered for cover and the badly hurt tribesman went forward toward his tormentor, taking more bullets and more but firing back even after he was dead.

For a second or two there was a respite, then to Erikki's shock Bayazid pulled the pin out of a grenade and tossed it through the doorway. The explosion was huge. Smoke billowed out into the corridor. At once Bayazid leaped through the opening, gun leveled, Erikki beside him.

The room was wrecked, windows blown out, curtains ripped, the carpet bed torn apart, the remains of the guard crumpled against a wall. In the alcove at the far end of the huge room, half-covered from the main bedroom, the table was upended, a serving maid moaning, and two inert bodies half buried under tablecloth and smashed dishes. Erikki's heart stopped as he recognized Azadeh. In panic he rushed over and shoved the debris off her—in passing noticed the other person was Hakim—lifted her into his arms, her hair flowing, and carried her into the light. His breathing did not start again until he was sure she was still alive—unconscious, only God knew how damaged, but alive. She wore a long blue cashmere peignoir that hid all of her, but promised everything. The tribesmen pouring into the room were swept by her beauty. Erikki took off his flight jacket and wrapped it around her, oblivious to them, "Azadeh . . . Azadeh . . ."

"Who this, pilot?"

Through his fog Erikki saw Bayazid was beside the wreckage. "That's Hakim, my wife's brother. Is he dead?"

"No." Bayazid looked around furiously. Nowhere else for the Khan to hide. His men were crowding through the doorway and he cursed them, ordering them to take up defensive positions at either end of the corridor and for others to go outside onto the wide patio and to guard that too. Then he scrambled over to Erikki and Azadeh and looked at her bloodless face and breasts and legs pressing against the cashmere. "Your wife?"

"Yes."

"She's not dead, good."

"Yes, but only God knows if she's hurt. I've got to get a doctor . . ."

"Later, first we ha—"

"Now! She may die!"

"As God wants, pilot," Bayazid said, then shouted angrily, "You said you knew everything, where the Khan would be, in the Name of God where is he?"

"I don't know. These . . . these were his private quarters, Agha, private, I've never seen anyone else here, heard of anyone else here, even his wife could only come here by invitation an—" A burst of firing outside stopped Erikki. "He's got to be here if Azadeh and Hakim are here!"

"Where? Where can he hide?"

In turmoil Erikki looked around, settled Azadeh as best he could, then rushed for the windows—they were barred, the Khan could not have escaped this way. From here, a defensible corner abutment of the palace, he could not see the forecourt or the chopper, only the best view of the gardens and orchards southward, past the walls to the city a mile or so distant below. No other guards threatening them yet. As he turned, his peripheral vision caught a movement from the alcove, he saw the automatic, shoved Bayazid out of the way of the bullet that would have killed him, and lunged for Hakim who lay in the debris. Before other tribesmen could react he had the young man pinioned, the automatic out of his hand, and was shouting at him, trying to get him to understand, "You're safe, Hakim, it's me, Erikki, we're friends, we came to rescue you and Azadeh from the Khan . . . we came to rescue you!"

"Rescue me . . . rescue me from what?" Hakim was staring at him blankly, still numb, still dazed, blood seeping from a small wound in his head. "Rescue?"

"From the Khan an—" Erikki saw terror come into the eyes, whirled and caught the butt of Bayazid's assault rifle just in time. "Wait, Agha, wait, it's not his fault, he's dazed . . . wait, he was . . . he was aiming at me not you, wait, he'll help us. Wait!"

"Where's Abdollah Khan?" Bayazid shouted, his men beside him now, guns cocked and ready to kill. "Hurry and tell me or you're both dead men!"

And when Hakim didn't answer at once, Erikki snarled, "For God's sake, Hakim, tell him where he is or we're all dead."

"Abdollah Khan's dead, he's dead . . . he died last night, no . . . the night before last. He died the night before last, near midnight . . ." Hakim said weakly and they stared at him with disbelief, his mind coming back slowly and he still could not understand why he was lying here, head pounding, legs numb, Erikki holding him when Erikki was kidnapped by tribesmen, when he was having breakfast with Azadeh, then guns exploding and diving for cover, guards firing, and then the explosion and half the ransom's already been paid.

Abruptly his mind cleared. "In God's name," he gasped. He tried to get up and failed. "Erikki, in God's name why did you fight in here, half your ransom's been paid . . . why?"

Erikki got up angrily. "There's been no ransom, the messenger's throat was cut, Abdollah Khan had the man's throat cut!"

"But the ransom—half was paid, Ahmed did it last night!"

"Paid, paid to whom?" Bayazid snarled. "What lies are these?"

"Not lies, half was paid last night, half paid by the new Khan as . . . as an act of faith for the . . . the mistake about the messenger. Before God, I swear it. Half's paid!"

"Lies," Bayazid scoffed, and aimed the gun at him. "Where's the Khan?"

"Not lies! Should I lie before God? I tell you before God! Before God! Send for Ahmed, send for the man Ahmed, he paid them."

One of the tribesmen shouted something, Hakim blanched and repeated in Turkish: "In the Name of God, half the ransom's already paid! Abdollah Khan's dead! He's dead and half the ransom was paid." A murmur of astonishment went through the room. "Send for Ahmed, he'll tell you the truth—why are you fighting here, there's no reason to fight!"

Erikki rushed in: "If Abdollah Khan's dead and half's been paid, Agha, other half promised, your honor's vindicated. Agha, please do as Hakim asks, send for Ahmed—he'll tell you who he paid and how."

Fear in the room was very high now, Bayazid and his men hating the closeness here, wanting to be in the open, in the mountains, away from these evil people and place, feeling betrayed. But if Abdollah's dead and half's paid . . . "Pilot, go and get his man Ahmed," Bayazid said, "and remember, if you cheat me, you will find your wife noseless." He ripped the automatic out of Erikki's hand. "Go and get him!"

"Yes, yes, of course."

"Erikki . . . first help me up," Hakim said, his voice throaty and weak.

Erikki was helplessly trying to make sense of all this as he lifted him easily and pushed through the men crowding near, and settled him on the sofa cushions beside Azadeh. Both saw her pallid face, but both also noticed her regular breathing. "God be thanked," Hakim muttered.

Then once more Erikki was half in nightmare, walking out of the room unarmed to the head of the stairs, shouting for Ahmed not to shoot, "Ahmed, Ahmed, I've got to talk to you, I'm alone . . ."

Now he was downstairs and still alone, still no firing. Again he shouted for Ahmed but his words just echoed off the walls and he wandered into rooms, no one around, everyone vanished and then a gun was in his face, another in his back. Ahmed and a guard, both nervous.

"Ahmed, quick," he burst out, "is it true that Abdollah's dead and there's a new Khan and that half the ransom's paid?"

Ahmed just gaped at him.

"For Christ's sake is it true?" he snarled.

"Yes, yes, that's true. But th—"

"Quick, you've got to tell them!" Relief flooding over him, for he had only half believed Hakim. "Quick, they'll kill him and kill Azadeh—come on!"

"Then the . . . they're not dead?"

"No, of course not, come on!"

"Wait! What exactly did th . . . . did His Highness say?"

"What the hell difference do—"

The gun jammed into Erikki's face. *"What did he say exactly?"*

Erikki searched his memory and told him as best he could, then added, "Now for the love of God, come on!"

For Ahmed time stopped. If he went with the Infidel he would probably die, Hakim Khan would die, his sister would die and the Infidel who was responsible for all this trouble would probably escape with his devil tribesmen. But then, he thought, if I could persuade them to let the Khan live and his sister live, persuade them to leave the palace, I will have proved myself beyond all doubt, both to the Khan and to *her*, and I can kill the pilot later. Or I can kill him now and escape easily and live—but only as a fugitive despised by all as one who betrayed his Khan. Insha'Allah!

His face creased into a smile. "As God wants!" He took out his knife and gave it and his gun to the white-faced guard and walked around Erikki. "Wait," Erikki said. "Tell the guard to send for a doctor. Urgently. Hakim and my wife . . . they may be hurt."

Ahmed told the man to do it and went along the corridor and into the hall and up the staircase. On the landing, tribesmen searched him roughly for arms then escorted him into the Khan's room, crowding after him, shoving him into the vast, empty space—Erikki they held at the door, a knife at his throat—and when Ahmed saw his Khan was truly alive, sitting bleakly on the cushions near Azadeh who was still unconscious, he muttered, "Praised be to God," and smiled at him. "Highness," he said calmly, "I've sent for a doctor." Then he picked out Bayazid.

"I am Ahmed Dursak the Turkoman," he said proudly, speaking Turkish with great formality. "In the Name of God: it's true that Abdollah Khan is dead, true that I paid half the ransom—5 million rials—last night on the new Khan's behalf to two messengers of the chief al-Drah of the village of Broken Tree, as an act of faith because of the unwarranted dishonor to your messenger ordered by the dead Abdollah Khan. Their names were Ishmud and Alilah and I hurried them north in a fine car." A murmur of astonishment went through the room. There could be no mistake, for all knew these false names, code names, given to protect the village and the tribe. "I told them, on behalf of the new Khan, the second half would be paid the moment the pilot and his air machine were released safely."

"Where is this new Khan, if he exists?" Bayazid scoffed. "Let him talk for himself."

"I am Khan of all the Gorgons," Hakim said, and there was a sudden silence. "Hakim Khan, eldest son of Abdollah Khan."

All eyes left him and went to Bayazid who noticed the astonishment on Erikki's face. He scowled, unsure. "Just because you say it doesn't mean th—"

"You call me a liar in my own house?"

"I only say to this man," Bayazid jerked a thumb at Ahmed, "that just because he says he paid the ransom, half of it, does not mean he paid it and did not then have them ambushed and killed—like my other messenger, by God!"

"I told you the truth, before God, and say again before God that I sent them north, safely with the money. Give me a knife, you take a knife, and I will show you what a Turkoman does to a man who calls him liar!" The tribesmen were horrified that their leader had put himself into such a bad position. "You call me liar and my Khan liar?"

In the silence Azadeh stirred and moaned, distracting them. At once Erikki began to go to her but the tribesman's knife never wavered, the tribesman muttered a curse, and he stopped. Another little moaning sigh that almost drove him mad, then he saw Hakim awkwardly move closer to his sister and hold her hand and this helped him a little.

Hakim was afraid, aching everywhere, knowing he was as defenseless as she was defenseless and needing a doctor urgently, that Ahmed was under siege, Erikki impotent, his own life threatened and his Khanate in ruins. Nonetheless he gathered his courage back. I didn't outfox Abdollah Khan and Najoud and Ahmed to concede victory to these dogs! Implacably he looked up at Bayazid. "Well? Do you call Ahmed a liar—yes or no?" he said harshly in Turkish so all could understand him and Ahmed loved him for his courage. All eyes now on Bayazid. "A *man* must answer that question. Do you call him a liar?"

"No," Bayazid muttered. "He spoke the truth, I accept it as truth." Someone said, "Insha'Allah," fingers loosened off triggers but nervousness did not leave the room.

"As God wants," Hakim said, his relief hidden, and rushed onward, every moment more in command. "More fighting will achieve nothing. So, half the ransom is already paid and the other half promised when the pilot is released safely. The . . ." He stopped as nausea threatened to overwhelm him but dominated it, easier this time than before. "The pilot's there and safe and so is his machine. Therefore I will pay the rest at once!"

He saw the greed and promised himself vengeance on all of them. "Ahmed, over by the table, Najoud's satchel's somewhere there." Ahmed shoved through the tribesmen arrogantly, to begin searching the debris for the soft leather purse. Hakim had been showing it to Azadeh just before the attack began, happily telling her the jewels were family heirlooms that Najoud had admitted stealing and, in complete contrition, had given him before she left. "I'm glad you didn't relent, Hakim, very glad," Azadeh had said. "You'd never be safe with her and her brood close to you."

I'll never be safe again, he thought without fear, watching Ahmed. I'm glad I left Ahmed whole, he thought, and glad we had the sense, Azadeh and I, to stay in the alcove under cover of the wall at the first sound of firing. If we'd been here in the room . . .

Insha'Allah. His fingers gripped her wrist and the warmth pleased him, her breathing still regular. "God be praised," he murmured, then noticed the men threatening Erikki. "You," he pointed imperiously at them, "let the pilot go!" Nonplussed the rough, bearded men looked at Bayazid who nodded. At once Erikki went through them to Azadeh, eased his heavy sweater away to give him readier access to the knife in the center of his back, then knelt, holding her hand, and faced Bayazid, his bulk protecting her and Hakim.

"Highness!" Ahmed gave Hakim Khan the purse. Leisurely he opened it, spilling the jewels into his hands. Emeralds and diamonds and sapphires, necklaces, encrusted golden bracelets, pendants. A great sigh went through the room. Judiciously Hakim chose a ruby necklace worth 10 to 15 million rials, pretending not to notice how all eyes were concentrated and the almost physical smell of greed that permeated the room. Abruptly he discarded the rubies and chose a pendant worth twice as much, three times as much.

"Here," he said still speaking Turkish, "here is full payment." He held up the diamond pendant and offered it to Bayazid who, mesmerized by the fire glittering from the single stone, came forward, his hand out. But before Bayazid could take it, Hakim closed his fist. "Before God you accept it as full payment?"

"Yes . . . yes, as full payment, before God," Bayazid muttered, never believing that God would grant him so much wealth—enough to buy herds and guns and grenades and silks and warm clothes. He held out his hand. "I swear it before God!"

"And you will leave here at once, in peace, before God?"

Bayazid pulled his brain off his riches. "First we have to get to our village, Agha, we need the airplane and the pilot."

"No, by God, the ransom's for the safe return of the airplane and the pilot, nothing more." Hakim opened his hand, never taking his eyes off Bayazid who now only saw the stone. "Before God?"

Bayazid and his men stared at the liquid fire in the rock-steady hand. "What's . . . what's to prevent me taking all of them, everything," he said sullenly, "what's to prevent me killing you—killing you and burning the palace and taking her hostage to force the pilot, eh?"

"Nothing. Except honor. Are Kurds without honor?" Hakim's voice rasped and he was thinking, how exciting this is, life the prize and death for failure. "This is more than full payment."

"I . . . I accept it before God as payment in full, for the pilot and the . . . and the airplane." Bayazid tore his eyes off the gem. "For the pilot and the airplane. But for you, you and the woman . . ." The sweat was trickling down his face. So much wealth there, his mind was shouting, so much, so easy to take, so easy but there is honor in this, oh, yes, very much. "For you and the woman there should be a fair ransom too."

Outside a car gunned its engine. Men rushed to the broken window. The car was racing for the main gate and as they watched, it hurtled through, heading for the city below.

"Quick," Bayazid said to Hakim, "make up your mind."

"The woman is worthless," Hakim said, afraid of the lie, aware that he had to bargain or they were still lost. His fingers chose a ruby bracelet and offered it. "Agreed?"

"To you the woman may be worthless—not to the pilot. The bracelet and the necklace, that one, together with the bracelet with the green stones."

"Before God that's too much," Hakim exploded, "this bracelet's more than enough—that's more than the value of the pilot and the airplane!"

"Son of a burnt father! This one, the necklace and that other bracelet, the one with the green stones."

They haggled back and forth, angrier and angrier, everyone listening intently except Erikki who was still locked in his own private hell, only concerned with Azadeh and where was the doctor and how he could help her and help Hakim. His hand was stroking her hair, his nerves pushed near the breaking point by the enraged voices of the two men as they reached the crescendo, the insults ever more violent. Then Hakim judged the moment right and let out a wail that was also part of the game of bargaining, "You're too good a negotiator for me, by God! You'll beggar me! Here, my final offer!" He put the diamond bracelet and the smaller of the emerald necklaces and the heavy gold bracelet onto the carpet. "Do we agree?"

It was a fair price now, not as much as Bayazid wanted but far more than he had expected. "Yes," he said and scooped up his prize and contentment filled the room. "You swear by God not to pursue us? Not to attack us?"

"Yes, yes, before God."

"Good. Pilot, I need you to take us home . . ." Bayazid said in English now and saw the rage soar into Hakim's face and added hastily, "I ask, not order, Agha. Here," he offered Erikki the gold bracelet, "I wish to hire your services, this's paym—" He stopped and looked off as one of his men guarding the patio, called out urgently, "There's a car coming up from the city!"

Bayazid was sweating more now. "Pilot, I swear by God I'll not harm you."

"I can't take you," Erikki said. "There's not enough gasoline."

"Then not all the way, halfway, just halfw—"

"There's not enough gasoline."

"Then take us and drop us in the mountains—just a little way. I ask you —ask not order," Bayazid said, then added curiously, "By the Prophet I treated you fairly and him fairly and . . . have not molested her. I ask you."

They had all heard the thread under the voice, perhaps a threat, perhaps not, but Erikki knew beyond any doubt that the fragile bubble of "honor" or "before God" would vanish with the first bullet, that it was up to him now to try to correct the disaster that the attack had become, chasing a Khan already dead, the ransom already half paid, and now Azadeh lying there, hurt as only God knows, and Hakim almost killed. Set-faced he touched her a last time, glanced at the Khan, nodded, half to himself, then got up, abruptly jerked the Sten gun out of the nearest tribesman's hands. "I'll accept your word before God and I'll kill you if you cheat. I'll drop you north of the city, in the mountains. Everyone in the chopper. Tell them!"

Bayazid hated the idea of the gun in the hands of this brooding, revenge-seeking monster. Neither of us has forgotten I threw the grenade that perhaps has killed a *houri*, he thought. "Insha'Allah!" Quickly he ordered the retreat. Taking the body of their dead comrade with them, they obeyed. "Pilot, we will leave together. Thank you, Agha Hakim Khan, God be with you," he said and backed to the door, weapon held loosely, but ready. "Come on!"

Erikki raised his hand in farewell to Hakim, consumed with anguish at what he had precipitated. "Sorry . . ."

"God be with you, Erikki, and come back safely," Hakim called out and Erikki felt better for that. "Ahmed, go with him, he can't fly and use a gun at the same time. See that he gets back safely." Yes, he thought icily, I've still a score to settle with him for the attack on *my* palace!

"Yes, Highness. Thank you, pilot." Ahmed took the gun from Erikki, checked the action and magazine, then smiled crookedly at Bayazid. "By God and the Prophet, on whose Name be praised, let no man cheat." Politely he motioned Erikki to leave, then followed him. Bayazid went last.

AT THE FOOTHILLS TO THE PALACE: 11:05 A.M. The police car was racing up the winding road toward the gates, other cars and an army truck filled with troops following. Hashemi Fazir and Armstrong were in the back of the lead car which skidded through the gate into the forecourt where an ambulance was already parked. They got out and followed the guard into the Great Room. Hakim Khan was waiting for them in his place of honor, pale and drawn but regal, guards around him, this part of the palace undamaged.

"Highness, God be praised you were not hurt—we've just heard about the attack. May I introduce myself? I'm Colonel Hashemi Fazir of Inner Intelligence and this is Superintendent Armstrong who has assisted us for years and is an expert in certain areas that could concern you—he speaks Farsi by the way. Would you please tell us what happened?" The two men listened intently as Hakim Khan related his version of the attack—they had already heard the rumored details—both of them impressed with his bearing.

Hashemi had come prepared. Before leaving Tehran yesterday evening he had meticulously gone through Hakim's files. For years both he and SAVAK had had him under surveillance in Khoi: "I know how much he owes and to whom, Robert, what favors and to whom, what he likes to eat and read, how good he is with gun, piano, or a knife, every woman he's ever bedded and every boy."

Armstrong had laughed. "What about his politics?"

"He has none. Unbelievable—but true. He's Iranian, Azerbaijani, and yet he hasn't joined any group, taken any sides, none, not said anything even a little seditious—even against Abdollah Khan—and Khoi's always been a festering bed of nettles."

"Religion?"

"Shi'ite, but calm, conscientious, orthodox, neither right nor left. Ever since he was banished, no, that's not quite true, since he was seven when his mother died and he and his sister went to live in the palace, he's been a feather wafted by his father's merest breath, waiting in fear for inevitable disaster. As God wants, but it's a miracle he's Khan, a miracle that that vile son of a dog died before doing him and his sister harm. Strange! One moment his head's on the block, and now he controls untold riches, untold power, and I've got to deal with him."

"That should be easy—if what you say's true."

"You're suspicious, always suspicious—is that the strength of the English?"

"Just the lesson an old cop's learned over the years."

Hashemi had smiled to himself and now he did it again, concentrating on the young man, Khan of all the Gorgons, in front of him, watching him closely, studying him for clues. What're your secrets—you've got to have secrets!

"Highness, how long ago did the pilot leave?" Armstrong was asking.

Hakim glanced at his watch. "About two and a half hours ago."

"Did he say how much fuel he had with him?"

"No, only that he would take them a little way and drop them."

Hashemi and Robert Armstrong were standing in front of the raised platform with its rich carpets and cushions, Hakim Khan dressed formally in warm brocades, a string of pearls around his neck with a diamond pendant four times the size of the one he had bartered their lives for. "Perhaps," Hashemi said delicately, "perhaps Highness, the pilot was really in league with the Kurdish tribesmen, and won't come back."

"No, and they weren't Kurds though they claimed to be, just bandits, and they'd kidnapped Erikki and forced him to lead them against the Khan, my father." The young Khan frowned, then said firmly, "The Khan my father should not have had their messenger killed. He should have bartered the ransom down, then paid it—and then had them killed for their impertinence."

Hashemi docketed the clue. "I will see they are all hunted down."

"And all my property recovered."

"Of course. Is there anything, anything at all, I or my department can do for you?" He was watching the young man closely and saw, or thought he saw, a flash of sardonic amusement and it rattled him. At that moment the door opened and Azadeh came in. He had never met her though he had seen her many times. She should be possessed by an Iranian, he thought, not by a rotten foreigner. How could she contain that monster? He did not notice Hakim scrutinizing him as intently. Armstrong did, watching the Khan without watching him.

She was dressed in Western clothes, gray green that set off her green-flecked eyes, stockings and soft shoes—her face very pale and made up just enough. Her walk was slow and somewhat painful, but she bowed to her brother with a sweet smile. "Sorry to interrupt you, Highness, but the doctor asked me to remind you to rest. He's about to leave, would you like to see him again?"

"No, no, thank you. You're all right?"

"Oh, yes," she said and forced a smile. "He says I'm fine."

"May I present Colonel Hashemi Fazir and Mr. Armstrong, Superintendent Armstrong—Her Highness, my sister, Azadeh."

They greeted her and she greeted them back. "Superintendent Armstrong?" she said in English with a little frown. "I don't remember 'Super-intendent' but we've met before, haven't we?"

"Yes, Highness, once at the French Club, last year. I was with Mr. Talbot of the British embassy and a friend of your husband's from the Finnish embassy, Christian Tollonen—I believe it was your husband's birth-day party."

"You've a good memory, Superintendent."

Hakim Khan smiled strangely. "That's a characteristic of MI6, Azadeh."

"Just of ex-policemen, Highness," Armstrong said easily. "I'm just a consultant to Inner Intelligence." Then to Azadeh: "Colonel Fazir and I were both so relieved that neither you nor the Khan was hurt."

"Thank you," she said, her ears and head still aching badly and her back giving her problems. The doctor had said, "We'll have to wait for a few days, Highness, although we will X-ray you both as soon as possible. Best you go to Tehran, both of you, they have better equipment. With an explosion like that . . . you never know, Highness, best to go, I wouldn't like to be responsible . . ."

Azadeh sighed. "Please excuse me for interrup—" She stopped abruptly, listening, head slightly tilted. They listened too. Just the wind picking up and a distant car.

"Not yet," Hakim said kindly.

She tried to smile and murmured, "As God wants," then went away.

Hashemi broke the small silence. "We should leave you too, Highness," he said deferentially, in Farsi again; "it was kind of you to see us today. Perhaps we could come back tomorrow?" He saw the young Khan take his eyes off the door and look at him under his dark eyebrows, the handsome face in repose, fingers toying with the jeweled ornamental dagger at his belt. He must be made of ice, he thought, politely waiting to be dismissed.

But instead Hakim Khan dismissed all his guards, except one he stationed at the door, well out of listening range, and beckoned the two men closer. "Now we will speak English. What is it you really want to ask me?" he said softly.

Hashemi sighed, sure that Hakim Khan already knew, and more than sure now that here he had a worthy adversary, or ally. "Help on two mat-ters, Highness: your influence in Azerbaijan could immeasurably help us to put down hostile elements in rebellion against the state."

"What's second?"

He had heard the touch of impatience and it amused him. "Second is somewhat delicate. It concerns a Soviet called Petr Oleg Mzytryk, an ac-quaintance of your father, who for some years, from time to time, visited here—as Abdollah Khan visited his dacha in Tbilisi. While Mzytryk posed as a friend of Abdollah Khan and Azerbaijan, in reality he's a very senior KGB officer and very hostile."

"Ninety-eight out of every hundred Soviets who come to Iran are KGB, therefore enemy, and the other two GRU, therefore enemy. As Khan, my father would have to deal with all manner of enemies"—again a fleeting sardonic smile that Hashemi noted—"all manner of friends and all those in between. So?"

"We would very much like to interview him." Hashemi waited for some reaction but there was none and his admiration for the young man increased. "Before Abdollah Khan died he had agreed to help us. Through him we heard the man intended secretly to come over the border last Saturday and again on Tuesday, but both times he did not appear."

"How was he entering?"

Hashemi told him, not sure how much Hakim Khan knew, feeling his way with greater caution. "We believe the man may contact you—if so, would you please let us know? Privately."

Hakim Khan decided it was time to put this Tehrani enemy and his British dog lackey in place. Son of a burnt father, am I so naive I don't know what's going on? "In return for what?" he said bluntly.

Hashemi was equally blunt. "What do you want?"

"First: all senior SAVAK and police officers in Azerbaijan put on suspension at once, pending review—by me—and all future appointments to be subject to my prior approval."

Hashemi flushed. Not even Abdollah Khan had ever had this. "What's second?" he asked dryly.

Hakim Khan laughed. "Good, very good, Agha. Second will wait until tomorrow or the next day, so will third and perhaps fourth. But about your first point, at 10:00 A.M. tomorrow bring me specific requests how I could help stop all fighting in Azerbaijan—and how you, personally, if you had the power, how you would . . ." He thought a moment, then added, "How you would make us safe against enemies from without, and safe from enemies from within." He turned his attention to Armstrong.

Armstrong had been hoping the exchange would go on forever, ecstatic that he was having the opportunity to witness this new Khan at firsthand going against a hardened adversary like Hashemi. Great balls of fire, if this little bugger can operate so confidently like this on day two of becoming Khan after being almost blown to kingdom come a couple of hours ago, Her Majesty's Government better put him high on the S danger list, "Slowly, slowly catchee monkee!" Now he saw the eyes fix on him. With an effort he kept his face bland, groaning inwardly: Now it's your turn!

"You're an expert in what certain areas that would concern me?"

"Well, Your Highness, I, er, I was in Special Branch and understand a little about intelligence and, er, counterintelligence. Of course good information, private information's essential to someone in your position. If you wanted, perhaps I could, in conjunction with Colonel Fazir, suggest ways to improve this for you."

"A good thought, Mr. Armstrong. Please give me your views in writing—as soon as possible."

"I'd be glad to." Armstrong decided to gamble. "Mzytryk could provide you rapidly with a lot of the answers you need, most of the important answers you need on the 'within and without' you mentioned, particularly if the Colonel could, er, chat with him in private." The words hung in the air. Beside him, he saw Hashemi shift his feet nervously. I'll bet my life you know more than you're letting on, Hakim, me lad, and bet my balls you didn't spend all those years just a bloody "feather"! Christ, I need a cigarette!

The eyes were boring into him and he would have loved to light up and say airily, For Christ's sake, stop all this sodding about and shit or get off the pot . . . Then his mind pictured this Khan of all the Gorgons squatting on a lavatory seat, everything hanging out, and he had to cough to stop his sudden laugh. "Sorry," he said, trying to sound meek.

Hakim Khan frowned. "How would I have access to the information?" he said, and both men knew that he was hooked.

"However you want, Highness," Hashemi said, "however you want."

Another small silence. "I'll consider what y—" Hakim Khan stopped, listening. Now they all heard the approaching putt-putt-putt of rotors and the sound of the jets. Both men started for the tall windows. "Wait," Hakim said. "One of you please give me a hand."

Astonished, they helped him stand. "Thank you," he said painfully. "That's better. It's my back. In the explosion I must have twisted it." Hashemi took some of his weight and between them he hobbled to the tall windows that overlooked the forecourt.

The 212 was coming in slowly, drifting down to her landing. As she got closer they recognized Erikki and Ahmed in the front seats but Ahmed was slumped down, clearly hurt. A few bullet holes in the airframe, a great chunk of plastic out of a side window. She settled into a perfect landing. At once the engines began to die. Now they saw the blood staining Erikki's white collar and sleeve.

"Christ . . ." Armstrong muttered.

"Colonel," Hakim Khan said urgently to Hashemi, "see if you can stop the doctor from leaving." Instantly Hashemi rushed off.

From where they were they could see the front steps. The huge door opened and Azadeh hobbled out and stood there a moment, a statue, others gathering beside her now, guards and servants and some of the family. Erikki opened his side door and got out awkwardly. Tiredly he went toward her. But his walk was firm and tall and then she was in his arms.

CHAPTER 56

IN KOWISS TOWN: 12:10 P.M. Ibrahim Kyabi waited impatiently in ambush for the mullah Hussain to come out of the mosque into the crowded square. He sat slumped against the fountain opposite the huge door, his arms cradling the canvas bag that camouflaged his cocked M16. His eyes were red-rimmed with tiredness, his whole body aching from his 350-odd-mile journey from Tehran.

Idly he noticed a tall European among the crowds. The man was following a Green Band, and wore dark clothes, parka, and peaked cap. He watched the two of them bypass the mosque and disappear into the alley beside it. Nearby was the maw of the bazaar. Its darkness and warmth and safety tempted him to leave the cold.

"Insha'Allah," he muttered automatically, then dully reminded himself to stop using that expression, pulled the old overcoat closer around him, and settled more comfortably against the fountain that, when winter's ice had gone, would once more trickle for passersby to drink or ritually to wash their hands and faces before going to prayers.

"What's this mullah Hussain like?" he had asked the street vendor who was ladling him a portion of the steaming bean horisht out of the cauldron that hung over the charcoal. It was morning then and he had just arrived after interminable delays, fifteen hours overdue. "What's he like?"

The man was old and toothless and he shrugged. "A mullah."

Another customer nearby swore at him. "May you be sacrificed! Don't listen to him, stranger, the mullah Hussain is a true leader of the people, a man of God, who owns nothing but a gun and ammunition to kill the enemies of God." Other customers echoed this unshaven youth and told about the taking of the air base. "Our mullah's a true follower of the Imam, he'll lead us into Paradise, by God."

Ibrahim had almost cried out in rage. Hussain and all mullahs deserve death for feeding these poor peasants such nonsense. Paradise? Fine raiments and wine and forty perpetual virgins on silk couches?

I won't think of loving, I won't think of Sharazad, not yet.

His hands caressed the hidden strength of the gun. This took away some of his fatigue and hunger, but none of his utter loneliness.

Sharazad. Now part of a dream. Better this way, much better: he had been waiting for her at the coffee shop when Jari had accosted him and muttered, "In the Name of God, the husband has returned. That which never began is finished forever," then had vanished into the crowds. At once he had left and fetched his gun and walked all the way to the bus station. Now he was waiting, soon to be martyred taking vengeance in the name of the Masses against blind tyranny. So soon now. Soon into blackness or into light, oblivion or understanding, alone or with others: prophets, imams, devils, who?

In ecstasy he closed his eyes. Soon I'll know what happens when we die and where we go. Do we, at long last, find the answer to the great riddle: Was Mohammed the last Prophet of God, or madman? Is the Koran true? Is there God?

In the alley beside the mosque, the Green Band leading Starke stopped and motioned toward a hovel. Starke stepped across the befouled joub and knocked. The door opened. "Peace be upon you, Excellency Hussain!" he said in Farsi, tense and on guard. "You sent for me?"

"Salaam, Captain. Yes, yes, I did," the mullah Hussain replied in English and motioned him to enter.

Starke had to stoop to go inside the one-room hut. Two babes were sleeping fitfully on their straw pallet on the dirt floor. A young boy stared back at him, hands clasped around an old rifle, and he recognized him as the same child at the fight between Hussain's men and Zataki's men. A well-serviced AK47 leaned against a wall. Over by the sink a nervous old woman in a black, stained chador sat on a rickety chair.

"These are my sons and this is my wife," Hussain said.

"Salaam." Starke hid his astonishment that she should be so old. Then he looked closer and saw the age was not in years.

"I sent for you for three reasons: First for you to see how a mullah lives. Poverty is one of a mullah's prime duties."

"And learning, leadership, and lawgiving. That apart, Agha, I know you're a hundred percent sincere in your beliefs," and trapped by them, Starke wanted to add, loathing this room with the terrible, never-ending poverty it represented, its stench and the helplessness that he knew need not be but would exist for all the days of the lives here—and in countless other homes of all religions, all the world over. But not with my family, thank God! Thank God I was born Texan, thank God ten billion trillion times that I know better and my kids won't, *won't, by God,* won't have to live in the dirt like these poor little critters. With an effort he stopped himself from brushing their flies away, wanting to curse Hussain for enduring that which need not be endured.

"You said three reasons, Agha?"

"The second is: Why are all but a few men scheduled to leave today?"

"They're long overdue leave, Agha. Work's slow at the base, this's a perfect time." Starke's anxiety increased. This morning, before he had been summoned here, there had already been three telexes and two calls on the HF from their HQ in Tehran, the last from Siamaki, now the ranking board member, demanding to know where Pettikin, Nogger Lane, and the others were. He had sluffed him off, saying that McIver would call him back the instant he arrived with Minister Kia, very conscious of Wazari's curiosity.

Yesterday had been the first he had heard of Ali Kia's visit. Charlie Pettikin, during his brief stopover outward bound for Al Shargaz, had told him what had happened to McIver and their fears about him. "Jesus . . ." was all he could mutter.

But yesterday had not been all bad. John Hogg had brought Gavallan's provisional schedule for Whirlwind with codes and times and coordinates of refueling alternates set up on the other side of the Gulf. "Andy said to tell you they've all been passed on to Scrag at Lengeh and Rudi at Bandar Delam and take into account the problems of all three bases," Hogg had told him. "Two 747 freighters are booked for Al Shargaz, dawn Friday. That'll give us plenty of time, Andy says. I'll bring another update when I come for the lads, Duke. The final button's not to be pressed until 7:00 A.M. Friday or same time Saturday or Sunday. Then it's no go."

None of Esvandiary's spies had been around so Starke had managed to squeeze another crate of very valuable 212 avionics aboard the 125. And there was more good luck: All their personnel exit permits were still valid, enough forty-gallon drums of fuel had been cached safely on the shore, and Tom Lochart had come in from Zagros on time, now a committed Whirlwind pilot. "Why the change, Tom? Thought you were dead set against it," he had said, perturbed by Lochart's manner. But his friend had just shrugged and he had left it at that.

Still, the thought of their 212s making a rush for it worried him very much. They had no real plan, just several possibilities. With an effort he concentrated, the room becoming increasingly claustrophobic. "They're overdue leave," he said again.

"When will their replacements be arriving?"

"Saturday, that's when they're scheduled."

"Esvandiary says you've been sending out many spares."

"Spares need replacement and checking from time to time, Agha."

Hussain studied him, then nodded thoughtfully. "What caused the accident that nearly killed Esvandiary?"

"The load shifted. It's a tricky operation."

Another small silence. "Who is this man Kia, Ali Kia?"

Starke was not expecting any of these questions, wondering if he was being tested again, and how much the mullah knew. "I was told he was a minister for Prime Minister Bazargan on a tour of inspection." Then added, "Also that he was, or is, a consultant to our joint partnership, IHC, maybe even a director, but I don't know about that."

"When is he arriving?"

"I'm not sure. Our director, Captain McIver, was ordered to escort him."

"Ordered?"

"Ordered, so I understand."

"Why should a minister be a consultant to a private company?"

"I imagine you'd have to ask him, Agha."

"Yes, I agree," Hussain's face hardened. "The Imam has sworn that corruption will cease. We'll go to the base together." He picked up the AK47 and slung it over his shoulder. "Salaam," he said to his family.

Starke and the Green Band followed Hussain along the alley to a side door of the mosque. There the mullah kicked off his shoes, picked them up and went inside. Starke and the Green Band did the same, except that Starke also took off his peaked hat. Along a passageway and through another door and then they were in the mosque itself, a single room under the dome, covered with carpets and no ornaments. Just decorative tiles, here and there, with exquisite inlaid Sanskrit quotations from the Koran. A lectern with an open Koran, nearby a modern cassette player and loudspeakers, wires carelessly strung, all electric lights bare and dim. From the loudspeakers came the muted singsong of a man reading from the Koran.

Men were praying, others gossiping, some sleeping. Those who saw Hussain smiled at him and he smiled back, leading the way to a columned alcove. There he stopped and put down his shoes and gun, waved the Green Band away. "Captain, have you thought any more about what we discussed at the questioning?"

"In what way, Agha?" Starke's apprehension soared, his stomach queasy.

"About Islam, about the Imam, God's peace upon him, about going to see him?"

"It's not possible for me to see him, even if I wanted to."

"Perhaps I could arrange it. If you saw the Imam, watched him talk, listened to him, you would find God's peace you seek. And the truth."

Starke was touched by the mullah's obvious sincerity. "If I had the chance I'd sure . . . I'd sure take it up, if I could. You said three things, Agha?"

"This was the third. Islam. Become Muslim. There is not a moment to lose. Submit to God, accept that there is only One God and that Mohammed is His Prophet, accept it and have life everlasting in Paradise."

The eyes were dark and penetrating. Starke had experienced them before and found them almost hypnotic. "I . . . I told you already, Agha, perhaps I will, in . . . in God's time." He pulled his eyes away and felt the dominating force lessen. "If we're going back, we'd better go now. I don't want to miss seeing my guys off."

It was almost as though he had not spoken. "Isn't the Imam the Most Holy of men, the most stalwart, the most relentless against oppression? The Imam is, Captain. Open your eyes and spirit to him."

Starke heard the underlying emphasis through the fervor and once more the seeming sacrilege disquieted him. "I wait, patiently." He looked back at the eyes that seemed to be looking through him, through the walls, into infinity. "If we're going, we'd better go," he said as gently as he could.

Hussain sighed. The light went out of his eyes. He shouldered his gun and led the way out. At the main door he stepped into his shoes, waited for Starke to do the same. Four more Green Bands joined them. "We're going to the base," Hussain told them.

"I parked my car just outside the square," Starke said, enormously relieved to be in the open again and out of the man's spell. "It's a station wagon, we can go in that if you like."

"Good. Where is it?"

Starke pointed and walked off, weaving through the stalls. He was almost a head taller than most of the crowd and now his mind was buzzing with thought and counterthought, sifting what the mullah had said, trying to plan what to do about Whirlwind.

"Goddamn," he muttered, swamped by the danger. I hope Rudi aborts, then I will, whatever Scrag does. Automatically his eyes were scanning as they would in a cockpit, and he noticed a commotion ahead by the fountain. Because of his great height he was the first to see the youth with the gun, the crowds scattering. He stopped, frozen with disbelief, Hussain coming alongside. But there was no mistake, the shrieking, berserk youth was charging through the people directly at him. "Assassin," he gasped, the men and women in front fleeing in terror, running, tripping, falling out of the man's path, and now the way was clear. Blankly he saw the man skid to a stop and point the gun directly at him.

"Look out!" But before he could dive for the ground and the cover of a stall, the impact of the first bullet spun him, slammed him back against one of the Green Bands. More bullets, someone nearby screamed, then another gun opened up, deafening him.

It was Hussain. His reflexes had been very good. At once he had realized the assassin attack was against him and the moment of respite that Starke had given him was enough. With one smooth movement he had swung his gun off his shoulder, aimed, and pulled the trigger, his mind shouting, "There is no other God but . . ."

His fire was coldly accurate and holed Ibrahim Kyabi, thrusting the life out of him, tearing the gun from the dead hands and putting him into the dirt. Numbly the mullah stopped firing and found he was still upright, disbelieving that he was not hit, impossible for the assassin to miss, impossible that he was not martyred and on the path to Paradise. Shakily he looked around in the pandemonium, wounded being helped, others wailing and cursing, one of his Green Bands splayed out, dead, many bystanders hurt. Starke was crumpled on the ground, half under the stalls.

"Praise be to God, Excellency Hussain, you're unhurt," a Green Band called out.

"As God wants . . . God is Great . . ." Hussain went over to Starke and knelt beside him. He saw blood was dripping from his left sleeve, his face was white. "Where are you hit?"

"I'm . . . I'm not sure. It's my . . . I think it's my shoulder or chest." It was the first time Starke had ever been shot. When the bullet had smashed him backward onto the ground, there was no pain but his mind was screaming: I'm dead, the bastard's killed me, I'll never see Manuela, never get home, never see the kids, I'm dead . . . Then he had had a blinding urge to run—to flee from his own death. He had wanted to jump to his feet but the pain tore the strength out of him and now Hussain was kneeling beside him.

"Let me help you," Hussain said, then to the Green Band, "Take his other arm."

He cried out as they turned him and tried to help him up. "Wait . . . for crissake . . ." When the spasm had passed he found he could not move his left arm at all, but his right worked. With his good right hand he felt himself, moved his legs. No pain there. Everything seemed to be working, except his left arm and shoulder, and his head was bleary. Gritting his teeth he opened his parka and pulled away his shirt. Blood seeped from the hole that was in the center of his shoulder but it wasn't pumping out, and there was no unbearable discomfort in his breathing, just a stabbing pain if he moved incautiously. "It's . . . I don't think it's . . . it's in my lungs . . ."

"Son of a burnt father, pilot," the Green Band said with a laugh. "Look, there's another hole in the back of your jacket, it's bleeding too, the bullet must've gone right through you." He started to probe the hole with a dirty finger and Starke cursed him violently. "Curse yourself, Infidel," the man said. "Curse yourself, not me. Perhaps God in his mercy gave you your life back, though why God would do that . . ." He shrugged and got up, looked at his dead comrade nearby and the other wounded, shrugged again, and sauntered over to Ibrahim Kyabi who lay in the dirt like a bag of old rags, and began to go through his pockets.

The crowd in the square was pressing forward, encroaching on the two of them, so Hussain got up and waved them away. "God is Great, God is Great," he shouted. "Keep back. Help those who are hurt!" When they had space again he knelt beside Starke. "Didn't I warn you your time was short? God protected you this time to give you another chance."

But Starke hardly heard him. He had found his handkerchief and was stuffing it against the hole, trying to stanch the blood, feeling the warm trickle down his back, muttering and cursing, now over his black terror, but not over the fear that he would still shame himself by running away. "What the hell was that bastard trying to kill me for?" he muttered. "Son of a bitch, goddamn crazy!"

"He was trying to kill me, not you."

Starke stared up at him. "Fedayeen, mujhadin?"

"Or Tudeh. What does it matter, he was an enemy of God. God killed him."

Another pain knifed into Starke's chest. He muffled a curse, hating all this God talk, not wanting to think about God but only about the kids and Manuela and normality and getting the hell out: I'm sick to death of all this madness and killing in the name of their own narrow version of God. "Sonsofbitches!" he muttered, his words swallowed in the noise. His shoulder was throbbing, the pain spreading. As best he could he balled the handkerchief, using it as a dressing, and closed his parka, muttering obscenities.

What the hell'm I gonna do now, for crissake? Goddamn crazy bastard, how the hell'm I gonna fly now? He shifted his position slightly. Pain dragged another involuntary groan from him and he cursed again, disgusted with himself, wanting to be stoic.

Hussain came out of his reverie, anguished that God had decided to leave him alive when, again, he should have been martyred. Why? Why am I so cursed? And this American, impossible for the spray of bullets not to have killed him also—why was he too left alive? "We'll go to your base. Can you stand up?"

"I'll . . . sure, just a moment." Starke readied. "Okay, careful . . . oh, sweet Jesus . . ." Even so he stood, weaving slightly, pain nauseating him. "Can one of your men drive?"

"Yes." Hussain called out to the Green Band kneeling beside Kyabi, "Firouz, hurry up!" Obediently the man came back.

"Just these coins in his pockets, Excellency, and this. What's it say?"

Hussain examined it closely. "It's a current Tehran University identity card."

The photo showed a handsome youth smiling at the camera. IBRAHIM KYABI, 3D YEAR, ENGINEERING SECTION. BIRTH DATE 12 MARCH 1955. Hussain glanced at the back of the card. "There's a Tehran address on it."

"Stinking universities," another young Green Band said. "Hotbeds of Satan and Western evil."

"When the Imam reopens them, God grant him peace, mullahs will be in charge. We'll stamp out all Western, anti-Islam ideas forever. Give the card to the komiteh, Firouz. They can pass it on to Tehran. Komitehs in Tehran will interrogate his family and friends, and deal with them." Hussain saw Starke looking at him. "Yes, Captain?"

Starke had seen the photo. "I was just thinking, in a few days he'd've been twenty-four. Kind of a waste, isn't it."

"God punished his evil. Now he is in hellfire."

NORTH OF KOWISS: 4:10 P.M. The 206 was cruising nicely over the Zagros foothills, McIver at the controls, Ali Kia dozing beside him. McIver was feeling very good. Ever since he had decided to fly Kia himself he had been light-headed. It was the perfect solution, the only one. So my medical's not current, so what? We're in a war operation, we have to take risks, and I'm still the best bloody pilot in the company.

He looked across at Kia. If you weren't such a horse's arse, I'd hug you for giving me the excuse. He beamed and clicked on the sender. "Kowiss, this is HotelTangoX ray at one thousand, heading 185 degrees inbound from Tehran with Minister Ali Kia aboard."

"HTX. Maintain heading, report at Outer Marker."

His flight and refueling at Isfahan International Airport had been uneventful, except for a few minutes after landing when excited, shouting Green Bands had surrounded the helicopter threateningly, even though he had had clearance to land and refuel. "Get on the radio and insist the station supervisor come at once," Kia had said to McIver, seething. "I represent the government!"

McIver had obliged. "The, er, the tower says if we're not refueled and away within the hour the komiteh will impound us." He added sweetly, delighted to pass on the message, "They, er, said, 'Foreign pilots and foreign airplanes are not welcome in Isfahan, nor running dogs of Bazargan's foreign-dominated government!' "

"Barbarians, illiterate peasants," Kia had said disgustedly, but only when they were safely airborne again, McIver enormously relieved that he had been allowed into the civilian airport and had not had to use the air force base where Lochart had refueled.

McIver could see the whole Kowiss air base now. On the far side of the field near their IHC complex he saw the company 125 and his heart did a flip. I told Starke to get the lads off early, he thought irritably. "IHC Control, HTX from Tehran with Minister Kia aboard."

"IHC Control. HTX, land on helipad 2. Wind's thirty to thirty-five knots at 135 degrees."

McIver could see Green Bands on the main gate, some near the helipad with Esvandiary and the Iranian staff. A group of mechanics and pilots was also collecting nearby. My reception committee, he thought, recognizing John Hogg, Lochart, Jean-Luc, and Ayre. No Starke yet. So I'm illegal. What can they do? I outrank them but if the ICAA find out they could be plenty bloody mad. He had his speech all ready, in case: "I apologize but the exigencies of Minister Kia's order necessitated an immediate decision. Of course it won't happen again." It wouldn't have happened at all if

Whirlwind wasn't planned. He leaned over and shook Kia awake. "We'll be landing in a couple of minutes, Agha."

Kia rubbed the fatigue out of his face, glanced at his watch, then straightened his tie, combed his hair and carefully readjusted his Astrakhan hat. He studied the people below, the neat hangars, and all the helicopters neatly lined up—two 212s, three 206s, two Alouettes—*my* helicopters, he thought with a glow. "Why was the flight so slow?" he said curtly.

"We're on time, Minister. We've had a bit of a headwind." McIver was concentrating on the landing, needing to make it very good. It was.

Esvandiary swung Kia's door open. "Excellency Minister, I'm Kuram Esvandiary, chief of IranOil in this area, welcome to Kowiss. Agha Managing Director Siamaki called to make sure we were prepared for you. Welcome!"

"Thank you." Ostentatiously Kia said to McIver, "Pilot, be ready to take off at 10:00 A.M. tomorrow. I may want to go around some oil sites with Excellency Esvandiary before going back. Don't forget, I have to be in Tehran for my 7:00 P.M. meeting with the prime minister." He got out and was bustled off to inspect the choppers. Immediately Ayre, Lochart, and the others ducked under the blades and came quickly alongside McIver's window. He disregarded their faces and beamed. "Hello, how're tricks?"

"Let me finish the shutdown for you, Mac," Ayre said, "we've a s—"

"Thanks, but I'm perfectly capable," McIver said crisply, then into the mike, "HTX closing down." He saw Lochart's face and sighed again. "So I'm slightly out of whack, Tom. So?"

"It's not that, Mac," Lochart said in a rush, "Duke's been shot." McIver listened appalled as Lochart told him what had happened. "He's in the infirmary now. Doc Nutt says his lung may be punctured."

"Christ Almighty! Then put him aboard the 125, go on Johnny, get g—"

"He can't, Mac," Lochart overrode him with the same urgency: "Hotshot's held up her departure till after Kia's inspection—yesterday old Duke tried every which way to get her in and out before you arrived but Hotshot's a sonofabitch. And that's not all, I think Tehran's rumbled us."

"*What?*"

Lochart told him about the telexes and the HF calls. "Siamaki's been bending Hotshot's ear, getting him worked up. I took Siamaki's last call— Duke had gone to the mullah's—and he was mad as a sonofabitch. I told him the same as Duke and sluffed him off saying you'd call when you got in, but Jesus, Mac, he knows you and Charlie've cleaned out your apartment."

"Ali Baba! He must've been a plant." McIver's head was reeling. Then he noticed the little gold St. Christopher that habitually he hung around the magnetic compass when flying. It was a present from Genny, a first

present, a war present, just after they'd met, he in the RAF, she a WAAF:
"Just so you don't get lost, me lad," she had said. "You don't have much of
a nose for north."

He smiled now and blessed her. "First I'll see Duke." He could see
Esvandiary and Kia wandering down the line of choppers. "Tom, you and
Jean-Luc see if you can chivy Kia along, butter the bugger up, flatter the
balls off him—I'll join you as quick as I can." They went off at once.
"Freddy, you spread the word that the moment we get the okay for the 125
to leave, everyone's to board fast and quietly. Is all the baggage aboard?"

"Yes, but what about Siamaki?"

"I'll worry about that bugger, off you go." McIver hurried away.

Johnny Hogg called out after him, "Mac, a word in your ear as soon as
poss."

The underlying urgency stopped him. "What Johnny?"

"Urgent and private from Andy: If this weather worsens he may postpone Whirlwind from tomorrow till Saturday. The wind's changed. It'll be
a headwind now instead of a tail—"

"You saying I don't know southeast from northwest?"

"Sorry. Andy also said, as you're here he can't give you the overriding yes
or no he promised."

"That's right. Ask him to give it to Charlie. What else?"

"The rest can wait. I haven't told the others."

Doc Nutt was in the infirmary with Starke. Starke lay on a cot, arm in a
sling, his shoulder heavily bandaged. "Hello, Mac, you have a good flight?"
he said witheringly.

"Don't you start! Hi, Doc! Duke, we'll get you out on the 125."

"No. There's tomorrow."

"Tomorrow'll take care of tomorrow and meanwhile you're on the 124—
125! For Christ's sake," McIver said irritably, his relief at having made the
flight safely and at seeing Starke alive peeled away his control, "don't act
like you're Deadeye Dick at the Alamo!"

"He wasn't at the goddamn Alamo," Starke slammed back angrily, "and
who the hell're you to act like Chuck Yeager?"

Doc Nutt said mildly, "If you both don't slow down, I'll order the two of
you bloody enemas."

Abruptly both men laughed and Starke gasped as pain rocked him. "For
crissake, Doc, don't make me laugh . . ." And McIver said, "Duke, Kia
insisted I accompany him. I couldn't tell him to push off."

"Sure." Starke grunted. "How was it?"

"Grand."

"What about the wind?"

"It's not a plus for tomorrow," McIver said carefully. "It can change back again just as quickly."

"If it stays this way it's a thirty-knot headwind or worse and we can't make it across the Gulf. There's no way we can carry enough fu—"

"Yes. Doc, what's the poop?"

"Duke should be X-rayed as soon as possible. Shoulder blade's shattered and there's some tendon and muscle damage, wound's clean. There might be a splinter or two in the left lung, he's lost a pint or so, but all in all he's been very bloody lucky."

"I feel okay, Doc, I'm mobile," Starke said. "One day won't make that amount of difference. I can still go along tomorrow."

"Sorry, old top, but you're shook. Bullets do that. You may not feel it now but in an hour or two you will, guaranteed." Doc Nutt was very glad he was leaving with the 125 today. Don't want to cope anymore, he told himself. Don't want to see any more fine young bodies bullet-torn and mutilated. I've had it. Yes, but I'll have to stick to it for a few more days, there're going to be others to patch up because Whirlwind's just not going to work. It's not, I feel it in my bones. "Sorry, but you'd be a hazard on any op, even a little one."

"Duke," McIver said, "it's best you go at once. Tom, you take one—no need for Jean-Luc to stay."

"And what the hell you figure on doing?"

McIver beamed. "Me, I'll be a passenger. Meanwhile, I'm just bloody Kia's very private bloody pilot."

IN THE TOWER: 4:50 P.M.   "I repeat, Mr. Siamaki," McIver said tightly into the mike, "there's a special conference in Al Sh—"

"And I repeat, why wasn't I informed at once?" The voice over the loudspeaker was shrill and irritated.

McIver's knuckles were white from the grip on the mike's stem, and he was being watched intently by a Green Band and Wazari whose face was still swollen from the beating Zataki had given him. "I repeat, Agha Siamaki," he said, his voice tidy, "Captains Pettikin and Lane were needed for an urgent conference in Al Shargaz and there was no time to inform you."

"Why? I'm here in Tehran. Why wasn't the office informed, where are their exit permits? Where?"

McIver pretended to be slightly exasperated. "I already told you, Agha, there was no time—phones in Tehran aren't working—and I cleared their exits with the komiteh at the airport, personally with His Excellency the mullah in charge." The Green Band yawned, bored, non-English-speaking, and noisily cleared his throat. "Now if you'll excu—"

"But you and Captain Pettikin have removed your valuables from your apartment. Is that so?"

"Merely a precaution to remove temptation from vile mujhadin and fedayeen burglars and bandits while we're away," McIver said airily, very conscious of Wazari's attention and sure that the tower at the air base was monitoring this conversation. "Now if you'll excuse me, Minister Kia requires my presence!"

"Ah, Minister Kia, ah, yes!" Siamaki's irritability softened a little. "What, er, what time do you both arrive back in Tehran tomorrow?"

"Depending on the winds . . ." McIver's eyes almost crossed as he had a sudden, almost overwhelming, desire to blurt out about Whirlwind. I must be going potty, he thought. With an effort he concentrated. "Depending on Minister Kia, the winds, and refueling, sometime in the afternoon."

"I will be waiting for you; I may even meet you at the airport if we know your ETA; there are checks to be signed and many rearrangements to be discussed. Please give Minister Kia my best wishes and wish him a pleasant stay in Kowiss. Salaam." The transmission clicked off. McIver sighed, put the mike down. "Sergeant, while I'm here I'd like to call Bandar Delam and Lengeh."

"I'll have to ask base," Wazari said.

"Go ahead." McIver looked out the window. The weather was deteriorating, the southeaster crackling the wind sock and the stays of the radio mast. Thirty knots, gusting to thirty-five on the counter. Too much, he thought. The upended mud tank that had crashed through the roof was only a few yards away. He could see Hogg and Jones patiently waiting in the 125 cockpit, the cabin door invitingly open. Through the other window he saw Kia and Esvandiary had finished their inspection and were heading this way, toward the offices directly below. Idly he saw that a connector on the main roof aerial was loose, then noticed the wire almost free. "Sergeant, you'd better fix that right smartly, you could lose all transmission."

"Jesus, sure, thanks." Wazari got up, stopped. Over the loudspeaker came: "This is Kowiss Tower. Request to call Bandar Delam and Lengeh approved." He acknowledged, switched frequencies, and made the call.

"This's Bandar Delam, go ahead Kowiss." McIver's heart picked up, recognizing Rudi Lutz's voice.

Wazari handed the mike to McIver, his eyes outside on the faulty connection. "Sonofabitch," he muttered, picked up some tools, opened the door onto the roof, and went out. He was still within easy hearing distance. The Green Band yawned, watching disinterestedly.

"Hello, Captain Lutz, McIver. I'm overnighting here," McIver said matter-of-factly, choosing the words very carefully. "Had to escort a VIP, Minister Kia, from Tehran. How're things at Bandar Delam?"

"We're five by five but if . . ." The voice stopped. McIver had heard the inrush of breath and concern, quickly bottled. He glanced at Wazari who was squatting beside the connector. "How long . . . how long're you staying, Mac?" Rudi asked.

"I'll be en route tomorrow as planned. Providing the weather holds," he added carefully.

"Understand. No sweat."

"No sweat. All systems go for a long and happy year. How about you?"

Another pause. "Everything five by five. All systems go for a long and happy year and *vive* the Imam!"

"Quite right. Reason for the call is that HQ Aberdeen urgently wants information about your 'updated impress file.'" This was code for Whirlwind's preparations. "Is it ready?"

"Yes, yes, it is. Where should I send it?" Code for: Do we still head for Al Shargaz?

"Gavallan's in Al Shargaz on an inspection trip so send it there—it's important you make a special effort and get it there quickly. I heard in Tehran there was a BA flight going into Abadan tomorrow. Get it on that flight for Al Shargaz tomorrow, all right?"

"Loud and clear. I've been working on the details all day."

"Excellent. How's your crew change situation?"

"Great. Outgoing crew've gone, incoming replacements due Saturday, Sunday at the latest. Everything's prepared for their arrival. I'll be on the next crew change."

"Good, I'm here if you want me. How's your weather?"

A pause. "Stormy. It's raining now. We've a southeaster."

"Same here. No sweat."

"By the way, Siamaki called Numir, our IranOil manager, a couple of times."

"What about?" McIver said.

"Just checking on the base, Numir said."

"Good," McIver said carefully. "Glad he's interested in our operations. I'll call tomorrow, everything's routine. Happy landings."

"You too, thanks for calling."

McIver signed off cursing Siamaki. Nosy bloody bastard! He looked outside. Wazari still had his back to him, kneeling beside the base of the aerial, near the skylight of the office below, totally concentrated, so he left him to it and made the call to Lengeh.

Scragger was quickly on the other end. "Hello, sport. Yes, we heard you were on the routine side trip escorting a VIP—Andy called from Al Shargaz. What's the poop?"

"Routine. Everything's as planned. HQ Aberdeen needs information of your 'updated impress file.' Is it ready?"

"Ready as she'll ever be. Where should I send it?"

"Al Shargaz, that's easiest for you. Can you get it over tomorrow?"

"Gotcha, old sport, I'll plan on it. How's your weather?"

"Southeasterly, thirty to thirty-five knots. Johnny said it might lighten tomorrow. You?"

"About the same. Let's hope she dies down. No problem for us."

"Good. I'll call tomorrow. Happy landings."

"Same to you. By the way, how's Lulu?"

McIver cursed under his breath, because in the excitement of the change of plan, having to escort Kia, he had totally forgotten his pledge to his car to save her from a fate worse than. He had just left her in one of the hangars as a further indication to the staff there he was returning tomorrow. "She's fine," he said. "How's your medical?"

"Fine. How's yours, old sport?"

"See you soon, Scrag." Wryly McIver clicked off the sender. Now he was very tired. He stretched and got up, noticed that the Green Band had gone and Wazari was standing at the doorway from the roof, his face strange. "What's the matter?"

"I . . . nothing, Captain." The young man closed the door, chilled, was startled to see the tower empty but for the two of them. "Where's the Green Band?"

"I don't know." Quickly Wazari checked the stairwell, then turned on him and dropped his voice: "What's going on, Captain?"

McIver's fatigue left him. "I don't understand."

"All those calls from Siamaki, telexes, guys leaving Tehran without permits, all the guys leaving here, spares going out, sneaked out." He jerked a thumb at the skylight. "Minister arriving all of a sudden."

"Crews need replacements, spares become redundant. Thanks for your help." McIver began to walk around him but Wazari stood in his way.

"Something's mighty goddamn crazy! You can't tell me th—" He stopped, footsteps approaching from downstairs. "Listen, Captain," he whispered urgently, "I'm on your side, I've a deal with your Captain Ayre, he's gonna help me . . ."

The Green Band came stomping up the stairs into the room, said something in Farsi to Wazari, whose eyes widened.

"What did he say?" McIver asked.

"Esvandiary wants you below." Wazari smiled sardonically, then went back out onto the roof again and squatted beside the connector, fiddling with it.

IN ESVANDIARY'S OFFICE: 5:40 P.M. Tom Lochart was frozen with rage, and so was McIver. "But our exit permits are valid and we've clearance to send personnel out today, right now!"

"With Minister Kia's approval the permits're held up until the replacements arrive," Esvandiary said curtly. He sat behind the desk, Kia beside him, Lochart and McIver standing in front of him. On the desk was the pile of permits and passports. It was nearing sunset now. "Agha Siamaki agrees too."

"Quite correct." Kia was amused and pleased at their discomfiture. Damned foreigners. "No need for all this urgency, Captain. Much better to do things in an orderly fashion, much better."

"The flight is orderly, Minister Kia," McIver said tight-lipped. "We've the permits. I insist the plane leaves as planned!"

"This is Iran, not England." Esvandiary sneered. "Even there I doubt if you could insist on anything." He was very pleased with himself. Minister Kia had been delighted with his pishkesh—the revenue from a future oil well—and had at once offered him a seat on the IHC board. Then, to his vast amusement, Kia had explained that exit permits should have fees attached to them: Let the foreigners sweat, the minister had added. By Saturday they will be most anxious of their own accord to press on you say three hundred U.S. dollars in cash, per head. "As the minister says," he said importantly, "we should be orderly. Now I'm busy, good aftern—"

The door swung open and now Starke was in the small office, his face blotchy, his good fist bunched, left arm in a sling. "What the hell's with you, Esvandiary? You can't cancel the permits!"

McIver burst out, "For God's sake, Duke, you shouldn't be here!"

"The permits're postponed, not canceled. Postponed!" Esvandiary's face contorted. "And how many times do I have to tell you ill-mannered people to knock? Knock! This isn't your office, it's mine, I run this base, you don't, and Minister Kia and I are having a meeting that you've all interrupted! Now get out, get out the lot of you!" He turned to Kia as though the two of them were alone and said in Farsi in a new voice, "Minister, I do apologize for all of this, you see what I have to deal with. I strongly recommend we nationalize all foreign airplanes and use our own p—"

Starke's jaw jutted. He bunched his fist. "Listen you sonofabitch."

"GET OUT!" Esvandiary reached into his drawer where there was an automatic. But he never pulled it out. The mullah Hussain came through the door, Green Bands behind him. A sudden silence pervaded the room.

"In the Name of God, what's going on here?" Hussain said in English, cold hard eyes on Esvandiary and Kia. At once Esvandiary got up and began to explain, speaking Farsi, Starke cut in with their side, and soon both men were getting louder and louder. Impatiently Hussain held up his hand. "First you, Agha Esvandiary. Please speak Farsi so my komiteh can understand." He listened impassively to the long-winded Farsi address, his four Green Bands crowding the door. Then he motioned to Starke. "Captain?"

Starke was carefully brief and blunt.

Hussain nodded at Kia. "Now you, Excellency Minister. May I see your authority to override Kowissi authority and exit permits?"

"Override, Excellency Mullah? Postpone? Not I," Kia said easily. "I'm merely a servant of the Imam, God's peace upon him, and of his personally appointed prime minister and his government."

"Excellency Esvandiary said you approved the postponement."

"I merely agreed with his wish for an orderly rearrangement of foreign personnel."

Hussain looked down at the desk. "Those are the exit permits with passports?"

Esvandiary's mouth went dry. "Yes, Excellency."

Hussain scooped them up and handed them to Starke. "The men and airplane will leave at once."

"Thank you, Excellency," Starke said, the strain of standing getting to him.

"Let me help." McIver took the passports and permits from him. "Thank you, Agha," he said to Hussain, elated with their victory.

Hussain's eyes were just as cold and hard as ever. "The Imam has said, 'If foreigners want to leave, let them leave, we have no need of them.'"

"Er, yes, thank you," McIver said, not liking to be near this man at all. He went out. Lochart followed.

Starke was saying in Farsi, "I'm afraid I have to go on the airplane too, Excellency." He told him what Doc Nutt had said, adding in English, "I don't want to go but well, that's it. Insha'Allah."

Hussain nodded absently. "You won't need an exit permit. Go aboard. I will explain to the komiteh. I will see the airplane leave." He walked out and went up to the tower to inform Colonel Changiz of his decision.

It took no time at all for the 125 to be filled. Starke was last to the gangway, legs very shaky now. Doc Nutt had given him enough painkillers to get him aboard. "Thank you, Excellency," he said to Hussain over the howl of the jets, still afraid of him yet liking him, not knowing why. "God's peace be with you."

Over Hussain now hung a strange pall. "Corruption and lies and cheating are against the laws of God, aren't they?"

"Yes, yes they are." Starke saw Hussain's indecision. Then the moment passed.

"God's peace be with you, Captain." Hussain turned and stalked off. The wind freshened slightly.

Weakly Starke climbed the steps, using his good hand, wanting to walk tall. At the top he held onto the handrail and turned back a moment, head throbbing, chest very bad. So much left here, so much, too much, not just choppers and spares and material things—so much more. Goddamn, I should be staying, not leaving. Bleakly he waved farewell to those who were left behind and gave them a thumbs-up, achingly aware that he was thankful not to be among them.

In the office Esvandiary and Kia watched the 125 taxiing away. God's curse on them, may they all burn for interfering, Esvandiary thought. Then he threw off his fury, concentrating on the vast feast that selected friends who desperately wished to meet Minister Kia, *his* friend and fellow director, had arranged, the entertainment of dancers to follow, then the temporary marriages . . .

The door opened. To his astonishment, Hussain came in, livid with rage, Green Bands crowding after him. Esvandiary got up. "Yes, Excellency? What can I d—" He stopped as a Green Band roughly pulled him out of the way to allow Hussain to sit behind the desk. Kia sat where he was, perplexed.

Hussain said, "The Imam, God's peace on him, has ordered komitehs to cast out corruption wherever it is to be found. This is the Kowiss air base komiteh. You are both accused of corruption."

Kia and Esvandiary blanched and both started talking, claiming that this was ridiculous and they were falsely accused. Hussain reached over and jerked the gold band of the gold watch on Esvandiary's wrist. "When did you buy this and with what did you pay?"

"My . . . my savings and—"

"Liar. Pishkesh for two jobs. The komiteh knows. Now, what about your scheme to defraud the state, secretly offering future oil revenues to corrupt officials for future services?"

"Ridiculous, Excellency, lies all lies!" Esvandiary shouted in panic.

Hussain looked at Kia who also had gone pasty gray. "What officials, Excellency?" Kia asked, keeping his voice calm, sure that his enemies had set him up to be trapped far away from the seat of his influence. Siamaki! It has to be Siamaki!

Hussain motioned to one of the Green Bands who went out and brought in the radio operator, Wazari. "Tell them, before God, what you told me," he ordered.

"As I told you earlier, I was on the roof, Excellency," Wazari said nervously; "I was checking one of our lines and overheard them through the skylight. I heard him make the offer." He pointed a blunt finger at Esvandiary, delighted for an opportunity for revenge. If it hadn't been for Esvandiary, I'd've never have been picked on by that madman Zataki, never been beaten and hurt, never been almost killed. "They were speaking English and he said, I can arrange to divert oil revenues from new wells, I can keep the wells off the lists and can divert funds to you . . ."

Esvandiary was appalled. He had carefully sent all the Iranian staff out of the office building and further, for safety, talked English. Now he was damned. He heard Wazari finish and Kia begin to speak, quietly, calmly, avoiding all complicity, saying he was only leading this corrupt and evil man on: "I was asked to visit here for just this purpose, Excellency, sent here by the Imam's government, God protect him, for just this purpose: to root out corruption wherever it existed. May I congratulate you on being so zealous. If you will allow me, the moment I get back to Tehran, I will commend you directly to the Revolutionary Komiteh itself—and of course to the prime minister."

Hussain looked at the Green Bands. "Is Esvandiary guilty or not guilty?"

"Guilty, Excellency."

"Is the man Kia guilty or not guilty?"

"Guilty," Esvandiary shouted before they could answer.

One of the Green Bands shrugged. "All Tehranis are liars. Guilty," and the others nodded and echoed him.

Kia said politely, "Tehrani mullahs and ayatollahs are not liars, Excellencies, the Revolutionary Komiteh not liars, nor the Imam, God save him, who perhaps could be called Tehrani because he lives there now. I just happen to live there too. I was born in Holy Qom, Excellencies," he added, blessing the fact for the first time in his life.

One of the Green Bands broke the silence. "What he says is true, Excellency, isn't it?" He scratched his head. "About all Tehranis?"

"That not all Tehranis are liars? Yes, that's true." Hussain looked at Kia, also unsure. "Before God, are you guilty or not?"

"Of course not guilty, Excellency, before God!" Kia's eyes were guileless. Fool, do you think you can catch me with that? *Taqiyah* gives me the right to protect myself if I consider my life threatened by false mullahs!

"How do you explain you're a government minister, but also a director of this helicopter company?"

"The minister in charge . . ." Kia stopped, for Esvandiary was blubbering loudly and mouthing accusations. "I'm sorry, Excellencies, as God wants, but this noise, it's difficult to speak without shouting."

"Take him outside!" Esvandiary was dragged away. "Well?"

"The minister in charge of the Civil Aviation Board asked me to join the IHC board as the government's representative," Kia said, telling the twisted truth as though he were imparting a state secret, adding other exaggerations equally importantly. "We're not sure of the loyalty of the directors. Also may I tell you privately, Excellency, that in a few days all foreign airplane companies are being nationalized . . ."

He talked to them intimately, modulating his voice for the most effect, and when he considered the moment perfect, he stopped and sighed, "Before God I confess I am without corruption like you, Excellency, and though without your great calling, I too have dedicated my life to serving the people."

"God protect you, Excellency," the Green Band burst out.

The others agreed and even Hussain had had most of his doubt pushed aside. He was about to probe a little more when they heard a distant muezzin from the air base calling to evening prayer, and he chided himself for being diverted from God. "Go with God, Excellency," he said, ending the tribunal, and got up.

"Thank you, Excellency. May God keep you and all mullahs safe to rescue us and our great Islamic nation from the works of Satan!"

Hussain led the way outside. There, following his lead, they all ritually cleansed themselves, turned toward Mecca, and prayed—Kia, Green Bands, office staff, laborers, kitchen workers—all pleased and content that once more they could each openly testify their personal submission to God and the Prophet of God. Only Esvandiary wept through his abject prayers.

Then Kia came back into the office. In the silence, he sat behind the desk and allowed himself a secret sigh and many secret congratulations. How dare that son of a dog Esvandiary accuse me! Me, Minister Kia! May God burn him and all enemies of the state. Outside there was a burst of firing. Calmly he took out a cigarette and lit it. The sooner I leave this dung heap the better, he thought. A squall shook the building. Drizzle spotted the windows.

LENGEH: 6:50 P.M.   The sunset was malevolent, clouds covering most of the sky, heavy and black-tinged. "It'll be closed in by morning, Scrag," the American pilot Ed Vossi said, his dark curly hair tugged by the wind that blew from the Hormuz up the Gulf toward Abadan. "Goddamn wind!"

"We'll be all right, sport. But Rudi, Duke, and the others? If she holds or worsens they'll be up shit creek without a paddle."

"Goddamn wind! Why choose today to change direction? Almost as though the gods're laughing at us." The two men were standing on the promontory overlooking the Gulf beneath their flagpole, the waters gray and, out in the strait, white-topped. Behind them was their base and the airfield, still wet from this morning's passing rain squall. Below and to the right was their beach and the raft they swam from. Since the day of the shark no one had ventured there, staying close in the shallows in case another lay in wait for them. Vossi muttered, "I'll be goddamn glad when this's all over."

Scragger nodded absently, his thoughts reaching into the weather patterns, trying to read what would happen in the next twelve hours, always difficult in this season when the usually placid Gulf could erupt with sudden and monstrous violence. For 363 or 364 days a year the prevailing wind was from the northwest. Now it wasn't.

The base was quiet. Only Vossi, Willi Neuchtreiter, and two mechanics were left. All the other pilots and mechanics and their British office manager had gone two days ago, Tuesday, while he was en route back from Bandar Delam with Kasigi.

Willi had got them all out to Al Shargaz by sea: "We had no trouble, Scrag, by God Harry," Willi had told him delightedly when he landed. "Your plan worked. Sending 'em by boat was clever, better than by chopper, and cheaper. The komiteh just shrugged and took over one of the trailers."

"They're sleeping on base now?"

"Some of them, Scrag. Three or four. I've made sure we feed them plenty of rice and horisht. They're not a bad group. Masoud's trying to keep in their good books too." Masoud was their IranOil manager.

"Why did you stay, Willi? I know how you feel about this caper, I told you to be on the boat, no need for you."

"Sure there is, Scrag, by God Harry, but you'll need a proper pilot along with you—you might get lost."

Good old Willi, Scragger thought. Glad he stayed. And sorry.

Since getting back from Bandar Delam on Tuesday, Scragger had found himself greatly unsettled, nothing that he could isolate, just a feeling that elements over which he had no control were waiting to pounce. The pain in his lower stomach had lessened, but from time to time there was still a flick of blood in his urine. Not forewarning Kasigi about the Whirlwind pullout had added to his unease. Hell, he thought, I couldn't have risked that, spilling Whirlwind. I did the best I could, telling Kasigi to go to Gavallan.

Yesterday, Wednesday, Vossi had taken Kasigi across the Gulf. Scragger had given Vossi a private letter to Gavallan explaining what had happened in Bandar Delam and his dilemma about Kasigi, leaving it to Gavallan to decide what to do. Also in the letter he had given details of his meeting with Georges de Plessey who was gravely concerned that troubles would again spill over into the Siri complex:

"Damage to pumping and piping at Siri's worse than first thought and I don't think she'll be pumping this month. Kasigi's fit to be tied as he's got three tankers due at Siri for uplifts in the next three weeks according to the deal he worked out with Georges. It's a carve-up, Andy. Nothing we can do. There's little chance of avoiding sabotage if terrorists really decide to have at them. Of course I haven't told Georges about anything. Do what you can for Kasigi and see you soonest, Scrag."

On this morning's routine call from Al Shargaz, Gavallan had said only he had received his report and was dealing with it. Otherwise he was noncommittal.

Scragger had not mentioned McIver, nor had Gavallan. He beamed. Bet my life Dirty Dunc flew the 206! Never would've bet old By the Book McIver'd've done it! Even so, bet my life he was like a pig in shit at the chance and no bloody wonder. I'd've done the same . . .

"Scrag!"

He glanced around. One look at Willi Neuchtreiter's face was enough. "Wot's up?"

"I just found out Masoud's given all our passports to the gendarmes—every last one!"

Vossi and Scragger gaped at him. Vossi said, "What the hell he do that for?" Scragger was more vulgar.

"It was Tuesday, Scrag, when the others left on the boat. Of course a gendarme was there to see them off, count them aboard, and that's when he asked Masoud for our passports. So Masoud gave them to him. If it'd been me I'd've done the same."

"Wot the hell did he want them for?"

Willi said patiently, "To re-sign our residence permits in Khomeini's name, Scrag, he wanted us to be legal—you've asked them enough times, haven't you?" Scragger cursed for a full minute and never used the same word twice.

"For crissake, Scrag, we gotta get 'em back," Vossi said shakily, "we gotta get 'em back, or Whirlwind's blown."

"I know that, sport." Blankly Scragger was sifting possibilities.

Willi said, "Maybe we could get new ones in Al Shargaz or Dubai—say we'd lost 'em."

"For crissake, Willi," Vossi exploded. "For crissake, they'd put us in the slammer so fast we wouldn't know which way was up! Remember Masterson?" One of their mechanics, a couple of years ago, had forgotten to renew his Al Shargaz permit and had tried to bluff his way through Immigration. Even though the visa was only four days out of date and his passport otherwise valid, Immigration had at once marched him into jail where he languished very uncomfortably for six weeks, then to be let out but banished forever: "Dammit," the resident British official had said, "you're bloody lucky to get off so lightly. You knew the law. We've pointed it out until we're blue in the face. . . ."

"Goddamned if I'll leave without mine," Vossi said. "I can't. Mine's loaded with goddamn visas for all the Gulf states, Nigeria, the UK and hell and gone—it'd take me months to get new ones, months, if ever . . . and what about Al Shargaz, huh? That's one mighty fine place but without a goddamn passport and their valid visa, into the slammer!"

"Too right, Ed. Bloody hell and tomorrow's Holy Day when everything's shut tighter'n a gnat's arse. Willi, you remember who the gendarme was? Was he one of the regulars—or a Green Band?"

After a moment Willi said, "He wasn't a Green Band, Scrag, he was a regular. The old one, the one with gray hair."

"Qeshemi? The sergeant?"

"Yes, Scrag. Yes, it was him."

Scragger cursed again. "If old Qeshemi says we've got to wait till Saturday, or Saturday week, that's it." In this area, gendarmes still operated as they had always done, as part of the military, without Green Band harassment, except that now they had taken off their Shah badges and wore armbands with Khomeini's name scrawled on them.

"Don't wait supper for me." Scragger stomped off into the twilight.

AT THE LENGEH POLICE STATION: 7:32 P.M. The corporal gendarme yawned and shook his head politely, speaking Farsi to the base radio operator, Ali Pash, whom Scragger had brought with him to interpret. Scragger waited patiently, too used to Iranian ways to interrupt them. They had already been at it for half an hour.

"Oh, you wanted to ask about the foreigners' passports? The passports are in the safe, where they should be," the gendarme was saying. "Passports are valuable and we have them locked up."

"Perfectly correct, Excellency, but the Captain of the Foreigners would like to have them back, please. He says he needs them for a crew change."

"Of course he may have them back. Are they not his property? Have not he and his men flown many mercy missions over the years for our people? Certainly, Excellency, as soon as the safe is opened."

"Please may it be opened now? The foreigner would appreciate your kindness very much." Ali Pash was equally polite and leisurely, waiting for the gendarme to volunteer the information he sought. He was a good-looking Tehrani in his late twenties who had been trained at the U.S. Radio School at Isfahan and had been with IHC at Lengeh for three years. "It would certainly be a kindness."

"Certainly, but he cannot have them back until the key reappears."

"Ah, may I dare ask where the key is, Excellency?"

The corporal gendarme waved his hand to the big, old-fashioned safe that dominated this outer office. "Look, Excellency, you can see for yourself, the key is not on its peg. More than likely the sergeant has it in his safekeeping."

"How very wise and correct, Excellency. Probably His Excellency the sergeant is at home now?"

"His Excellency will be here in the morning."

"On Holy Day? May I offer an opinion that we are fortunate our gendarmerie have such a high sense of duty to work so diligently? I imagine he would not be early."

"The sergeant is the sergeant but the office opens at seven-thirty in the morning, though of course the police station is open day and night." The gendarme stubbed out his cigarette. "Come in the morning."

"Ah, thank you, Excellency. Would you care for another cigarette while I explain to the captain?"

"Thank you, Excellency. It is rare to have a foreign one, thank you." The cigarettes were American and highly appreciated but neither mentioned it.

"May I offer you a light, Excellency?" Ali Pash lit his own too and told Scragger what had been said.

"Ask him if the sergeant's at home now, Ali Pash."

"I did, Captain. He said His Excellency will be here in the morning." Ali Pash hid his weariness, too polite to tell Scragger he had realized in the first few seconds that this man knew nothing, would do nothing, and this whole conversation and visit was a total waste of time. And of course gendarmes would prefer not to be disturbed at night about so insignificant an affair. What does it matter? Have they ever lost a passport? Of course not! What crew change? "If I may advise you, Agha? In the morning."

Scragger sighed. "In the morning" could mean tomorrow or the following day. No point in probing further, he thought irritably. "Thank him for me and say I'll be here bright and early in the morning."

Ali Pash obeyed. As God wants, the gendarme thought wearily, hungry and worried that another week had gone by and still there was no pay, no pay for months now, and the bazaari moneylenders were pressing for their loans to be repaid, and my beloved family near starving. *"Shab be khayr, Agha,"* he said to Scragger. "Good night."

"Shab be khayr, Agha." Scragger waited, knowing their departure would be as politely long-winded as the interview.

Outside in the small road that was the main road of the port town, he felt better. Curious bystanders, all men, surrounded his battered old station wagon, the winged S-G symbol on the door. "Salaam," he said breezily and a few greeted him back. Pilots from the base were popular, the base and the oil platforms a main source of very profitable work, their mercy missions in all weather well known, and Scragger easily recognizable: "That's the chief of the pilots," one old man whispered knowledgeably to his neighbor, "he's the one who helped young Abdollah Turik into the hospital at Bandar Abbas that only the highborn get into normally. He even went to visit his village just outside Lengeh, even went to his funeral."

"Turik?"

"Abdollah Turik, my sister's son's son! The young man who fell off the oil platform and was eaten by sharks."

"Ah, yes, I remember, the young man some say was murdered by leftists."

"Not so loud, not so loud, you never know who's listening. Peace be with you, pilot, greetings, pilot!"

Scragger waved to them cheerily and drove off.

"But the base is the other way, Captain. Where do we go?" Ali Pash asked.

"To visit the sergeant, of course." Scragger whistled through his teeth, disregarding Ali Pash's obvious disapproval.

The sergeant's house was on the corner of a dingy, dirt street still puddled from this morning's squall, just another door in the high walls across the joub. It was getting dark now so Scragger left the headlights on and got out. No sign of life in the whole street. Only a few of the high windows dimly lit.

Sensing Ali Pash's nervousness he said, "You stay in the car. There's no problem, I've been here before." He used the iron knocker vigorously, feeling eyes everywhere.

The first time he had been here was a year or so ago when he had brought a huge food hamper, with two butchered sheep, some sacks of rice, and cases of fruit as a gift from the base to celebrate "their" sergeant getting the Shah's Bronze Sepah Medal for bravery in action against pirates and smugglers who were endemic in these waters. The last time, a few weeks ago, he had accompanied a worried gendarme who wanted him to report at once the tragedy at Siri One, picking Abdollah Turik out of the shark-infested water. Neither time had he been invited into the house but had stayed in the little courtyard beyond the tall wooden door, and both times had been in daylight.

The door creaked open. Scragger was not prepared for the sudden flashlight that momentarily blinded him. The circle of light hesitated, then went to the car and centered on Ali Pash who almost leaped out of the car, half-bowed, and called out, "Greetings, Excellency Chief Officer, peace be upon you. I apologize that the foreigner disturbs your privacy and dares to c—"

"Greetings." Qeshemi overrode him curtly, clicked the light off, turning his attention back to Scragger.

"Salaam, Agha Qeshemi," Scragger said, his eyes adjusting now. He saw the strong-featured man watching him, his uniform coat unbuttoned and the revolver loose in its holster.

"Salaam, Cap'tin."

"Sorry to come here, Agha, at night," Scragger said slowly and carefully, knowing Qeshemi's English was as limited as his own Farsi was almost nonexistent. *"Loftan, gozar nameh. Loftan"*—Please, need passports. Please.

The gendarme sergeant grunted with surprise then waved a hard tough hand toward the town. "Passports in stat'ion, Cap'tin."

"Yes. But, sorry, there is no key." Scragger parodied opening a lock with a key. "No key," he repeated.

"Ah. Yes. Understand. Yes, no key. To'morrow. To'morrow you get."

"Is it possible, tonight? Please. Now?" Scragger felt the scrutiny.

"Why tonight?"

"Er, for a crew change. Men to Shiraz, crew change."

"When?"

Scragger knew he had to gamble. "Saturday. If I have key, go station and return at once."

Qeshemi shook his head. "To'morrow." Then he spoke sharply to Ali Pash who at once bowed and thanked him profusely, again apologizing for disturbing him. "His Excellency says you can have them tomorrow. We'd, er, we'd better leave, Captain."

Scragger forced a smile. *"Mamnoon am, Agha"*—Thank you, Excellency. *"Mamnoon am, Agha Qeshemi."* He would have asked Ali Pash to ask the sergeant if he could have the passports as soon as the station opened but he did not wish to agitate the sergeant unnecessarily. "I will come after first prayer. *Mamnoon am, Agha.*" Scragger put out his hand and Qeshemi shook it. Both men felt the other's strength. Then he got into the car and drove off.

Thoughtfully Qeshemi closed and rebolted the door.

In summertime the small patio with its high walls and trellised vines and small fountain was cool and inviting. Now it was drab. He crossed it and opened the door opposite that led into the main living room and rebolted it. The sound of a child coughing somewhere upstairs. A wood fire took off some of the chill but the whole house was drafty, none of the doors or windows fitting properly. "Who was it?" his wife called down from upstairs.

"Nothing, nothing important. A foreigner from the air base. The old one. He wanted their passports."

"At this time of night? God protect us! Every time there's a knock on the door I expect more trouble—rotten Green Bands or vile leftists!" Qeshemi nodded absently, but said nothing, warming his hands by the fire, hardly listening to her rattle on: "Why should he come here? Foreigners are so ill-mannered. What would he want passports for at this time of night? Did you give them to him?"

"They're locked in our safe. Normally I bring the key with me as always, but it's lost." The child coughed again. "How's little Sousan?"

"She still has a fever. Bring me some hot water, that'll help. Put a little honey in it." He set the kettle on the fire, sighed, hearing her grumbling: "Passports at this time of night! Why couldn't they wait till Saturday? So ill-mannered and thoughtless. You said the key's lost?"

"Yes. Probably that goathead excuse for a policeman, Lafti, has it and forgot to put it back again. As God wants."

"Mohammed, what would the foreigner want with passports at this time of night?"

"I don't know. Curious, very curious."

AT BANDAR DELAM AIRFIELD: 7:49 P.M. Rudi Lutz stood on the veranda of his trailer under the eaves, watching the heavy rain. *"Scheiss,"* he muttered. Behind him his door was open and the shaft of light sparkled the heavy raindrops. Soft Mozart came from his tape deck. The door of the next trailer, the office trailer, opened, and he saw Pop Kelly come out holding an umbrella over his head and slop through the puddles toward him. Neither noticed the Iranian in the shadows. Somewhere on the base a tomcat was spitting and yowling. "Hi, Pop. Come on in. You get it?"

"Yes, no problem." Kelly shook the rain off. Inside the trailer it was warm and comfortable, neat and tidy. The cover was off the built-in, reconnected HF that was on Standby, muted static mixing with the music. A coffeepot percolated on the stove.

"Coffee?"

"Thanks—I'll help myself." Kelly handed him the paper and went over to the kitchen area. The paper had hastily jotted columns of figures on it, temperatures, wind directions, and strengths for every few thousand feet, barometric pressures and tomorrow's forecast. "Abadan Tower said it was up to date. They claimed it included all today's incoming BA data. Doesn't look too bad, eh?"

"If it's accurate." The forecast predicted lessening precipitation around midnight and reduced wind strength. Rudi turned up the music, and Kelly sat down beside him. Rudi dropped his voice. "It could be all right for us, but a bitch for Kowiss. We'll still have to refuel in flight to make Bahrain."

Kelly sipped his coffee with enjoyment, hot, strong, with a spoon of condensed milk. "What'd you do if you were Andy?"

"With the three bases to worry about I'd . . ." A slight noise outside. Rudi got up and glanced out of the window. Nothing. Then again the sound of the tomcat, closer. "Damn cats, they give me the creeps."

"I rather like cats." Kelly smiled. "We've three at home: Matthew, Mark, and Luke. Two're Siamese, the other's a tabby; Betty says the boys're driving her mad to get 'John' to round it off."

"How is she?" Today's BA flight into Abadan had brought Sandor Petrofi for the fourth 212, along with mail from Gavallan, routed since the troubles through HQ at Aberdeen, their first for many weeks.

"Fine, super in fact—three weeks to go. The old girl's usually on time. I'll be glad to be home when she pops." Kelly beamed. "The doc says he thinks it's going to be a girl at long last."

"Congratulations! That's wonderful." Everyone knew that the Kellys had been hoping against hope. "Seven boys and one girl, that's a lot of mouths to feed." Rudi thought how hard he found it to keep up with the bills and school fees with only three children and no mortgage on the house—the house left to his wife by her father, God bless the old bastard. "Lots of mouths, don't know how you do it."

"Oh, we manage, glory be to God." Kelly looked down at the forecast, frowned. "You know, if I was Andy I'd press the tit and not postpone."

"If it was up to me I'd cancel and forget the whole crazy idea." Rudi kept his voice down and leaned closer. "I know it'll be rough for Andy, maybe the company'll close, maybe. But we can all get new jobs, even better paying ones, we've families to think of and I hate all this going against the book. How in the hell can we sneak out? Not possible. If we—" Car headlights splashed the window, the approaching sound of the high-powered engine growing then stopping outside.

Rudi was the first at the window. He saw Zataki get out of the car with some Green Bands, then Numir, their base manager, came from the office trailer with an umbrella to join him. *"Scheiss,"* Rudi muttered again, turned the music down, quickly checked the trailer for incriminating evidence, and put the forecast into his pocket. "Salaam, Colonel," he said, opening the door. "You were looking for me?"

"Salaam, Captain, yes, yes, I was." Zataki came into the room, a U.S. army submachine gun over his shoulder. "Good evening," he said. "How many helicopters are here now, Captain?"

Numir began, "Four 212s an—"

"I asked the captain," Zataki flared, "not you. If I want information from you I'll ask! Captain?"

"Four 212s, two 206s, Colonel."

To their shock, particularly Numir's, Zataki said, "Good. I want two 212s to report to Iran-Toda tomorrow at 8:00 A.M. to work under instructions of Agha Watanabe, the chief there. From tomorrow, you'll report daily. Have you met him?"

"Er, yes, I, er, once they had a CASEVAC and we helped them out." Rudi tried to collect himself. "Er, will . . . will they be working on, er, Holy Day, Colonel?"

"Yes. So will you."

Numir said, "But the Ayatollah sa—"

"He's not the law. Shut up." Zataki looked at Rudi. "Be there at 8:00 A.M."

Rudi nodded. "Er, yes. Can I, er, can I offer you coffee, Colonel?"

"Thank you." Zataki propped his submachine gun against the wall and sat at the built-in table, eyes on Pop Kelly. "Didn't I see you at Kowiss?"

"Yes, yes, you did," the tall man said. "That's, er, that's my normal base. I, er, I brought down a 212. I'm Ignatius Kelly." Weakly he sank back into his chair opposite him, as blown as Rudi, wilting under the searching gaze. "A night for fishes, isn't it?"

"What?"

"The, er, the rain."

"Ah, yes," Zataki said. He was glad to be speaking English, improving his, convinced that Iranians who could speak the international language and were educated were going to be sought after, mullahs or no mullahs. Since taking the pills Dr. Nutt had given him, he felt much better, the blinding headaches lessening. "Will the rain prevent flying tomorrow?"

"No, not—"

"It depends," Rudi called out quickly from the kitchen, "if the front worsens or improves." He brought the tray with two cups of sugar and condensed milk, still trying to cope with this new disaster. "Please help yourself, Colonel. About Iran-Toda," he said carefully, "all our choppers are on lease, are contracted to IranOil and Agha Numir here's in charge."

Numir nodded, started to say something, but thought better of it. "We've contracts with IranOil."

The silence thickened. They all watched Zataki. Leisurely he put three heaped teaspoons of sugar into his coffee, stirred, and sipped it. "It's very good, Captain. Yes, very good, and yes, I know about IranOil, but I have decided Iran-Toda takes preference over IranOil for the time being and tomorrow you will supply two 212s at 8:00 A.M. to Iran-Toda."

Rudi glanced at his base manager who avoided his eyes. "But . . . well, presuming this is all right with IranOil th—"

"It is all right," Zataki said to Numir. "Isn't it, Agha?"

"Yes, yes, Agha," meekly, Numir nodded. "I, I will of course inform Area Headquarters of your . . . your eminent instructions."

"Good. Then everything is arranged. Good."

It's not arranged, Rudi wanted to shout out in dismay. "May I ask how, er, how we'll be paid for the, er, new contract?" he asked, feeling stupid.

Zataki shouldered his gun and got up. "Iran-Toda will make arrangements. Thank you, Captain, I will be back after first prayer tomorrow. You will fly one helicopter and I will accompany you."

"Smashing idea, Colonel," Pop Kelly burst out suddenly, beaming, and Rudi could have killed him. "No need to come before 8:00 A.M., that'd be better for us—that's plenty of time to get there by, say, 8:15. Smashing idea to service Iran-Toda, smashing. We've always wanted that contract, can't thank you enough, Colonel! Fantastic! In fact, Rudi, we should take all four birds, put the lads into the picture at once, save time, at once, yes, sir, I'll set them up for you!" He rushed off.

Rudi stared after him, almost cross-eyed with fury.

NEAR AL SHARGAZ AIRPORT: 8:01 P.M. The night was beautiful and balmy, heavy with the smell of flowers, and Gavallan and Pettikin were sitting on the terrace of the Oasis Hotel, on the edge of the airfield on the edge of the desert. They were having a predinner beer, Gavallan smoking a thin cigar and staring into the distance where the sky, purple-black and star-studded, met the darker land. The smoke drifted upward. Pettikin shifted in his lounging chair. "Wish to God there was something more I could do."

"Wish to God old Mac was here, I'd break his bloody neck," Gavallan said and Pettikin laughed. A few guests were already in the dining room behind them. The Oasis was old and dilapidated, Empire baroque, the home of the British Resident when British power was the only power in the Gulf and, until '71, kept down piracy and maintained the peace. Music as ancient as the three-piece combo wafted out of the tall doors—piano, violin, and double bass, two elderly ladies and a white-haired gentleman on the piano.

"My God, isn't that *Chu Chin Chow?*"

"You've got me, Andy." Pettikin glanced back at them, saw Jean-Luc among the diners, chatting with Nogger Lane, Rodrigues, and some of the other mechanics. He sipped his beer, noticed Gavallan's glass was empty. "Like another?"

"No thanks." Gavallan let his eyes drift with the smoke. "I think I'll go over to the Met office, then look in on ours."

"I'll come with you."

"Thanks, Charlie, but why don't you stay in case there's a phone call?"

"Sure, just as you like."

"Don't wait for me to eat, I'll join you for coffee. I'll drop by the hospital to see Duke on my way back." Gavallan got up, walked through the dining room, greeting those of his men who were there, and went into the lobby that also had seen better days.

"Mr. Gavallan, excuse me, Effendi, but there's a phone call for you." The receptionist indicated the phone booth to one side. It had red plush inside, no air-conditioning and no privacy. "Hello? Gavallan here," he said.

"Hello, boss, Liz Chen . . . just to report we've had a call about the two consignments from Luxembourg and they'll arrive late." "Consignment from Luxembourg" was code for the two 747 freighters he had chartered. "They can't arrive Friday—they'll only guarantee Sunday 4:00 P.M."

Gavallan was dismayed. He had been warned by the charterers that they had a very tight schedule between charters and there might be a twenty-four-hour delay. He had had great difficulty arranging the airplanes. Obviously none of the regular airlines that serviced the Gulf or Iran could be approached and he had had to be vague about the reason for the charters and their cargo. "Get back to them at once and try and bring the date forward. It'd be safer if they'd arrive Saturday, much safer. What's next?"

"Imperial Air have offered to take over our position on our new X63s."

"Tell them to drop dead. Next?"

"ExTex have revised their offer on the new Saudi, Singapore, Nigerian contracts ten percent downward."

"Accept the offer by telex. Fix a lunch for me with the brass in New York on Tuesday. Next?"

"I've a checklist of part numbers you wanted."

"Good. Hang on." Gavallan took out the secretarial notebook he always carried and found the page he sought. It listed the present Iranian registration call signs of their ten remaining 212s, all beginning with "EP" stand-

ing for Iran, then "H" for helicopter, and the final two letters. "Ready. Off
you go."

"AB, RV, KI . . ."

As she read out the letters he wrote them alongside the other column.
For security he did not put the full new registration, "G" denoting Great
Britain, "H" for helicopter, just jotted the two new letters. He reread the
list and they tallied with those already supplied. "Thanks, they're spot on.
I'll call you last thing tonight, Liz. Give Maureen a call and tell her all's
well."

"All right, boss. Sir Ian called half an hour ago to wish you luck."

"Oh, great!" Gavallan had tried unsuccessfully to reach him all the time
he was in Aberdeen and London. "Where is he? Did he leave a number?"

"Yes. He's in Tokyo: 73 73 84. He said he'd be there for a while and if
you missed him he'd call tomorrow. He also said he'll be back in a couple of
weeks and would like to see you."

"Even better. Did he say what about?"

"Oil for the lamps of China," his secretary said cryptically.

Gavallan's interest picked up. "Wonderful. Fix a date at his earliest convenience. I'll call you later, Liz. Got to rush."

"All right. Just to remind you it's Scot's birthday tomorrow."

"Godalmighty, I forgot, thanks, Liz. Talk to you later." He hung up,
pleased to hear from Ian Dunross, blessing the Al Shargazi phone system
and distance dialing. He dialed. Tokyo was five hours ahead. Just after
1 A.M.

"*Hai?*" The Japanese woman's voice said sleepily.

"Good evening. Sorry to call so late but I had a message to call Sir Ian
Dunross. Andrew Gavallan."

"Ah, yes. Ian is not here for the moment, he will not be back until the
morrow, so sorry. Perhaps at ten o'clock. Please, can I have your number,
Mr. Gavallan?"

Gavallan gave it to her, disappointed. "Is there another number I can
reach him at, please?"

"Ah, so sorry, no."

"Please ask him to call me, call anytime." He thanked her again and
hung up thoughtfully.

Outside was his rented car and he got in and drove to the main airport
entrance. Overhead a 707 was coming around for final, landing lights on,
tail and wing lights winking.

"Evening, Mr. Gavallan," Sibbles, the Met officer said. He was British, a
small, thin, dehydrated man, ten years in the Gulf. "Here you are." He
handed him the long photocopy of the forecast. "Weather's going to be

changeable here for the next few days." He handed him three other pages. "Lengeh, Kowiss, and Bandar Delam."

"And the bottom line is?"

"They're all about the same, give or take ten or fifteen knots, a few hundred feet of ceiling—sorry, just can't get used to metrics—a hundred meters or so of ceiling. Weather's gradually improving. In the next few days the wind should come back to our standard, friendly northwesterly. From midnight we're forecasting light rain and lots of low clouds and mist over most of the Gulf, wind southeasterly about twenty knots overall with thunderstorms, occasional small turbulences," he looked up and smiled, "and whirlwinds."

Gavallan's stomach heaved, even though the word was said matter-of-factly and Sibbles was not party to the secret. At least, I don't think he is, he thought. That's the second curious coincidence today. The other was the American lunching at a nearby table with a Shargazi whose name he had not caught: "Good luck for tomorrow," the man had said with a pleasant smile, full of bonhomie, as he was leaving.

"Sorry?"

"Glenn Wesson, Wesson Oil Marketing, you're Andrew Gavallan, right? We heard you and your guys were organizing a . . . 'a camel race' tomorrow out at the Dez-al oasis, right?"

"Not us, Mr. Wesson. We don't go in much for camels."

"That a fact? You should try it, yes, sir, lotta fun. Good luck anyway."

Could have been a coincidence. Camel races were a diversion here for expats, a hilarious one, and the Dez-al a favorite place for the Islamic weekend. "Thanks, Mr. Sibbles, see you tomorrow." He pocketed the forecasts and went down the stairs into the terminal lobby, heading for their office which was off to one side. Neither a positive yes nor a positive no, he was thinking, Saturday safer than tomorrow. You pays your money and you takes your chances. I can't put it off much longer. "How're you going to decide?" his wife, Maureen, had asked, seeing him off at dawn the day before yesterday, Aberdeen almost socked in and pouring.

"Don't know, lassie. Mac's got a good nose, he'll help."

And now no Mac! Mac gone bonkers, Mac flying without a medical, Mac conveniently stuck at Kowiss and no way out but Whirlwind; Erikki still God knows where, and poor old Duke fit to be tied that he's off the roster but bloody lucky he came here. Doc Nutt had been right. X rays showed several bone splinters had punctured his left lung with another half a dozen threatening an artery. He glanced at the lobby clock: 8:27 P.M. Should be out of the anesthetic by now.

Got to decide soon. In conjunction with Charlie Pettikin I've got to decide soon.

He went through the NO ADMITTANCE EXCEPT ON OFFICIAL BUSINESS door, down the corridor, double-glazed windows the length of it. On the apron the 707 was being guided into its disembarking slot by a FOLLOW ME car, the sign in English and Farsi. Several Fokkerwolf forty-passenger prop feeders were parked neatly, a Pan Am jumbo that was part of the evacuation milk run to Tehran, and half a dozen private jets, their 125 among them. Wish it was Saturday, he thought. No, perhaps I don't.

On the door of their office suite was S-G HELICOPTERS, SHEIK AVIATION. "Hello, Scot."

"Hello, Dad." Scot grinned. He was alone, duty officer, and he sat in front of the HF that was on standby, a book in his lap, his right arm in a sling. "Nothing new except a message to call Roger Newbury at home. Shall I get him?"

"In a moment, thanks." Gavallan handed him the Met reports. Scot scanned them rapidly. The phone rang. Without stopping reading, he picked it up. "S-G?" He listened a moment. "Who? Oh, yes. No, he's not here, sorry. Yes, I'll tell him. 'Bye." He replaced the phone, sighed. "Johnny Hogg's new bird, Alexandra—'the Hot Tamale' Manuela calls her because she's certain he's going to get his pecker burned." Gavallan laughed. Scot looked up from the reports. "Neither one thing or the other. Could be very good, lots of cover. But if the wind picks up could be rotten, Saturday better than Friday." His blue eyes watched his father who stared out of the window at the apron traffic, passengers disembarking from the jet.

"I agree." Gavallan said, noncommittally. "There's someth—" He stopped as the HF came to life: "Al Shargaz, this is Tehran Head Office, do you read?"

"This is Al Shargaz, Head Office, you're four by five, go ahead," Scot said.

"Director Siamaki wants to talk to Mr. Gavallan immediately."

Gavallan shook his head. "I'm not here," he whispered.

"Can I take a message, Head Office?" Scot said into the mike. "It's a little late but I'll get it to him as soon as possible."

Waiting. Static. Then the arrogant voice Gavallan detested. "This is Managing Director Siamaki. Tell Gavallan to call me back tonight. I'll be here until 10:30 tonight or anytime after 9:00 A.M. tomorrow. Without fail. Understand?"

"Five by five, Head Office," Scot said sweetly. "Over and out!"

"Bloody twit," Gavallan muttered. Then more sharply, "What the devil's he doing in the office at this time of night?"

"Snooping, has to be, and if he plans to 'work' on Holy Day . . . that's pretty suspicious, isn't it?"

"Mac said he would clean the safe out of important stuff and throw his key and the spare into the joub. Bet those buggers have duplicates," Gavallan said testily. "I'll have to wait until tomorrow for the pleasure of talking with him. Scot, is there any way we can jam him listening to our calls?"

"No, not if we use our company frequencies which's all we've got."

His father nodded. "When Johnny comes in, remind him I may want him airborne tomorrow at a moment's notice." It was part of the Whirlwind plan to use the 125 as a high-altitude VHF receiver/transmitter to cover those choppers only equipped with VHF. "From seven o'clock onward."

"Then it's a go for tomorrow."

"Not yet." Gavallan picked up the phone and dialed. "Good evening, Mr. Newbury, please, Mr. Gavallan returning his call." Roger Newbury was one of the officials at the British consulate who had been very helpful, easing permits for them. "Hello, Roger, you wanted me? Sorry, you're not at dinner, are you?"

"No, glad you called. Couple of things: first, bit of bad news, we've just heard George Talbot's been killed."

"Good God, what happened?"

" 'Fraid it's all rather rotten. He was in a restaurant where there were some rather high-level ayatollahs. A terrorist car bomb blew the place to bits and him with it, yesterday lunchtime."

"How bloody awful!"

"Yes. There was a Captain Ross with him, he was hurt too. I believe you knew him?"

"Yes, yes, I'd met him. He helped the wife of one of our pilots get out of a mess at Tabriz. A nice young man. How badly was he hurt?"

"We don't know, it's all a bit sketchy, but our embassy in Tehran got him to the Kuwait International Hospital yesterday; I'll get a proper report tomorrow and will let you know. Now, you asked if we could find out the whereabouts of your Captain Erikki Yokkonen." A pause and the rustle of papers and Gavallan held on to his hope. "We had a telex this evening from Tabriz, just before I left the office: 'Please be advised in answer to your query about Captain Erikki Yokkonen, he is believed to have escaped from his kidnappers and is now believed to be with his wife at the palace of Hakim Khan. A further report will be forthcoming tomorrow as soon as this can be checked.' "

"You mean Abdollah Khan, Roger." Excitedly Gavallan covered the mouthpiece and whispered to Scot, "Erikki's safe!"

"Fantastic," Scot said, wondering what the bad news had been.

"The telex definitely says Hakim Khan," Newbury was saying.

"Never mind, thank God he's safe." And thank God another major hurdle against Whirlwind is removed. "Could you get a message to him for me?"

"I could try. Come in tomorrow. Can't guarantee it'll reach him, the situation in Azerbaijan is quite fluid. We could certainly try."

"I can't thank you enough, Roger. Very thoughtful of you to let me know. Terribly sorry about Talbot and young Ross. If there's anything I can do to help Ross, please let me know."

"Yes, yes, I will. By the way, the word's out." It was said flat.

"Sorry?"

"Let's say, 'Turbulences,' " Newbury said delicately.

For a moment Gavallan was silent, then he recovered. "Oh?"

"Oh. It seems a certain Mr. Kasigi wanted you to service Iran-Toda from yesterday and you told him you wouldn't be able to give him an answer for thirty days. So, er, we added two to two and with all the rumors got a bull's-eye, the word's out."

Gavallan was trying to get cool. "Not being able to service Iran-Toda's a business decision, Roger, nothing more. Operating anywhere in Iran's bloody now, you know that. I couldn't handle Kasigi's extra business."

"Really?" Newbury's voice was withering. Then, sharply, "Well, if what we hear is true we'd strongly, very strongly advise against it."

Gavallan said stubbornly, "You surely don't advise me to support Iran-Toda when all Iran's falling apart, do you?"

Another pause. A sigh. Then, "Well, mustn't keep you, Andy. Perhaps we could have lunch. On Saturday."

"Yes, thank you. I'd, I'd like that." Gavallan hung up.

"What was the bad?" Scot asked.

Gavallan told him about Talbot and Ross and then about "turbulences."

"That's too close to Whirlwind to be funny."

"What's this about Kasigi?"

"He wanted two 212s from Bandar Delam at once to service Iran-Toda—I had to stall." Their meeting had been brief and blunt: "Sorry, Mr. Kasigi, it's not possible to service you this week, or the next. I couldn't, er, consider it for thirty days."

"My chairman would greatly appreciate it. I understand you know him?"

"Yes, I did, and if I could help I certainly would. Sorry, it's just not possible."

"But . . . then can you suggest an alternative? I *must* get helicopter support."

"What about a Japanese company?"

"There isn't one. Is there . . . is there someone else to hold me over?"

"Not to my knowledge. Guerney'll never go back but they might know of someone." He had given him their phone number and the distraught Japanese had rushed off.

He looked at his son. "Damned shame but nothing I could do to help him."

Scot said, "If the word's out . . ." He eased the sling more comfortably. "If the word's out then it's out. All the more reason to press the titty."

"Or to cancel. Think I'll drop by and see Duke. Track me down if anyone calls. Nogger's taking over from you?"

"Yes. Midnight. Jean-Luc's still booked on the dawn flight to Bahrain, Pettikin to Kuwait. I've confirmed their seats." Scot watched him.

Gavallan did not answer the unsaid question. "Leave it like that for the moment." He saw his son smile and nod and his heart was suddenly overflowing with love and concern and pride and fear for him, intermixed with his own hopes for a future that depended on his being able to extract all of them from the Iranian morass. He was surprised to hear himself say, "Would you consider giving up flying, laddie?"

"Eh?"

Gavallan smiled at his son's astonishment. But now that he had said it, he decided to continue. "It's part of a long-term plan. For you and the family. In fact I've two—just between ourselves. Of course both depend on whether we stay in business or not. The first is you give up flying and go out to Hong Kong for a couple of years to learn that end of Struan's, back to Aberdeen for perhaps another year, then back to Hong Kong again where you'd base. The second's that you go for a conversion course on the X63s, spend six months or so in the States, perhaps a year learning that end of the business, then to the North Sea for a season. Then out to Hong Kong."

"Always back to Hong Kong?"

"Yes. China will open up sometime for oil exploration and Ian and I want Struan's to be ready with a complete operation, support choppers, rigs, the whole kit and caboodle." He smiled strangely. "Oil for the lamps of China" was code for Ian Dunross's secret plan, most of which Linbar Struan was not party to. "Air Struan'll be the new company and its area of responsibility and operation'd be China, the China Seas, and the whole China basin. Our end plan is that you'd head it."

"Not much potential there," Scot said with pretended diffidence. "Do you think Air Struan would have a future?" Then he let his smile out.

"Again this is all just between us—Linbar's not been given all the facts yet."

Scot frowned. "Will he approve me going out there, joining Struan's and doing this?"

"He hates me, Scot, not you. He hasn't opposed you seeing his niece, has he?"

"Not yet. No, he hasn't, not yet."

"The timing's right and we have to have a future plan—for the family. You're the right age, I think you could do it." Gavallan's eyes picked up light. "You're half-Dunross, you're a direct descendant of Dirk Struan, and so you've responsibilities above and beyond yourself. You and your sister inherited your mother's shares, you'd qualify for the Inner Office if you're good enough. That burk Linbar'll have to retire one day—even he can't destroy the Noble House totally. What do you say to my plan?"

"I'd like to think it over, Dad."

What's there to think over, laddie, he thought. "Night, Scot, I may drop back later." He gave him a careful pat on his good shoulder and walked out. Scot won't fail me, he told himself proudly.

In the spacious Customs and Immigration hall, passengers were trickling in from Immigration, others waiting for their baggage. The arrival board announced that the Gulf Air Flight 52 from Muscat, Oman's capital, had arrived on time and was due to leave in fifteen minutes for Abu Dhabi, Bahrain, and Kuwait. The newstand was still open so he wandered over to see what papers were in. He was reaching for the London *Times* when he saw the headline, PRIME MINISTER CALLAGHAN CITES LABOUR'S SUCCESSES, and changed his mind. What do I need that for? he thought. Then he saw Genny McIver.

She was sitting alone, near the boarding gate with a small suitcase beside her. "Hello, Genny, what are you doing here?"

She smiled sweetly. "I'm going to Kuwait."

He smiled sweetly back. "What the hell for?"

"Because I need a holiday."

"Don't be ridiculous. The button's not even pushed yet and anyway, there's nothing you can do there, nothing. You'd be in the way. You're much better off waiting here. Genny, for God's sake be reasonable."

The set smile had not even flickered. "Are you finished?"

"Yes."

"I am reasonable, I'm the most reasonable person you know. Duncan McIver isn't. He's the most misguided, misbegotten twit I've ever come across in all my born days and to Kuwait I am going." It was all said with an Olympian calm.

Wisely he changed tactics. "Why didn't you tell me you were going instead of sneaking off like this? I'd've been worried to death if you'd been missing."

"If I'd asked you you'd've shanghaied me. I asked Manuela to tell you later, flight time, hotel, and phone number. But I'm glad you're here, Andy. You can see me off. I'd like someone to see me off, hate seeing myself off—oh, you know what I mean!"

It was then he saw how frail she seemed. "You all right, Genny?"

"Oh, yes. It's just . . . well, I just must be there, have to be, I can't sit here, and anyway part of this was my idea, I'm responsible too, and I don't want anything—anything—to go wrong."

"It won't," he said and both of them touched the wooden seat. Then he slipped his arm through hers. "It's going to be all right. Listen, one good piece of news." He told her about Erikki.

"Oh, that's wonderful. Hakim Khan?" Genny searched her memory. "Wasn't Azadeh's brother, the one who was living in . . . blast, I've forgotten, someplace near Turkey, wasn't his name Hakim?"

"Perhaps the telex was right then and it is Hakim 'Khan.' That should be great for them."

"Yes. Her father sounded like an awful old man." She looked up at him. "Have you decided yet? If it's tomorrow?"

"No, not yet, not finally."

"What about the weather?"

He told her. "Not much of a decider, either way," she said.

"Wish Mac was here. He'd be wise in a situation like this."

"No wiser than you, Andy." They looked across at the departure board as the announcer called for passengers on Flight 52. They got up. "For what it's worth, Andy, all other things being equal, Mac's decided it's tomorrow."

"Eh? How do you know that?"

"I know Duncan. 'Bye, darling Andy." She kissed him hurriedly and did not look back.

He waited until she had vanished. Deep in thought he went outside, not noticing Wesson near the newsstand, putting his fountain pen away.

BOOK FOUR

BOOK FOUR

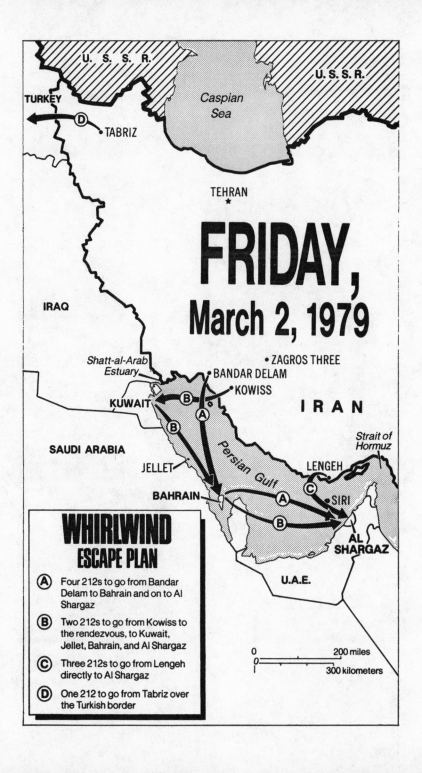

FRIDAY,
March 2, 1979

U. S. S. R.

U. S. S. R.

Caspian Sea

TURKEY

Ⓓ ● TABRIZ

TEHRAN ★

IRAQ

Shatt-al-Arab Estuary

● ZAGROS THREE

● BANDAR DELAM

Ⓑ ● KOWISS

Ⓐ

KUWAIT

I R A N

Strait of Hormuz

Ⓑ

SAUDI ARABIA

Persian Gulf

LENGEH

JELLET

Ⓒ

BAHRAIN

Ⓐ

● SIRI

Ⓑ

AL SHARGAZ

WHIRLWIND ESCAPE PLAN

Ⓐ Four 212s to go from Bandar Delam to Bahrain and on to Al Shargaz

Ⓑ Two 212s to go from Kowiss to the rendezvous, to Kuwait, Jellet, Bahrain, and Al Shargaz

Ⓒ Three 212s to go from Lengeh directly to Al Shargaz

Ⓓ One 212 to go from Tabriz over the Turkish border

U.A.E.

0 _____ 200 miles

0 _____ 300 kilometers

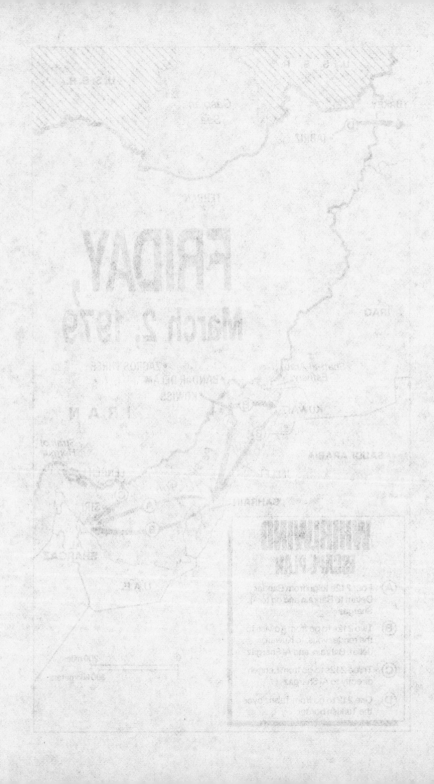

AL SHARGAZ—THE OASIS HOTEL: 5:37 A.M. Gavallan stood at his window, already dressed, night still heavy except to the east, dawn due soon now. Threads of mist came in from the coast, half a mile away, to vanish quickly in the desert reaches. Sky eerily cloudless to the east, gradually building to thick cover overall. From where he was he could see most of the airfield. Runway lights were on, a small jet already taxiing out, and the smell of kerosene was on the wind that had veered more southerly. A knock on the door. "Come in! Ah, morning, Jean-Luc, morning, Charlie."

"Morning, Andy. If we're to catch our flight it's time to leave," Pettikin said, his nervousness running the words together. He was due to go to Kuwait, Jean-Luc to Bahrain.

"Where's Rodrigues?"

"He's waiting downstairs."

"Good, then you'd best be on your way." Gavallan was pleased that his voice sounded calm. Pettikin beamed, Jean-Luc muttered *merde*. "With your approval, Charlie, I propose pushing the button at 7:00 A.M. as planned—provided none of the bases pull the plug beforehand. If they do we'll try again tomorrow. Agreed?"

"Agreed. No calls yet?"

"Not yet."

Pettikin could hardly contain his excitement. "Well, off we go into the wild blue yonder! Come on, Jean-Luc!"

Jean-Luc's eyebrows soared. *"Mon Dieu,* it's Boy Scouts time!" Then he went for the door. "Great news about Erikki, Andy, but how's he going to get out?"

"I don't know. I'm seeing Newbury at the Consulate first thing to try to get a message to him—to get out via Turkey. Both of you call me the second you land. I'll be in the office from six. See you later."

He closed the door after them. Now it was done. Unless one of the bases aborted.

AT LENGEH: 5:49 A.M. False dawn's light was barely perceptible through the overcast. Scragger wore a raincoat and trudged through the drizzle and puddles toward the cookhouse that had the only light on in the base. The wind pulled at his peaked flying cap, driving the soft rain into his face.

To his surprise Willi was already in the cookhouse, sitting near the wood stove drinking coffee. "Morning, Scrag, coffee? I've just made it." He motioned with his head into a corner. Curled up on the floor, fast asleep and near to the warmth, was one of the camp Green Bands. Scragger nodded and took off his raincoat.

"Tea for me, me son. You're up early, where's the cook?"

Willi shrugged and put the kettle back on the stove. "Late. I thought I'd have an early breakfast. I'm going to have some scrambled. How about if I cook for you too?"

Scragger was suddenly famished. "You're on! Four eggs for me and two pieces of toast and I'll go easy at lunch. We have any bread, sport?" He watched Willi open the refrigerator. Three loaves, plenty of eggs and butter. "Good oh! Can't eat eggs without buttered toast. They don't taste right." He glanced at his watch.

"Wind's veered almost south and up to thirty knots."

"My nose says she'll lessen."

"My arse says she'll lessen too but still she's shitty."

Scragger laughed. "Have confidence, mate."

"I'll be much more confident with my passport."

"Too right, so will I—but the plan still stays." When he had got back last night from the sergeant, Vossi and Willi had been waiting for him. Well away from prying ears he had told them what had happened.

Willi had said at once, and Vossi agreed, "We better alert Andy we may have to abort."

"No," Scragger said. "I figure it this way, sport: if Andy doesn't call for Whirlwind in the morning I've all day to get our passports. If he calls for Whirlwind, it'll be exactly at seven. That gives me plenty of time to get to the station at seven-thirty and back by eight. While I'm away you start the plan rolling."

"Jesus, Scrag, we been thr—"

"Ed, will you listen? We leave anyway but bypass Al Shargaz where we know we'd have trouble and duck into Bahrain—I know the port officer there. We throw ourselves on his mercy—maybe even have an 'emergency' on the beach. Meanwhile we radio Al Shargaz the moment we're clear of Iran skies for someone to meet us and bail us out. It's the best I can think of and at least we've covered, either way."

And it's still the best I can think of, he told himself watching Willi at the stove, the butter in the frying pan beginning to sizzle. "I thought we were having scrambled?"

"This's the way to scramble." Willi's voice edged.

"Bloody isn't, you know," Scragger said sharply. "You have to use water or milk an—"

"By God Harry," Willi snapped, "if you don't want the . . . *Scheiss!* Sorry, didn't mean to bite your head, Scrag. Sorry."

"I'm touchy too, sport. No problem."

"The, er, this way's the way my mother does them. You put the eggs in without beating them, the whites cook white and then, quick as a wink you put in a little milk and you mix her, then the white's white and the yolk's yellow . . ." Willi found himself not able to stop. He had had a bad night, bad dreams, and bad feelings and now with the dawn he felt no better.

Over in the corner the Green Band stirred, his nose filled with the smell of cooking butter and he yawned, nodded to them sleepily, then settled more comfortably and dozed off again. When the kettle boiled Scragger made himself some tea, glanced at his watch: 5:56 A.M. Behind him the door opened and Vossi wandered in, shook the rain off the umbrella.

"Hi, Scrag! Hey, Willi, coffee and two over easy with a side order of crisp bacon and hash brown for me."

"Get stuffed!"

They all laughed, their anxiety making them light-headed. Scragger glanced at his watch again. Stop it! Stop it, he ordered himself. You've got to keep calm, then they'll be calm. Easy to see they're both ready to blow.

AT KOWISS: 6:24 A.M. McIver and Lochart were in the tower looking out at the rain and overcast. Both were dressed in flight gear, McIver seated in front of the HF, Lochart standing at the window. No lights on—just the reds and greens of the functioning equipment. No sound but the pleasing hum and the not so pleasing whine of the wind that came in the broken windows, rattling the aerial stanchions.

Lochart glanced at the wind counter. Twenty-five knots, gusting thirty from the south-southeast. Over by the hangar two mechanics were washing down the already clean two 212s, and the 206 McIver had brought from Tehran. Lights on in the cookhouse. Except for a skeleton cookhouse staff, McIver had told the office staff and laborers to take Friday off. After the shock of Esvandiary's summary execution for "corruption" they had needed no encouragement to leave.

Lochart glanced at the clock. The second hand seemed interminably slow. A truck went by below. Another. Now it was exactly 6:30 A.M. "Sierra

One, this is Lengeh." It was Scragger reporting in as planned. McIver was greatly relieved. Lochart became grimmer.

"Lengeh, this is Sierra One, you're five by five." Scot's voice from Al Shargaz was clean and clear. Sierra One was code for the office at Al Shargaz airport, Gavallan not wanting to draw any more attention to the sheikdom than necessary.

McIver clicked on the HF transmit. "Sierra One, this is Kowiss."

"Kowiss, this is Sierra One, you're four by five."

"Sierra One, this's Bandar Delam." Both heard the tremble in Rudi's voice.

"Bandar Delam, this's Sierra One, you're two by five."

Now only static from the loudspeaker. McIver wiped his palms. "So far so good." The coffee in his cup was cold and tasted awful but he finished it.

"Rudi sounded uptight, didn't he?" Lochart said.

"I'm sure I did too. So did Scrag." McIver studied him, concerned for him; Lochart did not meet his eyes, just went over to the electric kettle and plugged it in. On the desk were four phones, two internal and two outside lines. In spite of his resolve, Lochart tried one of the outside phones, then the other. Both still dead. Dead for days now. Dead like me. No way of being in touch with Sharazad, no post.

"There's a Canadian consul in Al Shargaz," McIver said gruffly. "They could get through to Tehran for you from there."

"Sure." A gust rattled the temporary boarding over the broken window. Lochart paid the outside no attention, wondering about Sharazad, praying she would join him. Join me for what? The kettle began to sing. He watched it. Since he had walked out of the apartment, he had blocked the future out of his mind. In the night it had surged back, much as he tried to prevent it.

From the base came the first call of a muezzin. "Come to prayer, come to progress, prayer is better than sleep . . ."

AT BANDAR DELAM: 6:38 A.M. A sodden dawn, rain slight, wind less than yesterday. At the airfield Rudi Lutz, Sandor Petrofi, and Pop Kelly were in Rudi's trailer, no lights on, drinking coffee. Outside on the veranda, Marc Dubois was stationed on guard against eavesdroppers. No lights on elsewhere in the base. Rudi glanced at his watch. "Hope to God it's today," Rudi said.

"It's today or never." Kelly was very grim. "Make the call, Rudi."

"A minute yet."

Through the window Rudi could see the maw of the hangar and their

212s. None of them had long-range tanks. Somewhere in the darkness, Fowler Joines and three mechanics were quietly putting the last of the spare fuel aboard, finishing preparations begun cautiously last night while the pilots diverted the camp guards and Numir. Just before going to bed the four of them had individually made their range calculations. They were all within ten nautical miles of each other.

"If the wind holds at this strength, we're all in the goddamn sea," Sandor had said softly, difficult to talk over the music but not safe without it— earlier Fowler Joines had spotted Numir lurking near Rudi's trailer.

"Yes," Marc Dubois had agreed. "About ten kilometers out."

"Maybe we should blow Bahrain and divert to Kuwait, Rudi?"

"No, Sandor, we've got to leave Kuwait open for Kowiss. Six Iranian registered choppers all zeroing in there? They'd have a hemorrhage."

"Where the hell're the new registration numbers we were promised?" Kelly said, his nervousness growing every moment.

"We're being met. Charlie Pettikin's going to Kuwait, Jean-Luc to Bahrain."

"*Mon Dieu,* that's our bad luck," Dubois had said, disgustedly. "Jean-Luc's always late, always. Those Pieds Noirs, they think like Arabs."

"If Jean-Luc screws up this time," Sandor had said, "he'll be goddamn burger meat. Listen, about the gas, maybe we can get extra from Iran-Toda. It's gonna look mighty suspicious to be loaded with all that gas, just to go down there."

"Rudi, make the call. It's time."

"Okay, okay!" Rudi took a deep breath, picked up the mike. "Sierra One, this's Bandar Delam, do you read? This is . . ."

AT AL SHARGAZ HQ: 6:40 A.M.   ". . . Bandar Delam, do you read?"

Gavallan was sitting in front of the HF, Scot beside him, Nogger Lane leaning against a desk behind them, Manuela in the only other chair. All were rigid, staring at the loudspeaker, all sure the call meant trouble as the Whirlwind plan called for radio silence before 7:00 A.M. and during the actual escape, except in emergencies. "Bandar Delam, Sierra One," Scot said throatily. "You're two by five, go ahead."

"We don't know how your day is but we've some planned flights this morning and we'd like to bring them forward to now. Do you approve?"

"Standby One," Scot said.

"Damnation," Gavallan muttered. "It's essential all bases leave at the same time." Then again the airwaves crackled into life.

"Sierra One, this's Lengeh," Scragger's voice was much louder and clearer and more sharp. "We've flights too but the later the better. How's your weather?"

"Standby One, Lengeh." Scot glanced across at Gavallan, waiting.

"Call Kowiss," Gavallan said and everyone relaxed a little. "We'll check with them first."

"Kowiss, this's Sierra One, do you read?" Silence. "Kowiss, this's Sierra One, do you read?"

"This's Kowiss, go ahead." McIver's voice sounded strained and was intermittent.

"Did you copy?"

"Yes. Prefer firm forecast as planned."

"That decides it." Gavallan took the mike. "Sierra One, all bases, our weather's changeable. We will have your firm forecast at 0700."

"We copy," Scragger said.

"We copy." Rudi's voice was brittle.

"We copy." McIver sounded relieved.

Again the airwaves were silent. Gavallan said to no one in particular, "Better to stick to the plan. Don't want to alert ATC unnecessarily, or get that bugger Siamaki more difficult than usual. Rudi could have aborted if it was urgent, he still can." He got up and stretched, then sat down again. Static. They were also listening on the emergency channel, 121.5. The Pan Am jumbo took off rattling the windows.

Manuela shifted in her seat, feeling she was encroaching even though Gavallan had said, "Manuela, you listen with us too, you're the only Farsi speaker among us." The time did not weigh so heavily for her. Her man was safe, a little damaged but safe, and her heart was singing with joy for the blessed luck that brought him out of the maelstrom. "Because that's what it is, honey," she had told him last night at the hospital.

"Maybe, but without Hussain's help I'd still be in Kowiss."

If it wasn't for that mullah you would never've been hit, she had thought but did not say it, not wanting to agitate him. "Can I get you anything, darlin'?"

"A new head!"

"They're bringing a pill in a minute. Doctor said you'll be flying in six weeks, that you've the constitution of a roan buffalo."

"I feel like a bent chicken."

She had laughed.

Now she let herself drift comfortably, not having to sweat out the waiting like the others, particularly Genny. Two minutes to go. Static. Gavallan's fingers drumming. A private jet took off and she could see another airplane on final, a jumbo with Alitalia colors. Wonder if that'll be Paula's flight back from Tehran?

The minute hand on the clock touched twelve. At 7:00 A.M. Gavallan took the mike. "Sierra One to all bases: Our forecast's settled and we expect improving weather but watch out for small whirlwinds. Do you copy?"

"Sierra One, this's Lengeh." Scragger was breezy. "We copy and will watch for whirlwinds. Out."

"Sierra One, this's Bandar Delam, we copy, and will watch for whirlwinds. Out."

Silence. The seconds ticked by. Unconsciously Gavallan bit his lower lip. Waiting, then he clicked the transmit button. "Kowiss, do you read?"

AT KOWISS: 7:04 A.M.   McIver and Lochart were staring at the HF. Almost together they checked their watches. Lochart muttered, "It's an abort for today," wet with relief. Another day's reprieve, he thought. Maybe today the phones'll come back in, maybe today I can talk to her . . .

"They'd still call, that's part of the plan, they call either way." McIver clicked the switch on and off. The lights all checked out. So did the dials. "To hell with it," he said and clicked on the sender. "Sierra One, this's Kowiss, do you read?" Silence. Again, even more anxiously, "Sierra One, this's Kowiss, do you read?" Silence.

"What the hell's with them?" Lochart said through his teeth.

"Lengeh, this's Kowiss, do you read?" No answer. Abruptly McIver remembered and jumped to his feet and ran to the window. The main cable to the transmitter-receiver aerial was hanging loose, flapping in the wind. Cursing, McIver tore the door to the roof open and went out into the cold. His fingers were strong but the nuts were too rusted to move and he saw that the soldered wire ring was eaten away by rust and had fractured. "Bloody hell . . ."

"Here." Lochart was beside him and gave him the pliers.

"Thanks." McIver began to scrape the rust away. The rain had almost stopped but neither noticed it. A rumble of thunder. Sheet lightning flickered in the Zagros, most of the mountains clouded. As he worked hurriedly, he told Lochart how Wazari had spent so much time on the roof yesterday fixing the cable. "When I came on this morning I made a routine call so I knew she was working and we were loud and clear at 6:30 and again at 6:40. The wind must've pulled the wire between then and now . . ." The pliers slipped and he ripped a finger and cursed more.

"Let me do it?"

"No, it's fine. Couple of seconds."

Lochart went back into the tower cabin: 7:07. The base still quiet. Over at the air base some trucks were moving around but no airplanes. Down by the hangar their two mechanics still fiddled with the 212s, according to plan, Freddy Ayre with them. Then he saw Wazari cycling along the inside perimeter road. His heart flipped. "Mac, there's Wazari, coming from the base."

"Stop him, tell him anything but stop him." Lochart rushed off down the stairs. McIver's heart was thundering. "Come on, for God's sake," he said and cursed himself again for not checking. Check check and recheck, safety is no accident it has to be planned!

Again the pliers slipped. Again he applied them and now the nuts were moving down the bolt. Now one side was tight. For a second he was tempted to risk it, but his caution overcame his anxiety and he tightened the other side. A tentative pull on the cable. Tight. He hurried back, sweat pouring off him: 7:16.

For a moment he could not catch his breath. "Come on, McIver, for the love of God!" He took a deep breath and that helped. "Sierra One, this is Kowiss, do you read?"

Scot's anxious voice came back at once. "Kowiss, Sierra One, go ahead."

"Do you have any information on any weather for us?"

At once Gavallan's voice, even more anxious: "Kowiss, we sent out the following at exactly 0700: our forecast's settled and we expect improving weather but watch out for small whirlwinds. Do you copy?"

McIver exhaled. "We copy, and will watch for small whirlwinds. Did, did the others copy?"

"Affirmative . . ."

AT AL SHARGAZ HQ: ". . . I say again, affirmative." Gavallan repeated into the mike. "What happened?"

"No problem," McIver's voice came back, his signal weak. "See you soon, out." Now the airwaves were silent. A sudden cheer erupted in the room, Scot embraced his father and gasped as pain ripped up from his shoulder but no one noticed in the pandemonium. Manuela was hugging Gavallan, and she said, "I'm going to phone the hospital, Andy, I'll be back in a second," and ran off. Nogger was jumping up and down with glee and Gavallan said happily, "I think all nonpilots deserve a large bottle of beer!"

AT KOWISS: McIver switched off the set and slumped back in the chair, collecting himself, feeling strange—light-headed and heavy-handed. "Never mind that, it's a go!" he said. It was quiet in the tower except for the wind that creaked the door he had left open in his haste. He closed it and saw the rain had stopped, the clouds still gloomy. Then he noticed his finger was still bleeding. Beside the HF was a paper towel and he tore a piece off and wrapped it crudely around the wound. His hands were trembling. On a sudden impulse, he went outside and knelt beside the connecting wire. It took all his strength to pull it loose. Then he double checked the tower, wiped the sweat off his brow, and went down the stairs.

Lochart and Wazari were in Esvandiary's office, Wazari unshaven and grubby, a curious electricity in the air. No time to worry about that, McIver thought, Scrag and Rudi're already airborne. "Morning, Sergeant," McIver said curtly, aware of Lochart's scrutiny. "I thought I gave you the day off—we've no traffic of any importance."

"Yeah, Captain, you did but I, er, I couldn't sleep and . . . I don't feel safe over in the base." Wazari noticed McIver's flushed face and the crude paper bandage. "You okay?"

"Yes, I'm all right, just cut my finger on the broken window." McIver glanced at Lochart who was sweating as much as he was. "We'd better be going, Tom. Sergeant, we're ground-testing the 212s." He saw Lochart glance at him abruptly.

"Yes sir. I'll inform base," Wazari said.

"No need for that." Momentarily McIver was at a loss, then the answer came to him. "For your own sake, if you're going to hang around here, you'd better get ready for Minister Kia."

The color went out of the man's face. "What?"

"He's due shortly for the return flight to Tehran. Weren't you the only witness against him and poor bloody Hotshot?"

"Sure, but I heard them," Wazari flared, needing to justify himself. "Kia's a bastard and a liar and so's Hotshot and they had this deal cooking. Have you forgotten Hotshot was the one who ordered Ayre beaten up? They would have killed him, have you forgotten that? Esvandiary and Kia, everything I said was true, it was true."

"I'm sure it was. I believe you. But he's bound to be plenty bloody aggravated if he sees you, isn't he? So will the office staff, they were all very angry. They'll certainly give you away. Perhaps I can divert Kia," McIver said as a sop, hoping to keep him on their side, "perhaps not. If I were you I'd make myself scarce, don't hang around here. Come on, Tom." McIver turned to go but Wazari stood in his way.

"Don't forget I'm the one who stopped a massacre by saying Sandor's load shifted, but for me he'd be dead, but for me you'd all be up before a komiteh . . . you've got to help me . . ." Tears were streaming down his face now, "you gotta help me . . ."

"I'll do what I can," McIver said, sorry for him, and walked out. Outside he had to stop himself from running over to the others, seeing their anxiety, then Lochart caught up with him.

"Whirlwind?" he asked, having to hurry to keep alongside.

"Yes, Andy pressed the button on the dot at 0700 as planned, Scrag and Rudi copied and are probably already on their way," McIver said, the words tumbling over one another, not noticing Lochart's sudden despair. Now they reached Ayre and the mechanics. "Whirlwind!" McIver croaked and to all of them the word sounded like a clarion call.

"Jolly good." Freddy Ayre kept his voice flat, holding his excitement inside. The others did not. "Why the delay? What happened?"

"Tell you later, start up, let's get on with it!" McIver headed for the first 212, Ayre the second, the mechanics already jumping into the cabins. At that moment a staff car with Colonel Changiz and some airmen swung into the compound and stopped outside the office building. All the airmen carried guns, all wore green armbands.

"Ah, Captain, you're flying Minister Kia back to Tehran?" Changiz seemed a little flustered, and angry.

"Yes, yes, I am, at ten, ten o'clock."

"I had a message that he wants to bring his departure forward to eight o'clock but you're not to leave until ten as your clearance states. Clear?"

"Yes, but th—"

"I would have phoned but your phones are out again and there's something wrong with your radio. Don't you service your equipment? It was working then went off." McIver saw the colonel look at the three choppers lined up, begin to go toward them. "I didn't know you had revenue flights today."

"Just ground-testing one and the other has to test avionics for tomorrow's crew change at Rig Abu Sal, Colonel," McIver said hastily and to further divert him, "What's the problem with Minister Kia?"

"No problem," he said irritably, then glanced at his watch and changed his mind about inspecting the helicopters. "Get someone to fix your radio and you come with me. The mullah Hussain wants to see you. We'll be back in good time."

Lochart got his mouth moving. "I'd be glad to drive Captain McIver over in a minute, there're a few things here he sho—"

"Hussain wants to see Captain McIver, not you—now! You deal with the radio!" Changiz told his men to wait for him, got into the driver's seat, and beckoned McIver to sit beside him. Blankly, McIver obeyed. Changiz drove off and his driver wandered toward the office, the other airmen spread out, peered at the choppers. Both 212s were crammed with the last of the important spares, loaded last night. Trying to be nonchalant, the mechanics closed the cabin doors, started polishing.

Ayre and Lochart stared after the departing car. Ayre said, "Now what?"

"I don't know—we can't leave without him." Lochart felt nauseous.

AT BANDAR DELAM: 7:26 A.M. The four 212s were out of the hangar parked for takeoff. Fowler Joines and the other three mechanics were pottering in the back of the cabins, waiting impatiently. Unwieldy forty-gallon drums of reserve gasoline were lashed in place. Many crates of spares. Suitcases hidden under tarpaulins.

"Com' on, for effs sweet sake," Fowler said and wiped the sweat off, the air of the cabin heavy with gasoline.

Through the open cabin door he could see Rudi, Sandor, and Pop Kelly still waiting in the hangar, everything ready as planned except for the last pilot, Dubois, ten minutes late and no one knowing if Base Manager Numir or one of the staff or Green Bands had intercepted him. Then he saw Dubois come out of his door and almost had a fit. With Gallic indifference, Dubois was carrying a suitcase, his raincoat over his arm. As he strolled past the office, Numir appeared at the window.

"Let's go," Rudi croaked and went for his cabin as calmly as he could, clipped on his seat belt, and stabbed Engines Start. Sandor did likewise, Pop Kelly a second behind him, their rotors gathering speed. Leisurely, Dubois tossed his suitcase to Fowler, laid his raincoat carefully on a crate, and got into the pilot's seat, at once started up, not bothering with his seat belt or checklist. Fowler was swearing incoherently. Their jets were building nicely and Dubois hummed a little song, adjusted his headset, and now, when all was prepared, fastened his seat belt. He did not see Numir rush out of his office.

"Where are you going?" Numir shouted to Rudi through his side window.

"Iran-Toda, it's on the manifest." Rudi continued with the start-up drill. VHF on, HF on, needles coming into the Green.

"But you haven't asked Abadan for engine start an—"

"It's Holy Day, Agha, you can do that for us."

Numir shouted angrily, "That's your job! You're to wait for Zataki. You must wait for the col—"

"Quite right, I want to make sure my chopper's ready the instant he arrives—very important to please him, isn't it?"

"Yes, but why was Dubois carrying a suitcase?"

"Oh, you know Frenchmen," he said, saying the first thing that came into his head, "clothes are important; he's sure he's going to be based at Iran-Toda and he's taking a spare uniform." His gloved thumb hovered over the transmit switch on the column. Don't, he ordered himself, don't be impatient, they all know what to do, don't be impatient.

Then, behind Numir, through the haze, visibility down to a few hundred yards, Rudi saw the Green Band truck lumber through the main gate and stop, its noise covered by their jets. But it wasn't Zataki, just some of their normal Green Band guards and they stood there in a group watching the 212s curiously. Never before had four 212s been started up at once.

In his headphones he heard Dubois, "Ready, *mon vieux*," then Pop Kelly, then Sandor, and he clicked the send switch and said into the boom mike, "Go!," leaned closer to the window, and beckoned Numir. "No need for the others to wait, I'm waiting."

"But you were ordered to go in a group and your clearances . . ." The base manager's voice was drowned by the mass of engines shoved to full power, emergency takeoff procedure, conforming to the plan the pilots had secretly agreed on last night, Dubois going right, Sandor left, Kelly straight ahead like a covey of snipe scattering. In seconds they were airborne and away, staying very low. Numir's face went purple, "But you were told th . . ."

"This is for your safety, Agha, we're trying to protect you," Rudi called over the jets, beckoning him forward again, all his own needles in the Green; "this way's better, Agha, this way we'll do the job and no problem. We've got to protect you and IranOil." In his earphones he heard Dubois break mandatory radio silence and say urgently, "There's a car almost at the gates!"

At that instant Rudi saw it and recognized Zataki in the front seat. Maximum power. "Agha, I'm just going to take her up a few feet, my torque counter's jumping . . ."

Whatever Numir was screaming was lost in the noise. Zataki was barely a hundred yards away. Rudi felt the rotors biting into the air, then lift off. For a moment it looked as though Numir were going to jump onto a skid but he ducked out of the way, the skid scraping him, and fell as Rudi got forward momentum and lumbered away, almost bursting with excitement. Ahead, the others were in station over the marsh. He waggled his chopper from side to side as he joined them, gave them the thumbs-up, and led the rush for the Gulf four miles distant.

Numir was choked with rage as he picked himself up, and Zataki's car skidded to a halt beside him. "By God, what's going on?" Zataki said furiously, jumping out, the choppers already vanished into the haze, the sound of the engines dying away now. "They were supposed to wait for me!"

"I know, I know, Colonel, I told them but they . . . they just took off an—" Numir screamed as the fist smashed him in the side of the face and felled him. The other Green Bands watched indifferently, used to these outbursts. One of the men pulled Numir to his feet, slapped his face to bring him around.

Zataki was cursing the sky and when the spasm of rage had passed, he said, "Bring that piece of camel's turd and follow me." Storming past the open hangar he saw the two 206s parked neatly in the back, spares laid out here and there, a fan drying some new paintwork—all Rudi's painstaking camouflage to give them an extra few minutes. "I'll make those dogs wish they'd waited," he muttered, his head aching.

He kicked the door of the office open and stormed over to the radio transmitter and sat down near it. "Numir, get those men on the loud-speaker!"

"But Jahan, our radio operator isn't here yet and I do—"

"Do it!"

The terrified man switched on the VHF, his mouth bleeding and hardly able to talk. "Base calling Captain Lutz!" He waited, then repeated the order, adding, "Urgent!"

IN THE AIRPLANES: They were barely ten feet above the marsh-land and a few hundred yards away when they heard Zataki's angry voice cut in: "All helicopters are recalled to base, recalled to base! Report in!" Rudi made a slight adjustment to the engine power and to the trim. In the chopper nearest to him he saw Marc Dubois point at his headset and make an obscene gesture. He smiled and did likewise, then noticed the sweat running down his face. "ALL HELICOPTERS REPORT IN! ALL . . ."

AT THE AIRFIELD: ". . . HELICOPTERS REPORT IN." Zataki was shrieking into the mike. "ALL HELICOPTERS REPORT IN!"

Nothing but static answered him. Suddenly Zataki slammed the mike onto the table. "Get Abadan Tower! HURRY UP!" he shouted and the terrified Numir, blood trickling into his beard, switched channels, and after the sixth call, this time in Farsi, got the tower. "Here is Abadan Tower, Agha, please go ahead."

Zataki tore the mike out of his hand. "This is Colonel Zataki, Abadan Revolutionary Komiteh," he said in Farsi, "calling from Bandar Delam airfield."

"Peace be upon you, Colonel," the voice was very deferential. "What can we do for you?"

"Four of our helicopters took off without approval, going to Iran-Toda. Recall them, please."

"Just a moment, please." Muffled voices. Zataki waited, his face mottled. Waiting and waiting, then, "Are you sure, Agha? We do not see them on the radar screen."

"Of course I'm sure. Recall them!"

More muffled voices and more waiting, Zataki ready to explode, then a voice in Farsi said, "The four helicopters that left Bandar Delam are ordered to return to their base. Please acknowledge you are doing this." It was transmitted ineptly and repeated. Then the voice added, "Perhaps their radios are not functioning, Agha, the blessings of God upon you."

"Keep calling them! They're low and heading toward Iran-Toda."

More muffled voices, then more Farsi as before, then a sudden voice cut in in American English, "Okay, I'll take it! This is Abadan Control. Choppers on a heading of 090 degrees, do you read?"

IN DUBOIS'S COCKPIT: His compass heading was 091 degrees. Again the crisp voice in his earphones: "This is Abadan Control, choppers on a heading of 090 degrees one mile from the coast, do you read?" A pause. "Abadan Control, choppers on a heading of 090 switch to channel 121.9 . . . do you read?" This was the emergency channel that all aircraft were supposed to listen in on automatically. "Choppers on a heading of 090 degrees one mile from the coast return to base. Do you read?"

Through the haze Dubois saw that the coast was approaching fast, less than half a mile away, but flying this low he doubted if they could possibly be on radar. He looked left. Rudi pointed at his earphones and then a finger to his lips meaning silence. He gave him the thumbs-up and passed the message to Sandor who was on his right, turned to see Fowler Joines climbing in from the cabin to sit beside him. He motioned to the spare headset hanging above the seat. The voice was more brittle now: "All choppers outward bound from Bandar Delam to Iran-Toda return to base. Do you read?"

Fowler, connected now through the headset, said into their intercom, "Hope the effer drops dead!"

Then again the voice and their smiles faded: "Abadan Control to Colonel Zataki. Do you read?"

"Yes, go ahead."

"We picked up a momentary radar trace, probably nothing, but it could have been a chopper or choppers tightly bunched, heading 090 degrees"— the transmission was weakening slightly—"this would take them direct . . ."

AT THE AIRFIELD: ". . . Iran-Toda. Not requesting engine start and not being in radio contact is a serious violation. Please give us their call signs and names of the captains. Iran-Toda's VHF is still inoperative otherwise we would contact them. Suggest you send someone down there to arrest the pilots and bring them before the ATC Abadan komiteh at once for contravening air regulations. Do you copy?"

"Yes . . . yes, I understand. Thank you. Just a moment." Zataki shoved the mike into Numir's hands. "I'm going to Iran-Toda! If they come back before I get them, they're under arrest! Give Traffic Control what they want to know!" He stormed out, leaving three men on base with machine guns.

Numir began, "Abadan Control, Bandar Delam: HVV, HGU, HKL, HXC, all 212s. Captains Rudi Lutz, Marc Dubois . . ."

IN POP KELLY'S COCKPIT: ". . . Sandor Petrofi, and Ignatius Kelly, all seconded from IranOil by Colonel Zataki's order to Iran-Toda."

"Thank you, Bandar Delam, keep us advised."

Kelly looked right and gave an enthusiastic thumbs-up to Rudi who acknowledged . . .

IN RUDI'S COCKPIT: . . . and did the same to Dubois who also acknowledged. Then he peered into the haze once more.

The closely bunched choppers were almost over the coastline. Iran-Toda was to their left, about half a mile away, but Rudi could see none of it through the haze or mist. He accelerated slightly to get ahead, then turned from his heading of due south to due east. This gave them a deliberate direct course over the plant and he increased altitude only enough to clear the buildings. The complex rushed past but he knew that those on the ground would be well aware of their flight because of the howling suddenness of its appearance. Once past, he went down low again and held this same course, now heading inland for a little more than ten miles. Here the land was desolate, no villages nearby. Again, according to their plan, he turned due south for the sea.

At once visibility began to deteriorate. Down here at twenty feet, visibility was barely a quarter of a mile with a partial whiteout where there was no demarcation between sky and sea. Ahead, almost directly in their path, sixty-odd miles away, was Kharg Island with its immensely powerful radar and, beyond that, another two hundred and twenty miles, their landfall Bahrain. At least two hours of flying. With this wind more, the thirty-five southeasterly becoming a relative twenty-knot headwind.

Down here in the soup it was dangerous. But they thought they should be able to slip under radar if the screens were manned—and should be able to avoid fighter intercept, if any.

Rudi moved the stick from side to side waggling his chopper, then touched his HF Transmit button momentarily. "Delta Four, Delta Four," he said clearly, their code to Al Shargaz that all four Bandar Delam choppers were safe and leaving the coast. He saw Dubois point upward asking him to go higher. He shook his head, pointed ahead and down, ordering them to stay low and keep to the plan. Obediently they spread out and together they left the land and went into the deepening haze.

AT AL SHARGAZ HQ: Gavallan was on the phone to the hospital: "Quickly. Give me Captain Starke, please . . . Hello, Duke, it's Andy, I just wanted to tell you we received 'Delta Four' from Rudi a minute ago, isn't that marvelous?"

"Wonderful, great! Fantastic! Four out and five to go!"

"Yes, but it's six, don't forget Erikki . . ."

LENGEH: 8:04 A.M. Scragger was still waiting in the outer office of the police station. He sat disconsolately on a wooden bench in front of the gendarme corporal who looked down on him from a tall desk behind a chest-high partition.

Once again Scragger checked his watch. He had arrived at 7:20 in case the office opened early but the corporal had not arrived until 7:45 and waved him politely to the bench and invited him to wait. It was the longest wait he had ever had.

Rudi and the Kowiss lads must be airborne by now, he thought miserably, just like we'd've been if it wasn't for the bloody passports. Another minute then that's it. Daren't wait any longer—daren't; it'll still take us an hour or more to get away and sure to God there'll be a slipup somewhere between the three bases, bound to be some nosy parker who'll start asking questions and set the airwaves afire—apart from that burk, Siamaki. Last night Scragger had been on the HF and had monitored Siamaki's petulant calls to Gavallan at Al Shargaz, also to McIver at Kowiss telling him that he would meet him today at Tehran Airport.

Bloody burk! But I still think I was right not to call Andy and abort. Hell, we've got the easiest shot of all and if I'd put Whirlwind off until tomorrow there'd be something else, either with us or with one of the others, and there'd be no way old Mac could avoid flying back to Tehran today with bloody Kia. Can't risk that, just can't. Easy to hear Mac was as nervous as an old woman out to sea in a bucket.

The door opened and he looked up. Two young gendarmes came in, dragging a bruised young man between them, his clothes ripped and filthy. "Who's he?" the corporal asked.

"A thief. We caught him stealing, Corporal, the poor fool was stealing rice from the bazaari Ishmael. We caught him during our patrol, just before dawn."

"As God wants. Put him in the second cell." Then the corporal shouted at the youth, startling Scragger who did not understand the Farsi, "Son of a dog! How can you be so stupid to be caught? Don't you know it's no longer a simple beating now! How many times do you all have to be told? It's Islamic law now! Islamic law!"

"I . . . I was hungry . . . my . . ."

The terrified youth moaned as one of the gendarmes shook him roughly. "Hunger's no excuse, by God. I'm hungry, our families're hungry, we're all hungry, of course we're hungry!" They frog-marched the youth out of the room.

The corporal cursed him again, sorry for him, then glanced at Scragger, nodded briefly, and went back to his work. How stupid for the foreigner to be here on a Holy Day but if the old one wants to wait all day and all night until the sergeant comes tomorrow he can wait all day and all night.

His pen scratched loudly, setting Scragger's teeth on edge: 8:11. Grimly he got up, pretended to thank the corporal who politely pressed him to stay. Then he went for the door and almost bumped into Qeshemi. "Oh, sorry, mate! Salaam, Agha Qeshemi, salaam."

"Salaam, Agha." Qeshemi saw Scragger's relief and impatience. Sardonically he motioned him to wait as he went over to the desk, his shrewd eyes reading the corporal clearly. "Greetings, Achmed, God's peace on you."

"And on you, Excellency Sergeant Qeshemi."

"What trouble do we have today—I know what the foreigner wants."

"There was another Islamic-Marxist meeting near midnight down by the docks. One mujhadin was killed and we've another seven in the cells—it was easy, the ambush went easily, thanks be to God, and Green Bands helped us. What'll we do with them?"

"Obey the new rules," Qeshemi said patiently. "Bring the prisoners up before the Revolutionary Komiteh when they get here tomorrow morning. Next?" The corporal told him about the youth. "Same with him—son of a dog to be caught!"

Qeshemi went through the partition gate to the safe, pulled out the key, and began to open it.

"Thanks be to God, I thought the key was lost," the corporal said.

"It was but Lafti found it. I went to his house this morning. He had it in his pocket." The passports were on the boxes of ammunition. He brought them over to the desk, carefully checked them, signed the permit in the name of Khomeini, checked them again. "Here, Agha Pilot," he said, and handed them to Scragger.

"Mamnoon am, Agha, khoda haefez." Thank you, Excellency, good-bye.

"Khoda haefez, Agha." Sergeant Qeshemi shook the proffered hand, thoughtfully watched him leave. Through the window he saw Scragger drive off quickly. Too quickly. "Achmed, do we have gasoline in the car?"

"There was yesterday, Excellency."

AT BANDAR DELAM AIRPORT: 8:18 A.M.   Now Numir was running frantically from one mechanic's trailer to the next, but they were all empty. He rushed back to his office. Jahan, the radio op, looked at him startled.

"They've gone! Everyone's gone, pilots, mechanics . . . and most of their things are gone too!" Numir stuttered, his face still livid from the blow Zataki had given him. "Those sons of dogs!"

"But . . . but they've only gone to Iran-Toda, Excell—"

"I tell you they've fled, and they fled with our helicopters!"

"But our two 206s are there in the hangar, I saw them, and a fan's even drying the paint. Excellency Rudi wouldn't leave a fan on like tha—"

"By God, I tell you they've gone!"

Jahan, a middle-aged man wearing glasses, switched on the HF. "Captain Rudi, this's base, do you read?"

IN RUDI'S COCKPIT: Both Rudi and his mechanic Faganwitch heard the call clearly. "Base to Captain Rudi, do you read?" Rudi moved the trim a fraction then relaxed again, looking right and left. He saw Kelly motion at his headset, raise two fingers, and gesture. He acknowledged. Then his glee faded: "Tehran, this's Bandar Delam, do you read?" All pilots tensed. No answer. "Kowiss, this's Bandar Delam, do you read?" No answer. "Lengeh, this's Bandar Delam, do you read?"

"Bandar Delam, this's Lengeh, you're two by five, go ahead."

At once there was a spate of Farsi from Jahan that Rudi did not understand, then the two operators talked back and forth. After a pause, Jahan said in English: "Tehran, this is Bandar Delam, do you read?" Static. The call repeated. Static. Then, "Kowiss, do you read?" Then silence again.

"For the moment," Rudi muttered.

"What was all that about, Captain?" Faganwitch asked.

"We're pegged. It's barely fifty minutes since we took off and we're pegged!" There were fighter bases all around them and ahead was the big, very efficient one at Kharg. He had no doubt whatsoever that if they were intercepted they would be shot down like HBC. Correctly, he thought, sickened. And though they were safe enough at the moment down here just above the waves, visibility now less than a quarter of a mile, before long the haze would thin out and then they would be helpless. Again Jahan's voice, "Tehran, this is Bandar Delam, do you read?" Static. "Kowiss, this is Bandar Delam, do you read?" No reply.

Rudi cursed to himself. Jahan was a good radio op, persistent, and would keep calling until Kowiss or Tehran reported in. And then? That's their problem, not mine. Mine's to get my four out safely, that's all I have to worry about. I've got to lead my four out safely.

Ten to fifteen feet below were the waves, not yet white-topped but gray and nasty and the wind had not lessened. He looked across at Kelly and waved his hand from left to right, the signal to spread out more and not to try to keep visual contact if visibility got any worse. Kelly acknowledged. He did the same to Dubois who passed the message on to Sandor, on his extreme right, then settled down to squeeze maximum range with minimum fuel, straining his eyes to pierce the whiteout ahead. Soon they would be deep in the real sea lanes.

LENGEH, AT THE AIRFIELD: 8:31 A.M. "Jesus, Scrag, we thought you'd been arrested," Vossi burst out, Willi with him, intercepting his car, both of them weak with relief, their three mechanics also crowding around. "What happened?"

"I've got the passports, so let's get on with it."

"We gotta problem." Vossi was white.

Scragger grimaced, still sweating from the waiting and the ride back. "Now wot?"

"Ali Pash's here. He's on the HF. He came in as usual, we tried to send him off but he wouldn't go an—"

Impatiently, Willi butted in: "And for the last five minutes, Scrag, for the last five or ten minutes he's been by God Harry peculiar an—"

"Like he's got a vibrator up his ass, Scrag, never seen him like th—" Vossi stopped. Ali Pash came out onto the veranda of the office radio room and beckoned Scragger urgently.

"Be right there, Ali," Scragger called out. To Benson, their chief mechanic, Scragger whispered, "You and your lads all set?"

"Yessir." Benson was small, wiry, and nervous. "I got your stuff into the wagon just before Ali Pash came along. We scarper?"

"Wait till I get to the office. Ev—"

"We got Delta Four, Scrag," Willi said, "nothing from the others."

"Bonzer. Everyone wait till I give the signal." Scragger took a deep breath and walked off, greeting the Green Bands he passed. "Salaam, Ali Pash, g'day," he said, seeing the nervousness and anxiety. "I thought I gave you the day off."

"Agha, there someth—"

"Just a sec, me son!" Scragger turned and with pretended irascibility called out, "Benson, I told you if you and Drew want to go and picnic to go, but you'd better be back by two o'clock or else! And wot the hell're you two waiting for? Are you ground-checking or aren't you?"

"Yeah, Scrag, sorry, Scrag!"

He almost laughed seeing them fall over one another, Benson and the American mechanic, Drew, jumping into the old van and driving off, Vossi and Willi heading for their cockpits. Once inside the office he breathed easier, put his briefcase with the passports on his desk. "Now, wot's the problem?"

"You're leaving us, Agha," the young man said to Scragger's shock.

"Well, we, er, we're not leaving," Scragger began, "we're ground-test—"

"Oh, but you're leaving, you are! There's . . . there's no crew change tomorrow, there's no need for suitcases—I saw Agha Benson with suitcases —and why all the spares sent out and all the pilots and mechanics . . ." The tears began streaming down the young man's cheeks. ". . . it's true."

"Now listen here, me son, you're upset. Take the day off."

"But you're leaving like those at Bandar Delam, you're leaving today and what's going to happen to us?"

A burst of Farsi from the HF loudspeaker overrode him. The young man wiped away his tears and touched the transmit, replying in Farsi, then added in English, "Standby One," and said miserably, "That was Agha Jahan again repeating what he radioed ten minutes ago. Their four 212s have vanished, Agha. They've gone, Agha. They took off at 7:32 A.M. to go to Iran-Toda but didn't land there, just went inland."

Scragger groped for his chair, trying to appear calm. Again the HF, in English now: "Tehran, this's Bandar Delam, do you read?"

"He calls Tehran every few minutes, and Kowiss, but no answer . . ." More tears welled out of the young man's eyes. "Have Kowiss already gone too, Agha? Is Tehran empty of your people? What're we going to do when you've gone?" On the ramp the first of the 212s started up noisily, closely followed by the second. "Agha," Ali Pash said uneasily, "we're supposed to request engine start from Kish now."

"No need to bother them on their holiday, it's hardly a flight, just test-ing," Scragger said. He switched on the VHF and wiped his chin, feeling somehow dirty and greatly unsettled. He liked Ali Pash and what the young man had said was true. With them gone there was no job, no business, and for the Ali Pashes there was only Iran, and only God knew what would happen here. Over the VHF came Willi's voice: "My torque counter's acting up, Scrag."

Scragger took the mike. "Take her over to the cabbage patch and test her." This was an area some five miles inland, well away from the town where they tested engines and could practice emergency procedures. "Stay there, Willi, any problem call me, I can always fetch Benson if you need an adjustment. How you doing, Ed?"

"Dandy, real dandy. Scrag, if it's okay, I'd like to practice some engine outs, my license renewal's coming up soon—Willi can bird-dog me, huh?"

"Okay. Call me in an hour." Scragger went to the window, glad to have his back to Ali Pash and away from those sad, accusing eyes. Both choppers took off and headed inland away from the coast. The office seemed to be stuffier than usual. He opened the window. Ali Pash was sitting gloomily by the radio. "Why not take the day off, lad?"

"I have to reply to Bandar Delam. What should I say, Agha?"

"Wot did Jahan ask you?"

"He said Agha Numir wanted to know if I'd noticed anything strange, if anything strange had happened here, spares leaving, airplanes leaving, pilots and mechanics."

Scragger watched him. "Seems to me nothing strange's happened here. I'm here, mechanics've gone picknicking, Ed and Willi are off on routine checks. Routine. Right?" He kept his eyes on him, willing him to come over to their side. He had no way of persuading him, nothing to offer him, no pishkesh, except . . . "You approve of wot's happening here, me son?" he asked carefully. "I mean, what the future holds for you here?"

"Future? My future's with the company. If . . . if you leave, then . . . then I have no job, I won't . . . I can't afford to m . . . I won't, can't afford anything. I'm the only son . . ."

"If you wanted to leave, well, there'd be your job and a future if you wanted it—outside Iran. Guaranteed."

The youth gaped at him, suddenly understanding what Scragger was offering. "But . . . but what is guaranteed, Agha? A life in your West, me alone? What of my people, my family, my young bride-to-be?"

"Can't answer that, Ali Pash," Scragger said, eyes on the clock, conscious of time slipping by, the lights and the hum of the HF, readying to overpower the young man who was taller than he, bigger built, younger by thirty-five years, and then disable the HF and make a run for it. Sorry, me son, but one way or another you're going to cooperate. Casually he moved closer, into a better position. "Insha'Allah is your way of putting it," he said kindly, and readied.

Hearing that come from the mouth of this kind, strange old man he respected so much, Ali Pash felt a flood of warmth pervade him. "This is my home, Agha, my land," Ali Pash said simply. "The Imam is the Imam and he obeys only God. The future is the future and in God's hands. The past too is the past."

Before Scragger could stop him, Ali Pash called Bandar Delam and now was speaking Farsi into the mike. The two operators talked with one another for a moment or two, then abruptly he signed off. And looked up at Scragger. "I don't blame you for leaving," he said. "Thank you, Agha, for . . . for the past." Then, with great deliberation, he switched the HF off, took out a circuit breaker, and pocketed it. "I told him we . . . we were closing down for the day."

Scragger exhaled. "Thanks, me son."

The door opened. Qeshemi stood there. "I wish to inspect the base," he said.

AL SHARGAZ HQ: Manuela was saying, ". . . and then, Andy, Lengeh's operator, Ali Pash, said to Jahan, 'No, nothing's strange here,' then added, kinda abruptly, 'I'm closing down for the day. I must go to prayers.' Numir called him back at once, asking him to wait a few minutes but there was no answer."

"Abruptly?" Gavallan asked, Scot and Nogger also listening intently. "What sort of abruptly?"

"Like, like he kinda got fed up, or had a gun to his head—not usual for an Iranian to be that abrupt." Manuela added uneasily, "I might be reading something into it that wasn't there, Andy."

"Does that mean Scrag's still there or not?"

Scot and Nogger grimaced, appalled at the thought. Manuela shifted nervously. "If he was, wouldn't he have answered himself to let us know? I think I would have. Perhaps h—" The phone rang. Scot picked it up. "S-G? Oh, hello, Charlie, hang on." He passed the phone to his father. "From Kuwait . . ."

"Hello, Charlie. All's well?"

"Yes, thanks. I'm at Kuwait airport, phoning from Patrick's office at Guerney's." Though the two companies were rivals worldwide, they had very friendly relations. "What's new?"

"Delta Four, nothing else yet. I'll phone the moment. Jean-Luc's checked in from Bahrain—he's with Delarne at Gulf Air de France if you want him. Is Genny with you?"

"No, she went back to the hotel but I'm all set the moment Mac and the others arrive."

Gavallan said quietly, "Did you tell Patrick, Charlie?" He heard Pettikin's forced laugh.

"Funny thing, Andy, the BA rep here, a couple of other guys, and Patrick have this crazy idea we're up to something—like pulling all our birds out. Can you imagine?"

Gavallan sighed. "Don't jump the gun, Charlie, keep to the plan." This was to keep quiet until the Kowiss choppers were in the Kuwait system, then to trust Patrick. "I'll phone when I have anything. 'Bye— Oh, hang on, I almost forgot. You remember Ross, John Ross?"

"Could I ever forget? Why?"

"I heard he's in Kuwait International Hospital. Check on him when you're squared away, will you?"

"Of course, right away, Andy. What's the matter with him?"

"Don't know. Call me if you have any news. 'Bye." He replaced the phone. Another deep breath. "The word's out in Kuwait."

"Christ, if it's out th—" Scot was interrupted by the phone ringing. "Hello? Just a moment. It's Mr. Newbury, Dad."

Gavallan took it. "Morning, Roger, how're tricks?"

"Oh. Well, I, er, wanted to ask you that. How are things going? Off the record, of course."

"Fine, fine," Gavallan said noncommittally. "Will you be in your office all day? I'll drop by, but I'll call before I leave here."

"Yes, please do, I'll be here until noon. It's a long weekend, you know. Please phone me the moment you, er, hear anything—off the record. The moment. We're rather concerned and, well, we can discuss it when you arrive. 'Bye."

"Hang on a moment. Did you get word about young Ross?"

"Yes, yes, I did. Sorry but we understand he was badly hurt, not expected to survive. Damn shame but there you are. See you before noon. 'Bye."

Gavallan put the phone down. They all watched him. "What's wrong?" Manuela asked.

"Apparently . . . it seems young Ross is badly hurt, not expected to survive."

Nogger muttered, "What a bugger! My God, not fair . . ." He had regaled them all about Ross, how he had saved their lives, and Azadeh's.

Manuela crossed herself and prayed fervently to the Madonna to help him, then begged Her again and again to bring all the men back safe, all of them, without favor, and Azadeh and Sharazad, and let there be peace, please please please . . .

"Dad, did Newbury tell you what happened?"

Gavallan shook his head, hardly hearing him. He was thinking about Ross, of an age with Scot, more tough and rugged and indestructible than Scot and now . . . Poor laddie! Maybe he'll pull through . . . Oh, God, I hope so! What to do? Continue, that's all you can do. Azadeh'll be rocked, poor lassie. And Erikki'll be as rocked as Azadeh, he owes her life to him.

"I'll be back in a second," he said and walked out, heading for their other office where he could phone Newbury in private.

Nogger was standing at the window, looking out at the day and the airfield, not seeing any of it. He was seeing the wild-eyed maniac killer at Tabriz One holding the severed head aloft, baying like a wolf to the sky, the angel of sudden death who became the giver of life—to him, to Arberry, to Dibble, and most of all to Azadeh. God, if you are God, save him like he saved us . . .

"Tehran, this is Bandar Delam, do you read? Kowiss, Bandar Delam, do you read? Al Shargaz, Bandar Delam, do you read?"

"Five minutes on the dot," Scot muttered. "Jahan doesn't miss a bloody second. Didn't Siamaki say he'd be in the office from 0900 onward?"

"Yes, yes, he did." All their eyes went to the clock. It read 8:45.

AT LENGEH AIRPORT: 9:01 A.M. Qeshemi was standing in the hangar looking at the two parked 206s within. Behind him Scragger and Ali Pash watched nervously. A momentary shaft of sun broke the clouds and overcast and sparkled off the 212 that was waiting on the helipad fifty yards away, a battered police car and driver, Corporal Achmed, beside it. "Have you flown in one of those, Excellency Pash?" Qeshemi asked.

"The 206? Yes, Sergeant Excellency," Ali Pash said, giving the sergeant his most pleasing smile. "The captain sometimes takes me or the other radio operator when we're off duty." He was very sorry the Devil had moved his feet here today, worse than sorry because now he was inescapably involved in treason—treason to break rules, treason to lie to police, treason not to report curious happenings. "The captain would take you anytime you wished," he said pleasantly, his whole being concentrated now on extricating himself from the mire the Devil and the captain had put him into.

"Today would be a good day?"

Ali Pash almost broke under the scrutiny. "Of course, if you ask the captain, of course, Agha. You wish me to ask?"

Qeshemi said nothing, just moved out into the open, careless of the Green Bands, half a dozen of them, who watched curiously. To Scragger he said directly in Farsi, "Where is everyone today, Agha?"

Ali Pash acted as interpreter for Scragger, though he twisted the words, making them sound better and more acceptable, explaining that today being Holy Day, with no revenue flights, the Iranian staff had correctly been given the day off, the captain had ordered the 212s to their designated training area for testing, had allowed the remaining mechanics to go picnicking, and that he himself was leaving to go to the mosque as soon as His Excellency the sergeant had finished whatever he wished to finish.

Scragger was totally frustrated that he did not understand Farsi, and loathed being out of control of the situation but he was, completely. His life and those of his men were in the hands of Ali Pash.

"His Excellency asks, What do you plan for the rest of the day?"

"That's a bloody good question," Scragger muttered. Then the family motto came into his mind: "You hang for a lamb, you hang for a sheep, so you might as well take the whole bleeding flock"—the motto that had been handed down by his ancestor who had been transported for life to Australia in the early 1800s. "Please tell him as soon as he's finished, I'm going to the cabbage patch as Ed Vossi needs checking out. His license's due for renewal."

He watched and waited and Qeshemi asked a question that Ali Pash answered and all the time he was wondering what to do if Qeshemi said, Fine, I'm coming along.

"His Excellency asks if you would be so kind as to lend the police some gasoline?"

"Wot?"

"He wants some gasoline, Captain. Wants to borrow some gasoline."

"Oh. Oh, certainly, certainly, Agha." For a moment Scragger was filled with hope. Hold it, me son, he thought. The cabbage patch's not so far away and Qeshemi could want the gas to send the car there and still fly with me. "Come on, Ali Pash, you can give me a hand," he said, not wanting to leave him alone with Qeshemi, and led the way to the pump, beckoning the police car. The wind sock was dancing. He saw that the clouds aloft were building up, nimbus among them, traveling fast, shoved along by a contrary wind. Here below it was still southeasterly though it had veered even more southerly. Good for us but more of a bloody headwind for the others, he thought grimly.

IN THE HELICOPTERS, NEARING KISH ISLAND: 9:07 A.M.
Rudi's four choppers were in sight of each other, closer than before, cruising calmly just over the waves. Visibility varied between two hundred yards to half a mile. All pilots were conserving fuel, seeking maximum range, and again Rudi bent forward to tap his gas gauge. The needle moved slightly, still registering just under half full. "No problem, Rudi, she's working fine," Faganwitch said through the intercom. "We've plenty of time to refuel, right? We're on time and on schedule, right?"

"Oh, yes." Even so Rudi recalculated their range, always coming up with the same answer: enough to reach Bahrain but not enough for the legal amount of fuel in reserve. "Tehran, this is Bandar Delam, do you read?" Jahan's voice came in his headphones again, irritating him with its persistence. For a moment he was tempted to turn off but dismissed that as too danger—

"Bandar Delam, this is Tehran. We read you four by five, go ahead!"

Now a flood of Farsi. Rudi picked out "Siamaki" several times but little else as the two radio ops spoke back and forth and then he recognized Siamaki's voice, irritable, arrogant, and now very angry. "Standby One, Bandar Delam! Al Shargaz, this is Tehran, do you read?" Now even more angrily: "Al Shargaz, this is Director Siamaki, do you read?" No answer. The call repeated more angrily, then another spate of Farsi, then Faganwitch cried out, "AHEAD! Look out!"

The supertanker, almost a quarter of a mile long, was hurtling at them broadside through the haze, towering over them, dwarfing them, easing her way carefully upstream toward her Iraqi terminal, foghorn droning. Rudi knew he was trapped, no time to climb, no space to break left or right or he would collide with the others so he went into emergency stop procedure. Kelly on his left, banking perilously left, just made it past the stern, Sandor, extreme right, safe around the bow—Dubois not safe but instantly onto max power, stick right and back into a too steep climbing turn, tighter tighter tighter 50—60—70—80 degrees, bow rushing at him, not going to make it, *"Espèce de con . . ."* not going to make it, stick back, g force sucking him and Fowler down into their seats, the ship's gunwale racing at them, then they roared over the foredeck with millimeters to spare, the appalled deck crew scattering. Once safe, Dubois hauled her around into a 180 to go back for Rudi in the slight hope Rudi had managed to cushion the impact and had escaped into the sea.

Rudi had the stick back, nose up, power off, watching the airspeed tumble, nose a little higher, no time to pray, nose higher, side of the tanker closer and closer, nose higher still, stall warning howling, not going to make it, stall warning shrieking, any moment she'll fall out of the sky, tanker only yards away, seeing rivets, portholes, rust, paint peeling, closing on them but slowing, slowing, but too late, too late but maybe enough to soften the crash, now plummeting, stick forward, full power on momentarily to cushion the dreadful impact and fall and suddenly she was locked in hover five feet above the waves, the mushing blades barely inches from the side of the tanker that slid past gently. Somehow Rudi backed away a yard, then another, and hovered.

When his eyes could focus he looked up. On the bridge of the vessel so far above them he could see the officers staring down at them, most of them shaking their fists in rage. A purple-faced man had a loudspeaker now, and he was shouting at them, "Bloody idiot!" but they could not hear him. The stern passed them by, wake churning, the spray speckling them. The way ahead was clear.

"I'm . . . I'm going to hav'ta take a shit." Weakly Faganwitch began to crawl back into the cabin.

You can take one for me, Rudi was thinking, but he had no energy to say it. His knees were trembling and teeth chattering. "Careful," he muttered, then eased the throttle open, gained height and forward speed and soon he was quite safe. No sign of the others. Then he spotted Kelly coming round, looking for him. When Kelly saw him he waggled from side to side so happily, came into station alongside, gave him a thumbs-up. To save the others vital fuel coming back to search for the pieces, Rudi put his lips very close to the boom mike and hissed through his teeth, "Dot-dot-dot-dash, dot-dot-dot-dash, dot-dot-dot-dash," their privately agreed code for each to head for Bahrain independently, and to let them know he was safe. He heard Sandor acknowledge in the same simulated Morse, then Dubois who swooped alongside out of the haze, adding some self-generated static, and accelerated away. But Pop Kelly was shaking his head, motioning that he would prefer to stay alongside. He pointed ahead.

Once more in their headsets: "Al Shargaz, this is Agha Siamaki in Tehran, do you read?" Then more Farsi. "Al Shargaz . . ."

AT AL SHARGAZ HQ: ". . . This is Agha Siamaki . . ." Then another splurge of Farsi. Gavallan's fingers drummed on the desktop, outwardly calm, inwardly not. He had not been able to reach Pettikin before he left for the hospital and there was nothing he could do to choke Siamaki and Numir off the air. Scot adjusted the volume slightly, lessening the harangue, pretending with Nogger to be nonchalant. Manuela said throatily, "He's plenty mad, Andy."

AT LENGEH: 9:26 A.M. Scragger had the nozzle gushing gasoline into the police car. It frothed, overflowing, staining him. Muttering a curse he let the lever go, hung the nozzle back on the pump. Two Green Bands were nearby, watching closely. The corporal screwed the tank cap back into place. Qeshemi spoke to Ali Pash a moment. "His Excellency asks if you could spare him some five-gallon cans, Captain. Of course full ones."

"Sure, why not? How many does he want?"

"He says he could take three in the trunk and two inside. Five."

"Five it is."

Scragger found the cans and filled them and together they loaded the police car. She's a bloody Molotov cocktail, he thought. Storm clouds were building quickly. A flash of lightning in the mountains. "Tell him best not to smoke in the car."

"His Excellency thanks you."

"Anytime." Thunder came down from the mountains. More lightning. Scragger watched Qeshemi leisurely look around the camp. The two Green Bands were waiting. A few others were squatting in the lee of the wind, watching idly. Now he could stand it no longer. "Well, Agha, I better be off," he said, pointing at the 212 then into the sky. "Okay?"

Qeshemi looked at him strangely. "Okay? What okay, Agha?"

"I go now." Scragger motioned with his hand, pantomiming flying away, and kept his glazed smile. *"Mamnoon am, khoda haefez."* Thank you, good-bye. He held out his hand to him.

The sergeant stared at the hand then looked up at him, the shrewd hard eyes boring into him. Then the sergeant said, "Okay. Good-bye, Agha," and firmly shook hands.

The sweat was running down Scragger's face, and he forced himself not to wipe it away. *"Mamnoon am. Khoda haefez, Agha."* He nodded at Ali Pash, wanting to make it a good farewell, wanting to shake hands too but not daring to stretch their luck, so he just clapped him on the back in passing. "See you, me son. Happy days."

"Good landings, Agha." Ali Pash watched Scragger climb into the cockpit and get airborne and wave as he flew away. He waved back, then saw Qeshemi looking at him. "If I may be permitted, if you will excuse me, Excellency Sergeant, I will lock up and then go to the mosque."

Qeshemi nodded and turned back to the departing 212. How obvious they are, he was thinking, the old pilot and this young fool. So easy to read the minds of men if you're patient and watch for clues. Very dangerous to fly off illegally. Even more dangerous to help foreigners fly off illegally and stay behind. Madness! Men are very strange. As God wants.

One of the Green Bands, a barely bearded youth with an AK47, wandered closer, pointedly looked at the cans of gasoline in the back of the car. Qeshemi said nothing, just nodded to him. The youth nodded back, eyes hard, strolled off insolently to join the others.

The sergeant got into the driver's seat. Leprous sons of dogs, he thought sardonically, you're not the law in Lengeh yet—thanks be to God. "Time to go, Achmed, time to go." As the corporal climbed in beside him Qeshemi saw the helicopter go over the rise and vanish. Still so easy to catch you, old man, he told himself, bemused. So easy to alert the net, our phones are working and we've a direct link with Kish fighter base. Are a few gallons pishkesh enough for your freedom? I haven't decided yet.

"I'll drop you at the station, Achmed, then I'm off duty till tomorrow. I'll keep the car for the day."

Qeshemi let in the clutch. Perhaps we should have gone with the foreigners—easy to force them to take us, my family and I, but then that would have meant living on the wrong side of our Persian Gulf, living among Arabs. I've never liked Arabs, never trusted them. No, my plan's better. Quietly down the old coast road all today and all tonight, then my cousin's dhow to Pakistan with plenty of spare gasoline for pishkesh. Many of our people are there already. I'll make a good life for my wife and my son and little Sousan until, with the help of God, we can come home again. Too much hatred here now, too many years serving the Shah. Good years. As shahs go he was fine for us. We were always paid.

NORTH OF LENGEH: 9:23 A.M. The cabbage patch was ten kilometers northeast of the base, a desolate, barren rocky area in the foothills of mountains, and the two helicopters were parked, side by side, engines ticking over. Ed Vossi was standing at Willi's cockpit window. "I feel like throwing up, Willi."

"Me too." Willi shifted his headset slightly, the VHF on but, according to plan, not to be used unless in emergency, only listened to.

"You got something, Willi?" Vossi asked.

"No, just static."

"Shit. He must be in dead trouble. Another minute then I go look, Willi."

"We go look together." Willi watched the lightning in the hills, visibility about a mile with the clouds black and closing in. "No day for joy riding, Ed."

"No."

Then Willi's face lit up like a rocket and he pointed, "There he is!" Scragger's 212 was approaching at about seven hundred feet, dawdling along. Vossi took to his heels for his cockpit and got in. Now in their headphones: "How's your torque counter, Willi?"

"Not good, Scrag," Willi said happily, following their plan in case anyone was listening. "I asked Ed to take a look at her and he's not sure either—his radio's out."

"I'll land and we'll have a conference. Scragger to base, do you read?" No answer. "Scragger to base, we'll be on the ground awhile." No answer.

Willi gave the thumbs-up to Vossi. Both opened their throttles, concentrating on Scragger who was coming down in a leisurely landing approach.

At ground level Scragger checked his descent, and led the rush for the coast. Now the exhilaration was extreme, Vossi was shouting with glee, and even Willi was smiling. "By God Harry . . ."

Scragger went up over the ridge and down the other side and now he could see the coast and their small van parked on the rocky foreshore just above the waves. His heart missed a beat. A herd of goats with three herdsmen dotted his landing area. Fifty yards up the beach was a car with some people and children playing where never before had they seen anyone. Just out to sea a small powerboat was cruising along. Could be a fishing boat, could be one of the regular patrols against smugglers or escapees, for here with Oman and the pirate coast so close, historically there had always been great coastal vigilance.

Can't change now, he thought, heart racing. He saw Benson and the other two mechanics spot him, jump into the van, and drive toward his landing area. Behind him Willi and Vossi had throttled back to give him time. Without hesitation he went into his landing fast, goats scattering, herdsmen and picnickers transfixed. The moment his skids touched he shouted, "Come on!"

The mechanics needed no urging. Benson rushed for the cabin door and hurled it open, charged back to help the other two who had unlocked the van's tailgate. Together they pulled out suitcases and satchels and baggage and stumbled over to begin loading—the cabin already stuffed with spares. Scragger looked around and saw that Willi and Vossi had gone into hover, on guard. "So far so good," he said out loud, concentrating on the onlookers who were over their astonishment and were coming closer. His eyes searched all around. No real danger yet. Nonetheless he made sure his Very pistol was ready just in case, and willed the mechanics to hurry, worried that any moment the police car would come hurrying down the road. A second load. Then another, then the last, all three mechanics sweating, and now two clambered into the cabin, slammed the door. Benson fell into the front seat beside him, swore, and began to get out. "I forgot to switch off the van."

"To hell with that, here we go." Scragger opened up the throttles and got airborne, Benson locking the door, fixing his seat belt, and they were over the waves out into the haze of the Gulf. Scragger looked left and right. Willi and Vossi were flanking him tightly, and he wished he was HF equipped so he could report "Lima Three" to Gavallan. Never mind, we'll be there in a jiffy!

Once past the first of the rigs, he began to breathe easier. Hate leaving young Ali Pash like that, he thought, hate leaving Georges de Plessey and his lads, hate leaving the two 206s, hate leaving. Well, I've done me best. I've left recommendations and job promises for when we come back, if we come back, for Ali Pash and the others in the clerk's top drawer with all the money I had left.

He checked his course, heading southwest for Siri as though on their milk run in case they were on radar. Near Siri he would turn southeast for Al Shargaz and home. All being well, he thought, and touched the rabbit's foot Nell had given him so many years ago for luck. Past another rig to port, Siri Six. The electrical storm was crackling his headphones, then mixed with it loud and clear was: "Hey, Scragger, you and *les gars*, you're low, *n'est-ce pas?*"

It was the voice of François Menange, the manager of the rig they had just passed, and he cursed the man's vigilance. To close him down, he clicked on the transmit: "Mum's the word, François, quiet, eh? Practicing. Be quiet, eh?"

Now the voice was laughing. *"Bien sûr,* but you're crazy to practice low on a day like today. *Adieu."*

Sweat was beginning again. Four more rigs to pass before he could turn into the open sea.

They went through the first squall line, the wind buffeting them, rain loud on the windows, streaking them, plenty of sheet lightning all around. Willi and Vossi were tight on station and he was pleased to be flying with them. Forty times I thought Qeshemi was going to say, "You comealong-ame" and take me down to the pokey. But then he didn't and here we are and in an hour forty-odd minutes we'll be home and Iran only a memory.

AT KOWISS AIR BASE HQ: 9:46 A.M. The mullah Hussain said patiently, "Tell me more about Minister Kia, Captain." He sat behind the desk in the base commander's office. A hard-faced Green Band guarded the door.

"I've told you everything I know," McIver said exhaustedly.

"Then please tell me about Captain Starke." Polite, insistent, and unhurried as though there were all day and all night and all tomorrow.

"I've told you about him, too, Agha. I've told you about them both for almost a couple of hours. I'm tired and there's nothing more to tell." McIver got up from his chair and stretched and sat down again. No use trying to leave. He had done that once and the Green Band had silently motioned him back. "Unless you have something specific I can't think of anything to add."

He had not been surprised at the mullah probing about Kia and had repeated over and over how a few weeks ago Kia had suddenly been made a director out of nowhere, about his own limited dealings with him in the last few weeks, though not about the checks on banks in Switzerland that had greased the way for the 125 and got three 212s out of the cauldron. Damned if I'm going to do a Wazari on Kia, he had told himself.

Kia's understandable, but why Duke Starke? Where Duke went to school, what he eats, how long he's been married, one wife or more, how long with the company, is he Catholic or Protestant—anything and everything and then tell it all again. Insatiable. And always the same quiet, evasive answer to his question, Why?

"Because he interests me, Captain."

McIver looked out of the window. A speckle of rain. Clouds low. Distant thunder. There'd be updrafts and a few real whirlwinds in the thunderclouds eastward—great cover for the dash across the Gulf. What's happening with Scrag and Rudi and their lads? rushed back into the forefront of his mind. With an effort he pushed that away for later—and his weariness, and worry—and what the hell he was going to do when this interrogation finished. If it finished. Beware! Concentrate! You'll make a mistake if you're not a hundred percent, then you'll all be lost.

He knew his reserves were badly depleted. Last night he had slept badly and that had not helped. Nor had Lochart's enormous sadness over Sharazad. Difficult for Tom to face the truth, impossible to say it to him: Wasn't it bound to fall apart, Tom, old friend? She's Muslim, she's rich, you'll never be, her heritage's bound in steel, yours in gossamer, her family's her lifeblood, yours isn't, she can stay, you can't, and the final sword hanging over you, HBC. So sad, he thought. Did it ever have a chance? With the Shah, maybe. With the inflexibility of the new?

What would I do if I were Tom? With an effort he stopped his mind wandering. He could feel the mullah's eyes boring into him. They had hardly wavered once since Changiz had brought him here and had gone away.

Ah, yes, Colonel bloody Changiz. In the car coming over here and during the waiting he too had been probing. But his probing was just to establish exactly when and how often their 125 was scheduled for Kowiss, how many Green Bands were stationed on their side of the base, when they arrived, how many stayed on the base, and did they surround and guard the 125 all the time she was on the ground. The questioning had been casual, nothing asked that could not be more than just interest, but McIver was certain the real reason was to erect an escape route—if necessary. The final cement, the barter: "Even in a revolution mistakes happen, Captain. Friends are needed in high places more than ever, sad but true." You scratch my back or I'll claw yours.

The mullah got up. "I will take you back now."

"Oh. Very well, thank you." McIver guardedly studied Hussain. The brown-black eyes under the heavy eyebrows gave nothing away, skin stretched over his high cheekbones, a strange, handsome face masking a spirit of enormous resolution. For good or for bad? McIver asked himself.

IN THEIR RADIO TOWER: 9:58 A.M. Wazari was hunched down near the door to the roof, still waiting. When McIver and Lochart had left him in the office he had been torn between fleeing and staying, then Changiz and the airmen had arrived, almost simultaneously Pavoud with other staff, so he had sneaked up here unseen and ever since had been in hiding. Just before 8:00 A.M. Kia had driven up in a taxi.

From his vantage point up here he had seen Kia go into a paroxysm of rage because McIver was not waiting beside the 206, ready for takeoff. The green-banded airmen relayed what Changiz had ordered. Kia had protested loudly. More apologetic shrugs and Kia stormed into the building, loudly proclaiming he would phone Changiz and radio Tehran at once, but Lochart had intercepted Kia at the bottom of the stairs and told him the phones were out, the set malfunctioning, and no radio repairer available until tomorrow. "Sorry, Minister, there's nothing we can do about it—unless you want to go over to HQ yourself," Wazari had heard Lochart say. "I'm sure Captain McIver won't be long, the mullah Hussain sent for him." At once most of the bombast had gone out of Kia and that had pleased him but did not allay his grinding anxiety and he had stayed there in the wind and the cold, forlorn, lost, and in misery.

His temporary safety did nothing to cast off his anxieties or fears or suspicions, about Kia today and up before the komiteh again tomorrow—"You're needed for further questioning"—and why were those bastards Lochart and McIver so nervous, huh? Why did they lie to that sonofabitch turncoat Changiz about a crew change at Rig Abu Sal? No goddamn crew change needed there, not unless it was ordered in the night. Why're we down to three pilots and two mecs with a load of work starting Monday—why so many spares shipped out? Oh, God, get me to hell outta here.

It was so cold and blustery he came back inside the tower but left the door ajar for a quick retreat. Cautiously he looked out of the windows and through cracks in the boards. If he was careful he could see most of the base without being seen. Ayre, Lochart, and the mechanics were over by the 212s. The main gate was well guarded by regular Green Bands. No activity over at the base that he could see. A chill went through him. Rumors of another purge by the komiteh, that now he was high on their list because of his evidence against Esvandiary and Minister Kia: "By the Prophet, I heard they want to see you tomorrow. You took your life in your hands speaking out like that, don't you know the first rule of survival here for four thousand years has been to keep your tongue silent and your eyes closed on the doings of those above or, very soon, you'll have neither left in your head? Of course those above are corrupt, has it ever been different?"

Wazari moaned, helpless in the maelstrom and near breaking. Ever since Zataki had beaten him so badly, nose smashed—can't seem to breathe anymore—four teeth knocked out, and an almost perpetual headache, his spirit had left him and so had his courage. He had never been beaten before. So Hotshot and Kia were both guilty, so what, so what? What business was it of yours? And now your stupidity will consume you too.

Tears spilled down the bruises. "For crissake, for crissake, help, help me . . ." Then "malfunction" jumped into his head and he seized on it. What malfunction? The set was working fine yesterday.

He brushed the tears away. Making no sound, he slid over to the desk and quietly switched on the radio, keeping the volume to an absolute minimum. All seemed fine. Dials checked out. Lots of static from an electrical storm but no traffic. Unusual that there should be no traffic on the company frequency, someone somewhere should be sending. Not daring to turn the volume up, he reached into a drawer for a pair of headphones and plugged them in, bypassing the loudspeaker. Now he could have the signal as loud as he pleased. Curious. Still nothing. Carefully he switched out of the company channel to others. Nothing. Over to the VHF. Nothing, anywhere. Back to HF. He could not even pick up a routine, recorded weather report that still came out of Tehran.

He was a good radio operator and well trained and it took him no time to zero in on the fault. A look through the crack in the roof door confirmed the wire hanging free. Sonofabitch, he thought. Why the hell didn't I notice it when I was out there?

Carefully he switched off and crawled out again and when he was at the foot of the mast and saw that the wire had been sheared off but the rust at the end had been newly cleaned off, anger possessed him. Then excitement. Those bastards, he thought. Those hypocritical bastards, McIver and Lochart. They musta been listening and transmitting when I arrived. What the hell're they up to?

The connection was quickly repaired. HF on and instantly Farsi filled his ears on the company frequency: HQ at Tehran talking to Bandar Delam, then calling Al Shargaz and Lengeh and him at Kowiss, something about four choppers not going where they were supposed to go. Iran-Toda? Not one of our bases.

"Kowiss, this Bandar Delam, do you read?"

He recognized Jahan's voice from Bandar Delam. Automatically his finger went to the transmit switch, then stopped. No need to call back yet, he thought. The company airwaves were full now, Numir and Jahan from Bandar Delam and Gelani at Tehran, and Siamaki ranting and raving. "Sonofabitch," he muttered after a few minutes, everything falling into place.

IN THE HELICOPTERS OFF SIRI: 10:05 A.M.   Siri Island itself was a mile ahead, but before Scragger and his team could turn southeast for the international boundary, there were three more rigs to bypass. Like a bleeding minefield, Scragger thought. So far safe and no more shocks. All needles in the Green and the engines sounding sweet. His mechanic Benson, beside him, was staring at the waves rushing past just below them. Static in their earphones. From time to time, overflying international flights would report their positions to Kish radar, a checkpoint in their area, to be answered at once.

Into the intercom Benson said, "Kish're spot on, Scrag."

"We're under their radar. No sweat."

"I'm sweating. Are you?"

Scragger nodded. Kish was abeam of them, fifteen-odd miles to his right. He looked left and right. Vossi and Willi were alongside and he gave them a thumbs-up and they returned it—Vossi enthusiastically.

"Another twenty minutes and we're over the border," Scragger said. "Soon as we are, we'll go up to seven hundred."

"Good. Weather's improving, Scrag," Benson said. The cloud cover above had thinned appreciably, visibility about the same. In plenty of time they both saw the outward-bound, heavily laden tanker ahead. With Willi, Scragger banked astern of her with plenty to spare but Vossi exuberantly pulled up high over her, then leisurely came down into station alongside him.

At once in their headphones: "This is Kish Control, low-flying helicopter on a course 225, report height and destination!"

Scragger weaved from side to side to attract Willi and Vossi and pointed southwest and waved them off, commanding them to stay low and to leave him. He saw their reluctance, but he jabbed his finger southeast, waved a farewell, and pulled up in a climb, leaving them on the surface of the sea. "Hold on to your balls, Benson," he said, a weight in his stomach, then began transmitting, moving his boom mike back and forth from his mouth, simulating a bad signal: "Kish, this is chopper HVX out of Lengeh, inbound Siri Nine with spares, course 225. Thought I saw a capsized dhow but it was negative." Siri Nine was the farthest rig they normally serviced, just this side of the Iran-Emirate boundary, still under construction and not yet equipped with their own VHF. "Climbing back to seven hundred."

"Chopper HVX, you're two by five, your transmission intermittent. Maintain course and report seven hundred feet. Confirm you were informed of mandatory new regulations for start engines request at Lengeh." The operator's American-accented voice was five by five, crisp and professional.

"Sorry, Kish, this is the first day I've been back on duty." Scragger saw Willi and Vossi vanish into the haze. "Do I need to request engine start from Siri Nine after I've landed? I'll be there at least an hour." Scragger wiped a bead of sweat off. Kish would be within their rights to order him to land at Kish first to give him a roasting for breaking regulations.

"Affirmative. Standby One."

In the intercom, Benson said uneasily, "Now what, Scrag?"

"They'll be having a little conference."

"What're we going to do?"

Scragger beamed. "Depends on what they do." He clicked the sender: "Kish, HVX at seven hundred."

"Kish. Maintain course and altitude. Standby One."

"HVX." More silence. Scragger was sifting alternates, enjoying the danger. "This's better than flying a milk run, now isn't it, me son?"

"To be honest, it isn't. If I could get hold of Vossi, I'd strangle him."

Scragger shrugged. "It's done. We could've been in and out of radar ever since we left. Maybe Qeshemi reported us." He began whistling tonelessly. They were well past Siri Island now with rig Siri Nine five kilometers ahead. "Kish, this's HVX," Scragger said, still working the mike. "Leaving seven hundred on approach for Siri Nine."

"Negative HVX, maintain seven hundred and hold. Your transmission is intermittent and two by five."

"HVX—Kish, please say again, your transmission is garbled. I say again, am leaving seven hundred on approach for Siri Nine," Scragger repeated slowly, continuing to simulate bad transmission. Again he beamed at Benson. "Trick I learned in the RAF, me son."

"HVX, Kish. I say again maintain seven hundred and hold."

"Kish, it's bumpy and the haze's thickening. Going through six hundred. I will report on landing and call requesting engine start. Thanks and g'day!" he added with a prayer.

"HVX, your transmission is intermittent. Abort landing at Siri Nine. Turn 310 degrees, maintain seven hundred, and report direct to Kish."

Benson went white. Scragger belched. "Say again, Kish, you're one by five."

"I say again, abort landing at Siri Nine, turn to 310 degrees, and report direct Kish." The operator's voice was unhurried.

"Roger, Kish, understand we're to land Siri Nine and report Kish next. Going through four hundred for low-level approach, thank you and g'day."

"Kish, this is JAL Flight 664 from Delhi," broke in. "Overhead at thirty-eight thousand inbound Kuwait on 300. Do you read?"

"JAL 664, Kish. Maintain course and altitude. Call Kuwait on 118.8, good day."

Scragger peered through the haze. He could see the half-constructed rig, a work barge moored to one of its legs. Instrument needles all in the Green and—hey, wait a moment, temperature's up, oil pressure's down on number one engine. Benson had seen it too. He tapped the dial, bent closer. The oil pressure needle went up slightly then fell back again, temperature a few degrees above normal—no time to worry about that now, get ready! The deck crew had heard and seen them and stopped working, clearing away from the well-marked helipad. When he was fifty feet off the rig, Scragger said: "Kish, HVX landing now. G'day."

"HVX. Report direct Kish next. Request engine start. I repeat, report direct Kish next," all said clearly. "Do you read?"

But Scragger did not acknowledge, or land. At a few feet he just pulled into a hover, waved to the deck crew who recognized him and assumed it was just a practice of a familiarization-training run for a new pilot, a constant habit of Scragger's. A last wave, then he got forward motion, dropped neatly over the side, and hugging the sea, turned southwest at full throttle.

AT KOWISS AIR BASE: 10:21 A.M. The mullah Hussain was driving, and he stopped the car outside the office building. McIver got out. "Thank you," he said, not knowing what to expect now, for Hussain had been silent since they had left the office. Lochart, Ayre, and the others were over by the helicopters. Kia stalked out of the office, stopped on seeing the mullah, then came down the steps. "Good morning, Excellency Hussain, greetings, how pleasant to see you." He used a ministerial voice for an honored guest, but not an equal, then to McIver in English, curtly, "We should leave at once."

"Er, yes, Agha. Just give me a couple of minutes to get organized." Glad I'm not Kia, he told himself as he walked off, his stomach churning, and turned to Lochart. "Hello, Tom."

"You all right, Mac?"

"Yes." He added quietly, "We'll have to play this cautiously for the next few minutes. Don't know what the mullah's up to. Have to wait and see what he does about Kia, don't know whether Kia's in the creek or not. Soon as we know we can move." He dropped his voice even more. "I can't avoid taking Kia—unless Hussain grabs him. I plan to take him part of the way, just over the hills out of VHF range, pretend an emergency, and land. When Kia's out of the cockpit and cooling his heels, I'll take off and skirt this area and meet you at the rendezvous."

"Don't like that idea, Mac. Better let me do it. You don't know the place and those sand dunes are look-alikes for miles. I'd better take him."

"I've thought about that, but then I'd be flying one of the mecs without a license. I'd rather put Kia at risk than them. Besides, you might be tempted to keep on going back to Tehran. All the way. Eh?"

"Better that I drop him off and meet you at the rendezvous. Safer."

McIver shook his head, feeling rotten about putting his friend into a corner. "You'd go on, wouldn't you?"

After a strange pause, Lochart said, "While I was waiting for you, if I could've gotten airborne I'd've put him aboard and gone." He smiled a twisted smile. "The airmen said no way, to wait. Better watch them, Mac, some of them speak English. What happened to you?"

"Hussain just questioned me about Kia—and Duke."

Lochart stared at him. "Duke? What about?"

"Everything about him. When I asked Hussain why, all he'd say was: 'Just because he interests me.'" McIver saw a tremor go through Lochart.

"Mac, I think it's best if I take Kia. You might miss the rendezvous—you can go in tandem with Freddy. I'll get off first and wait for you."

"Sorry, Tom, can't risk that—you'll keep on going. If I were you I'd do the same and the hell with the risk. But I can't let you go back. To go back now'd be a disaster. It'd be a disaster for you—I'm sure of that, Tom—as well as for the rest of us. That's the truth."

"Hell with the truth," Lochart said bitterly. "All right, but by God, the moment we touch down at Kuwait, I'm on the month's leave I'm owed, or resigned from S-G, whichever you want—from the very second."

"Fair enough but it has to be from Al Shargaz. We'll have to refuel in Kuwait and get out of there as fast as we can—if we're lucky enough to get there and if they'll let us fly out."

"No. Kuwait's the end of the line for me."

"Please yourself," McIver said, hardening. "But I'll make sure you don't get a plane into Tehran, Abadan, or anywhere else in Iran."

"You're a bastard," Lochart said, sick that McIver had read his intentions so clearly. "Goddamn you to hell!"

"Yes, sorry. From Al Shargaz I'll help all I c—" McIver stopped, seeing Lochart mutter a curse. He turned around. Kia and Hussain were still conversing by the car. "What's the matter?"

"In the tower."

McIver looked up. Then he noticed Wazari, half-hidden by one of the boarded windows, beckoning them clearly. No way to pretend that they had not seen him. As they watched, Wazari beckoned them again and moved back into cover.

"Goddamn him," Lochart was saying. "I checked the tower just after you'd left to make sure he hadn't slipped up there and he hadn't so I thought he'd made a run for it." His face flushed with rage. "Come to think of it, I didn't go right up into the room so he could've hidden on the roof— the sonofabitch must've been there all the time."

"Christalmighty! Maybe he found the broken wire." McIver was rocked.

Lochart's face closed. "You stay here. If he tries to give us any trouble I'll kill him." He stalked off.

"Wait, I'll come too. Freddy," he called out, "we'll be back in a moment."

As they passed Hussain and Kia, McIver said, "I'm just going to ask for clearance, Minister. Takeoff in five minutes?"

Before Kia could answer, the mullah said cryptically, "Insha'Allah."

Kia said curtly to McIver, "Captain, you haven't forgotten I told you I must be in Tehran for an important meeting at 7:00 P.M.? Good," turned his back on them, again concentrating on Hussain. "You were saying, Excellency?"

The two pilots went into the office, seething at Kia's rudeness, bypassed Pavoud and the other staff, and headed for the tower staircase.

The tower was empty. Then they saw the door to the roof ajar and heard Wazari whisper, "Over here." He was just outside, crouched by the wall.

Wazari did not move. "I know what you're up to. There's no radio malfunction," he said, hardly able to contain his excitement. "Four choppers have pushed off from Bandar Delam and vanished. Your managing director Siamaki's screaming like a stuck pig because he can't raise Lengeh, us, or Al Shargaz and Mr. Gavallan there—they're just sitting tight, that's it, isn't it? Huh?"

"What's that got to do with us?" Lochart said tautly.

"Everything, of course everything, because it all fits. Numir at Bandar Delam says all expats've gone, there's no one left at Bandar. Siamaki says the same about Tehran, he even told Numir your houseboy, Captain McIver, your houseboy says most of your personal things and a Captain Pettikin's're out of the apartment."

McIver shrugged and went to switch on the VHF. "Safety precautions while Pettikin's on leave and I'm away. Been lots of robberies."

"Don't make a call yet. Please. Listen, for crissake, listen, I'm begging you . . . there's no way you can stop the truth. Your 212s and guys have gone from Bandar, Lengeh's silent, so they're the same, Tehran's closed down, the same, there's only here left and you're all set." Wazari's voice was curious and they could not tell yet what was under it. "I'm not gonna give you away, I want to help you. I want to help. I swear I want to help you."

"Help us do what?"

"Get away."

"Why should you do that, even if what you say's true?" Lochart said angrily.

"You were right not to trust me before, Captain, but I swear to God you can trust me now, I'm together now, earlier I wasn't but now I am and you're my only hope to get out. I'm up before the komiteh tomorrow and . . . and look at me, for crissake!" he burst out. "I'm a mess, and unless I

can get to a proper doctor I'll be a mess forever and maybe even a dead man
—there's something pressing here, hurts like hell," Wazari touched the top
of his mashed nose. "Since that bastard Zataki beat me my head's been
aching and I've been crazy, sure I have, I know it, but I can still help. I can
cover you from here if you'll take me with you, just let me sneak aboard the
last chopper—I swear I'll help." Tears filled his eyes. The two men stared at
him.

McIver clicked on the VHF sender. "Kowiss Tower, IHC testing, testing."

A long pause, then in heavily accented English, "This the tower, IHC,
you five by five."

"Thank you. We seem to have cleared the fault. Our 206 charter to
Tehran will leave in ten minutes, also our morning flight to rigs Forty, Abu
Sal, and Gordy with spares."

"Okay. Report airborne. Your Bandar Delam is been try to contact you."

McIver felt the sweat start. "Thanks, Tower. Good day." He looked at
Lochart, then switched on the HF. At once they heard Jahan's voice in
Farsi and Lochart began interpreting: "Jahan's saying the last sighting of
their flight was northeast, inland from the coast . . . that Zataki . . ."
For a moment his voice faltered, ". . . that Zataki had ordered the four
choppers to service Iran-Toda and should be at Iran-Toda by now and is
sure to call or send a message . . ." Then McIver recognized Siamaki.
Lochart was sweating. "Siamaki's saying he'll be off the air for half an hour
to an hour but he'll call when he gets back and to keep trying to raise us and
Al Shargaz . . . Jahan says okay and he'll wait out and if he has any news
he'll call."

Static for a moment. Then Jahan's voice in English: "Kowiss, this is
Bandar Delam, do you read?"

Lochart muttered, "If the tower's been picking all this up, why aren't we
all in the slammer?"

"It's Friday. No reason for them to monitor your company frequency."
Wazari wiped the tears away, back in control now. "Friday crew's minimal
and trainee—no flying, nothing happening, the komiteh sacked all radar
officers and five of the sergeants—sent them to the stockade." He shuddered then hurried on: "Maybe one of the guys picked up Bandar Delam
once or twice. So Bandar've lost contact with some of their choppers, so
what, they're foreigners and it happens all the time. But, Captain, if you
don't close Bandar and Tehran down, they've gotta . . . someone's gotta
get steamed up." He took out a grubby handkerchief and wiped a trickle of
blood from his nose. "If you switch to your alternate channel you'll be safe
enough, the tower don't have that."

McIver stared at him. "You're sure?"

"Sure, listen why don't y—" He stopped. Footsteps were approaching. Noiselessly he ducked back onto the roof into hiding. Kia stomped halfway up the stairs.

"What's keeping you, Captain?"

"I'm . . . I'm waiting for clearance to be confirmed, Minister. Sorry, I've been told to wait. Nothing I can do."

"Of course there is! We can take off and leave! Now! I'm tired of wait—"

"I'm tired too but I don't want my head blown off." McIver's temper snapped and he flared, "You'll wait! Wait! Understand? You bloody wait and if your bloody manners don't improve I'll cancel the whole trip and mention a pishkesh or two to the mullah Hussain I happened to forget at the questioning. Now get to hell out of here!"

For a moment they thought Kia was going to explode, but he thought better of it and went away. McIver rubbed his chest, cursing himself for losing his temper. Then he jerked a thumb at the roof and whispered, "Tom, what about him?"

"We can't leave him behind. He could give us away in a minute." Lochart looked around. Wazari was at the doorway.

"I swear I'll help," he whispered desperately. "Listen, when you take off with Kia, what d'you plan, to dump him, huh?" McIver did not answer, still unsure. "Jesus, Captain, you gotta trust me. Look, call Bandar on the alternate and chew Numir out like you did that bastard'n tell him you ordered all the choppers here. That'll take the heat off for an hour or two."

McIver glanced at Lochart.

Lochart said excitedly, "Why not? Hell, that's a good idea, then you take off with Kia and . . . and Freddy can get going. I'll wait here and . . ." The words trailed off.

"Then what, Tom?" McIver said.

Wazari came over and switched to the alternate channel, said quickly to Lochart, "You stall for a while, Cap, and when Cap McIver's gone and Ayre's out of the area, you tell Numir you're sure his four choppers've just switched off their HF, no need to use it, and they're on VHF. That gives you the excuse to get airborne and wander around, then you rush off to the fuel cache." He saw their look. "Jesus, Cap, anyone's gotta know you can't make it in one across the Gulf, no way, so you've gotta have stashed spare fuel somewheres. Onshore, or on one of the rigs."

McIver took a deep breath and pressed the transmit. "Bandar Delam, this is Captain McIver at Kowiss, do you read?"

"Kowiss—Bandar Delam, we've been trying to reach you for hours an—"

"Jahan, put Agha Numir on," McIver said curtly. A moment, then

Numir came on but before the IranOil manager could launch into a tirade, McIver cut in with his own. "Where are my four helicopters? Why haven't they reported in? What's going on down there? And why are you so inefficient that you don't know I ordered my helicopters and personnel here . . . ?"

AT AL SHARGAZ HQ: ". . . and why don't you remember that crew replacements are due in Bandar Delam after the weekend?" McIver's voice was faint but clear over the loudspeaker, and Gavallan, Scot, and Manuela were staring at it, aghast that McIver was still in place at Kowiss—did that mean Lochart, Ayre, and the others too?

"But we've been calling you all morning, Captain," Numir said, his voice fainter. "You ordered our copters to Kowiss? But why? And why wasn't I informed? Our copters were supposed to go to Iran-Toda this morning but never landed and have vanished! Agha Siamaki's also been trying to reach you."

"There's been a fault on our HF. Now listen here, Numir, I ordered *my* choppers to Kowiss. I never approved an Iran-Toda contract, know nothing about an Iran-Toda contract, so that's the end to it. Now stop creating a stink about nothing!"

"But they are our helicopters and everyone's left, everyone, mechanics and all pilots an—"

"Goddamnit, I ordered them all here pending an investigation. I repeat I am very dissatisfied with your operation. And will so report to IranOil! Now stop calling!"

In the office they were all still in shock. That McIver was still in Kowiss was a disaster. Whirlwind was going badly awry. It was 10:42 A.M. and Rudi and his three were overdue Bahrain. ". . . but we don't know their actual headwind, Dad," Scot had said, "or how long they'll take to inflight refuel. They could be three quarters to an hour late and still be okay—say an ETA at Bahrain of eleven to eleven-fifteen." But everyone knew that there could not safely be that amount of fuel on board.

Nothing yet from Scrag and his two but that's to be expected—they don't have HF aboard, Gavallan thought. Their flight to Al Shargaz should take about an hour and a half. If they'd left at say seven-thirty and did the pickup and got out without incident, say at seven-forty-five, their ETA's nine-fifteen whichever way you figure it. "No need to worry, Manuela, you understand about headwinds," he had said, "and we don't actually know when they left."

So many things to go wrong. My God, this waiting's rotten. Gavallan felt very old, picked up the phone and dialed Bahrain. "Gulf Air de France? Jean-Luc Sessonne, please? Jean-Luc, anything?"

"No, Andy. I've just called the tower and there's nothing in the system. *Pas problème*. Rudi'll be conserving fuel. The tower said they'd call me the instant they see them. Anything about anyone else?"

"We just found out Mac's still in Kowiss." Gavallan heard the gasp and the obscenities. "I agree. I'll call you." He dialed Kuwait. "Charlie, is Genny with you?"

"No, she's at the hotel. Andy, I—"

"We've just heard Mac's still at Kowiss an—"

"Christalmighty, what's happened?"

"Don't know, he's still transmitting. I'll call back when I've something definite. Don't tell Genny yet. 'Bye."

Again the nauseating waiting, then the HF came alive. "Tehran, this is Kowiss, Captain McIver. Go ahead."

"Kowiss, Tehran, we've been calling all morning. Agha Siamaki has been trying to reach you. He'll be back in about an hour. Please confirm that you ordered the four 212s to Kowiss."

"Tehran, this is Kowiss. Bandar Delam, you copy too." McIver's voice was slower and clearer but very angry. "I confirm, I have all my 212s—I repeat all my 212s—under my control. All of them. I will be unavailable to talk to Agha Siamaki as I am cleared to leave here for Tehran with Minister Kia in five minutes but will expect Agha Siamaki to meet the 206 at Tehran International. In a few moments we will be closing down for repairs—on orders from the authorities—and will be operating only on VFR. For your information Captain Ayre will be leaving in five minutes for rig Abu Sal with spares and Captain Lochart will remain on standby to meet my Bandar Delam 212s. Did you copy, Tehran?"

"Affirmative, Captain McIver, but can you please te—"

McIver cut in over him: "Did you copy, Numir, or are you more useless than ever?"

"Yes, but I must insist that we be infor—"

"I'm tired of all this nonsense. I'm managing director of this operation and as long as we operate in Iran that's the way it is going to be, simple, direct, and no fuss. Kowiss is closing down to make repairs as ordered by Colonel Changiz and will report as soon as we are on the air again. Remain on this channel but keep it clear for testing. Everything will proceed as planned. Over and out!"

Just then the door opened and Starke came in, an anxious young nurse with him. Manuela was dumbfounded. Gavallan leaped up and helped him to a chair, his chest heavily bandaged. He wore pajama bottoms and a loose terry dressing gown. "I'm okay, Andy," Starke said. "How are you, honey?"

"Conroe, are you crazy?"

"No. Andy, tell me what's happening?"

The nurse said, "We really can't take responsibil—"

Starke said patiently, "I promise only a couple of hours and I'll be real careful. Manuela, please take her back to the car, would you, honey?" He looked at her with that special look husbands have for wives and wives for husbands when it's not the time to argue. At once she got up and ushered the nurse out and when they had both gone, Starke said, "Sorry, Andy, couldn't stand it anymore. What's going on?"

AT KOWISS: 10:48 A.M.   McIver came down the tower steps, feeling sick and empty and not sure he would make it to the 206, let alone put the rest of the plan into effect. You'll make it, he told himself. Get yourself together.

The mullah Hussain was still talking to Kia, leaning against the car, his AK47 slung over one shoulder. "We're all set, Minister," McIver said. "Of course, if it's all right, Excellency Hussain?"

"Yes, as God wants," Hussain said, with a strange smile. Politely he put out his hand. "Good-bye, Minister Kia."

"Good-bye, Excellency." Kia turned and walked off briskly for the 206. Uneasily McIver offered his hand to the mullah. "'Bye, Excellency."

Hussain turned to watch Kia get into the cockpit. Again the strange smile. "It is written: 'The mills of God grind slowly, yet they grind exceeding small.' Don't they, Captain?"

"Yes. But why do you say that?"

"As a parting gift. You can tell your friend Kia when you land at Tehran."

"He's not my friend, and why then?"

"You're wise not to have him as a friend. When will you see Captain Starke again?"

"I don't know. Soon I hope." McIver saw the mullah glance back at Kia, and his disquiet increased. "Why?"

"I would like to see him soon." Hussain unslung the gun and got into the car and, with his Green Bands, drove off.

"Captain?" It was Pavoud. He was shaky and upset.

"Yes, Mr. Pavoud, just a minute. Freddy!" McIver beckoned Ayre who came at a run. "Yes, Mr. Pavoud?"

"Please, why are the 212s loaded with spares and luggage and all th—"

"A crew change," McIver said at once and pretended not to notice

Ayre's eyes crossing. "I've four 212s due here from Bandar Delam. You'd better get accommodations ready. Four pilots and four mechanics. They're due in about two hours."

"But we've no manifest or reason to h—"

"Do it!" McIver's tension boiled over again. "I gave the orders. Me! Me personally! I ordered *my* 212s here! Freddy, what the hell're you waiting for? Get going with your spares."

"Yessir. And you?"

"I'm taking Kia, Tom Lochart's in charge until I get back. Off you go. No, wait, I'll go with you. Pavoud, what the devil are you waiting for? Captain Lochart will be very bloody irritable if you're not ready in time." McIver stomped off with Ayre, praying that Pavoud was convinced.

"Mac, what the hell's going on?"

"Wait till we get to the others." When McIver reached the 212s he turned his back to Pavoud who still stood on the office steps and quickly told them what was going on. "See you at the coast."

"You all right, Mac?" Ayre said, very concerned with his color.

"Of course I am. Take off!"

OFF BAHRAIN: 10:59 A.M.   Rudi and Pop Kelly were still in tandem battling the headwind, nursing their engines—their fuel gauges reading empty, red warning lights on. Half an hour ago they had both gone into hover. The mechanics had swung the cabin doors open and leaned out, taking off the tank caps. Then they had uncurled the hoses and stuck the nozzle into the tank neck and come back into the cabin. With the makeshift pumps, laboriously they had pumped the first of the forty-gallon drums dry, then the second. Neither of the mechanics had ever refueled in the air like this. Both had been violently sick when they finished. But the operation was successful.

The haze was still strong, sea swell heavy under the wind, and since the near miss with the tanker all had been routine, grinding along, seeking maximum range, adjusting, always adjusting, and praying. Rudi had seen nothing of Dubois or Sandor. One of Rudi's jets coughed but picked up almost at once.

Faganwitch winced. "How far we got to go?"

"Too far." Rudi switched on his VHF, breaking their radio silence. "Pop, switch to HF, listen out," he said rapidly and switched over. "Sierra One, this is Delta One, do you read?"

"Loud and clear, Delta One," Scot's voice came back instantly, "go ahead."

"Off Boston"—their code for Bahrain—"at seven hundred, heading 185, low on fuel. Delta Two is with me, Three and Four on their own."

"Welcome from Britain to sunny lands, G-HTXX and G-HJZI, repeat G-HTXX and G-HJZI! Jean-Luc is waiting for you. We've no news yet of Delta Three and Four."

"HTXX and HJZI!" Immediately Rudi acknowledged with their new British call signs. "What about Lima Three and Kilo Two?" Lima for Lengeh's three, Kilo for Kowiss's two.

"No news yet except that Kilo Two is still in place." Rudi and Pop Kelly were shocked. Then they heard, "This is Tehran HQ, Al Shargaz, do you read?" quickly followed by Siamaki's voice: "This is Tehran, who is calling on this channel? Who is Kilo Two and Lima Three? Who is Sierra One?"

Scot's voice cut in loudly, "No sweat, HTXX, some twit's using our channel. Phone us on landing," he added to caution against unnecessary talk.

Pop Kelly butted in excitedly, "Sandbanks ahead, HTXX!"

"I see them. Sierra One, HTXX, we're almost at the coast now . . ."

Again one of Rudi's engines coughed, worse than before, but picked up, the rev counter needles spinning drunkenly. Then through the haze he saw the coast, a point of land and some sandbanks and now the beach and knew exactly where he was. "Pop, you deal with the tower. Sierra One, tell Jean-Luc I'm . . ."

AT AL SHARGAZ HQ: Gavallan was already dialing Bahrain and over the loudspeaker Rudi continued urgently, ". . . I'm at the northwest point at Abu Sabh beach, to the east . . ." a burst of static, then silence.

Gavallan said into the phone, "Gulf Air de France? Jean-Luc, please. Jean-Luc, Andy. Rudi and Pop're . . . Standby One . . ." Kelly's voice came in loudly: "Sierra One, I'm following Delta One down, he's engined out . . ."

"This is Tehran, who is engined out and where? Who's calling on this channel? This is Tehran who is call—"

AT THE BAHRAIN SHORE: The beach had good white sand, but was almost empty of people right here, many sailing boats and other pleasure craft out to sea, flocks of windsurfers in the fine breeze, the day balmy. Up the shore was the Hotel Starbreak, brilliant white, with palm trees and gardens and multicolored sunshades dotting the terraces and beaches. Rudi's 212 came out of the haze fast, rotors windmilling, jets coughing and no longer useful. His line of descent gave him little choice, but he was thankful that it would be a hard landing and not a sea landing. The beach was rushing toward them and he chose the exact point of landing just past a lonely sunshade slightly up the beach toward the road. He was into wind now and very close, steadied, then pulled the collective, altering the pitch of the blades to give momentary lift enough to cushion the fall and he skidded forward a few yards on the uneven surface, tipped a fraction but not enough to do any damage and they were safe.

"Bloody hell . . ." Faganwitch said, breathing again, heart working again, sphincter locked.

Rudi began the shutdown, the silence eerie, his hands and knees trembling now. On the beach ahead sunbathers and people on the terraces had got up and were looking at them. Then Faganwitch gasped, frightening him. He turned around and gasped too.

She wore dark glasses and little else under the lonely sunshade, topless, as good as bottomless, blond and beautiful and propped on one elbow watching them. Without hurrying she got up and slipped on the excuse of a bikini top.

"Christalmighty . . ." Faganwitch was speechless.

Rudi waved and called out throatily, "Sorry, I ran out of fuel."

She laughed, then Kelly came out of the sky and spoiled it all and they both cursed him, as the wash of his rotors tugged at the sunshade and her long hair, blowing her towel away and scattering sand. Now Kelly saw her too, politely backed downwind nearer the road and, as distracted as the others, promptly landed a foot high.

AT BAHRAIN INTERNATIONAL AIRPORT: 11:13 A.M. Jean-Luc and the mechanic Rod Rodrigues came out of the building at a run and headed across the tarmac toward a small tanker truck marked GAdeF— Gulf Air de France—that he had arranged to borrow. The airfield was busy, the modern terminal and allied buildings grand and gleaming white. Many jets of many nations loading or unloading, a JAL jumbo just landing.

"*On y va*, let's go," Jean-Luc said.

"Of course, Sayyid." The driver turned up the volume of the intercom, and with one smooth movement started the engine, got into gear, and was in motion. He was a slim, young Palestinian Christian wearing dark glasses and company overalls. "Where should we go?"

"You know Abu Sabh beach?"

"Oh, yes, Sayyid."

"Two of our choppers've landed there out of fuel. Let's go!"

"We are almost there!" The driver did a racing change and increased speed. Over his intercom loudspeaker came: "Alpha Four?" He picked up the hand mike and continued to drive flamboyantly one-handed. "This is Alpha Four."

"Give me Captain Sessonne."

Jean-Luc recognized the voice of Mathias Delarne, the Gulf Air de France manager for Bahrain—an old friend from French Air Force days and Algeria. "This's Jean-Luc, old friend," he said in French.

In French, Delarne said quickly, "The tower called me to say another chopper's just come into the system on your expected heading, Dubois or Petrofi, eh? Tower keeps calling her but cannot make contact yet."

"Just one?" Jean-Luc was abruptly concerned.

"Yes. She's on a correct VFR approach for helipad 16. The problem we discussed, eh?"

"Yes." Jean-Luc had told his friend what was really happening and the problem of the registrations. "Mathias, tell the tower for me she's G-HTTE in transit," he said, giving the third of his four allocated call signs. "Then phone Andy and tell him I'll send Rodrigues to deal with Rudi and Kelly. We'll deal with Dubois or Sandor—you and me—bring the second batch of stuff. Where do we meet?"

"My God, Jean-Luc, after this lot we'll have to join the Foreign Legion. Meet me in front of the office."

Jean-Luc acknowledged, hung the mike back on its hook. "Stop here!" The truck stopped instantly. Rodrigues and Jean-Luc almost went through the windshield. "Rod, you know what to do." He jumped out. "Off you go!"

"Listen I'd rather walk an—" The rest of it was lost as Jean-Luc ran back and the truck rushed off again with a screech of tires, out through the gate and onto the road that led to the sea.

AT KOWISS, IN THE TOWER: 11:17 A.M. Lochart and Wazari were watching McIver's distant 206 climbing up into the Zagros Mountains. "Kowiss, this is HCC," McIver was saying over the VHF, "leaving your system now. Good day."

"HCC, Kowiss. Good day," Wazari said.

Over the HF loudspeaker, in Farsi: "Bandar Delam, this is Tehran, have you heard from Kowiss yet?"

"Negative. Al Shargaz, this is Bandar Delam, do you read?" Static, then the call repeated, now silence again.

Wazari wiped his face. "You think Cap Ayre'd be at your rendezvous yet?" he asked, desperately anxious to please. It was not hard to sense Lochart's dislike of him, or his distrust. "Huh?"

Lochart just shrugged, thinking about Tehran and what to do. He had told McIver to send both mechanics with Ayre: "Just in case I get caught, Mac, or Wazari's discovered or betrays us."

"Don't do anything stupid, Tom, like going to Tehran in the 212, with or without Wazari."

"There's no way I could sneak back to Tehran without alerting the whole system and screwing Whirlwind. I'd have to refuel and they'd stop me."

Is there a way? he asked himself, then saw Wazari watching him. "What?"

"Is Cap McIver gonna give you a sign or call when he's dumped Kia?" When Lochart just looked back at him, Wazari said bleakly, "Goddamnit, don't you see you're my only hope to get out . . ."

Both men whirled, feeling eyes. Pavoud was peering at them through the stair banisters.

"So!" he said softly. "As God wants. You're both caught in your betrayals."

Lochart took a step toward him. "I don't know what's bothering you," he began, throat parched. "There's noth—"

"You're caught. You and the Judas! You're all escaping, running off with our helicopters!"

Wazari's face contorted and he hissed, "Judas, eh? You get your Commie ass up here! I know all about you and your Tudeh comrades!"

Pavoud had gone white. "You're talking nonsense! You're the one who's caught, you're th—"

"You're the Judas, you lousy Commie bastard! Corporal Ali Fedagi's my roommate and he's commissar on the base and he's your boss. I know all about you—he tried to get me to join the Party months ago. Get your ass up here!" And when Pavoud hesitated, Wazari warned, "If you don't I'm calling the komiteh and blowing you, Fedagi, along with Mohammed Berani and a dozen others an' I don't give a shit . . ." His fingers went to the VHF send switch but Pavoud gasped out, "No," and came onto the landing and stood there shakily. For a moment nothing happened, then Wazari grabbed the whimpering, petrified man and shoved him down into a corner, picked up a spanner to smash his head in. Lochart caught the blow just in time.

"Why're you stopping me, for crissake?" Wazari was shaking with fear. "He'll betray us!"

"No need . . . no need for that." Lochart had difficulty talking for a moment. "Be patient. Listen, Pavoud, if you keep quiet, we'll keep quiet."

"I swear by God, of course I'll ke—"

Wazari hissed, "You can't trust these bastards."

"I don't," Lochart said. "Quick. Write it all down! Quick! All the names you can remember. Quick—and make three copies!" Lochart shoved a pen into the young man's hand. Wazari hesitated then grabbed the pad and began to scribble. Lochart went closer to Pavoud who cringed from him, begging mercy. "Shut up and listen. Pavoud, I'll make a deal, you say nothing, we'll say nothing."

"By God, of course I won't say anything, Agha, haven't I faithfully served the company, faithfully all these years, haven't I been ev—"

"Liar," Wazari said, then added to Lochart's shock, "I've overheard you and the others lying and cheating and slobbering after Manuela Starke, peeping at her in the night."

"Lies, more lies, don't belie—"

"Shut up, you bastard!" Wazari said.

Pavoud obeyed, petrified by the venom, and huddled back into the corner.

Lochart tore his eyes off the quaking man and took one of the lists, put it into his pocket. "You keep one, Sergeant. Here," he said to Pavoud, shoving the third into his face. The man tried to back away, couldn't, and when the list was thrust into his hand, he moaned and dropped it as though it were on fire. "If we get stopped I promise you before God this goes to the first Green Band and don't forget we both speak Farsi and I know Hussain! Understand?" Numbly Pavoud nodded. Lochart leaned down and picked the list up and stuffed it into the man's pocket. "Sit down over there!" He pointed to a seat in the corner, then wiped his sweating hands on his trousers and switched on the VHF, picked up the mike.

"Kowiss calling inbound choppers from Bandar Delam, do you read?" Lochart waited, then repeated the call. Then, "Tower, this is base, do you read?"

After a pause a weary, heavily accented voice said, "Yes, we hearing you."

"We're expecting four inbound choppers from Bandar Delam that're only equipped with VHF. I'm going to get airborne and try to raise them. We'll be off the air until I get back. Okay?"

"Okay."

Lochart switched off. From the HF came: "Kowiss, this is Tehran, do you read?"

Lochart asked, "What about him?" Both of them looked at Pavoud who seemed to shrink into his chair.

The stabbing pain behind Wazari's eye was the worst it had ever been.

I'm gonna have to kill Pavoud, that's the only way I can prove I'm on Lochart's side. "I'll deal with him," he said and got up.

"No," Lochart said. "Pavoud, you're taking the rest of the day off. You walk downstairs, you tell the others you're sick, and you're going home. You say nothing else and leave at once. We can see you and hear you from here. If you betray us, by the Lord God, you and every man on this list'll be betrayed too."

"You swear you . . . you'll . . ." the words started to pour out, "you swear you'll tell no one, you swear?"

"Get out and go home! And it's on your head not ours! Go on, get out!" They watched him totter away. And when they saw him on his bicycle pedaling slowly down the road toward the town, they both felt a little easier.

"We should have killed him . . . we should have, Cap. I'd've done it."

"This way's just as safe and . . . well, killing him wouldn't solve anything." Nor help me with Sharazad, Lochart thought.

Again over the HF, again the nagging: "Kowiss, this is Bandar Delam, do you read?"

"It's not safe to leave those bastards broadcasting, Cap. Tower's gotta pick 'em up, however untrained and inefficient they are."

Lochart put all his mind on the problem. "Sergeant, get on the HF for an instant, pretend you're a radio mec who's pissed off with having his holiday screwed up. Tell 'em in Farsi to shut up, to stay the hell off our channel until we're repaired, that this lunatic Lochart's gone aloft to raise the four choppers on the VHF, perhaps one of them had an emergency and the others are with him on the ground. Okay?"

"Got it!" Wazari did it all, perfectly. When he switched off he held his head in his hands a moment, pain blinding him. Then he looked up at Lochart. "You trust me now?"

"Yes."

"I can come with you? Honest?"

"Yes." Lochart put out his hand. "Thanks for the help." He pulled the company HF frequency crystal out, mutilated it, and put it back, then pulled out the breaker of the VHF and pocketed it. "Come on."

In the office downstairs he stopped a moment. "I'm going aloft," he told the three clerks who stared at him strangely. "I'm going to try to raise the Bandar choppers on the VHF." The three men said nothing, but Lochart felt they knew the secret too. Then he turned to Wazari. "See you tomorrow, Sergeant."

"Hope it's okay to quit. My head hurts like hell."

"See you tomorrow." Lochart pottered in the office, conscious of the scrutiny, to give Wazari enough time to pretend to saunter off, actually to go around the hangar and sneak aboard: "Once you're out of the office you're on your own," Lochart had told him, "I won't check the cabin, I'll just take off."

"God help us all, Captain."

AT BAHRAIN AIRPORT: 11:28 A.M. Jean-Luc and Mathias Delarne were standing beside a station wagon near the helipad watching the incoming 212, shading their eyes against the sun, still unable to recognize the pilot. Mathias was a short, thickset man, with dark wavy hair, half a face, the other half badly burn-scarred when he had bailed out on fire not far from Algiers.

"It's Dubois," he said.

"No, you're wrong, it's Sandor." Jean-Luc waved, motioning him to land crosswind. The moment the skids touched, Mathias rushed under the rotors for the left cockpit door—paying no attention to Sandor who was shouting across at him. He carried a large paintbrush and a can of quick-drying airplane paint and he slapped the white paint over the Iran registration letters just below the door's window. Jean-Luc used the stencil they had prepared and black paint and his brush, then carefully peeled the stencil off. Now she was G-HXXI and legal.

Meanwhile, Mathias had gone to the tail boom and painted out IHC, ducked under the boom to do the same on the other side. Sandor just had time to move his arm out of the way of the door as, enthusiastically, Jean-Luc stenciled the second G-HXXI.

"*Voilà!*" Jean-Luc gave his material back to Mathias who went to the station wagon to stash it under a tarpaulin, while Jean-Luc wrung Sandor Petrofi's hand and told him about Rudi and Kelly and asked about Dubois.

"Don'know, old buddy," Sandor said. "After the pileup"—he explained about the near miss—"Rudi waved us off to head here independently. I never saw any of them again. Me, I put her into minimum consumption, stuck to the waves, and prayed. I've been on empty, warning lights on, for maybe ten goddamn minutes and crapping for twenty. What about the others?"

"Rudi and Kelly landed on Abu Sabh beach—Rod Rodrigues's looking after them—nothing yet on Scrag, Willi, or Vossi, but Mac's still at Kowiss."

"Jesusss!"

"*Oui,* along with Freddy and Tom Lochart, at least they were, ten or fifteen minutes ago." Jean-Luc turned to Mathias who came up to them, "Are you tuned into the tower?"

"Yes, no problem."

"Mathias Delarne, Sandor Petrofi—Johnson, our mec."

They greeted each other and shook hands. "How was your trip—*merde*, best you don't tell me," Mathias added, then saw the approaching car. "Trouble," he warned.

"Stay in the cockpit, Sandor," Jean-Luc ordered. "Johnson, back in the cabin."

The car was marked OFFICIAL and it stopped broadside to the 212 twenty yards away. Two Bahraini men got out, a uniformed Immigration captain and an officer from the tower, the latter wearing a long-flowing white dishdasha and headcloth with a twisted black coil holding it in place. Mathias went to meet them. "Morning, Sayyid Yusuf, Sayyid Bin Ahmed. This is Captain Sessonne."

"Morning," both said politely, and continued to study the 212. "And the pilot?"

"Captain Petrofi. Mr. Johnson, a mechanic, is in the cabin." Jean-Luc felt sick. The sun was glistening off the new paint but not the old, and the bottom of the *I* had a dribble of black from each corner. He waited for the inevitable remark and then the inevitable question, "What was her last point of departure?" and then his airy, "Basra, Iraq," as the nearest possible. But so simple to check there and no need to check, just walk forward and draw a finger through the new paint to find the permanent letters below. Mathias was equally perturbed. Easy for Jean-Luc, he thought, he doesn't live here, doesn't have to work here.

"How long will G-HXXI be staying, Captain?" the Immigration officer asked. He was a clean-shaven man with sad eyes.

Jean-Luc and Mathias groaned inwardly at the accent on the letters. "She's due to leave for Al Shargaz at once, Sayyid," Mathias said, "for Al Shargaz, at once—the very moment she's refueled. Also the others who, er, ran out of fuel."

Bin Ahmed, the tower officer, sighed. "Very bad planning to run out of fuel. I wonder what happened to the legal thirty minutes of reserve."

"The, er, the headwind, I expect, Sayyid."

"It is strong today, that's certain." Bin Ahmed looked out into the Gulf, visibility about a mile. "One 212 here, two on our beach, and the fourth . . . the fourth out there." The dark eyes came back onto Jean-Luc. "Perhaps he turned back for . . . for his departure point."

Jean-Luc gave him his best smile. "I don't know, Sayyid Bin Ahmed," he answered carefully, wanting to end the cat-and-mouse game, wanting to refuel and backtrack for half an hour to search.

Once more the two men looked at the chopper. Now the rotor stopped. The blades trembled a little in the wind. Casually Bin Ahmed took out a telex. "We've just received this from Tehran, Mathias, about some missing helicopters," he said politely. "From Iran's Air Traffic Control. It says, 'Please be on the lookout for some of our helicopters that have been exported illegally from Bandar Delam. Please impound them, arrest those aboard, inform our nearest embassy which will arrange for immediate deportation of the criminals and repatriation of our equipment." He smiled again and handed it to him. "Curious, eh?"

"Very," Mathias said. He read it, glazed, then handed it back.

"Captain Sessonne, have you been to Iran?"

"Yes, yes, I have."

"Terrible, all those deaths, all the unrest, all the killing, Muslim killing Muslim. Persia's always been different, troublesome to others who live in the Gulf. Claiming our Gulf as the Persian Gulf as though we, this side, did not exist," Bin Ahmed said, matter-of-factly. "Didn't the Shah even claim our island was Iranian just because three centuries ago Persians conquered us for a few years, we who have always been independent?"

"Yes, but he, er, he renounced the claim."

"Ah, yes, yes, that is true—and occupied the oil islands of Tums and Abu Musa. Very hegemonistic are Persian rulers, very strange, whoever they are, wherever they come from. Sacrilege to plant mullahs and ayatollahs between man and God. Eh?"

"They, er, they have their way of life," Jean-Luc agreed, "others have theirs."

Bin Ahmed glanced into the back of the station wagon. Jean-Luc saw part of the handle of a paintbrush sticking out from under the tarpaulin. "Dangerous times we're having in the Gulf. Very dangerous. Anti-God Soviets closer every day from the north, more anti-God Marxists south in Yemen arming every day, all eyes on us and our wealth—and Islam. Only Islam stands between them and world dominance."

Mathias wanted to say, "What about France—and of course America?" Instead he said, "Islam'll never fail. Nor will the Gulf states if they're vigilant."

"With the Help of God, I agree." Bin Ahmed nodded and smiled at Jean-Luc. "Here on our island we must be very vigilant against all those who wish to cause us trouble. Eh?"

Jean-Luc nodded. He was finding it hard not to look at the telex in the man's hand; if Bahrain had one, the same would have gone to every tower this side of the Gulf.

"With the Help of God we will succeed."

The Immigration officer nodded agreeably. "Captain, I would like to see the pilot's papers, and the mechanic's. And them. Please."

"Of course, at once." Jean-Luc walked over to Sandor. "Tehran's telexed them to be on the lookout for Iran registereds," he whispered hastily and Sandor went pasty. "No need for panic, *mon vieux*, just show your passports to the Immigration officer, volunteer nothing, you too, Johnson, and don't forget you're G-HXXI out of Basra."

"But, Jesus," Sandor croaked, "we'd have to've been stamped outta Basra, Iraq, and I got Iranian stamps over most every page."

"So you were in Iran, so what? Start praying, *mon brave*. Come on."

The Immigration officer took the American passport. Punctiliously he studied the photograph, compared it to Sandor who weakly took off his sunglasses, then handed it back without leafing through the other pages. "Thank you," he said and accepted Johnson's British passport. Again the studious look at the photograph only. Bin Ahmed went a pace nearer the chopper. Johnson had left the cabin door open.

"What's aboard?"

"Spares," Sandor, Johnson, and Jean-Luc said together.

"You'll have to clear customs."

Mathias said politely, "Of course he *is* in transit, Sayyid Yusuf, and will take off the moment he's refueled. Perhaps it would be possible to allow him to sign the transit form, guaranteeing he lands nothing and carries no arms or drugs or ammunition." He hesitated. "I would guarantee it too, if it was of value."

"Your presence is always of value, Sayyid Mathias," Yusuf said. It was hot on the tarmac and dusty and he sneezed, pulled out a handkerchief, and blew his nose, then went up to Bin Ahmed—still with Johnson's passport in his hand. "I suppose for a British plane in transit, it would be all right, even for the other two on the beach. Eh?"

The tower man turned his back on the chopper. "Why not? When those two arrive we'll set them down here, Sayyid Captain Sessonne. You meet them with the fuel truck and we'll clear them for Al Shargaz as soon as they're refueled." Again he looked out to sea and his dark eyes showed his concern. "And the fourth, when she arrives? What about her—I presume she's also British registered?"

"Yes, yes, she is," Jean-Luc heard himself say, giving him the new registration. "With . . . with your permission, the three will backtrack for half an hour, then go on to Al Shargaz." It's worth a try, he thought, saluting the two men with Gallic charm as they left, hardly able to grasp the miracle of the reprieve.

Is it because their eyes were blind or because they did not wish to see? I don't know, I don't know, but blessed be the Madonna for looking after us again.

"Jean-Luc, you'd better phone Gavallan about the telex," Mathias said.

OFFSHORE AL SHARGAZ: Scragger and Benson were staring at the oil and pressure gauges on number one engine. Warning lights were on, the needle of the temperature gauge at maximum, top of the red, oil pressure needle falling, almost at zero. Now they were flying at seven hundred feet, in good but hazy weather, past the international boundary with Siri and Abu Musa just behind them, and Al Shargaz directly ahead. The tower was three by five in their headsets, guiding traffic.

"I'm going to shut her down, Benson."

"Yes, don't want her seizing up."

Sound lessened and the chopper sank a hundred feet but when Scragger had increased power on number two and made adjustments she held her altitude. Still, both men were uneasy without the backup.

"No reason for her to go like that, Scrag, none at all. I did her check myself a few days ago. How we doing?"

"Just fine. Home's not too far ahead."

Benson was very uneasy. "Is there anywhere we could land in an emergency? Sandbanks? A rig?"

"Sure, sure there are. Lots," Scragger lied, eyes and ears seeking danger but finding none. "You hear something?"

"No . . . no, nothing. Bloody hell, I can hear every bloody parched cog."

Scragger laughed. "So can I."

"Shouldn't we call Al Shargaz?"

"Plenty of time, me son. I'm waiting for Vossi or Willi." They flew onward and every flicker of turbulence, decibel of pitch change from the engine, or tremble of a needle made the sweat greater.

"How far we got to go, Scrag?" Benson loved engines but hated flying, particularly in choppers. His shirt was clammy and chilled.

Then, in their headsets was Willi's voice: "Al Shargaz, this's EP-HBB inbound with EP-HGF at seven hundred, course 140 degrees. ETA twelve minutes," and Scragger groaned and held his breath, for Willi had automatically given their full Iranian call signs when they all had agreed to see if they could get away with the last three letters only. The very English voice of the controller came back loud and brittle: "Chopper calling Al Shargaz, we understand you're in transit, inbound on 140 and, er, your transmission was garbled. Please confirm you are, er, G-HYYR and G-HFEE? I say again. GOLF HOTEL YANKEE YANKEE ROMEO and GOLF HOTEL FOXTROT ECHO ECHO?"

Bursting with excitement, Scragger let out a cheer. "They're expecting us!"

Willi's voice was hesitant and Scragger's temperature went up twenty points: "Al Shargaz, this . . . this is G-HY . . . YR . . ." then Vossi excitedly cut in over him: "Al Shargaz, this is GolfHotelFoxtrotEchoEcho and GolfHotelYankeeYankeeRomeo reading you loud and clear; we'll be with you in ten minutes and request landing at the north helipad, please inform S-G."

"Certainly, G-HFEE," the controller said and Scragger could almost see the man's relief, "you're cleared for the north helipad and please call S-G on 117.7. Welcome! Welcome to Al Shargaz, maintain course and altitude."

"Yes, sir! Yessir indeedeee, 117.7," Vossi said. At once Scragger switched to the same channel and again Vossi: "Sierra One, this is HFEE and HYYR do you read?"

"Loud and wonderfully clear. Welcome all—but where's GolfHotelSierra VictorTango?"

AT AL SHARGAZ OFFICE: "He's in back of us, Sierra One," Vossi was saying.

Gavallan, Scot, Nogger, and Starke were listening on the VHF loudspeaker on their company frequency, the tower frequency also being monitored, everyone very conscious that any transmission could be overheard, particularly their HF by Siamaki in Tehran and Numir at Bandar Delam. "He's in back of us a few minutes, he, er, he ordered us to go on independently." Vossi was being pointedly careful. "We don't, er, we don't know what happened." Then Scragger cut in and they all heard the beam in his voice, "This is G-HSVT on your tails, so clear the decks . . ."

The room erupted in a sudden cheer, Gavallan mopped his brow, and muttered "Thank God," sick with relief, then jerked his thumb at Nogger, "Get going, Nogger!"

Gleefully the young man left and almost knocked over Manuela who, set-faced, was approaching from the corridor with a tray of cold drinks. "Scrag, Willi, and Ed are about to land," he called out on the run, by now at the far end. "Oh, how wonderful!" she said and hurried into the room. "Isn't that . . ." She stopped. Scragger was saying, ". . . am on one engine, so I'll request a straight in, best get a fire truck ready just in case."

Willi's voice at once: "Ed, do a 180 and join up with Scrag, bring him in. How're you on gas?"

"Plenty. I'm on my way."

"Scrag, this's Willi. I'll take care of the landing request and straight in. How're you for gas?"

"Plenty. HSVT, eh? That's a lot better than HASVD!" They heard his laugh and Manuela felt better.

For her the strain of this morning, trying to contain her fears, had been awful, hearing the disembodied voices so far away and yet so near, all of them related to persons that she liked or loved, or hated—those of the enemy: "That's what they are," she had said fiercely a few minutes ago, near tears because their wonderful friend Marc Dubois and old Fowler were missing missing missing and oh God it could have been Conroe and there may be others: "Jahan's enemy! Siamaki, Numir, they all are, all of them." Then Gavallan had said gently, "No, they're not, Manuela, not really, they're just doing their job . . ." But the gentleness had only goaded her, infuriated her, adding to her worry that Starke was here and not in bed at the hospital, the operation only last night, and she had flared: "It's a game, that's all Whirlwind is to all of you, just a goddamn game! You're a bunch a gung-ho glory boys and you . . . and you . . ." Then she had run out and gone to the ladies' room and wept. When the storm had passed she gave herself a good talking to for losing her control, reminding herself that men were stupid and infantile and would never change. Then she blew her nose and redid her makeup and fixed her hair and went to get the drinks.

Quietly Manuela put down the tray now. No one noticed her.

Starke was on the phone to Ground Control explaining what was necessary, Scot on the VHF. "We'll take care of everything, Scrag," Scot said.

"Sierra One. How's tricks?" Scragger asked. "Your Deltas and Kilos?"

Scot looked at Gavallan. Gavallan leaned forward and said dully, "Delta Three are fine, Kilo Two . . . Kilo Two are still in place, more or less."

Silence on the loudspeakers. On the tower frequency they heard the English controller clearing some inbounds. A bristle of static. Scragger's voice was different now. "Confirm Delta *Three*."

"Confirm Delta Three," Gavallan said, still in shock at the news about Dubois and the Bahrain telex that Jean-Luc had phoned in a few minutes ago, expecting an imminent explosion from their own tower, and from

Kuwait. To Jean-Luc he had said, "Air-sea rescue? We'd better call a May-day."

"We're the air-sea rescue, Andy. There isn't any other. Sandor's already taken off to search. As soon as Rudi and Pop are refueled they'll go too—I've worked out a block search for them—then they'll head direct Al Shargaz like Sandor. We can't hang around here, *mon Dieu*, you can't imagine how close we were to disaster. If he's afloat, they'll find him—there're dozens of sandbanks to land on."

"Won't that stretch their range, Jean-Luc?"

"They'll be okay, Andy. Marc didn't put out a Mayday so it must've been sudden or perhaps his radio failed or more probably he put down somewhere. There're a dozen good possibilities—he could have put down on a rig for fuel, if he went into the sea, he could've been picked up—any of a dozen things—don't forget radio silence was one of the primes. No sweat, *mon cher ami*."

"Very much sweat."

"Anything on the others?"

"Not yet . . ."

Not yet, he thought again and a twinge went through him.

"Who's Delta Four?" It was Willi asking.

"Our French friend and Fowler," Gavallan said matter-of-factly, not knowing who might be listening. "A full report when you land."

"Understand." Static, then, "Ed, how you doing?"

"Fine and dandy, Willi. Climbing to one thousand and doing fine. Hey, Scrag, what's your heading and altitude?"

"142, at seven hundred, and if you'd open your eyes and look two o'clock you'd see me 'cause I can see you."

Silence for a moment. "Scrag, you done it again!"

Gavallan got up to stretch and saw Manuela, "Hello, m'dear."

She smiled, a little tentatively. "Here," she said, offering a bottle, "you're entitled to a beer, and a 'sorry.'"

"No sorries, none. You were right." He gave her a hug and drank gratefully. "Oh, that's good, thank you, Manuela."

"How about me, darlin'?" Starke said.

"All you'll get from me, Conroe Starke, is water and a thick ear if you weren't plain muscle between the ears." She opened the bottle of mineral water and gave it to him, but her eyes were smiling and she rested her hand lightly on him, loving him.

"Thank you, honey," he said, so relieved that she was here and safe and others were safe, though Dubois and Fowler were question marks and many others still to go. His shoulder and chest were aching badly and he was becoming increasingly nauseated, his head throbbing. Doc Nutt had given him a painkiller and told him it was good for a couple of hours: "It'll hold you till noon, Duke, not much longer and perhaps less. You'd better be a noontime Cinderella or you'll be very bloody uncomfortable indeed. . . . I mean bloody as in hemorrhage." He glanced past Manuela at the clock: 12:04 P.M.

"Conroe, darlin', won't you please come back to bed, please?"

His eyes changed. "How about in four minutes?" he said softly.

She reddened at his look, then laughed and dug her nails lightly into his neck as a cat would when purring. "Seriously, darlin', don't you think—"

"I'm serious."

The door opened and Doc Nutt came in. "Beddy-bye, Duke! Say good night like a good boy!"

"Hi, Doc." Obediently Starke started to get up, failed the first time, just managed to cover his lapse, and stood erect, cursing inside. "Scot, we got a walkie-talkie or a radio with the tower frequencies?"

"Sure, sure we have." Scot reached into a side drawer and gave him the small portable. "We'll keep in touch—you've a phone by the bed?"

"Yes. See you later—honey, no I'm fine, you stay in case of the Farsi. Thanks," then his eyes focused out of the window. "Hey, look at that!"

For a moment all their cares were forgotten. The London–Bahrain Concorde was taxiing out, needle-sharp, peerless, her nose dropped for takeoff. Cruising speed, fifteen hundred miles per hour at sixty-five thousand feet, the forty-three-hundred-mile flight—three hours sixteen minutes. "She's gotta be the most beautiful bird alive," Starke said as he left.

Manuela sighed, "I'd just love to go in her once, just once."

"The only way to travel," Scot said dryly. "I heard they're stopping this run next year, aren't they?" Most of his attention monitoring Willi and Scragger and Vossi talking back and forth, no problem there yet. From his position he could see the truck with Nogger, mechanics, paint and stencils speeding for the helipad near the far end of the runway, a fire truck already standing by.

"They're bloody idiots," Gavallan said, talking to hide his grinding anxiety—his eyes seeking the incomers. "Bloody government doesn't know its arse from a hole in the ground, French the same. They should just write off research and development costs—they're written off already in actuality—then she's a perfectly viable business proposition for certain runs and priceless. LA to Japan's a natural, to Australia, Buenos Aires too . . . Anyone see our birds yet?"

"Tower's in a better position, Dad." Scot eased up the tower frequency.

"Concorde 001 you're next for takeoff. Bon voyage," the controller was saying. "When airborne call Baghdad on 119.9."

" 'Thank you, 119.9." Concorde was moving proudly, supremely confident that all eyes were on her.

"By God, she's worth looking at."

"Tower, this is Concorde 001. What's the fire truck for?"

"We've three choppers inbound for the north helipad, one on one engine . . ."

IN THE CONTROL TOWER: ". . . Would you like us to divert them until you're off?" the controller asked. His name was Sinclair and he was English, an ex-RAF officer like many of the controllers employed in the Gulf.

"No, no thanks, just curious."

Sinclair was a short, stocky, bald man, and he sat in a swivel chair at a low desk with a panoramic view. Around his neck hung a pair of high-powered binoculars. He put them to his eyes and focused. Now he could see the three choppers in V formation. Earlier he had positioned the one with the failed engine at the head of the V—he knew it was Scragger but pretended not to know. Around him in the tower was an abundance of first-class radar and communication equipment, telexes, with three Shargazi trainees and a Shargazi controller. The controller was concentrating on his radar screen, positioning the other six airplanes presently in the system.

Without losing the choppers in his binoculars, Sinclair clicked on his sender: "HSVT, this is the tower, how are you doing?"

"Tower, HSVT." Scragger's voice was clear and precise. "No problem. Everything in the Green. I see Concorde approaching for takeoff—would you like me to hold or hurry up?"

"HSVT, continue your direct approach at safety maximum. Concorde, go into position and hold." Sinclair called out to one of the trainees on the Ground Control, "Mohammed, soon as the chopper lands I turn him over to you, all right?"

"Yes, Sayyid."

"Are you in contact with the fire truck?"

"No, Sayyid."

"Then do it quickly! That's your responsibility." The youth started to apologize. "Don't worry, you made a mistake, that's over, get on with it!"

Sinclair adjusted the focus a hair. Scragger was fifty feet off, approach perfect. "Mohammed, tell the fire truck to get with it—come on for God's sake, those buggers should be ready with the foam hoses." He heard the young controller cursing the fire fighters again, then saw them piling out, readying their hoses. Again he moved the glasses over to the Concorde waiting patiently, lined up in the center of the runway, ready for takeoff, nowhere near any danger even if all three choppers blew up. Holding the Concorde for thirty seconds against a million-to-one chance her wake turbulence could cause a freak whirlwind for the wounded chopper was a small price. Whirlwind. Godalmighty!

The rumor that S-G was going to stage an illegal pullout of Iran had been all over the field for two days now. His binoculars went from the Concorde back to Scragger's chopper. Her skids touched down. The fire fighters closed in. No fire. "Concorde 001, you're cleared for takeoff," he said calmly, "HFEE and HYYR land when convenient, Pan Am 116 you're cleared to land, runway 32, wind twenty knots at 160."

Behind him a telex chattered. He paused a moment watching the Concorde take off, marveling at her power and angle of climb, then again centered on Scragger, deliberately not noticing the tiny figures ducking under the rotors with stencils and paint. Another man, Nogger Lane, who on Gavallan's instructions had privately given him advance notice of what was going on—though long after he already knew—was waving the fire truck away. Scragger was to one side retching, and the other man, he assumed the second pilot, was urinating monstrously. The other two choppers settled into their landings. Painters swarmed over to them. Now what on earth are they doing?

"Good," he murmured, "no fire, no fuss, no farting about."

"Sayyid Sinclair, you should read this telex perhaps."

"Uh?" Absently he glanced at the youth who was awkwardly trying to use the spare binoculars on the choppers. One look at the telex was enough. "Mohammed, have you ever used binoculars backward?" he asked.

"Sayyid?" The youth was perplexed.

Sinclair took the glasses from him, unfocused them, and gave them back reversed. "Train them on the choppers and tell me what you see?"

It took the youth a few moments to get the image centered. "They're so far away I can hardly make the three of them out."

"Interesting. Here, sit in my chair a moment." Puffed with pride the youth obeyed. "Now, call Concorde and ask for a position report."

The other trainees were filled with envy, all else forgotten. Mohammed's fingers trembled with excitement holding down the transmit. "Concorde, this . . . this is Bahrain Tower, please, your position report, please."

"Tower, 001, going through thirty-four thousand for sixty-two thousand, Mach 1.3 for Mach 2"—fifteen hundred miles per hour—"heading 290, leaving your area now."

"Thank you, Concorde, good day . . . oh, call Baghdad 119.9, good day!" he said beaming and when the time was correct Sinclair pointedly picked up the telex and frowned.

"Iranian choppers?" He gave the youth the spare glasses. "Do you see any Iranian choppers here?"

After examining the three incoming strangers very carefully, the youth shook his head. "No, Sayyid, those are British, the only others here we know are Shargazi."

"Quite right." Sinclair was frowning. He had noticed that Scragger was still slumped on the ground, Lane and some of the others standing around him. Not like Scragger, he thought. "Mohammed, send a medic and ambulance over to those British choppers on the double." Then he picked up the phone, dialed. "Mr. Gavallan, your birds are down safe and sound. When you have a moment could you drop by the tower?" He said it in the peculiarly casual, understated English way that only another Englishman would detect at once meant "urgently."

IN THE S-G OFFICE: Gavallan said into the phone, "I'll be there right away, Mr. Sinclair. Thanks."

Scot saw his face. "More trouble, Dad?"

"I don't know. Call me if anything happens." At the door, Gavallan stopped. "Damn, I forgot about Newbury. Call him and see if he's available this afternoon. I'll go to his house, anywhere—fix whatever you can. If he wants to know what's going on, just say, 'Six out of seven so far, one on standby and two to go.'" He hurried away with, "'Bye, 'bye, Manuela. Scot, try Charlie again and find out where the devil he is."

"Okay." Now they were alone, Scot and Manuela. His shoulder was aching and intruding more and more. He had noticed her depression. "Dubois'll turn up, you'll see," he said, wanting to sound very confident and mask his own fear they were lost. "And nothing could kill old Fowler."

"Oh, I do hope so," she said, her tears near. She had seen her husband stumble and was achingly aware of the extent of his pain. Soon I'm going to have to leave for the hospital and the hell with Farsi. "It's the waiting."

"Only a few more hours, Manuela, two more birds and five bods. Then we can celebrate," Scot added, hoping against hope, and thinking: Then the weight'll be off the Old Man too, he'll smile again and live a thousand years.

My God, give up flying? I love flying and don't want a desk job. Hong Kong for part of the year'd be fine but Linbar? I can't deal with Linbar! The Old Man'll have to deal with him—I'd be lost . . .

The old, nagging question leaped into his mind: What'd I do if the Old Man wasn't around? A chill went through him. Not if, when, it's going to happen someday. . . . It could happen any day. Look at Jordon, Talbot— or Duke or me. A fraction of an inch and you're dead—or you're alive. The Will of God? Karma? Joss? I don't know and it doesn't matter! All I'm sure of is since I was hit I'm different, my whole life's different, my certainty that nothing would ever touch me has vanished forever and all that's left is a God-cursed, icy, stench-ridden certainty of being very mortal. Christ Almighty! Does that always happen? Wonder if Duke feels the same?

He looked at Manuela. She was staring at him. "Sorry, I wasn't listening," he said and began to dial Newbury.

"I just said, 'Isn't it three birds and eight bods? You forgot Erikki and Azadeh—nine if you count Sharazad.'"

TEHRAN, AT THE BAKRAVAN HOUSE: 1:14 P.M. Sharazad stood in front of the long mirror in her bathroom, naked, examining the profile of her stomach, seeing if there was an added roundness yet. This morning she had noticed that her nipples seemed more sensitive and her breasts appeared tight. "No need to worry," Zarah, Meshang's wife, had laughed. "Soon you'll be like a balloon and in tears, you'll be wailing that you'll never be able to get into your clothes again and oh how ugly you look! Don't worry, you will—get into your clothes—and you won't look ugly."

Sharazad was very happy today, dawdling, and she frowned at herself and peered closer to see if she had any wrinkles, looking at herself this way and that, trying her hair up and down, bunched or to one side, contented and pleased with what she saw. The bruises were fading. Her body was quite dry from her bath and she powdered herself, stepped into her underclothes.

Jari bustled in. "Oh, Princess, aren't you ready yet? His Eminence your brother is expected back for lunch any minute and the whole house is frightened he'll be in another of his rages, oh, please hurry, we don't want to excite him now do we? . . ." Automatically she pulled the plug out of the bath, began tidying, all the time fussing and muttering and coaxing Sharazad along. In moments Sharazad was dressed. Stockings—no panty hose on sale for months now, even on the black market—no need for a bra. Warm blue cashmere dress of Paris cut with matching short-sleeved shawl coat. A quick brush and her naturally wavy hair was perfect, the barest touch of lip makeup, a line of kohl around her eyes.

"But, Princess, you know how your brother doesn't like makeup!"

"Oh, but I'm not going out, and Meshang's not . . ." Sharazad was going to say "my father" but stopped herself, not wanting to bring back that tragedy from the recesses of her mind. Father's in Paradise, she told herself firmly. His Day of Mourning, the fortieth day since he died, is still twenty-five days away and until then we must get on with living.

And loving?

She had not asked Jari what had happened at the coffee shop, the day she had sent her there to tell *him* her husband had returned and that what had never begun was ended. I wonder where he is, if he'll continue to visit me in my dreams?

There was a commotion downstairs and they knew Meshang had arrived. She checked herself a last time, then went to meet him.

After the night of his clash with Lochart, Meshang had moved back into the house with his family. The house was very big, Sharazad still had her rooms and was delighted that Zarah and her three children noised away the crushing silence and gloom that had previously been pervading it. Her mother was a recluse now, in her own wing, even eating there, served only by her own maid, praying and weeping most of the day. Never coming out, never inviting any of them in: "Leave me alone! Leave me alone!" was all she would whimper through the locked door.

During the hours that Meshang was in the house, Sharazad, Zarah, and others in the family were careful to cajole and flatter him. "Don't worry," Zarah had told her. "He'll be to heel soon enough. He thinks I've forgotten he insulted me and hit me and dares to flaunt the young whore that that vile son of a dog Kia tempted him with! Oh, don't worry, darling Sharazad, I'll have my revenge—it was unforgivable bad manners to treat you and . . . your husband like that. Soon we'll be able to travel again . . . Paris, London, even New York . . . I doubt if he'll have the time to go with us and then, ah, and then we'll kick up our heels, wear see-throughs, and have fifty suitors each!"

"I don't know about New York—putting oneself in so much danger of Satan," Sharazad had said. But in her secret heart she trembled with excitement at the thought. I'll go to New York with my son, she promised herself. Tommy will be there. Soon we'll be normal again, the power of the mullahs over Khomeini will be broken, may God open his eyes, their control of the Green Bands eliminated, the Revolutionary Komiteh disbanded, we'll have a true, fairly elected democratic Islamic government with Prime Minister Bazargan its leader under God, women's rights will never be touched again, the Tudeh no longer outlawed but working for all and there will be peace in the land—just as *he* said would happen.

I'm glad I am who I am, Sharazad thought. "Hello, darling Meshang, how nice you look today but so tired, oh, you mustn't work so hard for all of us. Here, let me pour you some more cool lemon and water, just the way you like it."

"Thank you." Meshang was lounging on the carpets, propped against cushions, his shoes off, already eating. A small brazier was ready to barbecue the kebabs, and twenty or thirty dishes of horisht and rice and vegetables and sweetmeats and fruit were within easy reach. Zarah was nearby and she beckoned Sharazad to sit on the carpet beside her.

"How do you feel today?"

"Wonderful, not the least bit sick."

Meshang's face became sour. "Zarah was sick all the time, and moping, not like a normal woman. Let's hope you're normal, but you're so thin . . . Insha'Allah."

Both women put on a smile, hiding their loathing, understanding each other. "Poor Zarah," Sharazad said. "How was your morning, Meshang? It must be terribly difficult for you with so much to do, so many of us to look after."

"It's difficult because I'm surrounded by fools, dear Sister. If I had efficient staff, trained as I am, it would all be so easy." And so much easier if you had not beguiled my father, twisted him, failed your first husband, and disgraced us with your choice of the second. So much anguish you've caused me, dear Sister, you with your consumptive-looking face and body and stupidity—me who has worked all hours to rescue you from yourself. Praise be to God my efforts have borne such fruits!

"It must be terribly hard for you, Meshang, I wouldn't know where to start," Zarah was saying and she was thinking, Simple to run the business providing you know where the keys are, the bank accounts, the debtors' paper—and all the skeletons. You don't want us to have equality and the vote because we'd easily work you into the joub and take the best jobs.

The rich lamb horisht and crisped golden rice was delicious, fragrantly spiced just as he liked, and he ate with enjoyment. Mustn't eat too much, he told himself. I don't want to get too tired before little Yasmin this afternoon. I never realized how succulent a zinaat could be, or lips so grasping. If she gets with child then I shall marry her and Zarah can rot.

He glanced at his wife. Immediately she stopped eating, smiled at him, and gave him a napkin to take the grease and dribbles of soup from his beard. "Thank you," he said politely and once more concentrated on his plate. After I've had Yasmin, he was thinking, after her I can sleep an hour and then back to work. I wish that dog Kia was back, we've much to talk about, much to plan. And Sharazad will ha—

"Meshang, dearest, did you hear the rumor the generals have decided to launch their coup," Zarah asked, "and that the army's ready to take over?"

"Of course, it's all over the bazaar." Meshang felt a twinge of anxiety. He had hedged as best he could in case it was true. "The son of Mohammed the goldsmith swears his cousin who is a telephone operator at army head-quarters overheard one of the generals saying they've waited to give an American task force time to get in range, and it'll be supported by an airborne landing."

Both women were shocked. "Parachutists! Then we should leave at once, Meshang," Zarah said. "It won't be safe in Tehran, we'd better go to our house in the Caspian and wait for the war to end. When could you leave? I'll start packing immed—"

"What house on the Caspian! We don't have any house on the Caspian!" Meshang said irritably. "Wasn't it confiscated along with all our other property that we worked generations to acquire? God curse the thieves after all we've done for the revolution and for mullahs over the generations?" He was red in the face. A dribble of horisht went into his beard. "And now . . ."

"Do forgive me, you're right, dearest Meshang, you're right as usual. Do forgive me, I spoke without thinking. You're right as usual but if it pleases you we could go and stay with my uncle Agha Madri, they have a spare villa on the coast, we could take that and we could leave tomorr—"

"Tomorrow? Don't be ridiculous! Do you think I won't have enough warning?" Meshang wiped his beard, somewhat mollified by her abject apology, and Sharazad thought how fortunate she had been with her two husbands who had never mistreated her or shouted at her. I wonder how Tommy's getting on at Kowiss or wherever he is. Poor Tommy, as if I could leave my home and family and go into exile forever.

"Of course we bazaaris will have warning," Meshang said again. "We're not empty-headed fools."

"Yes, yes, of course, dear Meshang," Zarah said soothingly. "I'm sorry, I only meant I was worried for your safety and wanted to be prepared." However foul he is, she thought, her insides fluttering, he's our only defense against the mullahs and their equally vile Green Band thugs. "Do you believe the coup will happen?"

"Insha'Allah," he said and belched. Either way I'll be prepared, with the Help of God. Either way, whoever wins, they'll still need us bazaaris, they always have and always will—we can be as modern as any foreigners, and smarter, some of us can be, certainly me. Son of a dog Paknouri, may he and his fathers be in hell for endangering us!

The Caspian! Her uncle Madri's a good idea, the perfect idea. I would have thought of it myself in a moment. Zarah may be used up and her zinaat as dry as summer's dust, but she's a good mother and her council—if you forget her foul humor—is always wise. "Another rumor's that our glorious ex-Prime Minister Bakhtiar is still in hiding in Tehran, under the protection and roof of his old friend and colleague, Prime Minister Bazargan."

Zarah gasped. "If the Green Bands catch him there . . ."

"Bazargan's useless. Pity. No one obeys him anymore, or even listens to him. The Revolutionary Komiteh would execute both of them if they're caught."

Sharazad was trembling. "Jari said there was a rumor in the market this morning that Excellency Bazargan has resigned already."

"That's not true," Meshang said shortly, passing on another rumor as though it were private knowledge. "My friend close to Bazargan told me he offered Khomeini his resignation but the Imam refused it, telling him to stay where he was." He held out his plate for Zarah to give him some more. "That's enough horisht, a little more rice."

She gave him the crisped part and he began to eat again, almost replete. The most interesting rumor today, whispered in enormous secrecy from ear to ear, was that the Imam was near death, either from natural causes or poisoned by Communist Tudeh agitators or mujhadin or CIA and, even worse, that Soviet legions were waiting just over the border ready to march into Azerbaijan again, and on to Tehran the moment he was dead.

Nothing but death and disaster're ahead if that's true, he thought. No, that won't happen, can't happen. The Americans will never let the Soviets conquer us, they can't allow them to take control of Hormuz—even Carter will see that! No. Let's just hope the first part's true—that the Imam is going to Paradise quickly. "As God wants," he said piously, waved the servants away, and when they were alone he turned his full attention onto his sister. "Sharazad, your divorce is all arranged, but for the formalities."

"Oh," she said, at once on guard, hating her brother for disturbing her calm, sending her brain into overdrive: I don't want to divorce, Meshang could easily have given us money from all the Swiss accounts and not been so nasty to my Tommy and then we could have gone—don't be silly, you couldn't leave without papers and exile yourself and Tommy left you, it was his decision. Yes, but Tommy said it would be for a month, didn't he, that he'd wait for a month? In a month so many things can happen.

"Your divorce presents no problem. Nor your remarriage."

She gaped at him, speechless.

"Yes, I've agreed to a dowry, much more than I expected for . . ." He was going to say for a twice-divorced woman carrying an Infidel's child, but she was his sister and it was a great match, so he did not. "The marriage will be next week and he's admired you for years. Excellency Farazan."

For a moment both women could hardly believe their ears. Sharazad felt a sudden flush, disoriented even more. Keyvan Farazan was from a rich bazaari family, twenty-eight, handsome, recently back from Cambridge University, and they had been friends all of her life. "But . . . I thought Keyvan's going to be ma—"

"Not Keyvan," Meshang said, irritated by her stupidity. "Everyone knows Keyvan's about to be betrothed. Daranoush! Excellency Daranoush Farazan."

Sharazad was transfixed. Zarah gasped and tried to cover her lapse. Daranoush was the father, recently widowed of his second wife who had died in childbirth like his first, a very wealthy man who owned the monopoly for the collection of waste in the whole bazaar area. "It's . . . it's not possible," she muttered.

"Oh, yes it is," Meshang said, almost glowing with pleasure, totally misreading her. "I never believed it myself when he broached the idea after hearing about your divorce. With his riches and connections, together we become the most powerful conglomerate in the bazaar, togeth—"

Sharazad burst out, "But he's loathsome and small and old, old and bald and ugly and he likes boys, and everyone knows he's a ped—"

"And everyone knows you're twice divorced, used, you're with child by a foreigner," Meshang exploded, "that you go on marches and disobey, your head's filled with Western nonsense and you're stupid!" He knocked over some of the plates in his fury. "Don't you understand what I've done for you? He's one of the richest men in the bazaar, I persuaded him to accept you—you're redeemed and now you—"

"But, Meshang, ha—"

"Don't you understand, you ungrateful bitch," he bellowed, "he's even agreed to adopt your child! By all the Names of God, what more do you want?"

Meshang was almost purple, quivering with rage, his fist bunched, shaking it in Sharazad's face, Zarah staring at her and then him, aghast at his fury as he ranted on.

Sharazad heard nothing, saw nothing, except what Meshang had decreed for her: the rest of her life joined to that little man, the butt of a thousand bazaari jokes, who stank perpetually of urine, fertilizing her once a year to bear and live and bear again until she died in childbirth or because of it—like his other two wives. Nine children from the first, seven from the second. She was doomed. Nothing she could do. Princess Night Soil until she died.

Nothing.

Nothing except I could die now, not by suicide, for then I'm forbidden Paradise and condemned to hell. Not suicide. Never. Never suicide but death doing God's work, death with God's name on my lips.

What?

KOWISS BASE: 1:47 P.M. Colonel Changiz, the mullah Hussain, and some Green Bands jumped out of their car. The Green Bands spread out over the base searching while the colonel and Hussain hurried into the office building.

In the office the two remaining clerks were in shock at the suddenness of the colonel's arrival. "Yes . . . yes, Excellency?"

"Where is everyone?" Changiz shouted. "Eh?"

"God knows we don't know anything, Excellency Colonel, except Excellency Captain Ayre is gone with spares to Rig Abu Sal and Excellency Captain McIver with Excellency Minister Kia to Tehran and Excellency Captain Lochart went to search for the incoming 212s an—"

"What incoming 212s?"

"The four 212s Excellency Captain McIver ordered here from Bandar Delam with pilots and other personnel and we're getting . . . we're getting ready to . . . to receive them." The clerk, whose name was Ishmael, wilted under the penetrating stare of the mullah. "As God knows, the captain went alone, to look alone for them as they've no HF and an airborne VHF could perhaps reach them."

Changiz was greatly relieved. He said to Hussain, "If the 212s are all coming here, there's been a panic for no reason." He mopped his brow. "When are they due?"

"I would imagine soon, Excellency," Ishmael said.

"How many foreigners are on the base now?"

"I . . . I don't know, Excellency, we've . . . we've been diligently busy trying to make up a manifest an—"

A Green Band ran into the office. "We can't find any foreigners, Excellency," he said to Hussain. "One of the cooks said the last two mechanics went with the big helicopters this morning. Iranian laborers said they heard replacement crews were due on Sunday or Monday."

"Saturday, Excellencies, tomorrow we were told, Excellencies," Ishmael interjected. "But with the incoming four 212s, they've mechanics on board as well as pilots and personnel, Excellency McIver said. Do you need mechanics?"

The Green Band was saying, "Some of the rooms—it looks as if the

Infidels packed hurriedly, but there are three helicopters still in the hangars."

Changiz turned on Ishmael. "What're those?"

"One . . . no two 206s and a French one, an Alouette."

"Where's Chief Clerk Pavoud?"

"He was sick, Excellency Colonel, he left sick just after noon prayers, and went home. Isn't that so, Ali?" he said to the other clerk.

"Yes, yes, he was sick and he left saying he would be back tomorrow . . ." the words trailed off.

"Captain McIver ordered the 212s here from Bandar Delam?"

"Yes, yes, Excellency, that's what he told Excellency Pavoud, I heard him tell him that exactly, with the pilots and other personnel, wasn't that so, Ali?"

"Yes, before God, that's what happened, Excellency Colonel."

"All right, that's enough." To Hussain the colonel said, "We'll radio Lochart." To the clerk he said, "Is Sergeant Wazari in the tower?"

"No, Excellency Colonel, he went back to the base just before Excellency Captain Lochart took off to search for the four 212s that should arr—"

"Enough!" Colonel Changiz thought a moment, then said rudely to the Green Band, "You! Get my corporal on the double to the tower."

The youthful Green Band flushed at the tone and glanced at Hussain who said coldly, "The colonel means, please find Corporal Borgali and bring him to the tower quickly."

Changiz started blustering, "I meant no impoliteness of cour—"

"Of course." Hussain stalked down the corridor toward the staircase that led to the tower. Very much chastened, Changiz followed.

Half an hour before, a telex had arrived at the air base from Tehran ATC asking for an immediate check on all IHC foreign personnel and helicopters at Kowiss: ". . . four 212s have been reported missing from IHC base at Bandar Delam by IHC Managing Director Siamaki, who believes they might have been illegally flown out of Iran to one of the Gulf states."

At once Changiz had been summoned by the duty Green Band who had already taken the telex to Hussain and the komiteh. The komiteh was in session on the base, painstakingly continuing investigations into Islamic reliability of all officers and men, and into crimes committed against God in the name of the Shah. Changiz felt nauseated. The komiteh was pitiless. No one who had been pro-Shah had yet escaped. And though he was commandant, appointed by the komiteh with Hussain's approval, confirmation from the all-powerful Revolutionary Komiteh had not yet arrived. Until that happened, Changiz knew he was on trial. And hadn't he taken an oath of allegiance to the Shah personally, like every man in the forces?

In the tower he saw Hussain staring at the equipment. "Can you work the radios, Colonel?" the mullah asked, his robes old but clean, turban white and freshly washed, but old too.

"No, Excellency, that's why I sent for Borgali." Corporal Borgali came up the stairs two at a time and stood to attention. "VHF and HF," the colonel ordered.

"Yessir." Borgali switched on. Nothing. A quick check and he found the mutilated crystal and that the VHF circuit breaker was missing. "Sorry, sir, this equipment's nonfunctioning."

"You mean sabotaged," Hussain said softly and looked at Changiz.

Changiz was numb. God burn all foreigners, he was thinking in despair. If it's deliberate sabotage . . . then this is proof they've fled and taken our choppers with them. That dog McIver must have known they were going to do it this morning when I was asking about the 125.

Prickles of ice needles went through him. No 125 now, no private escape route, no chance of taking Lochart or one of the other pilots hostage on a trumped-up charge, then secretly bartering the man's "escape from jail" for a seat for himself—if necessary. His entrails heaved. What if the komiteh finds out my wife and family are already in Baghdad, not as supposed at Abadan where my poor mother is "dying"? The nightmare devils were always jeering, shouting the truth: "What mother? Your mother's been dead for seven or eight years! You've planned to flee, you're guilty of crimes against God and the Imam and the revolution . . ."

"Colonel," Hussain said in the same chilling voice, "if the radios are sabotaged does it not follow that Captain Lochart is not searching for the other helicopters, he's not searching but has fled like the other one, and that McIver lied about ordering the other 212s here?"

"Yes . . . yes, Excellency, yes it does an—"

"And then it also follows that they have fled illegally and taken two helicopters from here illegally, apart from the four from Bandar Delam?"

"Yes . . . yes, that would be true too."

"As God wants, but you are responsible."

"But, Excellency, surely you must realize that it's not possible to have foreseen a secret, illegal operation like . . ." He saw the eyes and read them and his words faded away.

"So you've been duped?"

"Foreigners are sons of dogs who lie and cheat all the time . . ." Changiz stopped as a thought filled his mind. He grabbed the phone, cursed finding it inoperative. In a different voice he said quickly, "Excellency, a 212 can't fly across the Gulf without refueling, it's not possible, and McIver's got to refuel too to get to Tehran with Kia—he'll have to refuel too so we can catch them." To Borgali he said, "On the double, go back to our tower and find out where the 206 cleared for Tehran with McIver and Minister Kia is scheduled to refuel. Tell the duty officer to alert the base and arrest the pilot, detain the helicopter, and send Minister Kia on to Tehran . . . by road." He looked at Hussain. "You agree, Excellency?" Hussain nodded. "Good. Off you go!"

The corporal rushed down the stairs.

It was cold in the tower, the wind blustering. A small rain squall pelted the windows for a moment then passed by. Hussain did not notice it, his eyes on Changiz.

"We'll catch that dog, Excellency. Minister Kia will thank us."

Hussain did not smile. He had already arranged a reception komiteh for Kia at Tehran Airport, and if Kia could not explain all manner of curiosities in his behavior, soon the government would be less one corrupt minister. "Perhaps Kia is part of the plot and he's fleeing Iran with McIver, have you thought of that, Colonel?"

The colonel gaped. "Minister Kia? Do you think so?"

"Do you?"

"By God, it's . . . it's certainly possible, if you think so," Changiz replied cautiously, trying as never before to be alert. "I've never met the man in my life. You'd know better than me, Excellency, about Kia, you questioned him in front of the komiteh." And exonerated him, he thought with malicious delight. "When we catch McIver we can use him as a hostage to bring back the rest, we'll catch him, Excellency . . ."

Hussain saw the fear on the colonel's face and he wondered what the man was guilty of, was the colonel also part of the escape plan that had been obvious to him since he had questioned Starke yesterday and McIver this morning?

"And if it was obvious," he had imagined a religious superior asking, "why did you keep it secret and why didn't you prevent it?"

"Because of Starke, Eminence. Because I truly believe that somehow that man, though Infidel, is an Instrument of God and God-protected. Three times he prevented forces of evil giving me the blessed peace of Paradise. Because of him my eyes have been opened to the truth of God's wish that I must no longer seek martyrdom but must remain on an earthly path to become a relentless scourge for God and the Imam, against enemies of Islam and *his* enemies."

"But the others? Why allow them to escape?"

"Islam needs neither foreigners nor their helicopters. Should Iran need helicopters, in Isfahan there are a thousand others."

Hussain was completely sure he was right, as right as this pro-Shah,

American-supporting turncoat colonel was wrong. "So, Colonel, what about the two 212s, will you catch them too? How?"

Changiz went to the wall map quite sure that though both of them had been duped he was commandant and responsible if the mullah wanted to make him responsible. But don't forget this is the mullah who made a deal with Colonel Peshadi the night of the first attack on the base, this is the same one who befriended the American Starke and the odious maniac Zataki from Abadan. And am I not a supporter of the Imam and the revolution? Didn't I correctly give over the base to the soldiers of God?

Insha'Allah. Concentrate on the foreigners. If you can catch them, even one of them, you'll be safe from this mullah and his Green Band thugs.

Several standard flight paths were drawn on the map from Kowiss to various oil sites and to rigs out into the Gulf. "That dog clerk said spares to Abu Sal," he muttered. "Now if I were them, where would I refuel?" His finger stabbed the rigs. "One of these, Excellency," he said excitedly. "That's where they'd refuel."

"The rigs carry spare fuel?"

"Oh, yes, in case of an emergency."

"And how are you going to catch them?"

"Fighters."

ONSHORE AT THE RENDEZVOUS: 2:07 P.M. The two 212s were parked on the desolate, undulating beach in light rain. Dejectedly Freddy Ayre and Lochart sat in the open door of one of the cabins, their two mechanics and Wazari in the other, all of them tired from handling the big, cumbersome forty-gallon drums of fuel and taking turns pumping the gasoline into the tanks. Never had two 212s been refueled faster, nor full spares heaved aboard into each and secured faster, in case of an emergency. Freddy Ayre had arrived here about eleven-thirty, Lochart just after twelve, half an hour to refuel, and they had been waiting ever since.

"We'll give him another half an hour," Lochart said.

"Christ, you're acting as though we've all the time in the world."

"It's stupid for us both to wait, safer for you to go separately—how many times do I have to say it? Take everyone and I'll wait."

"When Mac arrives we can all g—"

"Goddamnit, take the mechanics and Wazari and I'll wait. That's what Mac'd say if he was here and you were waiting for me. For crissake, stop trying to play hero and push off."

"No. Sorry, but I'm waiting until he arrives or we both leave."

Lochart shrugged, his spirit as drab as the day. As soon as he had arrived he had worked out McIver's tentative schedule: "Freddy, Mac was safe out of the Kowiss system by eleven-twenty. Say at the very outside he flies on for another half an hour, then another half an hour, maximum, to fake the emergency, land and get rid of Kia, maximum an hour to get here, absolute max, at the very outside means one-thirty. My bet's he'll be here one to one-fifteen."

But it was after two and no Mac yet and maybe no Mac at all—there's got to've been a foul-up. He studied the clouds, seeking answers in the weather, and refining plans and counterplans. Empty drums were in a neat pile, another five still full. The drums had been brought here during routine runs to the rigs and cached under tarpaulins and camouflaged with sand and seaweed. Out to sea, barely visible, was a rig, high above the water level, perched on stilts.

He had had no trouble getting here from Kowiss. As soon as they were airborne and it was safe, Wazari had crawled forward. "Best you stay under cover until we're launched into the Gulf," Lochart had said. But once they had landed, Wazari had become very sick so he had changed his mind and told the others what had happened. Now Wazari had recovered and was accepted. But still considered suspect.

The shore stank of rotting fish and seaweed. Wind, steady at about thirty knots, throbbed the rotor blades, still adverse to their planned escape route to Kuwait. The murky ceiling had lowered, now down to about two hundred feet. But little of this registered on Lochart. More and more his mind was pulled northward to Tehran and Sharazad—while his hearing reached out over the wind and the waves for the sound of the 206. Come on, Mac, he prayed. Come on, don't let me down. Come on Mac, don't let me down . . .

Then he heard her. A few seconds to make sure, and he jumped out of the cabin, mouth slightly open to increase the strength of his hearing and directional ability. Now Ayre came out of his reverie and was beside him, both of them peering into the overcast, listening now, the engine growing louder, out to sea, then passing them by and Lochart cursed. "He's missed us!"

"VHF?" Ayre asked.

"Too goddamn dangerous . . . not yet . . . he'll make another pass, he's too good not to."

Again waiting, sound of the engines dying, dying, then the level holding. The engine sound grew. Again the chopper made a pass and missed them and began to die away, then once more turned back. Engine sounds growing and growing, then she came down through the murk half a mile up the beach, spotted them and began her approach. No doubt now that she was theirs, McIver the pilot and alone. They cheered.

IN THE 206 COCKPIT: McIver had had a very hard time finding the rendezvous, mud flats all looking the same, coastline the same, with conditions bad. Then he had remembered the nonworking rig just offshore and had eased out to find it and, using that as a marker, had come inland.

When his skids were solid on the ground he muttered, "Thank God for that," and exhaled, stomach aching and desperate to urinate, opened the cockpit door at once, and said over their questions, "Sorry, got to pee. Freddy, shut her down for me, will you?" Lochart, who was closer, said, "I'll do her, Mac."

"Thanks." McIver had unsnapped his seat belt, scrambled out, and hurried under the blades for the nearest dune. When he could speak he glanced around, saw Ayre waiting for him, the others over by the 212s. "My back teeth've been floating for an hour or more."

"I know how it feels."

McIver shook himself, zipped up, and noticed Wazari. "What the hell's he doing here?"

"Tom thought it best to bring him, safer than leaving him and he did help. We'd better get going, Mac. We're all refueled. What about the 206?"

"We'll have to leave her." She was not equipped with long-range tanks and it would take too much time to rig a temporary inflight refueling system. Even then, this adverse wind would gulp fuel and make the voyage not possible. McIver pointed out to sea, "I thought about parking her on the rig in the hope we could come back and pick her up, but that's a pipe dream. There's not enough space to land her and a 212 at the same time to pick me up. Bloody shame, but there you are."

"No problem with Kia?"

"No. He was a bit of a pain in the butt an—" He whirled. Behind them Lochart had gunned the 206 and now she was lifting and backing away. "For God's sake, Tom . . ." he bellowed and ran for the helicopter but Lochart backed faster and hauled her up twenty feet. "Tommmm!"

Lochart leaned out of the cockpit window. "Don't wait for me, Mac!" he shouted.

"But you're almost out of fuel . . ."

"There's plenty for the moment—I'll wait till you're gone then I'll refuel. See you in Al Shargaz!"

"What the hell's he playing at?" Ayre said dumbfounded.

"Sharazad," McIver said, cursing himself for forgetting. "He must've had fifty plans to take the 206, one way or another." Then he cupped his hands around his mouth and shouted, "Tom, you'll screw up Whirlwind for Christ's sake! You've got to come with us!"

"They'll never make me a hostage, Mac! Never! It's on my head, not yours . . . it's my decision, by God. Now push off!"

McIver thought a second, then bellowed, "Land now, we'll refuel for you, save you trouble." He saw Lochart shake his head, point at the 212s.

"I'm going back for Sharazad," Lochart shouted. "Don't try and stop me or wait me out . . . it's my neck not yours . . . Happy Landings." He waved then moved away to safety down the beach, turned into wind facing them and landed. But the engines were kept up, ready for instant takeoff.

"No way to rush him," McIver muttered, furious with himself for not being prepared.

"We . . . we could wait till he runs out of fuel," Ayre said.

"Tom's too smart to be trapped." Almost in panic McIver glanced at his watch, his mind giddy. "Bloody fools, me and Tom." He saw all the others looking at him.

"What're we going to do, Mac?" Ayre said.

McIver forced himself to think clearly: You're the leader. Decide. We're terribly late. Tom's decided after everything I said. That's his privilege. Sorry but that means he's on his own. Now think of the others. Erikki's got to be all right. Rudi and Scragger and their lads're safe—let's presume they're safe—so get into the 212 and begin the next leg.

He wanted to groan aloud, the thought of having to nurse a 212 to Kuwait at low level for the next two and a half hours plus almost crushed him. "Bloody hell," he muttered. The others still watched him. And waited. "Tom's going back to get his wife—we'll leave him to it."

"But if he gets caught, won't that screw Whirlwind?" Ayre asked.

"No. Tom's on his own. You heard what he said. We're leaving for Kuwait as planned. Everyone into Freddy's 212, I'll take Lochart's. Off you all go and we'll stay low and close. Radio silence until we're well across the line." McIver went for the other 212. Uneasily they looked at one another. They had all noticed his pallor and all knew about his lack of a medical.

Kyle, the short, lithe mechanic went after him. "Mac, no point in going alone, I'll fly with you."

"Thanks, but no. Everyone in Freddy's machine! Come on, get with it!"

Ayre said, "Mac, I'll go and talk to Tom. He must be crazy, I'll persuade him to come to Kuw—"

"You won't. If it was Gen, I'd be just as crazy. Everyone get aboard!" At that moment, the sound of two jet fighters at low level going through the sound barrier drowned the beach. The silence they left behind was vast.

"Jesus." Wazari shivered. "Captain, if you'll have me along, I'll fly with you?"

"No, everyone with Freddy, I'd prefer to fly alone."

"Your nonlicense makes no odds to me." Wazari shrugged. "Insha'Allah! I'll monitor the radio." He jerked his thumb skyward: "Those bastards won't speak English." He turned for the 212 and got into the left seat.

Ayre said, "It's a good idea, Mac."

"All right. We'll stay close and low as planned. Freddy, if one of us runs into trouble the other goes on." At Ayre's look, "I mean any trouble." A last look at Lochart, McIver waved again and went aboard. He was very glad not to be alone. "Thanks," he said to Wazari. "I don't know what'll happen at Kuwait, Sergeant, but I'll help all I can." He locked his seat belt and pressed Engine Start on Number One.

"Sure. Thanks. Hell, I got nothing to lose; my head's busting, I've had every aspirin outta the medical packs . . . What happened with Kia?"

McIver adjusted the volume of his headset, pressed Engine Start on Number Two, checking fuel tanks and instruments as he spoke. "I had to do the emergency a little later than I planned—landed about a mile from a village—but it went fine, too fine, the bugger fainted and then I couldn't get him out of the cockpit. Somehow he'd entwined himself in his seat and shoulder belts and I couldn't get him free. Didn't have a bloody knife to cut him loose. I tried every way, pushing and pulling, but the catch had stuck so I gave up and waited for him to come around. While I waited I got his luggage out and put it nearer to the road where he'd find it. When he came to, I had the hell's own job getting him to leave the cockpit." McIver's fingers went accurately from switch to switch. "Eventually I pretended we had a fire and jumped out, leaving him. That did it and he somehow got the catch undone and left in a hurry. I'd kept the engines running, bloody dangerous but had to chance it, and once he was clear, I rushed back and took off. Scraped a rock or two but no sweat . . ."

His heart had been pounding, his throat dry at the frantic takeoff, Kia clawing at the door handle, raving at him, hanging on, one foot on the skid, McIver afraid he would have to land again. Fortunately Kia's nerve failed and he let go and dropped back the few feet they were off the ground, and now McIver was free and away. He had circled once to make sure Kia was all right. The last he saw of Kia, he was shaking his fist and red with rage. Then he had set course for the coast, hugging the undulating trees and rocks. And though he was safe, the pounding in his chest did not lessen. Waves of nausea and heat began to sweep through him.

It's just the strain of the last week or so catching up, he had told himself grimly. Just strain and trying to haul that bugger out of the cockpit, along with worries over Whirlwind, and being scared fartless by the mullah's questioning.

For a few more minutes after leaving Kia, he had flown onward. Difficult to concentrate. Pain increasing. Controls unfamiliar. A spasm of nausea and he almost lost control so decided to land and rest a moment. He was still in the mountain foothills, rocks and clumps of trees and snow, the ceiling low and fairly thin. Through a haze of sickness he chose the first possible plateau and landed. The landing was not good and that, more than anything, frightened him very much. Nearby was a stream, partially frozen, the water frothing as it tumbled down the rocks. The water beckoned him. In bad pain he shut down, stumbled over to it, lay on the snow and drank deeply. The shock of the cold made him retch and when the spasm had passed he cleansed his mouth and drank sparingly. This and the cold of the air helped him. A handful of snow rubbed into the back of his neck and temples made him feel even better. Gradually the pain lessened, the tingling in his left arm went away. When it had almost gone he groped to his feet and, stumbling a little, made the cockpit, sank back in his seat.

His cockpit was warm and cozy and familiar—enclosing. Automatically he snapped his seat belt. Silence filled his ears and his head. Only the sound of the wind, and the water, no engines or traffic or static, nothing but the softness of the wind and water. Peacefulness. His eyelids were heavier than they had ever been. He closed them. And slept.

His sleep was deep and barely half an hour and very good. When he awoke he was revitalized—no pain, no discomfort, just a little light-headed as though he had dreamed the pain. He stretched gloriously. Tiny sound of metal clinking against metal. He looked around. Seated on a small mountain pony, watching him silently, was a youth, a tribesman. In a saddle sheath was a rifle and another was across his back with a bandolier of cartridges.

The two of them stared at each other, then the youth smiled and the plateau seemed to light up. "Salaam, Agha."

"Salaam, Agha." McIver smiled back, surprised that he was completely unafraid, somehow put at his ease by the wild beauty of the youth. *"Loftan befarma'id shoma ki hastid?"* He used one of his few stock phrases: May I ask who you are?

"Agha Mohammed Rud Kahani," and then some words McIver did not understand and he finished with another smile and, "Kash'kai."

"Ah, Kash'kai," McIver nodded, understanding that the youth was one of the nomadic tribes that spread across the Zagros. He pointed at himself. "Agha McIver," and added another stock phrase, *"Mota assef an, man zaban-e shoma ra khoob nami danam."* Sorry, I don't speak your language.

"Insha'Allah. America?"

"English. Englishman." He was watching himself and the other man. Helicopter and horse, pilot and tribesman, gulfs between them but no threat, one to the other. "Sorry, I must go now," he said in English, then parodied, flying away with his hands. *"Khoda haefez,"* good-bye, "Agha Mohammed Kash'kai."

The youth nodded and raised his hand in salute. *"Khoda haefez, Agha,"* then moved his horse to safety and stood there watching him. When the engines were up to power, McIver waved once and left. All the way to the rendezvous he had thought about the youth. No reason for that youth not to shoot me, or perhaps no reason to shoot me. Did I dream him, dream the pain? No, I didn't dream the pain. Did I have a heart attack?

Now, ready to leave for Kuwait, for the first time he faced the question. Disquiet returned and he glanced at Wazari who was staring disconsolately out the side window at the sea. How dangerous am I now? he asked himself. If I had one attack, even a mild one, I could have another, so am I risking his life as well as my own? I don't think so. I've only high blood pressure and that's under control, I take the two pills a day and no problem. I can't leave a 212 just because Tom's gone mad. I'm tired, but okay, and Kuwait's only a couple of hours. I'd be happier not to be flying. My God, I never thought I'd ever feel that. Old Scrag can have the flying, I'm done with it forever.

His ears were listening to the pitch of the engines. Ready for takeoff now, no real need to check the instruments. Through the rain speckles on his windshield he saw Ayre give him a thumbs-up, also ready. Down the beach he could see Lochart in the 206. Poor old Tom. Bet he's cursing us to hurry, anxious to refuel and rush north to a new destiny. Hope he succeeds—at least he'll have a following wind.

"Okay to switch on the VHF?" Wazari asked, distracting him. "I'll tune into military frequencies."

"Good." McIver smiled at Wazari, pleased to have him for company.

Lots of static in his headphones, then Farsi voices. Wazari listened awhile then said throatily, "It's the fighters talking to Kowiss. One of them said, 'In all the Names of God, how're we going to find two choppers in this pool of dog shit?'"

"They won't, not if I have anything to do with it." McIver tried to sound confident over a sudden tide of foreboding. He got Ayre's attention, pointed upward, indicating the fighters and motioned across his throat. Then he pointed a last time out into the Gulf and gave a thumbs-up. A glance at his watch: 2:21 P.M.

"Here we go, Sergeant," he said and twisted the throttles full open, "next stop Kuwait. ETA 4:40 P.M., or thereabouts."

AT KUWAIT AIRPORT: 2:56 P.M. Genny and Charlie Pettikin were sitting in the open-air restaurant on the upper level of the sparkling, newly opened terminal. It was a grand, sunny day, sheltered from the wind. Bright yellow tablecloths and umbrellas, everyone eating and drinking with enjoyment and gusto. Except for them. Genny had hardly touched her salad, Pettikin had picked at his rice and curry.

"Charlie," Genny said abruptly, "I think I'll have a vodka martini after all."

"Good idea," Pettikin waved for a waiter and ordered for her. He would have liked to join her but he was expecting to replace or spell either Lochart or Ayre on the next leg down the coast to Jellet Island—at least one refueling stop, perhaps two, before reaching Al Shargaz—God curse this sodding wind. "Won't be long now, Genny."

Oh, for Christ's sake, how many times do you have to say it, Genny wanted to scream, sick of waiting. Stoically she kept up her pretense of calm. "Not long, Charlie. Any moment now." Their eyes went seaward. The distant seascape was hazed, visibility poor, but they would know the instant the choppers came into Kuwait radar range. The Imperial Air rep was waiting in the tower.

How long is long? she asked herself, trying to pierce the heat haze, all her energy pouring out, seeking Duncan, sending prayers and hopes and strengths that he might need. The word that Gavallan had passed on this morning had not helped: "What on earth's he flying Kia for, Andy? Back to Tehran? What does that mean?"

"Don't know, Genny. I'm telling you as he said it. Our interpretation is that Freddy was sent to the fuel rendezvous first. Mac took off with Kia—he's either taking him to the rendezvous or he'll put him off en route. Tom's holding the fort for a time to give the others a breathing space, then he'll head for the RV. We got Mac's initial call at 10:42. Give him till 11:00 A.M. for him and Freddy to take off. Give them another hour to get to the RV and refuel, add two hours thirty flight time, they should arrive Kuwait around 2:30 at the earliest. Depending on how long they wait at the RV it could be anytime, from 2:30 onwards . . ."

She saw the waiter bringing her drink. On the tray was a mobile phone. "Phone call for you, Captain Pettikin," the waiter said as he put the glass in front of her. Pettikin pulled out the antenna, held the phone to his ear. "Hello? Oh, hello, Andy." She watched his face, "No . . . no, not yet . . . Oh? . . ." He listened intently for a long time, just an occasional grunt and nod, nothing showing outwardly, and she wondered what Gavallan was saying that she was not supposed to hear. ". . . Yes, sure . . . no . . . yes, everything's covered as far as we can . . . Yes, yes, she is . . . all right, hang on." He passed the phone over. "He wants to say hello."

"Hello, Andy, what's new?"

"Just reporting in, Genny. Not to worry about Mac and the others—no telling how long they had to wait at the RV."

"I'm fine, Andy. Don't worry about me. What about the others?"

"Rudi, Pop Kelly, and Sandor are en route from Bahrain—they refueled at Abu Dhabi and we're in contact with them—John Hogg's our relay station—their ETA here's in twenty minutes. Scrag's fine, Ed and Willi no problem, Duke's sleeping and Manuela's here. She wants to say hello . . ." A moment and then Manuela's voice: "Hi, darlin', how are ya, and don't say great!"

Genny smiled halfheartedly. "Great. Is Duke all right?"

"Sleepin' like a baby, not that babies sleep quiet all the time. Just wanted you to know we're sweating it out too. I'll pass you back to Andy."

A pause, then: "Hello, Genny. Johnny Hogg'll be in your area about now and he'll be listening too. We'll keep in touch. Can I speak to Charlie again, please."

"Of course, but what about Marc Dubois and Fowler?"

A pause. "Nothing yet. We're hoping they've been picked up—Rudi, Sandor, and Pop backtracked and searched as long as they could. No wreckage, there're lots of ships in those waters and platforms. We're sweating them out."

"Now tell me what Charlie's supposed to know but I'm not." She scowled into the dead silence on the phone, then heard Gavallan sigh.

"You're one for the book, Genny. All right. I asked Charlie if any telex had arrived from Iran yet, like the one we got here, in Dubai and Bahrain. I'm trying to pull all the strings I can through Newbury and our Kuwaiti embassy in case of a foul-up, though Newbury says not to expect much, Kuwait being so close to Iran and not wanting to offend Khomeini and petrified he'll send or allow a few export fundamentalists to stir up the Kuwaiti Shi'as. I told Charlie that I'm trying to get word to Ross's parents in Nepal and to his regiment. That's the lot." In a more kindly voice, "I didn't want to upset you more than necessary. Okay?"

"Yes, thanks. Yes, I'm . . . I'm fine. Thanks, Andy." She passed the phone back and looked at her glass. Beads of moisture had formed. Some were trickling. Like the tears on my cheeks, she thought and got up. "Back in a sec."

Sadly Pettikin watched her go. He listened to Gavallan's final instructions. "Yes, yes, of course," he said. "Don't worry, Andy, I'll take care of . . . I'll take care of Ross, and I'll call the very moment we have them on the screen. Bloody awful about Dubois and Fowler, we'll just have to think good thoughts and hope. Great about the others. 'Bye."

Finding Ross had shattered him. The moment he had got Gavallan's call this morning he had rushed to the hospital. Today being Friday, with minimum staff, there was just one receptionist on duty and he spoke only Arabic. The man smiled and shrugged and said, *"Bokrah,"*—tomorrow. But Pettikin had persisted and eventually the man had understood what he wanted, and had made a phone call. At length a male nurse arrived and beckoned him. They went along corridors and then through a door and there was Ross naked on a slab.

It was the suddenness, the totality of nakedness, of seeming defilement, and the obliteration of any shred of dignity that had torn Pettikin apart, not the fact of death. This man who had been so fine in life had been left like a carcass. On another slab were sheets. He took one and covered him and that seemed to make it better.

It had taken Pettikin more than an hour to find the ward where Ross had been, to track down an English-speaking nurse and to find his doctor.

"So very sorry, so very sorry, sir," the doctor, a Lebanese, had said in halting English. "The young man arrived yesterday in a coma. He had a fractured skull and we suspected brain damage; it was from a terrorist bomb we were told. Both eardrums were broken and he had a number of minor cuts and bruises. We X-rayed him, of course, but apart from binding his skull there was little we could do but wait. He had no internal damage or hemorrhage. He died this morning with the dawn. The dawn was beautiful today, wasn't it? I signed the death certificate—would you like a copy? We've given one to the English embassy—together with his effects."

"Did he . . . did he recover consciousness before he died?"

"I do not know. He was in intensive care and his nurse . . . let me see." Laboriously the doctor had consulted his lists and found her name. "Sivin Tahollah. Ah, yes. Because he was English we assigned her to him."

She was an old woman, part of the flotsam of the Middle East, knowing no forebears, part of many nations. Her face was ugly and pockmarked but she was not, her voice gentle and calming, her hands warm. "He was never conscious, Effendi," she said in English, "not truly."

"Did he say anything particularly, anything you could understand, anything at all?"

"Much that I understood, Effendi, and nothing." The old woman thought a moment. "Most of what he said was just mind wanderings, the spirit fearing what should not be feared, wanting that which could not be had. He would murmur 'azadeh'—azadeh means 'born free' in Farsi though it is also a woman's name. Sometimes he would mutter a name like 'Erri' or 'Ekki' or 'Kookri,' and then again 'azadeh.' His spirit was at peace but not quite though he never wept like some do, or cry out, nearing the threshold."

"Was there anything more—anything?"

She toyed with the watch she wore on her lapel. "From time to time his wrists seemed to bother him and when I stroked them he became calm again. In the night he spoke a tongue I have never heard before. I speak English, a little French, and many dialects of Arabic, many. But this tongue I have never heard before. He spoke it in a lilting way, mixed with wanderings and 'azadeh,' sometimes words like . . ." She searched her memory. "Like 'regiment' and 'edelweiss' and 'highlands' or 'high land,' and sometimes, ah, yes, words like 'gueng' and 'tens'ng,' sometimes a name like 'Roses' or 'Rose mountain'—perhaps it was not a name but just a place but it seemed to sadden him." Her old eyes were rheumy. "I've seen much of death, Effendi, very much, always different, always the same. But his passing was peaceful and his going over the threshold without hurt. The last moment was just a great sigh—I think he went to Paradise, if Christians go to Paradise, and found his Azadeh . . ."

CHAPTER 65

TABRIZ—AT THE KHAN'S PALACE: 3:40 P.M. Azadeh walked slowly along the corridor toward the Great Room where she was meeting her brother, her back still troubling her from the grenade explosion yesterday. God in heaven, was it only yesterday that the tribesmen and Erikki almost killed us? she thought. It seems more like a thousand days, and a light-year since Father died.

It was another lifetime. Nothing good in that lifetime except Mother and Erikki and Hakim, Erikki and . . . and Johnny. A lifetime of hatreds and killings and terrors and madness, madness living like pariahs, Hakim and I, surrounded by evil, madness at the Qazvin roadblock and that vile, fat-faced mujhadin squashed against the car, oozing like a swatted fly, madness of our rescue by Charlie and the KGB man—what was his name, ah yes, Rakoczy —Rakoczy almost killing all of us, madness at Abu Mard that has changed my life forever, madness at the base where we'd had so many fine times, Erikki and I, but where Johnny killed so many so fast and so cruelly.

She had told Erikki everything last night—almost everything. "At the base he . . . he became a killing animal. I don't remember much, just flashes, giving him the grenade in the village, watching him rush the base . . . grenades and machine guns, one of the men wearing a kookri, then Johnny holding up his severed head and howling like a banshee . . . I know now the kookri was Gueng's. Johnny told me in Tehran."

"Don't say any more now. Leave it until tomorrow, leave the rest until tomorrow, my darling. Go to sleep, you're safe now."

"No. I'm afraid to sleep, even now in your arms, even with all the glorious news about Hakim, when I sleep I'm back in the village, back at Abu Mard and the mullah's there, cursed of God, the kalandar's there and butcher's got his carving knife."

"There's no more village or mullah, I've been there. No more kalandar, nor butcher. Ahmed told me about the village, part of what had happened there."

"You went to the village?"

"Yes, this afternoon, when you were resting. I took a car and went there. It's a heap of burned rubble. Just as well," Erikki had said ominously.

In the corridor Azadeh stopped a moment and held on to the wall until the fit of trembling passed. So much death and killing and horror. Yesterday when she had come out onto the steps of the palace and had seen Erikki in the cockpit, blood streaming down his face and into his stubbled beard, more dripping from his sleeve, Ahmed crumpled beside him, she had died and then, seeing him get out and stand tall and walk to her, her own legs useless, and catch her up into his arms, she had come to life again, all her terrors had poured out with her tears. "Oh, Erikki, oh, Erikki, I've been so afraid, so afraid . . ."

He had carried her into the Great Room and the doctor was there with Hakim, Robert Armstrong and Colonel Hashemi Fazir. A bullet had torn away part of Erikki's left ear, another had scored his forearm. The doctor had cauterized the wounds and bound them up, injecting him with antitetanus serum and penicillin, more afraid of infection than of loss of blood: "Insha'Allah, but there's not much I can do, Captain, you're strong, your pulse is good, a plastic surgeon can make your ear look better, your hearing's not touched, praised be to God! Just beware of infection . . ."

"What happened, Erikki?" Hakim had asked.

"I flew them north into the mountains and Ahmed was careless—it wasn't his fault, he got airsick—and before we knew what was happening Bayazid had a gun to his head, another tribesman had one to mine and Bayazid said, 'Fly to the village, then you can leave.'

" 'You swore a holy oath you wouldn't harm me!' I said.

" 'I swore I wouldn't harm you and I won't, but my oath was mine, not of my men,' Bayazid said, and the man with a gun to my head laughed and shouted, 'Obey our Sheik or by God you will be so filled with pain you will beg for death.' "

"I should have thought of that," Hakim said with a curse. "I should have bound them all with the oath. I should have thought of that."

"It wouldn't have made any difference. Anyway it was all my fault; I'd brought them here and almost ruined everything. I can't tell you how sorry I am but it was the only way to get back and I thought I'd find Abdollah Khan, I never thought that *matyeryebyets* Bayazid would use a grenade."

"We're not hurt, through God's will, Azadeh and I. How could you know Abdollah Khan was dead, or that half your ransom was paid? Go on with what happened," Hakim had said and Azadeh noticed a strangeness under the voice. Hakim's changed, she thought. I can't understand what's in his mind like I used to. Before he became Khan, really Khan, I could but not now. He's still my darling brother but a stranger. So much has changed, so fast. I've changed. So has Erikki, my God how much! Johnny hasn't changed. . . .

In the Great Room, Erikki had continued: "Flying them away was the only way to get them out of the palace without further trouble or killing. If Bayazid hadn't insisted, I would have offered—no other way'd've been safe for you and Azadeh. I had to gamble that somehow they'd obey the oath. But whatever happened, it was them or me, I knew it and so did they, for of course I was the only one who knew who they were and where they lived and a Khan's vengeance is serious. Whatever I did, drop them off halfway or go to the village, they'd never let me go. How could they—it was the village or me and their One God would vote for their village along with them, whatever they'd agreed or sworn!"

"That's a question only God could answer."

"My gods, the ancient gods, don't like to be used as an excuse, and they don't like this swearing in their name. They disapprove of it greatly, in fact they forbid it." Azadeh heard the bitterness and touched him gently. He had held her hand. "I'm fine now, Azadeh."

"What happened next, Erikki?" Hakim asked.

"I told Bayazid there wasn't enough gasoline and tried to reason with him and he just said, 'As God wants,' stuck the gun into Ahmed's shoulder and pulled the trigger. 'Go to the village! The next bullet goes into his stomach.' Ahmed passed out and Bayazid reached over him for the Sten gun that had slipped to the floor of the cockpit, half under the seat, but he couldn't quite get it. I was strapped in, so was Ahmed, they weren't, so I shifted her around the skies in ways I didn't think a chopper could stand, then let her drop out and made a landing. It was a bad one; I thought I'd broken a skid but later I found it was only bent. As soon as we'd stopped I used the Sten and my knife and killed those who were conscious and hostile, disarmed the unconscious ones, and dumped them out of the cabin. Then, after a time, I came back."

"Just like that," Armstrong had said. "Fourteen men."

"Five, and Bayazid. The others . . ." Azadeh had her arm on his shoulder and she felt the shrug and the following tremor. "I left them."

"Where?" Hashemi Fazir had said. "Could you describe where, Captain?" Erikki had done so, accurately, and the colonel had sent men to find them.

Erikki put his good hand into his pocket and brought out the ransom jewels and gave them to Hakim Khan. "Now I think I would like to talk to my wife, if it pleases you. I'll tell you the rest later." Then she and he had gone to their own rooms and he said nothing more, just held her gently in his great embrace. Her presence soothed away his anguish. Soon to sleep. She slept barely at all, at once back in the village to tear herself in panic from its suffocating grasp. She had stayed quiet for a time in his arms, then moved to a chair and half dozed, content to be with him. He had slept dreamlessly until it was dark, then awoke.

"First a bath and then a shave and then some vodka and then we will talk," he had said, "I've never seen you more beautiful nor loved you more and I'm sorry, sorry I was jealous—no, Azadeh, don't say anything yet. Then I want to know everything."

In the dawn she had finished telling all there was to tell—as much as she would ever tell—and he his story. He had hidden nothing, not his jealousy, or the killing rage and the joy of battle or the tears he had shed on the mountainside, seeing the savagery of the mayhem he had dealt to the tribesmen. "They . . . they did treat me fairly in their village . . . and ransom is an ancient custom. If it hadn't been for Abdollah murdering their messenger . . . that might have made the difference, perhaps, perhaps not. But that doesn't forgive the killings. I feel I'm a monster, you married a madman, Azadeh. I'm dangerous."

"No, no, you're not, of course you're not."

"By all my gods, I've killed twenty or more men in half that number of days and yet I've never killed before except those assassins, those men who charged in here to murder your father before we were married. Outside of Iran I've never killed anyone, never hurt anyone—I've had plenty of fights with or without pukoh but never serious. Never. If that kalandar and the village had existed, I would have burned him and them without a second thought. I can understand your Johnny at the base; I thank all gods for bringing him to us to protect you and curse him for taking away my peace though I know I'm in his immortal debt. I can't deal with the killings and I can't deal with him. I can't, I can't, not yet."

"It doesn't matter, not now, Erikki. Now we've time. Now we're safe, you're safe and I'm safe and Hakim's safe, we're safe, my darling. Look at the dawn, isn't it beautiful? Look, Erikki, it's a new day now, so beautiful, a new life. We're safe, Erikki."

IN THE GREAT ROOM: 3:45 P.M. Hakim Khan was alone except for Hashemi Fazir. Half an hour ago Hashemi had arrived unbidden. He had apologized for the intrusion, handing him a telex. "I thought you'd better see this at once, Highness."

The telex read: "URGENT. To Colonel Fazir, Inner Intelligence, Tabriz: Arrest Erikki Yokkonen, husband of Her Highness, Azadeh Gorgon, for crimes committed against the State, for complicity in air piracy, hijacking, and high treason. Put him in chains and send him at once to my Headquarters here. Director, SAVAMA, Tehran."

Hakim Khan dismissed his guards. "I don't understand, Colonel. Please explain."

"The moment I'd decoded it, I phoned for further details, Highness. It seems last year S-G Helicopters sold a number of helicopters to IHC an—"

"I don't understand."

"Sorry, to Iran Helicopter Company, an Iranian company, Captain Yokkonen's present employer. Among them were—are—ten 212s including his. Today the other nine, valued at perhaps $9 million, were stolen and illegally flown out of Iran by IHC pilots—SAVAMA presumes to one of the Gulf states."

Hakim Khan said coldly, "Even if they have, this doesn't affect Erikki. He's done nothing wrong."

"We don't know that for certain, Highness. SAVAMA says perhaps he knew of the conspiracy—it certainly had to have been planned for some time because three bases are involved—Lengeh, Bandar Delam, and Kowiss —as well as their Tehran Head Office. SAVAMA are very, very agitated because it's also been reported that vast quantities of valuable Iranian spares have been whisked away. No mo—"

"Reported by whom?"

"The IHC managing director, Siamaki. Even more serious, all IHC foreign personnel, pilots and mechanics and office staff, have vanished as well. Everyone, so of course it was a conspiracy. It seems that yesterday there were perhaps twenty of them all over Iran, last week forty, today none. There are no S-G, or more correctly IHC foreigners left in all Iran. Except Captain Yokkonen."

At once the implication of Erikki's importance leaped into Hakim's mind and he cursed himself for allowing his face to give him away when Hashemi said blithely, "Ah, yes, of course you see it too! SAVAMA told me that even if the captain is innocent of complicity in the conspiracy, he's the essential means to persuade the ringleaders and criminals, Gavallan and McIver— and certainly the British government which must have been party to the treason—to return our airplanes, our spares, to pay an indemnity of very serious proportions, to return to Iran and stand trial for crimes against Islam."

Hakim Khan shifted uneasily on his cushions, the pain in his back surfacing, and wanted to shout with rage because all the pain and anguish had been unnecessary, and now, hardly able to stand without pain, he might be permanently injured. Put that aside for later, he told himself grimly, and deal with this dangerous son of a dog who sits there patiently like an accomplished salesman of precious carpets who has laid out his wares and now waits for the negotiation to begin. If I want to buy.

To buy Erikki out of the trap I shall have to give this dog a personal pishkesh, of value to him not SAVAMA, God curse them by any name. What? Petr Oleg Mzytryk at least. I could pass him over to Hashemi without a belch, if he comes, when he comes. He'll come. Yesterday Ahmed sent for him in my name—I wonder how Ahmed is, did his operation go well? I hope the fool doesn't die; I could use his knowledge for a while more. Fool to be caught off guard, fool! Yes he's a fool but this dog isn't. With the gift of Mzytryk and more help in Azerbaijan, and a promise of future friendship, I can buy Erikki out of the trap. Why should I?

Because Azadeh loves him? Unfortunately she is sister to the Khan of all the Gorgons and this is a khan's problem, not a brother's problem.

Erikki's a hazard to me and to her. He's a dangerous man with blood on his hands. The tribesmen, be they Kurds or not, will seek vengeance—probably. He's always been a bad match though he brought her great joy, still brings her happiness—but no children—and now he cannot stay in Iran. Impossible. No way for him to stay. I couldn't buy him two years of protection and Azadeh's sworn by God to stay here at least two years—how cunning my father was to give me power over her. If I buy Erikki out of the trap she can't go with him. In two years many estrangements could happen by themselves. But if he's no good for her, why buy him out? Why not let them take Erikki to checkmate a treason? It's treason to steal our property.

"This is too serious a matter to answer at once," he said.

"There is nothing for you to answer, Highness. Only Captain Yokkonen. I understand he's still here."

"The doctor ordered him to rest."

"Perhaps you would send for him, Highness."

"Of course. But a man of your importance and learning would understand there are rules of honor and hospitality in Azerbaijan, and in my tribe. He is my brother-in-law and even SAVAMA understands family honor." Both men knew this was just an opening gambit in a delicate negotiation—delicate because neither wanted SAVAMA's wrath on their heads, neither knew yet how far to go, or even if a private deal was wanted. "I presume many know of this . . . this treason?"

"Only me, here in Tabriz, Highness. At the moment," Hashemi said at once, conveniently forgetting Armstrong to whom he had suggested this phony telex this morning: "There's no way that son of a dog, Hakim, can expose it as a hoax, Robert," he had said, delighted with his own brilliance. "He's got to barter. We barter the Finn for Mzytryk at no cost to ourselves. That bloodthirsty maniac Finn can fly off into the sunset when we get what we want—until then we bottle him up."

"Say Hakim Khan won't agree, won't or can't deliver Mzytryk?"

"If he doesn't want to barter, we seize Erikki anyway. Whirlwind's bound to leak soon and I can use Erikki for all sorts of concessions—he's hostage at least for $15 million worth of planes . . . or perhaps I barter him to the tribesmen as a peace offering . . . The fact that he's a Finn helps. I could link him closely with Rakoczy and the KGB and cause the Soviets all sorts of mischief, equally the CIA, eh? Even MI6, eh?"

"The CIA've never harmed you. Or MI6."

"Insha'Allah! Don't interfere in this, Robert. Erikki and the Khan are an internal Iranian matter. On your own head, don't interfere. With the Finn I can get important concessions." But important only to me, Robert, not to SAVAMA, Hashemi had thought and smiled to himself. Tomorrow or the next day we will return to Tehran and then my assassin follows you into the night and then, poof, you're blown out like a candle. "He'll deliver him," he had said calmly.

"If Hakim gives up Erikki, he'll get hell and damnation and no peace from his beloved sister. I think she'd go to the stake for him."

"She may have to."

Hashemi remembered the glow of joy he had felt and now it was even better. He could see Hakim Khan's disquiet and was sure he had him trapped. "I'm sure you'll understand, Highness, but I have to answer this telex quickly."

Hakim Khan decided on a partial offer. "Treason and conspiracy should not go unpunished. Anywhere it is to be found. I've sent for the traitor you wanted. Urgently."

"Ah. How long will it take for Mzytryk to answer?"

"You'd have a better idea of that than me. Wouldn't you?"

Hashemi heard the flatness and cursed himself for making the slip. "I would be astonished if Your Highness wasn't answered very quickly," he said with great politeness. "Very quickly."

"When?"

"Within twenty-four hours, Highness. Personally or by messenger." He saw the young Khan shift painfully and tried to decide whether to delay or to press home his advantage, sure the pain was genuine. The doctor had given him a detailed diagnosis of the Khan's possible injuries and those of his sister. To cover every eventuality he had ordered the doctor to give Erikki some heavy sedation tonight, just in case the man tried to escape.

"The twenty-four hours will be up at seven this evening, Colonel."

"There is so much to do in Tabriz, Highness, following your advice of this morning, that I doubt if I could deal with the telex before then."

"You destroy the leftist mujhadin headquarters tonight?"

"Yes, Highness," now that we have your permission, and your guarantee of no repercussions from the Tudeh, Hashemi wanted to add but did not. Don't be stupid! This young man's not as three-faced as the dog Abdollah, may he burn in hell. This one's easier to deal with—providing you have more cards than he has and are not afraid to show your fangs when needed. "It would be unfortunate if the captain was not available for . . . for questioning this evening."

Hakim Khan's eyes narrowed at the unnecessary threat. As if I didn't understand, you rude son of a dog. "I agree." There was a knock on the door. "Come in."

Azadeh opened it. "Sorry to interrupt, Highness, but you told me to remind you half an hour before it was time to go to the hospital for X rays. Greetings, peace be with you, Colonel."

"And God's peace be with you, Highness." I'm glad such beauty will be forced into chador soon, Hashemi was thinking. She'd tempt Satan, let alone the unwashed illiterate scum of Iran. He looked back at the Khan. "I should be going, Highness."

"Please come back at seven, Colonel. If I've any news before then I'll send for you."

"Thank you, Highness."

She closed the door after him. "How're you feeling, Hakim, darling?"

"Tired. Lots of pain."

"Me too. Do you have to see the colonel later?"

"Yes. It doesn't matter. How's Erikki?"

"Asleep." She was joyous. "We're so lucky, the three of us."

IN TABRIZ CITY: 4:06 P.M.   Robert Armstrong checked the action of the small automatic, his face grim. "What're you going to do?" Henley asked, not liking the gun at all. He was also English, but much smaller, with a wispy mustache, and he wore glasses and sat behind the desk in the untidy, grubby office, under a picture of Queen Elizabeth.

"Best you don't ask that. But don't worry, I'm a copper, remember? This's just in case some villain tries to do me. Can you get the message to Yokkonen?"

"I can't go to the palace uninvited, what the hell'd be my excuse?" Henley's eyebrows soared. "Do I say to Hakim Khan, 'Terribly sorry, old boy, but I want to speak to your brother-in-law about getting a chum out of Iran by private helicopter.' " His banter vanished. "You're quite wrong about the colonel, Robert. There's no proof whatsoever the colonel's responsible for Talbot."

"If you had you wouldn't admit it," Armstrong said, angry with himself for exploding when Henley had told him about the "accident." Again his voice rasped. "Why the devil did you wait till today to tell me Talbot was blown up? For God's sake it happened two days ago!"

"I don't decide policy, I just carry messages and anyway we've just heard. Besides, you've been difficult to track down. Everyone thought you'd left, last seen boarding a British aircraft bound for Al Shargaz. Damn it, you've been ordered out for almost a week and you're still here, not on any assignment I know of, and whatever you've decided to do, don't, except kindly remove yourself from Iran because if you're caught and they get you to the third level, a lot of people are going to be very bloody peed off."

"I'll try not to disappoint them." Armstrong got up and put on his old raincoat with the fur collar. "See you soon."

"When?"

"When I bloody choose." Armstrong's face tightened. "I'm not under your authority and what I do and when I come and go is not up to you. Just see my report's kept in the safe until you've a diplomatic bag to pass it urgently to London, and keep your bloody mouth shut."

"You're not usually so rude, or so touchy. What the hell's up, Robert?"

Armstrong stalked out and down the steps and out into the cold of the day. It was overcast and promised to snow again. He went down the crowded street. Passersby and street merchants pretended not to notice him, presumed he was Soviet, and cautiously went about their own business. Though he was watching to see if he was being followed, his mind was sifting ways and means to deal with Hashemi. No time to consult his superiors, and no real wish to. They would have shaken their heads: "Good God, our old friend Hashemi? Send him onwards on suspicion he levitated Talbot? First we'd need proof . . ."

But there'll never be any proof and they won't believe about Group Four teams or about Hashemi fancying himself as a modern Hasan ibn al-Sabbah. But I know. Wasn't Hashemi bursting with happiness about assassinating General Janan? Now he's got bigger fish to skewer. Like Pahmudi. Or the whole Rev Komiteh, whoever they are—I wonder if he's pegged them yet? I wonder if he'd go for the Imam himself? No telling. But one way or another he'll pay for old Talbot—after we've got Petr Oleg Mzytryk. Without Hashemi I've no chance of getting him, and through him the sodding traitors we all know are operating up top in Whitehall, Philby's bosses, the fourth, fifth, and sixth man—in the Cabinet, MI5, or MI6. Or all three.

His rage was all possessive, making his head ache. So many good men betrayed. The touch of his automatic pleased him. First Mzytryk, he thought, then Hashemi. All that's left to decide is when and where.

BAHRAIN—AT THE INTERNATIONAL AIRPORT: 4:24 P.M.
Jean-Luc was on the phone in Mathias's office. ". . . No, Andy, we've
nothing either." He glanced at Mathias who listened, and gravely made a
thumbs-down to him.

"Charlie's beside himself," Gavallan was saying. "I just got off the phone
to him. Damn shame but nothing we can do but wait. Same with Dubois
and Fowler." Jean-Luc could hear the great weariness in Gavallan's voice.

"Dubois will turn up—after all he's French. By the way I told Charlie if
. . . when," he corrected himself hastily, "when Tom Lochart and Freddy
Ayre land, to tell them to refuel at Jellet and not come here, unless there's
an emergency. Mathias put the spare fuel on Jellet himself so we know it's
there. Andy, you'd better call Charlie and add your authority because
Bahrain could be difficult, I don't want to risk another confrontation—their
warning was clear whether we're flying on British registry or not. I still
don't know how we squeaked Rudi, Sandor, and Pop through. I'm certain
they'll impound any Iran registers, and the crews—and next time they'll
check the paint and papers."

"All right, I'll tell him at once. Jean-Luc, there's no reason for you to
come back to Al Shargaz; why not go direct to London tomorrow, then up
to Aberdeen? I'm posting you to the North Sea until we get sorted out, all
right?"

"Good idea. I'll report in Aberdeen on Monday," Jean-Luc said quickly,
stealing a free weekend. *Mon Dieu,* I've earned it, he thought, and changed
the subject to give Gavallan no time to argue. "Has Rudi arrived yet?"

"Yes, safe and sound. All three of them're bedded down. So're Vossi and
Willi too. Scrag's fine. Erikki's out of danger, Duke's mending slowly but
surely . . . if it wasn't for Dubois and Fowler, Mac, Tom and their lot
. . . Hallelujah! I've got to go, 'bye."

"Au revoir." Then to Mathias, *"Merde,* I'm posted to the North Sea."

"Merde."

"What's Alitalia's extension?"

"It's 22134. Why?"

"If I have to invoke the pope himself, I'm on the early flight to Rome
tomorrow with the connection to Nice—I need Marie-Christene, the kids,
and some decent food. *Espèce de con* on the North Sea!" Worriedly he
looked at the clock. *"Espèce de con* on this waiting! Where're our Kowiss
birds, eh?"

KUWAIT—OFFSHORE: 4:31 P.M. The red fuel-warning light came on. McIver and Wazari saw it instantly and both cursed. "How much we got left, Captain?"

"With this bloody wind, not much." They were just ten feet off the waves.

"How far we got to go?"

"Not far." McIver was exhausted and feeling terrible. The wind had freshened to nearly thirty-five knots, and he had been nursing the 212, trying to eke out their fuel, but there was not much he could do at this low level. Visibility was still poor, the overcast thinning rapidly as they neared the coast. He looked out of his window across at Ayre, pointed at his instrument panel, and gave a thumbs-down. Ayre nodded. His warning light had not yet come on. Now it did.

"Bloody hell," Kyle, Ayre's mechanic said. "We'll be in the open in a few minutes and sitting bloody ducks."

"Not to worry. If Mac doesn't call Kuwait soon, I'm going to." Ayre peered upward, thought he glimpsed the fighters above them, but it was just two seabirds. "Christ, for a moment . . ."

"Those bastards wouldn't dare follow us this far, would they?"

"I don't know." Since leaving the coast they had been playing hide-and-seek with the two jet fighters. Abeam Kharg, happily sneaking past in the rain and haze, not varying their height over the waves, he and McIver had been spotted: "This is Kharg radar control: choppers illegally outward bound on heading 275 degrees, climb to one thousand and hold—climb to one thousand and hold."

For a moment they were in shock, then McIver waved Ayre to follow him, turned 90 degrees due north away from Kharg, and went even lower to the sea. In a few minutes his earphones were filled with the Farsi from the fighters to air force control and back again. "They're being given our coordinates, Captain," Wazari gasped. "Orders to arm their rockets . . . now they're reporting they're armed . . .

"This is Kharg! Choppers illegally on course 270, climb to one thousand and hold. If you do not obey you will be intercepted and shot down; I repeat you will be intercepted and shot down."

McIver took his hand off the collective to rub his chest, the pain returning, then doggedly held the course as Wazari gave him snatches of what was being said, ". . . the leader's saying follow me down . . . now the wingman says all rockets armed . . . how're we going to find them in this shit . . . I'm slowing down . . . we don't want to miss them . . . Ground controller says, 'Confirm rockets armed, confirm kill . . .' Jesus, they're confirming rockets armed and on collision course with us."

Then the two jet fighters had come hurtling at them from out of the murk ahead but to the right and fifty feet above them and then they were past and vanished. "Christ, did they see us?"

"Jesus, Captain, I don't know but those bastards carry heat seekers."

McIver's heart was racing as he motioned to Ayre and went into hover, just above the waves, to throw the hunters off. "Tell me what they're saying, Wazari, for Christ's sake!"

"Pilots're cursing . . . reporting they're at two thousand, two hundred knots . . . one's saying there're no holes in the soup and the ceiling's around four hundred . . . difficult to see the surface . . . Controller's saying go ahead to international line and get between it and the pirates. . . . Jesus, pirates? Get between them and Kuwait . . . see if the cloud cover's any thinner . . . stay in ambush at two thousand . . ."

What to do? McIver was asking himself. We could bypass Kuwait and head direct Jellet. No good—with this wind we'd never make it. Can't turn back. So it's Kuwait and hope we can slither past them.

At the international line the clouds were just enough to hide them. But the fighters were lurking somewhere there in a holding pattern, waiting for a window, or for the clouds to thin, or for their prey to presume they were safe and climb up into regulation and approach height. For a quarter of an hour the military channel had been silent. They could hear Kuwait controllers now.

"I'm going to cut one engine to save gas," McIver said.

"You want me to call Kuwait, Skipper?"

"No, I'll do that. In a minute. You'd better go back into the cabin and prepare to hide. See if you can find some sea overalls, there're some in the locker. Use a sea safety coverall. Dump your uniform over the side and have a Mae West handy."

Wazari blanched. "We're going into the sea?"

"No. Just camouflage, in case we're inspected," McIver lied, not expecting to make the coast. His voice was calm and his head was calm though his limbs were leaden.

"What's the plan when we land, Skipper?"

"We'll have to play that as it happens. Do you have any papers?"

"Only my operator licenses, American and Iranian. Both say I'm Iran Air Force."

"Stay undercover, I don't know what's going to happen . . . but we'll hope."

"Skipper, we should climb out of this crap, no need to press our luck," Wazari said. "We're over the line, safe now."

McIver looked aloft. The cloud and haze cover was thinning very fast, now hardly any cover for them at all. The red warning light seemed to fill his horizon. Better climb, eh? Wazari's right, no need to press our luck, he thought. "We're only safe when we're on the ground," he said out loud. "You know that."

KUWAIT AIRPORT TOWER: 4:38 P.M.   The big room was fully staffed. Some British controllers, some Kuwaiti. The best modern equipment. Telex and phones and efficiency. The door opened and Charlie Pettikin came in. "You wanted me, sir?" he said anxiously to the duty controller, a rotund, florid-faced Irishman wearing a headset with a thin-tubed boom mike and single tiny earpiece.

"Yes, yes indeed I did, Captain Pettikin," the man said curtly, and at once Pettikin's anxiety increased. "My name's Sweeney, look!" He used his grease pencil as a pointer. On the outer periphery of his screen at the twenty-mile line was a small blip of light. "That's a chopper, possibly two. He, or they have just appeared, haven't reported in yet. 'Tis yourself who's expecting two inbounds, so I'm told, in transit from the UK, is that it now?"

"Yes," Pettikin said, wanting to cheer that, at long last, one or both were in the system—they had to be from Kowiss on such a course—at the same time achingly aware they were a long way yet from being safe. "That's correct," he said with a prayer.

"Perhaps they're not yours at all for, glory be, that's the deevil of a curious course to use, approaching from the east, if he or they're transiting from the UK." Pettikin said nothing under Sweeney's scrutiny. "Supposing he or they belong to yourself, now what would their call signs be?"

Pettikin's discomfort increased. If he gave the new British ones and the choppers reported in on their Iran registrations—as they were legally bound to do—they were all in trouble. The actual call letters had to be seen from the tower when the choppers came in to land—no way that controllers would not see them. But if he gave Sweeney the Iranian registrations . . . that would blow Whirlwind. The bastard's trying to trap you, he thought, a great emptiness inside him. "I'm sorry," he said lamely. "I don't know. Our paperwork's not the best. Sorry."

The phone on the desk purred softly. Sweeney picked it up. "Ah yes, yes, Commander? . . . Yes . . . no, not at the moment . . . we think it's two . . . yes, yes, I agree . . . no, it's fine now. It goes out from time to time . . . yes, very well." He hung up, once more concentrating on the screen.

Uneasily Pettikin looked at the screen again. The all-important blip did not seem to be moving.

Then Sweeney switched to maximum range and the screen picture reached out far into the Gulf, westward the few miles to the Kuwaiti border with Iraq, northwest to the Iraq–Iran border, both so very close. "Our long range's been out for a while or we'd've seen them sooner, now she's fine, glory be to God. Lots of fighter bases there," he said absently, his grease pencil indicating the Iran side of the Shatt-al-Arab border waterway toward Abadan. Then the pencil moved out into the Gulf on a line from Kowiss to Kuwait and poised over a blip. "These're your choppers, if there are two— and if they belong to yourself." The point moved north a little to two other rapidly moving dots. "Fighters. Not ours. But in our area." He looked up and Pettikin was chilled. "Unbidden and not cleared, so hostiles."

"What're they doing?" he asked, sure now he was being toyed with.

"That's what we'd all like to know, indeed we would." Sweeney's voice was not friendly. With his grease pencil he indicated two other blips, outward bound from the Kuwaiti military strip. "They're ours, going to have a look." He handed Pettikin a spare earpiece, clicked on his sender. "This is Kuwait: inbound chopper or choppers heading 274 degrees, what is your call sign and altitude?"

Static. The call repeated patiently. Then Pettikin recognized McIver's voice. "Kuwait this is chopper . . . this is chopper Boston Tango with chopper Hotel Echo in transit for Al Shargaz, going through six hundred for seven hundred." McIver had given only the last two letters of the Iranian registration, instead of all the letters required on the initial call, including the prefix EP for Iran.

Astonishingly Sweeney accepted the call: "Choppers Boston Tango and Hotel Echo report at outer marker," he said, and Pettikin saw that he was distracted, concentrating on the two hostile blips that were now closing on the choppers fast, tracking them with his pencil on the glass. "They're flat out," he muttered. "Ten miles eastern."

McIver's voice in their earphones: "Kuwait, please confirm outer marker. Request straight in, we're low on fuel."

"Straight in approved, report outer marker."

Pettikin heard the inflexibility and suppressed a groan. Sweeney began humming. The senior controller, a Kuwaiti, quietly got up from his desk and came over to stand behind them.

They watched the circling trace leaving a picture of the land and the blips of light in its wake, seeing them not as blips but as two hostile fighters and two far slower Kuwaiti interceptors still far away, two choppers helpless between them. Closer. The hostiles were almost merged with the choppers now, then they moved off and away, heading eastward back across the Gulf. For a moment all three men held their breath. Rockets took time to reach their targets. Seconds passed. Chopper blips remained. Kuwaiti interceptor blips remained, closing on the choppers, then they too turned back for home. Momentarily Sweeney switched into their channel and listened to the Arabic. He glanced up at the senior controller and spoke to him in Arabic. The man said, "Insha'Allah," nodded briefly at Pettikin, and went out of the room.

"Our interceptors reported seeing nothing," Sweeney said to Pettikin, his voice flat. "Except two choppers. 212s. They saw nothing." He went back into the regular band, airplanes reporting in and being channeled for takeoff and landing, then he switched the radar to closer range. Now the choppers were separated into two blips, still well out to sea. Their approach seemed interminably slow against the tracks of incoming and outgoing jets.

McIver's voice cut through the other voices, "Pan-pan-pan! Kuwait, this is chopper BT and HE, pan pan pan, both our warning lights are on, gauges empty, pan pan pan." The emergency call, one step below Mayday.

Sweeney said, "Permission to land on Messali Beach helipad directly ahead, near the hotel—we'll alert them and send you fuel. Do you copy?"

"Roger, Kuwait, thank you. I know the hotel. Please inform Captain Pettikin."

"Wilco, at once." Sweeney phoned and put their air-sea rescue helicopter on standby, ready for instant takeoff, sent a fire truck to the hotel, then held out his hand for Pettikin's earpiece, glanced at the door, and beckoned him closer. "Now listen to me," he hissed, keeping his voice down. " 'Tis yourself who'll meet them and refuel them, clear them through Customs and Immigration—if you can—and get them the deevil out of Kuwait within minutes or yourself and they and your high and mighty 'important' friends will all be in jail and good riddance! Holy Mother of God, how dare you jeopardize Kuwait with your madcap adventures against those trigger-happy Iran fanatics and make honest men risk their jobs for the likes of you. If one of your choppers was shot down . . . it was only the luck of the deevil himself stopped an international incident." He reached into his pocket and shoved a piece of paper into Pettikin's hand who was stunned by the venom and suddenness. "Read it, then flush it."

Sweeney turned his back and got on the phone again. Weakly, Pettikin went out. When it was safe he glanced at the paper. It was a telex. The telex. From Tehran. Not a photocopy. The original.

Christ Almighty! Did Sweeney intercept it and cover for us? But didn't he say, "clear them through Customs and Immigration—if you can"?

MESSALI BEACH HOTEL: The small fuel truck with Genny and Pettikin aboard swung off the coast road and into the vast hotel gardens, sprinklers going. The helipad was well west of the huge parking lot area. A fire truck already there and waiting. Genny and Pettikin jumped out, Pettikin with a shortwave walkie-talkie, both of them searching the haze out to sea. "Mac, do you read?"

They could hear the engines but not see them yet, then: "Two by five, Charlie . . ." much static . . . "but I . . . Freddy, you take the helipad, I'll go alongside." More static.

"There they are!" Genny cried. The 212s came out of the haze about six hundred feet. Oh, God, help them in . . .

"We have you in sight, Mac, fire trucks standing by, no problem." But Pettikin knew they were in deep trouble, no possibility of changing the lettering with so many people watching. One engine missed and coughed but they did not know which chopper. Another cough.

Ayre's voice, too dry, said, "Stand by below, I'm coming into the helipad."

They saw the left 212 detach slightly and start losing altitude, reaching for distance, engine spluttering. The fire fighters readied. McIver doggedly held course, maintaining altitude to give himself the best chance if his own engines cut.

"Shit," Pettikin muttered involuntarily, seeing Ayre coming in fast, too fast, but then he flared maximum and set her down in dead center, safe, McIver into emergency approach now—for Christ's sake, why's he flying alone and where the hell's Tom Lochart—committed now, no room to maneuver, no one breathing, and then the skids touched and at that moment the engines died.

Fire fighters, in radio contact with the airfield, reported, "Emergency over," began packing their gear, and now Pettikin was pummeling McIver's hand and he rushed over to Ayre to do the same. Genny stood beside McIver's open cockpit door, beaming at him.

"Hello, Duncan," Genny said, holding her hair out of her eyes. "Good trip?"

"Worst I've ever had, Gen," he said trying to smile, not quite with it yet. "In fact I never want to fly again, not fly myself, so help me! I'm still going to check Scrag—but only once a year!"

She laughed and gave him an awkward hug and would have released him but he held on to her, loving her—so relieved to see her and to be on ground again, his passenger safe, his bird safe, that he felt like crying. "You all right, luvey?"

That made her tears flow. He had not called her that for months, perhaps years. She hugged him even tighter. "Now look what you've made me do." She found her handkerchief, let him go, then gave him a little kiss. "You deserve a whisky and soda. Two large ones!" For the first time she noticed his pallor. "You all right, luv?"

"Yes. Yes, I think so. I'm a bit shook." McIver looked over her to Pettikin who was laughing and talking excitedly with Ayre, the truck driver already pumping fuel into the tanks. Beyond them an official-looking car was pulling in from the road. "What about the others, what's happened?"

"Everyone's safe—except Marc Dubois and Fowler Joines. They're still missing." She told him what she knew about Starke and Gavallan and Scragger, Rudi and his men. "One fantastic piece of news is that Newbury, he's a consulate man in Al Shargaz, got a message from Tabriz that Erikki and Azadeh are safe at her father's place but her father's dead, it seems, and now her brother's Khan."

"My God, that's wonderful! Then we've done it, Gen!"

"Yes, yes, we have—damn this wind." She pushed a strand of hair out of her eyes. "And Andy and Charlie and the others think Dubois has a good ch—" She stopped, her happiness evaporating, suddenly realizing what was wrong. She whirled and looked at the other 212. "Tom? Where's Tom Lochart?"

SOUTH OF TEHRAN: 5:10 P.M. The deserted oil well was in desolate hills about a hundred miles from Tehran. Lochart knew it from the old days, his 206 was parked beside the fuel pump and he had refueled manually, almost finished now.

It was a way station for helicopters serving this area, part of the great northern pipeline that, in normal times, housed an Iranian maintenance crew. In a rough hut were a few spare bunks for overnighting if you were caught in one of the sudden storms endemic here. The original British owners of the site had called it "D'Arcy 1908" to commemorate the Englishman by that name who had first discovered oil in Iran in that year. Now it belonged to IranOil but they had kept the name, and kept the fuel tanks topped up.

Thank God for that, Lochart thought again, the pumping tiring him. At the rendezvous on the coast, he had lashed two empty forty-gallon drums on the backseat against the possibility that D'Arcy 1908 would be open, and rigged a temporary pump. There was still enough fuel left at the shore to top up on the way out of Iran, and Sharazad could work the pump in flight. "Now we've a chance," he said out loud, knowing where to land, how to park safely, and how to sneak into Tehran.

He was confident again, making plans and counterplans, what to say to Meshang, what to avoid, what to tell Sharazad and how they would escape. There's got to be a way for her to get her rightful inheritance, enough to give her the security she needs . . .

Gasoline overflowed from the brimful tanks and he swore at his carelessness, capped them carefully, wiped the excess away. Now he was finished, the drums in the backseat already filled and the pump in place.

In one of the huts he had found some cans of corned beef and wolfed one of them—impossible to eat and fly, unless with his left hand, and he had been too long in Iran to do that—then picked up the bottle of beer he had set in the snow to chill, and sipped it sparingly. There was water in a barrel. He broke the ice and splashed water on his face to refresh himself but did not dare to drink it. He dried his face. The stubble of his beard rasped and again he swore, wanting to look his best for her. Then he remembered his flight bag and the razors there. One was battery-operated. He found it. "You can shave at Tehran," he said to his reflection in the cockpit window, anxious to go on.

A last look around. Snow and rocks and not much else. In the far distance was the Qom–Tehran road. Sky overcast but the ceiling high. Some birds circled far overhead. Scavengers. Vultures of some sort, he thought, buckling his seat belt.

TEHRAN—AT THE BAKRAVAN HOUSE: 5:15 P.M. The door in the outer wall opened and two heavily chadored and veiled women came out, Sharazad and Jari unrecognizable. Jari closed the door, hastily waddled after Sharazad, who walked away quickly through the crowds. "Princess, wait . . . there's no hurry . . ."

But Sharazad did not decrease her pace until she had turned the corner. Then she stopped and waited impatiently. "Jari, I'm leaving you now," she said giving her no time to interrupt; "don't go home but meet me at the coffee shop, you know the one, at six-thirty, wait for me if I'm late."

"But, Princess . . ." Jari could hardly talk, "but His Excellency Meshang . . . you told him we're going to the doctor's and there's n—"

"At the coffee shop about six-thirty, six-thirty to seven, Jari!" Sharazad hurried off down the street, cut dangerously into the traffic and across the road to avoid her maid who started to come after her, went into an alley, down another, and soon she was free. "I'm not going to marry that awful man, I'm not I'm not I'm not!" she muttered out loud.

The derision had already begun this afternoon, though it was only at lunch that Meshang had announced the great evil. Her best girlfriend had arrived an hour ago to ask if the rumors were true that Sharazad was going to marry into the Farazan family: "It's all over the bazaar, dearest Sharazad, I came at once to congratulate you."

"My brother has many plans, now that I am to be divorced," she had said carelessly. "I have many suitors."

"Of course, of course, but the rumor is that the Farazan dowry has already been agreed."

"Oh? First I've heard of it, what liars people are!"

"I agree, awful. Other vile rumormongers claim that the marriage is to take place next week and your . . . and the prospective husband is chortling that he outsmarted Meshang on the dowry."

"Someone outsmart Meshang? It has to be a lie!"

"I knew the rumors were false! I knew it! How could you marry old Diarrhea Daranoush, Shah of the Night Soil? How could you?" Her friend had laughed uproariously. "Poor darling, which way would you turn?"

"What does it matter?" Meshang had screeched at her. "They're only jealous! The marriage will take place, and tonight we will entertain him at dinner."

Perhaps I will, perhaps I won't, she thought seething. Perhaps the entertainment will not be what they expect.

Again she checked her directions, knees weak. She was going to *his* friend's apartment, not far away now. There she would find the secret key in the niche downstairs and go in and look under the carpet in the bedroom and take up the board as she had seen him do. Then she would take out the pistol and the grenade—God be thanked for the chador to cover them and keep me hidden—then carefully replace the board and the carpet and come home again. Her excitement was almost choking her now. Ibrahim will be so proud of me, going into battle for God, to be martyred for God. Didn't he go south to be martyred doing battle with evil in just the same way? Of course God will forgive his leftist silliness.

How clever of him to show me how to take off the safety catch and to arm the gun and to hold the grenade, to pull the pin, then throw it at the enemies of Islam, shouting "God is Great, God is Great . . ." then charging them, shooting them, being lifted into Paradise, this evening if I can, tomorrow at the latest, the whole city rife with rumors that leftists at the university have begun their expected insurrection. We will stamp them out, my son and I, we will, Soldiers of God and the Prophet on whose name be praised, we will!

"God is Great. God is Great . . ." Just pull the pin and count to four and throw it, I remember everything he said exactly.

KUWAIT—AT THE MESSALI BEACH HOTEL HELIPAD:
5:35 P.M.   McIver and Pettikin watched the two Immigration and Customs men, the first peering impassively at the airplane papers, the other poking about in the cabin of the 212. So far their inspections had been perfunctory though time-consuming. They had collected all passports and airplane papers, but had just glanced at them and asked McIver his opinion of the current situation in Iran. They had not yet asked directly where the helicopters had come from. Any moment now, McIver and Pettikin thought, waiting queasily.

McIver had considered leaving Wazari in hiding, but had decided against the risk. "Sorry, Sergeant, you'll have to take your chances."

"Who's he?" the Immigration man had asked at once, Wazari's complexion giving him away, and his fear.

"A radio-radar operator," McIver said noncommittally.

The official had turned away and left Wazari standing there, sweating in the heavy, seaproofed plastic coverall, Mae West half done up.

"So, Captain, you think there'll be a coup in Tehran, a military coup?"

"I don't know," McIver had told him. "Rumors abound like locusts. The English papers say it's possible, very possible, and also that Iran's caught up in a kind of madness—like the Terror of the French or Russian revolutions, the aftermath. May I get our mechanics to check everything while we wait?"

"Of course." The man waited while McIver gave the orders, then he said, "Let's hope the madness doesn't spread across the Gulf, eh? No one wants any trouble this side of the *Islamic Gulf.*" He used the word with great deliberation, all the Gulf states loathing the term Persian Gulf. "It is the Islamic Gulf, isn't it?"

"Yes, yes, it is."

"All maps will have to be changed. The Gulf is the Gulf, Islam is Islam and not just for the Shi'a sect."

McIver said nothing, his caution increasing, adding to his disquiet. There were many Shi'as in Kuwait and most of the Gulf states. Many. Usually they were the poor. Rulers, the sheiks, were usually Sunni.

"Captain!" the Customs officer in the doorway of the 212 cabin parked on the helipad was beckoning to him. Ayre and Wazari had been told to wait away from the helicopters in the shade until inspections were finished. Mechanics were busy ground-checking. "Are you carrying arms of any kind?"

"No, sir—apart from the regulation Very light pistol."

"Contraband of any kind?"

"No, sir. Just spares." All the usual questions, interminably, that would be repeated as soon as they were released to the airport. At length the man thanked him and motioned him away. The Immigration officer had gone back to his car with their passports. The radio transmitter had been left on and McIver could hear Ground Control clearly. He saw the man scratch his beard thoughtfully, then pick up the mike and talk into it in Arabic. This increased his concern. Genny was sitting in the shade nearby and he went over to her.

"Stiff upper lip," she whispered. "How's it going?"

"Wish to God they'd let us get on with it," McIver said irritably. "We'll have to endure another hour at the airport and damned if I know what to do."

"Has Charlie sa—"

"Captain!" The Immigration officer was beckoning him and Pettikin over to the car. "So you're in transit, is that it?"

"Yes. To Al Shargaz. With your permission, we'll leave at once," McIver said. "We'll go to the airport, file our flight plan, and take off as quickly as we can. Is that all right?"

"Where did you say you are in transit to?"

"Al Shargaz, via Bahrain for fuel." McIver was getting sicker by the minute. Any airport official would know they would have to refuel before Bahrain even without this wind, and all airports between here and there were Saudi, so he would have to file a flight plan for a Saudi landing. Bahrain, Abu Dhabi, Al Shargaz had all received the same telex. Kuwait too, and even if it had been intercepted here privately by a well-wisher, for whatever reason, the same would not be true of Saudi airports. Rightly, McIver thought, and saw the man look at the Iran registration letters under the cockpit windows. They had arrived under Iran registration, he would have to file the flight plan and leave under the same letters.

To their astonishment, the man reached into the pocket of his car and brought out a pad of forms. "I am inst— I will accept your flight plan here and clear you to Bahrain direct and you can leave at once. You can pay me the regulation landing fees and I'll stamp your passports too. There'll be no need to go to the airport."

"What?"

"I will accept your flight plan now and you can leave direct from here. Please make it out." He handed the pad to McIver. It was the correct form. "As soon as you've done it, sign it and bring it back." Some flies circling in the car were bothering him and he waved them away. Then he picked up the radio mike, pointedly waited until McIver and Pettikin walked off, and talked quietly into it.

Hardly able to believe what had happened, they went to lean against their truck. "Jesus, Mac, do you think they know and are just letting us go?"

"I don't know what to think. Don't waste time, Charlie." McIver shoved the pad into his hands and said more irritably than he meant to, "Just make out the flight plan before he changes his mind: Al Shargaz—if we happen to have an emergency on Jellet, that's our problem. For God's sake do it and let's get airborne as quick as we can."

"Sure. Right away."

Genny said, "You're not flying, are you, Duncan?"

"No, Charlie's going to do that."

Pettikin thought a moment, then took out a key and his money. "This's my room key, Genny. Would you get my stuff for me, nothing there of any importance, pay the bill, and catch the next plane. Hughes—he's the Imperial Air rep—he'll get you a priority."

"What about your passport and license?" she asked.

"Always carry them, frightened to death of losing them, and a $100 note —never know when you'll need some baksheesh."

"Consider it done." She pushed her dark glasses back onto the bridge of her nose, smiled at her husband. "What'll you do, Duncan?"

Without noticing it, McIver exhaled heavily. "I'll have to go on, Gen. Daren't stay here—doubt if they'd let me. They're desperate not to rock any boat and want to see the last of us. It's obvious, isn't it—who ever heard of being cleared from a beach? We're a bloody embarrassment and a threat to the state, of course we are. That's the truth! Do what Charlie says, Gen. We'll refuel at Jellet—change the registrations there and hope for the best —do you have the stencils, Charlie?"

"Brushes, paint, everything." Pettikin did not stop filling in the forms. "What about Wazari?"

"He's crew until someone asks a question. Put him down as radio operator. That's no lie. If they don't challenge him at Bahrain, they certain will at Al Shargaz. Perhaps Andy can work something out for him."

"All right. He's crew. That's it, then."

"Good. Gen, Jellet's easy from here, Bahrain too, and Al Shargaz. Weather's good, moon'll be out, so a night jaunt'll be fine. Do what Charlie says. You'll be there in good time to meet us."

"If you leave at once, you'll need food and some bottled water," she said. "We can get some here. I'll get them, Charlie. Come along, Duncan, you need a drink."

"Pour it for me at Al Shargaz, Gen."

"I will. But I'll pour you one now. You're not flying, you need it, and so do I." She went over to the Immigration officer and got permission to buy sandwiches and make a phone call.

"Back in a second, Charlie." McIver followed her into the hotel lobby and went straight for the toilet. There he was very sick. It took him some time to recover. When he came out she was getting off the phone.

"Sandwiches any second, your drink's poured, and I've booked you a call to Andy." She led the way out to a table on the sumptuous bar terrace. Three ice-cold Perriers with sliced lemon, and a double tot of whisky straight, no ice, just the way he liked it. He downed the first Perrier without stopping. "My God, I needed that . . ." He eyed the whisky but did not touch it. Thoughtfully he sipped the second glass of Perrier, and watched her. When it was half gone he said, "Gen, I think I'd like you to come along."

She was startled. Then she said, "Thank you, Duncan. I'd like that. Yes, yes, I would."

The lines in his face crinkled. "You'd've come anyway. Wouldn't you?"

She gave a little shrug. Her eyes dropped to the whisky. "You're not flying, Duncan. The whisky would be good for you. It would settle the tum."

"You noticed, eh?"

"Only that you're very tired. More tired than I've ever seen you, but you've done wonderfully, you've done a smashing job, and you should rest. You've . . . you've been taking your pills and all that rubbish?"

"Oh, yes, though I'll need a refill soon. No problem, but I felt pretty bloody a couple of times." At her sudden anxiety, "I'm fine now, Gen. Fine."

She knew better than to probe. Now that she was invited she could relax a little. Since he had landed she had been watching him very carefully, her concern growing. With the sandwiches she had ordered some aspirins, she had codeine-laced Veganin in her bag and the secret survival kit Dr. Nutt had given her. "What was it like flying again? Really?"

"From Tehran down to Kowiss was grand, the rest not so good. This last leg wasn't good at all." The thought of being hunted by the fighters and so near to disaster so many times made him feel bilious again. Don't think about that, he ordered himself, that's over. Whirlwind's almost over, Erikki and Azadeh're safe, but what about Dubois and Fowler, what the hell's happened to them? And Tom? I could bloody strangle Tom, poor bugger.

"You all right, Duncan?"

"Oh, yes, I'm fine. Just tired—it's been quite a couple of weeks."

"What about Tom? What'll you tell Andy?"

"I was just thinking about him. I'll have to tell Andy."

"That's one hell of a spanner in Whirlwind, isn't it?"

"He's . . . he's on his own, Gen. Maybe he can get Sharazad and sneak out again. If he's caught . . . we'll have to wait and see and hope," he said. But he was thinking *when* he's caught. McIver reached over and touched her, glad to be with her, not wanting to worry her more than she was now. Tough on her, all this. I think I'm going to die.

"Please excuse me, sahib, memsahib, your order's been taken out to the helicopter," the waiter said.

McIver handed him a credit card and the waiter left. "Which reminds me, what about your hotel bill, and Charlie's? We'll have to take care of them before we leave."

"Oh, I phoned Mr. Hughes while you were in the loo," she said, "and asked him if he'd take care of our bills and ship our bags and everything if I didn't call back in an hour. I've my handbag, passport, and . . . what're you smiling about?"

"Nothing . . . nothing, Gen."

"It was just in case you asked me. I thought . . ." She watched the bubbles in her glass. Again the tiny shrug and she looked up and smiled so happily. "I'm ever so glad you asked me, Duncan. Thank you."

AL SHARGAZ—ON THE OUTSKIRTS OF THE CITY: 6:01 P.M. Gavallan got out of his car and walked briskly up the steps toward the front door of the Moroccan-style villa that was enclosed by high walls.

"Mr. Gavallan!"

"Oh, hello, Mrs. Newbury!" He changed direction to join the woman who was half hidden, kneeling down, planting some seedlings near the driveway. "Your garden looks wonderful."

"Thank you. It's such fun and keeps me fit," she said. Angela Newbury was tall and in her thirties, her accent patrician. "Roger's in the gazebo and expecting you." With the back of her gloved hand she wiped the perspiration off her forehead and left a smudge in its wake. "How's it going?"

"Great," he told her, omitting the news about Lochart. "Nine out of ten so far."

"Oh, super, oh, that is a relief. Congratulations, we've all been so concerned. Wonderful, but for God's sake don't tell Roger I asked, he'd have a fit. Nobody's supposed to know!"

He returned her smile and walked around the side of the house through the lovely gardens. The gazebo was in a clump of trees and flower beds, with chairs, side tables, portable bar and phone. His joy faded, seeing the look on Roger Newbury's face. "What's up?"

"You're what's up. Whirlwind's what's up. I made it perfectly clear that it was ill advised. How's it going?"

"I've just heard our Kowiss two are safe in Kuwait and cleared on to Bahrain with no trouble, so that makes nine out of ten, if we include Erikki's one in Tabriz, Dubois and Fowler're still not accounted for but we're hoping. Now what's the problem, Roger?"

"There's hell to pay all over the Gulf with Tehran screaming bloody murder and all our offices on alert. My Fearless Leader and yours truly, Roger Newbury Esquire, are cordially invited at seven-thirty to explain to the Illustrious Foreign Minister why there's a sudden influx of helicopters here, albeit British registered, and how long they intend to stay." Newbury, a short lean man with sandy hair and blue eyes and prominent nose, was clearly very irritated. "Glad about the nine out of ten, would you like a drink?"

"Thanks. A light Scotch and soda."

Newbury went to fix it. "My Fearless Leader and I would be delighted to know what you suggest we say."

Gavallan thought a moment. "The choppers are out the moment we can get them aboard the freighters."

"When's that?" Newbury gave him the drink.

"Thanks. The freighters're promised by 6:00 P.M. Sunday. We'll work all night and have them off Monday morning."

Newbury was shocked. "Can't you get them out before that?"

"The freighters were ordered for tomorrow but I was let down. Why?"

"Because, old boy, a few minutes ago we had a friendly, very serious high-level leak that so long as the choppers weren't here by sunset tomorrow they might not be impounded."

Now Gavallan was also shocked. "That's not possible—can't be done."

"I'm suggesting that you'd be wise to make it possible. Fly them out to Oman or Dubai or wherever."

"If we do that . . . if we do that we'll be deeper in the mire."

"I don't think you can get any deeper, old boy. The way the leak put it was after sunset tomorrow you'll be in over your eyeballs." Newbury toyed with his drink, a lemon pressé. Blast all this, he was thinking. While we're obliged to help our important trading interests salvage what they can from the Iran catastrophe we've got to remember the long term as well as the short. We can't put Her Majesty's Government at risk. Apart from that, my weekend's ruined, I should be having a nice tall vodka gimlet with Angela and here I am, sipping slop. "You'll have to move them."

"Can you get us a forty-eight-hour reprieve, explain that the freighters are chartered but it's got to be Sunday?"

"Wouldn't dare suggest it, Andy. That would admit culpability."

"Could you get us a forty-eight-hour transit permit to Oman?"

Newbury grimaced. "I'll ask Himself but we couldn't feel them out until tomorrow, too late now, and my immediate reaction's that the request would correctly be turned down. Iran has a considerable goodwill presence there; after all they really did help put down Yemen-backed Communist insurgents. I doubt that they'd agree to offend a very good friend however much the present fundamentalist line might displease them."

Gavallan felt sick. "I'd better see if I can bring my freighters forward or get alternates—I'd say I've one chance in fifty." He finished his drink and got up. "Sorry about all this."

Newbury got up too. "Sorry I can't be more helpful," he said, genuinely sorry. "Keep me posted and I'll do the same."

"Of course. You said you might be able to get a message to Captain Yokkonen in Tabriz?"

"I'll certainly try. What is it?"

"Just from me that he should, er, should leave as soon as possible, by the shortest route. Please sign it GHPLX Gavallan."

Without comment Newbury wrote it down. "GHPLX?"

"Yes." Gavallan felt sure that Erikki would understand this would be his new British registry number. "He's not aware of, er, of certain developments so if your man could also privately explain the reason for haste I'd be very, very grateful. Thanks for all your help."

"For your sake, and his, I agree the sooner he leaves the better, with or without his aircraft. There's nothing we can do to help him. Sorry, but that's the truth." Newbury fiddled with his glass. "Now he represents a very great danger to you. Doesn't he?"

"I don't think so. He's under the protection of the new Khan, his brother-in-law. He's as safe as he could ever be," Gavallan said. What would Newbury say if he knew about Tom Lochart? "Erikki'll be okay. He'll understand. Thanks again."

CHAPTER

66

TABRIZ—AT THE INTERNATIONAL HOSPITAL: 6:24 P.M.
Hakim Khan walked painfully into the private room, the doctor and a guard following him. He was using crutches now and they made his walking easier, but when he bent or tried to sit, they did not relieve the pain. Only painkillers did that. Azadeh was waiting downstairs, her X ray better than his, her pain less than his.

Ahmed lay in bed, awake, his chest and stomach bandaged. The operation to remove the bullet lodged in his chest had been successful. The one in his stomach had done much damage, he had lost a great deal of blood, and internal bleeding had started again. But the moment he saw Hakim Khan he tried to raise himself.

"Don't move, Ahmed," Hakim Khan said, his voice kind. "The doctor says you're mending well."

"The doctor's a liar, Highness."

The doctor began to speak but stopped as Hakim said, "Liar or not, get well, Ahmed."

"Yes, Highness. With the Help of God. But you, you are all right?"

"If the X ray doesn't lie, I've just torn ligaments." He shrugged. "With the Help of God."

"Thank you . . . thank you for the private room, Highness. Never have I had . . . such luxury."

"It's merely a token of my esteem for such loyalty." Imperiously he dismissed the doctor and the guard. When the door was shut, he went closer. "You asked to see me, Ahmed?"

"Yes, Highness, please excuse me that I could not . . . could not come to you." Ahmed's voice was phlegmy, and he spoke with difficulty. "The Tbilisi man you want . . . the Soviet . . . he sent a message for you. It's . . . it's under the drawer . . . he taped it under the drawer there." With an effort he pointed to the small bureau.

Hakim's excitement picked up. Awkwardly he felt underneath the drawer. The adhesive bandages strapping him made bending difficult. He found the small square of folded paper and it came away easily. "Who brought it and when?"

"It was today . . . sometime today . . . I'm not sure, I think it was this afternoon. I don't know. The man wore a doctor's coat and glasses but he wasn't a doctor. An Azerbaijani, perhaps a Turk, I've never seen him before. He spoke Turkish—all he said was, 'This is for Hakim Khan, from a friend in Tbilisi. Understand?' I told him yes and he left as quickly as he arrived. For a long time I thought he was a dream. . . ."

The message was scrawled in writing Hakim did not recognize: "Many, many congratulations on your inheritance, may you live as long and be as productive as your predecessor. Yes, I would like to meet urgently too. But here, not there. Sorry. Whenever you're ready I would be honored to receive you, with pomp or in privacy, whatever you want. We should be friends, there's much to accomplish and we have many interests in common. Please tell Robert Armstrong and Hashemi Fazir that Yazernov is buried in the Russian Cemetery at Jaleh and he looks forward to seeing them when convenient." There was no signature.

Greatly disappointed, he went back to the bed and offered the paper to Ahmed. "What do you make of that?"

Ahmed did not have the strength to take it. "Sorry, Highness, please hold it so I can read it." After reading it, he said, "It's not Mzytryk's writing, I'd . . . I'd recognize his writing but it . . . I believe it genuine. He would have transmitted it to . . . to underlings to bring here."

"Who's Yazernov and what does that mean?"

"I don't know. It's a code . . . it's a code they'd understand."

"It is an invitation to a meeting, or a threat. Which?"

"I don't know, Highness. I would guess a meet—" A spasm of pain went through him. He cursed in his own language.

"Is Mzytryk aware that both the last times they were in ambush? Aware that Abdollah Khan had betrayed him?"

"I . . . I don't know, Highness. I told you he was cunning and the Khan your father very . . . very careful in his dealings." The effort of talking and concentrating was taking much of Ahmed's strength. "That Mzytryk knows they are in contact with you . . . that both of them are here now, means nothing, his spies abound. You're Khan and of course . . . of course you know you're . . . you're spied on by all kinds of men, most of them evil, who report to their superiors—most of them even more evil." A smile went over his face and Hakim pondered its meaning. "But then, you know all about hiding your true purpose, Highness. Not once . . . not once did Abdollah Khan suspect how brilliant you are, not once. If . . . if he'd known one hundredth part of who you really are . . . really are, he would have never banished you but made you . . . made you heir and chief counselor."

"He would have had me strangled." Not for a millionth of a second was

Hakim Khan tempted to tell Ahmed that he had sent the assassins whom Erikki had killed, or about the poison attempt that had also failed. "A week ago he would have ordered me mutilated, and you would have done it happily."

Ahmed looked up at him, eyes deep-set and filled with death. "How do you know so much?"

"The Will of God."

The ebb had begun. Both men knew it. Hakim said, "Colonel Fazir showed me a telex about Erikki." He told Ahmed the contents. "Now I have no Mzytryk to barter with, not immediately. I can give Erikki to Fazir or help him escape. Either way my sister is committed to stay here and cannot go with him. What is your advice?"

"For you it is safer to give the Infidel to the colonel as a pishkesh and pretend to her there's nothing you can do to prevent the . . . the arrest. In truth there isn't if the colonel wants it that way. He of the Knife . . . he will resist and so he will be killed. Then you can promise her secretly to the Tbilisi . . . But never give her to him, then you will control . . . then you may control him . . . but I doubt it."

"And if He of the Knife 'happens' to escape?"

"If the colonel allowed it . . . he will require payment."

"Which is?"

"Mzytryk. Now or sometime . . . sometime in the future. While He of the Knife lives, Highness, she will never divorce him—forget the saboteur, he was another lifetime—and when the two years are . . . are over she will go to him, that is if . . . if he allows her to . . . to stay here. I doubt if even Your Highness . . ." Ahmed's eyes closed and a tremor went through him.

"What happened with Bayazid and the bandits? Ahmed . . ."

Ahmed did not hear him. He was seeing the steppes now, the vast plains of his homeland and ancestors, the seas of grass from whence his forebears came forth to ride near the cloak of Genghis Khan, and then that of the grandson Kubla Khan and *his* brother Hulagu Khan who came down into Persia to erect mountains of skulls of those who opposed him. Here in the golden lands since ancient times, Ahmed thought, lands of wine and warmth and wealth and women of great doe-eyed beauty and sensuality, prized since ancient times like Azadeh . . . ah, now I will never take her like she should be taken, dragged off by the hair as spoils of war, shoved across a saddle to be bedded and tamed on the skins of wolves . . .

From a long way off he heard himself say, "Please, Highness, I would beg a favor, I would like to be buried in my own land and in our own fashion . . ." Then I can live forever with the spirits of my fathers, he thought, the lovely space beckoning him.

"Ahmed, what happened with Bayazid and the bandits when you landed?"

With an effort Ahmed came back. "They weren't Kurds, just tribesmen pretending to be Kurds and He of the Knife killed them all, Highness, with very great brutality," he said with strange formality. "In his madness he killed them all—with knife and gun and hands and feet and teeth, all except Bayazid who, because of his oath to you, would not come against him."

"He left him alive?" Hakim was incredulous.

"Yes, God give him peace. He . . . put a gun in my hand and held the Bayazid near the gun and I . . ." The voice trailed away, waves of grass beckoning as far as eyes could see . . ."

"You killed him?"

"Oh, yes, looking . . . looking into his eyes." Anger came into Ahmed's voice. "The son of a . . . a dog shot me in the back, twice, without honor, the son of a dog, so he died without honor and without . . . without manhood, the son of a dog." The bloodless lips smiled and he closed his eyes. He was dying fast now, his words imperceptible. "I took vengeance."

Hakim said quickly, "Ahmed, what haven't you told me that I need to know?"

"Nothing . . ." In a little while his eyes opened and Hakim saw into the pit. "There is no . . . no other God but God and . . ." A little blood seeped out of the side of his mouth. ". . . I made you Kh . . ." The last of the word died with him.

Hakim was uncomfortable under the frozen stare.

"Doctor!" he called out.

At once the man came in, and the guard. The doctor closed his eyes. "As God wills. What should we do with the body, Highness?"

"What do you usually do with bodies?" Hakim moved his crutches and walked away, the guard followed. So, Ahmed, he was thinking, so now you're dead and I'm alone, cut from the past and obliged to no one. Made me Khan? Is that what you were going to say? Did you know there were spy holes in that room too?

A smile touched him. Then hardened. Now for Colonel Fazir, and Erikki, "He of the Knife" as you called him.

AT THE PALACE: 6:48 P.M. In the failing light Erikki was carefully repairing one of the bullet holes in the plastic windshield of the 212 with clear tape. It was difficult with his arm in a sling but his hand was strong and the forearm wound shallow—no sign of infection. His ear was heavily taped, part of his hair shaved away for cleanliness, and he was mending fast. His appetite was good. The hours of talk that he had had with Azadeh had given him a measure of peace.

That's all it is, he thought, it's only a measure, not enough to forgive the killings or the danger that I am. So be it. That's what gods made me and that's what I am. Yes, but what about Ross and what about Azadeh? And why does she keep the kookri so close by her: "It was his gift to you, Erikki, to you and to me."

"It's unlucky to give a man a knife without taking money, at once, just a token, in return. When I see him I will give him money and accept his gift."

Once again he pressed Engine Start. Once again the engine caught, choked, and died. What about Ross and Azadeh?

He sat back on the edge of the cockpit and looked at the sky. The sky did not answer him. Nor the sunset. The overcast had broken up in the west, the sun was down and the clouds menacing. Calls of the muezzins began. Guards on the gate faced Mecca and prostrated themselves; so did those inside the palace and those working in the fields and carpet factory and sheep pens.

Unconsciously his hand went to his knife. Without wishing to, his eyes checked that the Sten gun was still beside his pilot's seat and armed with a full clip. Hidden in the cabin were other weapons, weapons from the tribesmen. AK47s and M16s. He could not remember taking them or hiding them, had discovered them this morning when he made his inspection for damage and was cleaning the interior.

With the tape over his ear he did not hear the approaching car as soon as he would have normally, and was startled when it appeared at the gate. The Khan's guards there recognized the occupants and waved the car through to stop in the huge forecourt near the fountain. Again he pressed Engine Start, again the engine caught for a moment, then shuddered the whole airframe as it died.

"Evening, Captain," the two men said, Hashemi Fazir and Armstrong. "How are you feeling today?" the colonel asked.

"Evening. With luck, in a week or so I'll be better than ever," Erikki said pleasantly but his caution was complete.

"The guards say that Their Highnesses are not back yet—the Khan expects us, we're here at his invitation."

"They're at the hospital being X-rayed. They left while I was asleep, they shouldn't be long." Erikki watched them. "Would you care for a drink? There's vodka, whisky, and tea, of course coffee."

"Thank you, whatever you have," Hashemi said. "How's your helicopter?"

"Sick," he said disgustedly. "I've been trying to start her for an hour. She's had a miserable week." Erikki led the way up the marble steps. "The avionics are messed. I need a mechanic badly. Our base's closed as you know and I tried to phone Tehran but the phones are out again."

"Perhaps I can get you a mechanic, tomorrow or the next day, from the air base."

"You could, Colonel?" His smile was sudden and appreciative. "That'd help a lot. And I could use fuel, a full load. Would that be possible?"

"Could you fly down to the airfield?"

"I wouldn't risk it, even if I could start her—too dangerous. No, I wouldn't risk that." Erikki shook his head. "The mechanic must come here." He led the way along a corridor, opened the door to the small salon on the ground floor that Abdollah Khan had set aside for non-Islamic guests. It was called the European Room. The bar was well stocked. By custom, there were always full ice trays in the refrigerator, the ice made from bottled water, with club soda and soft drinks of many kinds—and chocolates and the halvah he had adored. "I'm having vodka," Erikki said.

"Same for me, please," Armstrong said. Hashemi asked for a soft drink. "I'll have a vodka too, when the sun's down." Faintly the muezzins were still calling. *"Prosit!"* Erikki clinked glasses with Armstrong, politely did the same with Hashemi, and drank the tot in one swallow. He poured himself another. "Help yourself, Superintendent." Hearing a car they all glanced out the window. It was the Rolls.

"Excuse me a minute, I'll tell Hakim Khan you're here." Erikki walked out and greeted Azadeh and her brother on the steps. "What did the X rays show?"

"No sign of bone damage for either of us." Azadeh was happy, her face carefree. "How are you, my darling?"

"Fine. It's wonderful about your backs. Wonderful!" His smile at Hakim was genuine. "I'm so pleased. You've some guests, the colonel and Superintendent Armstrong—I put them in the European Room." Erikki saw Hakim's tiredness. "Shall I tell them to come back tomorrow?"

"No, no thank you. Azadeh, would you tell them I'll be fifteen minutes but to make themselves at home. I'll see you later, at dinner." Hakim watched her touch Erikki and smile and walk off. How lucky they are to love each other so much, and how sad for them. "Erikki, Ahmed's dead, I didn't want to tell her yet."

Erikki was filled with sadness. "My fault he's dead—Bayazid—he never gave him a chance. *Matyeryebyets!*"

"God's will. Let's go and talk a moment." Hakim went down the corridor into the Great Room, leaning more and more on the crutches. The guards stayed at the door, out of listening range. Hakim went to a niche, put aside his crutches, faced Mecca, gasped with pain as he knelt, and tried to make obeisance. Even forcing himself, he failed again and had to be content with intoning the Shahada. "Erikki, give me a hand, will you please?"

Erikki lifted him easily. "You'd better give that a miss for a few days."

"Not pray?" Hakim gaped at him.

"I meant . . . perhaps the One God will understand if you say it and don't kneel. You'll make your back worse. Did the doctor say what it was?"

"He thinks it's torn ligaments—I'll go to Tehran as soon as I can with Azadeh and see a specialist." Hakim accepted his crutches. "Thanks." After a moment's consideration he chose a chair instead of his usual lounging cushions and eased himself into it, then ordered tea.

Erikki's mind was on Azadeh. So little time. "The best back specialist in the world's Guy Beauchamp, in London. He fixed me up in five minutes after doctors said I'd have to lie in traction for three months or have two joints fused. Don't believe an ordinary doctor about your back, Hakim. The best they can do is painkillers."

The door opened. A servant brought in the tea. Hakim dismissed him and the guards, "See that I'm not disturbed." The tea was hot, mint-flavored, sweet and drunk from tiny silver cups. "Now, we must settle what you're to do. You can't stay here."

"I agree," Erikki said, glad that the waiting was over. "I know I'm . . . I'm an embarrassment to you as Khan."

"Part of Azadeh's agreement and mine with my father, for us to be redeemed and me to be made heir, were the oaths we swore to remain in Tabriz, in Iran, for two years. So, though you must leave, she may not."

"She told me about the oaths."

"Clearly you're in danger, even here. I can't protect you against police or the government. You should leave at once, fly out of the country. After two years when Azadeh can leave, she will leave."

"I can't fly. Fazir said he could give me a mechanic tomorrow, maybe. And fuel. If I could get hold of McIver in Tehran he could fly someone up here."

"Did you try?"

"Yes, but the phones are still out. I would have used the HF at our base but the office's totally wrecked—I flew over the base coming back here, it's a mess, no transport, no fuel drums. When I get to Tehran McIver can send a mechanic here to repair the 212. Until she can fly, can she stay where she is?"

"Yes. Of course." Hakim poured himself some more tea, convinced now that Erikki knew nothing about the escape of the other pilots and helicopters. But that changes nothing, he told himself. "There aren't any airlines servicing Tabriz or I'd arrange one of those for you. Still, I think you should leave at once; you are in very great danger, immediate danger."

Erikki's eyes narrowed. "You're sure?"

"Yes?"

"What?"

"I can't tell you. But it's not in my control, it's serious, immediate, does not concern Azadeh at the moment but could, if we're not careful. For her protection this must remain just between us. I'll give you a car, any one you want from the garage. There're about twenty, I believe. What happened to your Range Rover?"

Erikki shrugged, his mind working. "That's another problem, killing that *matyeryebyets* mujhadin who took my papers, and Azadeh's, then Rakoczy blasting the others."

"I'd forgotten about Rakoczy." Hakim pressed onward. "There's not much time."

Erikki moved his head around to ease the tension in his muscles and take away the ache. "How immediate a danger, Hakim?"

Hakim's eyes were level. "Immediate enough to suggest you wait till dark, then take the car and go—and get out of Iran as quickly as you can," he added deliberately. "Immediate enough to know that if you don't, Azadeh will have greater anguish. Immediate enough to know you should not tell her before you leave."

"You swear it?"

"Before God I swear that is what I believe."

He saw Erikki frown and he waited patiently. He liked his honesty and simplicity but that meant nothing in the balance. "Can you leave without telling her?"

"If it's in the night, nearer to dawn, so long as she's sleeping. If I leave tonight, pretending to go out, say to go to the base, she'll wait for me, and if I don't come back, it will be very difficult—for her and for you. The village preys on her. She'll have hysterics. A secret departure would be wiser, just before dawn. She'll be sleeping then—the doctor gave her sedatives. She'll be sleeping and I could leave a note."

Hakim nodded, satisfied. "Then it's settled." He wanted no hurt or trouble for or from Azadeh either.

Erikki had heard the finality and he knew beyond any doubt, now, that if he left her he would lose her forever.

IN THE BATHHOUSE: 7:15 P.M.   Azadeh lowered herself into the hot water up to her neck. The bath was beautifully tiled and fifteen yards square and many tiered, shallow at one end with lounging platforms, the hot water piped from the furnace room adjoining. The room was warm and large, a happy place with kind mirrors. Her hair was tied up in a towel and she rested against one of the tilted backrests, her legs stretched out, the water easing her. "Oh, that's so good, Mina," she murmured.

Mina was a strong, good-looking woman, one of Azadeh's three maidservants. She stood over her in the water, wearing just a loincloth, gently massaging her neck and shoulders. The bathhouse was empty but for Azadeh and the maidservant—Hakim had sent the rest of the family to other houses in Tabriz: "to prepare for a fitting Mourning Day for Abdollah Khan," had been the excuse, but all were aware that the forty days of waiting was to give him time to inspect the palace at his leisure and reapportion suites as it pleased him. Only the old Khanan was undisturbed, and Aysha and her two infants.

Without disturbing Azadeh's tranquillity, Mina eased her into shallower water and onto another platform where Azadeh lay full length, her head propped comfortably on a pillow, so that she could work her chest and loins and thighs and legs, preparing for the real oil massage that would come later when the water's heat had become deep-seated.

"Oh, that's so good," Azadeh said again. She was thinking how much nicer this was than their own sauna—that raw strong heat and then the frightful plunge into the snow, the aftershock tingling and life-giving but not as good as this, the sensuality of the perfumed water and quiet and leisure and no aftershocks and oh that is so good . . . but why is the bathhouse a village square and now it's so cold and there's the butcher and the false mullah's shouting, "First his right hand . . . stone the harlottttt!" She screamed soundlessly and leaped away.

"Oh, did I hurt you, Highness, I'm so sorry!"

"No, no, it wasn't you, Mina, it was nothing, nothing, please go on." Again the soothing fingers. Her heart slowed. I hope soon I'll be able to sleep without . . . without the village. Last night with Erikki it was already a little better, in his arms it was better, just being near him. Perhaps tonight it will be better still. I wonder how Johnny is. He should be on his way home now, home to Nepal on leave. Now that Erikki's back I'm safe again, just so long as I'm with him, near him. By myself I'm not . . . not safe, even with Hakim. I don't feel safe anymore. I just don't feel safe anymore.

The door opened and Aysha came in. Her face was lined with grief, her eyes filled with fear, the black chador making her appear even more emaciated. "Hello, Aysha dear, what's the matter?"

"I don't know. The world is strange and I've no . . . I'm centerless."

"Come into the bath," Azadeh said, sorry for her, she looked so thin and old and frail and defenseless. Difficult to believe she's my father's widow with a son and daughter, and only seventeen. "Get in, it's so good."

"No, no, thank you I . . . I just wanted to talk to you." Aysha looked at Mina then dropped her eyes and waited. Two days ago she would have just sent for Azadeh who would have come at once and bowed and knelt and waited for orders, as now she knelt as petitioner. As God wills, she thought; except for my terror for the future of my children I would shout with happiness—no more of the foul stench and sleep-shattering snores, no more of the crushing weight and moans and rage and biting and desperation to achieve that which he could but rarely. "It's your fault, your fault your fault . . ." How could it be my fault? How many times did I beg him to show me what to do to help, and I tried and tried and tried and yet it was only so rarely and then at once the weight was gone, the snoring would begin, and I was left awake to lie in the sweat and in the stink. Oh, how many times I wanted to die.

"Mina, leave us alone until I call you," Azadeh said. She was obeyed instantly. "What's the matter, Aysha dear?"

The girl trembled. "I'm afraid. I'm afraid for my son, and I came to beg you to protect him."

Azadeh said gently, "You've nothing to fear from Hakim Khan and me, nothing. We've sworn by God to cherish you, your son and daughter, you heard us, we did it in front of . . . of your husband, our father, and then again, after his death. You've nothing to fear. Nothing."

"I've everything to fear," the girl stammered. "I'm not safe anymore, nor is my son. Please, Azadeh, couldn't . . . couldn't Hakim Khan . . . I'd sign any paper giving up any rights for him, any paper, I only want to live in peace and for him to grow up and live in peace."

"Your life is with us, Aysha. Soon you will see how happy we'll all be together," Azadeh said. The girl's right to be afraid, she thought. Hakim will never surrender the Khanate out of his line if he has sons of his own—he must marry now, I must help find him a fine wife. "Don't worry, Aysha."

"Worry? You're safe now, Azadeh, you who just a few days ago lived in terror. Now I'm not safe and I'm in terror."

Azadeh watched her. There was nothing she could do for her. Aysha's life was settled. She was the widow of a Khan. She would stay in the palace, watched and guarded, living as best she could. Hakim would not dare to let her remarry, could not possibly allow her to give up a son's rights granted by the public will of the dying husband. "Don't worry," she said.

"Here." Aysha pulled a bulky manila envelope from under her chador. "This is yours."

"What is it?" Azadeh's hands were wet and she didn't want to touch it.

The girl opened the envelope and showed her the contents. Azadeh's eyes widened. Her passport, ID, and other papers, Erikki's also, all the things that had been stolen from them by the mujhadin at the roadblock. This was a pishkesh indeed. "Where did you get them?"

The girl was sure there was no one listening, but still lowered her voice. "The leftist mullah, the same mullah of the village, he gave them to His Highness, the Khan, to Abdollah Khan two weeks ago, when you were in Tehran . . . the same mullah as at the village."

Incredulously Azadeh watched her. "How did he get them?"

Nervously the girl shrugged her thin shoulders. "The mullah knew all about the roadblock and what happened there. He came here to try to take possession of the . . . of your husband. His Highness . . ." She hesitated, then continued in her halting whispers. "His Highness told him no, not until he approved it, sent him away, and kept the papers."

"Do you have other papers, Aysha? Private papers?"

"Not of yours or your husband's." Again the girl trembled. "His Highness hated you all so much. He wanted your husband destroyed, then he was going to give you to the Soviet, and your brother was to be . . . neutered. There's so much I know that could help you and him, and so much I don't understand. Ahmed . . . beware of him, Azadeh."

"Yes," Azadeh said slowly. "Did father send the mullah to the village?"

"I don't know. I think he did. I heard him ask the Soviet to dispose of Mahmud, ah, yes, that was that false mullah's name. Perhaps His Highness sent him there to torment you and the saboteur, and also sent him to his own death—but God intervened. I heard the Soviet agree to send men after this Mahmud."

Azadeh said casually, "How did you hear that?"

Aysha nervously gathered the chador closer around her and knelt on the edge of the bath. "The palace is a honeycomb of listening holes and spy holes, Azadeh. He . . . His Highness trusted no one, spied on everyone, even me. I think we should be friends, allies, you and I, we're defenseless, even you, perhaps you more than any of us and unless we help each other we're all lost. I can help you, protect you." Beads of sweat were on her forehead. "I only ask you to protect my son, please. I can protect you."

"Of course we should be friends," Azadeh said, not believing that she was under any threat, but intrigued to know the secrets of the palace. "You will show me these secret places and share your knowledge?"

"Oh, yes, yes, I will." The girl's face lit up. "I'll show you everything and the two years will pass so quickly. Oh, yes, we'll be friends."

"What two years?"

"While your husband is away, Azadeh."

Azadeh jerked upright, filled with alarm. "He's going away?"

Aysha stared at her. "Of course. What else can he do?"

IN THE EUROPEAN ROOM: Hashemi was handing Robert Armstrong the scrawled message from Mzytryk that Hakim had just given him. Armstrong glanced at it: "Sorry, Hashemi, I can't read Turkish."

"Ah, sorry, I forgot." Hashemi read it out in English. Both men saw Armstrong's disappointment. "Next time, Robert, we'll get him. Insha'Allah."

Not to worry, Armstrong thought. It was a long shot anyway. I'll get Mzytryk another time. I'll get him, and I'll get you, old friend Hashemi, rotten of you to murder Talbot. Why did you do that? Revenge because he knew many of your secrets? He'd done you no harm, on the contrary he put lots of bones of your way and smoothed lots of errors for you. Rotten! You didn't give him a chance, why should you have one? Soon as my passage out's arranged, you've had it. No reason to delay anymore now that Mzytryk knows I'm on to him and he's jeering from safety. Perhaps the Brass'll send Special Branch or a Special Air Services team into Tbilisi now we know where he is—someone'll get the bastard. Even if I don't . . .

He was distracted by Hakim Khan saying, "Colonel, what's this about Yazernov and Jaleh Cemetery?" and Hashemi answered smoothly, "It's an invitation, Highness. Yazernov's an intermediary Mzytryk uses from time to time, acceptable to both sides, when something of importance to both sides has to be discussed." Armstrong almost laughed, for Hashemi knew as well as he that it was a promise of a personal vendetta and of course an immediate Section 16/a. Clever of Mzytryk to use the name Yazernov and not Rakoczy.

" 'As soon as convenient' to meet Yazernov!" Hashemi said. "I think, Highness, we'd better return to Tehran tomorrow."

"Yes," Hakim said. Coming back in the car from the hospital with Azadeh, he had decided the only way to deal with Mzytryk's message and these two men was head-on. "When will you come back to Tabriz?"

"If it pleases you, next week. Then we could discuss how to tempt Mzytryk here. With your help there's much to do in Azerbaijan. We've just had a report that the Kurds are in open rebellion nearer to Rezaiyeh, now heavily provisioned with money and guns by the Iraqis—may God consume them. Khomeini has ordered the army to put them down, once and for all time."

"The Kurds?" Hakim smiled. "Even he, God keep him safe, even he won't do that—not once and for all."

"This time he might, Highness. He has fanatics to send against fanatics."

"Green Bands can obey orders and die but they do not inhabit those mountains, they do not have Kurdish stamina nor their lust for earthly freedom en route to Paradise."

"With your permission I will pass on your advice, Highness."

Hakim said sharply, "Will it be given any more credence than my father's—or my grandfather's—whose advice was the same?"

"I would hope so, Highness. I would hope . . ." His words were drowned as the 212 fired up, coughed, held for a moment, then died again. Out of the window they saw Erikki unclip one of the engine covers and stare at the complexity inside with a flashlight. Hashemi turned back to the Khan who sat on a chair, stiffly upright. The silence became complicated, three men's minds racing, each as strong as the other, each bent on violence of some kind.

Hakim Khan said carefully, "He cannot be arrested in my house or my domain. Even though he knows nothing of the telex, he knows he cannot stay in Tabriz, even Iran, nor may my sister go with him, even leave Iran for two years. He knows he must leave at once. His machine cannot fly. I hope he avoids arrest."

"My hands are tied, Highness." Hashemi's voice was apologetic and patently sincere. "It is my duty to obey the law of the land." Absently he noticed a piece of fluff on his sleeve and brushed it away. Armstrong got the signal at once. Brushing a left sleeve meant, "I need to talk to this man privately, he won't talk in front of you. Make an excuse and wait for me outside." Hashemi repeated with the perfect amount of sadness, "It's our duty to obey the law."

"I'm certain, quite certain, he was not part of any conspiracy, knows nothing about the flight of the others, and I would like him left alone to leave in peace."

"I would be glad to inform SAVAMA of your wishes."

"I would be glad if you would do what I suggest."

Armstrong said, "Highness, if you'll excuse me, the matter of the captain is not my affair, nor would I wish to rock any ship of state."

"Yes, you may go, Superintendent. When do I have your report on new security possibilities?"

"It will be in your hands when the colonel returns."

"Peace be with you."

"And with you, Highness." Armstrong walked out, then strolled along the corridors to the steps. Hashemi will roast the poor sod, he thought.

The evening was pleasant, nice nip in the air, a reddish tinge to the west. Red sky at night, shepherd's delight, red sky in the morning, shepherd's warning. "Evening, Captain. Between you, me, and the gatepost, if your bus was working I'd suggest a quick trip to a border."

Erikki's eyes narrowed. "Why?"

Armstrong took out a cigarette. "Climate's not very healthy around here, is it?" He cupped his hands around his lighter and flicked it.

"If you light a cigarette with all this gasoline around here, your climate and mine'll be not very healthy permanently." Erikki pressed the switch. The engine began winding up perfectly for twenty seconds, and again spluttered into silence. Erikki cursed.

Armstrong nodded politely and went back to the car. The driver opened the door for him. He settled back, lit the cigarette, and inhaled deeply, not sure if Erikki had got the message. Hope so. Can't give away the phony telex, or about Whirlwind, that'd put me against the nearest wall for treachery to Hashemi and the Khan for sticking my nose where it's clearly not invited—I was warned. Fair enough. It is internal politics.

Christ! I'm chocker with all this. I need a holiday. A long holiday. Where? I could go back to Hong Kong for a week or two, look up my old chums, the few who're left, or perhaps go up into the Pays d'Enhaut, the High Country, skiing. Haven't been skiing for years and I could use some good Swiss cooking, roesti and wurst and good coffee with thick cream and lots of wine. Lots! That's what I'll do. First Tehran, then Hashemi concluded, and off into the Wild Blue. Perhaps I'll meet someone nice . . .

But the likes of us don't come in from the cold, nor change. What the hell am I going to do for future money now that my Iranian pension's up the spout and my Hong Kong police pension's worth less and less every day? "Hello, Hashemi, how'd it go?"

"Fine, Robert. Driver, go back to HQ." The driver accelerated through the main gate and sped down the road toward the city. "Erikki'll sneak off in the early hours, just before dawn. We follow him until it pleases us and then we take him, outside Tabriz."

"With Hakim's blessing?"

"Private blessing, public outrage. Thanks." Hashemi accepted the cigarette, clearly pleased with himself. "By that time, the poor fellow will probably be no more."

Armstrong wondered what deal had been struck. "At Hakim's suggestion?"

"Of course."

"Interesting." That's not Hakim's idea. What's Hashemi up to now? Armstrong asked himself.

"Yes, interesting. After we've burned the mujhadins tonight and made sure that maniac Finn is netted, one way or another, we'll go back to Tehran."

"Perfect."

TEHRAN—AT THE BAKRAVAN HOUSE: 8:06 P.M. Sharazad put the grenade and pistol into the shoulder bag and hid it under some clothes in the drawer of her bureau. The clothes she would wear under her chador later, ski jacket and heavy sweater and ski pants, were already chosen. Now she wore a pale green silk dress from Paris that enhanced her figure and long legs perfectly. Her makeup too was perfect. A last check of the room and then she went downstairs to join the reception for Daranoush Farazan, her husband-to-be.

"Ah, Sharazad!" Meshang met her at the door. He was perspiring and covered his nervousness with pretended good humor, not knowing what to expect from her. When she had come back from the doctor's earlier, he had begun to harangue her and use dire threats, but, astonishingly, she had just dropped her eyes and said docilely, "There is no need to say any more, Meshang. God has decided, please excuse me, I will go and change." And now she was here, still docile.

And so she should, he thought. "His Excellency Farazan has been dying to greet you." He took her arm and led her through the twenty or so people in the room, mostly cronies of his and their wives, Zarah and some of her friends, none of Sharazad's. She smiled at those she knew and then turned all her concentration to Daranoush Farazan.

"Greetings, Excellency," she said politely and held out her hand. This was the first time she had ever been so close. He was shorter than she. She looked down on the few strands of dyed hair over his coarse pate, coarse skin, and even coarser hands, his bad breath infringing her space, his small black eyes glittering. "Peace be with you," she said.

"Greetings, Sharazad, and peace be with you, but please, please don't call me Excellency. How . . . how beautiful you are."

"Thank you," she said and watched herself take back her hand and smile

and stand beside him and run to fetch him a soft drink, skirts flying, and
bring it back as beautifully as it was possible to do, smiling at his droll
pleasantries, greeting other guests, pretending to be oblivious of their stares
and private laughter, never overdoing the performance, her mind centered
on the riot at the university that had already begun, and upon the Protest
March that had been forbidden by Khomeini but would take place.

Across the room Zarah was watching Sharazad, astonished with the
change but thanking God that she had accepted her lot and was going to
obey which would make all their lives easier. What else could she do?
Nothing! And nothing for me to do but accept that Meshang has a four-
teen-year-old whore who already has her fangs out, boasting that soon she'll
become his second wife.

"Zarah!"

"Oh! Yes, Meshang, my dear."

"The evening's perfect, perfect." Meshang mopped his brow and accepted a soft drink from the tray that also contained glasses of champagne
for those who cared for it. "I'm delighted that Sharazad got her senses back,
for of course it's a perfect match for her."

"Perfect," Zarah said agreeably. I suppose we should be thankful he
arrived alone and did not bring one of his fancy boys—it's true, he really
does smell of the ordure he sells. "You've arranged everything perfectly,
darling Meshang."

"Yes. Yes, it is. It's working out just as I planned."

NEAR JALEH: To reach the small grass airstrip, once the home of an
impoverished aero club now disused, Lochart had skirted the city and kept
low to come under any radar. All the way in from D'Arcy 1908 he had
tuned his radio to Tehran International but the airwaves were silent, the
airport closed down for Holy Day, no flights permitted. He had been careful
to arrive at sunset. When he cut the engine and heard the muezzins he was
pleased. So far so good.

The hangar door was rusty. With some difficulty he managed to open it
and wheeled the 206 inside. Then he reshut the door and began the long
walk. He wore his flight clothes and, if he was stopped, he planned to say
that he was an airline pilot whose car had broken down and was going to
spend the night with friends.

As he reached Tehran's outskirts, the roads became more and more
crowded, people going home or coming from the mosques, no color or
laughter among them, only a brooding apprehension.

There was not much traffic except army vehicles crammed with Green

Bands. No troops or uniformed police. Traffic wardens were young Green Bands. The city was coming back into order. Never a woman in Western dress, all chadors.

A few curses followed him, not many. A few greetings—his pilot's uniform gave him standing. Deeper into the city he found a good place to wait for a taxi near a street market. While he waited he bought a bottled soft drink, took a wedge of warm fresh bread and munched it. The night wind picked up a little but the brazier was cheerful and inviting.

"Greetings. Your papers, please."

The Green Bands were youths, polite, some with the beginnings of beards. Lochart showed them his ID that was stamped and current and they handed it back to him after some discussion. "Where are you going, may we ask?"

Deliberately in atrocious Farsi he said, "Visit friends, near bazaar. Car break down. Insha'Allah." He heard them talking among themselves, saying that pilots were safe, that this one was Canadian—isn't that part of the Great Satan? No, I don't think so. "Peace be with you," they said and wandered off.

He went to the corner and watched the traffic, the smell of the city strong—gasoline, spices, rotting fruit, urine, body odor, and death. His sharp eyes saw a taxi with only two men in the back and one in the front at an intersection now blocked by a truck making a turn. Without hesitation he ducked through the cars, shouldered another man out of the way, jerked the back door open, and crammed himself inside, apologizing profusely in good Farsi, and begged the occupants to allow him to accompany them. After some cursing, some haggling, the driver discovered the bazaar was directly on the route that he had arranged with the others, all individual travelers who had also fought their way in. "With the Help of God, yours will be the second stop, Excellency."

I've made it, he told himself exultantly, then allowed the other thought to surface: hope the others made it too. Duke and Scrag, Rudi, all of them, Freddy and good old Mac.

BAHRAIN—INTERNATIONAL AIRPORT: 8:50 P.M. Jean-Luc stood at the helipad and trained his binoculars on the two 212s that were over the end of the apron now, navigation lights winking. They had been cleared for a straight-in and approached fast. Beside him was Mathias, also using binoculars. Nearby was an ambulance, a doctor, and the Immigration officer, Yusuf. The sky was clear and star-filled, the night good with a warm fine wind.

The lead 212 turned slightly and now Jean-Luc could read the registration letters. G-HUVX. British. Thank God, they had time at Jellet, he thought, recognized Pettikin in the cockpit, then turned his glasses back to the other 212 and saw Ayre and Kyle, the mechanic.

Touchdown for Pettikin. Mathias and Jean-Luc converged, Mathias for Pettikin and Jean-Luc for the cabin door. He swung it open. "Hello, Genny, how is he?"

"He can't seem to breathe." Her face was white.

Jean-Luc caught a glimpse of McIver stretched out on the floor, a life jacket under his head. Twenty minutes before, Pettikin had reported to Bahrain Tower that one of his crew, McIver, seemed to be having a heart attack, urgently requested a doctor and ambulance meet them. The tower had cooperated instantly.

The doctor hurried past him into the cabin and knelt beside McIver. One look was sufficient. He used the hypodermic he had prepared. "This will settle him quickly and we'll have him in the hospital in a few minutes." In Arabic he called to the paramedics and they came on the run. He helped Genny down into the light, Jean-Luc now with them. "I'm Dr. Lanoire, please tell me what happened."

"Is it a heart attack?" she asked.

"Yes, yes, it is. Not a bad one," the doctor said, wanting to gentle her. He was half-French, half-Bahrain, very good, and they had been fortunate to get him at such short notice. Behind them the paramedics had McIver on a stretcher and were easing him gently out of the helicopter.

"He . . . my husband, he suddenly gasped and sort of croaked, 'I can't breathe,' then doubled over in pain and fainted." She wiped the sweat off her upper lip and continued in the same flat voice: "I thought it must be a heart attack and I didn't know what to do, then I remembered what old Doc Nutt had said when he gave all us wives a lecture once and I loosened Duncan's collar and we put him on the floor, then I found the . . . the capsules he'd given us and put one under his nose and crushed it . . ."

"Amyl nitrite?"

"Yes, yes that was it. Doc Nutt gave us each two of them and told us to keep them safe and secret and how to use them. It smelled awful but Duncan groaned and half came around then went off again. But he was breathing, kind of breathing. It was hard to hear or to see in the cabin but I thought he stopped breathing once and then I used the last capsule and that seemed to make it better again."

The doctor had been watching the stretcher. As soon as it was safely in the ambulance, he said to Jean-Luc, "Captain, please bring Madame Mc-

Iver to the hospital in half an hour, here's my card, they'll know where I am."

Genny said quickly, "Don't you think th—"

The doctor said firmly, "You'll help more by letting us do our job for half an hour. You've done yours, you've saved his life, I think." He rushed off.

CHAPTER 67

TEHRAN—AT THE BAKRAVAN HOUSE: 8:59 P.M. Zarah was at the dining table, making a last check that all was ready. Plates and cutlery and napkins of white linen, bowls of various horisht, meats and vegetables, fresh breads and fresh fruits, sweetmeats and condiments. Only the rice left to arrive and that would be brought when she called for dinner. "Good," she said to the servants and went into the other room.

Their guests were still chattering, but she saw that now Sharazad was standing by herself, near Daranoush who was deep in conversation with Meshang. Hiding her sadness, she went over to her. "My darling, you look so tired. Are you feeling all right?"

"Of course she's all right," Meshang called out with loud, brittle humor.

Sharazad put a smile on a face that had become very pale. "It's the excitement, Zarah, just all the excitement." Then to Farazan, "If you don't mind, Excellency Daranoush, I won't join you for dinner tonight."

"Why, what's the matter?" Meshang said sharply. "Are you sick?"

"Oh, no, dearest brother, it's just the excitement." Sharazad put her attention back on the little man. "Perhaps I may be allowed to see you tomorrow? Perhaps dinner tomorrow?"

Before Meshang could answer for him, Daranoush said, "Of course, my dear," and went closer, and kissed her hand, and it took all of her willpower not to heave. "We'll have dinner tomorrow. Perhaps you and Excellency Meshang and Zarah will honor my poor house." He chuckled. His face became even more grotesque. "*Our* poor house."

"Thank you, I will treasure the thought. Good night, peace be with you."

"And with you."

She was equally polite with her brother and Zarah, then turned and left them. Daranoush watched her walk away, the sway of her boyish hips and her buttocks. By God, look at her, he told himself with relish, imagining her naked, cavorting for him. I've made an even better arrangement than I imagined. By God, when Meshang proposed the marriage I was only persuaded by the dowry, along with the promises of political partnership in the bazaar—both substantial, which of course they should be for a woman pregnant with a foreigner's child. But now, by God, I don't think it will be so difficult to bed her, have her service me as I want to be served, and sometimes to make children of my own. Who knows, perhaps it will be as Meshang said, "Perhaps she'll lose the one she carries." Perhaps she will, perhaps she will.

He scratched absently until she left the room. "Now, where were we, Meshang?"

"About my suggestion for a new bank . . ."

Sharazad closed the door and ran lightly up the stairs. Jari was in her room, dozing in the big chair. "Oh Princess, how d—"

"I'm going to bed now, Jari. You can leave now and I'm not to be disturbed, Jari, by anyone for any reason. We'll talk at breakfast."

"But, Princess, I'll sleep in the chair and b—"

Sharazad stamped her foot, vexed. "Good *night*! And I am not to be disturbed!" Loudly she locked the door after her, even louder she kicked off her shoes, then, very quietly, changed quickly. Now the veil and chador. Cautiously she opened the French doors to the balcony and slipped out. Stairs went down to a patio garden and from there a passageway led to a back door. She eased off the bolts. The hinges creaked. Then she was out into the alley and had wedged the door shut. As she hurried away, her chador billowed out behind her like a great black wing.

In the reception room, Zarah glanced at her watch and walked over to Meshang. "Darling, would you like dinner to be served now?"

"In a moment, can't you see His Excellency and I are busy?"

Zarah sighed, then went off to talk to a friend, but stopped as she saw the doorkeeper come in anxiously, look around the room for Meshang, then hurry over to him and whisper. Blood drained out of Meshang's face. Daranoush Farazan gasped. She rushed over to them. "What on earth is it?"

Meshang's mouth worked but no sound came out. In the sudden hush, the frightened servant blurted out, "Green Bands're here, Highness, Green Bands with a . . . with a mullah. They want to see His Excellency at once."

In the great silence everyone remembered Paknouri's arrest and Jared's summons and all the other arrests, executions, and rumors of more terror, more komitehs, jails filled with friends and customers and relations. Daranoush was almost spitting with rage that he was here in this house at this time, wanting to rend his clothes because he had foolishly agreed to ally himself with the Bakravan family, already damned because of Jared's usury —the same usury that all bazaari moneylenders were guilty of but Jared was caught! Son of a burnt father and I've agreed publicly to the marriage and agreed in private to participate in Meshang's plans, plans I can see now oh

God protect me that are dangerously modern, dangerously Western, and clearly against the Imam's dictates and wishes! Son of a burnt father, there must be a back way out of this house of the damned.

Four Green Bands and the mullah were in the reception room the servant had shown them into, sitting cross-legged and leaning against the silk cushions. They had taken off their shoes and left them beside the door. The youths were wide-eyed at the richness of their surroundings, their guns on the carpets beside them. The mullah wore fine robes and a fine white turban and was an imposing man in his sixties with a white beard and heavy dark eyebrows, a strong face and dark eyes.

The door opened. Meshang tottered into the room like an automaton. He was pasty, and his head ached with the strength of his terror. "Greetings . . . greetings, Excellency . . ."

"Greetings. You are Excellency Meshang Bakravan?" Meshang nodded mutely. "Ah, then again greetings and peace be with you, Excellency, please excuse me that I arrive so late but I am the mullah Sayani and I come from the komiteh. We have just discovered about Excellency Jared Bakravan and I have come to tell you that though it was God's will, His Excellency was never condemned according to the law, was mistakenly shot, his property mistakenly appropriated, and that it will all be returned at once."

Meshang gaped at him, speechless.

"Islamic government is committed to uphold God's law." The mullah's brow darkened as he continued: "God knows we cannot control all zealots or simpleminded, misguided people. God knows there are some who through zeal make errors. And God knows too there are many who use the revolution for evil, hiding under the cloak of 'patriot,' many who twist Islam for their filthy purposes, many who will not obey the word of God, many who scheme to bring us into disrepute, even many who falsely wear the turban, many who do not merit the turban, even some ayatollahs, even them, but with the help of God we will tear off their turbans, cleanse Islam, and stamp out the evil, whoever they are . . ."

The words were not reaching Meshang. His mind was exploding with hope. "He . . . my father . . . I get our . . . property back?"

"Our Islamic government is the government of law. Sovereignty belongs to God alone. The law of Islam has absolute authority over everyone—including the Islamic government. Even the Most Noble Messenger, upon whom be peace, was subject to the law that God alone revealed, alone expounded by the tongue of the Koran." The mullah got up. "It was the

Will of God but Excellency Jared Bakravan was not judged according to the law."

"It's . . . it's true?"

"Yes, the Will of God, Excellency. Everything will be returned to you. Didn't your father support us lavishly? How can Islamic government flourish without bazaari help and support, how can we exist without bazaaris to fight the enemies of Islam, the enemies of Iran and the Infidel? . . ."

OUTSIDE THE BAZAAR: The taxi stopped in the crowded square. Lochart got out and paid the driver as two of a mass of would-be passengers, a woman and a man, fought their way into the space he had vacated. The square was full of people streaming into and out of the mosque and the bazaar and surrounding the street stalls. They paid little attention to him, his uniform and cap giving him free passage. The night was chill and overcast. The wind had picked up again and guttered the flames of the oil lamps of street vendors. Across the square was the street of the Bakravan house and he walked briskly, rounded the corner, and stepped aside to let the mullah Sayani and the Green Bands pass, then went on again.

At the door in the high wall he stopped, took a deep breath, and knocked loudly. Then knocked again. Then again. He heard footsteps, saw an eye behind the spy hole. "Doorkeeper, it's me, Excellency Captain Lochart," he called out happily.

The door swung open. "Greetings, Excellency," the doorkeeper said, still not over the shock of the abrupt arrival and departure of the mullah and Green Bands—bowed out humbly by Excellency Foul Temper himself, he thought in awe, who the very second the door was bolted had jumped up and down like a madman, drummed his feet on the ground, and rushed back silently into the house, and now here's another apparition, by God, the Infidel who once was married to the betrothed of Excellency Piss.

A squall blew dead leaves across the patio. Another pop-eyed servant stood at the open main door. "Greetings, Excellency," he mumbled, "I'll . . . I'll tell Excellency Meshang you've arrived."

"Wait!" Now Lochart could hear the excited buzz of voices coming from the dining salon, glasses clinking, laughter of a party. "Is my wife in there?"

"Your wife?" The servant collected himself with difficulty. "The, er, Her Highness, Captain Excellency, she's gone to bed."

Lochart's anxiety soared. "Is she sick?"

"She did not appear sick, Excellency, she went just before dinner. I'll tell Excellency Meshang th—"

"No need to disturb him and his guests," he said, delighted with the opportunity of seeing her alone first. "I'll see her, then come down and announce myself later."

The servant watched him go up the stairs, two at a time, waited until he was out of sight, then hurried to find Meshang.

Lochart went along a corridor into another. He forced himself to walk, relishing how surprised she would be and so happy and then they would see Meshang and Meshang would listen to the plan. At last he was at their door and turned the handle. When the door did not open, he tapped and called out softly, "Sharazad, it's me, Tommy." His spirit sang while he waited. "Sharazad?" Waiting. Knocking. Waiting. Then knocking a little louder. "Sharazad!"

"Excellency!"

"Oh, hello, Jari," he said, in his impatience not noticing that she was trembling. "Sharazad, darling, unlock the door, it's me, Tommy!"

"Her Highness said she was not to be disturbed."

"She didn't mean me, of course not! Oh! She's taken a sleeping pill?"

"Oh no, Excellency."

He put all of his attention on her. "What're you so frightened about?"

"Me? I'm not frightened, Excellency, why should I be frightened?"

Something's wrong, he thought. Impatiently he turned back to the door. "Sharazad!" Waiting waiting waiting. "This is ridiculous!" he muttered. *"Sharazad!"* Before he knew what he was doing he was hammering on the door. "Open the door, for crissake!"

"What are you doing here?"

It was Meshang, raw with rage. At the far end of the corridor, Lochart saw Zarah come into view and stop. "Good . . . good evening, Meshang," he said, his heart pounding, trying to sound reasonable and polite and why the hell doesn't she open the door and this isn't the way it's supposed to happen. "I came back to see my wife."

"She's not your wife, she's divorced, now get out!"

Lochart stared at him blankly. "Of course she's my wife!"

"By God, are you simple? She *was* your wife. Now leave my house!"

"You're crazy, you can't divorce her just like that!"

"GET OUT!"

"Get stuffed!" Again Lochart hammered on the door. "Sharazad!"

Meshang whirled on Zarah. "Go and get some Green Bands! Go on, get some Green Bands! They'll throw this madman out!"

"But, Meshang, isn't it dangerous to involve them in ou—"

"Get them!"

Lochart's temper snapped. His shoulder went into the door. It shuddered but did not give so he raised his foot, slammed his heel against the lock.

The lock shattered and the door burst open. "Get Green Bands!" Meshang shrieked. "Don't you understand they're on our side now, we're reinstated . . ." Then he rushed through the door too. Blankly he also saw the room was empty, bed empty, bathroom empty, nowhere else she could be. Both he and Lochart turned on Jari who stood at the doorway, staring with disbelief, Zarah cautiously behind her in the hall. "Where is she?" Meshang shouted.

"I don't know, Excellency, she never left here, my room is next door and I'm a light sleeper . . ." Jari howled as Meshang belted her across the mouth, the blow sending her reeling onto her hands and knees.

"Where's she gone?"

"I don't know, Excellency, I thought she was in be—" She shrieked as Meshang's toe went into her side. "By God, I don't know I don't know I don't know!"

Lochart was at the French doors. They opened easily, already unlatched. At once he went out onto the balcony, down the stairs, and to the back door. He came back slowly, in turmoil. Meshang and Zarah watched him from the balcony. "The back door was unlocked. She must've gone out this way."

"Gone where?" Meshang was flushed with rage, and Zarah turned on Jari who was still on her hands and knees in the bedroom, moaning and weeping with fear and pain. "Shut up, you dog, or I'll whip you. Jari! If you don't know where she's gone, where do you think she's gone?"

"I . . . I don't know, Highness," the old woman sobbed.

"Thinkkk!" Zarah shrieked and slapped her.

Jari howled. "I don't knowwww! She's been strange all day, Excellencies, strange, she sent me away this afternoon and went off by herself and I met her near seven o'clock and we came back together but she said nothing, nothing, nothing . . ."

"By God, why didn't you tell me?" Meshang shouted.

"What was there to tell, Excellency? Please don't kick me again, please!"

Meshang groped for a chair. The violent pendulum from total terror when the mullah and Green Bands were announced to total euphoria at his reprieve and reinstatement to fury finding Lochart here and Sharazad gone had momentarily unhinged him. His mouth moved but there was no sound and he saw Lochart questioning Jari but could not understand the words.

When he had rushed back into the dining room to stutter the God-given news there had been rejoicing, Zarah had wept with happiness and embraced him and so did the women, and the men had warmly wrung his hand. All except Daranoush. Daranoush was no longer there. He had fled. Out the back door. "He's gone?"

"Like a bag full of fart!" someone called out.

Everyone had started laughing, their private relief that they were no longer in any immediate danger of guilt by association, together with Meshang's totally unexpected rocket back to wealth and power, making them light-headed. Someone had shouted, "You really can't have Daranoush the Daring as a brother-in-law, Meshang!"

"No, no, by God," he remembered saying, quaffing a glass of champagne. "How could you trust such a man?"

"Not even with a bucket of piss! By the Prophet, I've always thought Dirty Daranoush overcharged for his services. The bazaar should rescind his contract!"

Another cheer and general agreement and Meshang had drunk a second glass of champagne, gloating over the glorious new possibilities opened up before him: the new contract for the bazaar's waste which he as the injured party would of course have, a new syndicate to finance the government under his guidance and greater profit, new associations with more important ministers than Ali Kia—where is that son of a dog?—new deals in the oil fields, monopolies to maneuver, a new match for Sharazad, so easy now for who would not want to be part of his family, *the* bazaari family? No need now to pay out a usurious dowry I agreed to only under duress. All my property back, the estates on the Caspian shores, streets of houses in Jaleh, apartments in the northern suburbs, lands and orchards and fields and villages, all of it back.

Then the servant destroying his elation, whispering that Lochart had returned, was already in his house, already upstairs. Rushing upstairs, and now helplessly watching the man he hated so much questioning Jari, Zarah listening as intently.

With an effort he concentrated. Jari was saying between sobs, ". . . I'm not sure, Excellency, she . . . she only . . . she only told me the young man that saved her life at the first Women's Protest was a university student."

"Did she ever meet him alone?"

"Oh, no, Excellency, no, as I said we met him at the march and he asked us to take coffee to recover," Jari said. She was petrified of being caught in the lie but more petrified of telling what had really happened. God protect us, she prayed. Where has she gone, where?

"What was his name, Jari?"

"I don't know, Excellencies, it might have been Ibrahim or . . . or Ishmael, I don't know. I already told you, he had no importance."

Lochart's head was pounding. No clue, nothing. Where would she have gone? To a friend's? To the university? Another protest march? Don't forget the rumors in the market about university students rioting again, more explosions expected tonight, more marches and countermarches, Green Bands versus the leftists, but all non-Imam-sponsored marches forbidden by the Komiteh and the Komiteh's patience ended. "Jari, you must have some idea, some way of helping us!"

Meshang said gutturally, "Whip her, she knows!"

"I don't I don't . . ." Jari wailed.

"Shut up, Jari!" Lochart turned on Meshang, his face pale and violence absolute. "I don't know where she's gone but I know the why: you forced the divorce, and I swear by the Lord God if she comes to harm, any harm, *you will pay!*"

Meshang blustered, "You left her, you left her penniless, you abandoned her and you're divorced, yo—"

"Remember, you will pay! And if you bar me from this house whenever I come back or she comes back, by God, be that on your head too!" On the edge of madness, Lochart stalked toward the French doors.

Zarah said quickly, "Where are you going?"

"I don't know . . . I . . . . To the university. Perhaps she's gone to join another march though why she'd run off to do that . . ." Lochart could not bring himself to articulate his real terror: that her revolt was so extreme that her mind was unhinged and she would kill herself—oh, not suicide, but how many times in the past had she said, "Never worry about me, Tommy. I am a Believer, I always try to do God's work and so long as I die doing God's work with God's name on my lips I will go to Paradise."

But what about our child-to-be? A mother wouldn't, couldn't, could she, someone like Sharazad?

The room was very still. For an eternity he stood there. Then, all at once, his being swept him into new waters. In a strange clear voice he said, "Bear witness for me: I attest that there is no other God but God and Mohammed is the Prophet of God . . . I attest that there is no other God but God and Mohammed is the Prophet of God . . ." and the third and last time. Now it was done. He was at peace with himself. He saw them staring at him. Stunned.

Meshang broke the silence, no longer in anger. "Allah-u Akbar! Welcome. But saying the Shahada is not enough, not by itself."

"I know. But it is the beginning."

They watched him vanish into the night, all of them spellbound that they had witnessed a soul being saved, an unbeliever transmuted into a Believer, so unexpectedly. All of them were filled with joy, degrees of joy. "God is Great!"

Zarah murmured, "Meshang, doesn't this change everything?"

"Yes, yes and no. But now he will go to Paradise. As God wants." Suddenly he was very tired. His eyes went to Jari, and she began to tremble again. "Jari," he said with the same calm, "you are going to be whipped until you tell me all the truth or you are in hell. Come along, Zarah, we mustn't forget our guests."

"And Sharazad?"

"As God wills."

NEAR THE UNIVERSITY: 9:48 P.M. Sharazad turned into the main road where Green Bands and their supporters were collecting. Thousands of them. The vast majority were men. All armed. Mullahs marshaled them, exorting them to maintain discipline, not to fire on the leftists until they were fired upon, to try to persuade them from their evil. "Don't forget they're Iranians, not satanic foreigners. God is Great . . . God is Great . . ."

"Welcome, child," an old mullah said gently, "peace be upon you."

"And upon you," she said. "We're marching against the anti-God?"

"Oh, yes, in a little while, there's plenty of time."

"I have a gun," she said proudly, showing it to him. "God is Great."

"God is Great. But better that the killing should cease and the misguided should recognize the Truth, renounce their heresies, obey the Imam, and come back to Islam." The old man saw her youth and resolution and was uplifted, and saddened. "Better the killing should cease but if those of the Left Hand do not cease to oppose the Imam, God's peace on him, then with the Help of God we will hurry them into hell. . . ."

TABRIZ—AT THE PALACE: 10:05 P.M. The three of them were sitting in front of the wood fire drinking after-dinner coffee and watching the flames, the room small and richly brocaded, warm and intimate—one of Hakim's guards beside the door. But there was no peace between them, though all had pretended otherwise, now and during the evening. The flames held their attention, each seeing different pictures therein. Erikki was watching the fork in the road, always the fork, one way the flames leading to loneliness, the other to fulfillment—perhaps and perhaps not. Azadeh watched the future, trying not to watch it.

Hakim Khan took his eyes off the fire and threw down the gauntlet. "You've been distracted all evening, Azadeh," he said.

"Yes. I think we all are." Her smile was not real. "Do you think we could talk in private, the three of us?"

"Of course." Hakim motioned to the guard. "I'll call if I need you." The man obeyed and closed the door after him. Instantly the mood of the room changed. Now all three were adversaries, all aware of it, all on guard and all ready. "Yes, Azadeh?"

"Is it true that Erikki must leave at once?"

"Yes."

"There must be a solution. I cannot endure two years without my husband."

"With the Help of God the time will pass quickly." Hakim Khan sat stiffly upright, the pain eased by the codeine.

"I cannot endure two years," she said again.

"Your oath cannot be broken."

Erikki said, "He's right, Azadeh. You gave the oath freely, Hakim is Khan and the price . . . fair. But all the killings—I must leave, the fault's mine, not yours or Hakim's."

"You did nothing wrong, nothing, you were forced into protecting me and yourself, they were carrion bent on murdering us, and as to the raid . . . you did what you thought best, you had no way of knowing the ransom was part paid or Father was dead . . . he should not have ordered the messenger killed."

"That changes nothing. I have to go tonight. We can accept it, and leave it at that," Erikki said, watching Hakim. "Two years will pass quickly."

"If you live, my darling." Azadeh turned to her brother who looked back at her, his smile still the same, eyes the same.

Erikki glanced from brother to sister, so different and yet so similar. What's changed her, why has she precipitated that which should not have been precipitated?

"Of course if I live," he said, outwardly calm.

An ember fell into the hearth and he reached forward and moved it to safety. He saw that Azadeh had not taken her gaze off Hakim, nor he off her. The same calm, same polite smile, same inflexibility.

"Yes, Azadeh?" Hakim said.

"A mullah could absolve me from my oath."

"Not possible. Neither a mullah nor I could do that, not even the Imam would agree."

"I can absolve myself. This is between me and God, I can ab—"

"You cannot, Azadeh. You cannot and live at peace with yourself."

"I can. I can and be at peace."

"Not and remain Muslim."

"Yes," she said simply, "I agree."

Hakim gasped. "You don't know what you say."

"Oh, but I do. I've considered even that." Her voice was toneless. "I've considered that solution and found it bearable. I will not endure two years of separation, nor will I endure any attempt on my husband's life, or forgive it." She sat back and left the battle for the moment, nauseous but glad she had brought the matter into the open but frightened all the same. Once more she blessed Aysha for forewarning her.

"I will not allow you to renounce Islam under any circumstances," Hakim said.

She just looked back at the flames.

The minefield was all around them, all mines triggered, and though Hakim was concentrating on her, his senses probed Erikki, He of the Knife, knowing the man was waiting too, playing a different game now that the problem was before them. Should I have dismissed the guard? he asked himself, outraged by her threat, the smell of danger filling his nostrils. "Whatever you say, Azadeh, whatever you try, for the sake of your soul I would be forced to prevent an apostasy—in any way I could. That's unthinkable."

"Then please help me. You're very wise. You're Khan and we have been through much together. I beg you, remove the threat to my soul and to my husband."

"I don't threaten your soul or your husband." Hakim looked at Erikki directly. "I don't."

Erikki said, "What were those dangers you mentioned?"

"I can't tell you, Erikki," Hakim said.

"Would you excuse us, Highness? We must get ready to leave." Azadeh got up. So did Erikki.

"You stay where you are!" Hakim was furious. "Erikki, you'd allow her to forswear Islam, her heritage, and her chance of life everlasting?"

"No, that's not part of my plan," he said. Both of them stared at him, bewildered. "Please tell me what dangers, Hakim."

"What plan? You have a plan? To do what?"

"The dangers, first tell me what dangers. Azadeh's Islam is safe with me, by my own gods I swear it. What dangers?"

It had never been part of Hakim's strategy to tell them, but now he was rocked by her intractability, aghast that she would consider committing the ultimate heresy, and further disoriented by this strange man's sincerity. So he told them about the telex and the pilots and airplanes fleeing, and his conversation with Hashemi, noticing that though Azadeh was as aghast as Erikki, her surprise did not seem real. It's almost as though she already knew, had been present, both times, but how could she possibly know? He rushed on: "I told him you could not be taken in my house or domain or in Tabriz, that I would give you a car, that I hoped you'd escape arrest, and that you would leave just before dawn."

Erikki was shattered. The telex's changed everything, he thought. "So they'll be waiting for me."

"Yes. But I did not tell Hashemi I had another plan, that I've already sent a car into Tabriz, that the moment Azadeh was asleep I wo—"

"You'd've left me, Erikki?" Azadeh was appalled. "You'd've left me without telling me, without asking me?"

"Perhaps. What were you saying, Hakim; please finish what you were saying."

"The moment Azadeh was asleep I planned to smuggle you out of the palace into Tabriz where the car is and point you toward the border, the Turkish border. I have friends in Khoi and they would help you across it, with the Help of God," Hakim added automatically, enormously relieved that he had had the foresight to arrange this alternate plan—just in case it was needed. And now it's happened, he thought. "You have a plan?"

"Yes."

"What is it?"

"If you don't like it, Hakim Khan, what then?"

"In that case I would refuse to allow it and try to stop it."

"I would prefer not to risk your displeasure."

"Without my help, you cannot leave."

"I'd like your help, that's true." Erikki was no longer confident. With Mac and Charlie and the rest gone—how in hell could they do it so fast? Why the hell didn't it happen while we were in Tehran but thank all gods Hakim's Khan now and can protect Azadeh—it's clear what SAVAK'll do to me if they catch me, when they catch me. "You were right about the danger. You think I could sneak out as you said?"

"Hashemi left two policemen on the gate. I think you could be smuggled out—somehow it should be possible to distract them—I don't know if there're others on the road down to the city but there may be, more than likely there would be. If they're vigilant and you're intercepted . . . that's God's will."

Azadeh said, "Erikki, they're expecting you to go alone, and the colonel agreed not to touch you inside Tabriz. If we were hidden in the back of an old truck—we only need a little luck to avoid them."

"You cannot leave," Hakim said impatiently, but she did not hear him. Her mind had leaped to Ross and Gueng and the previous escape, and how difficult those two had found it even though they were trained saboteurs and fighters. Poor Gueng. A chill went through her. The road north's as difficult as the one south, so easy to ambush us, so easy to put up road-blocks. Not so far in miles to Khoi, and past Khoi to the frontier, but a million miles in time and with my bad back . . . I doubt if I could walk even one of them.

"Never mind," she muttered. "We'll get there all right. With the Help of God we'll escape."

Hakim flared, "By God and the Prophet, what about your oath, Azadeh?"

Her face was very pale now and she held on to her fingers to stop the tremble. "Please forgive me, Hakim, I've told you. And if I'm prevented from leaving with Erikki now, or if Erikki won't take me with him, I'll escape somehow, I will, I swear it." She glanced at Erikki. "If Mac and all the others have fled, you could be used as a hostage."

"I know. I have to get out as fast as I can. But you have to stay. You can't give up your religion just because of the two years, much as I loathe leaving you."

"Would Tom Lochart leave Sharazad for two years?"

"That's not the point," Erikki said carefully. "You're not Sharazad, you're the sister of a Khan and you swore to stay."

"That's between me and God. Tommy wouldn't leave Sharazad," Azadeh said stubbornly, "Sharazad wouldn't leave her Tommy, she lov—"

"I must know your plan," Hakim interrupted coldly.

"Sorry, I trust no one in this."

The Khan's eyes narrowed to slits, and it took all of his will not to call the guard. "So there's an impasse. Azadeh, pour me some coffee, please." At once she obeyed. He looked at the huge man who stood with his back to the fire. "Isn't there?"

"Please solve it, Hakim Khan," Erikki said. "I know you to be a wise man and I would do you no harm, or Azadeh harm."

Hakim accepted the coffee and thanked her, watched the fire, weighing and sifting, needing to know what Erikki had in his mind, wanting an end to all this and Erikki gone and Azadeh here and as she always was before, wise and gentle and loving and obedient—and Muslim. But he knew her too well to be sure she would not do as she threatened, and he loved her too much to allow her to carry out the threat.

"Perhaps this would satisfy you, Erikki: I swear by God I will assist you, providing your plan does not negate my sister's oath, does not force her to apostasize, does not put her in spiritual danger or political danger . . ." He thought a moment, ". . . does not harm her or harm me—and has a chance of success."

Azadeh bridled angrily. "That's no help, how can Erikki possib—"

"Azadeh!" Erikki said curtly. "Where are your manners? Keep quiet. The Khan was talking to me, not you. It's my plan he wants to know, not yours."

"Sorry, please excuse me," she said at once, meaning it. "Yes, you're right. I apologize to both of you, please excuse me."

"When we were married, you swore to obey me. Does that still apply?" he asked harshly, furious that she had almost ruined his plan, for he had seen Hakim's eyes cross with rage and he needed him calm, not agitated.

"Yes, Erikki," she told him immediately, still shocked by what Hakim had said, for that closed every path except the one she had chosen—and that choice petrified her. "Yes, without reservation, provided you don't leave me."

"Without reservation—yes or no?"

Pictures of Erikki flashed through her mind, his gentleness and love and laughter and all the good things, along with the brooding violence that had never touched her but would touch anyone who threatened her or stood in his way, Abdollah, Johnny, even Hakim—particularly Hakim.

Without reservation, yes, she wanted to say, except against Hakim, except if you leave me. His eyes were boring into her. For the first time she was afraid of him. She muttered, "Yes, without any reservation. I beg you not to leave me."

Erikki turned his attention to Hakim: "I accept what you said, thank you." He sat down again. Azadeh hesitated, then knelt beside him, resting her arm on his knees, wanting the contact, hoping it would help to push away her fear and anger with herself for losing her temper. I must be going mad, she thought. God help me . . .

"I accept the rules you've set, Hakim Khan," Erikki was saying quietly. "Even so I'm still not going to tell you my pl— Wait, wait, wait! You swore you'd help if I didn't put you at risk, and I won't. Instead," he said carefully, "instead I'll give you a hypothetical approach to a plan that might satisfy all your conditions." Unconsciously his hand began stroking her hair and her neck. She felt the tension leaving her. Erikki watched Hakim, both men ready to explode. "All right so far?"

"Go on."

"Say hypothetically my chopper was in perfect shape, that I'd been pretending I couldn't start her properly to throw everyone off, and to get everyone used to the idea of the engines starting and stopping, say I'd lied about the fuel and there was enough for an hour's flight, easily enough to get to the border an—"

"Is there?" Hakim said involuntarily, the idea opening a new avenue.

"For the sake of this hypothetical story, yes." Erikki felt Azadeh's grip tighten on his knee but pretended not to notice. "Say in a minute or two, before we all went to bed, I told you I wanted to try to start her again. Say I did just that, the engines caught and held enough to warm her and then died, no one'd worry—the Will of God. Everyone'd think the madman won't leave well alone, why doesn't he quit and let us sleep in peace? Then say I started her, pushed on all power and pulled her into the sky. Hypothetically I could be away in seconds—provided the guards didn't fire on me, and provided there were no hostiles, Green Bands, or police with guns on the gate or outside the walls."

The breath escaped from Hakim's lips. Azadeh shifted a little. The silk of her dress rustled. "I pray that such a make-believe could come to pass," she said.

Hakim said, "It would be a thousand times better than a car, ten thousand times better. You could fly all the way by night?"

"I could, providing I had a map. Most pilots who've spent time in an area keep a good map in their heads—of course, this is all make-believe."

"Yes, yes it is. Well, then, so far so good with your make-believe plan. You could escape this way, if you could neutralize the hostiles in the forecourt. Now, hypothetically, what about my sister?"

"My wife isn't in on any escape, real or hypothetical. Azadeh has no choice: she must stay of her own accord and wait the two years." Erikki saw

Hakim's astonishment and felt Azadeh's instant rebellion under his fingers. But he did not allow his fingers to cease their rhythm on her hair and neck, soothing her, coaxing her, and he continued smoothly, "She is committed to stay in obedience to her oath. She cannot leave. No one who loves her, most of all me, would allow her to give up Islam because of two years. In fact, Azadeh, make-believe or not, *it is forbidden.* Understand?"

"I hear what you say, husband," she said through her teeth, so angry she could hardly speak and cursing herself for falling into his trap.

"You are bound by your oath for two years, then you can leave freely. It's ordered!"

She looked up at him, and said darkly, "Perhaps after two years I might not wish to leave."

Erikki rested his great hand on her shoulder, his fingers lightly around her neck. "Then, woman, I shall come back and drag you out by your hair." He said it so quietly with such venom that it froze her. In a moment she dropped her eyes and looked at the fire, still leaning against his legs. He kept his hand on her shoulder. She made no move to remove it. But he knew she was seething, hating him. Still, he knew it was necessary to say what he had said.

"Please excuse me a moment," she said, her voice like ice.

The two men watched her leave.

When they were alone Hakim said, "Will she obey?"

"No," Erikki said. "Not unless you lock her up and even then . . . No. Her mind's made up."

"I will never, never allow her to break her oath and renounce Islam, you must understand that, even . . . even if I have to kill her."

Erikki looked at him. "If you harm her, you're a dead man—if I'm alive."

AT THE NORTHERN SLUMS OF TABRIZ CITY: 10:36 P.M.

In the darkness the first wave of Green Bands rushed the door in the high wall, blew the locks off, and went into the inner patio with guns blazing. Hashemi and Robert Armstrong were across the square in the comparative safety of a parked truck. Other men lurked in the alley to cut off any retreat.

"Now!" Hashemi said into his walkie-talkie. At once the enemy side of the square was bathed in light from searchlights mounted on camouflaged trucks. Men were fleeing out of other doors but police and Green Bands opened up and the battle began. "Come on, Robert," Hashemi said and led a careful rush closer.

Informers had whispered that tonight there would be a high-level meeting of Islamic-Marxist leaders here and that this building was connected to others on either side by a rabbit warren of secret doors and passages. With Hakim Khan's assistance Hashemi had precipitated this first of a series of raids to deactivate extensive leftist opposition to the government, to seize the leaders and make a public example of them—for his own purposes.

The first group of Green Bands had cleared the ground floor and were charging up the stairs, careless of their safety. The defenders, now that they were over their surprise, fought back with equal ferocity, well armed and well trained.

Outside in the square there was a lull, no more defenders wishing to run the gauntlet or to join those pinned down helplessly among the cars, some already on fire. The alley behind the building was ominously quiet, police and Green Bands blocking both ends, well entrenched behind their vehicles. "Why do we wait here like stinking, cowardly Iraqis," one of the Green Bands said truculently. "Why don't we carry the battle to them?"

"You wait because that's what the colonel ordered," the sergeant of police said, "you wait because we can kill all the dogs safely and th—"

"I'm not subject to any dog colonel, only to God! God is greatttttttttt!" With that the youth cocked his rifle and rushed out of ambush toward the back door of the target building. Others followed him. The sergeant cursed them and ordered them back but his words were buried by the fusillade that came down on the youths from small windows high in the walls and slaughtered them.

Hashemi and others had heard the firing in the alley and presumed that a breakout had been attempted. "The dogs can't escape that way, Robert," Hashemi shouted gleefully, "they're trapped!" From where he was he could see that the attack on the main tenement was held up. He clicked on the sender: "Second wave into the HQ building." Immediately a mullah and another bunch of youths shrieked their battle cry and rushed across the square—Robert Armstrong appalled that Hashemi would order them out like that, floodlit, such easy targets. "Don't interfere, Robert! By God, I'm tired of you interfering," Hashemi had said coldly when he had made some suggestions on how to contain the raid before the attack had started. "Keep your advice to yourself, this is internal, nothing to do with you!"

"But, Hashemi, not all the buildings are hostile or Marxist, there're bound to be families, perhaps hundreds of innocen—"

"Keep quiet or, by God, I'll consider it treason!"

"Then I'll stay behind. I'll go back and watch the palace."

"I've said you'll come on the raid! You think you British're the only ones who can handle a few revolutionaries? You'll stay beside me where I can see you—but first give me your gun!"

"But, Hashem—"

"Your gun! By the Prophet, I don't trust you anymore. Your gun!"

So he had given it to him and then Hashemi had come out of his rage and had seemed to relax and laughed the encounter off. But he had not returned the gun and Armstrong felt naked in the night, afraid that somehow he had been betrayed. He glanced at him, saw again that strangeness in Fazir's eyes and the way his mouth was working, a little saliva at the corners.

A burst of heavy firing pulled his attention back to the tenement. The automatic fire was coming from the upper windows against the new attack. Many youths were cut down but some got inside, the mullah among them, to reinforce those fighters still alive. Together they pulled away the bodies blocking the stairs, and fought their way up onto the next floor.

In the square Hashemi was now ducked down behind a car, consumed with excitement and his sense of power. "More men into the HQ building!"

Never before had he been in control of a battle or even part of one. All his previous work had been secret, undercover, just a few men involved on each operation—even with his Group Four assassins all he had ever done was to give orders in safety and wait in safety, far from the action. Except the once that he had personally detonated the car bomb that had obliterated his SAVAMA enemy, General Janan. By God and the Prophet, his mind was shouting, this is what I was born for: battle and war!

"General assault!" he shouted into the walkie-talkie and then stood up and bellowed as loud as he could, "General assault!"

Men charged out of the night. Grenades over walls into patios and into windows indiscriminately. Explosions and billowing smoke, more firing, rifle and automatic and more explosions and then a giant explosion in the leftist headquarters as an ammunition and gasoline cache detonated, blowing off the top story and most of the façade. The wave of heat tore at Hashemi's clothes, knocked Armstrong down, and Mzytryk who had been watching through binoculars from the safety of an upstairs window on the other side of the square saw them clearly in the floodlight and decided the time was perfect.

"Now!" he said in Russian.

The sharpshooter beside him was already centered on the target through his telescopic sight, the rifle barrel resting on the window ledge. At once he flattened his index finger above the trigger guard, felt Mzytryk's finger on the trigger, and began the countdown as ordered: "Three . . . two . . . one . . . fire!" Mzytryk squeezed the trigger. Both men saw the dumdum bullet go into Hashemi's lower back, slam him spread-eagled against the car in front, then sprawling into the dirt.

"Good," Mzytryk muttered grimly, regretting only that his own eyes and hands were not good enough to deal with his son's murderers by himself.

"Three . . . two . . . one . . ." The gunsight wavered. Both of them cursed, for they had seen Armstrong whirl around, look in their direction for an instant, then hurl himself through a gap in the cars and disappear behind one of them.

"He's near the front wheel. He can't escape. Be patient—fire when you can!" Mzytryk hurried out of the room to the stairwell and shouted in Turkish to the men waiting below, "Go!" then rushed back again. As he came through the doorway, he saw the sharpshooter fire. "Got him," the man said with an obscenity. Mzytryk trained his binoculars but could not see Armstrong. "Where is he?"

"Behind the black car—he stuck his head around the front wheel for a second and I got him."

"Did you kill him?"

"No, Comrade General. I was very careful, just as you ordered."

"You're sure?"

"Yes, Comrade General, I got him in the shoulder, perhaps the chest."

The headquarters building burning furiously now, firing from the adjoining tenements sporadic, just pockets of resistance, attackers heavily outnumbering defenders, all of them whipped into a frenzy of brutality. Barbarians, Mzytryk thought contemptuously, then looked back at the sprawled body of Hashemi twitching and jerking and twitching again, half in and half out of the joub. Don't die too quickly, *matyeryebyets*. "Can you see him, the Englishman?"

"No, Comrade General, but I've both sides covered."

Then Mzytryk saw the broken-down ambulance arriving and men with Red Cross armbands fan out with stretchers to begin picking up the wounded, the battle mostly over now. I'm glad I came tonight, he thought, his rage not yet assuaged. He had decided to direct the retaliation personally the moment Hakim Khan's message had arrived yesterday. The barely disguised "summons"—together with Pahmudi's secret report of the manner of his son's death at the hands of Hashemi and Armstrong—had sent him into a paroxysm of rage.

Simple to arrange a helicopter and set down just outside Tabriz last night, simple to arrange a counterattack to ambush the two murderers. Simple to plan his vengeance that would cement relations with Pahmudi by removing his enemy Hashemi Fazir for him and at the same time save both his mujhadin and Tudeh much future trouble. And Armstrong, the elusive MI6 agent, another long-overdue elimination—curse that fornicator for appearing like a ghost after all these years.

"Comrade General!"

"Yes, I see them." Mzytryk watched the Red Cross men put Hashemi on a stretcher and carry him off toward the ambulance. Others went behind the car. The crossed lines of the telescopic sight followed them. Mzytryk's excitement soared. The sharpshooter waited patiently. When the men reappeared, they were half carrying, half dragging Armstrong between them. "I knew I'd hit the bastard," the sharpshooter said.

AT THE PALACE: 11:04 P.M. Silently the phosphorescent, red night-flying lights of the massed instrument panel came to life. Erikki's finger pressed Engine Start. The jets caught, coughed, caught, hesitated as he eased the circuit breakers carefully in and out. Then he shoved them home. The engines began a true warm-up.

Floodlights at half power were on in the forecourt. Azadeh and Hakim Khan, heavy-coated against the night cold, stood just clear of the turning blades, watching him. At the front gate a hundred yards or so away two guards and Hashemi's two police also watched but idly. Their cigarettes glowed. The two policemen shouldered their Kalashnikovs and strolled nearer.

Once more the engines spluttered and Hakim Khan called out over the noise, "Erikki, forget it for tonight!" But Erikki did not hear him. Hakim moved away from the noise, nearer to the gate, Azadeh following him reluctantly. His walk was ponderous and awkward, and he cursed, unused to his crutches.

"Greetings, Highness," the policemen said politely.

"Greetings. Azadeh," Hakim said irritably, "your husband's got no patience, he's losing his senses. What's the matter with him? It's ridiculous to keep trying the engines. What good would it do even if he could start them?"

"I don't know, Highness." Azadeh's face was white in the pale light and she was very uneasy. "He's . . . since the raid he's been very strange, very difficult, difficult to understand—he frightens me."

"I don't wonder! He's enough to frighten the Devil."

"Please excuse me, Highness," Azadeh said apologetically, "but in normal times he's . . . he's not frightening."

Politely the two policemen turned away, but Hakim stopped them. "Have you noticed any difference in the pilot?"

"He's very angry, Highness. He's been angry for hours. Once I saw him kick the machine—but different or not is difficult to say. I've never been near to him before." The corporal was in his forties and wanted no trouble.

The other man was younger and even more afraid. Their orders were to watch and wait until the pilot left by car, or any car left, not to hinder its leaving but to report to HQ at once by their car radio. Both of them realized the danger of their position—the arm of the Gorgon Khan had a very long reach. Both knew of the servants and guards of the late Khan accused by him of treason, still rotting in police dungeons. But both also knew the reach of Inner Intelligence was more certain.

"Tell him to stop it, Azadeh, to stop the engines."

"He's never before been so . . . so angry with me, and tonight . . ." Her eyes almost crossed in her rage. "I don't think I can obey him."

"You *WILL*!"

After a pause she muttered, "When he's even a little angry, I can do nothing with him."

The policemen saw her paleness and were sorry for her but more sorry for themselves—they had heard what had happened on the mountainside. God protect us from He of the Knife! What must it be like to marry such a barbarian who everyone knows drank the blood of the tribesmen he slaughtered, worships forest spirits against the law of God, and rolls naked in the snow, forcing her to do the same.

The engines spluttered and began to die and they saw Erikki bellow with rage and smash his great fist on the side of the cockpit, denting the aluminum with the force of his blow.

"Highness, with your permission I will go to bed—I think I will take a sleeping pill and hope that tomorrow is a better . . ." Her words trailed off.

"Yes. A sleeping pill is a good idea. Very good. I'm afraid I'll have to take two, my back hurts terribly and now I can't sleep without them." Hakim added angrily, "It's his fault! If it wasn't for him I wouldn't be in pain." He turned to his bodyguard. "Fetch my guards on the gate, I want to give them instructions. Come along, Azadeh."

Painfully he walked off, Azadeh obediently and sullenly at his side. The engines started shrieking again. Irritably Hakim Khan turned and snapped at the policemen, "If he doesn't stop in five minutes, order him to stop in my name! Five minutes, by God!"

Uneasily the two men watched them leave, the bodyguard with the two gate guards hurrying after them up the steps. "If Her Highness can't deal with him, what can we do?" the older policeman said.

"With the Help of God the engines will continue until the barbarian is satisfied, or he stops them himself."

* * *

The lights in the forecourt went out. After six minutes the engines were still starting and stopping. "We'd better obey." The young policeman was very nervous. "The Khan said five. We're late."

"Be prepared to run and don't irritate him unnecessarily. Take your safety catch off." Nervously they went closer. "Pilot!" But the pilot still had his back to them and was half inside the cockpit. Son of a dog! Closer, now up to the whirling blades. "Pilot!" the corporal said loudly.

"He can't hear you, who can hear anything? You go forward, I'll cover you."

The corporal nodded, commended his soul to God, and ducked into the wash of air. "Pilot!" He had to go very close, and touch him. "Pilot!" Now the pilot turned, his face grim, said something in barbarian that he did not understand. With a forced smile and forced politeness, he said, "Please, Excellency Pilot, we would consider it an honor if you would stop the engines, His Highness the Khan has ordered it." He saw the blank look, remembered that He of the Knife could not speak any civilized language, so he repeated what he had said, speaking louder and slower and using signs. To his enormous relief, the pilot nodded apologetically, turned some switches, and now the engines were slowing and the blades were slowing.

Praise be to God! Well done, how clever you are, the corporal thought, gratified. "Thank you, Excellency Pilot. Thank you." Very pleased with himself he imperiously peered into the cockpit. Now he saw the pilot making signs to him, clearly wishing to please him—as so he should, by God—inviting him to get into the pilot's seat. Puffed with pride, he watched the barbarian politely lean into the cockpit and move the controls and point at instruments.

Not able to contain his curiosity the younger policeman came under the blades that were circling slower and slower, up to the cockpit door. He leaned in to see better, fascinated by the banks of switches and dials that glowed in the darkness.

"By God, Corporal, have you ever seen so many dials and switches? You look as though you belong in that seat!"

"I wish I was a pilot," the corporal said. "I th—" He stopped, astonished, as his words were swallowed by a blinding red fog that sucked the breath out of his lungs and made the darkness complete.

Erikki had rammed the younger man's head against the corporal's, stunning both of them. Above him the rotors stopped. He looked around. No movement in the darkness, just a few lights on in the palace. No alien eyes or presence that he could sense. Quickly he stowed their guns behind the pilot's seat. It took only seconds to carry the two men to the cabin and lay them inside, force their mouths open, put in the sleeping pills that he had stolen from Azadeh's cabinet, and gag them. A moment to collect his breath before he went forward and checked that all was ready for instant departure. Then he came back to the cabin. The two men had not moved. He leaned against the doorway ready to silence them again if need be. His throat was dry. Sweat beaded him. Waiting. Then he heard dogs and the sound of chain leashes. Quietly he readied the Sten gun. The wandering patrol of two armed guards and the Doberman pinschers passed around the palace but did not come near him. He watched the palace, his arm no longer in the sling.

IN THE NORTHERN SLUMS: The ramshackle, canvas-colored ambulance trundled through the potholed streets. In the back were two medics and three stretchers and Hashemi lay on one, howling, hemorrhaging, most of the front of his loins torn out.

"In the Name of God, give him morphine," Armstrong gasped through his own pain. He was slumped on his stretcher, half propped against the swaying side, holding a surgical dressing tightly against the bullet hole in his upper chest, quite oblivious of the blood pumping from the wound in his back that was soaking the crude dressing one of the medics had stuffed through the rent in his trenchcoat. "Give him morphine. Hurry!" he told them again, cursing them in Farsi and English, hating them for their stupidity and rough handling—still in shock from the suddenness of the bullet and the attack that had come out of nowhere. Why why why?

"What can I do, Excellency?" came out of the darkness. "We have none of this morphine. It's God's will." The man switched on a flashlight and almost blinded him, turned it onto Hashemi, then to the third stretcher. The youth there was already dead. Armstrong saw they had not bothered to close his eyes. Another burbling scream came from Hashemi.

"Put out the light, Ishmael," the other medic said. "You want to get us shot?"

Idly, Ishmael obeyed. Once more in darkness, he lit a cigarette, coughed, and cleared his throat noisily, pulled the canvas side screen aside for a moment to get his bearings. "Only a few more minutes, with the Help of God." He leaned down and shook Hashemi out of his unconscious peace into waking hell. "Only a few more minutes, Excellency Colonel. Don't die yet," he said helpfully. "Only a few more minutes and you'll get proper treatment."

They all lurched as a wheel went into a pothole. Pain blazed through Armstrong. When he felt the ambulance stop, he almost wept with relief.

Other men pulled away the canvas tail cover and scrambled in. Rough hands grabbed his feet and dragged him down onto the stretcher and bound him with the safety straps. Through the hell mist of pain he saw Hashemi's stretcher being carried off into the night, then men lifted him carelessly, the pain was too much, and he fainted.

The stretcher bearers stepped over the joub and went through the doorway in the high wall, into the sleazy corridor and along it, down a flight of stairs, and into a large cellar that was lit with oil lamps. Mzytryk said, "Put him there!" He pointed to the second table. Hashemi was already on the first one, also strapped to his stretcher. Leisurely Mzytryk examined Armstrong's wounds, then Hashemi's, both men still unconscious.

"Good," he said. "Wait for me upstairs, Ishmael."

Ishmael took off the grimy Red Cross armband and threw it into a corner with the others. "Many of our people were martyred in the building. I doubt if any escaped."

"Then you were wise not to join the meeting."

Ishmael clomped upstairs to rejoin his friends who were noisily congratulating themselves on their success in grabbing the enemy leader and his running dog, the foreigner. All were trusted, hard-core Islamic-Marxist fighters, not a medic among them.

Mzytryk waited until he was alone, then took a small penknife and probed Hashemi deeply. The bellowing scream pleased him. When it subsided he lifted the pail of icy water and dashed it into the colonel's face. The eyes opened and the terror and pain therein pleased him even more. "You wanted to see me, Colonel? You murdered my son, Fedor. I'm General Petr Oleg Mzytryk." He used the knife again. Hashemi's face became grotesque as he howled, screaming and babbling incoherently, trying to fight out of his bonds.

"This's for my son . . . and this for my son . . . and this for my son . . ."

Hashemi's heart was strong, and he lasted minutes, begging for mercy, begging for death, the One God for death and for vengeance. He died badly.

For a moment Mzytryk stood over him, his nostrils rebelling against the stench. But he did not need to force himself to remember what these two had done to his son to drag him down to the third level. Pahmudi's report had been explicit. "Hashemi Fazir, you're repaid, you shiteater," he said and spat in his face. Then he turned and stopped. Armstrong was awake and watching him from the stretcher on the other side of the cellar. Cold blue eyes. Bloodless face. The lack of fear astonished him. I'll soon change that, he thought, and took out the penknife. Then he noticed Armstrong's right arm was out of the straps, but before he could do anything Armstrong had reached up for the lapel of his trenchcoat and now held the tip and the hidden cyanide capsule it contained near his mouth. "Don't move!" Armstrong warned.

Mzytryk was too seasoned to consider rushing him, the distance too far. In his side pocket was an automatic but before he could get it out he was sure that Armstrong's teeth would crush the capsule and three seconds left was not nearly enough time for vengeance. His only hope was that Armstrong's pain would make him faint, or lose concentration. He leaned back against the other table and cursed him.

When the stretcher bearers had tightened Armstrong's straps in the darkness of the ambulance, he had instinctively used his strength against the straps to give himself just enough space to pull out his arm—in case the pain became too much for him. Another capsule was secreted in his shirt collar. He had trembled through Hashemi's dying, thanking God for the respite that had allowed him to drag his arm free, the effort terrible. But once he had touched the capsule, his terror had left him and with it, much of his pain. He had made peace with himself at the edge of death where life is so utterly sublime.

"We're . . . we're professionals," he said. "We didn't murder your . . . your son. He was alive when . . . when General Janan took him away for Pahmudi."

"Liar!" Mzytryk heard the weakness in the voice and knew he would not have to wait much longer. He readied.

"Read the official . . . official documents . . . SAVAMA must have made some . . . and those of your God-cursed KGB."

"You think I'm such a fool you can set me against Pahmudi before you die?"

"Read the reports, ask questions, you could get the truth. But you KGB bastards never like the truth. I tell you he was alive when SAVAMA took him."

Mzytryk was put off balance. It wouldn't be normal for a professional like Armstrong—near death, one way or another, to waste time suggesting such an investigation without being certain of the outcome. "Where are the tapes?" he said, watching him carefully, seeing the eyes beginning to flicker, great tiredness from loss of blood. Any second now. "Where are the tapes?"

"There weren't any. Not . . . not from the third level." Armstrong's strength was ebbing. The pain had gone now—along with time. It took a bigger and bigger effort every second to concentrate. But the tapes must be protected, a copy already safely en route to London along with a special

report. "Your son was brave and strong and gave away nothing to us. What
. . . what Pahmudi hacked . . . hacked out of him I don't know . . .
Pahmudi's thugs . . . it was them or your own scum. He was al . . . alive
when your lot took him. Pahmudi told Hashemi."

That's possible, Mzytryk thought uneasily. Those motherless shiteaters in
Tehran messed up Iran, misread the Shah for years, and befouled our work
of generations. "I'll find out. By my son's head I'll find out but that won't
help you—comrade!"

"One favor deserves . . . one deserves ano . . . another. You knocked
off Roger, Roger Crosse, eh?"

Mzytryk laughed, happy to taunt him and exploit the waiting. "I arranged it, yes. And AMG, remember him? And Talbot, but I told Pahmudi
to use this shiteater Fazir for that 16/a." He watched the cold blue eyes
narrow and wondered what was behind them.

Armstrong was searching his memory. AMG? Ah, yes, Alan Medford
Grant, born 1905, dean of counterintelligence agents. In 1963, as Ian
Dunross's secret informant, he fingered a mole in the Noble House. And
another in my Special Branch who turned out to be my best friend. "Liar!
AMG was killed in a motorcycle accident in '63."

"It was assisted. We'd had a 16/a out on that traitor for a year or more—
and his Jap wife."

"He wasn't married."

"You bastards know nothing. Special Branch? Turd heads. She was Jap
Intelligence. She had an accident in Sydney the same year."

Armstrong allowed himself a little smile. The AMG motorcycle "accident" had been organized by the KGB but had been restaged by MI6. The
death certificate was genuine, someone else's, and Alan Medford Grant still
operates successfully though with a different face and different cover that
even I don't know. But a wife? Japanese? Was that another smoke screen,
or another secret? Wheels within wheels within . . .

The past beckoned Armstrong. With an effort he put his mind on what
he truly wanted to know, to check if he was right or wrong, no time to
waste anymore, none. "Who's the fourth man—our arch traitor?"

The question hung in the cellar. Mzytryk was startled and then he
smiled, for Armstrong had given him the key to have his revenge psycholog-
ically. He told him the name and saw the shock. And the name of the fifth
man, even the sixth. "MI6's riddled with our agents, not just moles, so's
MI5, most of your trade unions—Ted Everly's one of ours, Broadhurst and
Lord Grey—remember him from Hong Kong?—and not just Labour
though they're our best seeding ground. Names?" he said gloating, knowing
he was safe. "Look in *Who's Who*! High up in the banks, the City, in the

Foreign Office—Henley's another of ours and I've already had a copy of your report—up to Cabinet, perhaps even into Downing Street. We've half a thousand professionals of our own in Britain, not counting your own traitors." His laugh was cruel.

"And Smedley-Taylor?"

"Oh, yes, him too an—" Abruptly Mzytryk's gloating ceased, his guard slammed shut. "How do you know about him? If you know about him . . . Eh?"

Armstrong was satisfied. Fedor Rakoczy had not lied. All those names on the tapes already gone, already safe, Henley never trusted, not even Talbot. He was content and sad, sorry that he would not be around to catch them himself. Someone will. AMG will.

His eyes fluttered, his hand slid away from his coat lapel. Instantly Mzytryk rushed the space, moving very fast for such a big man, and pinioned the arm between the table and his leg, ripped the lapel away, and now Armstrong was powerless and at his mercy. "Wake up, *matyeryebyets*!" he said exultantly, the penknife out. "How did you know about Smedley?"

But Armstrong did not answer. Death had come quietly.

Mzytryk was enraged, his heart thundering. "Never mind, he's gone, no need to waste time," he muttered out loud. The mother-eating bastard went into hell knowing he was the tool of traitors, some of them. But how did he know about Smedley-Taylor? To hell with him, what if he told the truth about my son?

In the corner of the cellar was a can of kerosene. He began to slop it over the bodies, his rage dissipating. "Ishmael!" he called up the stairs. When he had finished with the kerosene he threw the can into the corner. Ishmael and another man came down into the cellar. "Are you ready to leave?" Mzytryk asked them.

"Yes, with the Help of God."

"And with the help of ourselves too," Mzytryk said lightly. He wiped his hands, tired but satisfied with the way the day and the night had gone. Now just a short ride to the outskirts of Tabriz to his helicopter. An hour—less— to the Tbilisi dacha and Vertinskya. In a few weeks the young puppy Hakim will arrive, with or without my pishkesh, Azadeh. If it's without, it will be expensive for him. "Start the fire," he said crisply, "and we'll be going."

"Here, Comrade General!" Cheerfully Ishmael threw him some matches. "It's your privilege to finish that which you began."

Mzytryk had caught the matches. "Good," he said. The first did not light. Nor the second. The third did. He backed to the stairs and carefully threw it. Flames gushed to the ceiling and to the wooden rafters. Then Ishmael's foot went into his back and sent him sprawling, headfirst, into the outskirts of the fire. In panic Mzytryk screamed and beat at the flames and he whirled and scuttled on his blackening hands and knees back toward the stairs, stopped a moment beating at his fur lapels, coughing and choking in the billowing black smoke and smell of burning flesh. Somehow he lurched to his feet. The first bullet smashed his kneecap, he howled and reeled backward into the fire, the second broke his other leg and hurled him down. Impotently he beat at the flames, his screams drowned by the gathering roar of the inferno. And he became a torch.

Ishmael and the other man jumped back up the stairs to the first landing, almost colliding with others who had rushed down. They gaped at the twitching body of Mzytryk, the flames now eating his boots. "What you do that for?" one of them said, aghast.

"My brother was martyred at the house, so was your cousin."

"As God wants, but, Ishmael, the comrade general? God protect us, he supplied us with money and arms and explosives—why kill him?"

"Why not? Wasn't the son of a dog an arrogant, ill-mannered Satanist? He wasn't even a Person of the Book," Ishmael said contemptuously. "Dozens more where they came from, thousands. They need us, we don't need them. He deserved to die. Didn't he come alone, tempting me?" He spat toward the body. "Important persons should have bodyguards."

A shaft of flames reached for them. They retreated hastily. The fire caught the wooden stairs and was spreading rapidly. In the street they all piled into the truck, no longer an ambulance. Ishmael looked back at the flames gutting the house and laughed uproariously. "Now that dog's a burnt father! May all Infidels perish as quickly."

IN THE PALACE FORECOURT: Erikki was leaning against the 212 when he saw the lights in the Khan's quarters on the second floor go out. A careful check on the two drugged policemen fast asleep in the cabin reassured him. Quietly he slid the cabin door closed, eased his knife under his belt and picked up the Sten. With the skill of a night hunter he moved noiselessly toward the palace. The Khan's guards on the gate did not notice him go—why should they bother to watch him? The Khan had given them clear orders to leave the pilot alone and not agitate him, that surely he would soon tire of playing with the machine. "If he takes a car, let him. If the police want trouble, that's their problem."

"Yes, Highness," they had both told him, glad they were not responsible for He of the Knife.

Erikki slipped through the front door and along the dimly lit corridor to the stairs leading to the north wing, well away from the Khan's area. Noiselessly up the stairs and along another corridor. He saw a shaft of light under the door of their suite. Without hesitation he went into the anteroom, closing the door silently after him. Across the room to their bedroom door and swung it open. To his shock, Mina, Azadeh's maid, was there too. She was kneeling on the bed where she had been massaging Azadeh who was fast asleep.

"Oh, your pardon," she stuttered, terrified of him like all the servants. "I didn't hear Your Excellency. Her Highness asked . . . asked me to continue as long as I could with . . . with the massage, then to sleep here."

Erikki's face was a mask, the oil streaks on his cheeks and on the taped bandage over his ear making him appear more dangerous. "Azadeh!"

"Oh you won't wake her, Excellency, she took a . . . she took two sleeping pills and asked me to apologize for her if you c—"

"Dress her!" he hissed.

Mina blanched. "But, Excellency!" Her heart almost stopped as she saw a knife appear in his hand.

"Dress her quickly and if you make a sound I'll gut you. *Do it!*" He saw her grab the dressing gown. "Not that, Mina! Warm clothes, ski clothes— by all the gods, it doesn't matter which but be quick!" He watched her, positioning himself between her and the door so she couldn't bolt. On the bedside table was the sheathed kookri. A twinge went through him and he tore his eyes away, and when he was sure Mina was obeying he took Azadeh's purse from the dressing table. All her papers were in it, ID, passport, driver's license, birth certificate, everything. Good, he thought, and blessed Aysha for the gift that Azadeh had told him about before dinner, and thanked his ancient gods for giving him the plan this morning. Ah, my darling, did you think I'd really leave you?

Also in the purse was her soft silk jewelry bag which seemed heavier than normal. His eyes widened at the emeralds and diamonds and pearl necklaces and pendants that it now contained. The rest of Najoud's, he thought, the same that Hakim had used to barter with the tribesmen and that I retrieved from Bayazid. In the mirror he saw Mina gaping at the wealth he held in his hand, Azadeh inert and almost dressed. "Hurry up!" he grated at her reflection.

AT THE AMBUSH ROADBLOCK BELOW THE PALACE: Both the sergeant of police and his driver in the car waiting beside the road were staring up at the palace four hundred yards away, the sergeant using binoculars. Just the dim lights on the outside of the vast gatehouse, no sign of any guards, or of his own two men. "Drive up there," the sergeant said uneasily. "Something's wrong, by God! They're either asleep or dead. Go slowly and quietly." He reached into the scabbard beside him and put a shell into the breech of the M16. The driver gunned the engine and eased out into the empty roadway.

AT THE MAIN GATE: Babak, the guard, was leaning against a pillar inside the massive iron gate that was closed and bolted. The other guard was curled up nearby on some sacking, fast asleep. Through the bars of the gate could be seen the snowbanked road that wound down to the city. Beyond the empty fountain in the forecourt, a hundred yards away, was the helicopter. The icy wind moved the blades slightly.

Babak yawned and stamped his feet against the cold, then began to relieve himself through the bars, absently waving the stream this way and that. Earlier when they had been dismissed by the Khan and had come back to their post, they had found that the two policemen had gone. "They're off to scrounge some food, or to have a sleep," he had said. "God curse all police."

He yawned, looking forward to the dawn when he would be off duty for a few hours. Only the pilot's car to usher through just before dawn, then relock the gate, and soon he would be in bed with a warm body. Automatically he scratched his genitals, feeling himself stir and harden. Idly he leaned back, playing with himself, his eyes checking that the gate's heavy bolt was in place and the small side gate also locked. Then the edge of his eyes caught a movement. He centered it. The pilot was slinking out of a side door of the palace with a large bundle over his shoulder, his arm no longer in the sling and carrying a gun. Babak hastily buttoned up, slipped his rifle off his shoulder, moved farther out of view. Cautiously he kicked the other guard who awoke soundlessly. "Look," he whispered, "I thought the pilot was still in the cabin of the helicopter."

Wide-eyed, they watched Erikki keep to the shadows, then silently dart across the open space to the far side of the helicopter. "What's he carrying? What's the bundle?"

"It looked like a carpet, a rolled-up carpet," the other whispered. Sound of the far cockpit door opening.

"But why? In all the Names of God, what's he doing?"

There was barely enough light but their vision was good and hearing good. They heard an approaching car but were at once distracted by the sound of the far cabin door sliding open. They waited, hardly breathing, then saw him dump what appeared to be two similar bundles under the belly of the helicopter, then duck under the tail boom and reappear on their side. For a moment he stood there, looking toward them but not seeing them, then eased the cockpit door open, and got in with the gun, the carpet bundle now propped on the opposite seat.

Abruptly the jets began and both guards jumped. "God protect us, what do we do?"

Nervously Babak said, "Nothing. The Khan told us exactly: 'Leave the pilot alone, whatever he does, he's dangerous,' that's what he told us, didn't he? 'When the pilot takes the car near dawn let the pilot leave.' " Now he had to talk loudly over the rising scream. "We do nothing."

"But we weren't told he would start his engines again, the Khan didn't say that, or sneak out with bundles of carpets."

"You're right. As God wants, but you're right." Their nervousness increased. They had not forgotten the guards jailed and flogged by the old Khan for disobedience or failure, or those banished by the new one. "The engines sound good now, don't you think?" They both looked up as lights came on at the second floor, the Khan's floor, then they jerked around as the police car came swirling to a stop outside the gate. The sergeant jumped out, a flashlight in his hand. "What's going on, by God?" the sergeant shouted. "Open the gate, by God! Where're my men?"

Babak rushed for the side gate and pulled the bolt back.

In the cockpit Erikki's hands were moving as quickly as possible, the wound in his arm inhibiting him. The sweat ran down his face and mixed with a trickle of blood from his ear where the taped bandages had become displaced. His breath came in great pants from the long run from the north wing with Azadeh bundled in the carpet, drugged and helpless, and he was cursing the needles to rise quicker. He had seen the lights go on in Hakim's apartments and now heads were peering out. Before he had left their suite he had carefully knocked Mina unconscious, hoping he had not hurt her, to protect her as well as himself so she would not sound an alarm or be accused of collusion, had wrapped Azadeh in the carpet and attached the kookri to his belt.

"Come on," he snarled at the needles, then glimpsed two men at the main gate in police uniforms. Suddenly the helicopter was bathed in a shaft of light from the flashlight and his stomach turned over. Without thinking, he grabbed his Sten, shoved the nose through the pilot's window, and pulled the trigger, aiming high.

The four men scattered for cover as bullets ricocheted off the gate masonry. In his panic the sergeant dropped the flash, but not before all had seen the two crumpled, inert bodies of the corporal and the other policeman sprawled on the ground and presumed them dead. As the burst stopped, the sergeant scrambled for the side gate and his car and his M16.

"Fire, by God," the driver policeman shouted. Whipped by the excitement, Babak squeezed the trigger, the shots going wild. Incautiously, the driver moved into the open to retrieve the flash. Another burst from the helicopter and he leaped backward. "Son of a burnt father . . ." The three of them cowered in safety. Another burst at the flashlight danced it, then smashed it.

Erikki saw his escape plan in ruins, the 212 a helpless target on the ground. Time had run out for him. For a split second he considered closing down. The needles were far too low. Then he emptied the Sten at the gate with a howling battle cry, slammed the throttles forward, and let out another primeval scream that chilled those who heard it. The jets went to full power, shrieked under the strain as he put the stick forward and dragged her airborne a few inches and now, tail high, she lurched ahead, skids screeching on the forecourt as she bounced and rose and fell back and bounced again and now was airborne but lumbering badly. At the main gate the driver tore the gun from a guard and went to the pillar, peered around it to see the helicopter escaping, and pulled the trigger.

On the second floor of the palace Hakim was blearily leaning out of his bedroom window, grasped from drugged sleep by the noise. His bodyguard, Margol, was beside him. They saw the 212 almost collide with a small wooden outhouse, her skids ripping away part of the roof, then struggle onward in a drunken climb. Outside the walls was the police car, the sergeant silhouetted in the beam of its headlights. Hakim watched him aim and willed the bullets to miss.

Erikki heard bullets zinging off metal, prayed they had touched nothing vital, and banked dangerously away from the exposed outer wall toward some space where he could slip behind the safety of the palace. In the wild turn the bundled carpet containing Azadeh toppled over and tangled with the controls. For a moment he was lost, then he used his massive strength to shove her away. The wound in his forearm split open.

Now he swerved behind the north wing, the chopper still only a few feet high, and headed toward the other perimeter wall near the hut where Ross and Gueng had been hidden. A stray bullet punctured his door, hacked into the instrument panel, exploding glass.

When the helicopter had disappeared from Hakim's view, he had hobbled across the huge bedroom, past the wood fire that blazed merrily, out into the corridor to the windows there. "Can you see him?" he asked, panting from the exertion.

"Yes, Highness," Margol said, and pointed excitedly. "There!"

The 212 was just a black shape against more blackness, then the perimeter floodlights came on and Hakim saw her stagger over the wall with only inches to spare and dip down behind it. A few seconds later she had reappeared, gaining speed and altitude. At that moment Aysha came running along the corridor, crying out hysterically, "Highness, Highness . . . Azadeh's gone, she's gone . . . that devil's kidnapped her and Mina's been knocked unconscious. . . ."

It was hard for Hakim to concentrate against the pills, his eyelids never so heavy. "What are you talking about?"

"Azadeh's gone, your sister's gone, he wrapped her in a carpet and he's kidnapped her, taken her with him . . ." She stopped, afraid, seeing the look on Hakim's face, ashen in this bleak light, eyes drooping—not knowing about the sleeping pills. "He's kidnapped her!"

"But that . . . that's not possible . . . not poss—"

"Oh, but it is, she's kidnapped and Mina's unconscious!"

Hakim blinked at her, then stuttered, "Sound the alarm, Aysha! If she's kidnapped . . . by God, sound . . . sound the alarm! I've taken sleeping pills and they . . . I'll deal with that devil tomorrow, by God, I can't, not now, but send someone . . . to the police . . . to the Green Bands . . . spread the alarm, there's a Khan's ransom on his head! Margol, help me back to my room."

Frightened servants and guards were collecting at the end of the corridor and Aysha ran tearfully back to them, telling them what had happened and what the Khan had ordered.

Hakim groped for his bed and lay back, exhausted. "Margol, tell the . . . tell guards to arrest those fools at the gate. How could they have let that happen?"

"They can't have been vigilant, Highness." Margol was sure they would be blamed—someone had to be blamed—even though he had been present when the Khan had told them not to interfere with the pilot. He gave the order and came back. "Are you all right, Highness?"

"Yes, thank you. Don't leave the room . . . wake me at dawn. Keep the fire going and wake me at dawn."

Gratefully Hakim let himself go into the sleep that beckoned so seductively, his back no longer paining him, his mind focused on Azadeh and on Erikki. When she had walked out of the small room and left him alone with Erikki, he had allowed his grief to show: "There's no way out of the trap, Erikki. We're trapped, all of us, you, Azadeh, and me. I still can't believe she'd renounce Islam, at the same time I'm convinced she won't obey me or you. I've no wish to hurt her but I've no alternative, her immortal soul is more important than her temporary life."

"I could save her soul, Hakim. With your help."

"How?" He had seen the tension in Erikki, his face tight, eyes strange.

"Remove her need to destroy it."

"How?"

"Say, hypothetically, this madman of a pilot was not Muslim but barbarian and so much in love with his wife that he goes a little more mad and instead of just escaping by himself, he suddenly knocks her out, kidnaps her, flies her out of her own country against her will, and refuses to allow her to return. In most countries a husband can . . . can take extreme measures to hold on to his wife, even to force her obedience and curb her. This way she won't have broken her oath, she'll never need to give up Islam, you'll never need to harm her, and I'll keep my woman."

"It's a cheat," Hakim had said bewildered. "It's a cheat."

"It's not, it's make-believe, hypothetical, all of it, only make-believe, but hypothetically it fulfills the rules you swore to abide by, and no one'd ever believe the sister of the Gorgon Khan would willingly break her oath and renounce Islam over a barbarian. No one. Even now you don't know for certain she would, do you?"

Hakim had tried to find the flaws. There're none, he had thought, astonished. And it would solve most of . . . wouldn't it solve everything if it came to pass? If Erikki was to do this without her knowledge and help . . . Kidnap her! It's true, no one'd ever believe she'd willingly break her oath. Kidnapped! I could deplore it publicly and rejoice for her in secret, if I want her to leave, and him to live. But I have to, it's the only way: to save her soul I have to save him.

In the peace of the bedroom he opened his eyes briefly. Flame shadows danced on the ceiling. Erikki and Azadeh were there. God will forgive me, he thought, swooping into sleep. I wonder if I'll ever see her again?

TEHRAN—NEAR THE UNIVERSITY: 11:58 P.M. In the chill darkness Sharazad stood with the phalanx of Green Bands protecting the front of the massed, shouting Islamics. They were packed together, chanting "Allahhhh-u Akbarrrr" in unison, a living barrier against the two to three thousand roaring, leftist students and agitators approaching down the road. Flashlights and burning torches, some cars on fire, guns, sticks, wooden clubs. Her fingers gripped the automatic in her pocket, grenade ready in her other pocket. "God is Great!" she shrieked.

The enemy was closing fast and Sharazad saw their clenched fists, the tumult growing on both sides, shouts more hoarse, nerves more stretched, anticipation rocketing—"There is no other God but God . . ." Now their enemies were so near she could see individual faces. Suddenly she realized they were not massed satanic revolutionaries, not all of them, but the vast majority students, men and women of her own age, the women bravely not chadored and shouting for women's rights, the vote, and all the sensible, God given, hard fought for, never-turning-back things.

She was transported back to the heady excitement of the Women's March, all of them in their best clothes, hair free, as free as their hair, with freedom and justice for all in their new Islamic republic where she and her son-to-be and Tommy would live happily ever after. But there again in front of her was the knife-wielding fanatic tearing the future away, but that didn't matter for her Ibrahim had stopped him, Ibrahim the student leader, he was there to save her. Oh, Ibrahim, are you here tonight, leading them now as you did with us? Are you here once more fighting for freedom and justice and women's rights or were you martyred in Kowiss as you wanted, killing your evil, two-faced mullah who murdered your father as mine was also murdered?

But . . . but Father was killed by Islamics, not leftists, she thought bewildered. And the Imam's still implacably for everything as it was in the Prophet's time . . . And Meshang . . . And Tommy forced out. And forced divorce and forced marriage to that foul old man and no rights!

"What am I doing here?" she gasped in the pandemonium. "I should be over there with them, I should be over there with them, not here . . . no, no, not there either! What about my child, my son-to-be, it's dangerous for him an—"

Somewhere a gun went off, then others and mayhem became general, those in the fore trying to retreat and those behind trying to get to the fight. Around Sharazad there was a mindless surge. She felt herself being crushed and carried forward, her feet hardly touching the ground. A woman beside her screamed and went under the feet. An old man stumbled, and vanished below mumbling the Shahada, almost bringing her down. Someone's elbow went into her stomach, she cried out in pain and her fear became terror. "Tommyyyy! Help meeeeee . . ." she shrieked.

A hundred yards or so ahead Tom Lochart was pressed against a shop front by the student marchers, his coat torn, peaked cap gone, more desperate than he had ever been. For hours he had been searching the groups of students hoping against hope to find her, sure she was somewhere among them. Where else would she go? Surely not to this student's apartment, the one Jari said she met, this Ibrahim or whatever his name was who meant nothing. Better she's there than here, he thought in despair. Oh, God, let me find her.

Chanting women passed, most in Western dress, jeans, jackets, and then he saw her. He fought alongside but once more he had made a mistake and he apologized and shoved his way to the side again, a few curses shouted after him. Then he thought he saw her on the far side of the roadway but again he was mistaken. The girl wore similar ski clothes to Sharazad and had the same hairstyle and was about her age. But she carried a Marxist-Islamic banner and, scourged by his disappointment, he cursed her, hating her for her stupidity. The shouts and countershouts were reaching him too, agitating him, and he wanted to pick up the cudgel and smash the evil out of them.

Oh, God, help me find her. "God IS great," he muttered, and though he was frantic with worry for her, at the same time his heart was soaring. Becoming Muslim will make all the difference. Now they will accept me, I'm one of them, I can go on the Hajj to Mecca, I can worship in any mosque, color or race means nothing to God. Only belief. I believe in God and that Mohammed was the Prophet of God, I won't be fundamentalist, or Shi'a. I'll be orthodox Sunni. I'll find a teacher and study and learn Arabic. And I'll fly for IranOil and the new regime and we will be happy, Sharazad and I . . .

A gun went off nearby, fires of a burning tire barricade soared into the air as small groups of screaming students were throwing themselves at the ranks of the Green Bands, other guns began firing, and now the whole street erupted into shouting, heaving bodies, the weak crushed underfoot. A berserk phalanx of youths dragged him with them toward the fighting.

Eighty yards away Sharazad was screaming, fighting for her life, trying to shove and kick and push her way to the side where there would be comparative safety. Her chador was torn away, her scarf vanished. She was bruised, pain in her stomach. Those around her were a mob now, hacking at those opposing it, all for themselves but wrapped into the mob beast. The battle waged back and forth, no one knowing who was friend or enemy, except mullahs and Green Bands who shouted, trying to control the riot. With an earsplitting roar, the Islamic mob hesitated a moment, then advanced. The weak fell and were crushed. Men, women. Screams and shouts and pandemonium, all calling on their own version of God.

Desperately the students fought back but they were swamped. Relentlessly. Many went down. Feet trampled them. Now the rest broke, the rout began, and the sides intermixed.

Lochart used his superior height and strength to batter his way to the side and now stood between two cars, protected by them for the moment. A few yards away he saw a small, half-hidden alleyway that led toward a broken-down mosque where there would be sanctuary. Ahead was a huge explosion as a car tank exploded, scattering flames. The fortunate were killed instantly, the wounded began to scream. In the flame light he thought he caught a glimpse of her, then a group of fleeing youths swarmed over him, a fist went into his back, others pummeled him out of the way, and he fell under their boots.

Sharazad was only thirty yards away, hair awry, clothes torn, still locked into the press of the mob, still pulled along by the juggernaut, still screaming for help, no one hearing or caring. "Tommyyyy . . . help meeeeee . . ."

The crowd parted momentarily. She darted for the opening, squeezing her way toward the barred and locked shops and parked cars. The tumult was lessening. Arms pushed for breathing space, hands wiped sweat and filth off, and men saw their neighbors. "You God-cursed Communist harlot," the man in her path shouted, eyes almost out of his sockets with rage.

"I'm not, I'm not, I'm Muslim," she gasped, but his hands had caught her ski jacket—the zipper wrecked—his hand went in and grabbed her breast.

"Harlot! Muslim women don't flaunt themselves, Muslim women wear chad—"

"I lost it—it was torn off me," she shrieked.

"Harlot! God curse you! Our women wear chador."

"I lost it—it was torn off me," she shrieked again and tried to pull away, "There is no oth—"

"Harlot! Whore! Satanist!" he shouted, his ears closed to her, the madness on him and the feel of her breast through her silk shirt and undershirt further inflaming him. His fingers clawed at the silk and ripped it away and now he held her roundness, his other hand dragging her closer to subdue her and strangle her as she kicked and screamed. Those nearby jostled them, or tried to move out of the way, hard to see in the darkness that was only rent by the light from fires, not know what was going on except someone had caught a leftist whore here in the ranks of the Godly. "By God, she's not a leftist, I heard her shouting for the Imam . . ." someone called out but cries ahead overrode him, another pocket of fighting flared up and men shoved forward to help or elbowed space to retreat and they left her and him together.

She fought him with her nails and feet and voice, his breath and obscenities choking her. With a final effort she called on God for help, hacked upward and missed and remembered her gun. Her hand grasped it, shoved it into him, and pulled the trigger. The man screamed, most of his genitals blown off, and he collapsed howling. There was a sudden hush around her. And space. Her hand came out of the pocket still holding the gun. A man near to her grabbed it.

Blankly she stared down at her attacker who twisted and moaned in the dirt.

"God is Great," she stuttered, then noticed her disarray and pulled her jacket together, looked up and saw the hatred surrounding her. "He was attacking me . . . God is Great, God is Great . . ."

"She's just saying that, she's a leftist . . ." a woman screeched.

"Look at her clothes, she's not one of us . . ."

Just a few yards away, Lochart was picking himself out of the dirt, head hurting, ears ringing, hardly able to see or to hear. With a great effort he stood upright, then shouldered his way forward toward the dark mouth of the alley and safety. Others had had the same thought and already the entrance was clogged. Then her voice, mingled with shouting, reached him and he turned back.

He saw her at bay, backed against a wall, a mob around her, clothes half torn off, the sleeve of her jacket ripped away, eyes staring, a grenade in her hand. At that second a man made a move at her, she pulled the pin out, the man froze, everyone began to back off, Lochart burst through the cordon to reach her and seized the grenade, keeping the lever down. "Get away from her," he roared in Farsi and stood in front of her, protecting her. "She's Muslim, you sons of dogs. She's Muslim and my wife and I'm Muslim!"

"You're a foreigner and she's a leftist by God!"

Lochart darted at the man and his fist now armored with the grenade crushed the man's mouth in, shattering his jaw. "God is Great," Lochart bellowed. Others took up the shout and those who disbelieved him did nothing, afraid of him but more afraid of the grenade. Holding her tightly with his free arm, half guiding, half carrying, Lochart went at the first rank, grenade ready. "Please let us pass, God is Great, peace be with you." The first rank parted, then the next, and he shoved through, muttering, "God is great. . . . Peace be with you," continually until he had broken out of the cordon and into the crowded alley, stumbling in the filth and potholes, bumping people here and there in the darkness. A few lights were on outside the mosque ahead. At the fountain he stopped, broke the ice, and with one hand scooped some water into his face, the torrent in his brain still raging. "Christ," he muttered and used more water.

"Oh, Tommyyyy!" Sharazad cried out, her voice far off and strange, near breaking. "Where did you come from, where, oh I . . . I was so afraid, so afraid."

"So was I," he stammered, the words hard to get out. "I've been searching for hours for you, my darling." He pulled her to him. "You all right?"

"Oh, yes, yes." Her arms were tight around him, her face buried in his shoulder.

Sudden firing, more shrieks back toward the street. Instinctively he held her tighter but sensed no danger here. Just half-seen crowds passing in the semidarkness, the firing becoming more distant and the noise of the riot decreasing.

We're safe at last. No, not yet, there's still the grenade—no pin to make it safe, no way to make it safe. Over her head and those of the passersby, he saw a burned-out building by the side of the mosque across the little square. I can get rid of it there safely, he persuaded himself, not thinking clearly yet, holding on to her and gathering strength from her embrace. The crowds had increased, now packing the alley. Until their numbers lessened it would be difficult and dangerous to dispose of the grenade across the square so he moved her closer to the fountain where the darkness was deeper. "Don't worry. We'll wait a second, then go on." They were talking English, softly—so much to tell, so much to ask. "You sure you're all right?"

"Yes, oh, yes. How did you find me? How? When did you get back? How did you find me?"

"I . . . I flew back tonight and went to the house but you'd gone." Then he burst out, "Sharazad, I've become Muslim."

She gaped at him. "But . . . but that was just a trick, a trick to get away from them!"

"No, I swear it! I really have. I swear it. I said the Shahada in front of three witnesses, Meshang and Zarah and Jari, and I believe. I do believe. Everything's going to be all right now."

Her disbelief vanished seeing the joy in him, his voice telling her over and over what had happened. "Oh, how wonderful, Tommy," she said, beyond herself with happiness, at the same time utterly certain that, for them, nothing would change. Nothing will change Meshang, she thought. Meshang will find a way to destroy us whether my Tommy's a Believer or not. Nothing will change, the divorce will stay, the marriage will stay. Unless . . .

Her fears vanished. "Tommy, can we leave Tehran tonight? Can we run away tonight, my darling?"

"There's no need for that, not now. I've wonderful plans. I've quit S-G. Now that I'm Muslim I can stay and fly for IranOil, don't you see?" Both were oblivious of the crowds passing, packed more tightly, anxious to be home. "No need to worry, Sharazad."

Someone stumbled and jostled him, then another, a pileup beginning that encroached on their little sanctuary. She saw him shove a man away and others began to curse. Quickly she took his hand, and pulled him into the mainstream. "Let's go home, husband," she said loudly in coarsened Farsi, cautioning him, holding on tightly, then whispered, "Speak Farsi," then a little louder, "We're not safe here and we can talk better at home."

"Yes, yes, woman. Better we go home." Walking was better and safer and Sharazad was here and tomorrow would solve tomorrow, tonight there would be a bath and sleep and food and sleep and no dreams or only happy ones.

"If we wanted to leave tonight secretly, could we? Could we, Tommy?"

Tiredness washed over him and he almost shouted at her that didn't she understand what he had just told her? Instead he held back the anger and just said, "There's no need to escape now."

"You're quite right, husband, as always. But could we?"

"Yes, yes, I suppose so," he said wearily, and told her how, stopping and starting again with the rest of the pedestrians as the alley narrowed, more claustrophobic every moment.

Now she was aglow, quite sure she could convince him. Tomorrow they would leave. Tomorrow morning I'll collect my jewels, we'll pretend to Meshang we'll meet him in the bazaar at lunchtime, but by then we will be flying south in Tommy's plane. He can fly in the Gulf states or Canada or anywhere, you can be Muslim and Canadian without harm, they told me when I went to the embassy. And soon, in a month or so we'll come home to Iran and live here forever . . .

Contentedly she went even closer to him, hidden in the crowd and by the darkness, not afraid anymore, certain their future would be grand. Now that he's a Believer he will go to Paradise, God is Great, God is Great, and so will I, and together, with the Help of God, we will leave sons and daughters behind us. And then, when we are old, if he dies first, on the fortieth day I will make sure his spirit is remembered perfectly, and then, afterward, I will curse his younger wife or wives and their children, then put my affairs in order and peacefully wait to join him—in God's time. "Oh, I do love you, Tommy, I'm so sorry that you've had so much trouble . . . trouble over me . . ."

Now they were breaking out of the alley into a street. The crowds were even heavier, swarming all over the roadway and in the traffic. But there was a lightness on them all, men, women, mullahs, Green Bands, young and old, the night well spent doing God's work. "Allah-u Akbar!" someone shouted, the words echoed and reechoed by a thousand throats. Ahead an impatient car lurched, bumped into some pedestrians who bumped into others who brought down others amid curses and laughter. Sharazad and Lochart among them, no one hurt. He had caught her safely and, laughing together, they rested on the ground a moment, the grenade still tight in his hand. They did not hear its warning hiss—without knowing it, in falling he had slackened the lever an instant, but just enough. For an infinity of time he smiled at her and she at him. "God is Great," she said and he echoed her just as confidently. And, the same instant, they died.

SATURDAY
March 3

AL SHARGAZ: 6:34 A.M. The tip of the sun crested the horizon and turned black desert into a crimson sea, staining the old port city and dhows in the Gulf beyond. From the minaret loudspeakers muezzins began but the music in their voices did not please Gavallan or any of the other S-G personnel on the veranda of the Oasis Hotel, finishing a hurried breakfast. "It gets to you, Scrag, doesn't it?" Gavallan said.

"Right you are, sport," Scragger said. He, Rudi Lutz, and Pettikin shared Gavallan's table, all of them tired and dispirited. Whirlwind's almost complete success was turning into a disaster. Dubois and Fowler still missing—in Bahrain, McIver not yet out of danger. Tom Lochart back in Tehran, God knows where. No news of Erikki and Azadeh. No sleep for most of them last night. And sunset today still their deadline.

From the moment yesterday when the 212s had started landing, they had all helped to strip them, removing rotors and tail booms for storing on the jumbo freighters when they arrived, if they arrived. Last night Roger Newbury had returned from the Al Shargaz palace meeting with the foreign minister in a foul humor: "Not a bloody thing I can do, Andy. The minister said he and the Sheik had been asked to make a personal inspection of the airport by the new Iranian representative or ambassador who had seen eight or nine strange 212s at the airport, claiming them to be their 'hijacked' Iran registereds. The minister said that of course His Highness, the Sheik, had agreed—how could he refuse? The inspection's at sunset with the ambassador, I'm 'cordially invited' as the British rep for a thorough check of IDs, and if any're found to be suspect, old boy, tough titty!"

Gavallan had been up all night trying to bring the arrival of the freighters forward, or to get substitutions from every international source he could conjure up. None were available. The best his present charterers could do was "perhaps" to bring forward the ETA to noon tomorrow, Sunday. "Bloody people," he muttered and poured some more coffee. "When you've got to have a couple of 747s there're none—and usually with a single phone call you can get fifty."

Pettikin was equally worried, also about McIver in Bahrain hospital.

No news was expected until noon today about the seriousness of McIver's heart attack. *Pas problème,* Jean-Luc had said last night. "They've let

Genny stay in the next room at the hospital, the doctor's the best in Bahrain, and I'm here. I've canceled my early flight home and I'll wait, but send me some money tomorrow to pay the bills."

Pettikin toyed with his coffee cup, his breakfast untouched. All yesterday and last night helping to get the helicopters ready so no chance to see Paula and she was off again to Tehran this morning, still evacuating Italian nationals, and would not be back for at least two days. Gavallan had ordered an immediate retreat of all Whirlwind participants out of the Gulf area, pending review. "We can't be too careful," he had told them all. "Everyone's got to go for the time being."

Later Pettikin had said, "You're right, Andy, but what about Tom and Erikki? We should leave someone here—I'd be glad to volun—"

"For Christ's sake, Charlie, give over," Gavallan had flared. "You think I'm not worried sick about them? And Fowler and Dubois? We have to do it one step at a time. Everyone who's not necessary is out before sunset and you're one of them!" That had been about 1:00 A.M. this morning in the office when Pettikin had come to relieve Scot who was still blearily manning the HF. The rest of the night he had sat there. No calls. At 5:00 A.M. Nogger Lane had relieved him and he had come here for breakfast, Gavallan, Rudi, and Scragger already seated. "Any luck with the freighters, Andy?"

"No, Charlie, it's still tomorrow noon at the earliest," Gavallan had said. "Sit down, have some coffee." Then had come the dawn and the muezzins. Now their singsong ceased. Some of the violence left the veranda.

Scragger poured himself another cup of tea, his stomach still upset. Another sudden chill zapped up from his bowels and he hurried to the bathroom. The spasm passed quickly with very little to show for it, but there was no blood therein, and Doc Nutt had said he didn't think it was dysentery: "Just take it easy for a few days, Scrag. I'll have the result of all the tests tomorrow." He had told Doc Nutt about the blood in his urine and the pain in his stomach over the last few days. To hide it would have been an unforgivable added danger, both to his passengers and to his chopper. "Scrag, best you stay here in hospital for a few days," Doc Nutt had said.

"Get stuffed, old cock! There's things to do and mountains to conquer."

Going back to the table he saw the brooding gloom upon everyone and hated it, but had no solution. Nothing to do except wait. No way to transit out because they would have to go through Saudi, Emirate, or Oman airspace and no possibility of a clearance for a few days. He had suggested, jokingly, they reassemble the helicopters, find out when the next British supertanker was outbound through Hormuz and then take off and land on her: ". . . and we just sail off into the Wild Blue and get off in Mombasa, or sail on around Africa to Nigeria."

"Hey, Scrag," Vossi had said in admiration, "that's wild-assed. I could use a cruise. How about it, Andy?"

"We'd be arrested and in the brig before the rotors had begun."

Scragger sat down and waved a fly away. The sun's birth color was less red now and all of them were wearing dark glasses against the glare.

Gavallan finished his coffee. "Well, I'm off to the office in case I can do something. If you want me I'm there. How soon'll you be finished, Rudi?"

Rudi was in charge of getting the choppers ready for transshipment. "Your target was noon today. It'll be noon." He swallowed the last of his coffee and got up. "Time to leave, *meine Kinder!*" Groans and catcalls from the others but mostly good-natured through their fatigue. A general exodus to transport waiting outside.

"Andy," Scragger said, "I'll come along with you if it's okay."

"Good idea, Scrag. Charlie, no need for you to be on Rudi's team as we're ahead of schedule. Why don't you come over to the office later?"

Pettikin smiled at him. "Thanks." Paula was not due to leave her hotel until 10:00 A.M. Now he would have plenty of time to see her. To say what? he asked himself, waving them good-bye.

Gavallan drove out of the gates. The airport was still partially in shadow. Already a few jets with their navigation lights on, engines winding up. The Iran evacuation was still priority. He glanced at Scragger, saw the grimace. "You all right?"

"Sure, Andy. Just a touch of gippy tummy. Had it bad in New Guinea—so I've always been careful. If I could get some of old Dr. Collis Brown's Elixir I'd be raring to go!" This was a marvelous and highly effective tincture invented by Dr. Collis Brown, an English army surgeon, to combat the dysentery that tens of thousands of soldiers were dying of during the Crimean War. "Six drops of the old magic and Bob's your unbloody uncle!"

"You're right, Scrag," Gavallan said absently, wondering if Pan Am Freighting had had any cancellations. "I never travel without Collis . . . wait a minute!" He suddenly beamed. "My survival kit! There's some there. Liz always sticks it into my briefcase. Collis Brown's, Tiger Balm, aspirins, a golden sovereign, and a can of sardines."

"Eh? Sardines?"

"In case I get hungry." Gavallan was glad to talk to take his mind off the looming disaster. "Liz and I have a mutual friend we met years ago in Hong Kong, fellow called Marlowe, a writer. He always carried a can with him, iron rations in case of famine—and Liz and I, we always laughed about it. It became kind of a symbol to remind ourselves how lucky we really are."

"Peter Marlowe? The one who wrote *Changi*—about the POW camp in Singapore?"

"Yes. Do you know him?"

"No. But I read that book, not the others, but I read that one." Scragger was suddenly reminded about his own war against the Japanese and then about Kasigi and Iran-Toda. Last night he had called other hotels to track Kasigi down and eventually had found him registered at the International and had left a message but as yet had not heard back. Probably he's chocker I let him down, he told himself, because we can't help him at Iran-Toda. Stone the crows! Bandar Delam and Iran-Toda seem a couple of years ago instead of just a couple of days. Even so, if it weren't for him, I'd still be handcuffed to that bleeding bed.

"Pity we don't all have our can of sardines, Andy," he said. "We really do forget our luck, don't we? Look how lucky we were to get out of Lengeh in one piece. Wot about old Duke? Soon he'll be fit as a fiddle. A fraction of an inch and he'd be dead but he isn't. Scot the same. Wot about Whirlwind! All the lads're out and so're our birds. Erikki's safe. Mac'll be all right, you wait and see! Dubois and Fowler? It's got to happen sometime, but it hasn't yet, so far as we know, so we can still hope. Tom? Well, he chose that and he'll get out."

NEAR THE IRAN-TURKISH BORDER: 7:59 A.M.   Some seven hundred miles northward, Azadeh shielded her eyes against the rising sun. She had seen something glint in the valley below. Was that light reflected off a gun, or harness? She readied the M16, picked up the binoculars. Behind her Erikki lay sprawled on some blankets in the 212's open cabin, heavily asleep. His face was pale and he had lost a lot of blood, but she thought he was all right. Through the lenses she saw nothing move. Down there the countryside was snow-locked and sparsely treed. Desolate. No villages and no smoke. The day was good but very cold. No clouds and the wind had dropped in the night. Slowly she searched the valley. A few miles away was a village she had not noticed before.

The 212 was parked in rough mountainous country on a rocky plateau. Last night after the escape from the palace, because a bullet had smashed some instrumentation, Erikki had lost his way. Afraid to exhaust all his fuel, and unable to fly and at the same time stanch the flow of blood from his arm, he had decided to risk landing and waiting for dawn. Once on the ground, he had pulled the carpet out of the cockpit and unrolled it. Azadeh was still sleeping peacefully. He had tied up his wound as best he could, then rewrapped her in the carpet for warmth, brought out some of the

guns, and leaned against the skid on guard. But much as he tried he could
not keep his eyes open.

He had awakened suddenly. False dawn was touching the sky. Azadeh
was still huddled down in the carpet but now she was watching him. "So.
You've kidnapped me!" Then her pretended coldness vanished and she
scrambled into his arms, kissing him and thanking him for solving the
dilemma for all three of them with such wisdom, saying the speech she had
rehearsed: "I know a wife can do little against a husband, Erikki, hardly
anything at all. Even in Iran where we're civilized, even here, a wife's
almost a chattel and the Imam is very clear on wifely duties, and in the
Koran," she added, "in the Koran and Sharia her duties are oh so clear. Also
I know I'm married to a non-Believer, and I openly swear I will try to escape
at least once a day to try to go back to fulfill my oath, and though I'll be
petrified and know you'll catch me every time and will keep me without
money or beat me and I have to obey whatever you order, I will do it." Her
eyes were brimming with happy tears. "Thank you, my darling, I was so
afraid . . ."

"Would you have done that? Given up your God?"

"Erikki, oh, how I prayed God would guide you."

"Would you?"

"There's no need now even to think the unthinkable, is there, my love?"

"Ah," he said, understanding. "Then you knew, didn't you? You knew
that this was what I had to do!"

"I only know I'm your wife, I love you, I must obey you, you took me
away without my help and against my will. We need never discuss it again.
Please?"

Blearily he peered at her, disoriented, and could not understand how she
could seem to be strong and have come out of the drugged sleep so easily.
Sleep! "Azadeh, I've got to have an hour of proper sleep. Sorry, I can't go
on. Without an hour or so, I can't. We should be safe enough here. You
guard, we should be safe enough."

"Where are we?"

"Still in Iran, somewhere near the border." He gave her a loaded M16,
knowing she could use it accurately. "One of the bullets smashed my compass." She saw him stagger as he went for the cabin, grope for some blankets, and lie down. Instantly he was asleep. While she waited for the daylight she thought about their future and about the past. Still Johnny to
settle. Nothing else. How strange life is. I thought I would scream a thousand times closed up in that vile carpet, pretending to be drugged. As if I
would be so stupid as to drug myself in case I would have to help defend us!
So easy to dupe Mina and my darling Erikki and even Hakim, no longer my

darling: ". . . her everlasting spirit's more important than her temporary body!" He would have killed me. Me! His beloved sister! But I tricked him.

She was very pleased with herself and with Aysha who had whispered about the secret listening places so that when she had stormed out of the room in pretended rage and left Hakim and Erikki alone, she had scurried to overhear what they were saying. Oh, Erikki, I was petrified you and Hakim weren't going to believe that I'd really break my oath—and frantic in case the clues I'd placed before you all evening wouldn't add up to your perfect stratagem. But you went one better than me—you even arranged the helicopter. Oh, how clever you were, I was, we were together. I even made sure you brought my handbag and jewel bag with Najoud's loot that I wheedled out of Hakim so now we're rich as well as safe, if only we can get out of this God-lost country.

"It is God-lost, my darling," Ross had said the last time she had seen him in Tehran, just before he had left her—she could not endure parting without saying good-bye so she had gone to Talbot to inquire after him and then, a few hours later, he had knocked on her door, the apartment empty but for them. "It's best you leave Iran, Azadeh. Your beloved Iran is once again bereft. This revolution's the same as all of them: a new tyranny replaces the old. Your new rulers will implant their law, their version of God's law, as the Shah implanted his. Your ayatollahs will live and die as popes live and die, some good men, some bad and some evil. In God's time the world'll get a little better, the beast in men that needs to bite and hack and kill and torment and torture will become a little more human and a little more restrained. It's only people that bugger up the world, Azadeh. Men mostly. You know I love you?"

"Yes. You said it in the village. You know I love you?"

"Yes."

So easy to swoop back into the womb of time as when they were young. "But we're not young now and there's a great sadness on me, Azadeh."

"It'll pass, Johnny," she had said, wanting his happiness. "It'll pass as Iran's troubles will pass. We've had terrible times for centuries but they've passed." She remembered how they had sat together, not touching now, yet possessed, one with the other. Then later he had smiled and raised his hand in his devil-may-care salute and he had left silently.

Again the glint in the valley. Anxiety rushed back into her. Now a movement through the trees and she saw them. "Erikki!" He was instantly awake. "Down there. Two men on horseback. They look like tribesmen." She handed him the binoculars.

"I see them." The men were armed and cantering along the valley bed, dressed as hill people would dress, keeping to cover where there was cover.

Erikki focused on them. From time to time he saw them look up in their direction. "They can probably see the chopper but I doubt if they can see us."

"They're heading up here?"

Through his aching and tiredness he had heard the fear in her voice. "Perhaps. Probably yes. It'd take them half an hour to get up here, we've plenty of time."

"They're looking for us." Her face was white and she moved closer to Erikki. "Hakim will have alerted everywhere."

"He won't have done that. He helped me."

"That was to escape." Nervously she looked around the plateau and the tree line and the mountains, then back at the two men. "Once you escaped he'd act like a Khan. You don't know Hakim, Erikki. He's my brother but before that he's Khan."

Through the binoculars he saw the half-hidden village beside the road in the middle distance. Sun glinted off telephone lines. His own anxiety increased. "Perhaps they're just villagers and curious about us. But we won't wait to find out." Wearily he smiled at her. "Hungry?"

"Yes, but I'm fine." Hastily she began bundling the carpet that was ancient, priceless, and one of her favorites. "I'm thirsty more than hungry."

"Me too but I feel better now. The sleep helped." His eyes ranged the mountains, setting what he saw against his remembrance of the map. A last look at the men still far below. No danger for a while, unless there are others around, he thought, then went for the cockpit. Azadeh shoved the carpet into the cabin and tugged the door closed. There were bullet holes in it that she had not noticed before. Another spark of sunlight off metal in the forest, much closer, that neither saw.

Erikki's head ached and he felt weak. He pressed the starting button. Wind up, immediate and correct. A quick check of his instruments. Rev counter shattered, no compass, no ADF. No need for some instruments— the sound of the engines would tell him when the needles would be in the Green. But needles on the fuel gauges were stuck at a quarter full. No time to check on them or any other damage and if there was damage, what could he do? All gods great and small, old and new, living or dead or yet to be born, be on my side today, I'll need all the help you can give me. His eyes saw the kookri that he remembered vaguely shoving in the seat pocket. Without conscious effort his fingers reached out and touched it. The feel of it burned.

Azadeh hurried for the cockpit, turbulence from the rotors picking up speed clawing at her, chilling her even more. She climbed into the seat and locked the door, turning her eyes away from the mess of dried blood on the seat and floor. Her smile died, noticing his brooding concentration and the strangeness, his hand almost near the kookri but not quite. Again she wondered why he had brought it.

"Are you all right, Erikki?" she asked, but he did not appear to have heard her. Insha'Allah. It's God's will he is alive and I'm alive, that we're together and almost safe. But now it's up to me to carry the burden and to keep us safe. He's not my Erikki yet, neither in looks nor in spirit. I can almost hear the bad thoughts pounding in his head. Soon the bad will again overpower the good. God protect us. "Thank you, Erikki," she said, accepting the headset he handed her, mentally girding herself for the battle.

He made sure she was strapped in and adjusted the volume for her. "You can hear me, all right?"

"Oh, yes, my darling. Thank you."

Part of his hearing was concentrated on the sound of the engines, a minute or two yet before they could take off. "We've not enough fuel to get to Van which's the nearest airfield in Turkey—I could go south to the hospital in Rezaiyeh for fuel but that's too dangerous. I'm going north a little. I saw a village that way and a road. Perhaps that's the Khoi–Van road."

"Good, let's hurry, Erikki, I don't feel safe here. Are there any airfields near here? Hakim's bound to have alerted the police and they'll have alerted the air force. Can we take off?"

"Just a few more seconds, engines're almost ready." He saw the anxiety and her beauty and once more the picture of her and John Ross together tumbled into his mind. He forced it away. "I think there are airfields all over the border sector. We'll go as far as we can; I think we've enough fuel to get over the border." He made an effort to be light. "Maybe we can find a gas station. Do you think they'd take a credit card?"

She laughed nervously and lifted up her bag, winding the strap around her wrist. "No need for credit cards, Erikki. We're rich—you're rich. I can speak Turkish and if I can't beg, buy, or bribe our way through I'm not of the tribe Gorgon! But through to where? Istanbul? You're overdue a fabulous holiday, Erikki. We're safe only because of you, you did everything, thought of everything!"

"No, Azadeh, you did." You and John Ross, he wanted to shout and looked back at his instruments to hide. But without Ross Azadeh'd be dead and therefore I'd be dead and I can't live with the thought of you and him together. I'm sure you lov—

At that moment his disbelieving eyes saw the groups of riders break out of the forest a quarter of a mile away on both sides of him, police among them, and begin galloping across the rocky space to head them off. His ears told him the engines were in the Green. At once his hands shoved full throttle. Time slowing. Creeping off the ground, no way that the attackers could not shoot them down. A million years of time for them to rein in, aim, and fire, any one of the dozen men. The gendarme in the middle, the sergeant, he's stopping, pulling the M16 out of his saddle holster!

Abruptly time came back at full speed and Erikki swung away and fled from them, weaving this way and that, expecting every second to be the last, then they were over the side, roaring down into the ravine at treetop level.

"Hold your fire," the sergeant shouted to the overexcited tribesmen who were at the lip, aiming and firing, their horses cavorting. "In the Name of God I told you we were ordered to capture them, to save her and kill him, not kill her!" Reluctantly the others obeyed and when he came up to them he saw the 212 was well away down in the valley. He pulled out the walkie-talkie and switched on: "HQ, this is Sergeant Zibri. The ambush failed. His engines were going before we got into position. But he's flushed out of his hiding place."

"Which way is he heading?"

"He's turning north toward the Khoi–Van road."

"Did you see Her Highness?"

"Yes. She looked petrified. Tell the Khan we saw the kidnapper strap her into the seat and it looked as though the kidnapper also had a strap around her wrist. She . . ." The sergeant's voice picked up excitedly. "Now the helicopter's turned eastward, it's keeping about two or three kilometers south of the road."

"Good. Well done. We'll alert the air force . . ."

TEHRAN—AT INNER INTELLIGENCE HQ: 9:54 A.M.

Group Four assassin Suliman al Wiali tried to stop his fingers from trembling as he took the telex from the SAVAMA colonel: "Chief of Inner Intelligence Colonel Hashemi Fazir was killed last night, bravely leading the charge that overran the leftist mujhadin HQ, together with the English adviser Armstrong. Both men were consumed by fire when the traitors blew up the building. (signed) Chief of Police, Tabriz."

Suliman was not yet over his fright at the sudden summons, petrified that this official had already found incriminating papers in Fazir's safe about Group Four assassins—the safe open and empty behind him. Surely my Master wouldn't have been that careless, not here in his own office! "The Will of God, Excellency," he said, handing the telex back and hiding his fury. "The Will of God. Are you the new leader of Inner Intelligence, Excellency?"

"Yes. What were your duties?"

"I'm an agent, Excellency," Suliman told him, fawning as would be expected, disregarding the past tense. His fear began to leave him. If these dogs suspected anything, I wouldn't be standing here, he reasoned, his confidence growing, I'd be in a dungeon screaming. These incompetent sons of dogs don't deserve to live in the world of men. "The colonel ordered me to live in Jaleh and keep my ears and eyes open and smoke out Communists." He kept his eyes blank, despising this lean-faced, pompous man who sat at Fazir's desk.

"How long have you been employed?"

"Three or four years, I don't remember exactly, Excellency, it's on my card. Perhaps it's five, I don't remember. It should be on my card, Excellency. About four years and I work hard and will serve you with all my power."

"SAVAMA is absorbing Inner Intelligence. From now on you will report to me. I'll want copies of your reports since you began."

"As God wants, Excellency, but I can't write, at least I write very badly and Excellency Fazir never required written reports," Suliman lied guilelessly. He waited in silence, shuffling his feet and acting dull-witted. SAVAK or SAVAMA, they're all liars and more than likely they arranged my Master's murder. God curse them—these dogs've ruined my Master's plan. They've done me out of my perfect job! My perfect job with real money and real power and real future. These dogs are thieves, they've stolen my future and my safety. Now I've no job, no pinpointed enemies of God to slay. No future, no safety, no protec—Unless!

Unless I use my wits and skills and take over where my Master was stopped!

Son of a burnt father, why not? It's the Will of God that he's dead and I'm alive, that he's the sacrifice and I'm not. Why not induct more teams? I know the Master's techniques and part of his plan. Even better, why not raid his house and empty the safe in the cellar he never knew I knew about. Not even his wife knows about that one. Now that he's dead it should be easy. Yes, and better I go tonight, get there first before these turd eaters of the Left Hand do it. What riches that safe could contain—should contain! Money, papers, lists—my Master loved lists like a dog loves shit! May I be sacrificed if the safe doesn't contain a list of the other Group Fours. Didn't my late Master plan to be today's al-Sabbah? Why not me instead? With assassins, real assassins who are already fearless of death and seek martyrdom as their guaranteed passport to Paradise . . .

He almost laughed aloud. To cover it he belched. "Sorry, Excellency, I'm not feeling well, can I leave, pl—"

"Where did Colonel Fazir keep his papers?"

"Papers, Excellency? May I be your sacrifice, Excellency, but what should a man like me know about papers? I'm just an agent, I reported to him and he sent me away, most times with a boot and a curse—it will be grand to work for a real man." He waited confidently. Now what would Fazir have wanted me to do? Certainly to be avenged which is clearly to dispose of Pahmudi who's responsible for his death—and this dog who dares to sit at his desk. Why not? But not until I've emptied the real safe. "Please can I go, Excellency? My bowels are overful and I've the parasite disease."

Distastefully, the colonel looked up from the card that told him nothing. No files in the safe, just money. A marvelous pishkesh for me, he thought, but where are his files? Fazir must have kept files somewhere. His home? "Yes, you can go," he said irritably, "but report to me once a week. Personally to me. And don't forget, unless you do a good job . . . we don't intend to employ malingerers."

"Yes, Excellency, certainly, Excellency, thank you, Excellency, I'll do my best for God and the Imam, but when should I report?"

"The day after Holy Day, every week." Testily the colonel waved him away. Suliman shuffled out and promised himself that before the next reporting day this colonel would be no more. Son of a dog, why not? Already my power reaches to Beirut and to Bahrain.

BAHRAIN: 12:50 P.M.   Due south, almost seven hundred miles away, Bahrain was balmy and sunny, the beaches full with weekend vacationers, windsurfers offshore enjoying the fine breeze, hotel terrace tables filled with men and women, scantily dressed to bask in the fine spring sunshine. One of these was Sayada Bertolin.

She wore a filmy sundress over her bikini and sipped a citron pressé and sat alone, her table shaded by a green umbrella. Idly she watched the bathers and the children playing in the shallows—one small boy a pattern of her own son. It'll be so good to be home again, she thought, to hold my son in my arms again and yes, yes, even to see my husband again. It's been such a long time away from civilization, from good food and good talk, from good coffee and croissants and wine, from newspapers and radio and TV and all the wonderful things we take for granted. Though not me. I've always appreciated them and have always worked for a better world and justice in the Middle East.

But now? Her joy left her.

Now I'm not just a PLO sympathizer and courier but a secret agent for Lebanese Christian militia, their Israeli overlords and their CIA overlords—thank God I was fortunate to overhear *them* whispering together when they thought I had already left after getting their orders to return to Beirut. Still no names, but enough to pinpoint their origin. Dogs! Filthy vile dogs! Christians! Betrayers of Palestine! There's still Teymour to be revenged. Dare I tell my husband who'll tell others in the Council? I daren't. *They* know too much.

Her attention focused out to sea and she was startled. Among the wind-surfers she recognized Jean-Luc, hurtling shoreward, beautifully balanced on the precarious board, leaning elegantly against the wind. At the very last second, he twisted into the wind, stepped off in the shallows, and allowed the sail to collapse. She smiled at such perfection.

Ah, Jean-Luc how you do love yourself! But I admit that had flair. In many things you're superb, as a chef, as a lover—ah, yes, but only from time to time, you're not varied enough or experimental enough for us Middle Easterns who understand eroticism, and you're too concerned with your own beauty. "I'll admit you're beautiful," she murmured, moistening pleasantly at the thought. In lovemaking you're above average, *chéri*, but no more. You're not the best. My first husband was the best, perhaps because he was the first. Then Teymour. Teymour was unique. Ah, Teymour I'm not afraid to think of you now, now that I'm out of Tehran. There I couldn't. I won't forget you, or what they did. I'll take revenge for you on Christian militia one day.

Her eyes were watching Jean-Luc, wondering what he was doing here, elated he was here, hoping he would see her, not wanting to make the first move to tempt fate but ready to wait and see what fate had in store. She glanced in her hand mirror, added a touch of gloss to her lips, perfume behind her ears. Again she waited. He started up from the beach. She pretended to concentrate on her glass, watching him in its reflection, leaving it up to chance.

"Sayada! *Mon Dieu, chérie!* What are you doing here?"

She was suitably astonished and then he was kissing her and she tasted the sea salt and smelled the sun oil and sweat and decided this afternoon would be perfect after all. "I just arrived, *chéri*. I arrived last night from Tehran," she said breathlessly, letting her desire fill her. "I'm wait-listed on Middle Eastern's noon flight to Beirut tomorrow—but what are you doing here, it's like a miracle!"

"It is, how lucky we are! But you can't go tomorrow, tomorrow's Sunday. Tomorrow we'll have a barbecue, lobsters and oysters!"

He was completely confident and Gallic and charmingly persuasive and she thought, Why not? Beirut can wait. I've waited so long one more day won't matter.

And he was thinking, How perfect! The weekend was going to be a disaster but now love this afternoon, then siesta. Later I'll choose a perfect dinner, then we'll dance a little and love tenderly and sleep soundly, ready for another perfect day tomorrow. "*Chérie*, I'm desolate but I must leave you for almost an hour," he said with the perfect touch of sadness. "We will lunch here—you stay at this hotel? Perfect, so do I: 1623. About one-thirty, quarter to two? Don't change, you look perfect. *C'est bon?*" He bent down and kissed her and let his hand stray to her breast, felt her tremor and was pleased.

AT THE HOSPITAL: 1:16 P.M.   "Good morning, Dr. Lanoire. Captain McIver, is it good or bad?" Jean-Luc said, speaking French to him— Anton Lanoire's father came from Cannes, his mother was Bahraini, a Sorbonne-trained daughter of an illiterate fisherman who still fished as he had always done, still lived in a hovel though he was a multimillionaire owner of oil wells.

"It's middling."

"How middling is that?"

The doctor steepled his fingers. He was a distinguished man in his late thirties, trained in Paris and London, trilingual, Arabic, French, and English. "We won't know with much accuracy for a few days; we still have to make several tests. We'll know the real good or bad when he has an angiogram a month from now, but in the meantime Captain McIver's responding to treatment and is not in pain."

"But is he going to be all right?"

"Angina is quite ordinary, usually. I understand from his wife he's been under very great stress for the last few months, and even worse for the last few days on this Whirlwind exercise of yours—and no wonder. What courage! I salute him and you and all those who took part. At the same time I'd strongly advise that all pilots and crews be given two or three months off."

Jean-Luc beamed. "May I have that in writing, please. Of course the three months sick leave should be with full pay—and allowances."

"Of course. What a magnificent job all of you did for your company, risking your lives—you should all get a well-deserved bonus! I wonder why more of you don't have heart attacks. The two months is to recuperate, Jean-Luc—it's essential you have a careful checkup before you continue flying."

Jean-Luc was perplexed. "We can all expect heart attacks?"

"Oh, no, no, not at all." Lanoire smiled. "But it would be very wise to be checked thoroughly—just in case. You know angina's caused by a sudden blockage of blood? A stroke's when the same happens to the brain. Arteries get clogged and that's it! Insha'Allah. It can happen anytime."

"It can?" Jean-Luc's discomfort increased. Piece of shit! It'd just be my luck to have a heart attack.

"Oh, yes," the doctor continued helpfully. "I've known patients in their thirties and early forties with perfectly normal blood pressure, normal cholesterol, and normal EKGs—electrocardiograms—and poof!" He parodied with his hands expressively. "Within a few hours—poof!"

"Poof! Just like that?" Jean-Luc sat down uneasily.

"I can't fly but I would imagine flying creates a lot of stress, especially somewhere like the North Sea. And stress is perhaps the biggest cause of angina, when part of the heart dies an—"

"My God, old Mac's heart died?" Jean-Luc was shocked.

"Oh, no, just a part. Every time you have an attack of angina, however mild, a part's lost forever. Dead." Dr. Lanoire smiled. "Of course you can go on quite a long time before you run out of tissue."

Mon Dieu, Jean-Luc thought squeamishly. I don't like this at all. North Sea? Bucket of shit, I'd better apply for a transfer before I even go there! "How long will Mac be in the hospital?"

"Four or five days. I would suggest you leave him today and visit tomorrow, but don't tax him. He must have a month's leave, then some further tests."

"What are his chances?"

"That's up to God."

Upstairs on the veranda of a pleasant room overlooking the blue waters, Genny was dozing in a chair, today's London *Times*, brought by BA's early flight, open on her lap. McIver lay comfortably in the starched clean bed. The breeze came off the sea and touched him and he woke up. Wind's changed, he thought. It's back to the standard northeasterly. Good. He moved to see better out into the Gulf. The slight movement awakened her instantly. She folded the paper and got up.

"How're you feeling, luv?"

"Fine. I'm fine now. No pain. Just a bit tired. Vaguely heard you talking to the doc, what did he say?"

"Everything seems fine. The attack wasn't bad. You'll have to take it easy for a few days, then a month off and then some more tests—he was very encouraging because you don't smoke, you're ever so fit, considering." Genny stood over the bed, against the light, but he could see her face and read the truth thereon. "You can't fly anymore—as a pilot," she said and smiled.

"That's a bugger," he said dryly. "Have you been in touch with Andy?"

"Yes. I called last night and this morning and will check again in an hour or so. Nothing yet on young Marc Dubois and Fowler but all our birds are safe at Al Shargaz and being stripped for freighting out tomorrow. Andy was so proud of you—and Scrag. I talked to him this morning too."

The shadow of a smile. "It'll be good to see old Scrag. You're okay?"

"Oh, yes." She touched his shoulder. "I'm ever so glad you're better— you did give me a turn."

"I gave me a turn, Gen." He smiled and held out his hand and said gruffly, "Thanks, Mrs. McIver."

She took it and put it to her cheek, then bent down and touched his lips with hers, warmed by the enormity of the affection in his face. "You did give me such a turn," she said again.

He noticed the newspaper. "That's today's, Gen?"

"Yes, dear."

"Seems years since I saw one. What's new?"

"More of the usual." She folded the paper and put it aside carelessly, not wanting him to see the section she had been reading in case it worried him. "Stock market collapse in Hong Kong." That'll certainly affect Struan's and that bastard Linbar, she thought, but will it touch S-G and Andy? Nothing Duncan can do, so never mind. "Strikes, Callaghan's messing up poor old Britain more than ever. They say he might call a snap election this year, and if he does Maggie Thatcher's got a good chance. Wouldn't that be super? Be a change to have someone sensible in charge."

"Because she's a woman?" He smiled wryly. "That'd certainly set the cat among the chickens. Christ Almighty, a woman PM! Don't know how she ever wangled the leadership away from Heath in the first place . . . she must have iron-plated knickers! If only the bloody Liberals'd stayed out of the way . . ." His voice trailed off and she saw him look out to sea, some passing dhows beautiful.

Quietly she sat down and waited, wanting to let him drift back into sleep, or talk a little, whatever pleased him. He must be getting better if he's already taking off after the Libs, she thought, bemused, letting herself drift, watching the sea. Her hair was moved by the breeze that smelled of sea salt. It was pleasant just sitting, knowing that he was all right now, "responding to treatment. No need to worry, Mrs. McIver." Easy to say, hard not to do.

There'll be a huge change in our lives, has to be, apart from losing Iran and all our stuff there, lot of old rubbish, most of it that I won't miss. Now that Whirlwind's over—I must've been mad to suggest it, but oh it worked so well! Now we've most of our lads out safely—can't think of Tom or Marc or Fowler, Erikki or Azadeh or Sharazad, God bless them all—and our best equipment and our face so we're still in business, our stake in S-G's got to be worth something. We won't be penniless and that's a blessing. I wonder how much we could get for our shares? I suppose we do have a share? But what about the "stock market collapse"? I hope that hasn't buggered us again.

It would be nice to have a little money, but I don't care so long as Duncan gets better. Perhaps he'll retire and perhaps he won't. I wouldn't want him really to retire, it would kill him. Where should we live? Near Aberdeen? Or Edinburgh near Sarah and Trevor, or London near Hamish and Kathy? Not London, nasty down there, and we shouldn't live too near either of the kids, don't want to bother them though it'd be ever so nice to be able to drop by from time to time, even baby-sit. Don't want to become the boring mother-in-law to Trevor or to young Kathy—such a lovely girl. Kathy, Kathleen, Kathy: Andrew and Kathy, and sometimes going to Castle Avisyard, and now Andrew and Maureen and tiny Electra. I wouldn't want to be alone, don't want Duncan to . . .

Don't want to relive the horror, the pounding, rattling darkness, not being able to see, jets howling, stink of petrol—my God, how do they stand the noise and the bouncing around hour after hour—and all the time Duncan gasping, not knowing if he was alive or dead, twice crying out, "He's dead, he's dead," but no one hearing and no one to help anyway and dear old Charlie flying here as fast as he could, the other man, the Iranian sergeant, what was his name, ah, yes, Wazari, Wazari nice but useless. Oh, God, that was awful, awful, and lasted forever . . . but now it's all right and thank God I was there. Duncan will be all right. He will be. He must be.

Wonder what'll happen to Wazari? He looked so frightened when the police took him off. Wait a moment, didn't Jean-Luc say he had heard they would probably release him into Andy's custody as a political exile if Andy guaranteed to take him out of Bahrain and give him a job?

Bloody revolution! Bloody nuisance I couldn't get back to collect some of my things. There was that old frying pan that'd never stick, and Grannie's teapot that made such a good cup of tea even out of filthy teabags and Tehran water. Ugh! Water! Soon no more squatting and using water instead of good soft paper. Ugh! If I never have to squat again it will be too soon. . . .

"What are you smiling about, Gen?"

"Oh, let me think! Oh, yes, I was thinking about having to squat, about all the bums in the early morning over the joubs and their bottles of water, poor people. It always looked so awful and at the same time funny. Poor people. No more squatting for us, me lad, it's back to Blighty." She saw his eyes change and her anxiety returned. "That's not bad, Duncan. Going home. It won't be, I promise."

After a pause, he nodded, half to himself. "We'll wait and see, Gen. We won't make any decision yet. No need to decide what we'll do for a month or two. First I'll get fit and then we'll decide. Don't you worry, eh?"

"I'm not worried now."

"Good, no need to worry." Once more his attention strayed to the sea. I'm not going to spend the rest of my life battling bloody British weather, that'd be awful. Retire? Christ, I'll have to think of something. If I've got to stop working I'll go mad. Maybe we could get a little place by the sea to winter in Spain or the south of France. I'll be buggered if I'm going to let Gen freeze and get old and bent before her time—that bloody awful salt-heavy wind off the North Sea! Never by God. We'll have more than enough money now Whirlwind's a success. Nine out of ten 212s! Wonderful! Can't think about Dubois or Fowler or Tom or Erikki, Azadeh or Sharazad.

His anxiety came back and with it a twinge that increased his anxiety and brought a bigger twinge . . .

"What're you thinking, Duncan?"

"That it's a beautiful day."

"Yes, yes, it is."

"Will you try Andy for me, Gen?"

"Of course." She picked up the phone and dialed, knowing it would be better for him to talk awhile. "Hello? Oh, hello, Scot, how're you—it's Genny." She listened then said, "That's good. Is your dad there?" Listening again, then, "No, just tell him I called for Duncan—he's fine and can be reached on extension 455 here. He just wants to say hello. Will you ask Andy to call when he comes back? Thanks, Scot . . . no he's really fine, tell Charlie too. 'Bye."

Thoughtfully she replaced the phone on its cradle. "Nothing new. Andy's out at the International with Scrag. They're seeing that Jap—you know the one from Iran-Toda—sorry, I wouldn't call him one to his face but that's what he is. Still can't forgive them for what they did in the War."

McIver frowned. "You know, Gen, perhaps it's time we did. Kasigi certainly helped old Scrag. The old 'sins of the fathers' bit doesn't add up. Perhaps we should start the new era. That's what we've got, Gen, like it or not, a New Era. Eh?"

She saw his smile and it brought tears near again. Mustn't cry, all's going to be well, the New Era will be good and he's going to get better, must get better—oh, Duncan, I'm so afraid. "Tell you what, me lad," she said brightly, "when you're super fit we'll go to Japan on holiday and then we'll see."

"That's a deal. We could even visit Hong Kong again." He took her hand and squeezed it and both hid their fear of the future, fear for the other.

AL SHARGAZ—INTERNATIONAL HOTEL: 1:55 P.M. Kasigi was weaving through the busy tables on the immaculate terrace overlooking the swimming pool. "Ah, Mr. Gavallan, Captain Scragger, so sorry to be late."

"No problem, Mr. Kasigi, please sit down."

"Thank you." Kasigi wore a light tropical suit and looked cool though he was not. "So sorry, I loathe being late but in the Gulf it's almost impossible to be on time. I had to come from Dubai and the traffic . . . I believe congratulations are in order. I hear your Whirlwind was almost a complete success."

"We're still short one chopper with two crew, but we were very lucky, all in all," Gavallan said, no joy in him or in Scragger. "Would you care for lunch or a drink?" Their lunch appointment, requested by Kasigi, had been for twelve-thirty. By prearrangement, Gavallan and Scragger had not waited and were already on coffee.

"A brandy and mineral water, tall, please, and another mineral water on the side. No lunch thank you, I'm not hungry." Kasigi lied politely, not wanting to embarrass himself by eating when they were finished. He smiled at Scragger. "So! I'm pleased to see you're safe with your airplanes and crew out. Congratulations!"

"Sorry I had to duck your questions but, well, now you'll understand."

"The moment I heard, I understood, of course. Health!" Kasigi drank the mineral water thirstily. "Now that Whirlwind's out of the way, Mr. Gavallan, perhaps you can help me solve my problems at Iran-Toda?"

"I'd like to, of course, but I can't. I'm very sorry but we can't. It's not possible. Just not possible, that must be obvious now."

"Perhaps it can be made possible." Kasigi's eyes did not waver. "I've heard that sunset tonight is a firm deadline to have your airplanes out or they will be impounded."

Politely Gavallan gestured with his hand. "Let's hope it's just another rumor."

"One of your embassy officials informed our ambassador that this was definite. It would be a tragedy to lose all your aircraft after so much success."

"Definite? You're certain?" Gavallan felt empty.

"My ambassador was certain." Kasigi put on a nice smile. "Say I could get your deadline extended from sunset tonight to sunset tomorrow, could you solve my problems at Iran-Toda?"

Both men stared at him. "Can you extend our deadline, Mr. Kasigi?"

"I can't but our ambassador might be able to. I have an appointment with him in an hour. I will ask him—perhaps he could influence the Iranian ambassador, or the Sheik, or both." Kasigi saw Gavallan's immediate interest and let that hang in the air, far too experienced a fisherman in Western waters not to know the bait. "I'm in Captain Scragger's debt. I haven't forgotten he saved my life, went out of his way to fly me to Bandar Delam. Friends shouldn't forget friends, should they? At Ambassador Level . . . perhaps it could be done."

The Japanese ambassador? My God, would it be possible—Gavallan's heart was racing with hope at the unexpected avenue. "There's no way ours can do anything, my contact was quite clear. I'd appreciate any help I could get, I certainly would. You think he'd help?"

"If he wanted to, I think he could." Kasigi sipped the brandy. "As you can help us. My chairman asked to be remembered to you and mentioned your mutual friend Sir Ian Dunross." He saw Gavallan's eyes react and added, "They had dinner together two nights ago."

"If I can help . . . just exactly what are your problems?" And where's the catch and what's the cost? Gavallan thought. And where's Ian? Three times I've tried to reach him and failed.

"I need three 212s and two 206s at Iran-Toda as soon as possible, under contract for a year. It's essential the plant gets completed and the local komiteh has promised me full cooperation—if we start at once. If not at once it will be disastrous."

Last night Chief Engineer Watanabe at Iran-Toda had sent him a coded telex. "Komiteh chief Zataki is like a mad shark over the S-G hijacking. His ultimatum: either we resume construction at once—for which we must have helicopters—or the whole plant will face immediate possession and nationalization and 'all foreigners here will face retribution for treason.' D hour is after sunset prayers Sunday fourth, when I am to appear before the komiteh. Please advise."

Urgent telephone calls most of the night to Osaka and Tokyo had only served to increase Kasigi's rage. "Yoshi, my dear friend," his cousin and overlord Hiro Toda had said with devastating politeness, "I've consulted the Syndicate. We all agree we're fortunate you're there on the spot. It's up to you. We're completely confident that you will solve these problems—before you leave."

The message was quite clear: solve it or don't come back.

He had spent the rest of the night trying to find a way out of his dilemma. Then, with the dawn, he had remembered a chance remark that the Japanese ambassador had made about the new Iranian ambassador that gave him a possible means to solve Gavallan's deadline and his own problem. "To be quite blunt and open, Mr. Gavallan," he said and almost laughed aloud at so stupid a remark—but so necessary in Western negotiations, "I need a plan by tomorrow sunset and answers by tomorrow sunset."

"Why then, may I ask?"

"Because I made commitments to a friend that I must honor which of course you'd understand," Kasigi said. "So we both have a deadline, the same one." Then he judged the time correct and struck hard to make sure the hook was firm. "If you can help me, I would forever appreciate it. Of course I'll do everything to persuade my ambassador to help you anyway."

"There's no point in offering any of our birds, they'd be impounded instantly, no point in offering you the 206s we left behind—they're sure to be *hors de combat* too. S-G's totally out, so's Bell, Guerney or any of the other companies. Could you get Japanese nationals who're helicopter pilots?"

"No. There're none trained." Not yet, Kasigi thought, again furious with the Syndicate for not having the foresight to train their own trustworthy people for the job. "The personnel will have to be foreign. My ambassador could smooth visas, and so forth—of course you know Iran-Toda's a National Project," he added, the exaggeration not bothering him. It soon will be when all the information I have gets into the right hands. "What about French or German crews?"

With an effort Gavallan tore his mind off how Ambassador Level could lead to his own men and choppers being safe, how he would then be out of Linbar's trap and free to deal with Imperial Helicopters in the North Sea, the Hong Kong crisis, the early retirement of Linbar, and positioning Scot for a future takeover. "So many wonderful possibilities," he said involuntarily, then covered himself quickly and concentrated on solving Iran-Toda. "There are two parts to the problem. First, equipment and spares: if you could provide a letter of credit at our usual monthly rate, renewable as long as you keep the planes—wherever I can get them from—with a guarantee that if the Iran authorities impound them you'll assume all lease payments in dollars outside of Iran and reimburse the owners against a total loss, I could get them to Iran-Toda within . . . within a week."

Kasigi said at once, "Our bankers are the Sumitomo; I could arrange a meeting with them here this evening. That's no problem. Where would you get the airplanes?"

"Germany or France—can't use British or American. Same for the pilots. Probably France's better because of their help to Khomeini. I might be able to get them through some friends at Aerospatiale. What about insurance? It'll be impossible for me to get you insurance in Iran."

"Perhaps I could do that from Japan."

"Good. I'd hate to fly uninsured birds. Next: Scrag, say we can get the aircraft, how many pilots and mecs'd you need?"

"Well, Andy, if you could get them, you'd best have eight to ten pilots, rostering, and ten to fourteen mecs, based outside Iran but close by."

"Who'd pay them, Mr. Kasigi? In what currency and where?"

"Whatever currency they wanted, wherever and however. Standard rates?"

"I'd think you'd have to offer a 'danger cost-of-living bonus,' Iran being what it is."

"Would you consider arranging the whole matter for me, Mr. Gavallan, the equipment and the personnel, for say a 10 percent override?"

"Forget percentages and remember our involvement'd have to be kept very quiet. I'd suggest this: your operation should be controlled—logistics, spares, and repairs—from Kuwait or Bahrain."

"Bahrain'd be better, Andy," Scragger said.

"Kuwait's much closer," Kasigi said.

"Yes," Scragger said, "so more liable for pressure from Iran or Iran-sponsored unrest. This side of the Gulf's due for a battering, I think. Too many Shi'as who're usually poor, too many sheiks who're Sunni. Short term or long term you're better off in Bahrain."

"Then Bahrain," Kasigi said. "Mr. Gavallan, can I have Captain Scragger's services for a year to run the operation—if it comes to fruition—at double his present salary?" He saw Scragger's eyes narrow and wondered if he'd gone too far too fast, so he added lightly, "If I ask you to give up your first love, my friend, it's only right you should be compensated."

"That's a great offer, but, well, I don't know. Andy?"

Gavallan hesitated. "It'd mean you'd have to quit S-G, Scrag, and quit flying. You couldn't run five ships and fly—and anyway you could never go back to Iran, no way."

That's right. Quit flying. So I'm at a crossroads too, Scragger was thinking. Don't try to pretend Mac's bad luck didn't give me a shaft to end all shafts. And why did I faint yesterday? Doc Nutt said it was just exhaustion. Balls, I've never fainted in my life before and wot do doctors know anyways? A year in Bahrain? That's better than a few months in the North Sea always bucking the next medical. No flying? My Gawd! Wait a minute, I could keep current and my hand in with a little local joyriding. "I'd have to think about that, but thanks for the offer, Mr. Kasigi."

"Meanwhile, Mr. Gavallan, could you organize the first month or so?"

"Yes. With a certain amount of luck, within the week I could get enough birds and crew there to get you started, the balance in a week or two for a renewable three-month contract." Gavallan added as delicately as he could, "So long as we beat our deadline."

Kasigi kept his satisfaction covered. "Good. Shall we meet here at nine? I'll bring Mr. Umura, who's president of the Sumitomo for the Gulf, to arrange the letters of credit in the form you want, Mr. Gavallan."

"Nine o'clock on the dot. Perhaps you could mention to your ambassador, even if tonight's sunset deadline passes, my freighters won't arrive till noon tomorrow and I won't be able to get them loaded and off before tomorrow sunset."

"You will keep 'Ambassador Level' just between us?"

"Of course. You have my word. Scrag?"

Kasigi heard Scrag say the same, and was, as always, astounded that Westerners could be so naive as to rely on someone's "word"—word of honor, whose honor, what honor? Hasn't it ever been that a secret shared is no secret and never will be again? Like Whirlwind, it had been so easy to smoke that one out. "Perhaps we could plan it this way: we settle finances and letters of credit tonight; you begin to arrange the helicopters and spares and crew, how to manage the operation from Bahrain, warehousing, and sum—everything subject to confirmation tomorrow sunset. If you've successfully extracted your own equipment by then, you guarantee Iran-Toda will have its helicopters within the week."

"You seem very confident you can eliminate our deadline."

"My ambassador can, perhaps. I'll phone and tell you what he says the moment I've left him. Captain Scragger, would it be possible for you to run a trainee program for Japanese pilots?"

"Easy, providing they speak English and have at least a hundred chopper hours. I'd have to get a training captain and . . ." Scragger stopped. It had suddenly occurred to him this was the perfect solution. "That's a beaut idea. I could be examiner—I can sign them out in type and that way I'd get enough flying under the right circs. Bonzer!" He beamed. "Tell you wot, sport, if Andy can fix it, I'm in." He stuck out his hand and Kasigi shook it.

"Thank you. Perfect. So Mr. Gavallan, do we 'give her a try'?"

"Why not?" Gavallan put out his hand and felt Kasigi's iron-hard grip and for the first time really believed there was a chance. Kasigi's smart. Very. Now he's got the standard modern Japanese company operating procedure in place: get foreign experts to train Japanese personnel on site, or to create the market in their own countries, then move in the trainees. We get the short-term profit, they get the long-term market. They're doing to us in business what they failed to do at war. In spades. So what? It is fair trading. And if Kasigi and his ambassador can extract me from my disaster, it's no skin off my nose to help him out of his. "We'll give her a try."

Kasigi smiled properly for the first time. "Thank you. I'll phone the moment I have any news." He half bowed, then strode off.

"You think he'll do it, Andy?" Scragger asked hopefully.

"Honest to God I don't know." Gavallan waved at a waiter for the bill. "How you going to solve him in time?"

Gavallan started to answer and stopped. He had just noticed Pettikin and Paula at a table by the swimming pool, their heads close together. "I thought Paula was off to Tehran this morning."

"She was. Maybe the flight was canceled or she took a sickie," Scragger said absently, afraid to be grounded.

"What?"

"That's Aussie. If it's a nice day and a sheila suddenly wants the afternoon off to swim or make love or just goof off, she calls in to the office during her lunch break and says she's feeling horrible. Sick. Sickie." Scragger's eyebrows soared. "Sheilas Down Under are very accommodating sometimes. That Paula's something else—Charlie's a goner."

Gavallan saw the pleasure on their faces under the umbrella, oblivious of the world. Apart from worry over Dubois, Erikki, and the others, he had read the piece in the morning's papers about the sudden stock market crash in Hong Kong: "Many of the major companies, headed by Struan's, Roth-well-Gornt, Par-Con of China, lost 30 percent of their value or more in the day, with the whole market plunging and no end in sight. The statement issued by the Taipan, Mr. Linbar Struan, saying that this was just a seasonal hiccup brought a slashing rebuff from the government and his rivals. The more sensational press was rife with widely circulated rumors of insider trading among the Big Four and manipulation by selling short to bring prices tumbling from their record high." That's got to be why I can't get hold of Ian. Has he gone to Hong Kong? Bloody Linbar! His balance sheet this year'll be red top to bottom.

With an effort he put brakes on his mind. He saw Pettikin reach over and cover Paula's hand. She did not take it away. "You think he'll pop the question, Scrag?"

"If he doesn't he's a mug."

"I agree." Gavallan sighed and got up. "Scrag, I'm not going to wait. You sign the bill, then go down and get Charlie, say I'm sorry but he's got to meet me in the office for an hour, then he's got the rest of the day off, then get hold of Willi and Rudi. I'll phone Jean-Luc, and between us we'll come up with what Kasigi needs, if he can deliver. Don't tell 'em why, just say it's urgent and to keep their mouths closed tighter than a gnat's bum." He walked off. "Hey, Mr. Gavallan!" stopped him. It was the American Wesson who jovially got up from his table and stuck out his hand. "You got time for a drink and to visit awhile?"

"Oh, hello, Mr. Wesson, thanks, but, er, can I take a raincheck? I'm in a bit of a hurry."

"Hell, yes, anytime." Wesson grinned at him and leaned closer, dropping his voice to a good-natured conspiratorial whisper, and for the first time Gavallan noticed the small hearing aid in the man's left ear. "Only wanted to say, congratulations, you sure as hell showed those jokers your heels!"

"We, er, we just got lucky. Sorry, got to dash. 'Bye."

"Sure, see you." Thoughtfully Wesson picked up his pen and put it in his pocket. So Kasigi is gonna try and bail out Gavallan, he thought, meandering toward the lobby. I'd never'd figured that one. Shit, there's no way the new regime'll cooperate. Kasigi's a pipe dreamer. Poor bastard must be going crazy, Iran-Toda's a mess, and hell, even if they start now it'll take years for that plant to be in production, and everyone knows Iran's oil spigot'll stay turned off, losing Japan 70 percent of her energy supply; there's gotta be another soar in world prices, more inflation . . . Japan's our only ally in the Pacific and the poor bastards're going to be nailed.

Jesus, with Gavallan's Lengeh op closed down, isn't the whole Siri field in jeopardy? How'll de Plessey operate Siri without chopper support? Ambassador, huh? Interesting. How's that gonna work? Who does what to whom? And how much do I pass on to old Aaron? The lot, that old bastard'll figure where it all fits if anyone can.

He wandered through the lobby and out to his car and did not notice Kasigi in a phone booth to one side.

". . . I quite agree, Ishii-san." Kasigi was speaking deferentially in Japanese, sweat on his brow. "Please inform His Excellency we'll get our equipment and crew, I'm sure of it—if you can arrange the rest." He kept the nervousness out of his voice.

"Ah, is that so? Excellent," Ishii from the embassy said. "I'll inform His Excellency at once. Now, what about the Iranian ambassador? Have you heard from him?"

The bottom dropped out of Kasigi's bottom. "He hasn't accepted the invitation?"

"No, so sorry, not yet, and it's almost three o'clock. Very distressing. Please join the meeting as we agreed. Thank you, Kasigi-san."

"Thank you, Ishii-san," he said, wanting to scream. Gently he replaced the phone.

In the air-conditioned lobby he felt a little better and went to the reception desk. There he collected his messages—two from Hiro Toda to phone —and went upstairs to his room and locked the door. He crushed the messages into a ball, threw them into the toilet, and began to urinate on them. "Dear stupid cousin Hiro," he said aloud in Japanese, "if I save your stupid neck which I have to do to save my own," then added a stream of English obscenities as there were none in Japanese, "your family will be in debt to mine for eight generations for all the trouble you're causing me."

He flushed the messages away, took off his clothes, showered, and lay naked on the bed in the cool breeze, wanting to gather energy and restore his tranquillity to prepare for the meeting.

The Japanese ambassador's chance remark that had initiated his whole scheme had been made to Roger Newbury at a British embassy reception a couple of days ago. The ambassador had mentioned that the new Iranian ambassador had been bewailing the closure of Iran-Toda that would have given the new Islamic state a tremendous position of economic power throughout the whole Gulf region. "His name's Abadani, university trained, majored in economics, of course fundamentalist but not rabidly so. He's quite young and not too experienced but he's a career officer, speaks good English, and was in the Kabul embassy . . ."

At the time the remarks had meant very little to Kasigi. Then Whirlwind happened. Tehran's telexes had spread throughout the Gulf, and then rumors of Abadani's demand for an inspection of Gavallan's helicopters fixed for this evening—an inspection that would obviously prove they had been Iranian registered: ". . . and that, Kasigi-san, will create an international incident," Ishii had told him late last night, "because now Kuwait, Saudi, Bahrain will be implicated—and that, I can assure you, one and all would prefer to avoid, most of all our Sheik."

In the dawn he had gone to see Abadani and had explained about Zataki and starting construction again, adding in great secrecy that the Japanese government was rearranging Iran-Toda as a National Project—therefore covering all future financing—and that with Excellency Abadani's cooperation he could also start work in Bandar Delam immediately.

"National Project? God be thanked! If your government is behind it formally, that would solve all financing forever. God be thanked. What can I do? Anything!"

"To restart immediately I need helicopters and expatriate pilots and crew. The only way I can get them quickly is with the help of S-G Helicopters and Mr. Gavall—"

Abadani had exploded.

After listening politely and seemingly agreeably to a tirade about air piracy and enemies of Iran, Kasigi had obliquely returned to the attack.

"You're quite right, Excellency," he had said, "but I had to choose between risking your displeasure by bringing it to your attention, or failing in my duty to your Great Country. Our choice is simple: If I don't get helicopters I cannot restart. I've tried Guerney's and others with no success and now I know I can only get them quickly through this dreadful man—of course only for a few months as a stopgap until I can make my own arrangements for Japanese personnel. If I don't restart at once that will precipitate this man Zataki, I assure you he and his Abadan komiteh is a law unto itself, making good his threat. That will shock and embarrass my government and cause them to delay implementation of total National Project financing and then . . ." He had shrugged. "My government will order Iran-Toda abandoned, and start a new petrochemical plant in a safe area like Saudi Arabia, Kuwait, or Iraq."

"Safe? Iraq? Those thieves? Saudi or Kuwait? By God, they're decadent sheikdoms ripe for overthrow by the people. Dangerous to attempt a long-term business with the sheiks, very dangerous. They don't obey God's law. Iran does now. Iran is in balance now. The Imam, God's peace on him, has rescued us. He has ordered oil to flow. There must be some other way of getting helicopters and crews! Gavallan and his mob of pirates have our property. I can't assist pirates to escape. Do you want pirates to escape?"

"Heaven forbid, I would never suggest that. Of course we don't know they are pirates, Excellency. I heard that these are just foul rumors spread by more enemies who want Iran hurt even more. Even if it were true, would you equate nine used airplanes against $3.1 billion already spent and another $1.1 billion my government might be persuaded to commit?"

"Yes. Piracy is piracy, the law is the law, the Sheik has agreed to the inspection, the truth is the truth. Insha'Allah."

"I totally agree, Excellency, but you know that truth is relative and a postponement until after sunset tomorrow would be in your national interests . . ." He had bitten back a curse and corrected his slip quickly, "in the interests of the Imam and your Islamic state."

"God's truth is not relative."

"Yes, yes, of course," Kasigi said, outwardly calm but inwardly gnashing his teeth. How can anyone deal with these lunatics who use their beliefs as a coverall and "God" whenever they wish to close a legitimate line of logic. They're all mad, blinkered! They won't understand as we Japanese do you've got to be tolerant about other people's beliefs, and that life is "from nothing into nothing," and heaven and hell and god merely opium smoke from an abberated brain—until *proven* otherwise!

"Of course you're right, Excellency. But they won't be his airplanes or crews—I just need his temporary connections." Wearily he had waited and cajoled and listened, then played his penultimate card: "I'm sure the Sheik and the foreign minister would consider it an immense favor if you'd postpone the inspection until tomorrow so they could go to my ambassador's special reception at eight this evening."

"Reception, Mr. Kasigi?"

"Yes, it's sudden but terribly important—I happen to know you're invited as the most important guest." Kasigi had dropped his voice even more. "I beg you not to mention where you got the knowledge but, again in private, I can tell you that my government is seeking long-term oil contracts that would prove astoundingly profitable to you if Iran can continue to supply us. It would be a perfect moment t—"

"Long-term contracts? I agree the Shah-negotiated contracts are no good, one-sided and must go. But we value Japan as a customer. Japan's never tried to exploit us. I'm sure your ambassador would not mind delaying his reception an hour until after the inspection. The Sheik, the foreign minister, Newbury, and I could go directly from the airport."

Kasigi was not sure how far he dared go. But, Mister Excuse for an Ambassador, he thought, if you don't postpone your inspection, I will be revenged because you will have made me commit the only sin we acknowledge: failure. "It's fortunate Iran's so well represented here."

"I will certainly come to the reception, Mr. Kasigi, after the inspection."

Kasigi's ultimate card had then been delivered with all the elegance needed: "I have a feeling, Excellency, you will soon be personally invited to my country to meet the most important, *most important* leaders there—for you of course realize how vital your Islamic state is to Japan—and to inspect facilities that would be valuable to Iran."

"We . . . we certainly need untainted friends," Abadani said.

Kasigi had watched him carefully and had seen no reaction, still the same pitiless eyes and inflexibility. "In these troubled times it's essential to look after friends, isn't it? You never know when disaster may strike you, whoever you are? Do you?"

"That's in the Hands of God. Only His." There had been a long pause, then Abadani had said, "As God warts. I will consider what you have said."

Now in the privacy of his hotel bedroom, Kasigi was very afraid. It's only essential to look after yourself. However wise or careful you are, you never know when disaster will strike. If gods exist, they exist only to torment you.

JUST INSIDE TURKEY: 4:23 P.M. They had landed just outside the village this morning, barely a mile inside Turkey. Erikki would have preferred to have gone farther into safety but his tanks were dry. He had been intercepted and ambushed again, this time by two fighters and two Huey gunships and had had to endure them for more than a quarter of an hour before he could duck across the line. The two Hueys had not ventured after him but remained circling in station just their side of the border.

"Forget them, Azadeh," he had said joyously. "We're safe now."

But they were not. The villagers had surrounded them, and the police had arrived. Four men, a sergeant, and three others, all in uniform—crumpled and ill fitting—with holstered revolvers. The sergeant wore dark glasses against the glare of the sun off the snow. None of them spoke English. Azadeh had greeted them according to the plan she and Erikki had concocted, explaining that Erikki, a Finnish citizen, had been employed by a British company under contract to Iran-Timber, that in the Azerbaijan riots and fighting near Tabriz his life had been threatened by leftists, that she, his wife, had been equally threatened, so they had fled.

"Ah, the Effendi is Finnish but you're Iranian?"

"Finnish by marriage, Sergeant Effendi, Iranian by birth. Here are our papers." She had given him her Finnish passport which did not include references to her late father, Abdollah Khan. "May we use the telephone, please? We can pay, of course. My husband would like to call our embassy, and also his employer in Al Shargaz."

"Ah, Al Shargaz." The sergeant nodded pleasantly. He was heavyset, close-shaven, even so the blue-black of his beard showed through his golden skin. "Where's that?"

She told him, very conscious of the way she and Erikki looked, Erikki with the filthy, bloodstained bandage on his arm and the crude adhesive over his damaged ear, she with her hair matted and dirty clothes and face. Behind her the two Hueys circled. The sergeant watched them thoughtfully. "Why would they dare to send fighters into our airspace and helicopters after you?"

"The Will of God, Sergeant Effendi. I'm afraid that on that side of the border many strange things are happening now."

"How are things over the border?" He motioned the other policemen toward the 212 and began to listen attentively. The three policemen wandered over, peered into the cockpit. Bullet holes and dried blood and smashed instruments. One of them opened the cabin door. Many automatic weapons. More bullet holes. "Sergeant!"

The sergeant acknowledged but waited politely until Azadeh had finished. Villagers listened wide-eyed, not a chador or veil among them. Then he pointed to one of the crude village huts. "Please wait over there in the shade." The day was cold, the land snowbound, the sun bright off the snow. Leisurely the sergeant examined the cabin and the cockpit. He picked up the kookri, half pulled it out of the scabbard, and shoved it home again. Then he beckoned Azadeh and Erikki with it. "How do you explain the guns, Effendi?"

Uneasily Azadeh translated the question for Erikki.

"Tell him they were left in my plane by tribesmen who were attempting to hijack her."

"Ah, tribesmen," the sergeant said. "I'm astonished tribesmen would leave such wealth for you to fly away with. Can you explain that?"

"Tell him they were all killed by loyalists, and I escaped in the melee."

"Loyalists, Effendi? What loyalists?"

"Police. Tabrizi police," Erikki said, uncomfortably aware that each question would pull them deeper into the quicksand. "Ask him if I can use the telephone, Azadeh."

"Telephone? Certainly. In due time." The sergeant studied the circling Hueys for a moment. Then he turned his hard brown eyes back to Erikki. "I'm glad the police were loyal. Police have a duty to the state, to the people, and to uphold the law. Gunrunning is against the law. Fleeing from police upholding the law is a crime. Isn't it?"

"Yes, but we're not gunrunners, Sergeant Effendi, nor fleeing from police upholding the law," Azadeh had said, even more afraid now. The border was so close, too close. For her the last part of their escape had been terrifying. Obviously Hakim had alerted the border area; no one but he had the power to arrange such an intercept so fast, both on the ground and in the air.

"Are you armed?" the sergeant asked politely.

"Just a knife."

"May I have it please?" The sergeant accepted it. "Please follow me."

They had gone to the police station, a small brick building with cells and a few offices and telephones near the mosque in the little village square. "Over the last months we've had many refugees of all sorts passing along our road, Iranians, British, Europeans, Americans, many Azerbaijanis, many —but no Soviets." He laughed at his own joke. "Many refugees, rich, poor, good, bad, many criminals among them. Some were sent back, some went on. Insha'Allah, eh? Please wait there."

"There" was not a cell but a room with a few chairs and a table and bars on the windows, many flies and no way out. But it was warm and relatively clean. "Could we have some food and drink and use the telephone, please?" Azadeh asked. "We can pay, Sergeant Effendi."

"I will order some for you from the hotel here. The food is good and not expensive."

"My husband asks, can he use the telephone, please?"

"Certainly—in due course."

That had been this morning, and now it was late afternoon. In the intervening time the food had arrived, rice and mutton stew and peasant bread and Turkish coffee. She had paid with rials and was not overcharged. The sergeant had allowed them to use the foul-smelling hole in the ground squatter, and water from a tank and an old basin to wash in. There were no medical supplies, just iodine. Erikki had cleaned his wounds as best he could, gritting his teeth at the sudden pain, still weak and exhausted. Then, with Azadeh close beside him, he had propped himself on a chair, his feet on another, and had drifted off. From time to time the door would open and one or other of the policemen would come in, then go out again. *"Matyeryebyets,"* Erikki muttered. "Where can we run to?"

She had gentled him and stayed close and kept a steel gate on her own fear. I must carry him, she thought over and over. She was feeling better now with her hair combed and flowing, her face clean, her cashmere sweater tidy. Through the door she could hear muttered conversation, occasionally a telephone ringing, cars and trucks going past on the road from and to the border, flies droning. Her tiredness took her and she slept fitfully, her dreams bad: noise of engines and firing and Hakim mounted like a Cossack charging them, both she and Erikki buried up to their necks in the earth, hooves just missing them, then somehow free, rushing from the border that was acres of massed barbed wire, the false mullah Mahmud and the butcher suddenly between them and safety and th—

The door opened. Both of them awoke, startled. A major in immaculate uniform stood there, glowering, flanked by the sergeant and another policeman. He was a tall, hard-faced man. "Your papers please," he said to Azadeh.

"I, I gave them to the sergeant, Major Effendi."

"You gave him a Finnish passport. Your Iranian papers." The major held out his hand. She was too slow. At once the sergeant went forward and grabbed her shoulder purse and spilled the contents onto the table. Simultaneously, the other policeman stalked over to Erikki, his hand on the revolver in his open holster, waved him into a corner against the wall. The major flicked some dirt off a chair and sat down, accepted her Iranian ID from the sergeant, read it carefully, then looked at the contents on the table. He opened the jewel bag. His eyes widened. "Where did you get these?"

"They're mine. Inherited from my parents." Azadeh was frightened, not knowing what he knew or how much, and she had seen the way his eyes covered her. So had Erikki. "May my husband please use the telephone? He wish—"

"In due course! You have been told that many times. In due course is in due course." The major zipped up the bag and put it on the table in front of him. His eyes strayed to her breasts. "Your husband doesn't speak Turkish?"

"No, no, he doesn't, Major Effendi."

The officer turned on Erikki and said in good English, "There's a warrant out for your arrest from Tabriz. For attempted murder and kidnapping."

Azadeh blanched and Erikki held on to his panic as best he could. "Kidnapping whom, sir?"

A flash of irritability washed over the major. "Don't try to play with me. This lady. Azadeh, sister to the Hakim, the Gorgon Khan."

"She's my wife. How can a hus—"

"I know she's your wife and you'd better tell me the truth, by God. The warrant says you took her against her will and flew off in an Iranian helicopter." Azadeh started to answer but the major snapped, "I asked him, not you. Well?"

"It was without her consent and the chopper is British not Iranian."

The major stared at him, then turned on Azadeh. "Well?"

"It . . . it was without my consent . . ." The words trailed off.

"But what?"

Azadeh felt sick. Her head ached and she was in despair. Turkish police were known for their inflexibility, their great personal power and toughness. "Please, Major Effendi, perhaps we may talk in private, explain in private?"

"We're private now, madam," the major said curtly, then seeing her anguish and appreciating her beauty, added, "English is more private than Turkish. Well?"

So, haltingly, choosing her words carefully, she told him about her oath to Abdollah Khan and about Hakim and the dilemma, unable to leave, unable to stay and how Erikki, of his own volition and wisdom, had cut through the Gordian knot. Tears streaked down her cheeks. "Yes, it was without my consent but in a way it was with the consent of my brother who helped Er—"

"If it was with Hakim Khan's consent then why has he put a huge reward on this man's head, alive or dead," the major said, disbelieving her, "and had the warrant issued in his name, demanding immediate extradition if necessary?"

She was so shocked she almost fainted. Without thinking Erikki moved toward her, but the revolver went into his stomach. "I was only going to help her," he gasped.

"Then stay where you are!" In Turkish the officer said, "Don't kill him." In English he said, "Well, Lady Azadeh? Why?"

She could not answer. Her mouth moved but made no sound. Erikki said for her, "What else could a Khan do, Major? A Khan's honor, his face is involved. Publicly he would have to do that, wouldn't he, whatever he approved in private?"

"Perhaps, but certainly not so quickly, no, not so quickly, not alerting fighters and helicopters—why should he do that if he wanted you to escape? It's a miracle you weren't forced down, didn't fall down with all those bullet holes. It sounds like a pack of lies—perhaps she's so frightened of you she'll say anything. Now, your so-called escape from the palace: exactly what happened?"

Helplessly Erikki told him. Nothing more to do, he thought. Tell him the truth and hope. Most of his concentration was on Azadeh, seeing the blank horror pervading her, yet of course Hakim would react the way he had—of course dead or alive—wasn't the blood of his father strong in his veins?

"And the guns?"

Once more Erikki told it exactly, about being forced to fly the KGB, about Sheik Bayazid and his kidnap and ransom and the attack on the palace, having to fly them off and then their breaking their oaths and so having to kill them somehow.

"How many men?"

"I don't remember exactly. Half a dozen, perhaps more."

"You enjoy killing, eh?"

"No, Major, I hate it, but please believe us, we've been caught up in a web not of our seeking, all we want to do is be let go, please let me call my embassy . . . they can vouch for us . . . we're a threat to no one."

The major just looked at him. "I don't agree, your story's too farfetched. You're wanted for kidnapping and attempted murder. Please go with the sergeant," he said and repeated it in Turkish. Erikki did not move, his fists bunched, and he was near exploding. At once the sergeant's gun was out, both police converged on him dangerously, and the major said harshly, "It's a very serious offense to disobey police in this country. Go with the sergeant. Go with him."

Azadeh tried to say something, couldn't. Erikki thrust off the sergeant's hand, contained his own impotent panic-rage, and tried a smile to encourage her. "It's all right," he muttered and followed the sergeant.

Azadeh's panic and terror had almost overwhelmed her. Now her fingers and knees were trembling, but she wanted so much to sit tall and be tall, knowing she was defenseless and the major was sitting there opposite her, watching her, the room empty but for the two of them. Insha'Allah, she thought and looked at him, hating him.

"You have nothing to fear," he said, his eyes curious. Then he reached over and picked up her jewel bag. "For safekeeping," he said thinly and stalked for the door, closed it after him, and went down the passageway.

The cell at the end was small and dirty, more like a cage than a room, with a cot, bars on the tiny window, chains attached to a huge bolt in one wall, a foul-smelling bucket in a corner. The sergeant slammed the door and locked it on Erikki. Through the bars the major said, "Remember, the Lady Azadeh's . . . 'comfort' depends on your docility." He went away.

Now, alone, Erikki started prowling the cage, studying the door, lock, bars, floor, ceiling, walls, chains—seeking a way out.

AL SHARGAZ—AT THE AIRPORT: 5:40 P.M.   A thousand miles away, southeast across the Gulf, Gavallan was in an HQ office anxiously waiting near the phone, an hour yet for sunset. Already he had a promise of one 212 from a Paris company and two 206s from a friend at Aerospatiale at reasonable rates. Scot was in the other office, monitoring the HF, with Pettikin on the other phone there. Rudi, Willi Neuchtreiter, and Scragger were at the hotel on more phones tracking down possible crews, arranging possible logistics in Bahrain. No word yet from Kasigi.

The phone rang. Gavallan grabbed it, hoping against hope for news about Dubois and Fowler, or that it was Kasigi. "Hello?"

"Andy, it's Rudi. We've three pilots from Lufttransportgesellschaft and they also promise two mecs. Ten percent over scale, one month on, two off. Hang on . . . a call on the other line, I'll call you back, 'bye."

Gavallan made a notation on his pad, his anxiety giving him heartburn, and that made him think of McIver. When he had talked to him earlier he had not mentioned any of the deadline problems, not wanting to worry him further, promising that as soon as their choppers were safely out he would be on the next connection to Bahrain to see him. "Nothing to worry about, Mac, can't thank you and Genny enough for all you've done . . ."

Through the window he could see the lowering sun. The airport was busy. He saw an Alitalia jumbo landing and that reminded him of Pettikin and Paula; no opportunity yet to ask him what was what. Near the far end of the runway in the freight area, his eight 212s looked raped and skeletal without their rotors and rotor columns, mechanics still crating some of them. Where the hell's Kasigi, for God's sake? He had tried to call him several times at the hotel but he was out and no one knew where he was or when he would return.

The door opened. "Dad," Scot said, "Linbar Struan's on our phone."

"Tell him to get stuffed . . . hold it," Gavallan said quickly. "Just say I'm still out, but you're sure I'll call him the moment I return." He muttered a string of Chinese obscenities. Scot hurried away. Again the phone rang. "Gavallan."

"Andrew, this is Roger Newbury, how are you?"

Gavallan began to sweat. "Hello, Roger, what's new?"

"Sunset's still the deadline. The Iranian insisted on coming by here to pick me up first so I'm standing by—we're supposed to go together to meet the Sheik at the airport. We'll arrive a few minutes early, then the three of us will go to the freight area to wait for His Nibs."

"What about the reception at the Japanese ambassador's?"

"We're all supposed to go after the inspection—God only knows what'll happen then but . . . well, ours not to reason. Sorry about all this but our hands are tied. See you soon. 'Bye."

Gavallan thanked him, put down the phone, and wiped his brow.

Again the phone. Kasigi? He picked it up. "Hello?"

"Andy? Ian—Ian Dunross."

"My God, Ian." Gavallan's cares dropped away. "I'm so glad to hear from you, tried to reach you a couple of times."

"Yes, sorry I wasn't available. How's it going?"

Gavallan told him guardedly. And about Kasigi. "We've about an hour to sunset."

"That's one reason I called. Damned bad luck about Dubois, Fowler, and McIver, I'll keep my fingers crossed. Lochart sounds as though he cracked, but then when love's involved. . . ." Gavallan heard his sigh and did not know how to interpret it. "You remember Hiro Toda, Toda Shipping?"

"Of course, Ian."

"Hiro told me about Kasigi and their problem at Iran-Toda. They're in a hell of a bind, so anything, anything you can do to help, please do."

"Got it. I've been working on it all day. Did Toda tell you Kasigi's idea about their ambassador?"

"Yes. Hiro called personally—he said they're more than anxious to help but it's an Iranian problem, and to be honest, they don't expect very much as the Iranians would be quite within their rights." Gavallan's face mirrored his dismay. "Help them all you can. If Iran-Toda gets taken over . . . well, strictly between us . . ." Dunross switched to Shanghainese for a moment: "The underbelly of a nobly thought of company would be slashed mortally." Then in English again. "Forget I mentioned it."

Though Gavallan had forgotten most of his Shanghainese he understood and his eyes almost crossed. He had had no idea that Struan's was involved —Kasigi had never even implied it. "Kasigi'll get his choppers and crew even if we miss our deadline and are impounded."

"Let's hope you're not. Next, did you see the papers about the Hong Kong stock exchange crash?"

"Yes."

"It's bigger than they're reporting. Someone's pulling some very rough stuff and Linbar's back is to the sea. If you get the 212s out and are still in business, you'll still have to cancel the X63s."

Gavallan's temperature went up a notch. "But, Ian, with those I can bust Imperial's hold by giving clients better service and better safety, an—"

"I agree, old chum. But if we can't pay for them you can't have them. Sorry, but there it is. The stock market's gone mad, worse than usual, it's bleeding over to Japan and we cannot afford to have Toda crash here either."

"Perhaps we'll get lucky. I'm not going to lose my X63s. By the way did you hear Linbar's giving Profitable a seat in the Inner Office?"

"Yes. An interesting idea." It was said flat and Gavallan could read neither positive nor negative. "I heard their side of the meeting in a round-about way. If today is a success, you're planning to be in London Monday?"

"Yes. I'll know better by sunset, or tomorrow sunset. If all goes well I'll drop by and see Mac in Bahrain, then head for London. Why?"

"I may want you to cancel London and meet me in Hong Kong. Something very bloody curious has come up—about Nobunaga Mori, the other witness with Profitable Choy when David MacStruan died. Nobunaga was burned to death a couple of days ago at his home at Kanazawa, that's in the country just outside Tokyo, in rather strange circumstances. In today's mail I got a very curious letter. Can't discuss it on the phone but it's plenty bloody interesting."

Gavallan held his breath. "Then David . . . it wasn't an accident?"

"Have to wait and see on that one, Andy, until we meet—either Tokyo or London, the very soonest. By the way Hiro and I had planned to stay at Kanazawa the night Nobunaga died but couldn't make it at the last moment."

"My God, that was lucky."

"Yes. Well, got to go. Is there anything I can do for you?"

"Nothing, unless you can give me an extension till Sunday night."

"I'm still working on that, never fear. Damned sorry about Dubois, Fowler, and McIver . . . that Tokyo number will take messages till Monday . . ."

They said good-bye. Gavallan stared at the phone. Scot came in with more news about possible pilots and planes but he hardly heard his son. Was it murder after all? Christ! Goddamn Linbar and his back to the wall and bad investments. Somehow or another I've got to have the X63s, got to.

Again the phone. The connection was bad and the accent of the caller heavy: "Long distance collect call for Effendi Gavallan."

His heart surged. Erikki? "This is Effendi Gavallan, I will accept the charge. Can you speak up, please, I can hardly hear you. Who is the call from?"

"One moment please . . ." As he waited impatiently he looked at the gate near the end of the runway that the Sheik and the others would use if Kasigi failed and the inspection took place. His breath almost stopped as he saw a big limousine with a Shargazi flag on its fender approaching, but the car passed by in a cloud of dust and a voice on the other end of the phone he could hardly hear said, "Andy, it's me, Marc, Marc Dubois . . ."

"Marc? Marc Dubois?" he stuttered and almost dropped the phone, cupped his hand over one ear to hear better. "Christ Almighty! Marc? Are you all right, where the hell are you, is Fowler all right? Where the hell are you?" The answer was gibberish. He had to strain to hear. "Say again!"

"We're at Kor al Amaya . . ." Kor al Amaya was Iraq's huge, half-mile-long, deep-sea oil terminal platform at the far end of the Gulf, off the mouth of the Shatt-al-Arab Estuary that divided Iraq and Iran, about five hundred miles northwest. "Can you hear me, Andy? Kor al Amaya . . ."

AT THE KOR AL AMAYA PLATFORM: Marc Dubois also had one hand cupped over his ear and was trying to be guarded and not to shout down the phone. The phone was in the office of the platform manager, plenty of Iraqi and expats in the office outside able to overhear. "This line's not private . . . *vous comprenez?*"

"Got it, for God's sake, what the hell happened? You were picked up?"

Dubois made sure he was not being overheard and said carefully, "No, *mon vieux*, I was running out of fuel and, *voilà*, the tanker *Oceanrider* appeared out of the *merde* so I landed on her, perfectly, of course. We're both fine, Fowler and me. *Pas problème!* What about everyone, Rudi and Sandor and Pop?"

"They're all here in Al Shargaz, everyone, your lot, Scrag's, Mac, Freddy, though Mac's in Bahrain at the moment. With you safe Whirlwind's got ten out of ten—Erikki and Azadeh are safe in Tabriz though . . ." Gavallan was going to say Tom's risking his life to stay in Iran. But there was nothing he or Dubois could do so instead he said happily, "How wonderful you're safe, Marc. Are you serviceable?"

"Of course, I, er, I just need fuel and instructions."

"Marc, you're British registry now . . . hang on a sec . . . it's G-HKVC. Dump your old numbers and put the new ones on. There's been hell to pay and our late hosts have splattered the Gulf with telexes asking governments to impound us. Don't go ashore anywhere."

Dubois's bonhomie had left him. "Golf, Hotel Kilo Victor Charlie, got it. Andy, *le bon Dieu* was with us because *Oceanrider*'s Liberian registry and her skipper's British. One of the first things I asked for was a pot of paint, paint . . . understand?"

"Got it, bloody marvelous. Go on!"

"As he was inbound Iraq I thought it best to keep quiet and stay with her until I talked with you and this is the first mo—" Through the half-opened door Dubois saw the Iraqi manager approaching. Much more loudly now and in a slightly different voice, he said, "This assignment with *Oceanrider*'s perfect, Mr. Gavallan, and I'm glad to tell you the captain's very content."

"Okay, Marc, I'll ask the questions. When is she due to finish loading and what's her next port of call?"

"Probably tomorrow." He nodded politely to the Iraqi who sat behind his desk. "We should be in Amsterdam as scheduled." Both men were having difficulty hearing.

"Do you think you could stay with her all the way? Of course we'd pay freighting charges."

"I don't see why not. I think you'll find this experiment will become a permanent assignment. The captain found the convenience of being able to lie offshore and yet get into port for a quick visit worthwhile but frankly the owners made an error ordering a 212. A 206'd be much better. I think they'll want a rebate." He heard Gavallan's laugh and it made him happy too. "I better get off the phone, just wanted to report in. Fowler sends his best and if possible I'll give you a call on the ship to shore as we pass by."

"With any luck we won't be here. The birds'll be freighted off tomorrow. Don't worry, I'll monitor *Oceanrider* all the way home. Once you're through Hormuz and clear of Gulf waters, ask the captain to radio or telex contact us in Aberdeen. All right? I'm assigning everyone to the North Sea until we're sorted out. Oh, you're sure to be out of money, just sign for everything and I'll reimburse the captain. What's his name?"

"Tavistock, Brian Tavistock."

"Got it. Marc, you don't know how happy I am."

"Me to. *À bientôt.*" Dubois replaced the phone and thanked the manager.

"A pleasure, Captain," the man said thoughtfully. "Are all big tankers going to have their own chopper support?"

"I don't know, m'sieur. It would be wise for some. No?"

The manager smiled faintly, a tall middle-aged man, his accent and training American. "There's an Iranian patrol boat standing off in their waters watching *Oceanrider.* Curious, huh?"

"Yes."

"Fortunately they stay in their waters, we stay in ours. Iranians think they own the Arabian Gulf, along with us, the Shatt, and the waters of the Tigris and Euphrates back to their source—a thousand and almost two thousand miles."

"The Euphrates is that long?" Dubois asked, his caution increasing.

"Yes. It's born in Turkey. Have you been to Iraq before?"

"No, m'sieur. Unfortunately. Perhaps on my next trip?"

"Baghdad's great, ancient, modern—so's the rest of Iraq, well worth a visit. We've got nine billion metric tons of proven oil reserves and twice that waiting to be discovered. We're much more valuable than Iran. France should support us, not Israel."

"Me, m'sieur, I'm just a pilot," Dubois said. "No politics for me."

"For us that's not possible. Politics is life—we've discovered that the hard way. Even in the Garden of Eden . . . did you know people have been living around here for sixty thousand years? The Garden of Eden was barely a hundred miles away; just upstream the Shatt where the Tigris and Euphrates join. Our people discovered fire, invented the wheel, mathematics, writing, wine, gardening, farming . . . the Hanging Gardens of Babylon were here, Scheherazade spun her tales to the Calif Harun al-Rashid, whose only equal was your Charlemagne, and here were the mightiest of the ancient civilizations, Babylonia and Assyria. Even the Flood began here. We've survived Sumerians, Greeks, Romans, Arabs, Turks, British, and Persians," he almost spat the word out. "We'll continue to survive them."

Dubois nodded warily. Captain Tavistock had warned him: "We're in Iraq waters, the platform's Iraqi territory, young fellow. The moment you leave my gangplank, you're on your own, I've no jurisdiction, understand?"

"I only want to make a phone call. I have to."

"What about using my ship to shore when we pass by Al Shargaz on the way back?"

"There won't be any problem," Dubois had t l him, perfectly confident. "Why should there be? I'm French." When ιe had made the forced landing on the deck, he had had to tell the captain about Whirlwind and the reasons for it. The old man had just grunted. I know nothing about that, young fellow. You haven't told me. First you'd better paint out your

Iran numbers and put G in front of whatever you like instead—I'll get my ship's painter to help. As far as I'm concerned if anyone asks me you're a one-shot experiment the owners foisted on me—you came aboard in Cape Town and I don't like you a bit and we hardly ever talk. All right?" The captain had smiled. "Happy to have you aboard—I was in PT boats during the war, operating all over the Channel—my wife's from the Île d'Ouessant, near Brest—we used to sneak in there from time to time for wine and brandy just like my pirate ancestors used to do. Scratch an Englishman, find a pirate. Welcome aboard."

Dubois waited now and watched the Iraqi manager. "Perhaps I could use the phone tomorrow again, before we leave?"

"Of course. Don't forget us. Everything began here—it will end here. Salaam!" The manager smiled strangely and put out his hand. "Good landings."

"Thanks, see you soon."

Dubois went out and down the stairs and out onto the deck, anxious to be back aboard the *Oceanrider*. A few hundred yards north he saw the Iranian patrol boat, a small frigate, wallowing in the swell. *"Espèce de con,"* he muttered and set off, his mind buzzing.

It took Dubois almost fifteen minutes to walk back to his ship. He saw Fowler waiting for him and told him the good news. "Effing good about the lads, effing bloody good, but all the way to Amsterdam in this old bucket?" Grumpily Fowler began to curse, but Dubois just walked to the bow and leaned on the gunwale.

Everyone safe! Never thought we'd all make it, never, he thought joyously. What a fantastic piece of luck! Andy and Rudi'll think it was planning but it wasn't. It was luck. Or God. God timed the *Oceanrider* perfectly to within a couple of minutes. Shit, that was another close one but over, so no need to remember it. Now what? So long as we don't run into bad weather and I get seasick, or this old bucket sinks, it'll be grand to have two to three weeks with nothing to do, just to think and wait and sleep and play a little bridge and sleep and think and plan. Then Aberdeen and the North Sea and laughing with Jean-Luc, Tom Lochart and Duke, and the other guys, then off to . . . off to where? It's time I got married. Shit, I don't want to get married yet. I'm only thirty and I've avoided it so far. It'd just be my bad luck to meet this Parisienne witch in angel's clothing who'll use her wiles to make me so smitten that she'll destroy my defenses and ruin my resolve! Life's too good, far too good, and dredging too much fun!

He turned and looked west. The sun, hazed by the vast pollution, was setting toward the land horizon that was dull and flat and boring. Wish I was at Al Shargaz with the guys.

AL SHARGAZ—INTERNATIONAL HOSPITAL: 6:01 P.M.

Starke sat on the second-floor veranda, also watching the lowering sun, but here it was beautiful over a calm sea below a cloudless sky, the great bar of reflected light making him squint even though he was using dark glasses. He wore pajama bottoms and his chest was strapped up and healing well and though he was still weak, he was trying to think and plan. So much to think about—if we get our birds out, or if we don't.

In the room behind him he could hear Manuela chattering away in a patois of Spanish and Texan to her father and mother in faraway Lubbock. He had already talked to them—and talked to his own folks and the children, Billyjoe, Little Conroe, and Sarita: "Gee, Daddy, when ya coming home? I got me a new horse and school's great and today's hotter'n a bowl of Chiquita's double chili peppers!"

Starke half smiled but could not pull himself out of his ocean of apprehension. Such a long way from there to here, everything alien, even in Britain. Next Aberdeen and the North Sea? I don't mind just a month or two but that's not for me, or the kids, or Manuela. It's clear the kids want Texas, want home, so does Manuela now. Too much's happened to frighten her, too much too quick too soon. And she's right but hell, I don't know where I want to go or what I want to do. Have to keep flying, that's all I'm trained for, want to keep flying. Where? Not the North Sea or Nigeria which're Andy's key areas now. Maybe one of his small ops in South America, Indonesia, Malaya or Borneo? I'd like to stay with him if I could but what about the kids and school and Manuela?

Maybe forget overseas and go Stateside? No. Too long abroad, too long here.

His eyes were reaching beyond the old city into the far distance of the desert. He was remembering the times he had gone out past the threshold of the desert by night, sometimes with Manuela, sometimes alone, going there just to listen. To listen to what? To the silence, to the night, or to the stars calling one to another? To nothing? "You listen to God," the mullah Hussain had said. "How can an Infidel do that? You listen to God."

"Those are your words, mullah, not mine."

Strange man, saving my life, me saving his, almost dead because of him then saved again, then all of us at Kowiss freed—hell, he knew we were leaving Kowiss for good, I'm sure of it. Why did he let us go, us the Great Satan? And why did he keep on telling me to go and see Khomeini? *Imam*'s not right, not right at all.

What is it about all this that's got to me?

It's the out there, the something of the desert that exists for me. Utter peace. The absolute. It's just for me—not for the kids or Manuela or my folks or anyone else—just me . . . I can't explain it to anyone, Manuela most of all, anymore'n I could explain what happened in the mosque at Kowiss, or at the questioning.

I'd better get the hell out or I'm lost. The simplicity of Islam seems to make everything so simple and clear and better and yet . . .

I'm Conroe Starke, Texan, chopper pilot with a great wife and great kids and that should be enough, by God, shouldn't it?

Troubled, he looked back at the old city, its minarets and walls already reddening from the setting sun. Beyond the city was the desert and beyond that Mecca. He knew that was the way to Mecca because he had seen hospital staff, doctors and nurses and others, kneeling at prayers in that direction. Manuela came out onto the veranda again, distracting his thought pattern, sat down beside him, and brought him partially back to reality.

"They send their love and ask when we're coming home. It'd be good to visit, don't you think, Conroe?" She saw him nod, absently, not with her, then looked where he was looking, seeing nothing special. Just the sun going down. Goddamn! She hid her concern. He was mending perfectly, but he wasn't the same. "Not to worry, Manuela," Doc Nutt had said, "it's probably the shock of being hit with a bullet, the first time's always a bit traumatic. It's that, and Dubois, Tom, Erikki, and all the waiting and worrying and the not knowing—we're all poised, you, me, everyone, but we still don't quite know for what—it's got to all of us in different ways."

Her worry was sinking her. To hide it she leaned on the railing, looking at the sea and the boats. "While you were sleeping, I found Doc Nutt. He says you can leave in a few days, tomorrow if it was real important, but you've got to take it easy for a month or two. At breakfast, Nogger told me the rumor is we'll all get at least a month's vacation, with pay, isn't that great? With that and the sick leave we got lots of time to go home, huh?"

"Sure. Good idea."

She hesitated, then turned and looked at him. "What's troubling you, Conroe?"

"I'm not sure, honey. I feel fine. Not my chest. I don't know."

"Doc Nutt said it's bound to be real strange for a bitty, darlin', and Andy said there's a good chance there'll be no inspection and the freighters are definite for noon tomorrow, nothing we can do, nothing more you can do . . ." The phone in the room rang and she went to answer it, still talking, ". . . nothing any of us can do more'n we're doing. If we can get out, us and our choppers, I know Andy'll get Kasigi's choppers and the crews then . . . Hello? Oh, hi, darlin' . . ."

Starke heard the sudden gasp and silence, his heart tweaked, then her explosion of excitement and she was calling out to him, "It's Andy, Conroe, it's Andy, he's got a call from Marc Dubois and he's in Iraq on some ship, he and Fowler, they force-landed with no sweat on some tanker an' they're in Iraq and safe. . . . Oh, Andy, that's great! What? Oh, sure, he's fine and I'll . . . but what about Kasigi? . . . Wait a mo— . . . Yes, but . . . Sure." She replaced the phone and hurried back. "Nothing from Kasigi yet. Andy said he was in a rush and he'd call back. Oh, Conroe . . ." Now she was on her knees beside him, her arms around his neck, hugging him but very carefully, her happiness spilling tears. "I've been so worried about Marc 'nd old Fowler, I was so afraid they were lost."

"Me too . . . me too." He could feel her heart pounding and his was too and some of the weight on his spirit lifted—his good arm holding her tightly. "Goddamn," he muttered, also hardly able to talk. "Come on, Kasigi . . . come on, Kasigi . . ."

AT AL SHARGAZ HQ: 6:18 P.M. Gavallan was at the office window watching Newbury's official car with the small Union Jack fluttering swing through the gate. The car hurried along the perimeter road toward the front of his building—uniformed chauffeur, two figures in the back. He half nodded to himself. From the tap on the hand basin he splashed a little cold water into his face and dried it.

The door opened. Scot came in, beside him Charlie Pettikin. Both were pale. "Not to worry," Gavallan said, "come on in." He strolled back to the window, trying to appear calm and stood there, drying his hands. The sun was near the horizon. "No need to wait here, we'll go to meet them." Firmly he led the way out into the corridor. "Great about Marc and Fowler, isn't it?"

"Wonderful," Scot said, his voice flat in spite of his resolve. "Ten birds out of ten, Dad. Can't do better than that. Ten out of ten."

Along the corridor and out into the foyer. "How's Paula, Charlie?"

"Oh, she . . . she's fine, Andy." Pettikin was astounded by Gavallan's sangfroid and not a little envious. "She . . . she took off for Tehran an hour ago, doesn't think she'll be back until Monday, though maybe tomorrow." God curse Whirlwind, he thought in misery, it's ruined everything. I know a faint heart never won a fair lady, but what the hell can I do? If they grab our choppers, S-G's down the sink, there's no job, I've almost no savings. I'm so much older than she is and . . . sod everything! In a sick, stupid way I'm glad—now I can't screw up her life and anyway she'd be crazy to say yes. "Paula's fine, Andy."

"She's a nice girl."

The foyer was crowded. Across it and out of the cool air-conditioning to the sunset's warmth and onto the entrance steps, Gavallan stopped astonished. Every one of the S-G contingent was there: Scragger, Vossi, Willi, Rudi, Pop Kelly, Sandor, Freddy Ayre, and all the others and all the mechanics. All were motionless, watching the approaching car. It swung up to them.

Newbury got out. "Hello, Andrew," he said, but now they were all transfixed, for Kasigi stood beside him, not the Iranian, and Kasigi was beaming, Newbury saying in a perplexed voice, "Really don't quite understand what's happening but the ambassador, the Iranian ambassador, canceled at the last minute, so did the Sheik, and Mr. Kasigi called for me to go to the Japanese reception so there'll be no inspection tonight . . ."

Gavallan let out a cheer and then they were all pummeling Kasigi, thanking him, talking, laughing, stumbling over each other and Kasigi said, ". . . and there won't be an inspection tomorrow even if we have to kidnap him . . ." and more laughter and cheers and Scragger was dancing a hornpipe. "Hooray for Kasigi . . ."

Gavallan fought his way through to Kasigi and gave him a bear hug, and shouted over the bedlam, "Thanks, thanks, by God. You'll have some of your birds in three days, the rest at the weekend . . ." then added incoherently, "Christ Almighty, give me a second, Christ Almighty I've got to tell Mac, Duke, and the others . . . celebration's on me . . ."

Kasigi watched him hurry away. Then he smiled to himself.

AT THE HOSPITAL: 6:32 P.M.   Shakily Starke put down the phone, glowing with happiness, and came back onto the veranda. "Goddamn, Manuela, goddamn, we made it, no inspection! Whirlwind made it; Andy doesn't know how Kasigi did it but he did it and . . . Goddamn!" He put his arm around her and leaned against the balustrade. "Whirlwind made it, now we're safe, now we'll get out and now we can plan. Goddamn! Kasigi, the son of a bitch, he did it! Allah-u Akbar," he added triumphantly without thinking.

The sun touched the horizon. From the city a muezzin began, just one, the voice peerless, beckoning. And the sound filled his ears and his being and he listened, all else forgotten, his relief and joy mingled with the words and the beckoning and the Infinite—and he went away from her. Helplessly she waited, alone. There in the going down of the sun she waited, afraid for him, sad for him, sensing the future was in balance. She waited as only a woman can.

The beckoning ceased. Now it was very quiet, very still. His eyes saw the old city in all its ancient splendor, the desert beyond, infinity beyond the horizon. And now he saw it for what it was. Sound of a jet taking off and seabirds calling. Then the puttputt of a chopper somewhere and he decided.

"Thou," he said to her in Farsi, "thou, I love thee."

"Thou, I love thee forever," she murmured, near tears. Then she heard him sigh and knew they were together again.

"Time to go home, my darlin'." He gathered her into his arms. "Time for all of us to go home."

"Home's where you are," she said, not afraid anymore.

AT THE OASIS HOTEL: 11:52 P.M.   In the darkness the telephone jangled discordantly, jerking Gavallan out of a deep sleep. He groped for it, switching on his side-table light. "Hello?"

"Hello, Andrew, this is Roger Newbury, sorry to call so late but th—"

"Oh, that's all right, I said to call up till midnight, how did it go?" Newbury had promised to phone and tell him what happened at the rest of the reception. Normally Gavallan would have been awake but tonight he had excused himself from the celebration just after ten and within seconds was asleep. "What about tomorrow?"

"Delighted to tell you His Excellency Abadani's accepted an invitation from the Sheik to spend the day hawking at Al Sal oasis, so it looks very good he'll be isolated all day. Personally, I don't trust him, Andrew, and we strongly advise you to get your planes and all personnel out as quickly and discreetly as possible, also to close down here for a month or two till we can give you the word. All right?"

"Yes, great news. Thanks." Gavallan lay back, a new man, the bed seductive, sleep beckoning. "I'd already planned to close down," he said with a mighty yawn. "Everyone's confirmed out before sunset." He had heard the nervousness in Newbury's voice but put it down to all the excitement, stifled another yawn, and added, "Scragger and I will be the last—we're on the plane to Bahrain with Kasigi to see McIver."

"Good. How the hell you managed Abadani I don't know—and I don't want to know either—but our collective hat's off to you. Now, er, now hate to bring bad tidings along with the good but we've just had a telex from Henley in Tabriz."

Sleep vanished from Gavallan. "Trouble?"

"Afraid so. It sounds bizarre but this's what it says." There was a rustle of paper, then, "Henley says: 'We hear there was some sort of attack yesterday or last night on Hakim Khan's life, Captain Yokkonen is supposed to be implicated. Last night he fled for the Turkish border in his helicopter, taking his wife Azadeh with him, against her will. A warrant for attempted murder and kidnapping has been issued in Hakim Khan's name. A great deal of fighting between rival factions is presently going on in Tabriz which is making accurate reporting somewhat difficult. Further details will be sent immediately they are available.' That's all there is. Astonishing, what?" Silence. "Andrew? Are you there?"

"Yes . . . yes, I am. Just . . . just, er, trying to collect my wits. There's no chance there'd be a mistake?"

"I doubt that. I've sent an urgent signal for more details; we might get something tomorrow. I suggest you contact the Finnish ambassador in London, alert him. The embassy number is 01-7668888. Sorry about all this."

Gavallan thanked him and, dazed, replaced the phone.

SUNDAY
March 4

AT THE TURKISH VILLAGE: 10:20 A.M. Azadeh awoke with a start. For a moment she could not remember where she was, then the room came into focus—small, drab, two windows, the straw mattress of the bed hard, clean but coarse sheets and blankets—and she recalled that this was the village hotel and last night at sunset, in spite of her protests and not wanting to leave Erikki, she had been escorted here by the major and a policeman. The major had brushed aside her excuses and insisted on dining with her in the tiny restaurant that had emptied immediately they had arrived. "Of course you must eat something to keep up your strength. Please sit down. I will order whatever you eat for your husband and have them send it to him. Would you like that?"

"Yes, please," she said, also in Turkish, and sat down, understanding the implied threat, the hackles on her neck twisting. "I can pay for it."

The barest touch of a smile moved his full lips. "As you wish."

"Thank you, Major Effendi. When can my husband and I leave, please?"

"I will discuss that with you tomorrow, not tonight." He motioned to the policeman to stand guard on the door. "Now we will speak English," he said, offering her his silver cigarette case.

"No, thank you, I don't smoke. When can I have my jewelry back, please, Major Effendi?"

He selected a cigarette and began tapping the end on the case, watching her. "As soon as it is safe. My name is Abdul Ikail. I'm stationed at Van and responsible for this whole region, up to the border." He used his lighter, exhaled smoke, his eyes never leaving her. "Have you been to Van before?"

"No, no I haven't."

"It's a sleepy little place. It was," he corrected himself, "before your revolution, though it's always been difficult on the border." Another deep intake of smoke. "Undesirables on both sides wanting to cross or to flee. Smugglers, drug dealers, arms dealers, thieves, all the carrion you can think of." He said it casually, wisps of smoke punctuating the words. The air was heavy in the little room and smelled of old cooking, humans, and stale tobacco. She was filled with foreboding. Her fingers toyed with the strap of her shoulder bag.

"Have you been to Istanbul?" he asked.

"Yes. Yes, once for a few days when I was a little girl. I went with my father, he had business there and I, I was put on a plane for school in Switzerland."

"I've never been to Switzerland. I went to Rome once on a holiday. And to Bonn on a police course, and another one in London, but never Switzerland." He smoked a moment, lost in thought, then stubbed out the cigarette in a chipped ashtray and beckoned the hotel owner who stood abjectly by the door, waiting to take his order. The food was primitive but good and served with great, nervous humility that further unsettled her. Clearly the village was not used to such an august presence.

"No need to be afraid, Lady Azadeh, you're not in danger," he told her as though reading her mind. "On the contrary. I'm glad to have the opportunity to talk to you, it's rare a person of your . . . your quality passes this way." Throughout dinner, patiently and politely, he questioned her about Azerbaijan and Hakim Khan, volunteering little, refusing to discuss Erikki or what was going to happen. "What will happen will happen. Please tell me your story again."

"I've . . . I've already told it to you, Major Effendi. It's the truth, it's not a story. I told you the truth, so did my husband."

"Of course," he said, eating hungrily. "Please tell it to me again."

So she had, afraid, reading his eyes and the desire therein, though he was always punctilious and circumspect. "It's the truth," she said, hardly touching the food in front of her, her appetite vanished. "We've committed no crime, my husband only defended himself and me—before God."

"Unfortunately God cannot testify on your behalf. Of course, in your case, I accept what you say as what you believe. Fortunately here we're more of this world, we're not fundamentalist, there's a separation between Islam and state, no self-appointed men get between us and God, and we're only fanatic to keep our own way of life as we want it—and other people's beliefs or laws from being crammed down our throats." He stopped, listening intently. Walking here in the falling light they had heard distant firing and some heavy mortars. Now, in the silence of the restaurant, they heard more. "Probably Kurds defending their homes in the mountains." His lips curled disgustedly. "We hear Khomeini is sending your army, and Green Bands, against them."

"Then it's another mistake," she said. "That's what my brother says."

"I agree. My family is Kurd." He got up. "A policeman will be outside your door all night. For your protection," he said with the same curious half smile that greatly perturbed her. "For your protection. Please stay in your room until I . . . I come for you or send for you. Your compliance assists your husband. Sleep well."

So she had gone to the room she had been given and then, seeing there was no lock or bolt on the door, had jammed a chair under the knob. The room was cold, the water in the jug icy. She had washed and dried herself, then prayed, adding a special prayer for Erikki, and sat on the bed.

With great care she slipped out the six-inch, steel hat pin that was secreted in the binding of her shoulder bag, studied it for a second. The point was needle sharp, the head small but big enough to grip for a thrust. She slid it into the underside of the pillow as Ross had shown her: "Then it's no danger to you," he had said with a smile, "a hostile wouldn't notice it, and you can get it easily. A beautiful young girl like you should always be armed, just in case."

"Oh, but, Johnny, I'd never be able to . . . never."

"You will when—if—the time ever comes, and you should be prepared to. So long as you're armed, know how to use the weapon whatever it is, and accept that you may have to kill to protect yourself, then you'll never, ever, need to be afraid." Over those beautiful months in the High Lands he had shown her how to use it. "Just an inch in the right place is more than enough, it's deadly enough . . ." She had carried it ever since, but never once had to use it—not even in the village. The village. Leave the village to the night, not to the day.

Her fingers touched the head of the weapon. Perhaps tonight, she thought. Insha'Allah! What about Erikki? Insha'Allah! Then she was reminded of Erikki saying, "Insha'Allah's fine, Azadeh, and a great excuse, but God by any name needs a helping earthly hand from time to time."

Yes. I promise you I'm prepared, Erikki. Tomorrow is tomorrow and I will help, my darling. I'll get you out of this somehow.

Reassured she blew out the candle, curled up under the sheets and covers still dressed in sweater and ski pants. Moonlight came through the windows. Soon she was warm. Warmth and exhaustion and youth led her into sleep that was dreamless.

In the night she was suddenly awake. The doorknob was turning softly. Her hand went to the spike and she lay there, watching the door. The handle went to the limit, the door moved a fraction but did not budge, held tightly closed by the chair that now creaked under the strain. In a moment the knob turned quietly back to its resting place. Again silence. No footsteps or breathing. Nor did the knob move again. She smiled to herself. Johnny had also showed her how to place the chair. Ah, my darling, I hope you find the happiness you seek, she thought, and slept again, facing the door.

Now she was awake and rested and knew that she was much stronger than yesterday, more ready for the battle that would soon begin. Yes, by

God, she told herself, wondering what had brought her out of sleep. Sounds of traffic and street vendors. No, not those. Then again a knock on the door.

"Who is it, please?"

"Major Ikail."

"One moment, please." She pulled on her boots, straightened her sweater and her hair. Deftly she disengaged the chair. "Good morning, Major Effendi."

He glanced at the chair, amused. "You were wise to jam the door. Don't do it again—without permission." Then he scrutinized her. "You seem rested. Good. I've ordered coffee and fresh bread for you. What else would you like?"

"Just to be let go, my husband and I."

"So?" He came into the room and closed the door and took the chair and sat down, his back to the sunlight that streamed in from the window. "With your cooperation that might be arranged."

When he had moved into the room, without being obvious she had retreated and now sat on the edge of the bed, her hand within inches of the pillow. "What cooperation, Major Effendi?"

"It might be wise not to have a confrontation," he said curiously. "If you cooperate . . . and go back to Tabriz of your own free will this evening, your husband will remain in custody tonight and be sent to Istanbul tomorrow."

She heard herself say, "Sent where in Istanbul?"

"First to prison—for safekeeping—where his ambassador will be able to see him and, if it's God's will, to be released."

"Why should he be sent to prison, he's done noth—"

"There's a reward on his head. Dead or alive." The major smiled thinly. "He needs protection—there are dozens of your nationals in the village and near here, all on the edge of starvation. Don't you need protection too? Wouldn't you be a perfect kidnap victim, wouldn't the Khan ransom his only sister at once and lavishly? Eh?"

"Gladly I'll go back if that will help my husband," she said at once. "But if I go back, what . . . what guarantee do I have that my husband will be protected and be sent to Istanbul, Major Effendi?"

"None." He got up and stood over her. "The alternate is if you don't cooperate of your own free will, you'll be sent to the border today and he . . . he will have to take his chances."

She did not get up, nor take her hand away from the pillow. Nor look up at him. I'd do that gladly but once I'm gone Erikki's defenseless. Cooperate? Does that mean bed this man of my own free will? "How must I cooperate? What do you want me to do?" she asked and was furious that her voice seemed smaller than before.

He half laughed and said sardonically, "To do what all women have difficulty in doing: to be obedient, to do what they're told without argument, and to stop trying to be clever." He turned on his heel. "You will stay here in the hotel. I will return later. I hope by then you'll be prepared . . . to give me the correct answer." He shut the door after him.

If he tries to force me, I will kill him, she thought. I cannot bed him as a barter—my husband would never forgive me, nor could I forgive myself, for we both know the act would not guarantee his freedom or mine, and even if it did he could not live with the knowledge and would seek revenge. Nor could I live with myself.

She got up and went to the window and looked out at the busy village, snow-covered mountains around it, the border over there, such a little way.

"The only chance Erikki has is for me to go back," she muttered. "But I can't, not without the major's approval. And even then . . ."

AT THE POLICE STATION: 11:58 A.M. Gripped by Erikki's great fists, the lower end of the central iron bar in the window came free with a small shower of cement. Hastily he pushed it back into its hole, looked out of the cage door and down the corridor. No jailer appeared. Quickly he stuffed small pieces of cement and rubble back around the base camouflaging it—he had been working on this bar most of the night, worrying it as a dog would a bone. Now he had a weapon and a lever to bend the other bars out of shape.

It'll take me half an hour, no more, he thought, and sat back on his bunk, satisfied. After bringing the food last evening, the police had left him alone, confident in the strength of their cage. This morning they had brought him coffee that had tasted vile and a hunk of rough bread and had stared at him without understanding when he asked for the major and for his wife. He did not know the Turkish for "major" nor the officer's name, but when he pointed at his lapel, miming the man's rank, they had understood him and had just shrugged, spoken more Turkish that he did not understand, and gone away again. The sergeant had not reappeared.

Each of us knows what to do, he thought, Azadeh and I, each of us is at risk, each will do the best we can. But if she's touched, or hurt, no god will help him who touched her while I live. I swear it.

The door at the end of the corridor opened. The major strode toward him. "Good morning," he said, his nostrils crinkling at the foul smell.

"Good morning, Major. Where's my wife, please, and when are you letting us go?"

"Your wife is in the village, quite safe, rested. I've seen her myself." The major eyed him thoughtfully, noticed the dirt on his hands, glanced keenly at the lock on the cage, the window bars, the floor, and the ceiling. "Her safety and treatment are dependent on you. You do understand?"

"Yes, yes, I do understand. And I hold you as the senior policeman here responsible for her."

The major laughed. "Good," he said sardonically, then the smile vanished. "It seems best to avoid a confrontation. If you cooperate you will stay here tonight, tomorrow I'll send you under guard to Istanbul—where your ambassador can see you if he wants—to stand trial for the crimes you're accused of, or to be extradited."

Erikki dismissed his own problems. "I brought my wife here against her will. She's done nothing wrong, she should go home. Can she be escorted?"

The major watched him. "That depends on your cooperation."

"I will ask her to go back. I'll insist, if that's what you mean."

"She could be sent back," the major said, taunting him. "Oh, yes. But of course it's possible that on the way to the border or even from the hotel, she could be 'kidnapped' again, this time by bandits, Iranian bandits, bad ones, to be held in the mountains for a month or two, eventually to be ransomed to the Khan."

Erikki was ashen. "What do you want me to do?"

"Not far away is the railway. Tonight you could be smuggled out of here and taken safely to Istanbul. The charges against you could be quashed. You could be given a good job, flying, training our fliers—for two years. In return you agree to become a secret agent for us, you supply us with information about Azerbaijan, particularly about this Soviet you mentioned, Mzytryk, information about Hakim Khan, where and how he lives, how to get into the palace—and anything else that is wanted."

"What about my wife?"

"She stays in Van of her own free will, hostage to your behavior . . . for a month or two. Then she can join you, wherever you are."

"Provided she's escorted back to Hakim Khan today, safely, unharmed and it's proved to me she's safe and unharmed, I will do what you ask."

"Either you agree or you don't," the major said impatiently. "I'm not here to bargain with you!"

"Please, she's nothing to do with any crimes of mine. Please let her go. Please."

"You think we're fools? Do you agree or don't you?"

"Yes! But first I want her safe. First!"

"Perhaps first you'd like to watch her spoiled. First."

Erikki lunged for him through the bars and the whole cage door shuddered under the impact. But the major stood there just out of range and laughed at the great hand clawing for him impotently. He had judged the distance accurately, far too practiced to be caught unawares, far too experienced an investigator not to know how to taunt and threaten and tempt, how to jeer and exaggerate and use the prisoner's own fears and terrors, how to twist truths to break through the curtain of inevitable lies and half-truths —to get at the real truth.

His superiors had left it up to him to decide what to do about both of them. Now he had decided. Without hurrying he pulled out his revolver and pointed it at Erikki's face. And cocked the pistol. Erikki did not back off, just held the bars with his huge hands, his breath coming in great pants.

"Good," the major said calmly, holstering the gun. "You have been warned your behavior gauges her treatment." He walked away. When Erikki was alone again, he tried to tear the cage door off its hinges. The door groaned but held firm.

AL SHARGAZ INTERNATIONAL AIRPORT: 4:39 P.M. From the driver's seat of his car Gavallan watched the loading hatch of a 747 freighter close on half the 212s, crates of spares and rotors. Pilots and mechanics were feverishly loading the second jumbo, just one more 212 carcass to get aboard, a dozen crates and piles of suitcases. "We're on schedule, Andy," Rudi, the loading master, said, pretending not to notice his friend's pallor. "Half an hour."

"Good." Gavallan handed him some papers. "Here are clearances for all mechanics to go with her."

"No pilots?"

"No. All pilots're on the BA flight. But make sure they're in Immigration by six-ten. BA can't hold the flight. Make sure everyone's there, Rudi. They've got to be on that flight—I guaranteed it."

"Don't worry. What about Duke and Manuela?"

"They've already gone. Doc Nutt went with them, so they're launched. I . . . that's about all." Gavallan was finding it hard to think.

"You and Scrag're still on the six-thirty-five to Bahrain?"

"Yes. Jean-Luc'll meet us. We're taking Kasigi to set up his op and get ready for his Iran-Toda birds. I'll see you all off."

"See you in Aberdeen." Rudi shook his hand firmly and rushed away. Gavallan let in the clutch, ground the gears and cursed, then went back to the office.

"Anything, Scrag?"

"No, no, not yet, sport. Kasigi called. I told him he's in business, gave him the chopper registrations, names of pilots and mecs. He said he's booked on our flight to Kuwait tonight, then he'll catch a ride to Abadan, then to Iran-Toda." Scragger was as perturbed as the others about the way Gavallan looked. "Andy, you've covered every possibility."

"Have I? I doubt it, Scrag. I haven't got Erikki and Azadeh out."

During the night, till very late London time, Gavallan had contacted everyone of importance he could think of. The Finnish ambassador had been shocked: "But it's impossible! One of our nationals couldn't possibly be involved in such an affair. Impossible! Where will you be this time tomorrow?" Gavallan had told him and had watched the night turn into dawn. No way to contact Hakim Khan other than through Newbury and Newbury was handling that possibility. "It's a bitch, Scrag, but there you are." Numbly he picked up the phone, put it down again. "Are you all checked out?"

"Yes. Kasigi'll meet us at the gate. I've sent all our bags to the terminal and had them checked in. We can stay here till the last moment and go straight over."

Gavallan stared at the airport. Busy, normal, gentle day. "I don't know what to do, Scrag. I just don't know what to do anymore."

AT THE POLICE STATION IN THE TURKISH VILLAGE: 5:18 P.M.

". . . just as you say, Effendi. You will make the necessary arrangements?" the major said deferentially into the phone. He was sitting at the only desk in the small, scruffy office, the sergeant standing nearby, the kookri and Erikki's knife on the desktop. ". . . Good. Yes . . . yes, I agree. Salaam." He replaced the phone, lit a cigarette, and got up. "I'll be at the hotel."

"Yes, Effendi." The sergeant's eyes glinted with amusement but, carefully, he kept it off his face. He watched the major straighten his jacket and hair and put on his fez, envying him his rank and power. The phone rang. "Police, yes? . . . oh, hello, Sergeant." He listened with growing astonishment. "But . . . yes . . . yes, very well." Blankly he put the phone back on its hook. "It . . . it was Sergeant Urbil at the border, Major Effendi. There's an Iran Air Force truck with Green Bands and a mullah coming to take the helicopter and the prisoner and her back to Ir—"

The major exploded. "In the Name of God who allowed hostiles over our border without authority? There're standing orders about mullahs and revolutionaries!"

"I don't know, Effendi," the sergeant said, frightened by the sudden rage. "Urbil just said they were waving official papers and insisted—everyone knows about the Iranian helicopter so he just let them through."

"Are they armed?"

"He didn't say, Effendi."

"Get your men, all of them, with submachine guns."

"But . . . but what about the prisoner?"

"Forget him!" the major said and stormed out cursing.

ON THE OUTSKIRTS OF THE VILLAGE: 5:32 P.M. The Iran Air Force truck was a four-wheel drive, part tanker and part truck, and it turned off the side road that was little more than a track onto the snow, changed gears, and headed for the 212. Nearby, the police sentry went to meet it.

Half a dozen armed youths wearing green armbands jumped down, then three unarmed, uniformed Iran Air Force personnel, and a mullah. The mullah slung his Kalashnikov. "Salaam. We're here to take possession of our property in the name of the Imam and the people," the mullah said importantly. "Where is the kidnapper and the woman?"

"I . . . I don't know anything about that." The policeman was flustered. His orders were clear: stand guard and keep everyone away until you're told otherwise. "You'd better go to the police station first and ask there." He saw one of the air force personnel open the cockpit door and lean into the cockpit; the other two were reeling out refueling hoses. "Hey, you three, you're not allowed near the helicopter without permission!"

The mullah stood in his path. "Here is our authority!" He waved papers in the policeman's face and that rattled him even more, for he could not read.

"You better go to the station first . . ." he stammered, then with vast relief saw the station police car hurtling along the little road toward them from the direction of the village. It swerved off into the snow, trundled a few yards and stopped. The major, sergeant, and two policemen got out, riot guns in their hands. Surrounded by his Green Bands, the mullah went toward them, unafraid.

"Who're you?" the major said harshly.

"Mullah Ali Miandiry of the Khoi komiteh. We have come to take possession of our property, the kidnapper, and the woman, in the name of the Imam and the people."

"Woman? You mean Her Highness, the sister of Hakim Khan?"

"Yes. Her."

" 'Imam'? Imam who?"

"Imam Khomeini, peace be on him."

"Ah, Ayatollah Khomeini," the major said, affronted by the title. "What 'people'?"

Just as toughly the mullah shoved some papers toward him. "The people of Iran. Here is our authority."

The major took the papers, scanned them rapidly. There were two of them, hastily scrawled in Farsi. The sergeant and his two men had spread out, surrounding the truck, submachine guns in their hands. The mullah and Green Bands watched them contemptuously.

"Why isn't it on the correct legal form?" the major said. "Where's the police seal and the signature of the Khoi police chief?"

"We don't need one. It's signed by the komiteh."

"What komiteh? I know nothing about komitehs."

"The Revolutionary Komiteh of Khoi has authority over this area and the police."

"This area? This area's Turkey!"

"I meant authority over the area up to the border."

"By whose authority? Where is your authority? Show it to me."

A current went through the youths. "The mullah's shown it to you," one of them said truculently. "The komiteh signed the paper."

"Who signed it? You?"

"I did," the mullah said. "It's legal. Perfectly legal. The komiteh is the authority." He saw the air force personnel staring at him. "What are you waiting for? Get the helicopter refueled!"

Before the major could say anything, one of them said deferentially, "Excuse me, Excellency, the panel's in a mess, some of the instruments are broken. We can't fly her until she's checked out. It'd be safer to g—"

"The Infidel flew it all the way from Tabriz safely by night and by day, landed it safely, why can't you fly it during the day?"

"It's just that it'd be safer to check before flying, Excellency."

"Safer? Why safer?" one of the Green Bands said roughly, walking over to him. "We're in God's hands doing God's work. Do you want to delay God's work and leave the helicopter here?"

"Of course not, of co—"

"Then obey our mullah and refuel it! Now!"

"Yes, yes, of course," the pilot said lamely. "As you wish." Hastily the three of them hurried to comply—the major shocked to see that the pilot, a captain, allowed himself to be overridden so easily by the young thug who now stared back at him with flat, challenging eyes.

"The komiteh has jurisdiction over the police, Agha," the mullah was saying. "Police served the Satan Shah and are suspect. Where is the kidnapper and the . . . the sister of the Khan?"

"Where's your authority to come over the border and ask for anything?" The major was coldly furious.

"In the Name of God, Imam Khomeini, this is authority enough!" The mullah stabbed his finger at the papers. One of the youths cocked his gun.

"Don't," the major warned him. "If you pull a single trigger on our soil, our forces will come over your border and burn everything between here and Tabriz!"

"If it's the Will of God!" The mullah stared back, dark eyes and dark beard and just as resolved, despising the major and the loose regime the man and uniform represented to him. War now or later was all the same to him, he was in God's hands and doing God's work and the Word of the Imam would sweep them to victory—over all borders. But now was not the time for war, too much to do in Khoi, leftists to overcome, revolts to put down, the Imam's enemies to destroy, and for that, in these mountains, every helicopter was priceless.

"I . . . I ask for possession of our property," he said, more reasonably. He pointed at the markings. "There are our registrations, that's proof that it is our property. It was stolen from Iran—you must know there was no permission to leave Iran, legally it is still our property. The warrant," he pointed to the papers in the major's hand, "the warrant is legal, the pilot kidnapped the woman, so we will take possession of them too. Please."

The major was in an untenable situation. He could not possibly hand over the Finn and his wife to illegals because of an illegal piece of paper—that would be a gross dereliction of duty and would, correctly, cost him his head. If the mullah forced the issue he would have to resist and defend the police station, but obviously he had insufficient men to do so, obviously he would fail in the confrontation. Equally he was convinced that the mullah and Green Bands were prepared to die this very minute as he himself was not.

He decided to gamble. "The kidnapper and the Lady Azadeh were sent to Van this morning. To extradite them you have to apply to Army HQ, not to me. The . . . the importance of the Khan's sister meant that the army took possession of both of them."

The mullah's face froze. One of the Green Bands said sullenly, "How do we know that's not a lie?" The major whirled on him, the youth jumped back a foot, Green Bands behind the truck aimed, the unarmed airmen dropped to the ground aghast, the major's hand went for his revolver.

"Stop!" the mullah said. He was obeyed, even by the major who was furious with himself for allowing pride and reflexes to overcome his self-discipline. The mullah thought a moment, considering possibilities. Then he said, "We will apply to Van. Yes, we will do that. But not today. Today we will take our property and we will leave." He stood there, legs slightly apart, assault rifle over his shoulder, supremely confident.

The major fought to hide his relief. The helicopter had no value to him or his superiors and was an extreme embarrassment. "I agree they're your markings," he said shortly. "As to ownership, I don't know. If you sign a receipt leaving ownership open, you may take it and leave."

"I will sign a receipt for our helicopter."

On the back of the warrant the major scrawled what would satisfy him and perhaps satisfy the mullah. The mullah turned and scowled at the airmen who hurriedly began reeling in the fuel hoses, and the pilot stood beside the cockpit once more, brushing the snow off. "Are you ready now, pilot?"

"Any moment, Excellency."

"Here," the major said to the mullah, handing him the paper.

"With barely concealed derision the mullah signed it without reading it. "Are you ready now, pilot?" he said.

"Yes, Excellency, yes." The young captain looked at the major and the major saw—or thought he saw—the misery in his eyes and the unspoken plea for asylum that was impossible to grant. "Can I start up?"

"Start up," the mullah said imperiously, "of course start up." In seconds the engines began winding up sweetly, rotors picking up speed. "Ali and Abrim, you go with the truck back to the base."

Obediently the two young men got in with the air force driver. The mullah motioned them to leave and the others to board the helicopter. The rotors were thrashing the air and he waited until everyone was in the cabin, then unslung his gun, sat beside the pilot, and pulled the door closed.

Engines building, an awkward liftoff, the 212 started trundling away. Angrily the sergeant aimed his submachine gun. "I can blow the motherless turds out of the sky, Major."

"Yes, yes, we could." The major took out his cigarette case. "But we'll leave that to God. Perhaps God will do that for us." He used the lighter shakily, inhaled, and watched the truck and the helicopter grinding away. "Those dogs will have to be taught manners and a lesson." He walked over to the car and got in. "Drop me at the hotel."

AT THE HOTEL: Azadeh was leaning out of the window, searching the sky. She had heard the 212 start up and take off and was filled with the impossible hope that Erikki had somehow escaped. "Oh, God, let it be true . . ."

Villagers were also looking up at the sky and now she too saw the chopper well on its way back to the border. Her insides turned over. Has he bartered his freedom for mine? Oh, Erikki . . .

Then she saw the police car come into the square, stop outside the hotel, and the major get out, straighten his uniform. Her face drained. Resolutely she closed the window and sat on the chair facing the door, near the pillow. Waiting. Waiting. Now footsteps. The door opened. "Follow me," he said. "Please."

For a moment she did not understand. "What?"

"Follow me. Please."

"Why?" she asked suspiciously, expecting a trap and not wanting to leave the safety of the hidden spike. "What's going on? Is my husband flying the helicopter? It's going back. Have you sent him back?" She felt her courage leaving her fast, her anxiety that Erikki had given himself up in return for her safety making her frantic. "Is he flying it?"

"No, your husband's in the police station. Iranians came for the helicopter, for him and you." Now that the crisis was over, the major felt very good. "The airplane was Iran-registered, had no clearance to leave Iran, so therefore they still had a right to it. Now, follow me."

"Where to, please?"

"I thought you might like to see your husband." The major enjoyed looking at her, enjoyed the danger, wondering where her secreted weapon was. These women always have a weapon or venom of some kind, death of some kind lurking for the unwary rapist. Easy to overcome if you're ready, if you watch their hands and don't sleep. "Well?"

"There are . . . there are Iranians at the police station?"

"No. This is Turkey, not Iran, no alien is waiting for you. Come along, you've nothing to fear."

"I'll . . . I'll be right down. At once."

"Yes, you will—at once," he said. "You don't need a bag, just your jacket. Be quick before I change my mind." He saw the flash of fury and it further amused him. But this time she obeyed, seething, put on her jacket and went down the stairs, hating her helplessness. Across the square beside him, eyes watching them. Into the station and the room, the same one as before. "Please wait here."

Then he closed the door and went into the office. The sergeant held out the phone for him. "I have Captain Tanazak, Border Station duty officer, for you, sir."

"Captain? Major Ikail. The border's closed to all mullahs and Green

Bands until further orders. Arrest the sergeant who let some through a couple of hours ago and send him to Van in great discomfort. An Iranian truck's coming back. Order it harassed for twenty hours, and the men in it. As for you, you're subject to court-martial for failing to ensure standing instructions about armed men!" He put the phone down, glanced at his watch. "Is the car ready, Sergeant?"

"Yes, Effendi."

"Good." The major went through the door, down the corridor to the cage, the sergeant following him. Erikki did not get up. Only his eyes moved. "Now, Mr. Pilot, if you're prepared to be calm, controlled, and no longer stupid, I'm going to bring your wife to see you."

Erikki's voice grated. "If you or anyone touches her I swear I'll kill you, I'll tear you to pieces."

"I agree it must be difficult to have such a wife. Better to have an ugly one than one such as her—unless she's kept in purdah. Now do you want to see her or not?"

"What do I have to do?"

Irritably the major said, "Be calm, controlled, and no longer stupid." To the sergeant he said in Turkish, "Go and fetch her."

Erikki's mind was expecting disaster or a trick. Then he saw her at the end of the corridor, and that she was whole, and he almost wept with relief, and so did she.

"Oh, Erikki . . ."

"Both of you listen to me," the major said curtly. "Even though you've both caused us a great deal of inconvenience and embarrassment, I've decided you were both telling the truth so you will be sent at once with a guard to Istanbul, discreetly, and handed over to your ambassador, discreetly—to be expelled, discreetly."

They stared at him, dumbfounded. "We're to be freed?" she said, holding on to the bars.

"At once. We expect your discretion—and that's part of the bargain. You will have to agree formally in writing. Discretion. That means no leaks, no public or private crowing about your escape or escapades. You agree?"

"Oh, yes, yes, of course," Azadeh said. "But there's, there's no trick?"

"No."

"But . . . but why? Why after . . . why're you letting us go?" Erikki stumbled over the words, still not believing him.

"Because I tested both of you, you both passed the tests, you committed no crimes that we would judge crimes—your oaths are between you and God and not subject to any court—and, fortunately for you, the warrant was illegal and therefore unacceptable. Komiteh!" he muttered disgustedly, then noticed the way they were looking at each other. For a moment he was awed. And envious.

Curious that Hakim Khan allowed a komiteh to issue the warrant, not the police who would have made extradition legal. He motioned to the sergeant. "Let him out. I'll wait for you both in the office. Don't forget I still have your jewelry to return to you. And the two knives." He strode off.

The cage gate opened noisily. The sergeant hesitated, then left. Neither Erikki nor Azadeh noticed him go or the foulness of the cell, only each other, she just outside, still holding on to the bars, he just inside, holding on to the bars of the door. They did not move. Just smiled.

"Insha'Allah?" she said.

"Why not?" And then, still disoriented by their deliverance by an honest man whom Erikki would have torn apart as the epitome of evil a moment ago, Erikki remembered what the major had said about purdah, how desirable she was. In spite of his wish not to wreck the miracle of the good he blurted out, "Azadeh, I'd like to leave all the bad here. Can we? What about John Ross?"

Her smile did not alter and she knew that they were at the abyss. With confidence she leaped into it, glad for the opportunity. "Long ago in our beginning I told you that once upon a time I knew him when I was very young," she said, her voice tender, belying her anxiety. "In the village and at the base he saved my life. When I meet him again, if I meet him, I will smile at him and be happy. I beg you to do the same. The past is the past and should stay the past."

Accept it and him, Erikki, now and forever, she was willing him, or our marriage will end quickly, not of my volition but because you'll unman yourself, you'll make your life unbearable and you'll not want me near you. Then I'll go back to Tabriz and begin another life, sadly it's true, but that's what I've decided to do. I won't remind you of your promise to me before we were married, I don't want to humiliate you—but how rotten of you to forget. I forgive you only because I love you. Oh, God, men are so strange, so difficult to understand, please remind him of his oath at once!

"Erikki," she murmured, "let the past stay with the past. Please?" With her eyes she begged him as only a woman can beg.

But he avoided her look, devastated by his own stupidity and jealousy. Azadeh's right, he was shouting at himself. That's past. Azadeh told me about him honestly and I promised her freely that I could live with that and he did save her life. She's right, but even so I'm sure she loves him.

Tormented he looked down at her and into her eyes, a door slammed inside his head, he locked it and cast away the key. The old warmth pervaded him, cleansing him. "You're right and I agree! You're right! I love you

—and Finland forever!" He lifted her off the ground and kissed her and she kissed him back, then held on to him as, more happy than he had ever been, he carried her effortlessly up the corridor. "Do they have sauna in Istanbul, do you think he'll let us make a phone call, just one, do you think . . ."

But she was not listening. She was smiling to herself.

BAHRAIN—THE INTERNATIONAL HOSPITAL: 6:03 P.M.

The muted phone rang in Mac's bedroom and Genny came out of her pleasing reverie on the veranda, Mac dozing in an easy chair beside her in the shade. She slipped out of her chair, not making a sound, not wanting to awaken him, and picked it up. "Captain McIver's room," she said softly.

"Oh, sorry to bother you, is Captain McIver free for a moment? This is Mr. Newbury's assistant at Al Shargaz."

"Sorry, he's sleeping, this is Mrs. McIver, can I take a message for him?"

The voice hesitated. "Perhaps you'd ask him to call me. Bertram Jones."

"If it's important, you'd better give it to me."

Again a hesitation, then, "Very well. Thank you. It's a telex from our HQ in Tehran for him. It says: 'Please advise Captain D. McIver, managing director of IHC, that one of his pilots, Thomas Lochart, and his wife have been reported accidentally killed during a demonstration.' " The voice picked up a little. "Sorry for the bad news, Mrs. McIver."

"Th—that's all right. Thank you. I'll see my, my husband gets it. Thank you." Quietly she replaced the phone. She caught sight of herself in a mirror. Her face was colorless, naked in its misery.

Oh, my God, I can't let Duncan see me or know or he'll ha—

"Who was it, Gen?" McIver said from outside, still half asleep.

"It . . . it'll wait, luvey. Go back to sleep."

"Good about the tests, wasn't it?" The results had been excellent.

"Wonderful . . . I'll be back in a second." She went to the bathroom and closed the door and splashed water on her face. Can't tell him, just can't . . . got to protect him. Should I call Andy? A glance at her watch. Can't, Andy'll be at the airport already. I'll . . . I'll wait till he arrives, that's what I'll do. . . . I'll go to meet him with Jean-Luc and . . . nothing to do till then . . . oh God oh God, poor Tommy, poor Sharazad . . . poor loves . . .

The tears poured out of her and she turned on the taps to hide the sound. When she came back onto the veranda McIver was contentedly asleep. She sat and looked at the sunset, not seeing it.

AL SHARGAZ INTERNATIONAL AIRPORT: Sunset. Rudi Lutz, Scragger, and all the others were waiting at their exit barrier, anxiously staring off toward the crowded foyer, arriving and departing passengers milling about. "Final call for BA 532 to Rome and London. All aboard, please."

Through the huge, plate-glass windows they could see the sun almost at the horizon. All were nervous. "Andy should've kept Johnny and the 125 as backup for God's sake," Rudi muttered testily to no one in particular.

"He had to send it to Nigeria," Scot said defensively. "The Old Man had no choice, Rudi." But he saw Rudi was not listening, so he half shrugged, absently said to Scragger, "You really going to give up flying, Scrag?"

The lined old face twisted. "For a year, only for a year—Bahrain's great for me, Kasigi's a beaut, and I won't give up flying completely, oh dear no. Can't, me son, gives me the creeps to think about it."

"Me too. Scrag, if you were my age would y—" He stopped as an irritable BA official came out through Security and strode up to Rudi: "Captain Lutz, absolutely your last call! She's already five minutes late. We can't hold her any longer! You've just got to board the rest of your party at once or we'll leave without you!"

"All right," Rudi said. "Scrag, tell Andy we waited as long as possible. If Charlie doesn't make it, throw him in the *Gottverdammstechen* brig! Goddamn Alitalia for being early. Everyone on." He handed his boarding pass to the attractive flight attendant and went through the barrier and stood on the other side, checking them through, Freddy Ayre, Pop Kelly, Willi, Ed Vossi, Sandor, Nogger Lane, Scot last and dawdling until he could wait no longer. "Hey, Scrag, tell the Old Man okay for me."

"Sure, sport." Scragger waved as he vanished into Security, then turned away, heading for his own gate the other side of the terminal, Kasigi waiting there already, brightened as he saw Pettikin running through the crowd, hand in hand with Paula, Gavallan twenty paces behind. Pettikin gave her a hurried embrace and rushed for the barrier.

"For Gawd's sake, Charlie . . ."

"Don't give me a hard time, Scrag, had to wait for Andy," Charlie said, almost out of breath. He handed over his boarding pass, blew a beaming kiss to Paula, went through the barrier, and was gone.

"Hi, Paula, wot's cooking?"

Paula was breathless too but radiant. She put her arm through his, gave him a little shrug: "Charlie asked me to spend his leave with him, *caro*, in South Africa—I've relations near Cape Town, a sister and her family, so I said why not?"

"Why not indeed! Does that mean th—"

"Sorry, Scrag!" Gavallan called out, joining them. He was puffing but twenty years younger. "Sorry, been on the phone for half an hour, looks like we've lost the bloody ExTex Saudi contract and part of the North Sea but to hell with that—great news!" He beamed and another ten years fell away, behind him the sun touched the horizon. "Erikki called as I was half out the door, he's safe, so's Azadeh, they're safe in Turkey and . . ."

"Hallelujah!" Scragger burst out over him, and from the depths of the waiting area past Security there was a vast cheer from the others, the news given them by Pettikin.

". . . and then I had a call from a friend in Japan. How much time have we?"

"Plenty, twenty minutes, why? You just missed Scot, he said to give you a message: 'Tell the Old Man okay.' "

Gavallan smiled. "Good. Thanks." Now he had regained his breath. "I'll catch you up, Scrag. Wait for me, Paula, won't be a moment." He went over to the JAL information counter. "Evening, could you tell me, please, when's your next flight out of Bahrain for Hong Kong?"

The receptionist tapped the keys of the computer. "Eleven forty-two tonight, Sayyid."

"Excellent." Gavallan took out his tickets. "Cancel me off BA's London flight tonight and put me on th—" Loudspeakers came to life and drowned him out with the all-pervading call to prayer. An immediate hush fell on the airport.

And high up in the vast reaches of the Zagros Mountains, five hundred miles northward, Hussain Kowissi slid off his horse, then helped his young son to make the camel kneel. He wore a Kash'kai belted sheepskin coat over his black robes, a white turban, his Kalashnikov slung on his back. Both were solemn, the little boy's face puffy from all the tears. Together they tethered the animals, found their prayer mats, faced Mecca, and began. A chill wind whined around them, blowing snow from the high drifts. The half-obscured sunset showed through a narrow band of sky under the encroaching, nimbus-filled overcast that was again heavy with storm and with snow. Prayers were soon said.

"We'll camp here tonight, my son."

"Yes, Father." Obediently the little boy helped with the unloading, a spill of tears again on his cheeks. Yesterday his mother had died. "Father, will Mother be in Paradise when we get there?"

"I don't know, my son. Yes, I think so." Hussain kept the grief off his face. The birthing had been long and cruel, nothing he could do to help her but hold her hand and pray that she and the child would be spared and that the midwife was skilled. The midwife was skilled but the child was stillborn, the hemorrhaging would not stop and what was ordained came to pass.

As God wants, he had said. But for once that did not help him. He had buried her and the stillborn child. In great sadness he had gone to his cousin—also a mullah—and had given him and his wife his two infant sons to rear, and his place at the mosque until the congregation chose his successor. Then, with his remaining son, he had turned his back on Kowiss.

"Tomorrow we will be down in the plains, my son. It will be warmer."

"I'm very hungry, Father," the little boy said.

"So am I, my son," he said kindly. "Was it ever different?"

"Will we be martyred soon?"

"In God's time."

The little boy was six and he found many things hard to understand but not that. In God's time we get to Paradise where it's warm and green and there's more food than you can eat and cool clean water to drink. But what about . . . "Are there joubs in Paradise?" he asked in his piping little voice, snuggling against his father for greater warmth.

Hussain put his arm around him. "No, my son, I don't think so. No joubs or the need for them." Awkwardly he continued cleaning the action of his gun with a piece of oiled cloth. "No need for joubs."

"That'll be very strange, Father, very strange. Why did we leave home? Where are we going?"

"At first northwest, a long way, my son. The Imam has saved Iran but Muslims north, south, east, and west are beset with enemies. They need help and guidance and the Word."

"The Imam, God's peace on him, has he sent you?"

"No, my son. He orders nothing, just guides. I go to do God's work freely, of my own choice, a man is free to choose what he must do." He saw the little boy's frown and he gave him a little hug, loving him. "Now we are soldiers of God."

"Oh, good, I will be a good soldier. Will you tell me again why you let those Satanists go, the ones at our base, and let them take away our air machines?"

"Because of the leader, the captain," Hussain said patiently. "I think he was an instrument of God, he opened my eyes to God's message that I should seek life and not martyrdom, to leave the time of martyrdom to God. And also because he gave into my hands an invincible weapon against the enemies of Islam, Christians and Jews: the knowledge that they regard individual human life sacrosanct."

The little boy stifled a yawn. "What's sacrosanct mean?"

"They believe the life of an individual is priceless, any individual. We know all life comes from God, belongs to God, returns to God, and any life only has value doing God's work. Do you understand, my son?"

"I think so," the little boy said, very tired now. "So long as we do God's work we go to Paradise and Paradise is forever?"

"Yes, my son. Using what the pilot taught, one Believer can put his foot on the neck of ten millions. We will spread this word, you and I . . ." Hussain was very content that his purpose was clear. Curious, he thought, that the man Starke showed me the path. "We are neither Eastern, nor Western, only Islam. Do you understand, my son?"

But there was no answer. The little boy was fast asleep. Hussain cradled him, watching the dying sun. The tip vanished. "God is Great," he said to the mountains and to the sky and to the night. "There is no other God but God . . ."

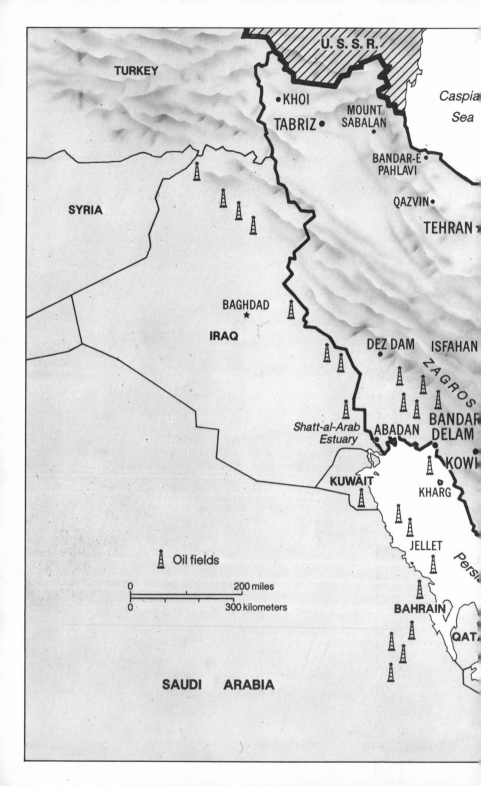